FIRST EDITION

THE READER'S DIGEST ASSOCIATION LIMITED
25 Berkeley Square, London W1X 6AB

THE READER'S DIGEST ASSOCIATION
SOUTH AFRICA (PTY) LTD
Nedbank Centre, Strand Street, Cape Town

Printed in Great Britain by Petty & Sons Ltd, Leeds

Original cover design by Jeffery Matthews F.S.I.A.D.

For information as to ownership
of copyright in the material in this book see last page

ISBN 0 340 27675 4

READER'S DIGEST

CONDENSED BOOKS

Reader's Digest
CONDENSED BOOKS

TORPEDO RUN
Douglas Reeman

BANNERS OF SILK
Rosalind Laker

MY LEFT FOOT
Christy Brown

TROJAN TREASURE
Robert L. Fish

COLLECTOR'S LIBRARY
EDITION

In this Volume:

TORPEDO RUN
by Douglas Reeman   (p.9)

Douglas Reeman returns with another thrilling adventure of naval warfare. In 1943 the control of the Black Sea, hinge of the Eastern Front, lies in German hands. To help the hard-pressed Russians, the British send in a flotilla of small but lethal motor torpedo boats. Led by the brilliant John Devane, the flotilla's formidable task is to break up and destroy the powerful enemy naval force patrolling the area. Then an old rival of Devane's, a wily German E-boat commander, appears on the scene, and the battle turns into a fierce duel.

Banners of Silk
by Rosalind Laker   (p.147)

The passion between Louise Vernet, a humble Parisian seamstress, and the dashing cavalry officer, Pierre de Gand, seemed doomed from the start. "I forbid the marriage," thundered Pierre's godfather, Emperor Napoleon III; and in the swirl of revolution their love was swept aside. Then Louise, a protegée of the renowned couturier, Charles Worth, took London society by storm with her own glamorous Parisian designs. This star-crossed romance is set against the elegant background of the nineteenth-century world of fashion.

MY LEFT FOOT *by Christy Brown (p.319)*

Born with cerebral palsy, Christy Brown had been unable to walk, speak, feed or dress himself—until, helped by his devoted mother, by his lively brothers and his friends, he found the key to his "prison". By learning to write with his left foot, the only part of his body he could at first control, he began a career that has been an inspiration to the disabled and to everyone who cares.

TROJAN TREASURE

by Robert L. Fish (p.395)

The fabulous lost treasure of ancient Troy suddenly turns up for international auction. But who is selling it—and why? And where has the priceless collection been since it disappeared during World War II?

Ruth McVeigh, head of the Metropolitan Museum of Art, is determined to solve the mystery. The bizarre treasure hunt leads her across Europe—into an unexpected romance, along dark paths of espionage, and under the threat of murder.

TORPEDO RUN

A CONDENSATION OF THE BOOK BY

Douglas Reeman

PAINTINGS BY MICHAEL TURNER   DRAWINGS BY JACK McCARTHY
PUBLISHED BY HUTCHINSON

In 1943 a tiny flotilla of British motor torpedo boats was transported overland to the Black Sea. Their mission: to help the Russians in a desperate campaign to recapture the Crimean Peninsula from the Nazi enemy. The Russians were hampered by the daring hit-and-run tactics of the German light naval force, but soon the experienced crews of the MTBs began to turn the tide of battle.

In command of the MTBs was John Devane, a battle-weary veteran at only twenty-seven. But just as his love for a beautiful navy widow began to add meaning to his lonely life, news reached him that an old adversary had arrived in the Black Sea. He discovered then that even in the midst of the impersonal savagery of modern high-speed battle, there could still be a duel between individuals.

Once again best-selling author Douglas Reeman has written an epic tale of the war at sea, and paid tribute to the courageous men who took part in it.

Recall

Lieutenant-Commander John Devane sat on a wooden bench and regarded the opposite wall. Grey rough concrete. You could even see where the first layer was tamped home. The brief professional interest passed and he sank back again, outwardly relaxed, but his mind busy with the distant sounds, the feeling of being off balance, lost.

The room was little more than a space curtained off from one of many such corridors beneath the Admiralty building in London. A far-off murmur was like the sea across a scattered reef, but it was traffic—red buses which still managed to make splashes of colour against the dust and rubble of wartime London, and taxis which never saw you when you needed them—and people on the move: endless, restless throngs, many in the uniforms of countries occupied by "them", as his mother called them. The enemy.

Devane glanced at his watch. It was eleven in the forenoon, a May day in 1943. But down here it could have been anywhere, any time. He thought briefly of his leave, interrupted by this unexpected summons to the Admiralty after only four days. Perhaps that was what you needed after the blood and guts of the Mediterranean war. Any longer and maybe you were too scared to go back.

The curtain was plucked aside by a small Wren. "Captain Whitcombe will see you shortly, sir."

Devane reached for his cap and stood up. He knew Whitcombe from way back, a bluff, red-faced captain who had been in retirement before the war and had been slotted into a desk job to allow someone else to take over a bridge at sea. Unlike some, Whitcombe had dropped into a niche which suited him perfectly.

Devane fell in step beside the Wren. She paused by a steel door labelled SPECIAL OPERATIONS which opened into another concrete box, with clattering typewriters, harsh lighting, and Wrens bustling about with signals and files.

A Wren second officer looked up from her desk. "Wait here, please. I'll tell Captain Whitcombe you've arrived."

He nodded and ran his fingers through his hair. It was as unruly as ever, and nearly four years of active service had not improved it. He thought about his last commission. The North African coast, sunshine and washed-out blue skies, or the fierce offshore winds which tore your face with dust and desert sand.

It had certainly been a long haul from those other days at home in Dorset when he had worked for his father as a fledgling architect. Looking back, it always seemed to have been spring or summer. Every weekend down to the coast in the sports car he owned jointly with his friend Tony. Sailing their old sloop round Portland Bill, pints afterwards in a pub at Weymouth. And later, more for a bet than anything, they had both joined the peacetime Royal Naval Volunteer Reserve.

Now the sloop and the car were gone. Tony too, for that matter, killed in a minesweeper within sight of the Portland Bill they had both loved so much.

He heard footsteps and muted voices. So there was someone else in with Whitcombe.

With a start he realized that all the typewriters had stopped, that several girls were looking at him. His eye fell on a carefully preserved newspaper which a Wren had taken from her desk.

Was it really him? Eyes squinting at the camera, battered cap all awry; some vague, grinning faces in the background with what he knew to be part of the old Maltese battery in the far distance.

The glaring headline still stunned him. DEVANE'S BATTLE SQUADRON STRIKES TERROR INTO THE RETREATING AFRIKA KORPS! THE LAST

10

GERMANS FLEE FROM TUNIS! There was more, a whole lot more. A voice said, "Will you come this way, sir," and as the door closed behind him Whitcombe strode to greet him. Still the same, thank God. Good old Tubby.

Whitcombe beamed. "Bloody good to see you again, John. This is Commander Kinross of our operations staff." Kinross gave a stiff nod. He looked a cold fish but extremely competent.

Whitcombe said, "Damn sorry about your leave." He smiled and glanced at the ribbon on Devane's jacket. "Another bar to your DSC. What does it feel like to be a hero and the public's darling?"

Feel like? Devane was twenty-seven years old and had been in the navy since the outbreak of war. He was a veteran, in the roaring, clattering world of motor torpedo boats, the war where you saw your enemy, sometimes even his fear, as the tracer cut him down and turned his boat into an inferno.

"I feel immensely old, sir." He grinned. It made him look like a youth.

They sat around the littered desk, and then Commander Kinross said abruptly, "I know your record, of course, your rise from first lieutenant in a Vosper MTB at Felixstowe to command a flotilla in the Med." He gave a wintry smile. "That sounds a bit brief for so active a life, but it was when you came to us with your command that I really had the opportunity to study your methods."

By "us", Kinross meant the special operations section, and more to the point, the special boat squadron which had achieved the impossible. From running guns to Tito's partisans and landing agents behind enemy lines, they had harried German convoys and communications from the Aegean to Tobruk, from embattled Malta to the Adriatic. Devane's handful of MTBs had tied down desperately needed patrol vessels and aircraft and, as the newspaper said, had indeed struck terror into the retreating Germans.

Whitcombe said, "Fact is, John, we need you back. God knows you've earned a break, but we're stretched to breaking point. We need experienced leaders as never before."

Kinross was impatient. "This year is the turning point. However we invade, northwards through Italy or the surrounding territory, it has to be soon. It's got to be right. One real failure now and we'll never get back." He stood up and moved to the great wall map, then pointed at the Mediterranean. "We have the whole North

11

African coast sewn up and the convoy routes covered by sea and air." His finger moved up further. "France next year, certainly no later, and then it will be one long slog all the way to Berlin." He turned and looked at Devane. "Of course, we'll not have it all our own way. But who would have believed that weather was as important as fuel and ammunition?"

Whitcombe interrupted. "Get on with it, William."

"Last winter, our Russian allies thought that the German armies on the Eastern Front would collapse in the snow and ice. But they didn't. Somehow the Germans stood firm. Incredible casualties on both sides, millions probably, acts of barbarism which make Attila the Hun seem like a bloody amateur."

Fascinated, Devane watched Kinross's finger on the move again. It came to rest on the Black Sea, then on the thrusting Crimean peninsula.

Kinross said distantly, "Brings back memories, eh? The Charge of the Light Brigade, Florence Nightingale." His tone sharpened. "Well, now it's the hinge of the whole front. The Germans took it from the Russians, and while they remain there in strength the Russians have no chance of thrusting as far as they must into Europe. If Hitler's generals can withstand another winter the Russians will have to begin all over again. We can say goodbye to our own invasion of northern France unless the enemy is completely involved on every front."

Whitcombe said, "The coastal forces flotillas, MGBs as well as your MTBs, have taken quite a hammering, so regrouping and remanning is top priority. The invasion of Sicily is set for July, so we don't have much time. A special MTB flotilla was sent to the Med a few weeks ago. All brand-new boats, five to be exact."

"Their senior officer is Lieutenant-Commander Don Richie, right?" Devane saw their startled exchange of glances. "You know the navy, sir, no secrets for long."

Whitcombe lit a cigarette carefully. "Of course, John, you and Richie served together at the beginning. In the Channel?"

"Yes. I know his wife too." Why had he said that?

"Well, Richie's special flotilla was put aboard some fast merchant ships, ex-passenger liners, at dead of night—men, torpedoes, everything—and whisked away. Through the canal and then up to Kuwait."

Nothing seemed to be making sense. Richie was the best there was. Another RNVR officer, who had become something of a legend. So why did they need *him?*

Whitcombe glanced at the wall clock. "Lunch soon, I think. Ask Mary to reserve us a table, William. She knows where."

Kinross left the room with obvious reluctance.

Whitcombe regarded Devane fondly. "I'll come to the point, John. Those five boats were taken overland and launched into the Caspian Sea. A rendezvous is being arranged for the whole flotilla to be carried overland again to the Black Sea. To work with the Russians against the enemy's flank. The Russians' one real weakness is on the water and they are keen for us to help, although I suspect they are hoping for more aid than we have to spare. I want you to command the flotilla, John. We need someone who is as well known and as respected as Richie."

So Don Richie was dead. Whitcombe did not have to tell him.

The tubby captain added slowly, "His wife was here this morning. She had already been told in the usual way, but we felt we owed it to her. After all he did, killed in action seems a small reward for her anyway." He looked round as Kinross's voice intruded through the door. "In fact, he shot himself." He gave a warning glance. "Enough said for now. We can talk some more later."

Devane followed the others, his mind grappling with what Whitcombe had disclosed. Richie dead. They all expected to die, but not like that. Why the *hell* had he done it?

AFTER LUNCH in a small club at the back of St James's, they had gone back to the Admiralty bunker where Whitcombe and Kinross had built up between them quite a picture of the new flotilla.

Now Devane studied a list of officers. The names were like small portraits of the men, for the new flotilla had been constructed from others which had been working in the Mediterranean, and Devane needed little to remind him.

One of the boats was commanded by George "Red" Mackay, transferred from a Canadian flotilla based at Alexandria. Devane smiled. Red had a loud, harsh voice and was terrific.

Another CO was Willy Walker, who looked rather like a disdainful heron.

"I notice there are extra people, five to a boat?" he said.

Whitcombe met his gaze. Devane's eyes were what you always remembered after you had met him, blue-grey, like the sea.

13

"Yes. Once you are in the Black Sea you'll be hard put to get replacements. So you'll have one officer and four ratings in addition to each normal complement. A tight squeeze, but there it is."

"When do you want me to leave, sir?"

"A few days' time. You'll be told. But it's absolutely top secret, John." Then he added, "You'll be working with Lieutenant-Commander Beresford, but you've done that before."

Another face. Intelligent but moody. One of the cloak-and-dagger brigade.

He replied, "Yes. Pretty good officer." He grinned at the old joke. "For a regular, that is."

Whitcombe seemed satisfied with his reactions. "Remember this, John, yours is an independent command. You'll have to rely on your own judgment most of the time. Beresford will be there to keep the Russians off your back. He's good at that kind of thing."

They all stood up. It was over. For the moment.

THE ROYAL NAVY had thoughtfully commandeered a small block of flats in a quiet square near to Harrods. Devane stood at his window and looked down at the square, his head ringing like an oil drum. After yesterday's meeting with Whitcombe and Kinross he should have gone straight to bed. He never slept well these days, but the gin bottle beside the bed, two-thirds empty, showed that it was no cure. He was drinking too much.

During breakfast, which had been brought to his bedside by a naval steward, he had re-read his folder of intelligence reports. He was going to the Black Sea, to a war he had only seen on the newsreels. The intelligence pack explained the technical side; about the five boats, all of which were of the latest design and had certain extras: power-operated guns, twin torpedo tubes, and a top speed of thirty-nine knots. Impressive.

Devane hoped there would be accommodation arranged ashore for the crews when they were in harbour. He smiled. *In Russia.* A seventy-one-foot-long MTB, with all the additional gear and ammunition for her extended patrol area, and barely room enough for her seventeen-man complement. Now there would be twenty-two! He could hear the moans already.

He re-examined the details of his own command. His first lieutenant, named Dundas, had a high recommendation. He was twenty-six, ex-merchant service. The third hand was a RNVR

14

lieutenant called Seymour. He was twenty-two, with two years in coastal forces. All it mentioned of his earlier existence was the title of journalist. It probably meant his local church magazine.

The boat's coxswain he did know. Petty Officer Tom Pellegrine, DSM and bar, who had been Richie's coxswain from the beginning. He was a regular, which was rare in coastal forces. Regulars were usually retained for ships more valuable than MTBs. But a good coxswain was vital. The bridge between officers and ratings. And when they were all packed in that little hull he would have his work cut out as a peacemaker.

There was not much in the pack about German naval forces in the area, except that they were a mixed collection of small craft which, like his own, had been carried across country, then floated down the Danube to their new killing ground.

Information about the Russians was even scarcer. Their naval squadron, the Azov Flotilla, was commanded by an officer called Sergey Gorshkov, but the man described as the real link with the British was Nikolai Sorokin, a full captain, who had already made his mark against the Germans in the Baltic.

The liaison would rest with Ralph Beresford. Devane had worked with him in the Mediterranean and on special missions amidst the Greek islands. He was most people's idea of the peacetime regular officer. Good-looking, dashing would be a better word. But Devane had seen the other side of the man. Tough, almost fanatical about each operation. He liked Beresford, or what he knew of him.

The telephone jangled. Devane sat down and picked it up. "Yes?"

"RPO 'ere, sir." He was one of the guardians of the lobby, "There's a lady 'ere, sir. To see you."

Devane sat bolt upright. "Can you put her on?" Somehow he was not surprised.

"John? This is Claudia."

He could see her as if she were right here with him. Dark, vivacious, lovely. She had always seemed so poised and confident, and he was shocked by the thought that she did not know how her husband had died. And he did.

"Hello. I'll come down. I—I heard you were in London." Half a lie was better than a whole one. "I'm terribly sorry about Don."

"Yes . . . I must talk to you, John." The line went dead.

Devane dialled the special number to Whitcombe's HQ and was told that he was not required to report again until 1500. Then he pulled on his jacket, and ran quickly downstairs to the lobby.

Claudia Richie was sitting on a bench by the door, her legs crossed, a cigarette in one hand. She turned and watched him. The movement of her lovely pale neck made him feel clumsy.

Devane took her arm. "How did you find this place?"

"Long time ago. With Don." She looked at him steadily. "Can we go somewhere?"

They walked into the warm sunlight and down towards Sloane Street. She slipped her hand through his arm.

"Where are you living, Claudia? Still at the farm?" Devane asked.

She nodded. "It's being run by conscientious objectors and Italian prisoners of war. Can you beat that?"

She looked at him, and Devane could see the pain in her brown eyes. Eyes so dark they seemed to fill her face.

She added, "But the farm really runs itself. They need all the food we can grow nowadays."

Devane thought about Don Richie, and how he had always seemed to be a typical gentleman farmer.

She appeared to read his mind. "Don never took much of an interest in it. Your Don and mine were different people, I expect. He needed to be a winner. Racing, sailing, everything. To him the MTBs were just an extension of his previous victories."

Devane glanced at her anxiously. She looked restless and lost, and in some odd way he felt responsible for her.

He asked, "Where are you staying in London?"

She stopped dead and disengaged her hand. "Why do you ask?"

"I'm sorry, Claudia. I just thought I'd take you there. I can guess what you're going through."

Her lip quivered. "I doubt that, John." She put out her hand impetuously. "I'm being stupid. Be a darling and get me a cab."

A taxi idled to the kerb. She said, "The Richmond Hotel, Chelsea, please." Devane opened the door and made to follow her.

She turned. "No. I'm sorry I dragged you out like this. I'm certain you've got plenty to do." She was pulling the door to.

Devane said, "Don't go. I'd like to talk. It's two years since we last met." He was conscious only of the fact she was leaving and added desperately, "Can I call you?"

Her mouth lifted for the first time in a small smile.

"If you want to. But what's the point?" She leaned forward and rapped the glass. "All right, driver!"

Devane watched the taxi edge into the traffic. She had wanted to tell him something and had changed her mind. Why? He glanced at his watch. What had he expected, for God's sake? She was probably wondering why a man like Don was dead and he was still in one piece.

He tried to laugh it off. Hurt pride, the fact that he was lonely. He had always had an eye for Claudia, of course, but who hadn't?

DEVANE FINISHED BUTTONING a clean shirt and then stared round his room. The blackout curtains were closed for, although it was still quite light outside, there was plenty of cloud about. The petty officer in the lobby had said, "They'll be over tonight, sir. Good cloud cover for the bastards."

Devane looked at the telephone. How many times had he done that since he had returned from the Admiralty, he wondered.

Whitcombe had filled him in on a few details about engineering staff for the boats' maintenance once they were delivered to the Black Sea, nothing very exciting. Then he had said abruptly, "I understand you saw Richie's widow this morning. What did she want?"

Devane had been both startled and angry to discover his moves were being recorded. Even when Whitcombe had added, "Just routine security, John," he had still felt resentful.

Whitcombe had changed tack. "See it this way. You are taking command of a new operational flotilla. It is no secret that all pendant numbers have been removed from the boats and the flotilla will be known only by the code name *Parthian*. You have five boats and some hundred and ten officers and ratings, to say nothing of Beresford's shore party, in your hands alone. A rash act, a break in security somewhere, and everything could fall apart before we begin."

Devane sat on the bed and played with his tie. Whitcombe had listened without further interruption as he explained what Claudia Richie had said, or had not said.

Then, surprisingly, Whitcombe had suggested, "Go and see her, John. Why not? It might calm her down, poor lass. It won't help us in operations to have her making inquiries. Some idiot might check up and spill the beans about Richie's suicide. Questions will be asked, and I shall have to delay *Parthian*."

"Oh, hell!" Devane stood up and reached for his jacket. She would probably pitch him out on his ear anyway. She might even have gone back to Devonshire already.

THE GIRL CLIPPIE on the bus called, "That's the Richmond, sir!" In the darkness Devane saw the reflected glitter of searchlights on water and knew the Richmond Hotel faced the Thames.

He groped for a door handle and found himself stumbling through some heavy curtains into a lobby, with an oak staircase turning above a small reception desk. A woman in a black dress behind the desk asked him, "May I help you, sir?"

"I was wondering if I could see Mrs. Richie."

"This *is* unexpected." Devane swung round and saw her standing at the foot of the stairway. She was carrying a coat over one arm.

"I was going for a walk along the embankment." She held out the coat to him. "Hold this for me." She turned into the coat easily. "It was me you came to see, I assume?"

He forced a smile. "I couldn't just walk away. You were upset. I wanted to help."

"Walk with me." As they crossed the darkened road to the embankment she added, "I'm better now. Sorry I made a scene. Not like me at all. But I felt sick. Fed up with all the solemn smiles, the evasiveness about Don."

She turned up her collar and paused momentarily to peer down at the swirling river. Then she moved off again and he fell in step beside her. He could smell her perfume.

"That's why I wanted to speak to you, John. Someone who knows what it's like."

"I can't tell you anything about Don's death. Really."

A searchlight sprang across the sky, an unending blue lance. Devane saw her face, pale in the glare, the moistness of her mouth.

She said, "I should like a drink. Very much." She looked across the road. "There's a place there somewhere."

It was then Devane realized. She was frightened of being alone, even more afraid of sympathy.

The pub was exactly right. Small, packed and full of noise and cheerful voices. The landlord peered through the smoke haze, his glance taking in Devane's rank and the girl's appearance. "Up this end, sir. Officers only." He winked. There was one vacant bar stool, wedged in a corner, and Devane helped her onto it.

"Two gins, right, sir?" the landlord said cheerfully.

More people pressed through the blackout curtains, and Devane had to shout to make himself heard. He was pressed against her knees but she made no obvious effort to move.

18

"I suppose you're taking Don's job?" She watched him. "Don't answer, not that you would anyway. But it doesn't take a genius to put two and two together. Your sort don't grow on trees. Don always said you were the best. Next to him, of course." She pushed her empty glass towards him and Devane signalled to the landlord.

"When you go back to Devon . . ." He got no further.

"I don't want to talk about it." She swallowed the gin in one gulp and grimaced at the taste. "You've not married, I hear. Don said you'd wait. He talked a lot about you, did you know that?"

Devane shook his head, afraid of breaking the spell. She was speaking freely now and one stupid remark could smash it. Outside an air-raid warning had droned for several minutes, but as usual it was ignored. It had become a part of daily life.

Devane had not known him that well, but when he thought of Richie, here in this crowded bar, he seemed more the way she had described him than he remembered him. *He needed to be a winner.*

She leaned forward and brushed something from Devane's sleeve. Her hair, almost jet black, fell across one cheek. "Tell me, when you go into action, do you have to clear your mind, wipe it clean so that you can cope? That's what Don said. Several times." She put her hand over his on the bar and tightened her grip in time with her words. "I should like to know."

"It's true. There's so much happening all at once." He could not take his eyes from her hand on his, it was so small and beautifully shaped. "Vigilance is everything. One moment of carelessness and it can cost lives, other people's as well as your own."

She nodded. "I needed to hear that. From you. Because if anyone in this damnable war knows about it, you do." Once more she nodded, the movement listless. "Thanks."

Devane took her other hand. "Tell me, Claudia. What is it?"

"Don is dead. It's over."

There was a long pause. Then she said in a tired voice, "We had a blazing row on that last leave before he went off to . . ." She took her hand from his and wiped her cheek with the back of it. Like a child. "He'd been at it too long, but would never admit it. He had to do better. To be the best!" She spoke the last words so loudly that several people stopped talking to listen. "I wanted to hurt him. To get back at him. I told him I was having an affair."

He stared at her, seeing Richie with the pistol in his hand.

"That was how we parted." She gave a shrug. "So you see, he was most likely killed because of me. That's what I had to ask you." The landlord's face loomed over the bar. "Everythin' OK, sir?" He glanced anxiously at the girl. "She looks a bit dicky." Devane's mind was frozen. He must get her out of here. He pushed himself from the bar and seized her by the shoulders. There was no time to explain. To say what he knew instinctively. "Hold me! For God's sake, hold on!" For a split second he felt her pressed against him, and then came the explosion.

It was more of a shock than a sound. He was falling and choking in dust and smoke, aware only that they were still clinging to each other and that the whole place was in darkness. As his senses returned he tried to free himself from the wood and brickwork across his shoulders. Voices yelled and echoed around him and he heard screams mingled with the desperate cries for help.

A bright column of fire spouted from the other side of the bar, and he guessed that either a gas main had caught fire or the kitchen stove had exploded. In the dancing blue flames he saw reeling figures, torn limbs, broken glass and rubble. The landlord was lying face downwards. There was blood everywhere. He found Claudia by the wall and pulled her to her feet, so that she hung against him lifelessly. She must have been stunned by the blast. He began to lift her over a broken beam, or was it the front of the bar?

Devane peered down at her and saw that her eyes were wide and staring. Then as her understanding returned she tried to turn her head, to see the smoky destruction.

Somewhere a bell rang loudly. Ambulances and fire engines were on their way. Two policemen crunched through the broken doors, their torches reflecting on their steel helmets.

Devane called, "In here. Six or seven still alive, I think."

The first policeman paused to peer at the girl. "She all right?"

She whispered to Devane, "Don't let them take me anywhere. I want to keep with you. Don't let them . . ." She fainted.

Devane slipped his arm beneath her legs, then, carrying her very carefully, he stepped through the collapsed doors and into the cool air. He heard voices calling instructions, and the clatter of spades and picks as rescuers searched amongst the wreckage for survivors.

She said huskily, "Put me down, please."

He lowered her to the pavement and she exclaimed, "I've lost a shoe!" Then she began to laugh, but no sound came, and Devane had to hold her against him until the paroxysm stopped.

Then she whispered, "Thanks. Very much. Near thing."

When he picked her up again she put her arm round his neck and rested her face against his cheek. "Don't leave me. Not yet."

An ambulance flashed past, its gong ringing frantically. Across the river there was a bright glow in the sky.

"I won't."

Back at the hotel, the woman he had spoken with at the desk exclaimed, "My God! Is she hurt?"

Someone switched on a small torch and Devane saw blood on the girl's leg. But it was already drying under a coating of dust.

Devane said, "I'm taking her to her room. If you have no objection?"

She shook her head. "N-no. Number eleven."

Devane started up the stairs. His body trembled as if he had a fever. It was always the same. He had made it. One more time.

The room, like the hotel, was old and musty. All different shades of brown. He sat her gently on the edge of the bed.

She said shakily, "There's some Scotch in the cupboard." Her hair was plastered to her forehead, her dress stained and crumpled.

"I brought it to bribe someone at the Admiralty." She tried to shrug but winced. "Ouch! I feel as if I've been in a scrum!"

Devane found the whisky but there was only one glass. He filled it carefully. She swallowed and almost choked. "Cheers!"

Then she handed him the glass and he took a long, careful drink. On an empty stomach it was like fire water.

She pulled up the skirt of her dress and examined her thigh.

21

There was a cut, but it looked clean enough. She said, "I'll just wash it and put a plaster on it. I'll not be long." She took down a dressing gown and paused by the door. "The bathroom is just two doors away. If the bombers come back you'll . . ."

"I'll come and get you. No matter what the management thinks!"

He sat down in the solitary chair and poured another drink. He could not leave her, but he should not stay.

The door opened and closed. She was wearing her robe and her skin looked pink and fresh. "A drink?" he asked.

She shook her head. Devane stood up and took her carefully in his arms. How long they stood like that he did not know or care.

She said unsteadily, "I should like you to kiss me."

Devane held her more tightly, half afraid that he might spoil the moment. As their mouths met he felt her body press against his. Then she slipped free and let her robe drop to the floor. She went to the bed and lay watching him as he tore off his clothes, nor did she speak until he was kneeling above her, her body taut under his exploring hands.

She whispered, "Take me now. I don't care about tomorrow."

They made love until they were completely spent, sparing each other nothing in their need and their awareness.

When the final All Clear wailed, Devane lay with her pressed against him, one of her legs thrown carelessly across his body. He listened to her gentle breathing, then turned to look at the grey light which filtered around the edges of the shutters.

Another day for each of them. And they were alive. *Alive*.

BESIDE A CAMP BED in a concrete bunker a telephone jangled, and Whitcombe yawned as he pressed it to his ear. "Yes?"

"Duty officer, sir. The signal has come through. *Parthian* has the go ahead. Shall I inform Lieutenant-Commander Devane, sir?"

"No. Give him another couple of hours." He thought of the girl with the sad, beautiful eyes and said, "It's the least we can do."

Parthian

Devane clung to the side of the wildly bucking car and wondered if any of his bones had been left unbroken. This was the final link in his bizarre journey from England. He seemed to have spent days changing from one military aircraft to the next, and with each hundred or so miles he travelled only the climate altered.

Often he thought of the dark-haired girl, as she had looked on that last morning, their *only* morning together after the air raid. What would become of her?

His final departure had bordered on the idiotic, he thought, with a carefully phrased telephone call to his parents in Dorset about a temporary shore job. And now, after all the hectic hustle and bustle, he was on dry land once more. He was actually in Russia, heading inland from the Caspian Sea as if the devil were after him.

The countryside was rugged and seemed untroubled. A few villages and several army encampments. Camouflage nets to hide ranks of armoured troop-carriers. Only the soldiers looked alien, even hostile.

There were two in the front of the car, the driver hunched behind the wheel and an army major. They spoke no English, and Devane's companion, a Lieutenant Kimber from Intelligence, had already explained, "Some do, but they don't advertise it."

Devane tried to estimate where the nearest Germans were. The Black Sea was about seven hundred miles from east to west, and maybe half that from north to south at its widest part. The Germans had long ago occupied Rumania and Bulgaria, and were now firmly rooted on the Crimean peninsula as well.

The major twisted round suddenly and said something to Devane's companion. Kimber replied in fluent Russian. Then he said, "A few more minutes. Your flotilla is up ahead of us."

Devane wanted to laugh. There was no sea for miles and miles, and yet this lieutenant had assured him that his flotilla, *Parthian*, was just up ahead. He could see nothing but a few flat-roofed, Moorish-looking buildings, some trees and two armed sentries with their hands in their pockets. A scout car edged through the dust, a long-barrelled machinegun swinging round to cover the car as it shivered to a halt. More throaty exchanges, papers examined, searching glances.

Devane said wearily, "Nice to feel welcome."

His companion glanced at him. "Most of the troops around this area are resting from the Eastern Front, sir. They stayed alive by mistrusting everyone but themselves."

Devane eyed him gravely. "That sounded like a rebuke."

"Sorry, sir. But it's like Alice through the looking glass out here.

You work things out, then change them round completely. Then you can think like a Russian."

Another camouflaged scout car rolled down a slight incline and stopped beside them. Its occupants, a squarely built Russian naval officer, and Lieutenant-Commander Ralph Beresford, climbed down, and Beresford said cheerfully, "Glad you made it, John. Allow me to introduce you. This is Captain Nikolai Sorokin."

The Russian thrust out his hand. "Welcome." He smiled and displayed strong, powerful teeth.

Beresford added casually, "Captain Sorokin is in command of local flotillas. We shall be working closely together."

There was the briefest hint of warning in his voice. Had Devane not worked with him before he might not have noticed it.

Beresford gestured to the car. "Come and meet your chaps."

The little car bounced round and up the incline to stop at the top of the rise. Below them were vans and armoured vehicles of every kind, with anti-aircraft guns, light and heavy, already manned and pointing at the evening sky. Soldiers busied themselves on every side, and the air above the great laager of vehicles was smoky with cooking fires and mobile kitchens.

But Devane's attention was riveted on the five MTBs. Out of the water, even a forty-four-ton boat looked like a battleship. But here they were toys, incidental to the great motorized carriers which were taking them from one sea to the other.

Soldiers were already hauling camouflage netting over the boats, and Devane guessed that when they were finished the whole encampment would look like just another hump of land from the air.

A Lavochkin fighter with bright red stars on its tapered wings droned towards the encampment from the next fold of hills, and the AA guns moved to cover it, as if sniffing for an enemy.

Beresford said quietly, "We've got good air cover. Without it, things could get distinctly nasty."

As the car moved forward again Devane automatically straightened his back, fatigue forgotten. This meeting would be a testing moment. Five MTBs, their crews and attendant maintenance staff had come all this way, knowing only a fraction of the truth, understanding even less of what was expected of them.

He relaxed as several figures emerged from amongst the parked load-carriers. The sight of British sailors, in this vast, strange country, made all the difference.

24

The lieutenant-commander in a stained boiler suit was Buckhurst, their "plumber", who had put together and patched up MTBs from Grimsby to Alexandria. He was a born fixer, and could make do with almost anything. He was a godsend, provided you could put up with his constant moaning. A lieutenant in battledress appeared, his bared head like a red mop. George Mackay, the Canadian. With him was Andy Twiss, the maniac who had once taken on five enemy armed trawlers single-handed, and had crawled back to Felixstowe, his boat like a pepper pot.

It was like entering an encampment of olden days. Inside were the familiar faces, outside were the aliens, watchful and unemotional. Devane returned their salutes, shook a hand here and there.

"You've not changed, Red."

Mackay grinned. "Hell, no, sir. Though much more of this an' I reckon I'll be about ready for the infantry!"

Buckhurst wiped his hand on his boiler suit before shaking Devane's hand.

"Russians!" He shot Sorokin a murderous glance. "They care as much for these boats as they do for their bloody sanitation!"

Sorokin ambled across the churned-up ground, still smiling, but his eyes were everywhere as he watched the sailors checking the lashings on their boats. Devane studied him. A hard nut. His record in the Baltic had read like the path of a whirlwind.

Sorokin spoke to Beresford, who translated. "The commanding officers and ourselves will dine with the Russians tonight, John." He did not even blink as he added, "That will mean champagne and caviar until it comes out of your ears. Very passable too."

Devane nodded. Champagne and caviar. It was further from Chelsea than he had imagined.

SOME OF THE BRITISH SEAMEN gave an ironic cheer as the third MTB came up tautly against her lines some thirty yards from the shore. For several days the great caravan of vehicles and supporting armour had moved ponderously westwards, heading for a safe place to launch the boats. Sometimes at night they had watched flashes lining the horizon and, although the fighting was many miles away, the clear, bright air made it appear close and threatening. There were other signs, too. Blackened and burned-out villages, deserted farmsteads, to mark the Luftwaffe's onslaught of the previous year.

Now Devane stood on the beach and watched the final unloading of the boats into their natural element. The operation was impressive. It was like seeing an amphibious invasion in reverse. Men scrambled over the gently swaying hulls while two destroyers cruised offshore, and the distant drone of a patrolling aircraft showed they were still under protection. Devane watched the blunt-bowed fuel lighter chugging towards the first MTB to be slipped into the water. It was just as well they had air and sea cover, he thought. For until *Parthian* reached the Russian naval base at Tuapse, which according to his map lay some one hundred miles to the northwest of where he now stood, they would be unarmed and defenceless.

The fourth MTB, commanded by Lieutenant Willy Walker, edged down the great ramps, guided by steel warps as thick as a man's wrist. He could see Walker fussing about below her bridge.

Then the last of the boats was moved slowly towards the water. Devane's. Where he would get to know the mettle of his small company and the strength of the flotilla he would now lead.

He had already met Dundas, his number one, and what he saw he liked, as he did the third hand Lieutenant Seymour, a willowy young man whose gentle appearance was totally at odds with his DSC and the hair-raising battle he had fought off Crete to win it.

Dundas had been the only man so far to mention Richie. He had been the one to find him dead in a cabin aboard the fast transport which had carried the new flotilla from the Mediterranean to the Gulf. Bitterly Dundas had said, "I never thought he was that sort. He was full of drive. I sometimes hated him for being so damned good at his job." He had made it sound like a betrayal.

Devane found he was clenching his fists as the boat came under the control of the line-handling parties and slewed round like a thoroughbred. Set against the deep blue water which rippled on her flared hull, she was a boat any man would give his arm to command. With her triple screws and three rudders she could accelerate from eight to thirty-nine knots in eleven seconds.

Even after her torpedoes had been fired each boat was still a deadly force to be reckoned with. In addition to her power-operated six-pounder forward and twin Oerlikons aft, she also carried a variety of machineguns and depth charges.

A great engine spluttered into life, and like tired monsters the big Russian carriers began to move up the beach towards the road. Devane heard boots squeaking in the sand and turned to see Sorokin watching the anchored flotilla with professional interest.

26

Devane spoke carefully. "Thank you, sir, for getting them here safely. It must have been a great responsibility."

Sorokin's mouth lifted slightly in a smile. "I would have hoped for more vessels." He shrugged. "But that is not your concern."

Beresford came striding down towards them. He glanced curiously at the Russian, before saying, "Ready, John?" Then he pointed towards an elderly launch idling close to the ramps. "That will take you out. I've had your gear sent across."

Devane nodded. "Thanks." He turned to say goodbye to Sorokin, but he was already climbing into his little scout car.

Beresford murmured, "Never mind that one, John. Your next meeting with him will probably be across a table, taking a bottling for having done something to offend the Soviets." He grinned. "*You* should worry."

They saluted each other formally, and Devane walked towards the launch. Dundas and Seymour were awaiting him on his boat. In the small open bridge he received a smart salute from Pellegrine, the coxswain. He was a sturdy man with a brick-red face. A mixture of sea-time and drink. Very soon now he would know them all. From Dundas down to an ordinary seaman named Metcalf, who was apparently a failed candidate for a commission.

As the reports of readiness were called from the deck or came up the various voicepipes, Devane pictured the petty officer in charge of the boat's powerful Packard engines. His name was Ackland, before the war a garage mechanic, so he should be all right.

Carroll, the leading signalman, was stooping down to push his flags into their lockers, and another leading hand with leather gauntlets to protect him from snags in the mooring wires was mustering a party ready to weigh anchor. His name was Priest. Devane was satisfied, names were falling into place already.

Carroll said, "The senior escort is signallin', sir!" He triggered an acknowledgement with his Aldis before peering at a hastily compiled list of local signals. "She's asking, '*Are you ready?*' "

Dundas asked, "Shall I call up the flotilla on the R/T sir? It'll save time."

Devane slung his binoculars about his neck and tugged his cap firmly over his eyes. "No. You do it, Bunts. The sooner we get used to a minimum of radio communicating the better."

Devane listened to the clack - - - clack of the signal lamp, then Carroll called, "All acknowledged, sir. Affirmative."

Devane walked to the forepart of the bridge and watched the easy pitch and roll of the bows. He ran his hand along the screen, savouring the moment. "Start up."

With a cough and a savage roar the five boats thundered into life, their hulls partially misted over by a curtain of high-octane vapour. Then, as they settled down to a steady rumble Devane said, "Up anchor. Bunts, signal the flotilla to form line astern and take station on the leading escort."

There was a clang from forward. "Anchor's aweigh!"

"All engines slow ahead." He glanced quickly at the coxswain. "Steer nor'west until we have station on Ivan."

The other boats followed him out in a tight curve, their guns covered and pointed impotently at the shark-blue sea.

Devane levelled his glasses on the leading destroyer. Toothless they might be, but they were back in the war.

DEVANE SAT AT his newly acquired desk and surveyed the flotilla's shore office without enthusiasm. It was partially underground and, like Whitcombe's HQ in London, had been constructed from gigantic slabs of concrete. The whole place throbbed with noises from the adjoining workshop, where Lieutenant-Commander (E) Hector Buckhurst had already set up his benches and drills, and from the strange, cavern-like dock beyond. The latter had originally been designed as a pen for Russian submarines, to protect them from bombing raids.

He thought of their arrival at Tuapse the previous day as darkness closed over the harbour. It had been a depressing sight, with many of the long, finger-like wharves savaged by bombings, and several ships showing only their masts above water.

Beresford had been waiting to greet them, and had been quick to shoot down any criticism from the various commanding officers. No bunks had so far been fitted in the concrete dock area, which meant the MTB crews would have to make the best of it in their already overcrowded hulls. And right now they were taking on ammunition and stowing extra belts and cannon shells throughout the hulls further to reduce the sleeping spaces.

There was no mail for anyone either. Someone should have thought how important it was to men away from home.

Dundas entered the concrete box and stood patiently by the desk while Devane made a note in the margin of a report.

Torpedo Run

"Ah, Number One. What can I do for you?"

Dundas looked like a sailor. Rugged, clear-eyed, he could have sailed with Drake. "We seem to be getting all we need for the boat, sir." He shivered. "It's the place, I suppose. No shore leave, the perimeter guarded as if we were POWs. It's not what I expected."

Devane looked up. "There have been raids every day. We must seem a bit pampered to them. But I want no friction. We're here to do a job, nothing more." He thought of the lieutenant's words in the car. *Alice through the looking glass*. Then he said, "It'll get better . . ."

A telephone buzzed.

It was Beresford. "Can you come to the main bunker, John?" He dropped his voice so that it was almost drowned by hissing static. "Bit of a flap on, so chop chop if you can."

Devane looked round for his cap. He had felt it in his bones as soon as he had arrived. A sense of urgency, even anxiety, which some people were at great pains to conceal. "Tell Red Mackay to take over until I get back, Number One. He's due for his half-stripe anyway. This will warn him what it'll be like."

Devane strode through the echoing workshop to where a Russian sailor was waiting to guide him to the command bunker. Sorokin was there with several other officers. He nodded companionably at Devane, but looked on edge.

Beresford hurried to meet him. "Glad you got here—"

He broke off as a thin voice said, "On behalf of Rear-Admiral Vasiliy Kasatonov"—the interpreter turned as if to bow to a forbidding figure seated on the far side of the table—"I am to welcome you to the struggle against the Nazi invaders."

Devane tried to remember something about Kasatonov. He was in command of the local defence, of the naval air forces, and had a significant political link with Moscow to uphold his authority. His whole presence gave an impression of immense determination.

The interpreter continued in the same sing-song tone, "The arrival of the British vessels is both a mark of progress and a sign of intent." He was staring at a point somewhere above Devane's shoulder. "Further intelligence has been received about the movement of enemy forces in this area, and we have learned that even larger . . ." He faltered and then said, "What *you* term 'E-boats' have been seen on patrol near Sevastapol."

Devane already knew something of the German naval strength in the Black Sea. It was a hotchpotch of small craft formed originally around their local minesweeping flotilla. Gunboats, armed launches, craft captured from the Russians, they had thrown everything into the battle to destroy and demoralize their enemies. A few E-boats had also been reported in the Black Sea. But this news of larger E-boats changed things. No wonder the Russians were disappointed by the size of the British offering.

The admiral spoke for the first time. A low, abrupt remark which made the interpreter stare at the ceiling as if for inspiration. He stammered, "While we have won one crushing victory after another, we have expected, *anticipated*, some sign that an invasion in the west was imminent. And now that the British at least have sent us this small group of torpedo boats we can feel the moment of final assault on Germany is not too far distant."

Devane thought of all the men he had seen die, the ships which had gone down in their efforts to carry food and supplies to Russia. Of the countries which had fallen to Hitler while Stalin had sheltered happily behind his non-aggression pact with Germany.

He realized the room was waiting for him to reply. There was no point in trying to describe his own country's record, they knew it as well as he did. *Through the looking glass.*

He said, "We are proud to be here. To put our skills, all of which have been gained in hard experience elsewhere, at the disposal of the Soviet navy and people. We will have some misunderstandings. That is common even in families. But we share the same enemy, and that is enough."

The admiral listened woodenly to the translation and then rose to his feet. With a curt nod to Beresford and Devane he strode from the bunker.

Sorokin embraced Devane. "He loves you, comrade! You found the *right* words!" He lit a cheroot. "Tonight you will leave harbour with some of my own"—he formed the word carefully—"flot-illa. I will give you later the details. Then we will fight like comrades!" He laughed as if it was a great joke.

"But first we drink. To seal our friendship, *da?*"

LIEUTENANT RODDY DUNDAS climbed onto the MTB's open bridge and groped his way to the forepart where Devane was peering abeam through his night glasses. "I've been right through the boat, sir. Not a chink of light anywhere."

Devane lowered the glasses. "How are the lads taking it?"

"Happy enough, sir." His teeth looked very white in the darkness. "Where are our allies?"

Devane thought about the brief, almost offhand meeting they had shared with the Russian flotilla's officers just before sailing. That had been two hours ago, and both groups of vessels had been heading due west since then.

There were ten craft in the Russian flotilla—three Italian-built gunboats, rather like small destroyers, two very old minesweepers and the remainder were converted motor launches. They were crammed with weapons of every sort, even multiple rocket launchers on loan from the Russian army. This flotilla, under its commander, a swarthy-faced officer named Orel, was steering about a mile off the starboard beam.

The object of their mission was a small but important convoy which was expected to pass along the southeast coast of the Crimean peninsula in twenty-four hours' time. Intelligence reports had stated that the convoy would be carrying valuable equipment for the enemy emplacements along that stretch of coast.

The German high command knew that an attempt would soon be made to retake the Crimea. A swift, well-handled convoy was a far better bet than risking the urgently needed supplies overland, when the Soviet air force would contest every yard of the way.

The two flotillas would head out to sea and rendezvous to the south of the convoy route. The enemy would then be unable to retreat, and could either scatter or continue on course until it eventually ran foul of other Russian patrols.

Devane had been irritated by the Russian commander's attitude. The British, despite having faster, more modern boats, would stand to seaward, and attack only if ordered. From Orel's tone, it sounded as if such an eventuality was considered unlikely.

Even at this reduced speed, which was making the MTBs yaw about uncomfortably, it would be a close thing, Devane thought. His flotilla carried enough fuel to allow for a cruising range of some five hundred miles. It was two hundred miles to the rendezvous. That did not allow much for a pitched battle and the homeward run. The Russian vessels were slower, but were converted for longer endurance. It was an interesting equation. Devane had said as much through the interpreter.

Orel had listened, then had picked up his cap and chart folder, and nodded curtly to Devane before murmuring something almost

31

inaudible. The interpreter said unhappily, "He says you are not to be afraid, Commander. His men have done it many times before."

Red Mackay had exploded. "Goddamn his bloody eyes! Let the bastards go alone, I say!"

"MORE COFFEE, SIR?"

Devane rubbed his eyes. Where had the day gone? The coffee tasted good. Scalding hot and as black as a boot. He searched abeam for the blurred shapes of the Russian vessels. All ten still there, and the speed now a miserable ten knots.

It had been a strange day, a limbo, a nothing of choppy water and no horizon, low cloud and a strange hazy light. It would be dark again soon.

Dundas joined him on the bridge and followed his gaze astern. The next boat back there was Willy Walker's, code name *Harrier*. The others were already merging into shadow.

Devane glanced at his watch. Soon, the Russian vessels would be curving away northwards to close the land. God, he hoped Orel knew what he was doing.

He thought about his own command. Five of the best MTBs available. Between them they could muster ten torpedoes and the firepower of a warship a dozen times their size.

Dundas handed his mug to the boatswain's mate and said, "This motion is making me dizzy."

Devane glanced at him. "But you were in the merchant service?"

Dundas grinned. "Yes. A million years ago. I'd just got my ticket. Never thought I'd end up in a little wooden box like this!"

"What about Seymour?"

"He's going to publish the great novel one day. Used to write for a living."

A brilliant light stabbed across the water, and Leading Signalman Carroll said, "The signal, sir! They're up and away!"

Devane nodded. A second earlier and Carroll would not have been on the bridge, nor was he required just yet. But he had already proved his worth. Before the war he had been a baker's roundsman. To see him now, glasses trained on the departing Russian flotilla, it was difficult to visualize Carroll with a horse and cart, a basket of bread on his arm.

Dundas said, "Shall I keep the guns covered, sir? I mean, there's not much chance of us being pounced on."

Devane smiled. "Probably not. But we'll go to action stations as planned. Never mind the grumbles. Go round yourself and check that there are extra magazines for the Oerlikons and plenty of spare belts for the MGs. I'm just going below to look at the chart again. Tell Seymour to take over the con, will you?"

He went down to the chartroom, and stooped over the table.

An hour later, as the five MTBs closed up at action stations, Devane said, "We will alter course now. Steer north by east. Revolutions for twenty knots. Warn the engine room." He could feel them staring at him through the darkness. "Tell the W/T cabin to inform the flotilla. After this we'll keep absolute silence."

Dundas spoke first. "But isn't that against what the Russians *want* us to do, sir?"

Devane climbed onto the gratings and gripped the screen. "Pass the word through the boat. Prepare for immediate action."

He heard Dundas's feet clattering down the short ladder from the bridge, a voice yelling orders from right aft.

As the throttles were opened and the bows rose in response to the sudden surge of power, Tom Pellegrine, the coxswain, gripped the wheel and rocked back on his heels as if he were riding and not steering the boat. Almost to himself he muttered, "Knew it. Knew somethin' was bloody wrong!"

The Glory Boys

Devane glanced up at the sky and saw the glimmer of stars through fast-moving cloud. He shivered as spray dashed over the bridge screen and pricked his skin. It was colder. Or was it? Maybe his nerves were playing up. He turned, angry with himself. "Stop engines. Do your stuff, Bunts."

Carroll blinked his shaded light astern, and the signal was repeated down the hidden line of boats. Devane gripped the rail as the motors faded into oppressive silence. The ridiculous feeling of vulnerability, when to stop and listen nearly always gave you an advantage.

The boat lifted and rolled in protest; here and there a man shifted restlessly at his station.

Devane heard the chartroom door open and close, and Dundas loomed up beside him. "I've checked our position again, sir. Even allowing for dead reckoning, I think we're just about where you wanted to be." He sounded uneasy. "The coast is approximately eight miles to the north of us. The Russians should be nearer and to the northeast. Maybe the convoy didn't come? Or that bloody Orel has lost it?"

Devane did not reply. He was seeing it in his mind, a triangle on a chart. The blacked-out convoy, Orel's ten antiquated vessels, and *Parthian*, stopped and drifting while every man in his flotilla probably thought he was raving mad to hang about rather than obey orders and hold to seaward of the Russians.

There was a chorus of gasps as the sky lit up to a brilliant white glare, followed instantly by faster, more deadly red flashes.

Seymour said, "They've found 'em." He sounded disappointed. "God, they've caught Jerry with his pants down by the look of it!"

The sounds seemed to take a long time to reach them and then Devane heard the dull boom of explosions, the rattle of machineguns. More star shells drifted eerily beneath the clouds, so that the sky appeared brighter than the sea below.

Devane gripped the screen. Orel was not having it all his own way, and he heard the occasional bang of a heavier gun as the convoy's armament fired back.

Dundas raised his mouth from a voicepipe. "Nothing from W/T. Orel doesn't need us anyway. And won't he crow about that!"

Pellegrine turned on his heels, his hands still grasping the wheel's spokes. "Sir!" His voice sounded urgent.

Devane moved to his side. "I know, Swain!" He felt icy fingers playing on his spine.

There it was. The unmistakable *thrum . . . thrum . . . thrum* of heavy diesels. E-boats, a whole bloody bunch of them, coming up fast astern of their convoy, judging to the minute what they thought the most dangerous part of the journey had to be. Orel and his mixed collection of gunboats were making such a din they would hear nothing until it was too late.

Devane saw faces lifting from gun mountings and hatchways, listening to the distant roar of engines. All down the line they would be preparing themselves. Unlike most flotillas, there were more veterans here than new volunteers. Even a single year in coastal forces made you a professional.

Pellegrine whispered, "They're crossin' our bows now, sir. I reckon 'bout two miles. No more."

34

Devane nodded. "Good lad. I agree." He spoke over his shoulder, hoping that Seymour was listening. "Pass the word, David. We shall be attacking in line abreast. Gun action." He heard Seymour move away, and added for the bridge's benefit, "Jerry is stalking his kill, he'll not expect a kick up the backside!"

The deck lifted sluggishly, as the combined wakes of the enemy vessels reached his flotilla, a miniature tidal wave. So they were well past now. He said, "Steer northeast. Maximum revs."

He craned forward, to catch the last of the sound from the enemy's engines. Feet shuffled behind him, he held out his hand and felt the leading signalman place the microphone firmly in his palm. Like a surgeon receiving the vital instruments, he thought vaguely.

He glanced at Dundas. "Start up!"

He snapped down the button. "*Parthian! Nuts* ahead! Line abreast to starboard! *Tally-ho!*"

The motors roared into life, and he heard the responding thunder from the other boats as they surged forward, swinging steeply from line astern to form up abeam of their leader.

Devane clutched the voicepipes for support, feeling the wind in his face as the torn spindrift came back from the bows like ragged arrows. Everything was shaking and rattling wildly, and he could sense the wildness around him like a rising madness.

Faster, faster. The clouds blinked in reflected flashes, and Devane saw a combined web of scarlet tracer arching from the E-boats towards their quarry. Fires leaped seemingly out of the sea itself as one, then two hidden vessels erupted into flames, spilling blazing fuel into the night like molten metal.

Devane ignored the quick intakes of breath, his mind concentrated on the dancing reflections, against which the E-boats stood out as starkly as if it were daylight. "*Open fire!*" he shouted.

Carroll yelled, "W/T signal from the Russkies, sir! 'Require assistance!' "

"Right on cue!"

Devane watched the two boats to starboard as they opened up on the wedgelike shapes ahead. If he had obeyed Orel's orders, the Russians would all have been dead before the MTBs could reach them.

The bridge shook violently as the six-pounder cracked out for the first time, joined immediately by the machineguns.

There were four large E-boats, and the one on Devane's port bow was weaving from side to side as if already out of control. One of her consorts was faring even worse, her low bridge and afterdeck spurting sparks and smoke.

Devane ducked as the weaving E-boat exploded with one tremendous flash. Pieces rained out of the sky, and feathers of spray shot up alongside as some of the fragments bracketed the MTB like gunfire. She must have been carrying mines.

The two unscathed E-boats were already coming about, firing blindly, their accuracy hampered by the drifting smoke.

Devane watched a line of tracer balls rising very slowly until they reached their final curve, and swept down towards him like comets. He heard metal hit metal and a man cry out as something smashed into the hull below the port torpedo tube.

The third MTB, Red Mackay's, roared out of the smoke, every gun firing, as one of the German boats presented her undefended side for just two precious minutes. Fragments flew from the E-boat and tracer shells rippled along her hull, crossing with those from Devane's boat in a tornado of steel and high explosive.

"Stand by, depth charges!" Devane clutched the screen to stay on his feet. "Hard a-port!"

The E-boat was still coming through the smoke, burning in several places, but closing the range until their combined speed was nearly sixty knots.

Bullets and shells ripped past the bridge or ricocheted from gun positions as the MTBs leaned over in a dramatic turn to port. From aft Devane vaguely heard shouts, and the clang of depth charges being lobbed across the enemy's bows. At minimum depth setting they exploded almost under the German's stern. The whole powerful hull seemed to leap out of the water, her bows pointing at the clouds. The depth charges had broken her in half and she was already on her way down. Men floundered in the seething bow waves as the MTBs tore past, others lifted their arms and sank out of sight rather than end their lives on those racing screws.

Devane peered abeam as they tore through the smoke. The others were still there, their guns silent as the devastated E-boats fell farther astern. The unscathed one had swung away to disengage, or to pick up survivors from *Parthian*'s murderous attack.

Other vessels loomed to meet them, and he tried to identify Orel's gunboat as they swept through the Russian flotilla and on

36

towards the convoy. There had apparently been four ships, one of which had been an anti-submarine vessel. Surprise, speed and the knowledge that they were being supported by the powerful E-boats had apparently been considered sufficient protection. The patrol vessel was already capsized, and two of the transports were burning or listing so badly they were unlikely to see another day. The one survivor was stern on, heading fast for the invisible shore.

"Half ahead." Devane wiped the sighting bar with his hand and peered at the ship's vague outline. "Stand by with torpedoes!"

He had seen the red blink of gunfire a long way off, but when the shells arrived, preceded by a thin, abbreviated whistle, they were no less of a surprise. A shore battery, probably using RDF to locate their remaining supply ship and pin down her attackers.

Another pair of waterspouts shot up close alongside, and Devane gritted his teeth as splinters punched into the lower hull.

"Fire." The torpedoes leaped from their tubes, the bows lifting slightly as the MTB increased speed again and began to turn away.

"Line astern! Steer southeast!"

Every face on the bridge lit up like waxworks as the torpedoes struck and exploded. A solid wall of flame shot up the vessel's side, picking out tiny details with stark clarity. A lifeboat, hanging in halves from its davits. The ship's scuttles gleaming like eyes in the reflected fires. Then a series of internal explosions changed the hull into an inferno.

Devane turned to watch as his boat speeded away from the smoke which stank of cordite and burning paintwork. "All engines, half ahead. Bunts, keep an eye open for a Russian forming-and-disposal signal. Call up the flotilla, Number One. Check for casualties and damage."

A light blinked across the water, as Seymour climbed back on the bridge. Carroll said, "From the Russians, sir. 'Return to base.'"

"What, Bunts, no please or thank you?"

Devane gripped the screen and tried to calm each muscle in turn. His stomach was screwed into a ball and he felt as if he were going to vomit.

"Very well. Acknowledge." He peered astern at the pall of smoke. "Now let's get the hell out of it." His voice had no strength and he was surprised that nobody turned to stare at him. He said tightly, "Fall out action stations, Number One. I'm going below."

Dundas watched him until he vanished through the little hatch, then he said quietly to Seymour, "Did you see that, David? Here's me, thought I was going to lose my guts back there, and the skipper just shrugs it off." He shook his head admiringly. "The Black Sea or the bloody Antarctic, he's the one for me!"

Pellegrine eased the wheel over and allowed his body to unwind. Nice and smooth, a copybook attack. He heard the clatter of mugs and knew that the kye, that thick, glutinous cocoa, would soon be handed round. It gave a man back his guts.

Able Seaman Irwin, the boatswain's mate, touched his arm. "I'm to relieve you, Swain."

Pellegrine released the wheel and was surprised just how hard he had been gripping it. "Southeast. Watch yer 'elm," he snapped.

He did not care for Irwin very much. A stroppy jack-ashore, always being dragged aboard stoned out of his mind by a shore patrol. But, like the kye, he was familiar, one of the family.

In the small wardroom Devane sat with his head in his hands, and wondered why he had not noticed it was happening to him. He had seen plenty of others go under in the same way. Usually they were hell-bent on destroying the enemy when, like a gun jamming when it was most needed, every muscle seemed to freeze.

He pushed himself away from the table and stared at the opposite bunks. It was like seasickness. In the navy there was no allowance for it. He stood up, jammed on his cap and made himself climb up into the keen air again.

From the W/T cabin, he heard the busy stammer of morse, and from forward he could smell something frying in the galley. Somewhere a man laughed and then began to whistle to himself.

By the time he had regained the bridge Devane was outwardly calm again. He nodded to the men on watch as they sipped their hot cocoa or munched the sandwiches which Dundas had had the sense to arrange before the action. Ordinary, everyday faces. In a London street, or in a crowded barracks, you would never notice any of them, but out here, they were special. They did not deserve to be let down.

He saw Seymour fixing up the ready-use chart table, and said, "Tell me about this book you're writing after the war, David."

Seymour waved his hand across the screen as if to embrace the flotilla. "Well, all this, sir. It's important. It should be written about." He almost blushed. "One day, I mean."

Devane nodded. The flotilla had fought for the first time together and had won. He thought of Kinross's severe features, and what he called his crews. "The Glory Boys". They had come through. Next time it might not be so easy.

LIEUTENANT-COMMANDER RALPH BERESFORD, Royal Navy, son of an admiral, and grandson of another, leaned back in a canvas chair and surveyed the flotilla's commanding officers with quiet amusement. If he had been worried that *Parthian*'s first sortie would go wrong in some way, he did not show it.

The flotilla's return had been managed without incident. Russian aircraft and two escorts had covered their final approach to the base at Tuapse. And damage had been minimal. Only one man had been injured, when he had fallen down a ladder and cut his head.

Orel had lost two vessels, and suffered casualties. Devane had tried to telephone Sorokin's HQ to break the ice, but had received only a polite acknowledgement from some junior aide.

Beresford was saying, "I think that a few more hit and runs on the enemy's coastal supply lines will change things completely. We could use a few extra boats though."

The other officers glanced at one another. Willy Walker, his long legs outstretched, sipped a mug of coffee, the yellow scarf that he always wore in combat still hanging from his neck.

Lieutenant Sydney Horne, a RNR officer like Dundas, commander of *Buzzard*, had been a fisherman with his father before the war. He had joined the navy when he had seen his father's little boat shot to matchwood by a German fighter. He was a broad, outwardly comfortable character, who was good with his men and liked by them in return. Unlike many of his more youthful companions, he was still a real sailor at heart, and found it hard to destroy ships and leave their hands to drown or burn.

Andrew Twiss, commanding officer of *Osprey*, was a real oddity. He had been an actor, although nobody had ever discovered what kind of theatre he had graced before the war. But whatever success he had found or lost, he had certainly discovered it in the navy. Maybe it was what he had always wanted to do, but Devane suspected he was really acting the part of his life. For Twiss was not just a young, hostilities-only lieutenant, he was the *British Naval Officer*. Always smartly turned out, which was almost a crime in coastal forces where battledress and old uniforms prevailed, he moved and spoke like a ghost from Jutland. Whenever they had pulled his leg about it, he had turned a haughty eye on them before claiming, "If we win this war, and with the companions I am doomed to serve alongside it seems unlikely, but *if*, gentlemen, there will be a far greater call for admirals in the acting profession than in the navy. And I shall be there!"

Devane knew Mackay, the Canadian, best. He was one of the warmest, and sometimes one of the most alarming, friends Devane had made. In battle, at close quarters or fanning across a heavily defended convoy with all hell breaking loose, he was like a rock. You never had to look astern to make sure he was covering your flank, he was sure to be there. When they got back from each sortie, his loud voice and grating laugh were equally forceful.

Mackay's first command had been sunk off Tobruk by a dive-bomber. Devane had detached his own boat from a patrol area nearby and gone to search for Mackay and any survivors. With an enemy-occupied coastline rising in the dawn light like a warning, Devane had found them. Six exhausted figures, squatting or clinging to a drifting life-raft, more like corpses than survivors.

Mackay had been one of them, but when the MTB had manoeuvred carefully against the little raft, and some of Devane's men had clambered down the scrambling nets to help them aboard, Mackay had called, "Not yet, John!" Sitting there on the raft, a seaman, no more than a boy, was dying slowly across his lap.

It had probably lasted minutes, but to the onlookers it had felt like hours. When it was over, Mackay had climbed aboard, refusing helping hands, saying nothing until he had joined Devane on the bridge. Then he had said bitterly, "His first trip with me."

It had been over a month before Devane had learned that the boy who had died in Mackay's arms was his kid brother.

Mackay was that sort of man.

Devane came out of his thoughts as Beresford said, "It would appear that our stay in the Black Sea may have to be prolonged." There were several groans but he ignored them. "Our chiefs of staff have been in constant contact with the Russians, and it seems likely that the proposed assault on the Crimea will be delayed until the beginning of winter."

Walker exclaimed, "But surely that will be *after* any Allied landings in southern Europe. I thought that the whole point of the Russians attacking when we did was to divide the German defences?"

40

Devane said, "The Russians must think that an assault on the Crimea in the colder weather will give them an advantage?"

Beresford nodded. "Something like that. But if the Germans are still there next spring, you can cross your fingers for a Normandy invasion. And you may as well know," he added, "that this operation will soon be taken over by a senior commander, with the necessary administrative and maintenance staff to support him."

Mackay frowned. "Just as well we weren't all wiped out the other night, the poor devil would have had nothing to command."

Beresford stood up. "That's all, gentlemen. Get some rest and report readiness for sea to your SO." He beckoned Devane to his side. "We're getting a Commander Eustace Barker, by the way. They obviously don't consider I'm senior enough to stand up to Sorokin. Barker will be just right. Not too lowly to invite bullying, nor high enough to excite accusations that we're trying to control this area."

Devane shook his head wearily. "Where are we going now?"

"To see Sorokin."

They found him behind a massive desk, a cheroot in his mouth, signing a procession of papers. He glanced up. "Be seated."

Eventually he sat back and scratched his ample stomach for several seconds. Then he came straight to the point. "Excuse my language, comrades, but I have too much haste for grammar." He looked at Devane. "Commander Orel told me what you did. That you did not obey his orders." He held up a massive hand as Beresford made to speak. "That with your superior speed and weapons you were able to destroy some of the enemy. Correct?"

"I acted as I saw fit, sir."

"Orel lost many comrades. Fifty-one to be perfect." He gave a great sigh, then he opened a desk drawer and took out a bottle of vodka. As an aide appeared with some glasses he added, "Fifty-one, you are thinking, Commander Devane? Not bloody many for a country like ours?" He said it as a joke but his words came out incredibly sad. "Orel has courage, but he lacks knowledge of this manner of warfare. On land Russia is invincible. For every soldier killed by the Nazi dogs, two fill his place. We will go on until our land is rid of them. For ever." He poured three large measures of vodka. "Now we drink a toast to you, Commander Devane, and your men." He held up his glass, like a thimble in his great fist. "And to the knowledge we need so badly!"

The vodka thrust through Devane like a hot bayonet. He began to see Sorokin's position differently. Sorokin was an officer of great experience and reputation. He was big enough to ignore the pitfalls of conflicting beliefs, of pride and jealousy, for one purpose only. To save his country and free it from the invaders.

But by taking such a stand on a short acquaintanceship he had shown his hand. Devane was moved by it, especially as he could guess what it would cost Sorokin if his faith and backing were condemned as misplaced by those more senior.

He could feel Sorokin's eyes boring into him, even as he poured another three glasses of vodka.

Devane said quietly, "I was thinking, sir." He ignored Beresford's warning glance. "It is only an idea, of course. In the past, your flotillas have attacked the enemy's coastal convoys. I think we should attack the E-boat base." He held his breath, wondering why he had deliberately offered his command like a sacrifice.

Sorokin stared at him. "Do you understand what you say?"

Devane found he was on his feet. "Yes. But it has to be soon. Before the enemy guesses what we are doing here."

"Your flotilla, *da*?"

"Well, sir, not exactly. I thought that a combined attack . . ."

Sorokin smiled slowly. It was like a sunrise. "Together."

"Yes, sir."

Sorokin looked at Beresford. "You have given me a tiger, *da*?" He lurched to his feet. "Leave now. I must think."

Before they reached the concrete dock Devane said, "Look, I'm sorry about that, Ralph. I'm not supposed to make suggestions. I didn't mean to interfere with your sphere of operations."

They stopped and looked at each other. Then Beresford said, "It's your neck, so why shouldn't you decide how to break it?" He clapped Devane's shoulder. "Actually, it's not a bad idea. It might bloody well come off, as Sorokin would put it!" He walked away.

Devane crossed to the edge of the concrete jetty and looked down at the five resting hulls, rocking gently in the oily water.

Parthian's future now seemed less certain than ever.

BERESFORD LEANED AGAINST one of the MTB's bunks, careful to keep out of Devane's way as he groped for his uniform.

Devane said, "It's only four in the morning, for God's sake! Couldn't it wait?"

42

Beresford smiled. "No, it can't." He was wide awake and maddeningly indifferent to the way Devane felt.

Devane stood up. "They'll have to see me without a bloody shave!"

They climbed up to the darkened deck, past armed sentries, and into another of the dank concrete corridors which linked Sorokin's command like underground tentacles.

The command bunker was in shadow, with only a central map table and a few figures around it brightly lit by an overhead cluster.

Commander Orel was speaking, but fell silent as the two British officers stepped into the glare.

Sorokin nodded to them. "Have some coffee."

A small man in a white jacket emerged with a tray and a steaming pot of coffee. It was piping hot and strong. Devane felt his tiredness moving away as he noticed that Orel's leather coat was stained with salt, that he was unshaven, with dark rings around his eyes. He looked desperately tired, and yet he was excited, more so than he could conceal.

Sorokin was weary too, his tunic open to his waist, and there were sweat stains on his shirt.

Beresford said evenly, "You remember the four E-boats which you engaged, John? Well, two were sunk, and another was badly holed and has been towed round to Sevastopol. Air reconnaissance think it's a full dockyard job. Now word has come in that the fourth E-boat was also damaged. Did you realize that?"

Devane recalled the zigzagging shapes in the smoke, the crackle of exploding ammunition, and the sheet of fire as one E-boat had been blown apart by his depth charges.

He replied, "Andy Twiss said he *thought* he had hit the fourth one. But it made off so fast he was not certain."

Commander Orel moved to the map table and slid an aerial photograph across so that Devane could see it.

Beresford said, "Russian Intelligence believes that the fourth boat is slipped for repairs. Just enough for her to return to her proper base." His finger touched the photograph. "See? Compare it with a previous picture. It must be camouflage netting. It wasn't there two weeks ago when the last recce was carried out." He added helpfully, "It's a very small island. There are some German troops there and an RDF station. But nothing to excite attention. Until now. Well, what d'you think?"

Devane studied the picture carefully. About the right size. And the fact that the fourth E-boat had not been sighted anywhere else made it possible. He straightened his back. If it was the missing E-boat and they could somehow seize her before she could put to sea, all kinds of possibilities would be presented.

Sorokin said something to Orel and after a moment's hesitation murmured, "Your idea of an attack on the German base, Commander. Would it not be easier if we had at our disposal a . . ." He searched his mind and then added, "A Trojan horse, yes?"

Beresford asked, "What do you think, John? It'll be your pigeon. If you say it's no go, then that's it."

Devane glanced at Orel and could feel the man's anxiety like a consuming force. His patrols must have begun this search immediately after the battle. No wonder he looked dead beat.

"What sort of place is it?" he asked.

Beresford said, "Commander Orel has described it as small and easy to defend. It is part of the minefield complex, but the Germans have laid the field so as not to inconvenience their own minor war vessels. An MTB should be safe enough. Captain Sorokin has suggested a raiding party be landed by submarine to knock out the RDF station. You could move in as soon as the attack gets going. That is, if you feel it's genuine."

Devane rubbed his chin and remembered he had not shaved. "We would need a diversion. The island is thirty miles from the mainland, and a long haul home for us. It will have to be good."

Voices buzzed around the table like trapped bees. Sorokin stared at Devane, his cheroot jutting like a black cannon.

"The admiral has promised support. An attack on the Kerch Straits from Azov. The Germans will think we are trying to force a landing on the Crimea." He turned slightly as Orel whispered across his shoulder, then said, "My Commander Orel insists he is capable of leading the attack."

Devane and Orel looked at one another, like fighters seeking an opening for that first blow. Devane said quietly, "Of that I am quite certain, sir. But, if this is the E-boat we think it is, could he take command?" He saw his words being fed into Orel's mind and then added simply, "Any more than I could control one of your submarines?"

Sorokin nodded heavily. "That is good sense."

Beresford remarked, "It could be costly."

Devane hardly heard him. "I think it's worth a damn good try. To capture one of their new E-boats would be a real bloody nose for Jerry." He nodded, and wondered suddenly if there had ever been any choice. "Yes. We should do it without delay."

"Two more days." Sorokin's great fist slammed down on the photograph. "Then we go!"

It was past dawn when Devane returned to the concealed dock. All five boats were alive with busy figures, the swish of mops and the muted purr of generators.

Dundas greeted him beside the bridge. "Flap on, sir?"

Devane smiled. "Nothing we can't handle, Number One." He saw Dundas relax. It was that easy. "Now, what about some breakfast?"

PARTHIAN'S OFFICERS SAT in the flotilla's newly acquired office and listened while Beresford explained the mission in detail.

Devane listened too, although he had gone over it more times than he could remember, had studied charts and aerial photographs, and examined pictures and silhouettes of German warships in the Black Sea to his brain's bursting point.

He glanced around the concrete office. Even it had changed in the time they had been here. Now, with duty boards and pin-ups, a half-burned German ensign hooked from the sea during the battle, it could have been in any theatre of war. Like all sailors they were settling in, making it like home. Wherever that was.

Beresford looked at their intent faces, their thoughtful expressions, as he said, "The Russian naval forces are making two strikes against the Crimea, one near the Kerch Straits, and another towards Balaklava. A lot will depend on German reactions, and what forces they move in against these strikes. Admiral Kasatonov is keen to cooperate, but he'll not want to pay a heavy price."

He looked at Devane. "It will be much like an Adriatic operation. Move in fast, and pull out before it gets too hot. I'll get the last details and met reports from Sorokin's HQ before you move." He smiled at Devane. "All yours."

Devane stood up. "I'll try not to flannel you. This could be a tough one. The island is no problem but, with two hundred miles there and back, we can expect trouble. To some of you this may seem an unworthy risk, but it is the kind of thing we are here to do. Keep probing and jabbing at the enemy's supply lines and coastal

45

defences, never give him time to rest or increase them. The final battle is a military one, it has to be. But as they call us the navy's infantry, we must play our part beforehand."

Whichever way you looked at it, there seemed to be no end to the fight. He felt a sudden despair as he recalled the night he had spent with Claudia. They had been overtaken by war, and their lives would never be the same again. Whenever he tried to see beyond the year he could find nothing. Just another operation, more risks and less odds in his favour each time.

He cleared his throat, cursing his self-pity. To them he was the leader of the flotilla, code name *Merlin* on the R/T, the man who would get them out of trouble. He said, "We shall put to sea at dusk. Rendezvous with Russian escorts at midnight."

Mackay stood up, his unlit pipe in his mouth. "Are the Russkies coming along with us, sir?"

"A raiding party. Twenty men to be carried in your boat." He silenced the groans. "Another twenty in mine. So tell your people to behave."

They began to leave, folding their notebooks. There was not one of them who looked apprehensive.

DUNDAS SLID INTO the MTB's bridge. "Communications tested, sir. Ready to proceed."

Devane adjusted an old towel around his neck beneath the collar of his waterproof suit. Nearby, the other boats prepared to leave the dock with a minimum of delay. To remain under the twenty feet of solid concrete with the Packard motors spewing out their high-octane fumes was like starting up a car in a sealed garage.

Seymour was on the forecastle with some seamen, waiting to cast off from the jetty. Down in his engine room, Petty Officer Tim Ackland, one-time mechanic at a garage on the Great North Road, watched the gauges and listened to his team tinkering with the machinery which within minutes would deafen him with its roar.

Lounging against the wheel, the coxswain, Petty Officer Pellegrine, tapped the compass with his finger and thought about his wife in Gosport. She had been so much nicer to him on that last leave. Usually she was placid, even dull, which was the way he liked her. She had seemed brighter, and he felt uneasy.

Maybe she was having it off with the local grocer, who seemed to be able to keep her very well supplied, whatever the shortages

46

were supposed to be. He would have to get to the bottom of it.

He came out of his brooding as a duffel-coated figure groped over the gratings to place freshly sharpened pencils in the little slot where the officer of the watch would find them. It was young Metcalf, the bane of the coxswain's life. "Come on, lad, jump about! You're supposed to be aft with Leading Seaman Hanlon!"

Metcalf mumbled something and vanished from the bridge. In the gloom, with his pale features framed in the hood of his coat, he looked like a furtive monk.

He paused on the ladder and watched Dundas talking with the commanding officer. Tears pricked his eyes as he relived the humiliation of being turned down for a commission. He should be on the bridge with them. He came from a good home, and had been at public school. Now all his friends were officers. It was so damned unfair. But he had a firm belief that in a small craft like an MTB he would discover another chance, show beyond doubt that his reversal was only temporary.

Leading Seaman Hanlon, a tough young man from the Liverpool docks, greeted him with, "Wot's up with you, wack? Lost yer bleeding ma?"

Metcalf ignored him and took his place with the others by the guardrails. He almost welcomed Hanlon's constant goading. It acted as a spur as well as a scourge. He would show them soon.

At the opposite end of the boat, his gauntleted fists hanging by his sides, was Leading Seaman Ted Priest, twenty-two years old and from Manchester. He had twice been demoted because of trouble ashore of one kind or another—brawls or women—but in an MTB he was happy and knew he was good at his job.

He was listening with patient boredom to the young two-ringer, Seymour, going on again about the book he was going to write one day. It had already become a bit of a joke on the mess deck. But he wasn't a bad bloke for an officer, Priest decided.

Standing on the gratings behind the screen, Devane heard Carroll whisper, "Lieutenant-Commander Beresford is coming aboard, sir."

Devane nodded and moved to the ladder, wondering what was bringing Beresford here.

He did not have long to wait.

Beresford sat in the wardroom, stale now with its deadlights screwed shut and the air heady with fuel. "You'll have to stand

47

down, John. I've just had a signal. Our new commander is arriving tomorrow. Operations are suspended until further orders."

"That's bloody ridiculous! We're doing what we came for. That signal makes us sound like the Home Fleet!"

Beresford shrugged. "Commander Barker is highly thought of, I'm told. Combined Ops, commando planning and that kind of thing."

Devane barely heard. "You know what the Russians will say, don't you? That we dreamed up this raid in the first place and then dropped them right in it once the plan was fixed." He nodded, satisfied. "I can see you overlooked that."

Beresford snapped, "What I think is hardly the bloody point, is it? I had a signal, and I've told you what it says."

"What's the time of origin?"

"It came in here twenty minutes ago."

Devane shouted up to the hatch, "Number One! See Commander Beresford over the side, will you?"

Beresford exclaimed, "You mad bastard! You're going anyway!"

Devane was halfway up the ladder. "You were too late to warn me. We'll be out of here like a dose of salts!"

Moments later, as Beresford stood beside Buckhurst, the engineer officer, and watched the boats swinging round from the moorings to churn the dock into a cauldron of waves, and smoke, he yelled, "Crazy idiot! Too late with the signal indeed!"

But Buckhurst, hands pressed over his ears as the concrete cavern quivered in the din of engines, did not hear him.

Beresford watched the last of the five boats vanish into the outer darkness of the dockyard and said resignedly, "Not that it would have made any difference. Not to him."

Attack

Devane levelled his glasses over the screen and watched the endless ranks of choppy whitecaps. The wind had risen quite suddenly from the west and the cloud had thinned considerably. Mackay's boat was steaming parallel some half-cable abeam, with Horne, Walker and Twiss following astern.

He moved to the after part of the bridge. It was mid-afternoon, the first full day at sea. They had sighted nothing all day. Sorokin's patrols had done their work well and, no matter what was happening closer to the land, the five MTBs were left to their own devices.

He saw the Russian assault troops muffled to the eyebrows in their padded uniforms. In spite of the crowded conditions in the boat, they had managed to remain entirely separate from the sailors. But there was nothing reserved about Commander Orel, who was in his element. He had spent hours creeping through the hull, and had fired question after question at Dundas until his interpreter had all but dried up. He repeatedly examined his maps, and Devane had noticed that he compared them with the chart on the table. He certainly took nothing for granted.

Devane glanced at his watch. Orel's people would begin their attack at 1700 hours. It would soon be time for another alteration of course. One more leg to take the boats northwards to the small island where it was hoped the damaged E-boat was still in hiding. "Take over, Number One." Devane walked to the ladder. "I'm going below for a few moments."

All at once he needed to get away from the frail atmosphere, the delicate balance between cooperation and downright hostility. In the deserted wardroom he sat against the vibrating bulkhead and listened to the swish of water past the hull. He went over it again, detail by detail. Plan of approach, observation, method, conclusion, *attack*. Just like the bloody tactical school.

He let out his breath slowly. It was really getting him down. Ashore, he was always frightened they were going to give him a job on the base. And at sea, he could only think of getting over the operation, putting it behind him with all the others.

The voicepipe shrilled and Devane snapped, "Yes?"

It was Dundas. "Time to alter course." There was a pause. "Everything all right, sir?"

"I'll come up." Devane sighed. "Everything's fine. And thanks."

On the bridge Dundas snapped down the voicepipe cover and climbed up beside the wheel. Thanks for what, he wondered? Soon he heard Devane behind him, the shuffling of feet as the Russians and the watchkeepers moved round in a crowded dance to let him through. Dundas saw that he looked calm and unruffled.

Over his shoulders Devane called to the interpreter, "Tell them to stop worrying, will you? It's a piece of cake." He grinned at Dundas. "Let's see what he makes of *that*."

But Seymour, who had nothing to do until the flotilla went to action stations, saw that Devane's hand was gripped so tightly around a voicepipe that the knuckles were white against the tanned skin, as if it was taking all his strength to hold him there.

Seymour looked away. It was like stumbling on a friend's secret.

Devane said, "Starboard twenty, Swain. Steer north by west."

Carroll's lamp clacked in time with his words, bringing the MTBs round together onto the new course.

They were committed. From this moment it was all a matter of timing and faultless execution. Right now, as Sorokin's ships were bombarding enemy positions along the Crimea, and fighter-bombers played havoc with ground positions, a submarine would be surfacing to put the first raiding party on the island. It was a backwater as far as the Black Sea battleground was concerned, but in a few hours it would become a small part of history.

Devane dragged his hand from the voicepipe and massaged his fingers. He saw Seymour watching him and made another effort. It would soon be over. "Action stations, Number One. Go round yourself. Keep them on top line."

Seymour relaxed as the alarm jangled through the boat. It was not good to steal another's secret.

"GO TO THE CHARTROOM and check those calculations, Number One." Devane wedged his elbows against the screen and trained his glasses beyond the port bow. It was supposed to be dusk, but the sea was already dark and vaguely menacing.

Dundas replied quietly, "They seem all right, sir. I checked them just now—"

"Do it again!"

Devane could feel the lieutenant's resentment as he groped his way to the ladder. But it was all taking far too long, and the sickening motion created by the boat's dead-slow progress for the past hour did not help.

Seymour said, "Zero hour, sir."

Devane moved his glasses another few inches. The little island was right there, blocking their path, or should be. It was unfair to take it out on Dundas. He was a damn good navigator.

Dundas returned. "It's dead ahead, sir. Four miles." He waited, expecting an outburst. "Commander Orel knows the place well, and his notes on the chart were a great help."

"Good." Devane lowered his glasses and rubbed his eyes. "The raiding party should be ashore by now."

He turned towards Orel, and then blinked as the Russian's features, the upper bridge and flapping ensign were suddenly illuminated by a vivid red glare. For a split second he thought that an enemy patrol had pinned them down with a star shell, or that some coastal battery had been tracking them with detection devices. But then came the explosion, crashing out of the glow like a thunderclap, and Devane knew it was something else.

The Russian interpreter was already explaining, but Devane said abruptly, "The Russian submarine. She's hit a mine."

As if a great hand had come out of the shadows to extinguish the glare, the sea became dark again. Voices murmured and flowed down either sidedeck as Seymour tried to restore order.

One thing, it was a quick death. Immediate. Like the bomb had been for those people in the pub. Either the submarine had lost her bearings in the minefield or she had struck a drifter. Either way, it did not make much difference now.

Provided the Russians had kept to their timetable, the raiding party would be ashore. The only thing which was not according to plan was that the whole island would be on the alert.

He snatched up the microphone. "*Parthian*, this is *Merlin*. We're going in! Start the attack!"

He glanced at Pellegrine. "Full ahead all engines!"

The bows rose several feet as the MTB leaped forward with a roar of motors. But surprisingly it broke the tension, the sudden anxiety that the explosion had thrown at them.

"Here comes the welcome!"

Red balls of tracer lifted as if from the sea and winged far abeam, and Devane thought he heard the heavier bark of artillery. But no telltale waterspouts shot upwards, and the tracer too stopped almost immediately.

Leading Signalman Carroll shouted, "There's the signal, sir!"

Devane nodded and watched the drifting flares. The Russian raiding party might still be wondering what was happening, or if they would ever be rescued now that their submarine had taken a last dive. But they had fired the flares, and would not have much longer to wait before they knew they were not alone.

Boots scraped on deck, and Devane heard shouted commands as the Russians crowded forward, weapons at the ready. Orel was

51

standing beside the coxswain, peering forward with one hand resting on Pellegrine's shoulder. They were rushing headlong into shadow, and only Orel really knew what this place was like.

"All engines half ahead! Starboard fifteen! Steady!" Devane gripped the rail beneath the screen for support as the deck tilted over. "Stand by to open fire!"

A solitary bullet thudded into the hull, and Devane found time to wonder who the marksman was. A startled sentry, most likely. On a tiny island, well clear of the war's main thoroughfare, the sight of five MTBs rushing out of the gloom straight for the solitary inlet would be enough to terrify anyone.

"Grenades exploding to port, sir."

But spray lancing over the flared bows hid the explosions. Devane saw a few dull flashes and imagined he heard the impartial stammer of automatic fire. Men were fighting out there. Hated enemies, with no quarter at the end of it.

Tracer flashed diagonally across the MTBs' approach and churned the sea into froth.

"Flares!" Devane shouted, and the anchorage leaped into stark outline beneath the drifting lights. It all seemed much smaller now, with no room for error or panic.

Devane winced as metal shrieked out of the gloom and ricocheted from the bridge. "Slow ahead all engines!"

He pounded the rail until the pain steadied his racing nerves. There it was. Pale, wedge-shaped and blurred in the dangling camouflage nets.

More tracer ripped past the bridge and then hammered the hull like massive boots.

Without realizing he was shouting, Devane called, "The bastards are on to us! Open fire! Knock that gun out!"

The bridge shook as the twin machineguns on the port side rattled into life, joined by the Oerlikons' sharper note, and then the full onslaught from Walker's boat which was following nose to tail.

Devane looked round for Dundas, but he had already gone to rally his boarding party.

He heard a sharp exchange of light automatic fire, the wild whooping of the Russians as they tensed themselves for the impact.

But the E-boat's cannon had ceased firing, and Devane guessed that its crew had probably been wiped out in the first barrage.

"Easy, Swain! More to starboard!"

Devane saw a dinghy drifting from its moorings, then felt the shudder as it was ground to fragments between the two hulls.

"All engines slow astern!"

There were yells from aft as grapnels were hurled onto the enemy's deck.

One of the seamen holding the spare ammunition belts gave a sharp cry and fell to his knees. He was trying to speak but it sounded as if he was drowning in his own blood. Devane gritted his teeth. *Now*. "All stop!"

As the motors died he heard the other sounds, gunfire and shouts, the stampeding boots of the troops, a grenade or two being hurled at some resistance on the shore. He saw Walker's boat, *Harrier*, edging up to the E-boat's stern, more men with lines and wires jumping down onto her deck like pirates in an Errol Flynn film. Some of them had been fighting with German E-boats for years, but he doubted if any had been as close as this to one before.

Devane watched the feverish preparations to get the E-boat ready for towing. She was big all right. Standing high from the water with her torpedoes and stores removed she looked twice as large as her captors.

He saw Dundas appear on the German's bridge, his gestures, even his expression very clear in the reflected gunfire and flares.

Seymour called, "There goes the second party of soldiers, sir!"

Mackay's boat was already reversing away from some kind of pontoon. Her cargo of soldiers were scampering into the gathering darkness, machineguns raking the shadows as they ran.

Carroll finished preparing his rockets. "I can fire the recall whenever you're ready, sir!"

Devane waved to Walker's boat as she turned crabwise to receive a towline. He saw Walker's yellow scarf waving like a banner. If they could move the E-boat under her own power that would really be something. But it was more likely the Germans had removed all her fuel before attempting any repairs.

Carroll hurried to a voicepipe and then said urgently, "Sir! W/T have a signal. *Most immediate!* Two enemy surface units approaching from northeast. Discontinue operation immediately."

Devane took precious seconds to consider it. Two surface units probably meant destroyers, and there would be more where they came from. He picked up the microphone handset. "*Kestrel*, this is *Merlin*. Do you read me?"

He heard Mackay's harsh voice as if he were here on the bridge. "This is *Kestrel*. Loud and clear".

"Take over, Red. Recall the soldiers and supply covering fire. Tell *Harrier* and *Osprey* to take charge of the tow. Make good use of the darkness. It'll be a long, long day tomorrow." They had all heard the signal and were probably wondering what he might do. "I'm taking *Buzzard* with me, got it?"

Mackay sounded grim. "Roger."

Seymour clung to the bridge ladder. "Are we pulling out, sir?"

"Yes. Cast off from the E-boat. Tell Number One to stay there in charge. You take over from him here." He swung round. "Bunts, call up *Buzzard*. Line astern on me. Fast as he can."

He pictured *Buzzard*'s commanding officer, the dependable ex-fisherman, Sydney Horne. No doubt he was weighing the odds at this moment. Two MTBs against two possible destroyers were hardly favourable.

"All gone forrard and aft, sir!"

"Very well. Slow astern all engines. Fend off forrard." Very carefully the MTB thrust through the drifting fragments of the dinghy. Smoke and vapour from the motors blended with that of explosions, and Devane could smell cordite, like the stench of death.

"All stop."

Carroll reported, "*Buzzard* has acknowledged, sir."

"Hard a-starboard, half ahead all engines. Stay close inshore, Swain, until Commander Orel indicates otherwise."

In the glow of distant gunfire, Devane thought he saw Dundas standing high on the E-boat's bridge, staring after his own boat as she continued to thrash clear of the inlet.

He heard feet dragging on the gratings and knew the dead seaman was being taken below. His name, what was it? Crookshank. That was it. A brief picture of a round, open face. A man he had not had time to know.

Seymour emerged from the chartroom. "Commander Orel says that the course to steer is north thirty-five east, sir. We shall skirt the minefield and keep it on our starboard hand for the next five miles."

"Thank you."

Devane watched the glow astern, the sudden flurry of fire and sparks as the Russian raiders blew up another objective. He looked for Seymour. "Check on damage, David. And ask the chief about fuel levels. Just in case."

As the MTB, with her shadowy consort close astern, settled on the new course, and some of the spare hands cleared away the empty magazines and spent cartridge cases, the Russian interpreter commented gravely, "You have done this kind of work before, I think."

Devane did not know whether to laugh or weep. "A few times." He patted the Russian's arm. "See if you can get me some coffee, there's a good chap."

The lieutenant stared, mystified. "Coffee? Yes."

Pellegrine had heard the Russian's remark and pursed his lips. A few times? My bloody oath!

DEVANE LICKED his lips and tasted the coffee which the Russian lieutenant had managed to obtain from somebody. That was an hour and a half ago. If the report was correct, contact with the two German ships would be soon. All the MTBs had were agility and speed. Surprise was out of the question, the Germans would very likely have radar.

Seymour said, "I've been round the boat, sir. All ready, guns and torpedoes."

"We've got to delay these two, no matter what. Otherwise they'll pick us off one by one. Have you ever fought with a destroyer, David?"

"No, sir."

Devane smiled. "We'll do this one our way. Check the chart and see if there are any navigation buoys hereabouts."

Seymour nodded. "There is, sir. Two miles to the north of this position. It's not in use, of course."

Devane searched his flimsy plan for any traps, then picked up the handset and pressed the switch. "This is *Merlin*. At slow speed, take station on the unused buoy, two miles to the north'rd. Silent routine."

He heard Horne's brief acknowledgement, saw the immediate flurry of white foam from the other boat's screws.

To Seymour he said, "Slow ahead. Direct the cox'n to steer for the buoy."

He felt the boat begin to tremble and respond to the thrust and triple rudders.

"Coming up to the buoy in five minutes, sir."

Devane nodded. Time was passing so swiftly it seemed only seconds ago that he had given his orders. Within minutes both MTBs were lying to on long slip ropes, with the gaunt navigation buoy swaying before their bows like a drunken bishop.

Devane searched the darkness with his glasses. And then . . .

"Sir! Port bow!" The lookout broke off, confused. "Thought I saw a light." He sounded relieved as he added, "*There*, sir!"

Devane steadied himself against the uneven roll of the deck. He had seen it, it was probably a ship's deadlight momentarily unfastened and swinging open to the same motion which was tossing the MTBs about. It was strangely comforting to realize that even the Germans could become careless.

Devane pushed his way across to the voicepipes and waited for the engine room to reply. "Chief? This is the captain. Any second now. Full revs. And hold on to your boots!" He heard Ackland laugh.

"Warn the fo'c's'le party, David. Slip the bowline the moment I sing out!"

The men around him tensed as Devane climbed onto the gratings again and gripped the rail. There it was. Like the sound of a fast car, far away. But it was the roar of fans which drowned even the engines and racing screws as the ship tore through the water. Moving from left to right. A copybook, diagonal attack.

"What the *hell!*"

A burst of red tracer ripped across the sea and vanished in the space of a second. Some fool in Horne's boat had forgotten a safety catch and fired by accident.

It was too late now.

"Slip! Starboard ten! All engines full ahead!"

The other MTB vanished astern in spray and smoke as Ackland threw open his throttles.

Devane held on tightly. A line of low-trajectory tracer tore past the port beam. "Port ten! Steady!"

Two shells exploded together, flinging up great columns of water which seemed to stand for minutes like white spectres before cascading back into the sea.

Splinters whined overhead, and two more guns shot out their scarlet tongues from another angle.

Two pairs. Devane tried to fix the other ship in his mind. "Stand by torpedoes!"

Devane watched the bright tracer plunging towards them, felt the deck tilt as Pellegrine expertly eased the boat in a tight zigzag towards the enemy. Two more shells burst nearby, the water falling across the afterpart with such violence that two seamen were knocked to the deck.

There was no sign of Horne's boat. Devane tried to clear his mind of everything but the patch of shadow beyond the searing light, the enemy's bow wave as he turned and charged towards them like a battering ram.

"Fire!"

The green and red tracers clawed at each other, then knitted together in a tight mesh until they ripped across steel and woodwork alike.

"Torpedoes running, sir!"

Devane yelled, "Hard a-port!"

He screwed his mind into a tight muscle as he tried to count the seconds. Splinters shrieked and clattered everywhere, and he heard a man cry out, a high, desperate sound as the breath was torn from his body.

Missed. They had missed the target with both torpedoes.

The enemy was still turning, and Devane could hear the great thresh of propellers and the roar of fans as she tilted hard over in pursuit.

More waterspouts, more great bangs and cascading spray.

Devane gasped, "Hard a-starboard! We'll try and cut across his stern!"

Another star shell lit the scene with a deadly, icy glare. A machinegun jammed, and Devane heard the seaman cursing as he tried to clear it. Forward of the bridge the six-pounder pivoted on its power-operated mounting, as it fired without a pause.

Carroll yelled, "We're losing way!" The engine room was in trouble. Devane pulled himself across the shaking bridge to seek out the other enemy ship. But there was only one after all. It made him despair to realize that, but for Horne's careless gunner, and this latest setback, they might have won.

Then a towering column of red and orange fire shot up seemingly to the clouds and Devane and his men saw their enemy for the first time. She was still charging in pursuit, but with half of her forecastle and her complete stern blasted away she was already ploughing deeper and deeper, driven down by the thrust of her engines.

In the glare of flames and exploding ammunition Devane saw the small shark's fin of the other MTB's bows far beyond the sinking ship, and knew that Horne had caught their attacker as she had turned for the kill.

Devane watched the other ship in her death agonies. Orel was watching too, peering into the night until the sea swallowed the broken hull and doused the last of the fires. Did he think it was all worth it, Devane wondered? A destroyer sunk, a submarine mined and lost with all hands, the death of an able seaman named Crookshank.

Carroll said, "*Buzzard*'s calling us up, sir. Do you require assistance?"

Devane gulped at the air as if it was water in a desert. "Assistance, Bunts? I think we *all* need it!"

IT FELT STRANGE to Devane to be idling along at a mere seven knots after the speed and chilling danger of the night. He stared beyond the stained screen. The sea was a darker blue and the sky devoid of cloud. From horizon to horizon there was nothing.

He listened to the occasional thump of hammers as the hands below deck dealt with another splinter hole in the hull's fabric. From aft and the engine-room hatch he heard the clatter of metal as Ackland and his men continued with their repairs.

Ackland had been forced to stop the port screw altogether. The shaft was damaged and to force more use from it might put it out of action for good.

Devane recalled the moment when dawn had opened up the sea around them. His feelings as he had ordered Red Mackay to take the rest of the flotilla and their captured E-boat back to base. As the senior officer of the flotilla it was arguable that he should have moved to another boat and left Seymour to cope as best he could. Now as the boat moved sluggishly over the dark water he was glad he had stayed behind.

Merlin had taken enough. One man killed outright, and another, a young stoker, clinging to life by a thread, had made a deep impact on their small company.

They had expected to be pounced upon as soon as it was full daylight. But now it was close on noon, and still nothing had happened. Just the painful progress, the boat steering almost crabwise in the water.

Seymour appeared on the bridge. "Stoker Duff's in a bad way, sir. Left thigh shot through. Tracer too."

Devane nodded, his eyes on the man at the wheel. Pellegrine was below with the wounded stoker. The coxswain was remarkable in many ways. His instincts about danger and the position of movements of an enemy in total darkness were uncanny. Now he was acting as ship's doctor, and doubtless he was good at that also.

Seymour appeared on the bridge. He removed his cap and pushed his fair hair from his forehead. "What about the flotilla, sir? Do you think they're home and dry yet?"

"Depends on their speed. Whether they've had additional help from Ivan. With Red Mackay making all the running, I'd say they've a better chance than most."

Leading Signalman Carroll moved up beside the helmsman. "I'll take over, Jimmy. You get some char."

Seymour nodded as the helmsman glanced at him seeking confirmation.

Devane looked at the sea as it slid slowly down the hull. They were a good team, he thought. Trusted and trusting.

He went down to the chartroom and leaned over the table, listening to the hull groaning, the restrained power of the motors.

He picked up the brass dividers and made a few swift calculations on the chart. They had come a long way. Another hour.

Devane jerked upright as a voice yelled from the bridge, "*Aircraft!* Aircraft bearing red four-five! Angle of sight one-five!"

The alarm bells jangled, and Devane ran for the ladder.

Covers were ripped from muzzles still blackened from the night's fighting. Hatches were slammed shut, men groped for ammunition.

Seymour was training his binoculars over the screen. "Two, sir. Look like Ju 88s."

The boatswain's mate said, "All guns closed up, sir."

Devane watched the two black silhouettes, so confident as they banked over and caught the sunlight on their cockpit covers.

He said, "Tell the engine room what's happening and better move the wounded man to the wardroom. He'll have a bit more protection over his head."

Pellegrine cursed as the hull tried to drag the bows off course "Not to bother, sir. He's bought it."

Devane rubbed his eyes and then searched for the two Junkers again. *Bought it*. So easily said. In England there would be another telegram, another heartbreak.

"Here they come." Devane wheeled round. "They'll close from starboard. Stand by all guns!"

The aircraft were wafer-thin above the water as they made a shallow approach towards the slow-moving MTB.

Devane heard cocking levers being pulled and the starboard machinegunner whistling through his teeth as he depressed both barrels to hold the enemy in his crosswires.

"Get up forrard, David, and supervise the six-pounder crew."

Their eyes met. Seymour did not need to be told why. Devane was sending him from the bridge in case the whole bunch of them were wiped out, leaving the boat without an officer or a coxswain.

Devane studied the oncoming aircraft. Coming out of the sun, as they always did, and accelerating. He held his breath as the cannon and machineguns stabbed out from the leader. Shells and bullets flailed the sea like whips, steel whimpered overhead and a great shadow roared above the mast.

"*Open fire!*"

The Oerlikons, already trained to port, sent two lines of tracer searing after the aircraft as it pulled away in a steep climb. Then they swung round again as the second attacker tore towards them.

"Hard a-starboard!"

Painfully the MTB slewed round, the six-pounder hammering violently as if to outpace the machineguns.

"Midships! Port fifteen! Steady!"

Devane had to stop himself from cringing as the Junkers 88 roared overhead. He saw smoke from the enemy's belly, and guessed the six-pounder had found a target. But these planes could take a lot of punishment.

The aircraft were dividing, one climbing slowly, the other turning in a wide circle almost brushing the water. They would come in from bow and beam, dividing the MTB's defences by their varied heights and bearings.

"Here come the bastards!"

Seymour was yelling, "Hold your fire! Easy, easy!" Like a man calming an excited horse.

The guns hammered into life, the tracers streaking away and crisscrossing the aircraft like a vivid web.

60

Splinters cracked and thudded across the hull, and a shell ripped through the flag locker and exploded above the sidedeck. Devane saw Pellegrine tug his battered cap more tightly across his slitted eyes as if to get better control of the wheel.

The second aircraft thundered across the sky, its great wings making it look like a bird of prey about to snatch them from the sea. More bullets and cannon shells ripped across the hull, and Devane saw a hole appear in the gratings within inches of his boot.

"Cease firing!"

He wiped his face with a piece of rag. As the two attackers turned away to prepare for another run, he shouted, "Report damage and casualties! More magazines, lively there!"

He licked his lips. They felt like parchment. Two more attacks like the last one, maybe just one, and they had had it. It was like fighting a tiger with an umbrella.

Carroll said in a hushed voice, "Engine room, sir."

Devane crossed to the voicepipe in two strides. So they were not even to have that last chance, that impossible gesture which had seen the end of so many battles.

"Yes?"

Ackland said, "I can give you fifteen knots, sir." He must have taken Devane's silence for disappointment. "On all three shafts."

Devane dimly heard the rising note of the aircraft as they turned towards the MTB once again. "Thanks, Chief. Bloody well done. And they say there are no more miracles."

Ackland sounded confused. "Sir?"

"Never mind, Chief. Give me all you've got, right now!" He snapped down the cover. "Hard a-starboard, Swain!" He felt the deck rising to the added thrust even as the wheel went over.

The leading Junkers swerved away as the MTB's wake broadened out in a rich white furrow. Fifteen knots was not much compared with nearly forty, but after their slow acceptance of the repeated attacks it felt like a new heart in the boat.

"On the first aircraft! Fire!"

Devane clung to the jerking bridge and watched as every weapon which would bear, even Orel's tommy gun, cracked out in unison.

Maybe the enemy pilot imagined the MTB had been shamming. But Devane had seen that dark line in the plane's belly, the bomb bay doors wide open and about to put an end to the impudent boat once and for all. The MTB's sudden increase of speed must have unnerved the German enough to make him change his approach.

Devane saw a ripple of flashes along the fuselage, the spurts of bright fire from one engine as cannon shells smashed into the exposed belly like a fiery claw. Then the plane exploded, blasted apart by her own bombs. Devane could feel the force of the explosion and its consuming heat until the fragments were scattered across the sea.

The other Junkers came in fast and low, but the attack was at arm's length, with only the machineguns spitting through the drifting pall. A few bullets hit the hull and some whined overhead, then the Junkers altered course away from them.

Leading Signalman Carroll was training his glasses towards the starboard bow and exclaimed huskily, "Here come the cavalry! No wonder the bastards made off!"

Devane could hear the vague throb of aircraft growing stronger and stronger. Sorokin had kept his word. They had made it.

He stared at his hands on the bridge rail, mesmerized by the red streak he had left on the grey paint with his fingers.

Seymour pounded up the ladder but stopped as he saw the shock on Carroll's face. Then he ran across the bridge and caught Devane in his arms as he began to fall.

For a few seconds they stood like statues, while three pairs of Russian fighters screamed overhead in pursuit of the Junkers.

Then Seymour said, "Help me with the captain! He's hit!" He lowered Devane to the gratings. "Bunts, tell W/T to make a signal to base. Require medical assistance."

Pellegrine handed over the wheel, dropped on his knees and opened Devane's jacket before slitting his shirt with his knife.

Seymour said tightly, "Lot of blood, Swain."

Pellegrine's hands were already busy with a dressing. "Yeh. And a lot of *man*, too, wouldn't you say, sir?"

Act of War?

The picture refused to become any clearer. It was like a steamy window. Devane felt sick and dizzy, and he guessed he had been pumped full of morphine on the passage back to base.

Where was he?

A square, low-ceilinged room, blurred and in shadow. Another bed on the far side of the room contained a motionless form, and sudden panic made Devane believe he was in fact dead and looking at himself.

He tried to remember what had happened. But he could recall little, except vague pictures of groping hands, anxious eyes.

A door opened somewhere and a white figure glided past the bed. It was a nurse, her eyes very dark above a kind of mask. She had bright red spots on her apron. Someone else's blood.

Devane moved his head painfully and watched her as she bent over the body on the opposite bed and examined some dressings.

Then she pulled the sheet over the body from head to toe and walked towards Devane, slipping aside her mask as she did so. She had a round, almost Mongolian face, ageless, although Devane guessed she was in her early twenties.

She checked his pulse. The room was so quiet he could hear her breathing, the soft squeak of starch as she bent over to feel his dressings.

"Am I going to live?"

She did not understand a word. She eyed him calmly and then pushed some hair from his forehead. Her hand very soft.

"Thanks." He tried to smile. "We don't understand a bloody word, do we? But I know you're helping me. I'm lucky. Not like the young stoker." His mind was straying. "Not like . . ." He saw her eyes move to the enamel tray with its jars and needles. She was going to put him out again.

Desperately he gripped her wrist and said, "Please, don't do that! I'll be quiet if that's what you want."

She released her wrist impassively then left the room.

Devane lay back. Voices ebbed and flowed beyond the door and he thought he heard some whistling.

Then he looked up and saw Beresford standing beside the bed, and realized he must have fainted or fallen asleep. He could see the other bed was empty and stripped clean.

Beresford smiled. "All right?" He squatted on a chair. "I've spoken to the doc. You'll be up and about in no time."

Devane closed his eyes. "Is it bad?"

"Should have been worse." Beresford reached across to the table and held up a star-shaped piece of metal. "This lump of Krupp steel must have ricocheted off something before it slammed into you. Otherwise . . ." He did not elaborate.

Beresford continued, "And in case you're worrying, the boats got back intact. Three killed, including your two, but otherwise it was a perfect operation. Everybody was hopping with delight!"

Delight. Devane thought of all those who had died in so short a time. Russians, Germans and three of his own.

Beresford said, "Barker's arrived, by the way."

Devane had to grapple with the name for several seconds. Commander Barker. "What does he say?"

Beresford grimaced. "Not much. He's a real book man. He and I are going to get along like a house on fire. I don't think. But the Russians made a big show for him, so maybe he'll settle in." He sounded unconvinced.

"Where *is* this place?"

"This?" Beresford looked round as if seeing the room for the first time. "It's a really cushy billet. Fifty miles from Tuapse. A commandeered farm, now a field hospital for the army."

Outside the door someone coughed, and Beresford stood up.

"Must dash. Can't have your nurse getting stroppy. She'd have me for breakfast!" He became serious again. "Everything's quiet. Red Mackay's half-stripe has been confirmed, so he's driving the flotilla until you return to the fold. Dundas, your Number One, is taking care of *Merlin*, and Ivan is gloating over the captured E-boat." He touched Devane's shoulder. "Take it easy, John. The war will still be there when you come back." Then he was gone.

The nurse entered the room.

"Damn, I forgot to ask him how long I'd been here!"

Devane felt her hands on his dressing again, the hot stab of pain as she disturbed the wound. That star-shaped splinter must have struck him in the back, just above his belt.

The nurse bent over him, her expression intent as she snipped away the bandages with her scissors and with a swift jerk pulled the last piece free. Devane gasped as the pain stabbed through him.

He said thickly, "You've got lovely eyes, did you know that?" He tensed his muscles to withstand the pain. "I know a girl with eyes like yours. Her name's Claudia. We made love, but I think I love her." He added unsteadily, "I don't suppose she even remembers me now. It was just one of those things." His eyes were stinging and he could not understand why. "Like the song you know. Just one of those crazy things."

She lowered him onto his back again and rearranged the sheet.

Devane murmured, "Sorry to be such a bloody nuisance. You must have a hell of a lot to do."

He watched her preparing the hypodermic needle but found that he had no resistance left in him.

She dabbed his arm and took it firmly in her grip, the needle poised like a dart.

Just for a moment she looked at him and smiled. "You are not a *bloody* nuisance, comrade, and my name is Ludmilla."

Devane was smiling as the darkness closed over him once again.

LIEUTENANT-COMMANDER RALPH BERESFORD watched Devane as he lowered himself from the camouflaged staff car and said, "I still think you should have stayed in hospital a bit longer."

Devane grinned. "They needed the bed." It was blinding sunlight, and the hammers inside his skull were worse than any hangover. He turned stiffly and nodded to the two army orderlies. They both beamed at him and then drove back along the pock-marked road.

Beresford said, "Barker's expecting you. He's a captain now, by the way." He made no attempt to hide his dislike. "I checked up on him. He's got quite a record in special operations. A planner, not a doer exactly. A year or so back he organized a raid behind German lines in North Africa. To bag Rommel or one of his top generals."

"I heard rumours about that. It was a shambles, I believe."

"Yes. The Krauts knew what was coming and were well prepared. Our lads were wiped out almost to a man. Including a young commando officer. Barker's son."

Beresford saw Devane's expression and exclaimed, "Don't be sorry for him. *Captain* Eustace Barker is proud of the fact!"

They continued in silence towards the concrete bunkers. Devane felt light-headed. He had been in the field hospital for twenty days. During the past week he had been allowed to take short walks, but by the time he reached Barker's new HQ, he thought he was going to pass out.

Beresford knocked and opened the door.

Captain Eustace Barker was standing against the opposite wall, as if he had been there some time, preparing for this moment. He was short but held himself so erect that he appeared much taller.

"Ah, Devane. You've arrived. Take a chair. No sense in wearing yourself out on the first day, what?"

His eyes were very sharp. Like his voice, sharp and incisive. Devane sat down carefully. "Thank you, sir. They patched me up extremely well."

He felt angry with himself for feeling so uneasy with the spruce little captain, as if he was apologizing for being wounded.

"Quite. Well, it's behind you now. And we've not been idle in your absence." He shot Beresford a quick smile. "Right, Ralph?"

Devane relaxed slightly. It had started. Barker's use of Beresford's name. To separate the regulars from the part-timers. God, he had imagined such stupid barriers had drowned for good at Crete.

Barker had been out of the navy between the wars, axed like so many others in the service cuts. But a navy stretched beyond the limit and officered by hastily trained volunteers had welcomed back the forgotten regulars like a gift from heaven. Some, like Whitcombe, had done very well. But there were others who used their arrogance to cover their own dismay at discovering that the peacetime years had left them too far behind to be of much use.

Beresford said evenly, "*Parthian* is at first-degree readiness, sir, and the captured E-boat is working up satisfactorily. We are sharing the maintenance with Captain Sorokin's staff, of course."

Barker raised one eyebrow. "I don't see why 'of course', Ralph." He sighed. "But then I was not here when the actual decision was made to undertake a raid." His clear eyes fixed on Devane. "A raid which I still consider to have been an unnecessary risk."

Devane said, "It was my decision, sir. The Russians are fighting the same war as ourselves. Any extra losses to the enemy must help all of us, surely? Captain Sorokin has said that the Russians will attack the Crimean peninsula in about four months' time. If the Germans continue to harry their convoys and shoot up their naval forces they'll be in no position to sustain an amphibious landing on the Crimea."

Barker smiled brightly. "Lesson over? Good show. Well, I know your record, naturally. Plenty of *dash*. But experience comes in handy too, especially when dealing with the Reds. I was in Odessa in 1919 and had plenty of chances to see what the damn Bolsheviks were like, and they've not changed, believe me!"

He added, "As it happens, I have been in regular contact with Admiralty and chiefs of staff. I have a mission in mind, and when it is out of the planning stage you will of course be briefed." His clear eyes moved between them. Like glass. "No pointless risks, gentlemen. Everything must be planned to the last degree. It's my way."

He moved to his desk and arranged two sheets of paper until they were exactly in line. Then he said, "There is the matter of Lieutenant-Commander Richie. It was a beastly business, of course. Bad for morale, especially at the beginning of *Parthian.*"

"Captain Whitcombe knows all about it, sir. It was decided—"

"Decisions can be wrong, Ralph. Likewise, they can be reversed. Lieutenant-Commander Richie's position is to be investigated and the true facts of his death will be released after the hearing." He glanced from Beresford to Devane. "You look surprised?"

Devane said, "He was listed as killed in action. His past achievements demand that—"

"*Demand?*" Barker leaned slightly towards him.

Beresford said quickly, "I feel the same, sir. Richie's widow will discover what happened. Is that necessary?"

"She will be told, of course. Their lordships are having her flown out. Under the circumstances it is her right to attend."

Devane heard himself ask, "Where is the inquiry to be, sir?"

"Port Said. Ralph and I will be going, naturally."

Beresford said, "I think Lieutenant-Commander Devane should attend, sir. His assuming command of *Parthian* might call for a few questions at any official hearing."

Barker stared at him. "You think so, Ralph?" He turned to Devane. "You *are* excused from active duty for the present, so I suppose . . ." He nodded. "Very well. Make a signal to that effect. Lieutenant-Commander Mackay will be left in command." He walked around his desk, apparently unwilling to sit down until they had left. "Send in my writer. I have some signals to dictate."

Outside the door Devane leaned against the cool concrete and took several deep breaths.

Beresford peered at him anxiously. "Bad?"

"No, just stunned. Can he really go off and leave *Parthian?*"

Beresford took his arm and they walked down the corridor in silence. Devane asked, "Do you know what the inquiry is about?"

Beresford did not reply directly. "Richie was engaged in the North Sea a year ago. Dropping and picking up agents from Norway. It has something to do with that."

Devane saw Dundas hurrying to meet them, obviously delighted to see him. "You look *fine,* sir!" They stood on the jetty and looked at the moored boats. "I expect we'll be off again soon, sir." It sounded like a question. "I heard from the Russians that the Germans have stopped searching for their E-boat."

"How can they be certain?"

Dundas looked uncomfortable. "Sorry, I thought you'd know. Captain Sorokin had an old motor launch taken to sea and scuttled near to the German minefield. When we took the E-boat there were fifteen Germans on board, if you remember. Sorokin's men made certain they were still aboard when the launch was scuttled, and wearing life jackets. It wouldn't take a genius to discover the corpses were from the E-boat's original crew."

Devane turned away, sickened. The Germans would imagine their E-boat had tried to return to base and had hit a stray mine.

Sorokin had needed to keep a secret. In his war there was only one way to do it.

BERESFORD OPENED the wooden shutters and winced as the sunlight gouged across his face.

"Phew! At least they managed to find us a fairly good billet," he said. "What I know of Port Said, it's like trying to open an oyster with a bus ticket to get a decent room."

Devane lay back in a cane chair and nodded. It was oppressively hot, but at least in the room there was an illusion of coolness.

Through the partly open shutters Beresford could see the masts and funnels which lined the waterfront, could hear the murmur of voices, street-cries and the occasional blast of a car horn. Tuapse and its bomb-shattered dockyard seemed lost in distance and time.

He closed the shutters and lifted a gin bottle, frosted with moisture, from a bucket of ice. Devane watched as he made two pink gins, large ones even by naval standards.

"Cheers!"

Devane moved his body gingerly against the chair. The scar was healing well, but hurt like hell whenever he forgot to guard it against sudden contact.

Beresford said, "Richie's widow is being flown in today. She's got a room at *the* hotel. That's what they call it."

Up to this moment Devane had expected, even hoped, that she would not come. She might not want to. But he was deluding himself, clinging to the impossible dream. As usual.

Beresford closed his eyes and swallowed some more iced gin. "Remember Korvettenkapitän Lincke?"

Devane stared. "Lincke. Of course. Why, has he been killed?"

It was strange how a man's name could become as strong as the man, or a memory. Korvettenkapitän Lincke had first proved his ability in the Channel when in command of an E-boat. As soon as the dust of Dunkirk had settled, his name had begun to appear in intelligence packs, sometimes with blurred newspaper photographs pinned inside for recognition purposes. Shaking hands with Grand Admiral Raeder, or receiving an Iron Cross from Hitler himself, Lincke had lived a charmed life. A survivor like himself.

Inevitably their paths had crossed. Lincke had commanded an Italian naval unit in the Adriatic.

Beresford did not open his eyes. "No, not killed. Intelligence seems pretty sure Lincke's in the Black Sea."

It was very possible. Especially if the German high command had got wind of *Parthian* and its true purpose.

Devane said, "It's too much of a coincidence. Lincke's arrival and Barker's proposed operation."

Beresford looked at him. "I agree. I also discovered that Vice-Admiral Talents, my overall boss, was at Dartmouth with Eustace Barker. I can smell the workings of the Old Pals' Act."

Devane laughed. "I'm glad I'm a simple soul."

"You?" Beresford leaned forward with the bottle. "That'll be the day!" He stood up. "I'm going to find a shower somewhere. Get your head down while you can. We assemble at 0900 tomorrow."

Devane nodded, his mind dulled by the gin. Beresford's disclosure about Lincke did not fool him for a moment. He must face it. Lincke was in the Black Sea for one purpose above all others.

Devane said it aloud. "He's going to get me, if he can."

He poured another gin. He should feel flattered. Maybe Beresford had let it out so casually, to give him a chance to stand down. To plead unfitness due to the stress of constant action.

If they thought that about him, they would have to think again.

WHEN DEVANE ARRIVED at the shabby building where the inquiry was being conducted, he was astonished to see the familiar figure of Captain Whitcombe. God knows why they had brought him here for an inquiry which could have been completed in Whitehall. Nevertheless, he was glad to see him in some strange way.

Whitcombe beamed at him. "You look well, John, damn well. Considering. How is it, by the way?"

Devane answered, "Doesn't hurt much now. I was wondering—"

"Later." Whitcombe took him aside as more officers arrived. "I'm sorry about all this, for Richie's sake, and for his widow's, of course. But my coming out here will help *us* to complete our plans for the Black Sea strategy without attracting too much attention. Mrs. Richie has the right, after the hearing, to claim the body. It's in the military hospital."

Devane looked away. He had imagined Richie was buried at sea. What might it do to her when she was told? To know that Richie was lying in an iced vault while she had made love in a Chelsea hotel.

Whitcombe was watching him worriedly. "Beresford's told you about Lincke. My guess is that he was being sent anyway, as soon as the Germans picked up the news that Richie was on his way. You or Richie would affect Lincke in the same fashion."

"I know." He glanced at the clock above a military policeman's head. "But before we go in, sir, is this inquiry really necessary, even to cover up our future operations? Richie was wrong to shoot himself, but it happens. Brave men should never crack under the strain, but they do." He waved his hand towards the white and khaki uniforms. "This is a farce."

"Cowardice doesn't come into it. Richie was already being investigated, and he knew it."

Devane saw a car carrying a Swedish flag stop outside the building. Two men with neat briefcases got out.

"Take your places, gentlemen."

The doors opened and Devane followed the others into the room. It could have been anywhere, but for the outdated fans and a native servant who was putting out ashtrays on a long trestle table.

The court consisted of an elderly commander, two lieutenant-commanders and a bespectacled lawyer from the Judge Advocate's department. At another table sat Whitcombe and Barker, the latter shining in a suit of white drill. The two Swedish visitors were seated at another table.

The commander at the trestle table surveyed the room at large. "Governed by the same rules of secrecy as before, this court of inquiry is reopened." He nodded to the two Swedes and added, "And may I offer my greetings to our, er, guests."

He went on briskly, "Before we get down to the matter concerned in this inquiry, I have something to announce. This very morning the Allied forces made several successful landings on the island of

70

Sicily. Enemy resistance was overcome and all first objectives taken."

If they could have cheered, Devane knew they would have done so. After all the waiting, the setbacks and losses in four years of war, this was the first step on the long way to victory.

The commander continued, "The evidence in the case of Lieutenant-Commander Donald Jason Richie, Distinguished Service Cross and Bar, Royal Navy Volunteer Reserve, is as follows."

Devane could feel the tension around him.

The commander continued, "Our distinguished guests from the Swedish committee for the investigation of welfare into the conditions of prisoners of war and enemy occupied territories have played no small part in this investigation. On the date stated in my final report, Lieutenant-Commander Richie was employed on a special operation on the Norwegian coast. He was in temporary command of a motor gunboat. Whilst ashore with three of his men, Richie surprised a squad of six German soldiers and three civilians. He took the Germans prisoner, one of his own men having been killed in the brief exchange of fire. It transpired that the three civilians were Norwegians who were being taken into custody for interrogation." He glanced severely around the room. "Richie disarmed his prisoners but made no effort to question either the German soldiers or the civilians. Having ordered his two remaining men to carry their dead companion back to the landing place, he shot all nine men with a machine-pistol."

The quiet words plummeted into the room like grenades. "One of the Norwegians, who was in fact a member of the Resistance, managed to crawl away, and eventually crossed into Sweden for safety. From his evidence, and as a result of more recent investigations, the facts have become fully documented."

Devane heard the murmur of voices flowing around him. He could see it all. Perhaps Richie had already passed the danger point, and the sight of an enemy, flesh and blood at close quarters, had been too much for him. But to disarm them, then gun them down like beasts, had been premeditated.

The commander folded a page on his file and signed it with a flourish. "These are the facts and so shall they be recorded."

He rose and replaced his cap. "The court is dismissed."

Devane stood up, his mind grappling with what he had heard. Richie's name was ruined. He must have known that Barker was on his way to Tuapse and once there would complete the investigation which would destroy him.

Beresford was waiting for him, his eyes hidden behind dark glasses.

Devane asked harshly, "You knew that too, I suppose?"

"Not all of it. Some I guessed."

Captain Whitcombe joined them and grunted, "Let's have a noggin. I need it after that."

Barker walked lightly towards them. "Went pretty well, I thought. No loose ends." He nodded to Devane. "I'll talk with you later." He nodded again. "No loose ends. That's what I like to see."

Devane murmured quietly, "Bastard!"

Whitcombe said uneasily, "I didn't hear that. Oh, damn!" He turned as a lieutenant hurried towards him with something to sign. "Won't keep you."

But Devane was looking across to the other end of the corridor. She stood out like a bright picture, dressed all in white, her dark hair and eyes seeming to accentuate her poise, her defiance.

He saw the lieutenant leave Whitcombe and push through towards her, a book held out as if for an autograph. Whitcombe explained heavily, "That's the release permit for her husband's body."

But Devane did not hear, he was already thrusting past the others. He said, "Hello. It's me."

She swung towards him. "You made me jump. I had no idea . . . ."

He squeezed her arm gently, and guided her towards the door. "Let's get away from here."

As they walked arm in arm along the crowded waterfront, she turned to him and said, "Everyone kept apologizing, as if they were genuinely sorry. Don can't be buried at sea with naval honours because of all this." Her chin lifted with sudden anger. "He really messed it up this time! And I thought it was because I said I was having an affair!"

Devane heard himself ask, "Were you?" He added quickly, "That was unforgivable. Don't say anything."

She answered without hesitation. "You were the affair. I invented it. You were the only friend I ever heard Don praise. That meant he envied you . . ." She looked at him searchingly. "I know it's very wrong. But in a strange way I'm happy. And I am very glad to see you. I hope it shows."

WHITCOMBE PAUSED at the top of the steps as a staff car pulled up for him, and he climbed in.

His thoughts turned to Barker's plan. It was almost foolproof. As safe as any of their crackpot schemes could ever be. He almost wished that he had been able to find a flaw in it before giving the signal to go ahead.

For months the Russian and German naval forces had been playing a cat-and-mouse game. Hitting a convoy here, attacking a shore position there, with the casualties too often outweighing the value of each operation. It was a stalemate, and while it lasted there was no hope of a major military advance on the Eastern Front with the resulting drain of German forces in the west.

A German supply ship lay in a Rumanian port, safe from attack, protected more by a false neutrality than anything with real teeth. The captured E-boat would be able to enter the harbour without difficulty. A suitable diversion elsewhere could make it a knock-out punch. In and out, job done. It made sense.

There was a flaw, but not one strong enough to move the chiefs of staff. Even the PM had given the mission his blessing.

Whitcombe opened a file and frowned at the photograph of a smiling German naval officer. Korvettenkapitän Gerhard Lincke.

If Captain Bloody Barker had thought of the plan, then so too might he.

DEVANE OPENED THE DOOR and stood in the darkness, listening.

The hotel was small and scruffy, and but for the massive movement of servicemen to the new battlefields in Sicily he knew there would have been no accommodation left, even to sit down.

"Where have you been?" Her voice came out of the darkness. "I was worried."

Devane walked to the window and opened a shutter very slightly. It was hard to believe there was a great canal out there, ships and people, a lifeline from one sea to the next.

"It took time. But it's done." He tugged open his shirt. "God, it's so hot."

She said, "Come here. Tell me about it."

He felt his way to the bed and sat down beside her. "I had to see several people." He kept his voice steady. "They've agreed to a burial at the military cemetery tomorrow. I've arranged for the army padre to do it."

Her voice was husky, and for an instant he thought she was crying. "You're good to me, John. I don't know what I'd have done." She reached up and touched his face. "You know that, don't you?"

He saw her dark hair framed by a pillow. Her bare shoulders gave a faint glow, like silk, and he wanted to take her in his arms, to love her and to lose himself in her and tell her everything.

"I know that I love you, Claudia." He bent over and kissed her. "This isn't just a passing thing. Not to me. I want you to accept that. If anything happens, I need to know you understand, even if you can't share all that I feel."

She whispered, "I'm so happy." She pulled him down and kissed him hard, as if she wanted to make each moment last a lifetime.

He said softly, "I shall be leaving tomorrow."

"I see. One night. Like the last time." She clung to his neck, pulling herself up to him. "You must come back, John. I need you so. If only . . ."

The rest was lost as they came together as one.

74

THE ROOM WAS SMALL and square with a tiny window near the ceiling.

Korvettenkapitän Gerhard Lincke lay on his back, fingers interlaced behind his head, as he stared unseeingly at the ceiling and thought of the speech he would make that afternoon to the combined crews of his new command, *Gruppe Seeadler*. Seven boats, some with officers and men new to their elite service. He would probably make the same speech as usual. In Germany and Holland, in France and North Africa, Italy and Greece.

This time it was Russia, but the enemy, like the speech, was the same. The thought made him smile, so that he looked younger than his twenty-eight years.

He threw his legs over the side of the bed and stood up. He wore a white singlet and pale cream trousers. Matched against them, his fair hair and tanned arms and face made him look more like an athlete than a naval officer.

On a small scrubbed table lay a massive folder. It was strange to learn that some of his old enemies from the Channel and Mediterranean were here also. He walked to the table and leafed open the folder. It would be like a clean canvas for him. He had the backing of the grand admiral and of the Führer himself. He would cause resentment, even hatred, but he was used to that. The war would be won. *Must* be won. His recent meeting with Hitler had inspired him beyond belief. Perhaps it was because of the different attitude. His admirals had praised him for his victories at sea, but they respected him as a weapon, whereas Hitler had made him feel like a man, a German officer.

He scanned the neat writing of the admiral's secretary, the comment about the British flotilla leader named Richie. *Dead*. But not in action. That was strange. Perhaps they would soon learn more. When you fought a fast-moving war in little ships you needed to know your opponents far better than details of weapons and endurance.

Lincke never believed in luck or coincidence. He had studied the reports on the unexpected destruction of the torpedo boat escort to the Crimean convoy, the devastating attack launched by British MTBs which were not even supposed to be in the Black Sea.

One surprise was never enough. The same unit had seized a German *schnellboot*, and even though it had broken free, only to be destroyed in their own minefield, it would not stop there.

He examined a newspaper photograph of Lieutenant-Commander John Devane. Not a new name to Lincke. He was one of the reservist officers who had caused so much amusement in Kiel in those first heady days of war and one victory after another.

They should have known better. An island race like the British had always relied on their amateur sailors. Dunkirk proved that.

The door opened, and Max, his orderly, servant and faithful guardian, peered in at him. "They are waiting, sir," he said.

Lincke dressed with care. Korvettenkapitän Gerhard Lincke, holder of the Knight's Cross and Oak Leaves, and three other decorations, leader of the newly formed *Gruppe Seeadler*, was ready.

He frowned at his reflection in the mirror. There had been something missing in the folder. What was it? Devane troubled him. There was some clue or explanation which went beyond their old score.

Max stood aside to let him pass. He had known Lincke for a long time. Often in the past he had imagined he might die for Gerhard Lincke. Now, as he heard the assembled crews stamp to attention to receive their commander, he was quite certain of it.

MOORED TO THE DOCKSIDE, lying apart from the smaller British craft, the captured German E-boat presented a picture of strength and power. A few shaded lights hung from the dripping concrete roof of the pen, so that the E-boat's hull appeared to glow eerily, the effect magnified by her strange interwoven camouflage of dazzle paint, blue and grey, with stark black stripes striking back from her bows like the markings of a tiger.

Commander Felip Orel moved slowly about the deserted bridge, pausing to examine the compass, the torpedo sighting-bar, anything which was of interest but unfamiliar to him.

The two sentries on the jetty were watching him. One British, the other one of his own men. It was past midnight, and in the bunker-like pen it was as silent as a tomb. Just the slap of oily water between the moored hulls, the occasional creak of lines and fenders.

Orel always found it easier to think at moments like these. He considered the operation in the Rumanian port which Captain Sorokin had outlined that afternoon. It made good sense, but if things went against them the whole Russian force could be destroyed and supply routes along the Black Sea coast left unguarded.

He admired Sorokin for several reasons. His ability to keep ahead of the powerful staff in Moscow, and to stand up for his command whenever its achievements were criticized. He could even accept some of the things which his superior thought necessary to the needs of war. Stern-faced, Sorokin's photograph had appeared in many a front-line newspaper, his camouflaged combat coat often smudged with the blood of wounded comrades he had just visited.

Orel had seen him strip off that same coat to reveal an immaculate uniform as he strode, cheroot in hand, into his HQ to share champagne and caviar with his staff. An enigma, a hypocrite, it was hard to decide.

He thought too of the newly arrived British. He had always understood that the British were different from his own people. Spoilt, over confident and arrogant. And yet so far these failings had not shown themselves. But the British captain, Barker, was the exception. He was *exactly* what he had expected.

He slid from the chair and walked to the side of the bridge. She was a superior boat, he decided. With her three great Daimler-Benz diesels she could manage forty-two knots without difficulty, and four torpedoes and powerful twenty- and forty-millimetre cannon put her well ahead of the British boats.

If the enemy had seen right through Sorokin's ruse, they might be ready and waiting. His swarthy face hardened as he pictured the man who commanded the new *Gruppe Seeadler*. A German officer of great ability, but one who thought nothing of shooting hostages or burning a coastal village. Moscow had a complete file on Lincke.

Orel lowered himself from the bridge and walked aft. The Russian sentry stamped to attention and banged his rifle to the ground. The

77

British seaman dragged his heels together and watched Orel pass without interest. He only saluted his own officers anyway, and certainly not at night. He gave a great yawn. Bloody foreigners.

DEVANE LAY ON HIS BACK, his face turned towards the shuttered window, outlined now by the dawn's strengthening light.

He had dreaded this morning more than any he could recall, and yet in some strange way he felt reborn and cleansed.

The girl lay beside him. He felt her stir, her hand sliding across his chest, and was instantly reminded of their discovery, their love which each had believed was only a momentary need.

Now it was too late for doubt, and there was no chance of turning it aside even if they wanted to.

He saw that her eyes were open, watching him, her lips slightly parted and moist in the pale light. He kissed her, knowing that he should go, knowing he would crack if he prolonged the parting.

He whispered into her hair, "I never want to lose you, but . . ."

"No buts, John. We love each other. Come back to me, darling."

He dragged on his drill uniform, then, or so it seemed, he was in the street and walking quickly away from the hotel. But still the pain did not come. With sudden realization Devane understood why. He was no longer alone.

Barker's War

Captain Barker thrust his hands into the pockets of his reefer jacket, the thumbs protruding forward at matching angles, while he regarded the assembled officers.

"The plan of attack is virtually complete, gentlemen." His pale eyes gleamed in the overhead lights. "Our captured E-boat has finally been supplied with torpedoes. The remainder of the necessary equipment will be taken aboard in the next twenty-four hours."

Devane sat to one side of the captain's desk and watched the other officers' reactions. If there was any show of real enthusiasm amongst them it was one of eagerness to get the job done.

They had all seemed genuinely glad to see him back as the flotilla's senior officer, and even Red Mackay had said cheerfully, "Thank God I didn't have to take this lot to sea without you!"

Barker snapped, "It will be a hard one, gentlemen, but I want it to go like a clock! A lot will depend on timing."

Devane glanced at Beresford, who was slumped in another chair with only a tapping foot to show he was awake.

The target was a small Rumanian port called Mandra, some forty miles north of the Bulgarian border. With both countries completely under German control and influence, it was obviously a careful choice.

Barker's voice droned on, lifting only occasionally as he completed a sentence with a sharp snap. "And now the matter of distinguishing marks." He glanced at his watch. "I want all boats to paint on a pendant number forthwith. The time for stealth is over. The enemy will know *Parthian* is here, he will *not* know what we are doing."

Devane found he was clenching and unclenching his fists. Barker was probably right, but why bother at this stage?

Barker was saying, "The senior boat will be number one, of course," He gave a thin smile. "And the rest painted in seniority."

Devane controlled his breathing with an effort. *Number one.* It was like having a target painted on the boat. There was enough to worry about . . . He shook himself angrily. He was overreacting. Counting his past missions and matching them against the growing chances of disaster. He had seen plenty of others do it. He stared hard at the floor between his feet. *Not me. Not now.*

Beresford cleared his throat. "We have invitations from several Russian messes, sir. I thought we might relax the non-fraternization at this stage."

Barker stared at him. "This is a combat flotilla on special operations. Do I have to spell it out? The Reds have no love for us. They need us, which is entirely different in my book."

Beresford nodded and said no more.

Devane guessed that some of the others had been getting onto him about taking leave in the town and accepting invitations to dine with the local forces.

Barker squared his shoulders and looked around their faces.

"Return to your boats and tell your people. But I suggest you keep your pep-talks to a minimum. Some of the ratings seem pretty rebellious from what I've seen of them. Their records suggest they've occupied the detention quarters more than sea-going ships!" He nodded curtly. "Carry on."

The officers left the concrete room and made their various ways back to the jetty. More than one of them paused to study the moored E-boat with her tiger stripes and newly painted eagle insignia.

LIEUTENANT-COMMANDER RALPH BERESFORD leaned on the E-boat's chart table and looked directly at Devane. The hull was throbbing around them, adding to the illusion of a great beast about to be slipped from a leash. It was dusk outside. No more waiting.

"Well, how do you feel, John? Now that it's time to go?"

Devane scribbled another note on his pad and then sat back in the chair. He had been almost continuously in the German boat for two days, trying to get her measure. But she still felt unfamiliar, just as Barker's final plan lacked a sense of reality.

He shrugged. "It'll be better when we get there." He tried to sound convincing for Beresford's sake, and added, "It should be a quiet passage to the enemy coast. If we're spotted we'll have to break off the mission anyway. No sense in stirring up the hornets in advance."

The captured E-boat, code-named *Trojan*, was to enter the enemy-occupied port of Mandra and carry out a single-handed attack on a large supply ship which had been moored there for several months. She was the local German admiral's HQ as well as the repair and mother ship for the E-boat flotillas. She had probably serviced this very craft on arrival in the Black Sea.

It was the kind of operation which if properly executed would put *Parthian* right in the headlines, and the effect on local enemy shipping would resound from one end of the Black Sea to the other.

Only one MTB, *Buzzard*, now with a crimson number 4 painted on her hull, would be escorting the E-boat, to provide covering fire in the withdrawal from Mandra.

Barker had insisted that the E-boat should be crewed by selected officers and ratings from the rest of the flotilla. Horne, *Buzzard's* CO, was to be Devane's second-in-command. He was very competent and experienced, and Devane guessed he had been picked specially just in case he himself should be killed. The third hand was a Canadian named Bill Durston, Mackay's first lieutenant. To share the honour fairly, as Barker had commented.

Pellegrine was to be Devane's coxswain, and Petty Officer Ackland had charge of the E-boat's engine room. The remainder of

the British ratings were mostly engine-room hands, while Barker
had reluctantly conceded that the gunnery should be handled by a
Russian contingent. A total company of thirty-six officers and
ratings, whereas the E-boat's normal complement was twenty-
three.

Devane said, "Provided we can get in without too much bother,
we should be out again before daylight. Ivan can provide air cover
for the home run to base."

The E-boat was equipped with her own powerful cannons, but
the replaced torpedoes, with hasty modifications, were Russian.
Her full cargo of mines were also from the local armaments dump.
What with that and her mixed crew she was one of the freaks of
naval warfare, Devane thought.

Beresford gathered up his papers and prepared to leave. He said
suddenly, "Take care, old son. In the past few days I've come to
believe that Churchill, Stalin and Hitler don't count. This is
Barker's war, and we're not allowed to forget it! So keep your head
down."

Devane took an envelope from his pocket. "If anything goes
wrong, would you send this letter for me?"

Beresford's eyes flickered down to it. "Sure. I'll see she gets it."
With a nod he turned and clattered up the ladder.

Horne and Durston entered immediately. Horne banged his
hands together and said, "My own boat is loaded to the deck beams
with extra fuel. But with me aboard here with you, sir, my number
one'll not dare to lose contact!"

He gave a great guffaw. In spite of all his active service Horne still
looked like a fishing skipper.

Durston grinned. "Red was glad to see the back of me!"

They looked at each other like conspirators, then Devane said,
"Make the signal."

He could hear the Russian lieutenant mustering his gun crews.
He spoke very little English but they all knew what to do.

Pellegrine touched his cap. "All engines standin' by, sir."

Devane smiled at him. "They sound fine."

The signalman called, "Signal acknowledged, sir. 'Proceed when
ready.' "

"Tell *Buzzard* to start up."

Devane walked to the rear of the bridge and watched their
solitary escort vanish momentarily into a cloud of high-octane gas as

she roared into life. Mooring lines snaked aboard, and through the din Devane heard the crews of the other MTBs cheering. He saw Horne waving to his own boat as she turned towards the bunker's mouth, and guessed he was probably more worried about handing over command to his number one than he was about the raid.

Durston had already gone forward and could be heard yelling at the seamen fore and aft as they prepared to cast off the mooring ropes. His warm Canadian voice sounded strangely reassuring.

"Slow astern starboard outer."

Soon the jetty was sliding slowly past. Big and powerful she might be, but the E-boat turned her one hundred and fifteen feet like a London taxi.

Pellegrine murmured, "I can see the markers, sir."

Devane patted his arm. "She's all yours. Slow ahead, port and starboard outer."

Around him men started to relax. Wires and ropes were stowed away and the guardrails stripped to give every gun a full arc of fire. Down in his engine room Ackland was already busy amongst the glistening machinery, oblivious to everything but the care of the three great diesels, which to him at least were beautiful.

Horne crossed the bridge, his broad figure muffled against the evening air in a duffel coat. "We'll be clear of the harbour limits in twenty-five minutes, sir." His eyes lit up briefly as a lamp blinked across from the MTB which was beating round to take station astern.

The signalman said, "From *Buzzard*, sir. 'We are following father.' "

Devane moved away as Horne replied, "Make to them. 'Stay close and learn how it's done.' "

Devane left them to it. They were all professionals here. They only needed him when the attack began. He went below.

Horne watched him climb down from the bridge and waited for Durston to join him on the gratings.

"He seems cool." The Canadian levelled his glasses on a half-submerged wreck as it slid past, a bell-buoy tolling mournfully.

Horne grunted. "Yes. He'll do me. The best."

Durston persisted, "This place we're doing. D'you reckon we'll pull it off?"

Horne glared. "For God's sake, go and rustle up a hot drink. I'll tell you about bloody Mandra when we're back here again!"

The lieutenant strolled away, chuckling.

At the wheel Pellegrine kept his eyes on the will-o'-the-wisp light of the launch which was guiding him out. As always he was weighing up his chances. They had a good team, but the E-boat was different. He pictured the necklace of mines around the decks, the extra drums of fuel, the torpedoes. A floating bomb. One mistake and his wife in Gosport could do what she bloody well liked. He frowned into the shadows. Not if he could help it.

Below in the deserted cabin Devane sat with his legs outstretched, his ear within inches of the bridge telephone. He took out the star-shaped splinter from his pocket and turned it over in his fingers. Then abruptly he stood up and climbed swiftly to the bridge.

Horne was startled to see him reappear so quickly. He said carefully, "I was sorry to hear about Lieutenant-Commander Richie."

"Yes." Devane took out the star-shaped splinter and sent it spinning over the side. "But that's all in the past. There's just us now. Right, Swain?"

Pellegrine showed his teeth. "True, sir. Like all of them other times. Us against the bloody world!"

Devane climbed to the forepart of the bridge and stared beyond the bows. Perhaps Lincke was out there somewhere. In Mandra maybe?

It had to happen one day, so why not there?

He tried to shrug it off. They had nearly lost the desert war because Rommel had become almost super-human in the eyes of the Eighth Army soldiers. If he let Lincke affect him in a similar fashion he could end up losing his life.

Torpedoman Pollard appeared with a steaming fanny of tea. "Char up, gents!"

Pellegrine said, "I thought we'd got shot of you, Geordie!"

Devane took the mug of sweet tea and was suddenly grateful. With men like Pollard and Pellegrine, Horne and Ackland around he had a far stronger weapon than Lincke would ever possess.

HORNE TURNED as he sensed Devane's presence on the bridge.

"About to alter course to south seventy west, sir. Dawn will be up in about fifteen minutes."

"Good." Devane moved to the forepart of the bridge, his legs taking the E-boat's uneven plunge as she pushed across the low ranks of wavelets. No boat designed for speed was expected to enjoy this painful crawl but fifteen knots was economical.

Horne said quietly, "This is the first op I've done where I've set off knowing there's not enough fuel to get me home again. I just hope Captain Barker and the Russians have got a fuelling rendezvous worked out. We'll be down to a cupful of diesel by then."

Devane nodded. They all knew the score.

"We *must* conserve fuel. This time tomorrow we'll be in the thick of it. After that . . ." He shrugged. "We'll manage somehow."

Horne chuckled. "Most of the lads are too sick with the motion to care. As for the Russkies, they seem as happy as sandboys. They know their gunnery too. Just as well."

Devane raised his glasses and moved them carefully from bow to bow. Black horizon, the sea confined to a few pale crests, and a jagged edge of spray from the stem.

He thought of the long, endless day while they had cruised closer and closer to the western end of the Black Sea. The nearer they got, the hazier the plan of attack seemed to become.

The seaman on the wheel stood to one side as Pellegrine appeared yawning and rubbing his eyes. He seemed to sense each alteration of course and trusted nobody but himself to handle it.

The watchkeepers changed, the gun crews checked their magazines. A leading torpedoman appeared from nowhere and began a methodical inspection of the starboard tube. To an onlooker it would appear as if each man had been aboard for years instead of hours.

Then Devane got his first glimpse of the MTB bouncing gracelessly astern. Cracking on speed for the final part of the attack would seem like a relief after this.

Lieutenant Durston lurched onto the bridge and squinted at the brightening sky. "Breakfast's ready," he said brightly.

"*Aircraft*! Bearing red four-five! Moving right to left. Angle of sight two-oh!"

Horne leaped across the bridge. "God!"

Devane raised his glasses. Against a filmy bank of cloud the tiny black dot appeared to be motionless. "Call up *Buzzard*. Tell them—"

"She's seen it, sir."

Horne breathed out fiercely. "Good thinking. If my number one had used a lamp instead of flags I'd have murdered him!"

"Dead slow all engines. Tell the chief what's happening." Devane concentrated on the little dot. Even at this speed their wake could be seen for miles by a vigilant airman.

"Aircraft's altered course, sir. Heading due south."

Durston muttered, "Anti-submarine patrol maybe. Too near land to be German."

It will make no difference, Devane thought grimly. If the plane was Turkish the enemy would hear of their presence just as quickly.

The lookout, crouched over his massive search-binoculars, shifted them slightly on their mounting. "No change, sir," he reported.

"Now what?" Horne did not look directly at Devane.

Devane let the glasses fall to his chest. It was his decision. Press on, or abort now and hope for another chance later on?

A German pilot would fly exactly as this one was doing. He would remain on course, do nothing to show he had seen the two white wakes on the sea below. He would make his signal later.

But suppose it was a Turk? Unskilled in the craft of modern warfare, he might be too curious to stay away. On the other hand . . .

Devane jammed his fist into his pocket. "Disregard. Resume cruising speed in ten minutes. Inform *Buzzard*."

Just like that. It was all it took to make a decision. One which might kill every man aboard within the hour.

He continued with the pretence. "Now about breakfast . . ." He saw them relax and grin at each other.

The skipper's not bothered. No panic. He could almost hear them.

"COURSE NORTH TWENTY WEST, sir." Pellegrine's eyes glowed faintly in the shaded compass light. "Revolutions for eighteen knots."

"Very good." Devane tugged at his jacket. With the steel shutters shut, and all but the observation slits closed around the E-boat's bridge, the air was clammy and oppressive.

Lieutenant Horne stood beside the coxswain, his thick figure rising and falling easily to the motion.

Devane felt the tension around him. The hourly expectation of discovery or an ambush following the sighting of that aircraft had taken a toll of their nerves. But they were less than twenty miles from the inlet and, thank God, they were making better headway now.

Devane said, "Test communications. And post two more lookouts on the upper bridge." He peered round in the gloom. "Interpreter?"

"Here, sir."

"Come and join me. If we have to speak to a patrol, you'd better be ready with the loudhailer."

The interpreter groped from the rear of the wheelhouse, and Devane heard Pellegrine mutter, "Gawd, you again?"

It was Metcalf. Devane had left it to Beresford to select a convincing interpreter, but he had not expected to see the young seaman who had failed to get his commission.

Like most of the hands he was wearing a white sweater, the nearest thing to a German's sea-going gear, without actually wearing the uniform of a dead sailor.

Metcalf gripped the bridge rail and said fiercely, "Ready, sir."

Horne called, "Communications tested and correct, sir. All guns loaded."

Devane peered at his watch. Even that was German. Soon now.

Metcalf whispered, "Will I have to speak, sir?"

"Not likely. There'll be a challenge, and provided the Russkies have got it right, we should be able to flash the correct reply." He tore his mind from the mental picture he had formed of the little port, Mandra. "Feeling all right, Metcalf?"

Metcalf shivered. "Yessir. Fine." It was true. He had never felt better. Even the other seamen had studied him with more respect once they had discovered he could speak German.

Horne yelled, "Port lookout reports a light at red four-five."

Devane snapped, "Alter course. Steer north thirty west."

It would take only minutes to make up for the alteration of course. But to steer straight past the mysterious light would be inviting trouble. It might be an enemy patrol lying offshore.

The rating at the voicepipe said in a hushed tone, "Lookout reports the light again, sir. Low down. Could be a torch."

"Torch?" Devane crossed the bridge and wrenched open one of the steel shutters.

As he levelled his powerful night glasses he heard Horne say, "Fisherman, most likely. Fouled a net."

But whoever it was would probably have a radio and two unlit craft might make him nervous. It was the Turkish aircraft all over again, except now they were an hour from their objective.

86

The rating at the voicepipe said, "Another flash, sir. Fine on the port bow now, sir."

"Slow ahead all engines." And let's hope the MTB is awake and doesn't run up our backside.

"Bunts, get aloft to the searchlight. Train it on the bearing and when I give the word . . ."

The signalman grinned. "On me way, sir."

Devane rested his back against the signal locker. "Warn all guns to stand by." Instinct, some latent warning? "Searchlight!"

The beam cut across the sea like something solid, pinning down the other vessel and transforming her into solid ice.

Horne murmured, "Fishing, right enough!"

"Bloody hell!" Devane jumped to the voicepipes. "Full ahead!"

With her great engines roaring, the E-boat crashed across the water like a battering ram. Devane saw tiny figures mesmerized and unreal in the unwavering beam of light, and a tiny patch of colour beyond the fisherman's battered hull.

A grey tripod mast, the glint of steel. A patrol boat. It was probably a routine search of local Rumanian vessels.

Horne shouted, "Open fire, sir?"

"No!" Devane wheeled round to seize Metcalf's arm. "All set, lad?" The youth nodded jerkily. "Steer round the other side of them, Swain!" He gestured sharply at Horne. "Reduce speed. Twelve knots."

Devane dare not take his eyes from the oncoming boats. One slip now and they could be blown to fragments, or at best crippled.

Devane said, "Call him up, Metcalf. 'What ship?' "

A German E-boat would make a challenge without hesitation. He listened to Metcalf's voice, harsh and distorted in the loudhailer. When he rested his hand on his shoulder he could feel Metcalf's whole body quivering. But it was not fear. He was wildly excited.

Devane said, "Alongside, starboard side to. Warn Lieutenant Durston. Get the fenders ready, we'll grapple if possible."

Pellegrine eased the wheel over so that the fishing boat, with the launch tied alongside, seemed to pivot round on its beam.

Devane said, "Tell W/T to listen for any squawks from Jerry. We'll lob a depth charge under his keel if he tries anything."

Metcalf lowered the loudhailer. "No reply, sir."

He levelled his glasses and watched some German seamen shielding their eyes from the searchlight as they lowered rope fenders over the side. The suddenness, the casual challenge, each had played a vital part. The next three minutes were critical.

A heaving line snaked across the disturbed water and was caught deftly by a German.

"Boarders away!" A whistle shrilled, and even as the E-boat surged alongside the smaller craft the first seamen leaped across the slit of water. A shot cracked out, and the searchlight above the bridge exploded like a hand grenade. Above the throbbing engines Devane heard the Canadian lieutenant's voice, the sudden clatter of automatic fire, then complete silence.

Horne exclaimed thickly, "Both boats taken, sir. The Russkies shot down a few by the look of it. Bastards."

Devane nodded and seized Metcalf's arm again. "Go across and tell Lieutenant Durston to take charge of the patrol boat and follow us in. Disable the fishing boat and leave her. Fast as he can, right?"

Metcalf nodded. "Y-yes, sir."

Devane found he could even smile. "You did well, by the way. Now off you go and keep your head down."

Pellegrine chuckled, "Better watch out, sir. 'E'll 'ave your job!"

Horne came back. "All secure, sir. But I'm afraid Bunts has bought it." They looked up as a thin dark line ran down from the searchlight mounting. In daylight that stain would be red.

"Cast off." Devane strode to the ladder. "I'm going up. See that our flags are hoisted for the final run in."

Horne watched him climb up the short ladder and heard him snap open the voicepipes. He could see it clearly in his mind. Devane outwardly calm, risking his life on the exposed upper bridge to guide his little flotilla through hell if need be. Sharing his position with a dead signalman whose name he had never known.

As the light filtered towards the land to separate sea from sky, shore from shadows, the flags were hoisted to either yard, the white ensign and the blue and white Russian flag.

A searchlight on shore, already feeble in the dawn light, swung across the water and hesitated above the three approaching boats.

From another bearing a lamp blinked out a curt challenge, and just as quickly a reply was flashed by Durston's unexpected command. Devane realized that the signal was different from the one he had been instructed to use. Fate was still watching over him.

He licked his lips, his mouth suddenly like ashes. "Full ahead all engines! Start the attack!"

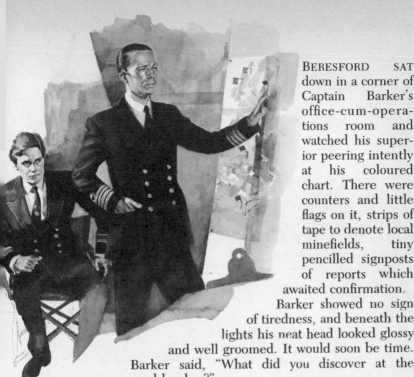

BERESFORD SAT down in a corner of Captain Barker's office-cum-operations room and watched his superior peering intently at his coloured chart. There were counters and little flags on it, strips of tape to denote local minefields, tiny pencilled signposts of reports which awaited confirmation. Barker showed no sign of tiredness, and beneath the lights his neat head looked glossy and well groomed. It would soon be time.

Barker said, "What did you discover at the command bunker?"

"I saw Sorokin and his staff, sir. It all seemed spot on." He added, "*Parthian* has regrouped and Lieutenant-Commander Mackay is taking the four boats on a sweep to the west sector."

"Lieutenant Kimber from Intelligence should be here too."

"I left him with Sorokin, sir. Our link with the Russians, just in case things get a bit hectic later on."

"*Things* will soon change, be assured of that." Barker looked around his little HQ. "I shall have my own staff, communications, intelligence, operations, everything I need. I'm not playing messenger boy for the Reds, believe me!" The telephone jangled and Beresford lifted it swiftly. It was Kimber.

"Everything is quiet, sir. Sorokin has received several reports about the diversions. The Germans are running a convoy towards Sevastopol. They are bound to expect an attack on it. Commander Orel is in charge." He lowered his voice as if others were nearby. "The Germans are using F-lighters unfortunately."

Barker snapped testily, "Is this a private conversation?"

Beresford put down the telephone. "The diversionary attack is under way, sir. But Kimber has discovered that Jerry is using F-lighters." He saw the shutters drop behind Barker's pale eyes and added, "F-lighters are fairly fast and carry heavy armament. They also hump cargo, so they are in fact both convoy *and* escort. Another worrying factor is that they are too shallow draught for a torpedo attack. I've run up against them in the Med."

Barker walked to another wall map. "Well, I *know* that, Ralph. You're not the only one with combat experience!"

Beresford turned away. *You lying bastard. You hadn't a clue!*

The door opened and Kimber entered, his face pale and tired.

Barker glared. "Why are you here?"

"Captain Sorokin thought I should be with you, sir. He will keep us informed." He laid some counters on the chart. "*Parthian*'s approximate position, sir."

Barker leaned over the chart. "What the hell is *Merlin* doing?"

Kimber shifted uncomfortably. "Sorokin requested that a boat be detached to search for the crew of one of their aircraft which has ditched, sir. Lieutenant Dundas in *Merlin* was at the end of the patrol area and so the nearest. I thought—"

Barker said sharply, "You thought, did you? That makes a bloody change around here!" He swung on Beresford. "I instructed Mackay to stay in position, I ordered him to remain in his sector until after the attack on Mandra was completed! Well, did I not?"

Beresford felt a touch of anxiety. Barker was really worried about something. There was sweat on his upper lip.

"You also ordered *Merlin* to patrol on the flotilla's extreme westerly flank, sir. She would be the obvious choice to search for survivors. If you like, I'll go and speak to Sorokin myself—"

"No. I want you here." Surprisingly, he began to hum to himself. "Ring Sorokin's operation staff and find out all you can about enemy movements." He stared at the clock. "Well, Devane will be in position about now." He could not resist adding, "Provided he has not forgotten how to obey orders too!"

Beresford spoke to an officer he had already met at the Russian HQ. He said, "The attack on the German convoy has begun, sir. It seems as if the Germans were expecting it."

"What about *Parthian*? Is Mackay still in his sector?"

"South of the Crimea the weather has closed in a bit, sir. Sea mist, poor visibility."

"I did not ask for a weather report!"

90

"Lieutenant-Commander Mackay has maintained radio silence, sir. As ordered."

"Yes. Yes, I see." Barker's hum rose and fell like a disturbed bee. "Keep that line open. Any news of *Merlin* and . . ." He shut his mouth and returned to the chart table.

Beresford gripped the telephone tightly. It could not be. Surely not even Barker would set up Dundas's boat as the bait for Lincke? He shook himself angrily. He was too tired, too rattled to think clearly. It was ridiculous. He tried again, his eyes moving to the nearest wall map.

German coastal forces *had* to be drawn away from the Rumanian port of Mandra. The Russians had therefore mounted a spirited diversionary attack on a legitimate target. But an old hand like Lincke would be looking further afield, searching for flaws, taking counter-measures, particularly after *Parthian*'s previous success.

Beresford had started to sweat. It was unnerving. Barker had foreseen this and had sent Dundas to the extreme boundary of the so-called safe patrol area. Safe? He must be raving mad.

If Lincke decided to investigate, *Parthian* would be in the vicinity. Beresford could see it exactly. The MTB with the new number 1 painted on her hull would be like a bone to a terrier to Lincke.

But things had gone badly wrong. A plane had ditched, and Dundas had been requested to make a search for its crew. As the Russians were laying on such a massive attack to draw the fire from Devane, it was the least they could do.

Barker snapped, "Anything?"

"No, sir."

Kimber was on the other telephone. "Russian Intelligence reports that the attack on Mandra has begun." His eyes lifted to the clock. "Allowing for the delays, they should almost be clear away by now." Or dead, his voice seemed to suggest.

Beresford watched Barker as he moved another little counter on his chart. He thought of the letter Devane had given him.

Come on, John, fight your way home. Just like the other times. It's not just us who need you now.

The telephone came to life against his ear. "Dundas has picked up faint radio signals. Probably from a life-raft. He passed the information on R/T to a Russian patrol boat before investigating."

Barker stared at him for several seconds. "Good. Fine. Dundas

91

should be able to get a fix on it and return to *Parthian*'s sector without further delay."

Beresford watched the colour returning to Barker's face.

It was true. He had staked out Dundas like a goat for a tiger.

Even Barker could not hide his relief, knowing that Dundas would be within call of *Parthian* once he had found the airmen.

Beresford wanted to hurl the telephone at Barker's complacent, arrogant head. In the end there were no victors. Only survivors.

ONE HUNDRED AND FIFTY MILES west of the cramped bunker where Barker and Beresford waited for news, the motor torpedo boat code-named *Merlin* idled through a swirling maze of mist.

Lieutenant Roddy Dundas crossed the bridge and trained his glasses abeam in a hopeless attempt to find the horizon or the sky. The distress signal was feeble but identifiable as the kind used by airmen in rubber dinghies. But for the eerie mists which passed through the rigging like pieces of torn shrouds they would surely have sighted something by now.

He swore under his breath. The boat felt so different. Like an hotel whose guests have all departed. Able Seaman Irwin, boatswain's mate, was on the wheel, not the redoubtable Pellegrine.

Leading Signalman Carroll murmured, "I reckon we'll see something soon, sir."

Dundas grimaced. "Hope so."

It was comforting to have Carroll anyway. He swung round as Lieutenant Seymour appeared on the bridge.

"I've been all round, Number One." Seymour grinned. "I suppose I should call you 'sir' as you are temporarily in command."

"That's right." Dundas turned away, then added, "Sorry I snapped, David." He felt foolish, idiotic. Seymour had done as much as anyone. There was certainly no cause to take it out on him.

Carroll said, "Sparks reports a strong signal, sir. Same bearing."

Dundas sighed. "Get up forrard, David, with three good hands. Have a scrambling net and a grapnel ready. I'll stop everything when you pass the word." He gave a rueful grin. "Bloody Russians. I just hope they're grateful, that's all!"

Seymour clambered to the deck and walked carefully forward, his feet slipping on the wet deck as the MTB pitched uneasily.

He saw Leading Seaman Priest by the six-pounder. He grinned through the mist. "Net an' fish 'ook ready, sir!"

Seymour clutched the rim of the forward hatch and knelt down, his eyes on the drifting mist.

Priest asked, "D'you think there'll be some mail waitin' when we get back, sir?"

Seymour smiled. "Don't tell me you're in more trouble at home?"

He stiffened as he saw the incredulous expression on Priest's face. When he swung round to follow the seaman's gaze, he felt as if his heart and lungs were being crushed in a vice.

A small breeze had lifted the mist slightly, so that it floated above the water like a canopy. And there, dead ahead, her black and white stripes stark against the sea, was an E-boat.

Apprehension and despair flashed through Seymour's mind, and the chilling understanding that this was no chance meeting in the mist. He was able to record each part of it. The yellow dinghy lashed to the E-boat's side, two dead airmen still dangling towards the water like puppets. The trap which they had sprung.

Something snapped inside him and he twisted round, his mouth shaping the words, the warning, even though it was too late.

Then came the cannon and machinegun fire, crashing into the boat like iron flails; smoke and wood splinters ripping through the air, engulfing Seymour, and hurling him to the deck.

He dimly realized that Priest was running towards the six-pounder, that a seaman was rolling over and over, his clothing smoking and then blazing before he vanished over the side.

Seymour managed to lurch to his feet, agony closing around him as he tried to stagger aft. He heard someone screaming, the sound scraping his skull until he collapsed against the six-pounder's shield and tried to press his hands over his ears.

In those terrible seconds Seymour knew that the screaming was his own, and that he could not shut it out, for both of his hands had gone. Then, mercifully, all sound and pain stopped.

The Bright Face of Danger

Lieutenant Horne exclaimed thickly, "I just don't believe it!" He stared across the port side of the bridge as a spur of land swept abeam. "They must be fast asleep!"

Pellegrine tucked his jaw firmly into the neck of his sweater and concentrated on the shifting patterns beyond the bows where the inlet's sheltered water jostled with the sea. He was not sure what he had been expecting. At the briefing, Beresford had told them about the German supply and HQ ship, *Potsdam,* which had to be destroyed at all costs. She was a cargo liner of some twenty thousand tons which in peaceful times had traded between Hamburg and the South Americas.

As she loomed through the shadows at the far side of the inlet, he could not imagine how she had picked up her moorings without running aground. She was huge, vast like a block of tenements.

He found that he was sweating. The engines were growling confidently at half-speed, the bow wave rolling away towards the shore to port and rocking some sleeping fishing boats to starboard. Surely to God someone would sound the alarm?

He heard Devane say, "Signal Durston to take the lead." His voice grew louder. "Boom ahead. Prepare for some excitement."

That was all. No doubts, no uncertainty.

Pellegrine took a firmer grip on the wheel. To the seaman at his side he said, "If I catch one, take over at the double, got it?"

The man nodded. "What if I get clobbered, Swain?"

"Then we'll both sit on a bleedin' cloud and watch the rest make a potmess of it!"

On the upper bridge Devane watched the German launch sliding ahead, some vague shapes crowded in her open cockpit. Lieutenant Harry Rodger in the MTB had dropped well astern, but for all the interest being shown after their brief exchange of signals they could have gone in line abreast with a band playing, he thought.

Two Russians hurried to the forepart of the bridge and cocked their submachineguns. One of them was using the dead signalman to steady his gun. Devane lifted his glasses and examined the great wall-sided HQ ship. She looked as if she was never intended to move again. Catwalks and derricks, pontoons alongside, even a tug nestling against her fat flank. She was damn big.

"Slow ahead all engines." The enemy would be expecting them to reduce speed about now while the boom was opened. He could see it well in the strengthening light. A long line of buoys, no doubt with anti-torpedo nets strung between them. There was no chance of a submarine getting in. She would hit bottom in no time.

Thank God Durston had managed to seize the local code book before the crew of the German launch could fling it overboard. He saw the blink of a hand lamp, the responding flicker from the ship.

Faintly he heard a clatter of machinery and saw the boom begin to open, a blue light bobbing on the end of the unmoving part.

He said sharply, "Stand by, torpedoes! Signal Durston to remain in the boom entrance. We'll pick him up as we leave."

The blue light was passing them now, they were already through the line of buoys. It was no longer a suggested attack, another crackbrained operation, nor was it next week or the day after tomorrow. It was now!

Devane gripped a stanchion, his eyes watering with concentration as he tried to estimate the exact bearing of the target. Not that he could miss. Provided the Russian torpedoes worked properly . . . .

A searchlight swept across the inlet. It seemed confused until it settled on the launch by the open boom and rebounded to the two fluttering flags above the approaching E-boat.

A single shot echoed flatly around the inlet, and Devane heard the shell hiss almost apologetically above the E-boat. Fired on a fixed bearing, probably because the gun-layer, hauled bodily from his bunk, still did not understand what was happening.

Devane shouted, "All guns, *open fire!*"

His words were drowned by the instant crash and rattle of gunfire. Tracer tore across the water and into moored craft like liquid fire. Smoke, then flames belched from one of the anchored vessels, and Devane saw more tracer, its trajectory almost flat on the water as it cracked past him, burst along the shoreline to add to the confusion. That was Rodger in *Buzzard* doing his stuff.

A launch loomed from beyond the flared bows, and Devane saw light flood from its wheelhouse as figures stumbled on deck, only to be met by the terrifying clatter of machineguns and cannon fire.

A Russian seaman whooped gleefully and poured a burst from his tommy gun into the launch as he thrust past. The lights went out, and the scrambling figures dropped and lay still as the big forty millimetre raked it from aft and turned it into a furnace.

Devane pressed his face to the sighting-bar, knowing that Horne would be copying his every move. Just in case. Steady . . . steady . . . steady now.

Tracer lifted from the shore at long last and shrieked overhead like hornets. Splashes and violent bumps alongside showed that some German gunners were finally alert to what was happening.

"*Fire!*" Devane felt the deck kick slightly, saw the brief splashes beyond the bows.

"Torpedoes running, sir!"

"Hard a-starboard! Revs for twenty knots!"

Vaguely from one corner of his eye Devane saw the British MTB tearing past, the sea boiling aside from her upraised bows like solid snow. A searchlight settled on her, but vanished as one of Rodger's Oerlikons smashed it into oblivion.

The explosions were almost unnoticeable against the roar of the E-boat diesels and the clatter of gunfire. Great white columns of water shot up the *Potsdam's* side, hurling pontoons, small boats, catwalks high into the air. When the torrents cascaded down again the wreckage came too, pockmarking the anchorage with leaping fountains of spray.

Devane felt a shockwave boom across the inlet and lift the deck beneath him.

Fire, smoke and columns of sparks were already rising above the great ship as the MTB curtsied round, fighting with rudders and screws to get clear from the danger. Both of Rodger's torpedoes also exploded on target, the smoke rolling and twisting round a scarlet centre as the devastation continued.

Devane felt steel hacking the deck, saw the Russian gunner

thrown hard against the dead signalman, as bullets hammered across them into the dense smoke.

Another series of explosions burst across the inlet, joined instantly by another, even greater one, as fire reached something vital deep in the *Potsdam*'s hull.

"Dead slow all engines!" Devane had to gasp out the order twice before Pellegrine heard and repeated it. "Stand by to pick up our party from the launch! Incendiary grenade as we pull clear!"

More savage crashes and explosions made the hillside show itself clearly as if it was bright sunlight instead of early dawn. When Devane glanced astern he saw a great black shadow rising through the smoke, like something from a nightmare. Higher and higher, shining now in the reflected flames. He realized it was the bottom and keel of the capsizing ship, whose full length was rocked constantly by internal detonations.

Bullets whined and cracked around him. The second Russian gunner had vanished overboard. Stooping figures ran doubled-over towards the port bow as the launch emerged from a wall of smoke.

"All stop!" Devane pounded the rail. This was the most dangerous moment. Come on, for God's sake. *Shift yourselves*.

He saw Durston clambering up last, ducking as a seaman hurled a grenade into the disabled launch. Splashes too, as its German crew abandoned the craft and started to swim for the shore. Machinegun fire spattered amongst them, from the Russians or some of his own men, Devane could not see.

The grenade exploded prematurely as the launch bobbed clear, burning and crackling fiercely, a solitary corpse sitting in the cockpit as if to await his own cremation.

Devane ducked down as tracer swept across from starboard. Bright green balls, lifting gently and then tearing towards him with frightening speed.

He felt the deck buck and kick, heard someone cry out in agony as the torrent of cannon fire found a target. More tracer slashed out from forward and aft as the Russian gun crews accepted the duel, the vivid reds and greens locking with each other and making the towering pall of smoke glow like a volcano.

Devane shouted, "I'm coming down! Half ahead all engines!" He clambered down the ladder to the deck beside the wheelhouse, wrenched open the door and almost fell into the bridge.

Horne yelled, "Mining party ready, sir!"

A stray bullet whined through a slit in the shutters and ricocheted around the bridge like a maddened hornet. There was hard slapping sound, and a seaman fell dead at Devane's feet.

Devane stepped over him and swept paint chippings and broken glass from the chart table as he peered down at the madly vibrating bearings and figures.

He jabbed the chart with his dividers. "*Here.* Alter course now. Steer north thirty east. Start dropping the mines in ten minutes."

Horne stared at him fixedly, oblivious to the noise and the savage cracks against the hull. "It'll take too long! They'll pin us down as soon as it's daylight!"

Devane replied sharply, "*Do it.* The mines will keep the local shipping held up for weeks." He turned away. "Signal *Buzzard* to take station astern."

The mention of his own boat seemed to steady Horne, and he barked off his orders without further argument.

"Casualties?"

A seaman by the voicepipes, his forehead speckled with red droplets from flying glass, called, "Six, sir. All dead."

A dull boom shivered around the hull as the E-boat headed along her new course. It was the HQ ship finally surrendering to the onslaught of internal explosions. The shallow inlet had helped to contain and expand each one, and half of the waterfront would also be in ruins.

Six dead, the seaman had said. Looking back at the smoke and leaping fires it was a marvel anyone had come through.

At the prescribed position the mines were released over the E-boat's stern at regular intervals. With luck they might bag a German warship or supply vessel, but even if they caught nothing the delays and shortages they would cause would more than make up for it.

"Last one, sir!"

"Very well. Increase to twenty knots." He ducked as a shell screamed over the bridge and burst far out to sea. "Zigzag, Swain. Make that twenty-five knots until *Buzzard* has finished her part."

The MTB carried only a few mines, but they might still bring home a catch or two. The Rumanians' faith in their German landlords would be badly shaken after this, Devane thought grimly.

The deck swayed this way and that as the E-boat turned and forged towards the bright water. The land astern was still blurred, concealed in smoke and a layer of morning mist. But somewhere a coastal battery was wide awake and out for revenge.

Another shell burst to seaward, throwing up a thin column of spray, to be followed almost at once by another. Fired from a slightly different bearing as the German gunnery officer tried to trap the runaway E-boat in crossfire.

"*Buzzard* has increased speed!" Horne gulped as a shell exploded within half a cable of the MTB. But she was already opening her throttles, a smoke container spewing out a dense tail to confuse the artillery spotters. He shouted, "Get the hell out of it, Harry!"

Pellegrine said, "Don't think your number one can 'ear you, sir!" He was actually grinning.

Devane heard a faint whine and pressed himself against the side of the bridge. The explosion seemed to be somewhere else, and for an instant he thought the MTB had received a direct hit.

In the next second he felt himself lifted from his feet, the whole wheelhouse and bridge deck bursting upwards and outwards, flinging bodies about, knocking them senseless, while others groped like blind men as smoke and sparks belched amongst them.

Devane realized his hearing had gone in the explosion, but as it returned he regained his feet, his eyes stinging and burning as he tried to reach the forepart of the bridge. There was smoke and grit everywhere, and the diesels sounded as if they too were in terrible agony, rising and dropping in a succession of roars.

Devane slipped and almost fell on a sprawled body. It was the seaman with the cut face, his staring eyes fixed and angry, while blood pumped between his outflung legs as if it would never stop.

"Must slow down! She'll break up!" Devane was almost sobbing as he gripped the voicepipes and realized for the first time he was alone. There was smoke coming from two of the voicepipes as if it was being forced through by a pump.

"God!" Devane dragged the engine-room telephone from its clip and pressed it to his ear. Nothing. He jabbed one of the communications buttons; it blew the switchboard to fragments.

"Right then, me lads. What's all this then?" It was Pellegrine, his voice slurred like a drunk as he climbed painfully to his feet. He saw the dead seaman and grunted, " 'E was supposed to take over if I copped it!" He peered short-sightedly at Devane. "You OK, sir?"

Devane nodded. To see Pellegrine's brick-red face, to know he

100

was not alone, almost tipped the scales. He answered shakily, "Yes. Near thing. I'm not sure what . . ."

A frail figure came swaying through the smoke. It was Metcalf.

Devane said, "Take the wheel. I'll give you a course—"

Pellegrine blew his nose violently. "Compass 'as burst, sir."

Devane saw the young seaman staring at him, his face white with shock. "Take it anyway, Metcalf. Try to keep the boat from chasing her tail." He turned to Pellegrine before the youth could protest. "Get aft. See what you can do. Fetch help." He winced as another shell exploded brightly on the port beam.

"Where the hell is . . . ? Get going, Swain. Find the chief."

Pellegrine picked up his battered cap. "I'll deal with it. Mr. 'Orne's in a bad way, sir."

Devane picked his way across the broken deck and upended gratings. There were two more dead men. One British, the other Russian. Apparently unmarked, killed by blast or shock, they sat side by side and seemed to watch him as he moved past.

Horne lay in a corner, his leg pinioned by a steel plate. If only the engines would stop. They were coughing and roaring intermittently, shaking the whole hull with each revolution. But the boat was slowing down. Not from Ackland's doing. She was going under.

Horne opened his right eye and blinked. The other side of his face had been torn away. Nothing. Horne whispered, "My boat OK?"

"Fine."

He felt Horne groping for his hand. He must have been hit in the side too. He was bleeding terribly. Dying.

Devane gripped the man's rough hand and squeezed it. "You did bloody well."

Horne looked at him, his voice clear and calm. "It's over, isn't it?"

"We're getting out." He heard feet sliding and crunching through the destruction, Torpedoman Geordie Pollard's voice as he yelled for more hands to come to the bridge. "You just lie still."

Horne's eye watched him gravely. "Over for me, I meant."

Devane shook with uncontrollable sobs.

Horne whispered fiercely, "Take hold, sir. People are coming. If they see you give in, what chance do they have?" He added, "Back there"—he took two painful breaths—"I was the one who nearly cracked up. But you knew, didn't you?"

Devane nodded brokenly.

"Well then."

Lieutenant Durston lunged through the smoke and gasped, "I've told the chief to stop engines, sir. The pumps are bloody useless. We're taking water fast. Did I do right?"

Devane reached out and closed Horne's eye. Then he gently removed his hand from the ex-fisherman's grasp and stood up.

"You did right. Tell the cox'n to muster hands, starboard side. Be prepared for ditching." Another explosion shattered the stillness but it no longer mattered. "Lieutenant Horne has just died."

"God Almighty." Durston stared at the dead man, then at the shattered bridge. "You were damn lucky, sir."

Devane looked at him despairingly, knowing the worst was over. That Horne had saved his sanity. Perhaps it had helped him to die without fear? He replied, "I know that now."

Metcalf called, "*Buzzard's* coming alongside, sir!"

Devane walked to the door and wrenched it back. The gunfire had stopped, and the land was hidden by an endless bank of smoke. But there was an airfield less than twenty miles away. They must not waste time. He glanced at his weary, filthy men, as they watched the MTB surging alongside.

Here was Petty Officer Ackland, soaked in oil, almost unrecognizable until he smiled at Pellegrine, his friend. Devane heard himself say, "Well done, Chief. Did you get all your people out?"

"Didn't lose one, sir." Ackland stared along the pitted, listing deck. "Jerry or not, I'd have liked to get her back to base."

Devane watched the MTB making fast, the busy purpose of the seamen as they carried the wounded sailors to their own boat. He heard steps behind him and somehow knew it was Lieutenant Rodger. Devane said, "She's sinking fast now. No need for a demolition charge." He turned and looked at the lieutenant. "Get us out of here. You're in command now."

He followed Rodger across to the other boat. As the MTB's screws thrashed the sea into lively froth he climbed to the bridge and watched the two hulls, the old enemies, drift apart.

Alone, in spite of the men around him, Metcalf sat on a hatch cover and stared at the E-boat as she dipped further and further, the sea flowing towards her bridge as if moving uphill.

He had been there. On that bridge and at the wheel. The captain had trusted him. Even the grumpy old coxswain.

The MTB gathered speed and headed swiftly away from the land. Astern of her the sea was empty once again.

CAPTAIN BARKER STOOD in his office, smiling. The smile weakened as Devane entered the room with Beresford.

Being here was almost the worst part, Devane thought. Incredibly, the passage back to Tuapse had gone without incident, and even the carefully prepared rendezvous with a force of Russian patrol boats and aircraft had worked like clockwork.

At any other time he would have been jubilant, the success of the operation rising to soften the hurt, the pain of those who had died in battle.

He was so fatigued he felt like dropping, and yet he was afraid of what sleep would bring to torment him. The longest part of the journey back had been right here in Tuapse. The walk from the jetty to this office, past the other MTBs at their moorings, their companies waving and cheering.

Beresford had fallen in step beside him. "Before you see Captain Barker, John," he said, "*Parthian* was out to help with the patrols. Your own boat ran into a Jerry."

They both stopped dead.

"What happened?" Devane gripped his arm fiercely. "Tell me!"

Beresford described the incident with brief clarity. The signal from the ditched airmen, *Merlin*'s search through the sea mist, and the pounce by the E-boat. "It could have been a whole lot worse, John. But a Russian submarine surfaced in the vicinity, quite by accident, with battery trouble, and she whistled up air support. The Jerry raked *Merlin* from bow to stern and then made off like a bat out of hell."

Together they had walked to the small dock where Buckhurst's men were working busily on the dried-out MTB. The signs of the encounter were starkly visible: the splintered mahogany planking, the dark stains where men had been cut down by flying metal. He had stared at the boat as he listened to Beresford's description of the aftermath. Lieutenant David Seymour very badly wounded; a seaman named Nairn missing; the helmsman, Able Seaman Irwin, critically wounded, who had died on the way back to base.

"I must see David," was all he could say as Beresford led him away from the dock. "Did you know he was going to be a writer?"

"Everyone did." Beresford forced a smile.

"No hands, you say. Poor David."

Now, as he stood beneath Barker's glaring lights, he felt bitter and cheated.

Barker said crisply, "Good to see you back! God, the whole place is talking about it. The HQ ship destroyed and at least two warehouses of military equipment blown up as well. I wish to high heaven I had been there to see it! There are strong indications that the German commandant of the base was killed in the raid!"

Devane looked at him emptily. "I'm glad of that." He ignored Beresford's warning glance. "We lost a lot of good men. Lieutenant Horne was one." He wanted to look at the ground but did not dare in case his control broke. "He saved my life, did you know that?"

Barker's smile looked unreal. "How could I? But the job was *done*, and that's the main thing." He rubbed his hands together. "We'll drink to it later on. It's a bit early for me just now."

Devane said, "Not for me. I think I shall probably get very drunk. After I've discovered what happened to *Merlin*, that is."

Barker fiddled with some signals on his desk. "Bad business. But it happens. Two boats meeting. One always has to be the first to act. Pity it wasn't ours."

"It was Lincke. It must have been."

Barker pouted. "Well, we can't be certain."

Beresford said, "I think we can, sir. Russian Intelligence insist he was sighted in the area. On his own too. Unusual."

"Very." If only the tiredness would let go. Devane tried again. "We need more boats. We must have support."

"I've been telling Ralph here the same thing." Barker tried to relax. "A proper staff, minds working as one to—"

They jumped as Devane slammed his hand down on the table. "I said boats, not bloody desk warriors, sir!" He stared at his own hands, grimy with oil, with another man's blood. The dirt of war.

He hurried on without waiting for Barker to recover. "I hear the Germans have got F-lighters now, and probably more E-boats. Well, if they can get reinforcements, and God knows they're fighting on two fronts as it is, surely we can too?"

He moved to a wall chart and stared at it unseeingly. "It was Lincke. It's got his stamp. He's worked it all out for himself!"

Barker said sharply, "The operation at Mandra was a complete success. If indeed Lincke's attack on *Merlin* was planned, it hardly makes up for the destruction of their support base, does it?"

"Lincke won't care. He's out to destroy *Parthian*. It's personal to him. So we must get replacements. Now, if you don't mind, I've things to do. Letters to write, a report to be completed."

He stood in the doorway, the room swaying before his eyes. "More boats, sir. This is only the beginning. Lincke never gives up. I know him like I know myself." He jammed his stained cap on his head. "Well, I don't give up either."

The door slammed and Barker stared at Beresford.

Beresford said quietly, "Let it drop, sir. He's had about all he can take. You can't go on for ever, mission after mission, and still be expected to say 'sir' in the right places."

Barker sounded unconvinced, but he smiled brightly. "Enough said. Get Kimber. I must word my dispatch very carefully."

Beresford walked into the small office used by the flotilla's senior officer. Devane was sitting at the table, his face flat on his forearm. It was the first time Beresford had ever seen him give in like this and he felt strangely moved.

He crossed to his safe, unlocked it, took out a full bottle of Scotch and a glass, and put them on the table. He said softly, "Best medicine in the world. I'm just sorry it's all I can do for you, old son."

Then he closed the door and walked away.

Drifter

The two MTBs drifted about half a cable apart, their weapons like burnished copper in the strange sunset. There was a late breeze, but not enough to break the regular swell into whitecaps.

Devane rested his elbows below the screen and stared at the horizon. Waiting and listening. The deadly game which never ended.

Ever since the raid on the Rumanian anchorage Devane had shifted from one boat to the next in his small flotilla. So that he would get to know his command better, and they him. This was *Harrier*, Lieutenant Willy Walker's boat. His own boat, *Merlin*, was still in dock at Tuapse, and Dundas was with her.

Devane glanced abeam at the other boat as she lifted and dipped in a web of her own phosphorescence. *Buzzard*, with her scarlet number 4 painted on her hull, Harry Rodger in command. Horne had died nearly two months ago. It did not seem possible.

It was now October, and along the Eastern Front the two great armies had stirred, as if each dreaded the merciless grip of ice and slush which the winter would soon bring to them. Dogfights by day, the clouds blinking to artillery duels by night.

But at sea the war was different. Searching for scattered convoys, rounding them up and escorting them to safety. Hunting the enemy's light forces, exchanging rapid fire, then fading into the night even before a kill could be confirmed.

The news of the Allied landings in Italy at Salerno had changed little here. They had become too involved with their own restricted war, and from their isolation had grown a fanatical determination to seek out and destroy the enemy at every opportunity.

They had had successes. F-lighters sunk in a fight which had been at less than twenty yards range. Two heavy transports stalked and torpedoed within a mile of a safe harbour. This boat had shot down a German bomber, Mackay's *Kestrel* had sunk two converted gunboats and a lighter filled with oil.

But each move made by *Parthian* seemed to be matched by Lincke's *Seeadler*. The Germans had become adept at using a single E-boat to cause panic amongst a Russian convoy, then, while the escorts struggled to restore order, Lincke's striped E-boats thundered out of the darkness and painted the sea with fire and livid explosions.

Devane thought of Claudia, as he often did during moments of illusory peace like this. She had written twice to him, and he had written to her, but what was there to tell? She knew better than many what their war was about.

Perhaps she had found someone else? Devane allowed the thought to hurt him again. And why not? A moment of love in some cheap hotel was hardly an offer for a girl like Claudia.

Walker stepped up beside him, his familiar yellow scarf pale against the water abeam.

"All quiet, Willy?"

Walker sucked on an unlit pipe and nodded. "Might get a sniff tonight, sir. Jerry's been pushing storeships into the Crimea. Getting jumpy about Ivan making an attempt to retake the bloody place, I expect."

The enemy-occupied coast was only forty miles away. Soldiers and equipment, airstrips and camouflaged field guns. All facing south and east. Waiting for it. Dreading it.

To the north the German armies were in retreat. Only here, in the Crimea, the hinge of the war, were they holding fast. If the

106

Russian army could force the Kerch Strait and gain a beach-head on the peninsula, the whole front would crumble. But the Russian high command still seemed unwilling to use the Allied successes in Sicily and Italy for that final, necessary pivot. They spoke of waiting for the coming winter to wear down the last German resistance.

Barker's promised expansion had made a modest beginning. A couple of lieutenants for his operations section, another engineer to Buckhurst's department, and some spare ratings for the boats themselves.

As Pellegrine had dourly commented, "All we want is a few Wrens an' it'll be just like bloody 'ome!"

The boats were beginning to feel it—leaks, wear and tear, shortages of spare parts—and Buckhurst was full of complaints and moans. But no more boats had been earmarked for the Black Sea's forgotten war. They were needed elsewhere. In the Med, and in the Channel, too, where they would already be preparing for the big one. The invasion of Northern Europe.

Devane thought suddenly of his visit to the military hospital to see David Seymour. The Russian medical staff had been confident that he would recover. But it had been difficult not to look at the bandages where his hands had once been, not to search for the youthful confidence which he had always shown in the past.

Now he was on his way home. To what?

Devane said, "We'll do a listening watch for a while, then sweep to the nor'west, keeping well south of the enemy minefield. Might bag one of their coastal craft if we're lucky."

After this patrol he would be returning to *Merlin*, and Barker had promised a new officer for him. Devane pushed Barker from his thoughts and added, "Not much visibility tonight, Willy. I think we'll move in now. We can still rendezvous with Red Mackay at the end of his sector."

Walker showed his teeth in a grin. He understood. Impatient to move, frightened of no decision rather than the wrong one.

"I'll pass the word."

Alone again, Devane wiped his night glasses with some tissue, already damp in the cloying air.

Two torpedoes, twenty-two young men, some very young, and the power and grace of a thoroughbred. No wonder they were never short of volunteers.

"Ready, sir."

"Signal *Buzzard* to take station astern of us."

"*Buzzard*'s acknowledged, sir."

Devane felt the seaman next to him stiffen. "Sir! Dead astern!"

Devane pushed past him. How perfectly the other MTB showed her lines, even in this mist. Almost every detail, from her small mast and white ensign to her squat bridge. He could even see the heads of the men behind the low screen.

Between the two boats the sea was like black glass laced with silver, but all Devane saw was the tiny, bobbing dot which lay in direct line with the other boat's stem.

He shouted, "Call up *Buzzard* on R/T!" He swung round as Walker ran to see what was happening. "Tell them there's a drifter dead ahead of them!"

Feet skidded on the wet gratings and Devane heard the sharp exchange between Walker and his telegraphist. And all the while he kept his eyes on the fading little dot.

Walker snapped. "Full ahead! Starboard fifteen! No sense in risking the boat!"

Then came the explosion. One great searing flash with a red centre, and other vague, more distorted sounds as fuel, ammunition and depth charge detonated as one huge bomb.

The explosion was extinguished with terrible suddenness, snuffed out as if the MTB had never existed. For what seemed like endless moments pathetic fragments of wreckage continued to fall in a great circle, and a few tiny flames burned on the sea itself until they, too, vanished.

Harrier cruised round the place where Rodger's first command had hit a drifting mine. But there was not even a life-raft left to mark the place.

Walker looked at Devane. "Return to base, sir?"

"No. We'll rendezvous with *Kestrel* and *Osprey*." He could sense their hurt, their resentment. Hatred even. As if he had killed that MTB himself with his bare hands.

He walked to the forepart of the bridge again. A whole MTB's company wiped out. He found that he was holding his breath, keeping his whole frame tense, until slowly at first, then out of discipline and routine, the others responded to their tasks. *Not your turn. Not yet.*

"Have a mug of kye, sir." It was Walker again, his voice normal.

"Thanks, Willy. A kind thought." He held the hot, steaming mug to his lips and watched the sky over the rim. "Near thing that time, Willy."

Walker nodded dully. "And then there were four."

LIEUTENANT-COMMANDER RED MACKAY, leaning against the dripping wall of the bunker, straightened up as Devane left the operations room.

"Everything OK?"

Devane shrugged, holding back tiredness. "Yes." The fact that Barker had listened to his report of the patrol and the loss of *Buzzard* without any sort of criticism had only just occurred to him.

Mackay fell in step beside him, and together they walked to the little dock. Devane looked down at the repaired *Merlin* and saw Dundas talking to a lanky officer in blue battledress. Seymour's replacement, no doubt.

"I'll leave you then." Mackay rubbed his stubbled chin. "I'm going to take a bath. If I can find one." He blurted out, "They may offer you another command. It's on the cards, it must be. With the landings in Italy, the big flap at home as to when we'll invade France, they'll need experienced leaders as never before."

"What's up, Red? You want my job here?"

Mackay refused to be deflected. "If you stay with *Parthian* we *might* just come through. If you go, and who could blame you with your record, I reckon that bloody Lincke will have us for breakfast." He stuck out his chin. "I've said my piece. Bill Durston, my number one, told me how you held them all together during the Mandra raid. And he's not easily impressed, the big-headed bastard. The fact is, no matter what Captain Barker imagines, we're out of our league here. This is an army war. We're just a necessary nuisance."

Devane nodded. "I've no intention of going, Red. Not unless they order me out."

"That suits me fine." Mackay grinned and strode towards his boat.

Dundas saluted Devane as he walked slowly down the brow. "Good to have you back, sir." He looked as if he had not slept for days. "This is the new third hand, Lieutenant Chalmers."

Chalmers also saluted, the movement stiffly mechanical. He was tall and angular, very tanned, with a hawkish face and a pair of bright blue eyes. At a guess he was about twenty-five.

He said, "Transferred from the base at Alexandria, sir. My last boat bought it during the Sicily invasion."

Dundas said quickly. "He's been in hospital, sir."

Devane held out his hand, "Glad to have you here. What's your first name?"

"David, sir."

The lanky lieutenant had the same name as Seymour. His grip felt hard, like a glove. Without dropping his eyes Devane guessed that Chalmers had been badly burned. Now he was back to be retested.

"Well, David, get to know the boat, then see Lieutenant-Commander Beresford about local operations, right?"

Dundas interrupted. "There's some mail for you, sir. In the wardroom." He fidgeted with his buttons. "Sorry about *Buzzard*."

"Yes. Bloody waste." He nodded to Pellegrine whose brick-red face had just appeared around the side of the bridge. "Hello, Swain, how are things?"

Pellegrine grimaced. " 'Ad a letter from the old woman, sir. If she's not up to somethin' I'll give up me pension, so 'elp me." Then he smiled. "Still, that can wait, eh, sir?"

Devane lowered himself down into the small wardroom. It was clean, and there was a smell of fresh paint everywhere.

He took down the letters from the rack and examined them. Two from his mother, a bill from Gieves and . . . he hesitated as he saw her writing on the last one.

He threw off his waterproof coat and poured himself a glass of brandy. Someone, probably Dundas, had left it ready for him.

His mother would understand, he thought vaguely, and in any case . . . His hand shook as he opened Claudia's letter.

My darling John . . . .

WHEN DUNDAS ENTERED the wardroom half an hour later he found Devane sitting as before, the glass of brandy untouched.

Nothing had gone, everything was as he had dreamed and prayed. She loved him. She had cried when she had received his letters. And there was a lot more, too, which he would read and re-read.

"All right, sir?"

Devane nodded and pushed the bottle across the table. "Join me in a drink, Number One. I'm afraid I'm back to plague you again."

Dundas reached for another glass. "We've all missed you, sir." The glass hovered momentarily in mid-air. "And I'm damned sorry about what happened. To David. To the others."

110

"You'll get over it. You must. Anyway, I've recommended you for a command of your own."

He saw the astonishment and the gratitude in Dundas's eyes and was glad he had told him.

My darling John. Devane swallowed the brandy and felt its warmth. For the first time in many months he was drinking because he wanted to enjoy it. Not because he needed it as a shield against himself. What had Willy Walker said? *And then there were four.*

Well, if necessary, they would be enough.

"WHERE THE HELL are we going?" Devane clung to the door of the army staff car and tried to prepare for each jarring wrench.

Beresford grinned. "To Captain Barker's villa. You've not been before?"

"Never been asked." Devane watched the feeble glow from the shuttered headlights swing past some fallen trees and two lounging sentries. The whole area to the east of Tuapse was in the hands of the army. "What's all this in aid of, Ralph?"

Beresford glanced at the Russian driver and said quietly, "Ivan is going all out for the big push." He spoke more easily as the driver began to hum to himself. "*Parthian* is going to take part." He shot a quick glance at him. "I think Barker's been scheming for something of the sort since he arrived."

Devane accepted the information calmly. Before, he would have been on the edge of his seat. Suspicious, apprehensive, waiting for the bad news. Could her letter do so much for him?

He said, "Another raid, is that it?"

Beresford smiled and lit a cigarette. "Piece of cake to you, John. No bother. You've changed, you know. Maybe you've got your second wind?" When Devane remained silent he added, "Anyway, the Russians will go through Jerry's defences like the proverbial steamroller. But Barker needs us here, if only to put on a show."

Devane thought about it. It would certainly explain Barker's reception after *Buzzard*'s loss. His mind had been elsewhere.

"We can't do much with just the four boats." Devane looked at his companion. "Are we getting reinforcements at long last?"

"Nothing in the pipeline. But then we'll be the last to hear."

The car butted between two collapsed gates and turned into a small courtyard. It was a low-roofed villa, built probably for some party official. Now it was Barker's.

111

"One thing, John." Beresford touched his arm as the car quivered to a halt. "Go easy with Barker. He's been a long time on the beach, remember? He'll do almost anything to help his career." He gave his arm a quick nudge. "D'you follow, old son?"

They climbed out into the darkness. The place smelt of damp and the countryside. But you could still hear the faint murmur of artillery even here.

Devane was not sure what to expect, but as they were guided through two doors and a blackout curtain he was almost blinded by the bright lights and the uniformed figures in the long room.

White-jacketed stewards or Russian orderlies bustled amongst the officers with trays of glasses, and somewhere there was lively music and a clatter of dishes.

Beresford grinned. "Well, well. Most impressive. Here he comes."

Barker was tiny in stature when compared with many of the Russian officers at this gathering. But somehow he seemed to rise above all of them as he strode to meet the two lieutenant-commanders.

"Good show. Right on time." He ran a quick glance over Devane's uniform. "You *could* have worn a bow tie, but still . . ." He swung round as one of his new operations officers whispered to him.

Sorokin stood in the entrance while two orderlies stripped off his shabby coat. As he turned to the lights his dress uniform and medals transformed him into an impressive figure.

He nodded to Barker and took a glass of champagne before saying, "Commander Devane. You did some brave work my staff tells me. Pity you lose a little ship, but . . ." He gave an eloquent shrug.

Barker rocked forward on his toes. Even so, his chin barely reached Sorokin's shoulder. "Which is why I was gratified to hear that your people are almost ready to attack." Barker wanted Sorokin to understand that he was already conversant with the prepared plans, that he was trusted by the chiefs of staff in London.

Sorokin beamed. "I would have told you the full details later, naturally."

Barker's pale eyes flickered, "Naturally."

Beresford said, "The fact is, it's going to take a lot of organization if the Russian army is to cross the Kerch Strait from the mainland to the Crimea. To support such an advance, the army will need

112

constant supplies, unimpeded convoys. Commander Orel's gun-boats and support craft are familiar with those waters of course."

Sorokin's great head swivelled towards him. "You are saying that the Germans will forestall such a landing? That Comrade Orel's forces will not *withstand* the German flotillas?"

Barker said curtly, "Nobody wants your attack to fail, Captain Sorokin. Least of all your Admiral Kasatonov, I imagine."

Devane watched the game pass again to Beresford who said smoothly, "Captain Barker has a plan, sir. A commando raid immediately *before* the main assault across the Kerch Strait." He gave a winning smile. "I hasten to add the men involved would be your own, sir."

Sorokin breathed out slowly. "And what would be the object of this *solitary* deed?"

Barker moved in. "Up to now, *Parthian* has been employed well, but only as an extension of your overall command, so to speak, instead of a single, vital weapon." He gave a slight cough. "Which I am sure your chiefs of staff would agree with mine was the intended object, right?"

Devane took another glass from a tray and listened with amazement. Four MTBs, and Barker was discussing them as if they were a cruiser squadron. But it meant that the Russians must be worried, far more than Sorokin admitted.

Sorokin nodded ponderously. "That has some sense."

Barker rocked back again onto his heels, his hands wedged into his pockets with the thumbs protruding.

"*Parthian* will execute the raid. Four boats, under cover of night and with *certain* help from your patrols, a landing force of a hundred men, and we can cause such disruption behind the German defences it will give your assault every chance of success."

Sorokin's jaw tightened. "Not possible. My people have fought and died, starved and suffered to win back our country and crush the fascists once and for all!"

Barker was impatient. "Orel does not have the right vessels at his disposal. I do." He brushed an invisible speck from his sleeve. "Furthermore, if Korvettenkapitän Lincke, who is not unknown to you, I believe, throws his E-boats amongst your landing craft and supply ships at the moment of attempting to retake the peninsula, your whole campaign may have to be curtailed."

Devane waited for the Russian to explode, but Sorokin merely bit his lip. "*Parthian* will draw Lincke away, is that what you are saying?"

Devane tensed. It was not such a bad plan, provided they could get more MTBs, and that Lincke did not have ideas of his own.

Barker looked sharply at Devane. "My study of Lincke's past behaviour leaves me in no doubt as to his intentions. Lieutenant-Commander Devane has met with him before, and will back me up."

Devane stared at him. He could recall exactly how Barker had scoffed at the remotest possibility of Lincke's vendetta with *Parthian*, and more particularly, with its new senior officer.

"And where is this place you intend to launch your attack?" Sorokin sounded dangerously calm.

"My team is working out the final details with the intelligence people. I cannot say too much." He eyed Sorokin blandly. "Security is everything, as you will appreciate, I'm sure."

Devane put down his glasses. It was incredible. Sorokin had backed down. If Barker's raid failed, the enemy would be roused and ready for a major attack. But if he was refused permission to carry out his plan, the Russians were in worse trouble. Lincke's flotilla and the other small naval units would see to that.

Beresford said almost humbly, "Everything will be done to help your raiding party achieve success, sir. The place we have selected is largely occupied by Russian soldiers who changed sides when the German armies were advancing. I—" He got no further.

Sorokin's champagne glass shattered in his grip, droplets of blood ran down the front of his impeccable uniform. "Those *swine!*" he exclaimed fiercely. "Those soft-bellied scum!" A vein throbbed on his forehead. He stared down at Barker's impassive features for a long moment. "You shall have your wish, Comrade Barker!"

He swung Barker around by his elbow and bellowed to the room at large. Soon everyone was clapping and cheering.

Beresford explained in a loud whisper, "He is telling them that we, his allies, are going to stand shoulder to shoulder against the common enemy." He grinned. "Very melodramatic, although I think our captain is still smouldering at being classed as a comrade!"

Devane said, "What about his plan? Is it really any good?"

"I've no idea. But it could shorten the war on this front."

As Barker hurried across to meet another senior Russian officer, Devane said, "You must realize that *Parthian* stands no chance at all if it hits real opposition."

Beresford shrugged. "It's your job to lead, no matter what the odds might be. It's never been any different."

"It hasn't, but I thought *you* were different. I was wrong. You use people, they don't matter to you."

Beresford grinned uneasily. "Here, steady on."

"Why didn't you tell me how Dundas got jumped by Lincke? Tell me that Barker had set up my boat, knowing that Lincke would go after it, thinking it was me? Did you bloody well imagine I wouldn't work it out for myself?" He looked round the room, hating the faces, the laughter. "David lost his hands because of it."

"We don't know for certain. You're guessing."

Devane did not conceal his contempt. "Tell Barker not to worry. I'll get Lincke. Or he'll get me. Now I'm going back to the base."

As he turned on his heel Beresford called anxiously after him, "You're just tired, John."

Devane took his cap from a Russian servant. "Not tired, *sick!*"

Outside in the cool, damp air he watched a few pale stars.

My darling John. The words hung in his mind as if she had spoken them from the shadows.

But there was no future now. He shook himself angrily, as a staff car jerked towards him. *What did you expect? Nobody lives for ever.*

The little villa was soon out of sight, and the sea was waiting for him. As usual.

MANY MILES from the villa, Devane's adversary, the man he had never met, stood by the window and contemplated the dawn. It was cold and damp, like the accursed country.

Korvettenkapitän Gerhard Lincke listened to the far-off wail of a siren. The Eastern Front never rested for long, but Lincke had taught himself to keep his mind clear of unnecessary diversions. He would inspect the whole of *Gruppe Seeadler* this morning. There was no substitute for routine.

He heard the girl moan in her sleep and turned to look at her. She was an interpreter, described as Polish. But Lincke knew from her record sheet that she had been born a Russian, and had lost her family in the revolution. He had taken her to his bed not from lust or affection. It was just another part of his routine. Necessary . . .

He shivered and stood back from the window. Today the new admiral would come and inspect the naval forces here. He would replace the one killed in *Parthian*'s attack on the *Potsdam*. Lincke gave a tight smile as he recalled how some of his brother officers had expected him to be enraged by such an impudent attack.

Quite the reverse. Lincke had been seeking the last clue in the pattern of events. He knew that Devane commanded the handful of motor torpedo boats named *Parthian*. He had studied his background, and knew him better than some of his own subordinates.

He thought of the coming Russian offensive, and the thought troubled him. It could not be delayed much longer.

He looked down at the girl. In the grey light she looked almost beautiful. Lincke never considered the possibility of Germany losing the war. But should any of these patriots, or traitors, whichever way you saw them, fall into Russian hands, God help them.

Lincke stood stock still, suddenly ice-cold. All that study of intelligence material and it had been right there in front of his face. He almost laughed aloud. It was so devious. So British.

The girl stirred and opened her eyes. She murmured something but Lincke ignored her. His heart was beating faster as he considered telling his new superior of his discovery but discarded it instantly. *He* commanded *Seeadler*, not some admiral who knew nothing of these people.

His second-in-command could inspect the boats today. Max would drive him to where the Russians were quartered, the ones who wore the uniforms of the Reich.

Time was running out fast. If Lincke knew it, so would the man Devane. He had stayed alive too long to be a fool.

Lincke shouted for Max, his orderly.

When the door burst open and Max, dishevelled in a watch-coat, peered in, Lincke said calmly, "I need a bath and a shave."

It was going to be a better day after all.

"Max, we are going to lay a trap for the Englishman." He left the room, laughing.

Cat and Mouse

Lieutenant Dundas climbed onto the gratings in the forepart of the bridge and said, "Signal received from Russian escort commander, sir. He is withdrawing as ordered."

"Very well." Devane peered abeam, but the escorting warships had already melted into the darkness. "Signal *Kestrel* and tell Red to make sure the launches are on station. I want a tight formation all the way."

He leaned against the corner of the pitching bridge, his ears taking in the labouring motors, throttled down to slow speed, the sluice of the sea against the hull and the boat's sluggish response. Packed with fuel and extra ammunition, depth charges and spare Russian machineguns, the MTB felt heavy in the water.

November. Four months since he had taken over command of *Parthian*. It seemed an eternity. It was as if all the rest, even Horne's death, were a working-up for this last operation. Not weeks away now, but a matter of hours.

During the preparation for this hit-and-run assault on the Crimean shoreline, Devane had waited for news of his enemy, Lincke. There had been practically nothing. A few sighting reports from Russian air patrols, but they could have been wrong anyway as the Germans had a lot of small craft working the coastal waters. Then again, Lincke might already guess what *Parthian* was doing, and might be biding his time.

The fact that Sorokin had sent his four fastest and most modern launches to carry the one hundred Russian shock troops proved how much he valued Barker's plan.

Devane thought of the men around him. He heard Carroll humming softly to himself, a lookout whispering to the boatswain's mate. Lieutenant Chalmers was on the forecastle, checking Leading Seaman Priest's six-pounder. He never seemed to rest or sleep, as if he was driven by some terrible urge or memory.

A seaman had the helm, and he guessed that Pellegrine was below in his mess, preparing himself as he always did before an action. A real old sweat. Money and paybook in an oilskin pouch. A small flask of rum in one pocket, a spare bulb for his life-jacket lamp. Ready for anything, was the coxswain.

He heard Leading Seaman Hanlon's hard Liverpool accent. "Come on, la, what's up with yer? You're like a spare part at a bleedin' weddin'." He was probably having a go at Ordinary Seaman Metcalf again. Those two seemed to hate each other more than the enemy.

Dundas came back rubbing his hands. "All checked, sir. Boats on station. Feels a bit lively. We may be in for a blow."

117

Four MTBs making a tight box formation, with the launches close astern. Eight low shapes heading towards the land. Orel's supporting gunboats were closing in from the southeast, like the jaws of a trap. If Lincke took the bait, Orel would catch him. If he did not, the raid would cause enough panic anyway to help the main Russian thrust across the Kerch Strait.

The point of attack was a small niche in the Crimean coast named Suzrov, some twenty miles northeast of Krasnoarmeisk. It was a safe part of the peninsula as far as the enemy were concerned. There was an extension to the minefield, and the area was known to be zeroed in for two artillery batteries, controlled by a RDF station which the Germans had positioned in a bombed church.

A straightforward attack. They had done it several times in the Med and the Adriatic.

Pellegrine's untidy shape appeared on the bridge, and he grunted as he took over the wheel.

"Course, north twenty west, Swain."

Dundas peered at his watch. "Action stations, sir?"

"Yes. Most of them will be there already anyway." It was always the same. Not easy to rest with only three planks of mahogany between you and the sea.

Someone gave a little cry as the sky was bathed in deep red. Later, much later it seemed, there was the sullen rumble of guns. Miles away a night attack had been disturbed or scattered.

"Two minutes past midnight, sir. *Parthian* at action stations." Then the age-old chestnut, "Enemy coast in the vicinity."

Devane smiled and shrugged his shoulders deeper into his waterproof suit. It was so easy to let your mind drift. Like a man will fall asleep quite happily and freeze to death, or a motorist will doze off at the wheel. It was always there, waiting to tempt him. Claudia's arms around him, pulling him closer . . . .

A dull thud jerked him back to the present. A hatch slamming shut.

Dundas hovered by his elbow. "I'll get down aft, sir."

Devane saw that Chalmers had come to the bridge. In a stunt like this one, it would be safer to have Dundas working with men he knew and who trusted him. Chalmers could take over the bridge if his CO bought it.

"Warn the engine room. Minimum revs in about ten minutes." He could feel the towel which he had tucked around his neck

118

getting damp with spray, or was it the sweat of fear? He realized Dundas was still there. "Something wrong, Number One?"

Dundas fumbled with the heavy pistol-belt he had donned. "Good luck, Skipper. In case . . ." He sounded awkward.

Devane was moved. "Keep your head down." He felt shocked by his own words. What Beresford had often said. It sounded like a betrayal. They had barely spoken since that evening.

"One more time." Devane looked at Chalmers. Poised, taut like a spring. Searching the darkness ahead.

Pellegrine shifted his seaboots. "What wouldn't I give now for a few jars at the Nelson, then back 'ome for a bit of the other."

Metcalf, who was acting as spare hand on the bridge, asked, "The other what, Cox'n?"

Pellegrine glared at the darkness. "Gawd Almighty!"

The minutes ticked past and nothing happened. The sea's motion became less violent, and Devane knew it was because land was creeping out on the port bow to shield them from open water. But no flares burst overhead, no tracer ripped past to destroy their challenge.

"Dead slow. Tell the first lieutenant to keep a close watch astern for the launches."

Another dull glow lit up the sky, but with a difference. The bottom of it was black and uneven, something solid.

"Enemy coast ahead, sir!" No jokes this time.

"All guns stand by." Devane licked his lips. They felt as if they were glued together. *Come on, Jerry. What the hell's got into you?*

The motors sounded louder now, and he wondered if anyone on the shore had heard them yet. Guns manned and pointing at *Parthian*, at him. The local airfield alerted so that even the survivors would be strafed into oblivion.

Devane thought of Lincke and was suddenly calm. It did not matter how either of them felt. They had to prove something. To settle a score which had already cost too many lives.

"Here come the launches, sir."

Four low sinister shapes, darker than the water which held them, they overtook their escorts and swept towards the shore. Not a sound or a glint of metal betrayed them.

Devane had seen the soldiers, tough and hard-faced, being mustered to collect their weapons and equipment. The other Russians who had changed sides because of the old hatred left by the revolution would find no quarter there.

119

A seaman said fiercely, "God, how much bloody longer?"

Pellegrine snapped, "Silence! As long as it takes, see?"

Devane readjusted his night glasses. In a matter of hours the big push across the Kerch Strait would begin. Russian troops on the Crimea for the first time since the big retreat when hundreds of thousands of them, Russian and German, had frozen to death.

Far to starboard a flare burst against the clouds. But it was over the land and no immediate threat. Devane saw the familiar faces suddenly clear and pale in the light. Another flare, even further to starboard. Someone was getting nervous, or suspicious.

The port machinegunner nestled more firmly against his twin guns and repeated over and over, "Come on, yew bastards! Let's be 'avin' yew!"

Devane knew they were as near as they could expect to get. They would have to stop and take stock of their bearings soon. Once again he was amazed that it had been so easy.

Carroll said in a whisper, "The Russkies *must* be ashore by now!"

Devane could picture them creeping up into the rugged darkness with their weapons out and ready. A knife for the throat of an unwary sentry, grenades for the weapon slits and blockhouses, burp-guns and mortars for the real work.

A launch glided past and Devane let out a slow breath. It was empty. At least twenty-five men were ashore and undiscovered.

The tension was unbearable, and when something metallic clattered across the engine room Devane thought for an instant it would make the machinegunners overreact with a burst of tracer.

A second launch moved abeam, and Devane saw a figure waving a white flag or a handkerchief as he passed.

Chalmers said bitterly, "He's well out of it."

Devane turned his head to look at him when the whole bridge and foredeck lit up with a single explosion. He thought for a moment that they had been tracked by a shore battery. Then he saw the flashes along the shoreline, sharp and deadly, as grenades were flung into dugouts and bunkers. The first explosion had barely died when it flared up again with livid brightness. Great flames leaped towards the clouds, and Devane saw what he guessed to be blazing fuel running down a slope like molten lava.

"Starboard ten. Slow ahead all engines."

The deck vibrated as Ackland opened his throttles. There was a lot of firing now, small arms and light automatic weapons which

120

seemed to fan out from the landing point, the progress marked by little stabs of fire and the occasional bright star of a grenade. Devane heard the dull crump of bombs exploding further inland, the slow response from a German artillery position until it too was bombed into silence. Then a tall, tree-shaped burst of flame lit up the water's edge, and Devane guessed that the raiders had blown up the RDF station.

"Twenty minutes past midnight, sir."

"Very well. Remind me at the half-hour, Bunts."

Across the water, Devane heard a grinding roar of tracks, magnified by the sloping wedge of land. Tanks or troop-carriers rushing to the scene, but still a long way to travel.

"There's supposed to be a road at about red four-five. Any armour will come from the town. We'll have the advantage over them."

Chalmers said quietly, "For a while anyway."

The raid was spreading in both directions, and Devane could imagine the alarm changing to terror as the defenders heard Russian voices like their own right amongst them.

An explosion rocked the hull, and Devane heard fragments falling on the deck and splashing alongside. "On helmets, everyone!"

Pellegrine steadfastly ignored the call. He had never been known to wear a "battle bowler" as he called it.

The raiders must have discovered another fuel dump, for that too was blazing fiercely, and some of it was running down to the sea's edge to make a small fiery barrier.

Metcalf said, "They're throwing supplies into the fire, sir."

Devane lowered his glasses, sickened. Metcalf was mistaken. In the powerful lenses he had seen the kicking bodies, some of them burning like torches as they were hurled into the river of fuel.

"Time, sir." Carroll sounded hoarse.

"Right. Make the signal for recall. Tell *Kestrel* by R/T to execute phase two." He heard the men moving about, grateful to have something to do to disperse the terrible spectacle.

The boatswain's mate said, "Still, I suppose if it was our country an' they was fighting for the Nazis—"

"Hold your noise, damn you!" Chalmers's face was wild in the reflected glare. "You don't know what it's like!" He bent over as if he were going to vomit. "I saw my chaps die like that. We were swimming, making for a destroyer which had been hit by a bomb but was still afloat. As I swam I could hear the burning fuel coming

121

after me." He pushed his knuckles into his mouth. "I could hear it! The fire took all but three of us."

Devane touched his arm. "Go and relieve the first lieutenant."

As Chalmers made to leave the bridge the boatswain's mate blocked his path. "Sorry for what I said, sir. No 'arm intended."

Chalmers looked at him. "I know. I'm the one to apologize."

Devane thrust his hands deep into his jacket as the green flare exploded to recall the raiders to the beach.

Carroll said, "First launch loaded and away, sir."

Devane nodded. *Kestrel* and *Harrier* were already moving out to open waters. *Merlin* and *Osprey* would screen the final withdrawal.

After that it would be a matter of a few hours before they knew if Barker's ruse had worked or not.

Dundas appeared on the bridge. "Ready to move, sir."

"Very well."

Star shells exploded across the glittering water, but the cloud was low and the smoke too dense for them to be of any use.

He saw another launch gathering speed as it throbbed past. There were a lot of bandaged heads and limbs in that one, and he saw a corpse rolled over the side and left to float astern like so much rubbish. We shall never understand the Russians, he thought. Not in a thousand years.

"Last one clear, sir. No casualties to us." Dundas grinned. "Makes a change."

Devane looked up as another star shell exploded directly overhead. "And if Orel's gunboats are in the right place at the right time, we should keep it that way." It was an easy lie, an expected one. *Parthian* would be badly mauled even if the ruse had worked. But at least it would be over. For the lucky ones. The few.

"Ready to take up new course, sir. North seventy east. *Osprey* on station astern."

"Carry on. Increase revolutions for twenty knots."

The land had already dipped into the shadows again, but a few fires still flickered, and a pattern of sparks circled above the beach where men had perished for their treachery. Or their beliefs.

Devane settled himself in his corner. So now we wait.

CAPTAIN BARKER STOOD with his hands in his reefer pockets, and surveyed his operations room. It was larger now that he had had a wall removed and an adjoining store transformed into an extension.

The lights were very bright, so that charts and wall maps, coloured markers and flags stood out like parts of a pattern.

A seaman was collecting empty teacups, and Barker's new officers were by their telephones, pencils and signal pads within reach.

Only Beresford looked out of place, he thought. He was slumped at his own table, his hair tousled as if he had just got out of his bunk.

Barker snapped, "The attack must be working. We'd have heard otherwise."

A telephone jangled and was snatched up by one of the lieutenants. He spoke carefully in Russian and replaced it.

"From Russian HQ, sir. The first attack across the Kerch Strait has been launched. Heavy fighting reported."

Beresford stirred. "Orel's six gunboats will be in position to support *Parthian*." He looked at the clock. "I wonder what Lincke makes of all this?"

"He'll not be in the strait, be certain of that." Barker's pale eyes gleamed. "Even if he suspects Devane's raid is a sprat to catch a mackerel, he can't afford to ignore it."

The telephone interrupted him. The lieutenant spoke for several seconds and then covered the mouthpiece with his hand. "It's all a bit confusing, sir. I—I don't really know what's going on."

Beresford was on his feet and over to the other table. He snatched the telephone from the lieutenant and spoke rapidly.

When he had put the handset down he said, "That was Captain Sorokin himself." His voice shook momentarily. "*Parthian*'s attack worked. The enemy has started to move men and armour along the coast before the main Russian assault."

"Well? Spit it out, man!" Barker's face was suddenly pale.

Beresford said quietly. "Sorokin's been removed from his command. By order of Admiral Kasatonov. He's in disgrace."

"I don't see what that has to do with *us*?"

"You don't?" Beresford walked to the plot table. "The admiral is withdrawing the bulk of Orel's covering force. He says he needs it at the strait. You know the story." He glanced at the lieutenant. "I'm not surprised you couldn't understand. I think Sorokin's drunk, or halfway there. But he *tried* to explain. Orel has left two of his gunboats. The rest are already running for the strait."

Barker stared at him. "*Two?*"

"Yes, sir. *Two gunboats*. They might as well have taken the lot."

Barker rubbed his eyes. "Now. Let me think." He began to hum busily. "This is where it counts, eh, Ralph? Thinking caps on, what? We must not overreact. *Seeadler* may also be heading for the strait, had you thought of that?"

Beresford ignored him. To Lieutenant Kimber he said flatly, "Make a signal to *Parthian*. Get it off immediately. Top priority. Tell *Parthian* that Orel's covering force has been withdrawn. Two supporting vessels only are in vicinity."

Barker said sharply, "That's unnecessary! We don't know—"

"We don't *know* anything, sir. I just want John Devane to get a chance to run for it."

"Run? Is that what he'll do?" Barker was barely able to control his agitation as he watched Kimber hurry away.

"Of course he won't. But he's got to be told. To have a chance, no matter how slight."

Barker swung round and saw a rating enter with a fresh tray of tea. "Don't stand there gawping, you useless idiot!" He was almost screaming. "Get me Russian HQ on the telephone *at once!*"

A door was opened by a sentry and Sorokin lurched into the harsh lights, his uniform coat unbuttoned and stained. He was obviously very drunk. He saw Beresford and nodded. "I come to you. I come to say sorry. That is not an easy thing for me, but I am ashamed."

Beresford said gently, "Here, sir. Sit down."

He gestured to the seaman with the tea but Sorokin shook his massive head and slumped down heavily. He dragged a flask from his pocket and drank for several seconds.

Then he said thickly, "They are sending me to a new place. Siberia probably, my friend, *da?*"

Beresford said, "What happened?"

"Nothing. Politics. Enemies. What is the difference? Maybe you are to blame, for being here, for being seen as my friends."

Beresford said sadly, "I understand. About *Parthian*, sir . . ."

Sorokin tried to rise, but fell down again. "I gave a last order. There is another gunboat in the base. It was just repaired. You go and help your friend. There is only few men on board." He dragged an envelope from his breast pocket. "Here is authority."

Beresford said quietly, "It is two hundred miles. We'll never reach the rendezvous. Already it may be too late."

"No matter. Your friend will know you have tried. And I will not feel like a traitor." He got to his feet and gripped Beresford's arm like a vice. "Leave now." He lumbered to the door.

124

Barker said abruptly, "God! I've never seen anything like it! No pride in the man!"

Beresford opened his drawer and took out a pistol. As Kimber reappeared he said, "Muster all the spare hands and march them to the dockyard. Give the OOD this authority to board the gunboat. Take all the medical gear you can find. Steal it if need be."

Barker interrupted sharply, "Am I hearing you correctly, Ralph? Take a Russian gunboat, to do what, for God's sake?"

Beresford clipped his pistol-belt in place. "I am a good officer, sir. If you order me to stay here, to leave your people to be *wiped out* to prove some idiotic theory, then stay I will. But by God I shall make certain everybody knows why I stayed. You can say goodbye to promotion after that!"

"How *dare* you!"

Beresford eyed Barker coldly. "Then I'm leaving. Now. It may be a useless gesture, but I'll feel cleaner."

The telephone shattered the tension.

The lieutenant stammered, "From Russian HQ, sir." He was staring at Beresford. "Their troops are on the peninsula and pushing inland. Intelligence reports that *Gruppe Seeadler* has been sighted heading northeast from Balaklava."

Beresford nodded. "Thank you. So Lincke was not where we anticipated. He intends to jump *Parthian* from astern." To the startled lieutenant he added, "Make a signal to *Parthian* to that effect."

He walked to the door, then turned. "Add to the signal, 'Keep your head down.'" His voice broke. "'Old son.'"

The door shut and they all stared at Barker.

Barker was humming tunelessly. He said suddenly, "I must draft a signal to Vice-Admiral Talents. To tell him about the raid's success. But for it, the Russian attack might never have begun."

He glanced at his brightly lit command, but this time nobody was looking at him.

Sunset

"Ease down to fifteen knots." Devane dabbed his face with a towel and winced. His skin felt raw from the spray which came buffeting back from the bows. "No sense in shaking ourselves to bits."

Around him binoculars and gun muzzles probed the darkness, as men strained to get a first hint of danger.

Lieutenant Chalmers seemed to have recovered from his outburst, and was standing aft by the twin Oerlikon mounting, his arms folded, as the pitching deck quivered and plunged beneath him.

Dundas emerged from the chartroom and said, "We may have missed them, sir."

Devane pictured his four MTBs strung out in pairs, the Russian launches managing as best they could somewhere astern. Their part was over. "We'll stop soon and listen. You never know."

Feet clattered on the wet gratings, and Carroll called, "Signal from W/T, sir. 'Most immediate, Russian covering force Romeo is withdrawn. Two vessels only in your vicinity.'" He hesitated, then finished, "'Russian attack has begun. Ends.'"

Devane stood motionless. What were the Russians playing at? Perhaps they knew that Lincke was already in the strait, harrying the Russian troop transports, and no longer constituted a danger?

Dundas muttered, "Of all the luck!"

The boatswain's mate asked, "Fall out action stations, sir?"

Devane thought rapidly as he felt the tension moving away, the dangerous air of relaxation growing about him.

"No." He spoke sharply, "We're not out of the woods yet." He heard the quick whispers. *The skipper's round the bend*. Well, they could think what they bloody well liked.

He swung round. "Number One, Signal *Osprey* to fall back and cover the launches. Remainder of *Parthian*, line abreast." As Dundas groped his way aft he added, "After that, R/T silence."

Devane gripped the wet screen, silently cursing the chorus of sea and wind. Why should Orel's gunboats pull away?

"*Osprey*'s acknowledged, sir. Andy Twiss will love being lumbered as an escort!"

Devane barely heard him. The signal had sounded different. Like Beresford, and yet . . .

Carroll said tersely, "Another signal from W/T, sir. 'German E-boats closing from southwest.'"

Dundas jumped for the voicepipes. "Bloody hell!"

Devane remained by the screen, his fingers numb from the force of his grip. "That all?"

"It finishes, 'Keep your head down, old son.'"

"Thanks, Bunts." Devane released his hold gently. It was almost

126

better this way. Like the moment when the cell door opens and the prisoner knows there is no reprieve.

He said, "Stand by to alter course. Steer south sixty west. Signal *Parthian*, Bunts. Hand lamp."

He heard the swift clack . . . clack of Carroll's lamp. The other boats would have monitored Beresford's signal, would know they would get the order to turn and fight. It was what they had come for, Russian help or not.

"Acknowledged, sir." Carroll's voice was a whisper.

"Very well. Execute. Warn the engine room to be prepared for maximum revs."

The three hulls turned gracefully. Line abreast, each one shining in spray, facing an invisible enemy.

Devane wiped his glasses for the hundredth time and tried to find some small comfort. The sighting report could be mistaken. Perhaps it was not *Seeadler* anyway. It would be just like Barker's lot to dramatize everything. But the comfort evaded him.

"Bunts? Time check."

"Five minutes past one, sir."

Soon. Even allowing for their alteration of course and speed. It must be. Stealth was the only thing they had left.

"Stop engines. Warn all hands." Devane felt the deck slide forward and down as the boat lost way. "Well, Swain?" Devane glanced at Pellegrine's battered cap. It was all he could distinguish in the darkness. "Don't let me down now."

Pellegrine rested on his spokes. "Should 'ave sighted our launches by now. I just 'ope Mr. Twiss don't mistake *us* for Krauts."

Carroll murmured, "I'm ready with the lamp, Swain. No bother there."

Pellegrine continued to listen. *No bother there.* But the commanding officer of the MTB which they had detached to escort the Russian launches had been an actor. Pellegrine grimaced. It would be just our luck if he saw this as his greatest role.

Metcalf whispered, "There! Engines!"

Devane listened. It was no mistake. The regular *thrum . . . thrum . . . thrum* of heavy diesels.

Pellegrine called, "There's another MTB out there too, sir. Starboard bow."

Devane bit his lip hard. Twiss had probably gone back to round up a straggler or to take one of them in tow. The E-boats were

127

closing fast astern. Just as they would have been on *Parthian* but for Beresford's signal.

Dundas said, "I'll call up *Osprey*, sir. Andy might hold them off until we join him."

Devane peered at the luminous compass. "Negative. They'll cut us up piecemeal. This is our one and only chance, can't you see that? *Osprey's* lookouts may spot the danger in time."

Dundas stared at him. "But he'll not stand a bloody earthly!"

Devane lowered his glasses. "Get aft and send Chalmers up here. Gun action. Depth charges if we get the slightest opening."

Dundas nodded jerkily. "Yes. I see." He was groping for the bridge ladder when Devane called him back.

"It's the only way. Do you imagine I wanted it like this?" It was suddenly important that Dundas should understand.

Dundas faltered, one foot in the air. "I'm just glad I don't have to decide, sir."

"You will, Roddy. You will, one day." But his words were lost as the night split apart in a galaxy of flares and tracer shells.

Lurking like assassins in the shadows beyond the blinding flares, the three MTBs started their motors and moved slowly towards the brightly lit arena. In the centre of the crisscrossing balls of tracer, and pinned down by the enemy's flares, the isolated MTB was already increasing speed, snarling round to face the E-boats which had burst out of the night.

A low shape rippled past the savage exchange of shots, and then burst into flames as cannon fire transformed one of the troop launches into a pyre in a moment.

Chalmers was here now, glasses levelled, cap tugged low over his hawklike nose, as he snapped, "Six E-boats. Moving right to left." This time he did not even blink as another explosion painted the sea like blood. "There's the leader. Red four-five."

In the angry glow the tiger stripes were even clearer.

"*Osprey's* stopping and on fire, sir! Two E-boats closing her."

Twiss's boat was almost stopped, and was being raked by the enemy without mercy. But Twiss's gunners were still firing back at a range of some twenty-five yards.

Now or never. Devane raised his voice. "All ahead full! Open fire!" In a tight arrowhead the three hulls raced from the shadows with every gun which would bear ripping into the circling E-boats and churning the sea into a white froth.

128

Above the clatter of machineguns and the heavier bang of Priest's six-pounder, Devane heard the mounting roar of motors as the boat tore across the swell like an avenging devil.

"A *hit*! Got the bastard!" Another voice, cracked with anxiety. "Watch that one!" Then the terrible thud and shriek of metal as the German gunners at last realized that *Osprey* was not alone.

Devane saw *Harrier* butting into the lead, Walker's yellow scarf whipping out above the screen like a lance pennant.

Tracer flashed over the bridge, and Devane heard the clatter of falling rigging and the ping of splinters against a gunshield. Somewhere a man was croaking for help and a machinegunner was swearing at his loader as he fumbled to serve the smoking breeches, oblivious to everything except the need to keep firing.

The E-boats had split into two sections, their long hulls gleaming in the fires as they tilted hard over. One of them had stopped dead, smoke gushing from aft and tiny figures falling in crossfire as they tried to find safety.

"Tell *Kestrel* to finish that one!"

Mackay's *Kestrel* came bouncing across the torn waters, guns blazing, barely leaving enough room to cross the damaged E-boat's stern as he lobbed his depth charges alongside.

Two more E-boats were coming head on through the smoke, but one swerved aside as she collided with the capsized hull of a Russian launch. Men were floundering in the water but vanished as they were sucked bodily into the racing propellers.

The E-boat which had hit the half submerged wreck veered away, engines coughing and roaring.

Devane yelled, "Steer straight for him!"

He felt nothing as tracer lifted from the oncoming E-boat and then tore down towards him. Priest's return fire plus an onslaught from Walker's gunners were enough. The E-boat swung away, guns still firing.

A tremendous explosion lit the sky, and with horror Devane saw Twiss's boat blasted apart, the torpedoes adding to the destruction as a passing E-boat dealt the death blow. He turned away, unable to watch the pieces of hull and men dropping amongst the churned wakes of the antagonists.

Chalmers yelled, "Three of us to four of them now, the sods!"

Devane held on to Chalmers's words. The odds were better. One E-boat sinking, another damaged and out of the fight. But for the

129

Germans' attention being riveted on Twiss and his launches, they would have stood no chance at all. Twiss, the actor who had intended to play the parts of admirals after the war.

He shouted, "Nuts to starboard! Tell Red to watch his quarter!"

Devane heard Carroll using the R/T, the insane rattle of guns as Briton and German tried to knock out the resistance, just long enough, seconds even, to make the kill.

Chalmers yelled, "*Harrier*'s in trouble!"

Devane touched Pellegrine's hunched shoulder. "Close on *Harrier*."

A gunner shouted wildly, "Got the bastard!" Walker's six-pounder must have raked the enemy's bridge even as the two boats charged headlong on a converging course. Coxswain, officers, cut down in a scythe of splinters and tracer.

Metcalf paused, gasping, as he hauled more ammunition to the machineguns, and cried desperately, "They're going to collide!"

Devane snatched the handset from Carroll's fingers. "*Harrier*! This is *Merlin*! Break off! For God's sake, Willy, *break away*!"

In the flickering gunfire he saw men crouching on the MTB's side-deck, stricken at the sight of the E-boat charging blindly towards them.

Devane levelled his glasses. He could see Walker's face in the bucking lenses, his teeth bared in agony as he tried to pull himself to the wheel. He had just time to notice that nobody else moved on the MTB's bridge, that Walker's scarf was bloody, before both boats struck and exploded.

Devane wiped his face with the back of his glove. "Oh God, Willy." It was all he could say.

Pellegrine called sharply, "Enemy's regrouping, sir!" He spun the wheel and narrowly avoided another overcrowded launch which had somehow stayed afloat throughout the encounter.

"Stand by! Gun action!"

Devane pulled himself out of his stunned disbelief and ran to the opposite side. There was *Kestrel*, foam surging beneath her keel as she roared up to join her leader. *Then there were two*.

Carroll was peering at him. "You all right, sir?"

Devane nodded. There was wreckage everywhere, flung back and forth as E-boats and MTBs tore through it. A few men were swimming, others floated with the untroubled languor of the dead.

And then all at once the sea was quieter, the roaring, incessant clatter of engines and gunfire moving away like a terrible storm.

"They've gone." Chalmers stared at the darkness with amazement. "We've driven the bastards off!"

Devane dragged his thoughts from the sights and the pain. "Reduce speed. Report damage and casualties. Tell Number One to get forrard and look for survivors." He saw the other MTB slowing down, her decks alive with busy figures as empty shell cases and spent cartridges were swept to one side.

That was all he had left of *Parthian*. And Lincke was still alive. *Seeadler* remained, not intact, but a ready weapon. The despair and the shock of what had happened welled up inside him like terrible anger, white-hot, all-consuming.

Devane glanced over the screen and saw a life-jacket drifting past. But the corpse in it was beyond care.

Pellegrine gestured to the boatswain's mate. "You go an' make some cocoa. Put a tot in it for luck."

Dundas pulled himself up to the bridge. "Only one casualty. Able Seaman Bridges. Splinter in the foot. Damage, a few holes aft, and the rigging shot away. I don't know how we did it. Picked up one survivor. Just one. Out of all that mess." He gave what could have been a laugh. Or a sob. "A Jerry, would you believe?"

The thick, glutinous kye, well laced with illicit rum, did more good than a banquet. Devane took the handset from its rack. "Hello, Red. Damage and casualties?"

The Canadian's voice sounded dull. "Two men cut by splinters. No major damage to speak of. After what happened just now I can't . . ." He did not finish it.

It *was* a miracle.

"Alter course, and tell the Russian launches we'll head for the rendezvous." There were only two launches left.

Devane looked at the sky. The fact they had survived was not enough. It was unfinished. Even when the first dawn light found the two scarred MTBs and their overloaded consorts, the men on watch, or those plugging leaks and overhauling the guns, did not speak, for in their hearts they knew they had only won a reprieve.

All through the day, as the boats pushed steadily to the east, the single German survivor sat on the upper deck and stared at the tossing water. Once, Devane saw Geordie Pollard offer the German a cup of something hot. They did not smile nor speak, but the German took the proffered cup as if it was something precious.

At dusk they met Beresford's commandeered gunboat, the remaining vessels of the force having returned to base apparently on the assumption that there would be no survivors to escort.

Beresford crossed to the stopped MTB, to meet Devane on the bridge amongst the dirt and the litter of battle. He said quietly, "You've done more than enough. I was afraid. I wanted to help."

Devane smiled. The gunboat looked like a relic from the Kaiser's war. "In *that* thing?"

Beresford looked across at Mackay's MTB. "And this is all that's left of *Parthian*?" He shook his head.

"I'll need fuel, Ralph." Devane swilled some tea round his mug and examined it thoughtfully. "And all the ammo you can spare."

"I've got fuel and ammunition. I thought you might need some, but now . . ." His eyes sharpened. "You're not going after him?"

"I've no instructions. Remember the last time I sailed without 'hearing' Barker's orders?"

Beresford nodded slowly, feeling Devane's pain, understanding him perhaps for the first time ever. "I'm coming with you," he said.

Devane smiled gravely. "Then we can both keep our heads down."

"Where are we going?"

Devane had thought about it. "The only place where Lincke can get his boats repaired now. Back to Mandra. He'll take on fuel first. That will keep him busy tonight. So with luck we'll get to Mandra first and be waiting for him. By the way, why *did* the Russians pull out from the rendezvous?"

"The admiral fired Sorokin."

It sounded so ridiculous they both smiled.

Then Devane said abruptly, "Well, let's go and prove Sorokin was right in his trust."

Three hours later, as the launches and the ancient gunboat turned towards Tuapse, the MTBs headed in the opposite direction.

"Sunset in three hours, sir." Chalmers looked at the sky, his eyes red-rimmed, his lean features telling the strain.

Devane took another mug from Metcalf. Coffee, cocoa, tea? It all tasted the same now.

"Very well. See if you can arrange another meal for the lads."

All that day they had ploughed their way westward, alone but for

132

Mackay's boat which was cruising two miles off the port beam. Even at that distance he had heard the thud of hammers, the rattle of drills as Mackay's men carried out repairs. The Canadian had signalled that the underwater damage was worse than he had realized. But he had promised his best.

It still seemed incredible that the others had all gone, that the sea could be so desolate and empty. If no contact was made before nightfall they, too, would have to scuttle for home. Even then they might run dry of fuel, in spite of the extra load.

He saw Dundas on the swaying forecastle with Leading Seaman Priest and the AB named Bridges who had got a splinter in his foot. He was hobbling along with one foot bandaged. He could have gone back to Tuapse in the old gunboat, but he had asked to stay.

The sea was unbroken but for an occasional patch of white. Great purple swells of water, with the sky streaked in dark clouds like tattered banners. He rubbed his stubbled chin and tried not to think of a hot bath and bed. A bed with Claudia to take him in her arms and soothe away the pain and the terrors.

A fish jumped nearby and fell with a splash. Torpedoman Geordie Pollard waved a handful of empty mugs and yelled, "Just right for me tea, that kipper!" There were a few tired grins.

Petty Officer Ackland climbed stiffly into the bridge. He looked paler than usual, and his face and hands were smeared with grease.

"All right, Chief?"

"Not bad, sir. Pumps are playing up a bit, and I think the starboard outer screw has got a nick or two from splinters." He saw his friend Pellegrine squatting on an ammunition box and munching a massive sandwich. "Lazy devil."

Pellegrine chuckled. "We've been workin', lad. Not like your cushy job in the bloody cellar!"

Ackland yawned and spread his arms. "Did you want me, sir?"

Devane nodded. "Just to say thanks. I don't know how you keep this boat going, but I appreciate it."

Ackland grinned. "You keep us afloat, sir. I'll do the rest."

Carroll called, "From *Kestrel*, sir. 'Losing fuel. Request permission to reduce speed.'"

"Affirmative, Bunts. Revs for eight knots."

Ackland observed, "He's got a good chief, sir. They'll cope."

Devane glanced at the clouds. The visibility was poor. Sunset or not, it would be dark earlier than they wanted.

Ackland said, "I'll get my head down, sir. My winger can watch the motors. I'd like to talk about promotion for him later on."

Devane clapped his shoulder. "We'll do that, Chief."

He moved restlessly about the bridge. Beresford appeared from somewhere, hatless, his hair blowing in the breeze. "Anything?"

"No. Not even a recall from Barker. Not that I'd hear it."

They grinned, the tension held at bay by the old familiarity.

Beresford said, "Barker will know by now. He'll be for the chop after this cock-up. Or a knighthood!"

Devane walked to the chartroom. It was dark and cool in there, with the MTB's own smells of oil and high-octane, of coiled rope and damp woodwork. He switched on the chart light and studied the Rumanian coast. There was not much time left. They might be spotted by an air patrol, or even a surface vessel of some kind. He jerked back as his head lolled over the chart. Sleep threatened.

He stood up and groped for the door to the bridge. *I've had it. Had it.*

On the bridge he found Chalmers and Beresford with their glasses trained on the other boat. "Trouble?"

Chalmers nodded. "They've stopped, sir. They just signalled that they've almost finished with the leak."

Devane looked at Pellegrine. "Take the wheel, Swain. Port fifteen. Close to loudhailer distance. Rig a bowline and hoist a lookout up the mast. It'll give him an extra few feet." He glanced at Metcalf. "You're the youngest. Up you go. Bunts, give him a hand."

As the other boat came closer, Devane switched on the loudhailer and said, "I think the bird has flown, Red. We'll return to base as soon as it's dark."

Above the bridge, his legs wrapped painfully around the stumpy mast, Ordinary Seaman Metcalf moved his binoculars in a complete circle before giving his arms a rest. It was cold, and his body ached from the hours of waiting and watching, remembering the swift horror of the battle, the corpses. But somehow the ordeals had given him strength, and a new hope. Not just for getting a commission. Somewhere along the way he had grown up. He was no longer a stranger amongst his messmates. Well, hardly a stranger.

Metcalf peered down at the square bridge beneath his seaboots. Devane was right below him, waving to the other CO as the boats edged apart. Lieutenant-Commander John Devane. What a man.

134

Metcalf gave a great yawn and raised his glasses again. He felt sick. It was impossible, but *there was a ship*. It had not been there before. Surely? He shouted, *"Ship! Starboard quarter!"*

He was close to panic as he tried to identify it. An old tramp steamer of the three-island type, with a pair of derricks and one funnel, which at such a distance looked as thin as a matchstick.

Above the upsurge of voices, he heard Devane's shout. "What course?"

Metcalf struggled frantically with the bearing. "I—I think she's heading south, sir!"

The lenses misted over momentarily, and when he looked again he saw a tiny patch of colour on the old freighter's side. Red, with some sort of insignia in the centre.

He shouted down the information and heard Carroll call crisply, "Turkish, sir."

Devane said, "That follows. She may not have seen us though. Heading for Istanbul probably."

Mackay's voice, frustrated and angry, echoed across the water. "I can't move yet! It's worse than my chief thought!"

Devane waved to him across the darkening water. It was too late anyway. Lincke had done it again. When he came looking for them in the future it would be another story. "Get that lad down. An MTB's mast is hardly suited for lookout duty," he said.

Metcalf eased his leg from the yard and took a last glance at the Turkish ship. She was pouring out a long trail of black, greasy smoke which hung over her wake like a tail.

Carroll shouted, "Come on, boy! Jump about! I'm still holding the bloody line for you!"

Metcalf could not speak. And for an instant longer he thought his eyes were playing tricks. Then in a remarkably steady voice he shouted, "Three vessels, sir! Same bearing as the ship! Closing fast!" He was vaguely conscious of the sudden silence, the immensity of his discovery. "I—I believe they're E-boats, sir!"

He almost fell headlong as Carroll lowered him to the bridge and Devane beckoned him to the side.

"Sure?"

Metcalf nodded. "Three, sir. You'll not be able to see them now. They're beyond the freighter. Two very close together."

Beresford said, "One of them's towing the damaged boat." They looked at each other. "The third will be Lincke."

135

"Tell *Kestrel*. Make it quick." Devane stepped into the forepart of the bridge. "Bring her about, Swain." A precious second to check the compass. "Steer north eighty east. Stand by all engines."

Beresford pounded his fist below the screen. "What the *hell* is holding *Kestrel*?"

"Never mind him. I'm going all out for that freighter. She's our only chance. If she signals the Jerries we're in for trouble." He bared his teeth. "What about the odds now?"

Beresford was cocking a German Luger which he had brought aboard. "Three to one, if Red stays out of it. Not good at all."

"Steady on north eighty east, sir." Pellegrine was completely absorbed. He paused to glance at Metcalf by his side. "All your fault, this is. It's me bloody birthday too!"

Carroll said dryly, "Happy Birthday, Swain!"

Devane stared directly ahead. He could see the old ship more clearly now. There was so much smoke, the other boats might be anywhere.

He made up his mind. "All ahead full!"

He gripped the rail and bent his knees as the hull lifted violently to the surge of power. It was like riding a living thing, as she tore across the swell, hurling aside banks of foam like a plough through snow.

Beresford asked breathlessly, "What d'you want me to do?"

"No passengers here, Ralph!" Devane laughed. "Bridges has an injured foot. Give him a hand on the port MG mounting. You'll be nice and handy if anything unpleasant happens in here!"

He turned towards the freighter again, shutting out all of them except for Priest and his six-pounder. It was as if they were charging headlong to ram the old Turkish tramp steamer. Like Twiss, a crash, a great fireball, then nothing.

A seaman yelled, "Come on, old girl! Shift yerself!" The man sounded excited, as if it were the greatest thing in his life.

Devane gripped the rail more tightly to suppress his sudden despair. Dear God, I don't want to lose her now. *Claudia.*

Pellegrine said, "I'll bet we're makin' those Turks sweat!"

The MTB with the scarlet number 1 painted on her rearing bows was flashing towards the freighter at thirty-nine knots, and when Devane glanced astern he could not see Mackay's boat at all.

He watched as the rusty old ship appeared to slide towards the starboard bow. Tiny faces peered down from the open flying bridge.

Devane let the glasses fall to his chest and felt the spray sting his face like hail. If the rudders jammed now they would blow the neutral ship sky-high.

"Across her stern!" He darted another glance at his men. Taut faces, slitted eyes, bodies stooped as if to withstand the shock as they hit the great pall of black smoke.

The high stern loomed above them and there were more vague pictures. A man in a chef's hat waving and yelling soundlessly, the smoke making Chalmers cough, the nearness of collision which Pellegrine had judged so finely that Devane could have sworn their keel left the sea as they bounded over the other ship's wake.

"E-boat! Port bow!"

"Open fire!"

Guns banged and rattled into life, the cone of tracer lashing across and settling on the leading E-boat like a web. Devane saw the other two Germans moving apart as the towline was slipped and the other commander hurried to support his leader.

It took an age, or so it seemed, for the Germans to react. Devane could hear his men yelling and cursing as they fired and reloaded until the gun muzzles were shimmering with the heat.

He imagined how he would have felt. So close to safety. Just a battered freighter, and then, like an avenger, the MTB had burst through the smoke, every gun firing. Casualties often occurred when a ship was homeward-bound. Now it was happening to Lincke. They could not defeat three E-boats, but he would get Lincke.

Tracer whipped overhead and cut past the old freighter which had made a frightened turn to avoid being hit.

Devane pointed at the leading E-boat. "That one, Swain!"

Everyone near him knew what he meant, and from aft he heard the sudden crack of the twin Oerlikons as the damaged E-boat, parted from her tow, began to drift across the sights.

"Hard a-starboard! Steady. Hard a-port!"

Zigzagging and rolling wildly, the MTB swung towards the second E-boat, and Devane saw the shells and tracer bursting along her bridge and then hurling buckled plating into the air like paper.

The leading E-boat was turning swiftly in an attempt to cut him off from the damaged one, but as they tore past Devane heard the clang of depth charges being lobbed over the quarter and tensed as they exploded together, one almost alongside the drifting boat.

The damaged boat was tilting steeply, and some rubber dinghies were already paddling away. *Two to one.*

Devane was knocked from his feet as shells hammered into the chartroom and exploded against the bridge structure. The cracks and bangs were deafening, and Devane saw blood on his legs and thought he was wounded. But it had been the boatswain's mate who had been hit, killed outright.

The hull jumped and quivered again as more shells ripped through the planking, some exploding in the PO's mess, others going on to shatter the W/T cabin and kill the telegraphist even as he tried to reach a fire extinguisher.

"Hard a-port!" Devane clenched his jaw as bullets clattered around the bridge.

Leading Seaman Priest was crawling away from the six-pounder, and Devane saw Beresford slide behind the controls to replace him. Priest rolled over and lay on his back, waiting to die as his blood pumped steadily into the scuppers.

The second E-boat was streaming smoke and slowing down as the Oerlikon guns cracked over her in twin lines of tracer, smashing down gun crews and wounded alike, and setting fire to some ammunition which turned the upper deck into a death trap.

Devane dashed the spray and sweat from his eyes and stared wildly at the remaining E-boat. She was turning again at full speed, her forward guns spewing balls of tracer towards him as she levelled off on a converging course. He saw the insignia on her bridge, the tiger stripes and the little Union Jacks and Red flags painted on the bridge to display Lincke's "kills".

Now they were meeting at last.

The gratings bounced under Devane's seaboots, and he saw smoke spurt through the planks. A fire had started between decks.

He saw Chalmers staring at it with sick fascination and yelled, "Get down there and *put that fire out!*"

A bullet smacked through the flag locker and Carroll stared at the neat hole it had left within six inches of his thigh. He exclaimed, "I'll go too!"

Chalmers staggered to the bridge gate. "No! I'm all right!" Then he was gone, half falling into the smoke as Pellegrine put the boat into another fierce turn.

"Hard a-starboard!" The smoke was getting worse. Devane squinted at the veering shape of the enemy. "Depth charges!"

But Lincke was ready. As two more charges exploded, hurling up twin columns of spray, he swung away, the E-boat's hull barely splashed as the water cascaded down again.

Pellegrine grunted with pain as a splinter, gouged from the bridge, struck him in the forehead like a barbed dart. When Metcalf tried to help him he snarled, "Leave it be! I'm still alive!"

Metcalf ducked as more splinters of steel and wood shrieked above the bridge, and then heard Devane yell, "Help Bunts!"

Carroll had fallen awkwardly, with one leg bent double beneath him. Between clenched teeth he gasped, "Shot right through! Get a dressing, mate!" Then he fainted.

As the MTB thrashed round yet again, matching burst for burst with the E-boat, her company fought their individual battles throughout her small hull.

In the blazing galley Lieutenant Chalmers and a youthful stoker used axes and extinguishers to quell the fire and to free a wounded seaman who had been carried below for safety. The engine room, half filled with smoke and fumes, was punctured in several places, but the three motors were still holding their revolutions as Ackland, his boiler suit soaked in water from a leaking pump, darted around them. His young helper, whom Ackland had earmarked for promotion, rolled in the bilge waste and leaking oil, his arms outspread as if he had been crucified. A heavy bullet had hit him in the back and he had died alone, his cries unheard in the roar of motors he had served so well.

The Oerlikon gunner, too, was dead, and had to be dragged bodily from his harness before Torpedoman Pollard could take his place.

Lieutenant Dundas rushed to the bridge. "We're taking water, sir!" he exclaimed.

Devane did not answer. The E-boat was turning again. Lincke had dropped a smoke float as an additional shield as he prepared for another attack.

The starboard machineguns fell silent and he heard the seaman blaspheming as he struggled to deal with the stoppage. The weapons had overheated, had fired almost every belt of ammunition.

Dundas ran to the voicepipe and then repeated, "Chief says the starboard rudder is sheered off and the starboard outer shaft is overheating fast!"

"Stop starboard outer, Swain."

Devane felt it like a wound in his body. It was all for nothing. He saw the E-boat's striped outline moving rapidly through the drifting smoke, passing over two swimmers and forcing them under as she headed straight for the MTB.

"Belay that order! I want full revs!"

Devane ignored the startled glances and ran to the opposite side. Lincke was there. Still coming. *Let him come.*

"Straight for him!" Devane ducked as bullets cracked into the bridge. One hit Carroll, killing him as he lay unconscious from his wound.

In his engine room Ackland watched his gauges and knew that the speed was already dropping away. Outside, in that other world of death and stark colour, he knew the moment was close. He thought of the garage where he had worked on the Great North Road, the day-trippers in the sunshine, the bad days when nobody came. Devane wanted full speed. It would destroy the motors and probably the whole bloody boat. What the hell. They were all done for anyway.

Dundas shouted, "Power's dropping!"

Devane nodded, his eyes smarting from the smoke, from the despair, as he accepted that it was almost done. The big E-boat had turned yet again, and appeared to be at right angles to the port bow. Her guns were still flashing, although her after-weapons were badly damaged and firing only in spasmodic bursts.

"Six-pounder's jammed, sir." Metcalf stood looking down at the forecastle, his voice husky and unsteady.

Devane looked past him, expecting to see Beresford dead. But he was sitting with one hand on the gun. Its power had gone. It was useless.

Devane watched the slowly moving E-boat. Lincke was that confident. It was time for the kill, and he was savouring it. He could even see Lincke's white cap on the bridge as he climbed up to watch.

He's not even going to let me surrender. Would I have done the same for him?

Devane watched the E-boat's forward guns train round until they seemed to be pointing directly at him. He felt the motors slowing down, heard the uneven rattle from the damaged shaft.

Shoot, you bastard! It's what you wanted. A sitting duck.

The snarl of racing engines cut above the other sounds, and Devane saw Mackay's MTB tearing through the smoke, her guns

140

flashing vividly as she cut through the wall of smoke like a rocket.
Devane saw it all in a split second. Lincke's figure swing round,
his hat flung from his head as the bridge was raked by tracer.

Lincke's boat had been more badly damaged than he had
realized. As Mackay's MTB tore past with all her weapons firing, the
E-boat's forward guns, which had been pointing so confidently
seconds before, lifted slowly towards the sky and stayed there.

After what seemed like an eternity, someone hoisted a scrap of
white bunting over Lincke's bridge, and a few figures emerged from
below, their hands held high above their heads while they waited
beside their dead and wounded.

Devane stared at Dundas for several seconds. "Stop engines.
Report on damage."

He removed his cap and stood on the gratings to watch the other
MTB moving alongside the surrendered E-boat. Mackay's chief had
been a good one, just as Ackland had said. Another minute, seconds
even, and . . .

Devane looked at his battered command, at the survivors who
were picking their way over the torn planking and broken guns. But
no better than any of mine. No better.

He glanced at Metcalf, shaking now with shock and the surprise
at being alive. At Pellegrine, worn out and leaning on the wheel, a
wooden splinter still bloodily implanted in his forehead. He saw
Chalmers, black from head to toe, leaning against the side of the
bridge, his burned hands resting at his sides. He had beaten the fire
and, with it, his fear.

Beresford climbed up beside him. "Red cut it a bit fine." He tried
to light a cigarette, then grimaced. "Sorry. This place stinks of
petrol!"

Dundas returned. "The chief can get the pumps working, sir, but
he can't manage more than ten knots."

Devane turned as the other MTB thrashed astern from the
motionless E-boat. Mackay had placed demolition charges, and the
German survivors would have to manage on their rubber rafts until
help arrived.

Then Dundas asked him, "Didn't you want to go over and see
Lincke, sir?"

"He's dead." Devane watched the MTB turning towards him.
"It's better not to see your enemies, Roddy. They often look too
much like us."

A light blinked across the water. Dundas triggered off the Aldis and then said, "From *Kestrel*. 'What orders?' "

They looked at each other, and did not even turn when the demolition charges in Lincke's E-boat exploded deep in the hull.

"Tell Red Mackay, 'Thank you very much for your timely help!' " He looked up at the sky, almost dark now. "Orders? We're going home. Just tell him that."

Petty Officer Pellegrine stood back stiffly and fingered the splinter gingerly. " 'Ere, young Metcalf. Take the wheel. Keep station on *Kestrel*. I'm goin' to sit down." He gave a slow grin. "You did well, son."

Devane gripped the screen and felt *Merlin* shivering to life again. *So did you.*

The clouds touched the horizon, and soon the two little ships were lost in darkness. Going home.

Douglas Reeman

When Douglas Reeman describes naval battles from the vantage point of motor torpedo boats, he writes from vivid first-hand experience, for his own wartime service was in MTBs.

Reeman, the author of thirty immensely popular books about the war at sea, both modern and historical, compares MTB warfare with that of Nelson's day. Both were characterized by close contact with the enemy, and were fought at a fast and furious pace. Yet in contrast Reeman can recall with dread the endless hours he spent drifting on the tide, with all engines stopped, listening for the low drumming of a stalking German E-boat's engines.

He seems to have led a charmed life throughout his active service, surviving the sinking of no less than three MTBs. On the third occasion his boat was hit by mortar shells off the coast of Normandy. The craft caught fire and exploded, and Reeman was lucky to escape with his life.

He has never lost his affection for the people with whom he shared the constant dangers of sea warfare. "They were a mixed bunch," he says, "more so than in any other branch of the navy." Since the average age of the sailors was only nineteen, a real devil-may-care attitude existed among the close-knit crews. The comradeship that so naturally developed then is still strong, and Reeman regularly meets fellow veterans at reunions of the MTB Association. There is one problem: at times they find it difficult to remember if they actually served together, or whether they merely met at the last reunion!

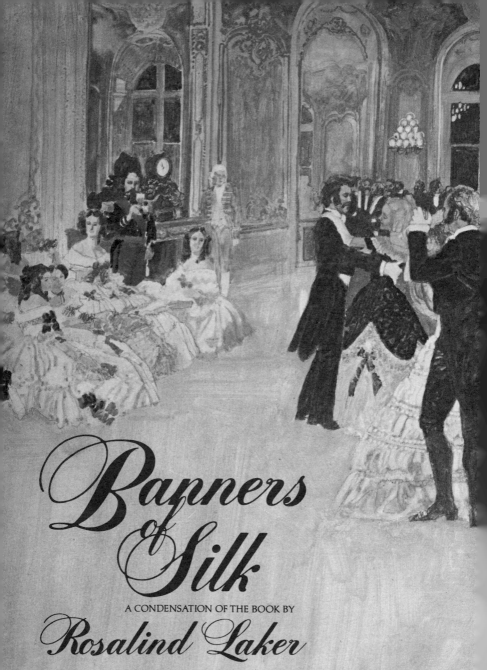

Banners
of Silk

A CONDENSATION OF THE BOOK BY

Rosalind Laker

ILLUSTRATED BY CHUCK HAMRICK
PUBLISHED BY EYRE METHUEN

The lonely orphan shivering in the Paris night seemed destined for a life of poverty. Instead, Louise Vernet's magical skill with needle and thread took her from squalor to the grand salon of the English couturier, Charles Worth, perhaps the greatest dress designer of all time.

There, amid the pageantry and brilliance of Napoleon III's Second Empire, she fitted gowns for the most elegant women of the day. And there Louise lost her heart to the dashing cavalry officer, Pierre de Gand. Though his wealth and high rank stood in the way of happiness, and Louise's own career was to take her from Paris to London, their passion drew them together like a golden thread, shining and unbreakable.

Chapter One

She sat huddled in the darkness, young, afraid, and alone. It was quiet in the paupers' burial ground. Beyond its encompassing railings, lofty buildings shut off all sound of the night throb of Paris. In the rue de Richelieu, only a stone's throw over the rooftops, no echo came of the clatter of the hoofs on the cobbles by high-stepping carriage horses in the frosty January night. Nothing disturbed the stillness in the child's vicinity except the shiver of grass around the newly turned patch of earth, and sometimes the scuttling of rats in the garbage that littered the corners and gutters nearby. It was the fifth consecutive night that Louise Vernet had kept her vigil there. She was ten years old, and all she had to defend herself and the place she guarded was an old kitchen knife.

Fear kept her from tears. A blurring of vision could prevent her from sighting an intruder. Those unidentifiable figures who took a shortcut along the dark path through the churchyard had not seen her in the velvet shadows, and whatever business had them abroad in the night hours was not for the purpose of disturbing the recently buried.

Others who passed by, at the earlier hour of eight o'clock, were the workers who came from a building farther down the unlit back street. These were the grisettes, the seamstresses employed by a certain Madame Camille, one of the leading couturières in Paris in that year of 1843. The child looked forward to their comfortable femininity surging into her bleak surroundings at the end of their long working day. Eagerly she would watch for the first rays of the little lanterns they carried. As they streamed past, thirty or more in

147

number, the glowworm light flickered on weed and branch and sometimes on the thin face of the child herself. In her desolation she yearned to be part of their company, to keep close to the skirts of the motherly older women while joining in the giggles of the younger ones.

Now, on this fifth night, they had come and gone. Nothing would relieve her quaking fear of the night watch until dawn dispersed the danger that she dreaded. Suddenly she heard the faint screech of hinges. Somebody was coming through the far gate, but without an honest light to show the way. She swallowed hard and rose slowly to her feet, the knife shaking in her clasp.

The grisette coming into the churchyard had a lantern, but the flame had nearly gone out, and she cursed it under her breath as she tried to coax the wick back into life. Moreover, she was hampered by the box of outwork that she carried over her arm. She and the other grisettes used the paupers' path, as it was called, because it provided a shortcut to the square, and it was safer than going through the narrow alleyways, where more than one murder had been committed in the past year. In the burial ground there was room to run if need be, and Catherine Allard, soft and round and buxom in her twenty-eighth year, could move swiftly enough when she wanted to.

She felt her way along the path in the darkness, unaware that she was increasing the rigid terror of one from whom she was hidden by bushes. Then at last the wick of the lantern flared high, and Catherine's dazzled eyes caught the gleam of a knife blade. Screaming, she dropped the lantern in the very second that she registered the gaunt, half-demented visage of the child clutching the weapon. She leaped forward, knocked the knife flying, and then snatched it up from the path. Grabbing the child by the collar, Catherine shook her with a violence that made her own auburn ringlets tumble about.

"All right, you little vixen! Who put you up to this? Where are the others?"

"What others, mademoiselle?" Louise cried frantically.

"The rest of the young hooligans waiting to rob an honest citizen. I know the tricks." She bawled into the darkness. "Come out, or your accomplice will feel this blade between her ribs!"

Louise gave a screech of fright. "I'm alone, I swear it! And I wouldn't rob anyone."

148

Catherine released her captive with a thrust that sent the child sprawling. She retrieved her lantern and found to her relief that it was not broken. After tossing the knife into the bushes, she fully expected the misdemeanant to take to her heels. Instead, the child rose to her feet and stood stubbornly, though her shoulders heaved with sobs.

Catherine made a threatening gesture. "Be off with you! Or I'll call on the law to decide fit punishment for you."

"Don't send me away from here." The sobs made it difficult to catch the child's words. "If the medical students come with spades, there'll be nobody to raise the alarm."

Catherine gaped. Then comprehension dawned, and she raised her lantern. Its rays leaped out across a new grave, and her anger and her sympathies were switched. Without doubt this *misérable* had been the victim of a cruel joke. "Who sent you to guard this place?" she demanded.

"No one. There is no one else and never has been. Just my *maman* and me. I'm here to keep her from being taken away."

A gush of compassion overwhelmed Catherine. She was by nature intensely emotional, able to love and hate with equal ease. Her origins stemmed from the district of Les Halles, where the market folk were renowned for their generosity and good humour as well as for their foul language and lusty appetites. Her own mother had been one of the *dames des Halles*, a warmhearted, boisterous woman who had concerned herself in her lifetime with many a waif and stray.

Catherine was filled with remorse. "You poor lamb." She put aside her box and the lantern and crouched down to bring her face on a level with the child's. "Tell me what happened." With gentle hands she tucked the strands of tangled black hair back under the bonnet and smoothed away the tears.

The sobs subsided, and amid sniffs and gulps the tale was told. Louise's widowed mother, Anne-Madeleine Vernet, one of the many weavers in Paris who used their homes as workshops, had fallen ill, a misfortune that had brought the most terrible hardships in its wake. Everything that could be sold went to raise funds, and finally a pauper's funeral ended the sorry tale. Catherine filled in for herself the details of what had followed for Madame Vernet's daughter, with no food except what could be stolen or scrounged, and four terrible nights spent in a churchyard. It was said that medical students helped themselves from new graves when their allotted supplies ran short, but how much truth was in it Catherine did not know. At least it was a danger safely removed from any grave more than twenty-four hours old. As tactfully as she could, Catherine explained why the violation Louise feared would not now take place.

"So you see, there's no need for you to remain here any longer," she concluded comfortingly.

Louise nodded slowly, suddenly at a loss, with nothing left to distract her from the gnawing hunger that now seemed to overcome her. She folded her arms and huddled into herself. Catherine recognized the child's state and sighed.

"You had better come home with me, Louise Vernet," she said resignedly, gathering up the lantern and her box again. "I'll find you a bit of supper." It was not really convenient to have a stranger in her quarters, but she remembered how she had felt as a child when her own mother had died. "You can bed down by the cooking stove for the night," she added generously.

Louise's face became radiant and she sprang into activity, scooping up a bundle of her own belongings and insisting on taking the parcel from her benefactress and carrying it. Catherine was uncomfortably aware of the child's rapt expression. It was best to make the situation perfectly clear.

"I can't do with you under my roof for more than a night." The statement was firm. "You must get yourself off early in the morning even if it is Sunday." She shook an admonishing finger. "And no begging at my door afterwards."

"No, mademoiselle."

As they walked, Catherine volunteered some personal information. "My name is Allard. Catherine Allard."

"It is a pleasure to make your acquaintance, mademoiselle."

"Hmm." Catherine eyed Louise with a sideways glance. "Your mother taught you to be polite, I'll say that for her. It should stand you in good stead. If you tidy yourself up and present yourself at a convent door somewhere, you'd stand a chance of being taken in as a future novice. Otherwise you had better try to get yourself into an orphanage."

They were hurrying across the square and Catherine did not notice that there was no acknowledgment of her advice. Louise's mind was racing, and the idea that she should present herself at any institution did not come into her plans. She had decided to be a grisette. From an early age she had been taught to sew, and she had an exceptional flair with a needle. It had been a foregone conclusion that one day she would earn a living by it. Now she saw Mademoiselle Catherine as a vital link with her dreams, a link that must not be severed.

Like so many other grisettes, Catherine had cheap garret accommodation, hers in a tall, half-timbered house on the rue du Fouarre. As always when she climbed the stairs, one flight after another, she wondered why she was not as thin as a rake with the daily haul of it. But nothing made any difference to her figure, which even in lean times stayed amply curved, a pleasure to those men who had come in and out of her life over the years.

"Here we are." She set a key in the lock, but it was unfastened, and she gave a little cry of surprise as she pushed the door open. Louise, following her, saw that the sharply sloping roof formed a large, wedge-shaped room that served as both kitchen and parlour. Expectantly Catherine darted across to the bedroom door and swung it wide.

"Marcel, *chéri!*" she exclaimed breathlessly.

Louise, craning her neck, saw a young man lower the newspaper that he was reading. He sat in silken shirt sleeves at the end of the bed. There was a scowl on his boyish features.

"You're late," he complained harshly in reply to the woman's greeting. "You're usually home long before this."

"If I had known you would be here—" Catherine broke off, removing her bonnet as she spun around to Louise. "Help yourself to something to eat. I'll be entertaining my gentleman friend until late. You'll find a coverlet in the cupboard." She swept into the bedroom, closing the door behind her.

Louise set down the box of sewing and looked about her. Spotting a candle, she lit it and soon found some food and a bit of poor-quality coffee. She helped herself to a modest share of bread, cheese, and cold meat. With her hunger lessened, she turned her attention to the box she had carried for Catherine. She lifted the lid, interested to see the work that it contained. She caught her breath at the sheen of yellow satin lying within. There was a note stating that the satin had to be turned up a certain number of millimetres. In the morning she would offer to sew every stitch. Had she not been so tired, she would have started on it immediately.

She found the coverlet and spread it in a corner by the stove, then tumbled thankfully into its folds. She was already drifting into sleep when she felt it being tucked more cosily around her. Catherine's bare feet padded away, and the chink of glasses and a wine bottle being taken from the shelf told of her purpose in coming out of the other room.

Louise was up and dressed and had been stitching the yellow satin for more than two hours when the young man emerged from the bedroom, thrusting his arms into a well-cut coat. He gave the child a sharp glance and without a word took his hat from a peg, arranging it at a modish angle before a looking glass. About to depart, he reached into his pocket for a key, which he weighed contemplatively on his palm for a few seconds before tossing it into a wooden dresser. The door closed behind him, and his footsteps faded quickly down the stairs.

It was past noon when Catherine emerged, roseate with sleep. Stretching luxuriously, she looked beatifically at Louise.

"Still here, are you? I thought you would have gone long . . ." Her voice trailed off in a gasp of horror as she saw how Louise had been occupying the time. "Oh, no! What have you done?"

She leaped forward in a frenzy to snatch up one petal-shaped piece of satin after another, and shrieked at Louise in panic and fury. "You wicked, vindictive little wretch! One small scrap of that satin would cost more than your life is worth."

Ashen, not knowing what she had done wrong, Louise managed to dodge the blows aimed at her. "I did it to help. To repay you. My hemming is perfect. *Maman* always said that, and I washed my hands to keep it clean."

"But it wasn't to be turned up that way!" Catherine screamed. In lunging at Louise again, she happened to catch her hip on the edge of the rickety dresser, which rocked wildly. A couple of plates danced loose and smashed to the floor, accompanied by the clang of a key. Seeing it among the debris, she seemed instantly to forget all else. Her hand went unsteadily to her throat. "Where did that key come from?" she questioned.

Louise said shakily, "The gentleman left it when he went away."

All colour drained from Catherine's face; bending double and throwing her arms over her head, she collapsed on her knees to the floor. "I can't bear it. I love Marcel. How can I live without him? I'll die! I'm going to die, die, die."

Her grief was terrible to see, all self-control gone. With a child's instinct to comfort, Louise went and put her arms around the woman, who turned blindly to cling to her. Half smothered by fleshy weight, Louise endured the embrace stoically until she could ease Catherine up into a chair.

"I'll make some coffee," she said consolingly. "It will do you good."

When she had poured a cup she carried it to Catherine. The grisette sipped at it gratefully, her eyes shut. Louise busied herself unpicking some stitches from a piece of the satin, and after a while she brought it to Catherine for inspection.

"Do look. It hardly shows where my hemming was. A gentle press with a flatiron will put it completely right."

Catherine blinked red and swollen eyes. There was no denying that the satin would be as good as new again. "You're quite the young needlewoman, aren't you?" she admitted warily.

"My mother taught me."

"Taught you to read other people's instruction notes too, did she?" There was an edge to Catherine's voice that was lost on the child.

"Yes, she did," Louise replied innocently. "My father taught her to read and she taught me. How did you learn?"

Catherine wiped her wet lashes with the back of her hand. "One of my gentlemen paid for me to have reading and writing lessons. He missed me when he travelled on business, and wanted me to write letters to him."

"He sounds agreeable."

Catherine heaved a deep sigh. "I was really fond of him, although he was three times my age. I had a comfortable little apartment then on the rue de Soissons, but he died suddenly and I was turned out by his wife's lawyers."

"Were you a grisette then?"

"Yes. I worked not because I needed the money, but because it gave me an excuse to see the other girls. The first two or three months with him I nearly went mad with loneliness. Believe me, there's nothing worse in the whole world than being on your own, waiting for a man you care about to slot you into his life for an hour or two." She saw how starkly her listener was regarding her. "Don't look so upset. It needn't be like that for you. Keep out of bad ways that your late *maman* wouldn't like, and one day you'll find a nice young man to marry you."

153

"Why are you not married?"

At any other time Catherine would have resented the question, but now it did her good to talk. "The men I would have liked to marry either had wives already or didn't want to marry me."

The memories brought a bitter frown to her brow, and Louise hastily sought to divert her. "I'll finish unpicking all the hems that I've done."

Catherine answered almost automatically. "Take each stitch out with a needle point. No tugging or catching of threads."

Louise seized the chance presented. "It will take hours to do that. I'll have to stay on till tomorrow."

A vague nod. "Very well. Just get things right." Catherine looked towards the stove. "Have you been cooking? Something smells good."

"I made some soup out of a few scraps I found in the cupboard." Although it was the beginning and end of her culinary achievements, Louise did have the gift of making tasty soup, with plenty of seasoning, herbs, and fried onions. Towards the end of her mother's life she had had to forage for any food she could find, and most of it was suitable only for a soup pot.

"Fetch two bowls from the cupboard," Catherine said. "I'm sure you're as hungry as I am."

They had an unexpectedly companionable meal. At Louise's prompting, Catherine talked readily about her work, rating her employer, Madame Camille, high among the renowned dressmakers of Paris. Much of the work done was commonplace, the customers having already decided what style they wanted. Sometimes, for economy, they provided a discarded silk dress for lining. Such was the number of dressmakers in Paris that even Madame Camille had to compete fiercely in price. In contrast to this mundane confection work, as it was called, there was the sought-after sewing of ball gowns and wedding garments, together with masses of voluminous petticoats. Yet even for this elaborate work customers were prepared to pay only a low sum, so no fortunes were made, and the wages of the grisettes were abysmally low.

"We work twelve hours a day," Catherine said between spoonfuls of soup. "Except between seasons, when we can be turned off at a moment's notice. Then there are times when we have to work right through the night. Some customers won't order a dress until the day before a big occasion, so that no one else finds out what they're wearing. They never give a thought to the likes of us stitching away by lamplight until dawn to get it ready." She sighed. "The workrooms get hot and stuffy with the oil lamps overhead, but at the same time the chill from the flagstones goes right up the thighs, which is why most of us have our own wooden slats in front of our chairs." She tilted her head. "We like to wear pretty caps and clean silk aprons, and give the men of Paris something to think about when we trip by." A little smile touched her mouth. She knew it had been said many a time that it was the grisettes of Paris who made it a city to see. She took another spoonful of soup. "I like the work, no matter if things aren't all that they should be. I suppose the truth is that sewing lovely garments is the next best thing to wearing 'em."

Louise had made herself deaf to the more dismal aspects of being a seamstress that Catherine had mentioned. In her mind's eye the life held storybook colours. "I'd want to wear those beautiful clothes," she burst out.

Catherine frowned across the table. "Wanting to and being able to are two different things. Only the rich can do what they want." A thought struck her. "How was it that nobody in your *maman's* family gave her a helping hand?"

"She didn't have folks of her own any more, and she was too proud to ask the Vernet family. *Maman* had never met them, you see. She was a silk weaver in the city of Lyons when she met and married my father. There was trouble over it, but what sort she never told me. Then, a few days before I was born, my father died with consumption of the lungs."

"Hmm." Catherine peered at her in sudden concern. "You don't have a cough, do you?"

"No. Just the stomach ache when I'm hungry."

Catherine was relieved. "Madame Camille gets rid of anyone who has a persistent cough. I wouldn't want to catch anything."

With the meal finished, Catherine gave Louise a helping hand with the unpicking of the satin pieces, not realizing that her assistance was not welcomed. By early evening all but one piece still held by Louise was done. Catherine heated a pair of flatirons on the stove and carefully pressed out the material. Then she sat down again, and with nimble fingers began to fasten the hems as they should have been done in the first place. The opaque side of the satin was the right one and used uppermost, while the shiny surface was brought over into a hem to make a handsome edging to each petal piece and fastened with an embroidery stitch. Happening to glance up, she saw Louise transfixed with fascination, and she explained why the satin was being thus prepared.

"All these separate pieces will be put into layers on a skirt, making it look like a big, upside-down rose, but first each section must be stitched like this"—she leaned forward in order that the child could see better—"and then like that."

Louise breathed out in awe. "No wonder I did it wrong."

It was then that Catherine realized the child was spinning out the task. She voiced a niggling worry that had been plaguing her. "What shall you do if there's no getting into an orphanage?"

Louise looked up with a composed expression. "I could come back and sew outwork for you."

Catherine stared. "What a sauce you've got! It would cost me my job at Madame Camille's if anyone suspected that the outwork I took home went into other hands." She tapped her chest importantly. "I'm privileged as it is. It's not every seamstress who's allowed to earn a little extra."

Louise shrugged her narrow shoulders, dismissing the argument. "You can check every stitch I do. All I ask in return is that you let me live here until I can get taken on as an apprentice at Madame Camille's."

Catherine laughed. "You couldn't get the job of picking up pins in any dressmaking establishment of consequence until you're at least fourteen years old."

Louise was undeterred. "Then I've lots of time to practise. Meanwhile, I'll keep this place clean for you, collect firewood, carry water up, and cook your meals. All I want is that one day I'll be a seamstress just like you."

Catherine's soft heart could not harden itself against such an appeal. Moreover, the conditions were to her advantage. She could always bring home petticoat frills and understiffening to be hemmed, as well as other straightforward items that normally she did not bother with, choosing more complicated work that paid better. Nobody need know she had not done the work herself, and she would let nothing go by that was not perfectly executed. "We'll see how it goes," she said cautiously. "In the meantime, you can forget about leaving tomorrow."

Louise gave a long sigh of thankfulness.

156

IT WAS NOT Catherine's intention to exploit Louise's willingness to work, but she accepted without much thought the new leisure time that was given her. No more going to market unless it suited her convenience; no more carrying water buckets or scrubbing floors or preparing vegetables. In addition, there was the extra money that Louise's outwork brought in, the payment mounting up better than Catherine had anticipated.

Louise had been in her new home two months when Catherine awoke one night to see candlelight flickering under the door. Thinking that Louise must have forgotten to extinguish the candle, she rose to nip the wick. The sight that met her was not what she expected. Louise sat, still fully dressed, at the table, asleep over her sewing. With consternation Catherine realized just how the abundance of work had been completed. She shook Louise gently by the shoulder.

"Wake up," she said softly. "You can't sit in this chair all night. I don't suppose the floor is very comfortable either. I'll see about getting a truckle bed for you tomorrow."

Louise knew then that Catherine would never send her away.

A year and more went by, and Louise settled completely into her surroundings. Catherine talked about having a narrow space under the eaves made into a bedroom for her, but the money could not be spared. Instead, a patched and faded curtain was rigged up around the truckle bed to give some degree of privacy.

For all her emotional instability and often foolhardy behaviour, Catherine was steadfast in looking after Louise. If the child had any complaint, it was that Catherine gave too much thought to what she believed the late Anne-Madeleine Vernet would have wanted for her daughter. Many a clout or reprimand had been delivered for a lapse of manners, or just for coming home late from an errand and giving cause for anxiety. It often seemed to Louise that had she been a novice in a nunnery she could not have been kept on a stricter path.

Every Sunday after church they would go for a walk, mingling with the crowds, enjoying their escape from the labours of the week. It was then that the people came into their own, making the city theirs. The Bois de Boulogne made a leafy setting for thoroughbred horses and their riders, while the fashionable boulevards held a constant stream of elegant equipages. At times a sense of pure carnival prevailed. Professional entertainers would gather under the bordering trees: jugglers and beggar bards, fortune-tellers, strong men breaking chains, and those with dancing bears or performing monkeys.

Occasionally Catherine and Louise caught a glimpse of King Louis Philippe when the royal coach went bowling by. Their country's constitutional monarch was not a popular figure, and over the years he had become the butt of ridicule and scorn. Lampoonists depicted him as a dumpy figure looking more like a provincial shopkeeper than a royal personage, the umbrella he invariably carried exaggerated out of all proportion. A sword in place of an umbrella would have been much more to the liking of many Frenchmen, who yearned to see France restored to the heights of power and glory of the Empire days. Nevertheless, Louis Philippe was a fervent admirer of Napoleon I. He had seen the emperor's body brought home from Saint Helena and had had the great man's statue reinstated on its column in the Place Vendôme. Catherine made her own laurel wreath every year to add to those that adorned the railings at the base of the statue, not so much in tribute to the past but in hope for the future. Many people thought that Prince Louis Napoleon Bonaparte, imprisoned for conspiracy, was the emperor's son and not just his nephew. Catherine was one among a host of others who believed that France would not be France again until a Bonaparte held the reins once more.

Catherine and Louise had planned to take a walk to the rue de Richelieu one Sunday when a heavy shower sent them scurrying into the Louvre. Catherine shook the raindrops from her shawl and stepped back to gape at a large painting, not noticing the man close behind her who had also come in out of the rain.

"La! Your pardon," she exclaimed as she bumped into him. Turning, she saw a stocky man of medium height with a squarish face, roguish eyes, and a knowing mouth curled into a smile.

"It was my fault entirely, mademoiselle. I should have seen how absorbed you were in that masterpiece. You obviously have a real taste for all this." He gestured towards the treasures around them. "Perhaps I could prevail upon you to explain their merits to me." He caught his breath in affected apology. "Forgive me. I am Henri Berrichon, and I've been in Paris but three months. And you, mademoiselle?"

Introductions took place. Louise half expected to be ignored, having observed that men favoured with Catherine's smiles rarely had eyes for anyone else; but he bowed to her and inquired after her health and was altogether a thoroughly pleasant man. Before long the three of them were drinking hot chocolate at a café on the Boulevard des Italiens. The sun had come out again, creating a rainbow over the city and striking the same colours in the drops that ran from the scalloped edge of the awning under which they sat. This is what it is like to be rich, Louise thought, letting the hot chocolate roll over her tongue.

When they left the café, Henri Berrichon bought Louise a paper twist full of caramels from a street hawker, and then he purchased a bunch of violets from a flower seller for Catherine, saying that they matched her eyes. By the close of that momentous Sunday Catherine was in love again.

Henri was a horse dealer by trade, and like many to whom money is easy come, easy go, he was generous to the point of being extravagant, taking pleasure in spoiling Catherine with little gifts. Louise was never left out, receiving a hair ribbon or a handkerchief trimmed with lace. Henri also had a keen sense of humour and was able to reduce them to helpless mirth with his endless quips, which suited Catherine, who liked a jolly atmosphere.

Louise was delighted to see how happy he and Catherine were together. She had never witnessed anything more touching than the blissful way they held hands, the loving manner in which they cuddled. At the end of the summer Henri had proposed, and Catherine, overcome, had put her arms around Louise and wept with joy.

It seemed only sensible that they should continue to live in the garret for the time being, so Henri bought timber and mixed plaster to construct the long-awaited room under the eaves. He made it much larger than Catherine had thought possible, which made her decide that it should be their room, while Louise would move into the smaller one when the day came.

The wedding dress was sewn from a length of russet silk that Henri had bought, and it lay in shining folds over a chair beside the prettiest bonnet Catherine had ever owned. One evening there came a demanding knock on the garret door. Catherine, tidying a stray curl back into a ringlet with one hand, opened the door to a tight-faced woman standing on the threshold.

The woman looked Catherine up and down and said, "So you're the latest. Where's my husband? I'm Madame Henri Berrichon."

The truth came out. Catherine sank into a chair and sat completely stunned. Henri Berrichon had been through a bigamous marriage during the six years that had elapsed before his wife traced him to Catherine's door. Although the woman waited until late that night and called again next morning, Henri did not appear. He had slipped from his wife's grasp once more. Neither Catherine nor Louise saw him again.

There followed a winter as gloomy as the summer had been joyous. Louise was convinced that Henri had truly loved Catherine, but in her anguish Catherine clapped her hands over her ears and would not listen to any words of comfort. The russet silk dress and the bonnet were packed away, and with a gesture that symbolized the end of all zest for life, Catherine turned the key on the new room and all that was in it.

CHAPTER TWO

The winter passed. In the spring of 1845 the key still remained turned in the door of the spare room. Louise had no objection to sleeping behind the curtain on the truckle bed, but she did think they should supplement their income by taking in a lodger. Catherine, who had not ceased to mope, refused to discuss the suggestion. Louise kept the room clean, and as she aired the good straw mattress that Henri had bought, she was irritated by the unused space. On all the other floors every available nook and cranny was sublet, accommodation at a low rent always being in demand. For the first time she did her outwork with some resentment. It grated on her that Catherine should be unnecessarily improvident.

The return of warmer days brought stuffiness to the garret, but with a window open wide Louise could sew in the breezes that skimmed the rooftops. One day she heard somebody mounting the stairs to the top landing. A knock came. She put aside her sewing and answered the door to a stranger.

He was about twenty, tall and lithely built, his topcoat well fitting, and he had set down beside him a small, brass-cornered trunk, which he must have carried on one broad shoulder up the stairs. He was not far from being handsome, with crisp dark hair, alert brown eyes, and a determined chin.

"*Bonjour*, mademoiselle." He was smiling in a friendly manner, and Louise realized with some embarrassment that she was staring at him. He had a phrase book in his hand and he read a sentence from it haltingly. "Have—you—a—room—to—rent?" he inquired in tortured French.

She knew by his accent that he was an Englishman. "You have come to the wrong door, monsieur," she replied. "A lodger on the floor below is leaving."

He looked at her blankly, then thrust the phrase book forward for her to point out the translation of her reply. As she sought out the answer she had second thoughts. Catherine would have to face up to opening the room sooner or later. Without further hesitation she indicated the sentence that stated a room was available, then found a currency table and showed him what the rent would be. The young man nodded to show that the terms were acceptable if the room should suit him.

"Come in," she invited gravely.

He shouldered his trunk and then removed his stovepipe hat politely with his free hand. Looking around, he was relieved to see that the place was clean. Personally fastidious, he could live in poverty, but not in squalor.

Louise unlocked a recessed door and stood aside for him to enter. He set down his trunk and found himself in a typical attic room, with barely enough space to get past the wide bed, but it was clean and smelled faintly of newish timber and whitewash. A narrow window gave light onto a small round table and a chair which, with a chest of drawers and a chipped enamel basin, made up the room's only other furniture. He put his hat on a peg by the door to show that he was satisfied with the accommodation. Oddly, the girl looked both pleased and scared by his decision, and he thought he had better make himself known to put her at her ease.

"My name is Worth," he said slowly and clearly. "Charles Frederick Worth, to be exact."

She comprehended and gave a quick bob. "Louise Vernet."

He thought the way she had spoken her name quite enchanting.

161

He would have to master the Gallic inflection that came hard to an Englishman, while at the same time learn the language as fast as he could, or he would never find employment in the trade in which he was qualified.

"I'm honoured to make your acquaintance, Louise," he said. When she held out her hand he would have taken her fingers to bow formally over them, had not her palm been turned uppermost to receive the first month's payment in advance.

When the door closed after her, he strode swiftly to the window and flung it wide. Paris at last! The monotonous view of rooftops stretching into the distance did not disappoint him. His artistic eye enabled him to appreciate the russets and greenish greys of the slates set at crazy angles amid crooked chimney pots.

He breathed the air in deeply, wanting to become a physical part of the city in which he had arrived less than two hours ago. How well the journey had gone! First boarding the Channel packet at London Bridge and sailing away down the Thames. A good crossing to Boulogne, and then an outside seat on a coach, where he had cheerfully viewed the soft green flatness of the French countryside. With the coming of dawn the windmills on the hill of Montmartre were sighted, and not long afterwards, with a thunder of wheels over cobbles, he had been swept into Paris. How eagerly he had twisted on his seat to look in one direction and then another as the city stirred in the rising sunlight.

As the coach lumbered on, he smelled the true Paris in the aromas from cafés and wineshops, in the fragrance of cigar shops, in the spit and polish of glossy carriages taking home all-night revellers. Fountains were being turned on, sparkling streams gushing from the mouths of iron fish and cupids and gargoyles. All kinds of handcarts rumbled along with produce for market, vegetables and fruit brimming the baskets.

Not far from the Arc de Triomphe the mud-splashed diligence had set down its passengers. Trying to appear as nonchalant as if he travelled abroad every day of his life, he was nevertheless thankful when a fellow passenger gave him some advice about where to look for accommodation. And he had found it. One garret room and—he leaned out of the window and looked down—the use of an outdoor privy in the courtyard below.

It did not take him long to unpack. On the table he placed his Bible, from which he read every morning, and beside it his

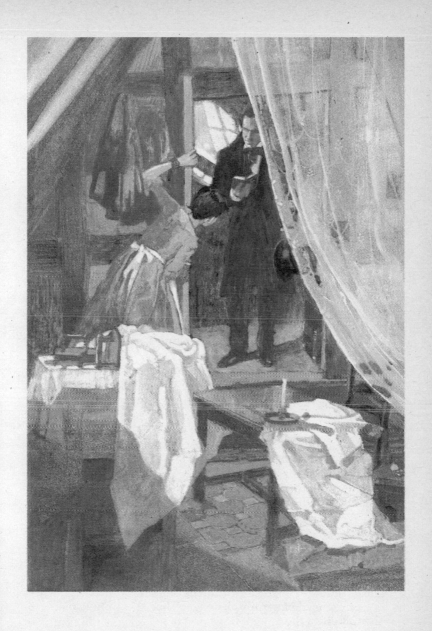

sketching materials. The last items from the trunk were his tools of trade, consisting of a tape measure and a large pair of sharp shears necessary to a draper's shop assistant. Louise had brought him a ewer of hot water, and after washing away the dust of the journey he pulled his cuffs neatly into place and glanced about with a satisfied air. Now to settle the emptiness of his stomach at the cheapest café he could find, and afterwards he would start looking for work.

As he came from his room, he saw the girl was sitting by the window hemming a length of cambric. He tried out the phrase he had rehearsed in French. "I am going out to luncheon."

To his surprise Louise repeated it, correcting his pronunciation, and gratefully he took note. "*Merci*'" he said with a flourish.

She nodded. "*Bon appétit*, Monsieur Worth."

He went out and down the rickety flight of twisting stairs, swinging his new cane. He hoped he would not be forced to defend himself with the blade that flicked out of the end of the cane when a button in the top was depressed. Before he had left London, his friends had presented him with this memento, certain he would need it in a city where the unlit streets were notoriously dangerous.

In the days when he and his brother had lived in the comfortable house at Bourne in Lincolnshire, his father had had a collection of elegant canes, several having concealed blades. He could see them now in his mind's eye, their tops made of gold and silver and ebony, initialled W. W. and engraved with feathery designs. William Worth was a lawyer and gentleman who, when Charles was still a young boy, had been brought to ruin by a passion for gambling. The house, the horses and carriages, the staff, and all that had made up a secure family life had gone, all gone. To Charles the despair of his mother overshadowed everything else. She had never recovered from the loss of his two sisters in infancy, and it grieved him to see her misfortunes increased as she was turned out of her home. He would never forgive his father for that.

Mrs. Worth, deserted by her husband, was at a loss to know where to go. Her elder son had received his law training while there was still money to foot the bills, but she was determined not to make herself and her youngest child a burden to him. She sought refuge with a branch of the family who enjoyed the high standard of living to which she had been accustomed from birth, having been a Quincy of Quincy before her marriage. They agreed to take her in, but she was given the ignominious post of housekeeper in return for her keep and an annual pittance that was barely enough to keep her in working stockings. "But nothing for the boy," her ill-graced benefactor said in tones that brooked no argument. "Take him from school and set him to work."

Then eleven years old, Charles found himself sent away from all that was dear and familiar to him, working from dawn until darkness in a printer's shop, sleeping at night under one of the presses. Each day he awoke to a new loathing of the ink mixing and the sweeping up and the turning of roller handles. He did his best, but as time went by his health began to be affected. He had been a year in the printing trade when he faced his mother at breaking point.

"I'm not made to be a printer, Mama." He caught her hand as if he were drowning. "If I don't get away, I'll die."

Suddenly she believed that he would. It seemed to her he was gaining that hollow-eyed look that all too frequently heralded the dreaded consumption. She came close to panic. "We must find something else for you, but where?" she asked helplessly.

He beamed at her. "Somewhere that has material finer than paper to handle. In a draper's shop, Mama." Eagerness flooded his voice. "Not a small, local business, but one of the renowned establishments in London, where there would be the chance of promotion after apprenticeship."

She took his face between her hands, thinking how he never failed to amaze her, as practical as he was aesthetic in his tastes.

Mrs. Worth humbled herself completely in order to persuade her influential cousin to write to the Drapers' Guild on Charles's behalf, and the letters were duly forthcoming. Charles was given a seven-year apprenticeship at the esteemed linen drapers, Swan and Edgar, and during that time he would serve a twelve-hour day, live on the premises, and obey to the letter the rules laid down for good behaviour. At the end of it he would be a fully-fledged salesman with knowledge of every department, able to deal with all types of customers, and ripe for advancement should he prove himself possessed of exceptional ability.

Charles arrived in a London that was just getting accustomed to having a new young queen on the throne. It was a larger and more confusing and exciting place than he had ever imagined possible, its streets crowded with traffic. Somewhat overcome, he presented himself at 45-51 Regent Street and was at once absorbed into the drapery business.

165

The living quarters for the apprentices were spartan, furnished with only the barest necessities; and the food, while ample and sustaining, was far from tasty. He, like all of his workmates, was addressed solely by his surname. He became so used to being called Worth that it set a pattern for the rest of his life.

For the first year an apprentice was everyone's dogsbody, but Worth's interest and quickness were soon observed by Mr. Edgar, and before long he was assigned to selling the fine materials, shawls, and mantles that the shop retailed. Since he had been reared as a gentleman, it was natural for Worth to greet customers courteously at all times, and he had the ability to judge exactly the colour and style best suited to a customer's complexion or her hair or her eyes.

The ladies who shopped at leading stores expected the best of attention whether they made a purchase or not, and the handsome young apprentice salesman at Swan and Edgar's was without equal in his service. His charm, his genuine interest, his way of looking at a woman as if she eclipsed all others, made them seek him out at whichever counter he happened to be. Inevitably temptations came his way, but he turned a blind eye to subtle blandishments. He was not aware of having high principles, but the waywardness of his father's behaviour had given him an aversion to self-indulgence.

He received no wages as an apprentice, which barred him from theatres and concerts and even the humble pub. The small amount of money that his mother was able to send him went towards such necessities as soap and shoe repairs. Yet the whole panorama of London was his, including the galleries of paintings and sculpture where there was no charge for admission. On one visit to the National Gallery he had come face to face with the famous portrait of Queen Elizabeth wearing the flame-coloured gown with its design of eyes and ears that proclaimed her omnipotence, seeing and hearing everything as sovereign of the land. The luxury of the heavy velvet outmatched anything Worth had ever seen. "If ever I'm rich enough," he had promised himself, "I'll have that fabric copied."

In the galleries he took careful note of the way the women of the past had adorned themselves. It intrigued him to see how velvet enhanced a creamy bosom, how silk was gathered to diminish a waist, the way merino was cut for an eighteenth-century riding habit, and the manner in which gauze and other gossamer fabrics were used, particularly by Gainsborough, for ethereal effect. Each time he emerged from a gallery his eye was offended afresh by the daunting rigidity of silhouette in which women of the present day were encased. The bonnet, the shawl or mantle, and the dome-shaped skirt made them as uniform as pawns on a chessboard. Worth came to the conclusion that fashion should free and beautify women, not imprison them.

His apprenticeship drew to a close. He went to work for a while at Lewis and Allenby, the silk mercers, also in Regent Street. His intelligence and business acumen were noticed by Mr. Allenby, and promotion would soon have come his way, but the idea of going to Paris had recently laid a hold on him. Paris, the centre of fashion that influenced every piece of merchandise that passed through his hands. Worth could think of nothing else, and he wrote to his mother. Would she lend him the money for the fare?

Mrs. Worth once more sought her cousin's aid. After a certain amount of procrastination a reluctant purse was opened on condition that the sum be repaid to the last farthing. Mrs. Worth was able to send her son his fare, with just enough extra to guarantee his keep for a short while until he found employment.

And now he was in Paris at last. Worth swung his cane as he walked on the rue de Rivoli. He was full of optimism.

When Catherine came home, she flew into a rage at the thought of another man occupying the room that was to have been her nuptial chamber.

"Monsieur Worth is nice," Louise insisted stoutly. "He will make a good tenant, I'm sure of it. And he paid a month's rent in advance." She dived her hand into her apron pocket and held out the attractive display of money.

"Very well," Catherine mumbled reluctantly. It would be madness to reject the income. But the high colour remained in her cheeks. She was never to take to Charles Worth. He had appeared to her an intruder, and she could not forgive him for not being Henri Berrichon, irrational though it was.

Although the dressmaking business was in the summer doldrums, Catherine was kept on to sew a wedding gown for stock. Normally everything was made to suit each customer's individual require-ments, but it was always necessary to keep two or three bridal dresses on hand for those marriages that had to take place with undue haste. There was nothing like an elaborate wedding gown that must have taken months of preparation to quash any hint of scandal about the occasion.

At home, Louise, now quite accomplished, utilized her skills in making a new dress for herself out of two old ones. She used the material of one to inset bands into the other that increased in width as they passed down from waist to hem in what was known as pyramid trimming. Daily she sewed, and daily Worth went out searching for employment. One look at his face when he returned would tell her the result.

"Never mind, Monsieur Worth," she would say. "Tomorrow is another day."

They talked together every evening before Catherine came home, which was an invaluable aid to him in improving his French. His stumbling attempts at the language were closing doors to him, and on one occasion he had been openly ridiculed for an error of speech. Each setback only strengthened his determination. He sat in his room studying his French by candlelight far into the night.

Louise suspected that he was not getting enough to eat. She would gladly have given him her portion any time, but she knew that Catherine, whose dislike of Worth was noticeable, was watching for an excuse to be rid of him. And Louise could not endure the thought of Worth's being told to leave.

At first she was not aware of being in love. The sweet and tender emotion that welled up in her at the thought of Worth was so utterly new and strange that she was bewildered by it. Later she did wonder how one said *je t'aime* in English. She had no desire to confess her feelings, shying away from sharing that intimacy with him, but for her own sake she wanted to know how the most beautiful words in any language were expressed in his tongue.

"You are looking very elegant," he said admiringly when she was wearing the finished dress with the pyramid trimming.

She was overwhelmed by the compliment, smoothing the gathers over her lap when she sat and drawing her shabby market-stall boots back under her chair. Out of embarrassment she sought to deprecate the garment she had made. "Do you really like it? It looks what it is, two old dresses made into one."

"But you have made a charming *châle*." It was an incorrect word, and as he sought the true one in his mind he leaned forward on the bench where he was sitting and touched the scallops around the neckline. "This ornamentation."

She swallowed hard. His fingertips had brushed her flesh, and it was as if fire had shot through her. "*Collerette*," she said.

168

He struck his forehead in exasperation. "Of course. I should have known. The English word is basically the same. Why do I have to add stupidity to everything else?"

She was indignant. "You're not stupid. You're very clever. Only a short time in France and already you're able to say so much that I can understand."

He chuckled ruefully. "Not everyone has your patience with me. I find it so much easier to converse with you than with strangers."

"You do?" She held her breath, lowered her lashes and concentrated on lacing her trembling fingers in her lap. She feared with her whole being that he would become aware of her love for him.

His face drew into a thoughtful expression, kindness in his eyes. He knew of and respected her youthful devotion, and with the inner eye of an artist he could see beyond the hesitant girl that she was now to the handsome woman she would become. She already possessed those indefinable depths of mystery without which beauty itself was a veneer that meant nothing. Such a creature could wear clothes to perfection. Even her simple dress needed only a minor adjustment to enhance her graceful arms and hands.

"I know what should be done to your dress," he said. He jumped up and went into his room, returning with pencil and sketch pad. With a few swift lines he changed the whole appearance of the dress by adding a loose falling cuff to the sleeves in the same pattern as the pyramid trimming. "*Voilà!* What do you think of that?"

All tension left her as she appraised the simple innovation. "That's clever! Those cuffs would make all the difference."

He smiled, handing her the sketch to keep. "I can't take all the credit. I saw similar cuffs on a *comtesse* in a portrait in the Louvre."

Louise gave back a smile. "Then I'll be in grand company."

She made up the sleeves out of some leftover material and was delighted with the result. They gave the dress considerable style, and she basked in Worth's praise when he said how well she had carried out his idea.

Before long Worth ran out of money. He was behind with the rent, and each day he feared that Mademoiselle Allard would tell him to leave. Then miraculously his luck changed. He happened to notice a small draper's shop called La Ville de Lyons, which had quality goods in its windows. He marched in with an air of perfect confidence and asked in his much-improved French if there was a vacancy for an assistant.

"There might be." The proprietor himself came from behind the counter. "Do you have letters of reference?"

Worth presented his papers, and the proprietor glanced over them. Swan and Edgar. Lewis and Allenby. He knew London, and the names stood out. "Hmm," he said. "Come into my office, Monsieur Worth. We'll have a little talk."

It was soon settled. Within half an hour Worth had served his first customer at La Ville de Lyons and made a very successful sale. When the shop closed at eight o'clock, he cheerfully tidied the stock on the shelves and swept up. He walked home with a buoyant step, ran up the flights to the garret floor, and there he stopped in dismay. Outside the door was his trunk and a pile of his books. He hammered on the door.

Catherine's voice shouted from within. "If that's Monsieur Worth, go away. Your rent is ten days overdue and your accommodation here is terminated."

His pride prevented him from telling her he had work. Instead, his anger surged. "So be it. Whatever is owing shall be paid to you before long. Is Louise there?"

"No, I've sent her out. You've turned her head enough. Goodbye to you, Monsieur Worth."

He shouldered his belongings and went down the stairs and away from the rue du Fouarre. Out of his first week's wages he sent the outstanding rent by messenger. Catherine sent him back a receipt. She did not ask the messenger where he was.

FOR A LONG TIME Louise looked for Worth wherever she went, but she never saw him. In a city of over a million people it was no wonder. Gradually she became more resigned to the state of things, and the day came when she could go out on an errand without making it a search for him.

They had moved from their garret, Catherine having decided that they should make a fresh start in new surroundings, and taken a room with two sleeping alcoves above a warehouse in the rue Saint-Martin. The accommodation was no less mean than before, but it did have a view of the river, and Louise never tired of watching the traffic on the water. Catherine was more impressed by the lower rent, although they were soon aided in their financial situation by a state event in another country.

There was to be a double wedding in the Spanish royal family, the

170

young Queen Isabella II and her sister, the Infanta, having decided that it should be a joint ceremony. The Infanta's bridegroom was to be one of King Louis Philippe's sons, the Duc de Montpensier, and French couturières were to make all that would be required by the royal brides. Madame Camille was chosen to make Queen Isabella's wedding gown as well as over fifty dresses for the royal trousseau. The needlewomen of every dressmaker of repute were soon working night and day to complete the orders that poured in from ladies of the Spanish aristocracy as well as those of the French and foreign courts who were to be guests. Needles flashed, scissors cut, and thousands of metres of silk *chinée*, satin *broché*, damasks and taffetas were measured out. All were made up in the fashion of stiff, dagger-pointed corsage, with huge skirts stiffened beneath with a horsehair material known as crinoline. Louise did the nail-breaking work of sewing the cumbersome crinoline onto underskirts. But she was thankful to be so busy, and soon memories of the Englishman were pushed even farther back in her mind.

Worth had left La Ville de Lyons. It had served him well, enabling him to establish himself in the French drapery trade while exercising the language, which he now spoke fluently. But when he learned of a vacancy for a qualified assistant at Maison Gagelin, on the fashionable rue de Richelieu, he wrote a letter applying for the post. A few days later a reply advised him of the time when he should present himself for consideration.

In his black broadcloth frock coat and stovepipe hat he arrived at the grand establishment of Maison Gagelin. He looked with intense satisfaction at the ornate entrance and inside at the Persian carpet, all tawny and russet. Through high-flung arches he could see how one section of the shop opened into another, each illumined by crystal chandeliers. Garlands and swags framed the windows, and damask panels lined the walls. There were impressive mahogany counters and plentiful arrangements of hothouse flowers. Display of the merchandise itself was limited to a tasteful glimpse here and there of cashmere shawls and ready-made mantles and cloaks, as well as swaths of handsome materials. Worth had long ago noted that opulence of any kind gave off a peculiarly sensuous aroma, and it hung in the air about him, soft and scented and heady like an exotic incense.

He was shown to the proprietor's office. Behind the desk Monsieur Gagelin sat squarely, rigid and stern, with a gold watch

171

chain looped across his well-cut waistcoat. His moustache was large, as befitted his importance, his side-whiskers abundant. He gestured for Charles to be seated and picked up the letter of application.

"Monsieur Worth, in spite of the comprehensive account you have given me of your time in the drapery business, I would like to hear from you why you should be considered a worthy applicant."

Worth was well aware that his fluency in French was being tested, but had no qualms as he pointed out that customers from the British Isles and the United States would welcome the attention of an assistant able to deal with their requirements in their own tongue. A quarter of an hour later he left the shop in high good humour. He was to start work the following Monday at the material counters, where he would cut lengths for couturières as well as for individual customers choosing fabrics for themselves. There would be a small improvement in his wages, and with the debt paid at last to his mother's cousin, he should be marginally better off.

When Monday morning came he was fitted with a new frock coat and trousers, then taken on a round of the shop by one of his fellow assistants. As always before shop doors opened, a bustle of activity prevailed as shelves and counters were dusted and merchandise uncovered. There were a number of young women assistants, and introductions took place. The tour continued on through the stockrooms and the sewing rooms, where seamstresses were already at work making up or altering garments.

In the weeks that followed, Worth heaved and carried his stock, unrolled it, matched it, measured it, changed one fabric for another, and ran out the billowing, undulating metres yet again. Long experience had taught him how to guide a customer into making up her mind, and his skilful salesmanship did not go unnoticed. He was summoned one morning to Monsieur Gagelin's office.

"You have been promoted to the counter selling mantles and capes and so forth," Monsieur Gagelin informed him with a nod of approval. "Your salary will be adjusted accordingly. Your fellow assistant is a *demoiselle de magasin*, Mademoiselle Vernet."

Worth closed the door of the office behind him and fingered his dark silk cravat thoughtfully. *Vernet!* Surely not Louise Vernet! At once he realized the folly of such speculation. Louise would never have reached so exalted a position, *demoiselles de magasin* being young women from good backgrounds, whose parents paid for the privilege of having them trained in business. As he hurried in the direction of his new counter, he looked forward to meeting the young woman with whom he was to work.

She was busily arranging the folds of an embroidered shawl as he came through the connecting archway. When she saw him her shoulders stiffened, and he wondered with some dismay if she resented having to work with a new partner.

"Mademoiselle Vernet? I'm Charles Worth. We are to serve at this counter together, I've been told. May I say that the profound honour is mine."

"It is a pleasure to become acquainted with you, Monsieur Worth." She had a quiet, melodious voice, and Worth sensed that, far from being hostile, she was simply an extremely shy young woman. Her face was oval and sweet-mouthed, the lower lip full, and her chin was rounded. Her curly hair was rich chestnut. Under the well-defined curve of her brows her eyes were a most unusual sapphire blue. But it was her arresting carriage that made the greatest impact on him. Few women had that indefinable poise that would have enabled them to wear sackcloth with dignity, but he recognized that Mademoiselle Vernet was blessed with it. Her black silk dress appeared extraordinarily stylish, though it was little different from those worn by the other young women assistants.

"I'm sure we shall get on well together," he assured her agreeably. "Have you been at Gagelin's long?"

Her tranquil blue eyes regarded him steadily. "Five years."

Too late he realized that his question had been tantamount to asking her age, since *demoiselles de magasin* started their apprenticeships at the age of sixteen. So she was twenty-one. His age. The faint glaze of rose along her cheekbones had deepened its tint, but otherwise she still stood calmly, completely in charge of herself. Without doubt a most unusual young woman.

"Then you must be more than familiar with this counter," he said in a businesslike manner. "I'd be obliged if you would tell me about the stock and where the items are located."

She dealt efficiently with his request and soon observed his flair for selling when the first customer of the day came to the counter. The lady wanted a short cape, and after she had tried on any number of them, the choice was whittled down to two.

"Which is it to be?" the woman said over and over again. She turned in melting appeal to Worth. "Tell me what you think."

Marie Vernet felt sympathy for him. She knew how difficult it was

173

to point such dithering customers to a choice. But Worth merely smiled and tilted the cheval glass to a better angle.

"Match your eyes, madame," he advised. "In *your* case, whenever in doubt, always match your eyes."

She looked from him to her own wide-eyed reflection with every show of pleasure. "Yes, of course," she agreed a trifle breathlessly, letting the olive-coloured cape slide to the counter while retaining the dark brown velvet. "Yes, indeed."

Marie hid her astonishment. The lady did have handsome eyes, but it would never have occurred to Marie or, she was sure, to any other assistant to compel a decision from the customer by means of a subtle compliment. As the day went on, her respect grew for the selling talents of her new fellow assistant. She could only hope that she would prove an adequate partner at what was now his counter. It would also be prudent, she thought, to guard herself against his apparently irresistible charm.

It took Worth a little while to discover her Christian name, and then it was not Marie herself but another young lady assistant who let it slip in conversation. He would have liked to call her by it whenever customers were not present, but Marie retained a polite formality which made the taking of such a liberty out of the question. They worked together in perfect harmony, but once the dustcovers were placed over the goods for the night, communication was at an end. As the weeks went by he became more and more tantalized by the distance she retained between them.

Marie and Worth had had a particularly busy morning at their counter when a customer swept into the shop with bonnet plumes rearing imperiously, cape floating, and hands clasped in a sable muff. She was Madame Marie-Thérèse de Gand, a rich and powerful widow who often visited Paris from her château in the Loire Valley to attend to matters of business and pleasure, the latter including the lavish replenishment of her wardrobe. On this occasion she had come to attend the graduation at the École Militaire of her only son, Pierre, and she wanted an evening shawl of jewel-like brilliance to set off her new black velvet gown at the Opéra that evening.

She was escorted to one of the gilded chairs set by the appropriate counter. Worth, already engaged in serving at the other end of the counter, glanced at the formidable widow out of the corner of his eye. He recognized instantly the most dreaded of all customers, the woman set on being impossible to please.

174

Marie tirelessly displayed shawl after shawl in the colours requested, carmine and emerald and golden yellow, cobalt and acid pink and shimmering coral. The soft silk and lace mounds grew on the polished mahogany surface, but her efforts were in vain. Madame de Gand continued to shake her head disdainfully at everything she was shown.

Worth, whose own customer had departed, observed the scene closely. Madame de Gand had become bored, and it was obvious that Marie was not going to make a sale. He could imagine Marie's anxious feelings. She knew that Monsieur Gagelin would be far from pleased if this grand customer went from the shop dissatisfied. Quickly opening a drawer, Worth took from it a particularly beautiful snow-white shawl. Sweeping the others aside, he held up its silken spread. "The opera house has colour enough, madame. Don't compete with it. Outshine it! Your gown is to be black velvet and your jewels are to be diamonds. So what could be more outstanding than the sophistication of pure white?"

She saw immediately that he was right. As well as the gilt and crimson of the opera house and the splendour on the stage, the gentlemen in her party would be in military uniform, and she had thought to dazzle against their brilliance. Instead, with a coloured shawl, she would be swamped into the background.

"I am not sure," she declared, not ready yet to be won over.

Worth turned to Marie. "Let me place this shawl around your shoulders to show Madame de Gand the effect it will have." He drew her to the front of the counter and told her to walk up and down. "Go a few yards this way and that."

Marie was dismayed. She was used to displaying shawls behind the counter, but never in front of it. She was aware that not only were Madame de Gand's steely eyes glued on her, but other customers were watching as well. All her life she had hated being the centre of attention. "Go on," Worth prompted gently.

Inwardly she quaked, but she began to walk. In no way did her shyness show as she took one graceful step after another, her head gloriously poised and her back straight. On Marie's prettily shaped shoulders and against the black silk of her dress, the shawl took on an immeasurable splendour.

Worth, watching her, thought again that he had never seen a woman better suited to set off clothes. As she went the full length of the Persian carpet and swung slowly about to retrace her steps, several ladies drifted away from counters to stare at her. Marie, not daring to glance right or left, kept her gaze on Worth, and his eyes held her in a compelling look of encouragement and admiration.

"Once more," he said as she came within earshot. She obeyed, but with inner trepidation, and the shawl, slipping from her shoulders, was further enhanced by a deepening of its folds.

Madame de Gand rose to her feet. "The white shawl will do," she said imperiously. "Send it to my suite at the Hôtel Dauphine, to arrive not later than four o'clock."

Worth bowed and escorted her out to her carriage. When he returned there was no sign of Marie. Jubilant at their shared triumph, he searched about, and after a few minutes he found her leaning against the wall in one of the stockrooms, an arm across her eyes. He pulled the velvet curtain across the doorway as he went to her. "What's the matter? Are you feeling faint?"

She lowered her arm, shaking her head. "It's nothing."

He saw she was trembling, her face open and vulnerable. He reached for a glass of water. "Here. Drink this."

She sipped the water, then adopted a light note that was at variance with the tremor in her voice.

"All went well with the shawl, due to your salesmanship."

He regarded her with pride. "The credit is entirely yours. The customer viewed you in the shawl and thought she could look the same. But never in a thousand years could another woman match you for elegance."

Her cheeks glowed at Worth's extravagant praise. In the emotion of the moment she was aware of how close he was to putting his arms about her. A delicious, slightly delirious panic seized her, and she turned to go back into the counter area. Over her shoulder her gaze came to rest on him with a look of pure affection.

"I have never been paid a more moving compliment. It meant more to me than you could possibly know." And she walked away.

Worth began to realize that he was falling in love with her.

FOR THE FIRST FEW WEEKS Worth made no headway with his courtship. It was hampered by Marie's inherent shyness that also made her so loath to parade in shawls and mantles for customers. This was an innovation in the clothing trade and he now made it a regular practice, finding that nothing sold a piece of apparel more quickly than when Marie displayed it on her person. He was certain

176

that with time she would become used to being admired, and he merely loved her all the more for her modesty.

Then a new development brought Marie still further into the public eye. She needed a new work dress, and knowing Worth was an expert on silk, she asked him to help in its selection. She purchased the fabric he suggested and took it to the sewing room to be made up. The next day was Sunday, and she emerged from church to find Worth outside with a folder under his arm.

He doffed his hat. "I've been waiting to invite you to have coffee with me. I have sketches of your new dress to show you."

At a corner table in a nearby café he ordered the coffee and then opened the folder for her. It contained sketches of a dress viewed from the front, back, and sides. It was beautiful, simple in line, with intricate tucking across the bodice and a discreet piping of velvet highlighting the standing collar and cuffs.

Marie gazed at it in awe. "It's wonderful. I adore it. But the seamstresses at Gagelin's would be at a loss with all those tucks."

His face had become suffused with pleasure at her praise. "My apprenticeship included some instruction in tailoring, and I have the pattern worked out for them to follow down to the last detail. And I'll supervise the fittings myself."

"Fittings? I never have more than one. Nobody does."

"Ah, but you will with my dress. It has to be perfect. Human beings are not geometrically formed, and from what I have observed, dressmakers make up garments as if they were."

"Yes, I think that's true," she agreed. "Tell me, have you done other designs?"

He grinned cheerily. "I jot them down all the time."

She hesitated. "May I see them? Not to choose another for myself," she said quickly. "I'm just extremely interested."

He seized his chance. "Suppose we meet again next Sunday, and then I could show them to you. Afterwards we'll go for a walk and have luncheon somewhere."

She accepted. The following Sunday was a momentous occasion for Worth. It was the first time he had revealed his collection of sketches to another's gaze. Marie gave little gasps of delight as she took up one design after another. When she had seen them all she sat back, marvelling at the originality and grace of the dresses.

"I've never seen anything like them," she declared. "If only they could be made up, they would captivate all who saw them."

178

He smiled, closing the folder. "I'm very glad you like them. If the day should come when they take form, I would want you to be there to wear the best of them."

At this she blushed. It was the first hint he had given of serious intentions towards her. He said no more about the possible future of their relationship then, but launched into his long-held ideas on the subject of fashion. He told her how he deplored fashion's stalemate, declaring that it should be solely for the enchantment of individual women, the present rigidity discarded in favour of a great flowering of beauty. Marie was enthralled. In wordless admiration she rested a hand on his arm. Immediately he covered it with his own, looking into her eyes. He was aware of a special bond between them.

They left the café and took a stroll down the Boulevard des Italiens. After eating in a small restaurant, they went to the Jardin des Plantes, where they sat on a park bench.

When their time together was over, he escorted her back to the Maison Gagelin, where she and the other female assistants had their lodgings. Worth pressed Marie's hand lightly. "Say you'll come out with me again next Sunday."

"That would be most pleasurable."

THE FIRST FITTING of Marie's dress took place in the deserted sewing room after shop hours. The seamstress had left it for her, and when she had put it on she called Worth. She turned one way and then the other to view her reflection in a long mirror.

"How splendid it looks! I've never had such a dress. . . ." Her voice trailed away when she saw his disappointment.

"Those ham-fisted women haven't begun to get it right!" he stormed. "Look at the set of that sleeve!" He ripped it away from its seam. "The darts are too high, and the gathering at the waist is not even!" He snatched up a pair of scissors and began snipping.

"No! Please don't!" she gasped, trying to hold the dress together.

"It has to be repinned and retacked. I'll do it myself now." More stitches parted. Gathers gave way to show her petticoat.

"I beg you! No more!"

The desperation of her plea made him halt. With a start he saw that he had exposed her shoulder, and she was clutching the front of the bodice to the low neckline of her lace-trimmed chemise. Worth stared at her. She was lovely beyond belief.

"The repinning won't take long," he said dazedly.

179

He went to work on the dress, and all the time Marie stood with her lashes downcast. The self-control Worth was exerting made his brow glisten as he slid his fingers under the cloth to protect her from the pins. Marie in her petticoats had ignited an adoring passion in him that was to last the rest of his life.

The next fitting went smoothly. Nothing was needed but a minuscule adjustment to one cuff. On the morning that Marie appeared in the dress for the first time, her fellow *vendeuses* came from every quarter, exclaiming and complimenting her. As the day continued, customers began to make inquiries, but were disappointed to learn that the garment was not available to them.

The comments continued, and Worth finally went to his employer with a suggestion as to how this keen interest in his dress could be commercialized. Enthusiastically he made his point to Monsieur Gagelin and the new partner in the business, Monsieur Opigez. "You could have a collection of dresses made up from my designs in muslin, and customers could choose from the materials that you sell. I'm sure that there would be a ready sale."

Monsieur Gagelin was outraged. "You would turn this distinguished house into a common dressmaker's!" His voice shook. The hierarchy in trade was clearly defined, and to slip down by one fraction could change the whole class of one's customers. He turned to his partner. "Do you not agree, monsieur?"

"Let us hear no more of the matter," he endorsed inflexibly.

Worth was both angered and exasperated by the shortsighted rejection, but Marie soothed him and bade him be patient. She was his joy. They spent every Sunday together. She had shown him in countless small ways that she was aware of his feelings towards her, although he had not yet dared to voice his longing.

It was a warm Sunday afternoon in May when they set out to visit the Palace of Versailles to see the recently restored picture and sculpture galleries. When they arrived they turned by mutual, unspoken consent in the direction of the gardens. The air was as soft as a feathered fan, and their feet made no sound on the lush grass. A kind of magic possessed the day.

They came upon an ancient stone seat under a veritable canopy of purple lilac. He drew her down on it beside him and took both her hands. She could scarcely breathe, her heart hammering in her breast. She saw such tenderness in his gaze that she knew the words he would say before he uttered them.

"I love you, Marie. With all my heart and soul and for all eternity I'll love only you."

She melted into his arms. "I love you, dearest Charles. This is truly the happiest day of my life."

They could make no plans for the future. They knew that circumstances and their low wages prevented any talk of marriage for an unforeseeable length of time. Their consolation was that they would be in each other's company every day. Only one shadow was to mar their time together. No matter how hard she tried, Marie could not overcome her dislike of promenading up and down to show merchandise and avoided it whenever she could. It was the only point about which they ever had a disagreement.

Worth designed another work dress for her, this one with fluted inlets in the graceful skirt. Customers took one look at it and wanted such a dress for themselves. When thwarted, they made their displeasure known to the proprietors, who were at a loss to comprehend why some of their most esteemed ladies wanted the dresses worn by a lowly *vendeuse!*

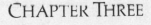

CHAPTER THREE

When Louise Vernet reached the age of fifteen she realized to her relief that she had stopped growing. She was taller than average, with a slender waist and long, well-shaped legs. Her face had changed little, not even Catherine, who was always biased as far as Louise was concerned, was able to say that her looks were remarkable. Only her eyes had real quality, ever changing from golden brown to amber according to the variance of light as well as mood. Her blue-black hair was straight and heavy, and she wore it coiled at the nape of her long white neck.

Over the past months she had presented herself, with samples of her sewing work, at fine dressmaking establishments, but such doors were shut firmly in the faces of those who had not served their apprenticeship. Louise knew that at anything less than the best establishments she would learn nothing, and earn less than she gathered in from her sewing at home, making simple dresses for the wives and daughters of tradesmen. This work had become a necessity. The failure of the corn harvest and the blighting of the potato crop the previous year had made the price of foodstuffs soar, and Louise frequently sewed a whole dress for less than the price of a loaf of bread. Because of a decline in trade, the outwork that Catherine had once brought home had come to an end long ago.

The desperate economic crisis resulted in innumerable clashes between political groups and the gendarmerie. Posters demanding work, food, and wider suffrage appeared overnight, only to be torn down by officialdom in the morning. One night when Catherine was hurrying home from work, she was knocked to the ground by a demonstrator and injured in a scuffle. The next morning, when she tried to get up, she kept fainting away. As she became more and more anxious about getting to work, the swooning spells increased.

Louise donned Catherine's cap and shawl. "I'm going in your place," she said. "After all you've taught me, I'll get by."

"You mustn't go!" Catherine groaned, putting a hand to her aching head. "You'll be spotted, and I'll end up getting the boot."

"You'll get it anyway if you don't appear," was the crisp reply. "Wish me luck."

When Louise reached the throng of grisettes making their way to work, she explained the circumstances to two of Catherine's workmates, Berthe and Aude, who soon spread the word to the others.

"You keep with us," said Berthe. "We might get away with it."

With Catherine's cap pulled well down over her hair, Louise followed Berthe through the patternmaking, pressing, and cutting rooms before she reached those set aside for the needlewomen. A vast table occupied the centre of each sewing area, and after collecting Catherine's work for the day, Louise squeezed into the chair between Berthe's and Aude's.

"Thread your needle and get started," Aude advised. "It don't do to look idle for a second."

The work Louise had in hand was gauging seven breadths of shot taffeta onto a waistband, the secret being to keep it even. As she slipped on her thimble she caught the encouraging nods and smiles of other seamstresses around the table, and then all heads bent over their work. Talk was discouraged by the supervisor, Madame Rousseau, a thin, energetic woman with a pale complexion and dyed red hair. However, when she was out of earshot, chatter buzzed around the table.

Louise commented to Berthe, "Everybody's sewing such sombre shades. Not at all what I had expected."

Berthe snipped a thread with her scissors. "The court is still in mourning for the king's sister. It's only a couple of months since she died, and for a while all the ladies' new clothes will be in grey or purple. If it had been King Louis Philippe himself, we would have been up to our necks in black for a year."

When Louise had finished the last of the gauging, a work supplier brought over five widths of taffeta to be made into ruffles for a skirt. Louise set to work again, feeling some sympathy for the eventual wearer of the garment, who with her many petticoats and under-skirts stiffened with crinoline would have a considerable weight to carry around.

"Mademoiselle Allard! Are those ruffles finished?"

Louise looked up with a start. Madame Rousseau, a little distance away, was checking a list that she held.

"Almost," Louise mumbled, drawing back in her chair.

"You're slow today. What has been the delay?"

Louise froze, hearing the clack of footsteps bent on investigation. Then there came a gasp of astonishment, and the cap was whipped from her head. "Where have you come from?" the woman exploded. "How long have you been on these premises? Who *are* you?"

Louise gave her name and explained about Catherine's injury, but the inquisition did not end there. In the supervisor's office, Louise's work was spread out and examined for defects and faults, but none of consequence was found. Madame Rousseau sat down in her chair at the desk, facing Louise sternly. "I do not know who is the most to blame, Mademoiselle Allard or you."

"I am. She didn't want me to come, but I hoped to save her from losing her job."

"I have never dismissed a seamstress yet for being genuinely indisposed, although naturally I have to suspend them from employment during any illness. However, Madame Camille expects her seamstresses to keep out of street brawls and political upris-ings." There was a pause. "How old are you?"

"Almost sixteen."

The supervisor's long fingers beat a thoughtful tattoo on the desk. "You are remarkably young to have reached the standard of sewing that you have shown today."

"Thank you, madame." Louise set her shoulders and came out boldly with her request. "Would Madame Camille take me as an apprentice on the merits of my work?"

Madame Rousseau answered without hesitation. "Out of the question." She saw disappointment strike the girl's expressive face. "However," she added, "all is not lost. Do you know what it means to be an improver?"

Louise blinked, hardly daring to hope. "Yes. Improvers are those who have served a dressmaking apprenticeship and are ready to take on more varied and extended work."

"Correct. I happen to think that you have reached that stage." Madame Rousseau took up a pen and dipped it in the inkwell. "In view of your accomplishments, I feel justified in creating such a niche for you. Tell me your name again." She wrote it down. "You will inform Mademoiselle Allard that she may have one more day's rest, and she is to bring you with her when she returns."

Louise set off to run all the way home, but she had not gone far before she realized that something serious was afoot in the city. The air was charged and electric, and several times she had to skirt throngs of men, their voices angry in political discourse. Many times she heard shouts of *"Vive la réforme!"* When she reached the safety of her own door, Catherine fell upon her in relief.

"Thank heavens you're safely home. I heard neighbours saying that the government has banned the political rally that was to be held tomorrow, and heaven knows what will happen now."

All the anxiety could not quell Catherine's reaction to the good news that Louise had to tell, and she insisted on opening a bottle of wine. They drank two toasts, the first to Louise's future and the second to the future of France.

"May we see our country restored to the glory of the Empire," Catherine said, raising her glass towards a tricolour on the wall. "Let the exile of Prince Louis Napoleon Bonaparte soon be over."

Later that evening thirty demonstrators were shot down by the National Guard. The slaughter was the signal for a great uprising and a state of armed mob rule. The next day King Louis Philippe and his queen fled Paris with only the clothes they wore. They reached the coast and immediately took ship for England. In Paris a Second

184

French Republic was declared under a provisional government.

The following morning, as soon as it was safe to venture out, Catherine and Louise hurried through streets bearing the scars of the short and violent overthrow to reach Madame Camille's workshop. They found the gates padlocked, and took their turn with other silent and subdued grisettes to read the notice displayed. FEBRUARY 25, 1848. MADAME CAMILLE REGRETS THAT IN THE PRESENT UNCERTAIN CIRCUMSTANCES THIS ESTABLISHMENT WILL REMAIN CLOSED UNTIL FURTHER NOTICE.

It was not only Madame Camille who had put up her shutters. Stocks had fallen, and there had been a run on the banks. Foreigners, who normally crowded the city of pleasure, had departed, causing many hotels to close. Catherine and Louise were among thousands deprived of a livelihood.

By May, the Second French Republic was failing to provide the work for which so many were desperate. Starvation was rife. In June, a hundred thousand hungry men rose up in vengeful revolt, and once again Paris was a city of guns and flames. Troops were rushed in, and for four terrible days the battle was fought, with no mercy shown on either side. The dead numbered in the thousands, and the gutters ran with blood.

The rebellion was finally quelled, but its aftermath brought still greater hardships to the citizens of Paris. Businesses collapsed in bankruptcy, shops closed, and elegant carriages became a rare sight in the streets. Ladies made do with the dresses they had, and little work came the couturières' way.

Neither Catherine nor Louise had work of any kind. Unable to pay their rent, they removed their belongings under cover of darkness and took one small room in a hovel near the bread market. Louise went back to her well-remembered methods of foraging for food, returning to the haunts of her childhood and her old tricks of snatching anything edible from stalls or passing carts.

Whenever she went out on her sorties she saw posters concerned with the forthcoming elections. They advocated votes for Louis Napoleon, whose name seemed to be working magic on thousands who were to vote for the first time. In December he was brought into power, voted by universal suffrage President of the French Republic.

Louise and Catherine went to see him on his triumphant ride through Paris. Louise picked some pale winter rosebuds from the garden of an empty house and carefully removed every thorn from the stalks as she waited at Catherine's side near the Élysée Palace, the new president's official residence. It was a crisp, sunny day, and her spirits were high, for she had managed to obtain a little sewing work from a shopkeeper's wife.

The drumming of regimental music heralded the coming of the prince-president. Along the rue du Faubourg Saint-Honoré there rode into view a splendid escort of cavalry. Among the most spectacular were the cuirassiers, their scarlet and blue tunics set off by white breeches and black knee boots pressed against the sheen of their dapple-grey horses. The crowd pressed forward excitedly, those at the forefront being pushed almost into the cavalry's path. Louise tried to draw back, and in the same instant a young officer's white-gauntleted hand swept down and snatched the rosebuds from her. She gasped, caught totally unawares, and saw the cuirassier's face above her as he leaned in the saddle. He had a tanned, firm-jawed face and low-lidded, grey-green eyes lively with laughter.

"Flowers for me?" he quipped wickedly. "Ever at your service, mademoiselle!"

Helplessly she watched him bear her rosebuds away in triumph, his glance sliding back recklessly to hold her gaze until he could look no longer.

She plucked at Catherine's sleeve. "Did you see what happened to my flowers!" she exclaimed, but Catherine did not hear.

"There he is!" Catherine's cry burst exuberantly from her throat. *"Vive le président!"*

Louise, her thoughts still full of the cuirassier, watched the new ruler of France's destiny ride into view, acutely conscious of having no roses to throw in his path. Mounted on a magnificent chestnut charger, his gold epaulets dancing, Prince-President Louis Napoleon, in his mid-forties, bore a strong resemblance to his emperor uncle, whose statue he was shortly to pass in the Place Vendôme. A superb horseman, he was a long-bodied, short-legged man, with a prominent forehead, a large nose, and a wax-ended moustache and goatee beard that many Frenchmen were already emulating. Louise joyfully joined in the cheers until he had gone by, continuing his path of acclaim through the city.

That same evening Lieutenant Pierre de Gand of the Sixth Cuirassiers, off duty and no longer in uniform, returned to the rue du Faubourg Saint-Honoré and reached the place where he had

snatched the rosebuds from a pair of reluctant hands. He sauntered along, a determined thrust to his chin, as he scrutinized the area in the faint hope that he might see the girl again somewhere in the vicinity.

Who was she? he pondered. Did she make bonnets for a milliner or sell bread in a *boulangerie*? Not since his cadet days had he thought to consort with a pretty shopgirl, but the magnetism emanating from her had gripped him in those few extraordinary moments.

There were a few passers-by in the street, but no figure that he recognized. He frowned impatiently at the whim that had brought him there. He had better things to do with his time. A hackney cab was coming along the street and he hailed it, giving the address of a café where he knew his fellow officers would be.

Week followed week, and the prince-president's influence on the economy gradually made itself felt. Hotels reopened. Shutters were taken down from shops, and here and there a coat of fresh paint made an optimistic splash of colour. Trade began to revive, and Madame Camille opened her workshop again. Among her sewing hands was the young improver named Louise Vernet.

BY THE TIME she was seventeen Louise had been promoted, by way of a brief spell at Catherine's table, to the embroiderers' room, where the perfection of her stitches was put to full glory. Leaves and flowers and classic motifs sprang forth in her multi-coloured silks to trail in abundance over ball gowns and day dresses, wedding mantles and sweeping trains.

Louise and Catherine moved from their hovel into quarters similar to those they had shared before, their frugal standard of living raised fractionally by Louise's wages. The seasonal rise and fall in trade, however, still prevented the smallest extravagance.

From her first day of employment Louise had absorbed everything that would stand her in good stead in her dressmaking career. At the present time she was expanding her range of knowledge by taking lessons in patternmaking from the newly hired cutter at Madame Camille's. His name was Will Russell. It was the second time an Englishman had entered her life.

A male cutter was something of an innovation. Most couturières preferred women for this task, believing they produced feminine lines better suited to the air of gentility and helplessness necessary

188

to a lady's garments. But Madame Camille had become aware of the evolving trend towards lines of extreme smartness to express the uncompromising assertion of Frenchwomen in the aftermath of the 1848 revolution. With this new emphasis in mind, she sought an English cutter to interpret her clothes, because none could deny that the best tailoring in the world came from across the English Channel.

Will Russell had gained experience in a London cloth mill and was working for the renowned Paris tailor Ebeling when Madame Camille found him.

"I must point out," he informed Madame Camille in his excellent French, "that at Ebeling's I have already expended some of the time I allotted to being in Paris. I intend to go back to England as soon as my two years are up."

"I do not see any great problem there," she replied cautiously. It was not that point which made her hesitate to employ him. It was the effect that his powerfully masculine presence would have on her needlewomen that concerned her. With his rebellious fair hair, his arrogant look, and his powerful body, it was obvious that Will Russell was, at the age of twenty-seven, in his full and lusty prime. But there was no denying his professional skill, and she came to the reluctant conclusion that her needlewomen would have to look out for themselves. "Very well, Mr. Russell. The rest of your time in France shall be in my employ."

Will Russell moved into the cutting room with all the dedicated upheaval of a new broom. He extended the tables with his own carpentry and put up shelves. He rearranged the oil lamps to give maximum light with reflectors he had made himself, being something of an inventor in his spare time. From the start he made it clear that he considered the cutting room his domain, and he kept very much to himself.

A number of the women fancied him, but even those who twitched their petticoats harder than most gained no more than an appreciative grin. They concluded that he had decided to live by the old bachelor adage of never soiling one's own doorstep.

Will had been born in England, the son of a Portsmouth sea captain. His mother was Welsh, and it was from her side of the family that he inherited his rugged good looks and his deep singing voice. At times he felt more Welsh than English, and the musical speech of Wales had fastened itself on his tongue with steadfastness.

It amused Louise to imitate his undulating foreign accent for the entertainment of the other grisettes, until one day they fell silent, choking back their giggles, and stared in embarrassed consternation towards the doorway. There he stood, with muscular arms folded ominously. Louise, struggling not to laugh, lowered her needlework. "La! Monsieur Russell! I didn't see you there."

He glowered at her. "When you can speak English better than I can speak French, you'll have the right to mock, but not before."

Her quick wits reacted instantly. She sprang up from her chair and faced him, arms akimbo. "*Bon!*" Then she added in what little English she could summon, "You may teach me. Yes?"

For a second or two he looked dumbfounded, then an answering glint danced in his narrowed eyes. "I'll teach you, Mademoiselle Whatever-your-name-is. But I'm warning you that I'll tolerate nothing less than the best of results."

Running a hand through his thick hair, he returned to the cutting room, and Louise collapsed back into her chair, convulsed with mirth.

After that day Will Russell never saw Louise without speaking some words of English to her. She bought a French-English phrase book and rehearsed sentences to practise on him, and he was merciless in his corrections. Gradually she began to build on the bare bones of the language she had gained from Worth, and eventually was able to converse with some fluency.

Louise had begun to feel that all that was missing in her dressmaking skills was a masterly touch in cutting patterns. Long ago Catherine had taught her how to make a garment pattern from any picture, but even Catherine did not have Will Russell's ability with the shears. The quality of his lines and the adept way he could adjust a pattern for perfection of fit were what Louise wanted to acquire. He heard out her request, then nodded.

"Very well. You'll have to be here a quarter of an hour earlier in the mornings, and I can spare you a short time during the midday break."

She proved to be an enthusiastic pupil, and Madame Rousseau did not disallow the instruction, since no time was taken for it from Madame Camille. Louise was teased by the other grisettes about Will, but untouched and physically unawakened, she tripped in and out of his company without the least consideration of the effect she might be having upon him.

190

MADAME ROUSSEAU announced her retirement. Her successor was Mademoiselle Nenette Deneuve, who was small, dark-haired, youngish, and a veritable martinet. She altered everything, rearranged the seating in order to separate talkers, and started a battle with Will that was to rage unceasingly. She tried to exercise her power over him, and he stubbornly refused to change his method of work. When she attempted to reorganize the cutting room, he ordered her out. She retaliated by criticizing his cutting, but it continued to leave his hands as faultless as ever.

Louise fell an early victim to the battle and was forbidden entry to the cutting room, on the old rule of segregation of the sexes. Her instruction had reached a point where Madame Rousseau had told her she could make a full pattern and cut from it under Will's supervision, but now that chance was snatched from her. She fumed and threw up her hands and stamped her foot, her Gallic blood aroused, and finally she went to the cutting-room doorway to break the news to Will.

"The supervisor has refused permission for me to cut a garment!" she exclaimed.

Will straightened up from laying out a pattern "Well now, don't you worry." He came strolling across to her, smiling. "There's more ways of killing a cat than drowning it."

She gave a vexed little laugh. "What do you mean?"

He had no chance to tell her. Down the corridor a sharp voice echoed against the walls. "Mademoiselle Vernet, must I warn you again? Monsieur Russell! Back to work!"

Louise rolled up her eyes and shot away to the embroiderers' room. Will did not move from the doorway, but merely folded his arms, the tawny hairs glinting below the rolled-up sleeves of his smock. There came an angry clack of heels, and Mademoiselle Deneuve was facing him, her lips drawn tight. "Are you deaf as well as insolent?"

Without expression he began to sing under his breath. Her temper increased. She began to accuse him of laziness, acidly criticizing his work, as she had done so often before. He heard none of it, and neither did anyone else, for as he turned back to his table he drowned her tirade in an old song of the Welsh valleys. Mademoiselle Deneuve stamped from the room.

From that day forward Louise became the target of the supervisor's most vicious criticism. Throughout each verbal attack Louise

191

seethed inwardly, her teeth gritted, her eyes fixed on her embroidery. There were evenings when she went home pale from her ordeal. Catherine was indignant.

"I've met her sort before. Jealous women always try to belittle the skills of others and deride their achievements."

"Why should she be jealous of me?" Louise asked.

"If you don't know, then I'm not telling you."

One morning Will caught up with Louise near the entrance to Madame Camille's and told her to come to the cutting room some evening after everyone else had gone. She was overjoyed, but said nothing to Catherine, who would have argued against it.

The opportunity came when Catherine went out to supper with a beau. Louise took the path through the paupers' burial ground and climbed the wall with the aid of a stout wooden crate that Will had concealed in the long grass. Once at Madame Camille's she tapped on the shutters of the cutting room, then darted around to the workshop door, where Will let her in.

"Isn't this fun!" she exclaimed excitedly, and sprang ahead of him into the brightly lit cutting room, shedding her shawl and bonnet. She pirouetted gleefully between the tables. "Where do I start?"

"Take the next design off the pattern pile and set to work."

Her face sparkled as she took the top design from the shelf. The instructions stated that it was for a grey silk carriage dress with a tight bodice and high neck, trimmed with fancy buttons and tassels, the sleeves ending in small cuffs, the skirt having multiple flounces. The design was not easy, but she resolved to complete it to perfection.

While Will continued with the velvet he had been cutting, Louise set to work at the long table allotted to her, making the pattern according to the design and to the customer's measurements. Neither spoke to the other. She was deft and accurate in her work, but every part of the dress needed the most careful charting, and she smiled when it was finished.

"There! The pattern is done." She brushed back a fallen strand of hair from her heat-dampened brow. It was stifling in the room, and she had unbuttoned the top of her dress a few inches. She was unaware how often Will had glanced across at her. He was half dizzy with her presence.

"Congratulations," he answered automatically, his mind dwelling on the allure of her. "You did that first stage in good time."

She unrolled the bolt of grey silk, the rich fabric shimmering along the table. Will did not help her spread it out, not wanting to risk the slightest physical contact with her. All he could think about was holding her in his arms.

They worked on in silence. When Will had done all he needed to do that night, he folded into a work tray the last garment he had cut and cleared his table in readiness for the morning. Louise cut her last flounce and straightened up. She had lost all track of time and blinked dazedly.

"It's midnight," Will said, extinguishing all the lamps but one.

"I've kept you late," she apologized contritely.

"No. On the contrary. I usually work to one or two o'clock. Now I'll escort you home. Leave everything just as it is."

Tired and deliriously happy at what she had achieved, Louise swayed towards him, smiling, intending to thank him. His senses snapped. He crushed her to him and kissed her passionately.

They fell apart, breathless. Louise stared at him like an awakening sleepwalker. When he reached for her again, she did not draw back but responded ardently and put her arms around his neck. Neither heard the distant jingle of a key ring outside as the gates opened. Then the door of the cutting room shivered as someone entered the building. For a few seconds they froze.

"I mustn't be found here!" Louise said in panic.

Will released her, listening intently. It was a light, familiar step that was approaching.

"It's the Deneuve woman!" he exclaimed. "Quick, the window!"

Louise snatched up her bonnet and shawl as he crossed to the window and threw the outside shutters wide. Effortlessly he picked her up in his arms and helped her through the opening. Her feet touched the ground, and then she was off into the darkness. He only had time to refasten the window before the door opened.

Nenette Deneuve glared at him from the threshold. Suspiciously her eyes came to rest on the window. "Why have the shutters been opened at this late hour?"

"A breath of air, mam'selle."

She charged across the room, the silk fringe on her mantle swinging, and pulled open the window to look out for a few seconds before slamming it shut again. She swung about, and her swift gaze took in the disorder of the cutting table. "Have you been alone here this evening?" she questioned acidly.

193

"Am I not always alone?"

In a burst of fury she hammered a fist on the table. "Stop deceiving me! I heard the thud of the shutters as I drew near. You've had the effrontery to let one of my needlewomen into this place with you. It was that contrary baggage, Louise Vernet!"

His expression was impassive. "Are you sure your imagination isn't running away with you?"

She jerked up her chin viciously. "Indeed it is not. In gross defiance of my instructions you have allowed Vernet to tamper with costly material that has most surely been ruined. Madame Camille shall hear of this first thing in the morning."

"No, she won't," he said, his quiet tone implacable, "and there are two good reasons why. Firstly, I don't expect any mistakes to be found in what has been cut. Secondly, you can't denounce anyone without involving me, and you don't want to run the risk of seeing me thrown out."

"I don't know what you're talking about."

His eyes held hers compellingly. "You're more angry about finding out that I haven't been alone here than about the flouting of your discipline."

Her neck was taut. "I only came to check that all was in order."

He raised an eyebrow. "At midnight? About the hour when you judged my work to be almost done?"

Her face was patchy as she retorted, "You are as conceited as you are uncouth." She swept from the room, and Will heard the gates clang behind her.

WHEN DAWN CAME, Louise was hollow-eyed and anxious. Did trouble await her? She had not dared a backward glance in order to see if Will had been right as to the identity of the intruder. Getting home shortly before Catherine, she had lain in bed and thought about all that had passed between Will and her. Yet this morning she did not want to see him or to meet his eyes. As she took her place at the embroiderers' table, the sound of his voice addressing somebody else sent such colour soaring into her face that she felt it must surely scorch the edge of her frilled linen cap. She bent her head low over her stitching and worked at double her normal pace.

For a while it seemed that it was to be a day like any other. Then late in the afternoon there appeared to be some confusion at Catherine's table in the sewing room. The grisette sitting opposite

194

Louise tilted her chair to catch a glimpse of what was going on. "Looks like trouble with some grey silk," she said.

Louise went ice-cold. She could not conceive that anything might be wrong with the pattern she had cut. Out of the corner of her eye she saw Mademoiselle Deneuve come to the threshold of the embroiderers' room, the tray containing the carriage dress supported on her hip by one hand. Louise lifted her head. Without a word the woman beckoned her ominously. "Come with me."

Mademoiselle Deneuve led the way through a hallway and up a flight of stairs that led to Madame Camille's office. Louise was left in an anteroom while the woman went in.

Mademoiselle Deneuve soon reappeared and said, "This way." Louise drew breath and followed. There, in the small, much ornamented salon, stood Madame Camille, whose plumpish visage was irate.

She shook the half-tacked bodice of the carriage dress at Louise. "Did you cut this silk?"

Louise stood very still and straight. "Yes, madame."

"How *dare* you!" Madame Camille hurled what she held to the floor. "Mademoiselle Deneuve has reported to me that you had the audacity to give Monsieur Russell some falsified story of having received permission to cut a garment in full. You have ruined a length of an important customer's silk which cannot be replaced."

Louise scarcely knew what to say. "What is wrong with the dress, madame?"

"Everything!" Madame Camille thundered her reply. "It was not cut according to the customer's measurements, it has been caused to fray, and the cuffs are uneven!"

Louise was aghast. "I can't believe it. I took such care."

Madame Camille seemed scarcely able to control her rage. "You are dismissed! Never mention your time in this house in applying for work elsewhere, because it will be my duty to warn any employer of your destructive and inexcusable behaviour. Go!"

Throughout it all, Nenette Deneuve had not moved. Now, with lids lowered to hide the gleam of satisfaction in her eyes, she bobbed to Madame Camille and once again led the way for Louise, who was as stunned by her own miscutting of the dress as by her dismissal. Where had she gone wrong? What miscalculations had she made? Within minutes she found herself outside the gates, completely rejected after two years of employment. She began to walk, taking no heed of direction, merely walking in a daze of shock.

At the workshop it was more than an hour before Will heard that she had gone. When one of the grisettes told him, he went straight to Nenette Deneuve's office.

"Why has Louise been dismissed?" he demanded.

She gave him a thin smile. "It is perfectly simple. Louise Vernet did not cut the stuff as expertly as you appear to have imagined. It was so full of errors that nothing could be salvaged."

He leaned across the desk and seized her by the shoulders. "You recut that silk! You went in early this morning and snipped off enough here and there to destroy that garment!"

She jerked herself free and rose to her feet. "I did no such thing. You're making excuses for that girl."

He continued fiercely, as if she had not spoken. "What you did not take into account was that I had checked it all." The corners of his mouth lifted derisively at her startled glance. "After you left I went over her work and found it perfect."

Nenette Deneuve gripped the back of the chair by which she was standing. "Think what you like," she spat. "I will deny everything, and in my position of trust I shall not be doubted. Go back to your workroom, Monsieur Russell. Too much of this day has been wasted already."

He took a step away from the desk, his gaze on her cynical and scornful. "As you say, much time has been wasted."

He returned to his workroom, collected his shears and the various small gadgets he had set up to aid him in his work, and tied them all into a bundle. Then he put on his coat, took up the bundle, and made his way upstairs to find Madame Camille. She was amazed to see him in her own precincts, and was still more taken aback by what he had to say.

"I regret that I have to give you my immediate resignation, madame."

"But why this sudden decision?" she questioned in bewilderment. "Is it the dismissal of that foolish seamstress? Mademoiselle Deneuve explained everything to me. You are in no way to blame for what happened."

"On the contrary, madame. I'm entirely responsible. I should have locked her work away when I knew it to be faultless, and given no one a chance to interfere with it. Mademoiselle Vernet should be reinstated without delay."

Madame Camille held up her hand. "Do not try to shift the blame. I will not discuss the matter further." She was remembering her first doubts about employing him; perhaps it was as well that this Englishman was leaving. "I accept your resignation," she said, inclining her head. "Your work has always been of the highest standard. You may call upon me for a reference whenever you should need it."

"I doubt if I'll ever find it necessary. Goodbye, madame."

When Louise came home, the hour was late. She found Will waiting for her with Catherine. They both sprang up to greet her, Catherine alternately weeping and raging over the injustice of her dismissal. When Louise had calmed her down she faced Will, who told her that he had no doubt at all that Mademoiselle Deneuve had taken shears to the grey silk.

Louise, overcome, sank into a chair, shaking with relief. "But you're out of work because of me," she said remorsefully.

Will smiled at her, an arm resting on the table by which they sat. "It was time I left anyway. I'm going home to start my own clothing business. I've patented my version of the sewing machine and I intend to train hands to use it."

Catherine looked dubious. "Ladies wouldn't like anything that wasn't hand-sewn right through."

"The machines won't eliminate hand-sewing," Will said. "But they will accelerate the production of ready-made clothes." He regarded Louise assessingly. "What are you going to do?"

She tilted her head, her eyes brightly optimistic as she outlined her plan. She would apply for work, giving the impression that she had only recently returned to France after working as a dressmaker in England. "I'll try to get into one of the shop sewing rooms where garments are made up for stock. After I re-establish myself, I'll go forth again with my reputation unsullied."

Will was impressed by her initiative. "I'll write a testimonial as to the high standard of your work," he offered.

"That would be a great help to me," Louise said, and rushed to fetch writing materials for him.

When the letter was signed he made his farewells. "Perhaps we shall meet again one day," he said in the doorway.

"I hope so, Will."

For a second or two she thought that he was going to kiss her, but he gave her a long look, then disappeared down the stairs.

197

CHAPTER FOUR

In exasperation Louise tumbled her dresses about as she tried to decide what she should wear. After watching her for a while, Catherine went to a chest in the corner of the room and drew out the russet silk dress, shaking it free from its folds.

"Here you are," she said in an odd voice. "Alter it to the latest mode, and you'll look fresh out of a bandbox. The bonnet has never been worn either."

Louise felt a lump in her throat. "Dear, dear Catherine. I can't take that from you."

"It's high time some use was made of it." Catherine was blinking rapidly to hide the glistening of her eyes. "Henri paid a lot for the silk." Resolutely she picked up a pair of scissors. "If I give you a hand, we should have it ready by tomorrow."

For the rest of that Sunday they unpicked and pressed and recut and stitched. The result dazzled both of them. Louise had never worn anything so fine; the russet silk moulded her form and accentuated her waist. Catherine saw clearly that Louise was, at the age of eighteen, a handsome, striking creature.

"Now for the bonnet," Louise said eagerly. She put it on, tied the ribbons, and swung around to present herself for Catherine's approval. "What do you think? Do I look like a high-class seamstress who has learned her skills abroad?"

Catherine felt compelled to be honest. "You look nice, that's for sure. As to the rest of it, I don't know. Monsieur Worth never had any luck getting work on the strength of what he had done in England."

"It was his French that was against him," Louise said. Her face flashed defiance. "It will be different for me!"

The next morning she set out in a mood to conquer all bastions. She was conscious of heads turning to watch her go by, her russet silk ashimmer in the sun.

When she had no luck at the shops in the rue de Rivoli, she turned in the direction of the rue de Richelieu. Upon entering number 83, she gazed around at the velvets and silks draped like hangings in a potentate's palace, the brocades and damasks set taut like exotic sails, and the gauzes and tulles and muslins that were allowed to waft and billow enticingly.

"Is anyone attending you, mademoiselle?"

She turned and stared into the face of Worth. She saw his incredulous look. "Louise!"

The old tenderness swept over her, and she knew then that first love could never be truly banished. "How are you, dear Worth?" she asked emotionally. "I can scarcely believe that it is you."

"Nor I that it is my little friend from my first days in Paris." He took her hands and looked her up and down in admiration. "You've grown into a beautiful woman. And such elegance!"

She laughed happily, withdrawing her fingers from his clasp. "This dress is donated finery which I remodelled. I'm hoping that Messieurs Gagelin and Opigez will employ me on the strength of it as an example of my professional skill."

"So you have continued with your sewing?" He took her by the elbow and drew her out into the centre of the floor. "Walk up and down. Let me see how well the dress hangs and if it fits you as perfectly in motion as it appears to while you are standing still." As she hesitated he flapped his hands as if shooing geese. "Walk! Walk!"

Not at all sure that he had not taken leave of his senses, she walked a short distance. When she retraced her steps he was standing with feet apart and arms folded, observing her critically. Before she could reach him, he had spoken to an assistant over some matter and had directed two customers to a distant counter, never once taking his gaze from her.

"You are the *premier commis!*" she exclaimed with awe. Head salesman at Maison Gagelin was an extremely exalted position.

A flicker of surprise crossed his face, as if he had forgotten she could not possibly know about it. "Yes, I am. A recent but welcome promotion. As a matter of fact, I have some voice in connection with the sewing room, and since I cannot fault your dress, except that I would prefer a larger bow crushed more dramatically at the throat, you have obtained the employment you were looking for. All that remains is for Monsieur Gagelin or Monsieur Opigez to authorize your appointment."

She stared at him. "You can't recommend me," she burst out. "It could put you in a bad light. I came here ready to let it be thought I had spent the last two or three years in England. I—"

He interrupted, drawing her out of earshot of anyone who happened to be standing nearby. "Now," he said, "how could you make such a claim? And why?"

She told him everything and when she had finished he stroked his chin thoughtfully. "Give me Mr. Russell's letter," he said. She took it from her drawstring purse, and he read it. "This is recommendation enough. Wait here."

He was back a few minutes later. "All is well," he informed her. "I gave my personal guarantee as to your character, and my request to take you on as a sewing hand was granted immediately."

Louise felt weak with relief and thankfulness. "You'll never regret giving me this chance, I promise you. I'll work so hard."

He gazed at her kindly. "You always did. I used to think how industrious you were for a young girl. Now I'll put you in the charge of someone who can show you where you'll be working and tell you the rules to be observed. As a matter of fact, she is your namesake."

Louise thought later that had she been wearing anything but the russet silk she would have felt as ill-clad as a country wench before Marie Vernet's chic appearance.

Marie greeted her with a charming smile. "Charles has told me how he stayed at your home when he first came to Paris!" Marie exclaimed. "I hope we shall be good friends and that you will be happy working here."

"I'm sure I shall, Mademoiselle Vernet," Louise replied, smiling. "How strange that we should both have the same surname."

Worth looked down at Marie fondly. "The surname should not be Vernet very much longer. We hope to marry soon."

The colour drained from Louise's face as remembered dreams and longings that she had not realized still lingered within her were swept away. "I wish you both happiness," she said quietly.

"Thank you, Louise." Marie did not notice the paleness. She was full of what had happened in recent months to bring their chance of marrying nearer. "You see, so many customers wanted dresses like those Charles designed for me that our employers finally allowed him to have a few toiles on hand—muslin replicas of his designs that could be made up in the customer's choice of material." She gave an enchanting little laugh. "Far from satisfying the demand, the

200

availability of the toiles increased it. Now Charles has widened the range, and designs each garment with a particular fabric in mind."

"How wise," Louise murmured, thankful to lose herself in admiration of Worth's initiative. Then Marie took her companionably by the arm and led her away to the sewing room.

Once more Louise found herself working twelve hours a day at a sewing table. Conditions were better than they had been at Madame Camille's and her wages higher. Moreover, there was no danger of being turned out in case of a slump, because ready-made garments were always being sewn for stock. In addition, the proprietors decided that a number of Worth's designs should be made up for display at the Great Exhibition held in the Crystal Palace in London, which had been instigated by Prince Albert, consort to Queen Victoria. Louise was proud that much of the sewing that went into the dresses was hers. She had never seen anything more beautiful and original than these designs. In them she discovered Worth's preference for elusive colours that could shade from one into another like the depths of water, tantalizing the eye with the question as to whether it was mulberry or mauve, grey or blue.

On the twenty-first of June, just seven weeks after the opening of the Great Exhibition, Louise was one of the guests at the wedding of Marie Vernet and Charles Frederick Worth. After that day Worth's adoration of Marie reached new and glorious heights. Everything he was to design in the years ahead was in reality a paean to his wife.

By the time the Great Exhibition closed in October, the Worth dresses had commanded a tremendous amount of attention and Maison Gagelin won a gold medal for France. But long before that summer of 1851 had ended, buyers of many nationalities had come to Paris to see the clothes designed by this extraordinarily imaginative young Englishman, and the proprietors of Maison Gagelin finally bowed to the opening of a dressmaking department within their hallowed precincts.

The venture was an immediate success and dresses were ordered by the most esteemed customers. For Marie Worth it meant a drastic change. She was thrust completely into the public eye by being called upon to promenade around the salon in all of her husband's latest creations. She would have preferred that all the garments be shown on wicker frames, which was the established method of display, but that would no longer have suited the customers at Maison Gagelin. Her joy in her husband's triumph helped to ease the strain, but the old shyness returned when she had to enter from behind curtains in his most breathtaking designs. Usually these were ball gowns, and since a décolletage was not acceptable in daytime, Marie had to wear an undertop of black silk to cover her arms, shoulders, and bosom.

For Louise the weeks and months seemed to slip past with a speed that matched the pace of her needle. It was a tremendous day for her when Worth, who had observed her work closely, promoted her from a first sewing hand to a fitter. He soon realized that she had a unique understanding of what he wanted in the fit of a dress, and in the early summer of 1852 he promoted her to be his premier fitter. In a black silk dress with a white velvet pincushion fastened to a ribbon around her wrist, she became completely at home in a sphere where women ran the whole gamut of emotions from tantrums to ecstatic bliss over a dress. Time and time again she saw them change from discontented creatures in petticoats at the first fittings to satisfied and preening ladies in the finished creations.

Worth, flouting convention, supervised all the fittings himself, and Louise found him a demanding master. Most dressmakers pandered to the customers' dislike of the rigours of a fitting and kept them to a minimum. Worth aimed for one or two, but did not hesitate to command as many as he deemed necessary. He would make Louise repin a hundred times if need be. Worth's enthusiasm for perfection reached out to the rest of the dressmaking department. None of the women ever begrudged him a minute of the endless work involved.

NOVEMBER CAME damply to Paris that year, bringing early-morning mists that lay over the city like silvery gauze. Madame de Gand complained of the weather to her son when he arrived at her hotel to escort her on a shopping expedition.

"You shall come with me to the rue de Richelieu," she declared as they went out to her waiting carriage. "I am ordering a gown from Gagelin and Opigez to take to Fontainebleau." She sat down in the carriage, and as Pierre took the seat beside her, she thought how the uniform of the cuirassiers suited him.

"I suggest, Mother," he said as the carriage began to bowl along, "that since we are both going to this house party at Fontainebleau we travel there together."

"That would be most agreeable."

Marie-Thérèse de Gand was looking forward to the prince-president's house party for her own particular reasons. When she was only a girl her parents had given shelter to the seven-year-old Louis Napoleon and his mother, Hortense, ex-queen of Holland, on their flight from Paris. Madame de Gand still remembered the tragic beauty of the woman when she arrived by night with her youngest son, escorted by a single adjutant, her face marked by all she had been through. Louis Napoleon, who had been devoted to his mother, never forgot those who had befriended him in time of trouble. Throughout the years he had kept in touch with Marie-Thérèse de Gand and was godfather to her son. One of his godfatherly obligations was to be fulfilled at Fontainebleau, but it was a secret between Louis Napoleon and Madame de Gand. Lost in thought, Madame de Gand gave a start as he spoke again.

"Did you know that the prince-president rarely rides out these days without hearing shouts of 'Vive l'empereur?' "

She nodded. "Is it not thrilling? They say that the plebiscite at the end of this month is a foregone conclusion." She tapped his arm playfully. "That is why I'm most interested to see this Spanish noblewoman who will be with us at Fontainebleau. I want to see if she will make a suitable empress."

Pierre smiled. From what he had heard, it was not as a wife that his godfather wanted Eugénie de Montijo, but it seemed that the lady was resisting his advances.

As Pierre entered Maison Gagelin at his mother's side he was prepared for boredom, but a sense of filial duty had prevented him from getting out of the shopping expedition. In the salon, they were shown to gilded chairs. Worth came through a draped archway and bowed to the new arrivals. He had waited on Madame de Gand several times in the serving of minor accessories since the occasion when he had sold her the white shawl.

"I require a satin ball gown in rose red or deep pink," she told him. "My servant will be delivering one of my dresses shortly. That will be a guide to you as to my measurements and the style I wish. It must be finished and delivered to my hotel by tomorrow morning. All that remains is for you to show me a choice of satins in the colours that I mentioned."

This was the established method of dealing with a dressmaker, and Worth knew it would be a long time before women became accustomed to the new gospel of fit and fashion that he was preaching.

"Provided you do not object to fittings going late into the night," he answered easily, "there will be no problem in making a dress in such a limited time."

Her brows drew together ominously. "I do not need a fitting if you are as good a couturier as you are claimed to be. I have told you clearly enough what I want."

"I would never rely on measurements from a garment that could not possibly fit as I would fit you, madame. I also suggest that a garnet red would enhance your alabaster skin far better than the shades you mentioned. Now, Madame Worth will show you a range of dresses to choose from."

The curtains parted, and Marie emerged in a ball gown of emerald-green satin, with a skirt consisting entirely of latticed strips of the material.

Anything Madame de Gand had been about to say was lost in her throat. She sat leaning slightly forward in her chair. Pierre, watching Marie appreciatively and deploring the daytime necessity of the black silk covering of her arms and bosom, indulged his mother in a little flattery.

"Nobody would look at Eugénie de Montijo at Fontainebleau if you wore that dress, Mother."

Marie displayed several more dresses, but Madame de Gand decided on the first one, to be made in shadings of garnet red. Worth led her towards a fitting room, outside of which the fitter waited. Pierre could see her. A young woman with raven-black hair and a lovely throat. She happened to turn her head, and their eyes met. To each came instant recognition clouded with puzzlement as neither remembered at once where they'd met. Then he knew her. She was the girl of the winter rosebuds.

Swiftly she disappeared into the fitting room with his mother and remained out of sight. Whether she had evaded him deliberately or not, he did not know. He would most certainly take steps to find out.

Madame de Gand thought her son was being unusually attentive when he returned that same afternoon with her for her first fitting, and again in the early evening for the second. As if that were not enough, he escorted her there at midnight for the final one. Then Monsieur Worth allowed him into the fitting room to see how fine

204

his mother looked while the fitter made an alteration of about a millimetre to the hem.

"Goodnight, Pierre," Madame de Gand said contentedly when he handed her into her carriage, not accompanying her back to the hotel. "Until tomorrow."

It was three o'clock in the morning when the activity in the dressmaking room came to a halt. Louise followed the seamstresses down the corridor to the door. Outside, she paused to take a deep breath of the night air, thankful for its chill against her face. She had been in a state of turmoil ever since she had seen the cuirassier officer again. Pierre, his mother had called him. Pierre de Gand. During the final fitting, each time she had looked up, his eyes had been waiting for hers, reflected in the looking glasses that lined the room. And her stupid heart had been hammering all the time.

"Good evening—or should I say good day, Mademoiselle Louise."

She smothered her startled cry by clapping a hand over her mouth. Pierre had been waiting in the shadows, and now he moved into the light of the street lantern. "You frightened me!"

"I apologize. That was not my intention. I'm leaving Paris today for about a week, and I wanted to renew our acquaintanceship before I left."

"I was not aware that we shared one." She began to walk on purposefully, and he immediately fell into step at her side.

"I've looked for you ever since I took your roses," he said.

"I make sure that I don't stand at the front of a crowd any more," she replied crisply.

"Forgive me," he persisted, "and let us make a new beginning. I'm Pierre de Gand, as you know, having heard my name as I heard yours. I want to be sure that you will see me when I return." He was eyeing her sideways with a twinkling glance. "Please. I swear never again to take tribute intended for another."

She forced back a smile. "No, Lieutenant de Gand. The work I do extends to all hours, often without warning, and I never make promises that I can't be sure of keeping. Goodnight."

She broke into a run to catch up with the seamstresses.

The next morning found Louise as busy as usual in the fitting rooms. She was handing a dress to the chief sewing hand when Worth appeared.

"Mademoiselle Louise," he said, his tone unexpectedly severe.

"Kindly inform your swain, whoever he is, not to have his tokens delivered to this house and—worse—to my department!" He held out a bouquet of cream rosebuds in a silver frill, dripping with satin ribbons.

Again Pierre had caught her off guard. No silk petticoat, no gewgaws proclaiming an ulterior motive, but an offering as beguiling as a valentine. She inhaled the fragrance of the buds, and some part of her heart was touched for the first time.

AT THE PALACE of Fontainebleau, Pierre was given comfortable rooms overlooking the huge horseshoe staircase that gave access to the grand entrance. He was anticipating a pleasurable few days. There would be riding to hounds and, in the evenings, dancing and theatricals and cards, plenty to distract him from an impatience to return to Paris. He could not remember when he had been so smitten. He had barely refreshed himself and changed his clothes after the journey when a servant brought word that Louis Napoleon wished to see him.

Entering the salon where he was to wait, Pierre found he was not alone. Standing in front of the tall windows, her back to him, was a girl looking out at the fading November day. She wore a dark blue dress that combined with the wintry gloom to make her smooth white-gold hair shine with the brightness of a candle flame. She started at the click of the double doors behind Pierre, and swung about to regard him steadily and assessingly with fine hazel eyes. "You must be Pierre de Gand." Her voice was light and pleasing.

"You have me at a disadvantage, mademoiselle."

"Don't be alarmed. Your memory isn't failing you. We have never met, although we share the same godfather in the prince-president. No, wait a moment." She gave her head a little shake. "I will rephrase what I said, since the restoration of the Empire is almost accomplished. You and I rejoice in the emperor, Napoleon III, as our mutual godfather."

He walked towards her. "But you haven't told me your name."

"I'm Stéphanie Casile. This is my first visit to this part of the country; I haven't seen Paris yet. Isn't that sad? To have reached the age of seventeen and never to have seen Paris."

He smiled. "Are you to visit Paris while you are here?"

She sighed. "No, I must go back to the convent school until the summer. Then my godfather has promised that I shall come to court." Her eyes sparkled. "That will be at the Palace of the Tuileries! What state occasions I shall see! What balls I shall attend!"

Pierre chuckled quietly. "It can be guaranteed that at the Palace of the Tuileries you'll be able to make up for all the social deprivation of your school days."

"That is what I'm counting on." She turned as the door opened again and Louis Napoleon came into the room. Stocky and dapper, his hair smoothed into a curling side quiff with macassar oil, his moustache ends waxed to needle points, and his goatee immaculately trimmed, he smiled benignly at seeing them together.

"So you have made each other's acquaintance." He spread his arms as if to encompass them both. "I felt this would be an opportunity to spend a little time with my children of the church." He kissed Stéphanie on both cheeks, then turned to Pierre. "This charming young lady is the daughter of a good friend, Joseph Casile, who stood by me in less happy days. Now, alas, he and his dear wife are no longer in this world, denied the chance to see the new dawning of France's greatness." Louis Napoleon looked from one to the other of them. "But you, in all the splendour of your youth, symbolize the future of our country. I know you will both be a credit to France always, and to me."

Stéphanie was deeply moved. "You are too kind, Monseigneur."

Louis Napoleon led them to chairs and there followed a convivial hour of conversation. Both Pierre and Stéphanie could see that he wished to cement their friendship with one another. When Louis Napoleon finally left them, Pierre was less than pleased to realize that he had been inveigled into looking after Stéphanie during the sojourn at Fontainebleau.

That evening he danced with her dutifully, but was glad when other partners took her off his hands for a while. There was one woman present with whom he wanted to dance above all the rest. It was Eugénie de Montijo, Countess of Teba, who illumined the gathering with her extraordinary beauty. Her features were classically moulded, her eyes were an exceptional hyacinth blue, and her magnificent titian hair was worn in thick coils around the crown of her head, needing little imagination on anyone's part to see it as an empress's red-gold diadem. She was twenty-five years old, the daughter of a Spanish grandee, and fiery in disposition, for all the porcelain docility of her expression. She knew Louis Napoleon was avid for her, but while trying to seduce her he was searching the royal houses of Europe for a lady more suited by rank to become an emperor's bride. For herself, she had suffered two devastating disappointments in love, and this made her less than easy to win. When Pierre de Gand asked her to dance with him, she accepted in her customary gracious manner, gliding onto the floor in a drifting of water-green tulle.

"Your godfather mentioned that you are in the cavalry," she remarked as they rotated around the shining floor amid the other dancers. "Were you escorting him when he rode back into Paris after his triumphal tour of the country two weeks ago?"

"I was. You saw the procession, did you?"

"I watched from an apartment window along the route. Such a splendid sight!" Her curiously oblique eyebrows, which gave such interest to her ravishing face, rose in marvel at what she had observed. There was no doubt in Pierre's mind that Eugénie had the most exquisite looks he had ever seen.

He was up early for the hunting next morning, and Stéphanie was there in the forecourt before him, mounted on a black mare, neat and purposeful in a riding habit that was as lacking in style as the dress she had worn the previous evening. But her face was merry and excited.

"Do you ride as well as you have undoubtedly been taught to pray?" Pierre chaffed irreverently, bringing his horse alongside.

She laughed and made a face at him. "You'll see, Lieutenant High-and-Mighty."

As she spoke, Eugénie made her appearance. Stéphanie saw Pierre's eyes go from her to the Spanish noblewoman, and she had to admit to herself that no one could have offered much competition to the strikingly clad horsewoman approaching on a high-spirited thoroughbred. Scorning a sidesaddle, Eugénie rode astride with a full skirt covering grey trousers, which were tucked, Spanish fashion, into high-heeled leather boots. Her felt hat was shaped like a matador's, an ostrich feather pinned to it with a diamond brooch. Her eyes were ashine with anticipation of the chase.

"Good morning, ladies. Good morning, gentlemen," she greeted the company, saluting them with her short, pearl-handled whip. Louis Napoleon leaned forward in the saddle to speak to her, and it was not hard to guess the ardour of his compliment by the way she lowered her lashes bewitchingly.

Stéphanie had hoped to impress Pierre that day, for she rode exceedingly well, but none could compete with Eugénie, who eclipsed everyone else with her superb horsemanship. She crowned it all by being first in at the kill.

The following day, causing gossip to reach new heights, Louis Napoleon gave to Eugénie the Andalusian thoroughbred that she had ridden so splendidly. Eugénie seemed a trifle embarrassed by the munificent gift, but Louis Napoleon's generosity did not end there. During a walk by the lake, Eugénie and Stéphanie and some other ladies were discussing clothes and favourite colours.

"Coral in all its shades," Stéphanie said.

"I like green myself," Eugénie remarked. "Strong, clear shades— like this spread of clover leaves." She stooped and picked a leaf as Louis Napoleon detached himself from the gentlemen and came to her side. "Look," she said in quiet wonder at the beauty of the simple leaf. "See how the dew hangs on it like a tear."

That evening she wore another gift from him, one brought from Paris by a special messenger. It was a spray of clover leaves fashioned in emeralds. Stéphanie was enchanted by the romantic gesture. How long could Eugénie continue to resist his amorous pursuit?

The next day the party broke up, and people went their separate ways. In the vestibule, Pierre bade Stéphanie farewell. She wore an ugly plaid cape and an outmoded bonnet.

"It has been an honour to make your acquaintance," he said to her. "I wish you a safe journey back to the convent."

She felt despair at his conventional farewell and the uninterested look in his eyes that showed his mind was on other matters. She would *make* him remember her! Completely without warning, she flung her arms about his neck and fastened her mouth on his in a kiss not be expected of any well-bred girl.

Sheer astonishment paralysed him for no more than a second, and then he took full advantage of her unexpected behaviour. A pretty girl was always a pretty girl. She could not know that he liked her well enough, but that his thoughts were centred on seeing Louise again. When he released her, it was she who had been roundly kissed, and it amused him to see she was abashed.

"*Au revoir*, Pierre." She regained her poise and extended her hand to him, as she should have done originally.

He took it and bowed. "Until we meet again, Stéphanie."

LOUISE EDGED her way through the throng. In her hand was a card allotting her a seat on a stand at the Champ de Mars. From it she would view the military parade in honour of the bestowing of the title of emperor on Louis Napoleon. All shops and businesses were closed, and Paris was a sight never to be forgotten. Bunting and flags adorned public buildings and private houses, and hundreds of banners bearing the imperial eagle whipped in the wintry air. The most ornamental of the fountains ran with wine, and garlands of evergreens were looped around posts.

Louise had not seen Pierre since the night she had left him near the shop, but his consideration in sending her an invitation showed that he had no intention of giving up his pursuit. Her front-row seat was a grand one. Before her stretched the sandy parade area and the stone military buildings, the only spot of colour a crimson-carpeted dais where Napoleon III would shortly take his place. Louise wore brilliant yellow silk flowers on her bonnet and a shawl in the same sharp colour. It would not be her fault if Pierre failed to see her.

He did see her. As he rode in line with his fellow officers he spotted her bright face, but on such an important state occasion there was nothing he could do to direct her attention towards him.

Louise could not see Pierre, yet she felt a certain pride when his regiment received the imperial eagle, which Louis Napoleon was handing out to his loyal troops. Then a military band struck up *"Partant pour la Syrie,"* which had been composed by Hortense Bonaparte, the emperor's mother, and the spectators rose to their feet to honour the Second Empire of France.

The last notes of the new anthem faded away, and around Louise everyone gradually departed. She sat on alone, wondering how long it took an officer to change from dress uniform. She thought an hour should be plenty. If he had not appeared in that time, she would go.

It took him half an hour to change and reach the stand where she sat. He came to a halt and saluted her smartly. Only then did he allow a grin to steal across his face. "I'm pleased that you waited," he said with intense satisfaction. "Otherwise how on earth should I have found you in Paris on this day of days?"

"Or I discover a means to thank you for the ticket to the parade, to say nothing of the beautiful rosebuds, Captain de Gand." She had noticed his promotion immediately in his insignia.

He was pleased with his rise in rank. Many honours and promotions had been handed out to coincide with the rise of another

Bonaparte to imperial power, and it had been extremely gratifying to find he was listed. He offered her his arm. "The rest of the day is ours, Mademoiselle Louise. There never was such a day as this one for celebrations and beginnings." His look was serious and his words struck deep. As she put her hand into the crook of his elbow she was confident and unafraid.

Thousands of troops released from duties added the splendour of their uniforms to the colourful crowds that surged up and down the Champs-Élysées, filling the cafés and spending money as if an emperor in the Tuileries was the guarantee of a gold-filled purse for all. Louise found herself swept into an expensive café for some refreshment. The place was full, but miraculously, as soon as Pierre was sighted by the headwaiter, there appeared to be space after all.

"This way, Captain de Gand. I trust this table by the window will be to your satisfaction."

By the window! Louise caught her breath with excitement and peered out at the merry flow of humanity in the boulevard below. Pierre asked her what she would like, and she turned her gaze to him. "Hot chocolate with cream would be most pleasant."

He was intrigued by her restrained request. It was an old adage that a grisette could be won with a lobster salad, a visit to the theatre, and a ride on a fairground switchback. Pierre ordered coffee for himself and watched her enjoyment of the chocolate as they talked. Her appearance pleased him greatly. Her dress was dark brown wool with stitching that looked amazingly intricate, enhancing the seductive shape of her shoulders.

"Have you ever spoken to the emperor?" Louise asked him.

He hesitated for a moment. "On occasion. The cuirassiers have always had special favour with him."

"Did you always want to go into the army?"

He leaned his arms on the table, looking across at her. "Yes, I did, which was lucky for me, since I had little choice in the matter. There is a tradition of army service in the de Gand family." His lips parted in a slow smile. "I was the youngest in a houseful of females. I have six sisters, and I believe my parents had begun to despair of ever begetting a soldier for France."

"La! You must have been spoiled!" Louise exclaimed with a soft laugh.

"So they say," he agreed amicably, his eyes crinkling.

When they left the café he managed to hail a fiacre, and they rode

212

about the city in the early dusk. He had taken her hand into his as the carriage began to move, but she withdrew it after a few moments, and the classic advances he had planned were neatly nipped in the bud. He decided that he would dismiss a candlelit supper for two and further their relationship in surroundings more suited to the mood of the fête day. He ordered the carriage to drive them to the Grande-Chaumière on the Boulevard du Montparnasse, a favourite haunt of his cadet days.

It was hot and crowded inside. Waiters darted hither and thither with trays held high, and a band tried to compete against the clatter of knives and forks and the noisy laughter. Louise and Pierre were guided to an alcove, where the cloth was whipped from the table and a clean one shaken from its crackling folds and spread across it. Outside, the gardens were full of people dancing riotously.

After wine had been brought and their order given, they went out to join the dancers. Feet flashing, Louise's petticoats tossing, it was the first of many times they danced that night. They had come to a breathless halt at the final chord of a polka when suddenly the sky was filled with bright pink stars, and one firework followed another in a splendid end to the day. Pierre put his arm around Louise.

When they arrived at her house, Louise stopped in the foyer to part from Pierre. "Never have I known such a fête day," she declared, resting her body in blissful weariness against the wall.

"Nor I." They had already arranged to meet the following Saturday, which was the one day of the working week when Maison Gagelin closed at five o'clock instead of eight. "I'll get tickets for the Conservatoire de Musique, if you like."

"I should like that very much." She smiled in anticipation. "Now I must bid you goodnight."

She found her way barred by his outstretched arm. Her eyes rose to meet his. "Not yet," he implored softly. "Not quite yet."

He leaned forward and kissed her very lightly, a smile in his eyes. Almost in the same instant he caught her about the waist, pulling her to him. There was no more gentleness in his kissing, the pressure of his mouth on hers hard and ardent. Her arms wrapped about his shoulders. It was as if they had merely been passing time until this moment.

She drew away from him, breathless, her eyes very bright. He was reluctant to let her go, and she paused on the lowest stair to kiss him lightly again. "Goodnight, Pierre. Goodnight."

His voice followed her up the flight, echoing in the stairwell. "Goodnight, *chérie*."

In her room, she whirled exultantly around and around, her arms upflung. Then she threw herself backwards onto the bed, merrily kicking off her shoes. He was the man for her and she the woman for him. No brief and shadowed *affaire* for them, only the exchange of true and lasting love.

Louise decided not to tell Catherine about Pierre. She remembered Catherine's disapproval when Worth had been the object of her unrequited love. Instead, she confided in Marie Worth.

Marie was expecting a baby, but she had maintained her service and efficiency in the shop. One evening, just after the shop had closed, Louise sought Marie's aid. She was going to the theatre with Pierre for the first time and was wearing the russet silk dress she had altered, cutting the neckline into a low décolletage. She needed Marie's help in fastening on the roses she had made from a piece of discarded material.

Marie pinned on the roses. "I hope you enjoy the play," she said. She had misgivings about Louise and her officer, and it echoed in her tone. The girl often chatted happily about her evenings with Pierre, and it was difficult to tell whether she realized that his distinguished origins must bar any future for them.

Worth appeared in the doorway. Shaking his head, he stepped forward and swivelled Louise abruptly about to face him. "Not *three* flowers on the décolletage. Only one. That's enough for emphasis." Oblivious to the amused glances being exchanged between the women, he unpinned two of the roses.

"Louise is going to see *La Dame aux Camélias*," Marie informed her husband, handing him needle and thread.

Concentrating, Worth stitched the rose into place. His fingers brushing against her skin no longer had the effect on Louise they once had. She was barely aware of them as she stood patiently, hoping Pierre would think her dress was a new one.

"There!" Worth handed the needle back to Marie and then gave Louise a long look. "The play is a sad one. Most of the women in the audience weep, so go prepared, Louise."

She did not weep, though she understood that Worth had wanted her to see a parallel between the famous courtesan, barred by class and status from marrying the man she loved, and her own relationship with Pierre. But she was no Marie Duplessis, doomed

214

to go down under pressure from outside influences. All her life she had been no stranger to opposition, but now her star was in the ascendant, and she was resolved that it should not fall.

Always now when Pierre took Louise home he would see her to her door, although she had never asked him in. On this night, when she inserted the key in the lock, he put his hand over hers.

"Let me see where you live, Louise. I want to be able to picture you in your surroundings when you are away from me."

She had no choice but to let him across the threshold. She slipped off her shawl and lit a lamp, the pearly light rising up over her face. He looked about him with interest, noticing the simple furnishings, the neatness. Then he looked again at Louise. Never had he desired a woman more. "Louise—"

Like an echo a voice called sleepily from the other room. "Louise? Is that you?"

She moved across to the door. "Yes, it is. Goodnight, Catherine." She turned to Pierre, whose expression showed annoyance. "Catherine always likes to know that I'm safely home."

"Don't you find that oppressive?"

"Sometimes," she admitted, "but I owe everything to her."

As he made his way out of the house, Pierre decided on the course of action he would take. He had given thought before to getting a place of his own in Paris, and now he would see about obtaining one without delay. He needed somewhere to be alone with Louise. Louise, Louise. He had never been more in love.

The next day Louis Napoleon announced his forthcoming marriage to Eugénie de Montijo, and startled everyone with the information that the civil ceremony would take place a week later and the religious ceremony the day after. Many thought such haste unseemly, but others who knew the imperial bridegroom were aware that his passion for the lady was almost at breaking point. For those who had to organize the procession and refurbish the state coaches, seven days was a perilously short span of time in which to get everything completed. For the dressmakers and suppliers of fine fabrics the announcement meant a rush of business. At Maison Gagelin it was the impetus needed to make Worth's employers capitulate to his insistence that the dressmaking department be hugely expanded, and in the meantime he and Marie, with Louise and the rest of the sewing team, worked around the clock to get the orders completed.

The civil ceremony was a private affair, but the religious ceremony at the Cathedral of Notre-Dame brought vast crowds to pack themselves behind the hedge of blue-coated infantrymen that lined the route from the Tuileries. Louise and Catherine had secured a good viewing place, and it was Pierre whom Louise wanted to see even more than the new empress.

Luck was with her that day. As the cavalry clattered past in a jingling of harness, she spotted him. He faced rigidly ahead, the sunshine flashing on the chin strap that fastened the fine helmet. Soon afterwards came the red and gold glass coach in which the emperor and the empress sat side by side, acknowledging the cheering and the endless shouts of *"Vive l'empereur! Vive l'impératrice!"* Eugénie's diamond coronet, which had once adorned the Empress Josephine, flashed multi-coloured fire. Already the new empress was loved. The path she intended to tread had revealed itself in her donation of Paris's own wedding gift to the founding of a children's home and a hospital for the incurable. Tales of her kindnesses were legion. No emperor ever had a more worthy bride.

CHAPTER FIVE

Baron Georges Haussmann had been commissioned by the emperor to create a Paris that was to surpass all other cities in beauty. Pierre de Gand heard about the grandiose plans when his godfather occasionally invited him to spend an hour or two in conversation over a drink and a cigar.

"It is a long-held dream of mine," the emperor confided once. "The rebuilding of Paris will supply work for hundreds of thousands of men and eliminate one of the main causes of unrest." His eyes shone with enthusiasm through the smoke rising lazily from his cigar. "Down will come the ugly and dilapidated property where dens of troublemakers have festered, and up will go houses of grace and dignity to face wide boulevards. Along the avenues will be strategically placed military barracks to ensure law and order. Never will the world have seen such a city."

All splendid talk, but to an officer seeking accommodation in which to co-habit with the girl he loved, it was irritating to see row after row of property go down in rubble as boulevards were widened to breathtaking dimensions.

It was by sheer chance that he happened to hear of an apartment in a building being retained for its architectural value, and upon inspection it proved to be altogether suitable. Craftsmen were employed to redecorate and refurbish, and when all was near completion, he sent for some fine pieces of his own from the château to complete the furnishings. He had told Louise nothing about his acquisition. He had made her more than aware of his feelings for her, however, and now he was simply awaiting the right moment to mention the apartment.

Life had rarely been more agreeable. His hours of duty at the Tuileries were anything but tedious, as the empress had thought it fitting that her husband's godson should be her personal escort, riding beside her carriage when she took her afternoon drives.

She and the emperor took keen interest in bringing forth a great renaissance of France's past glory. As a result of the state balls at the Tuileries, the banquets and receptions and other splendid functions, the imperial court was being spoken of as the most brilliant in Europe, set to outglitter even that of St. Petersburg. Fashion was on the crest of a wave of prosperity, and the newest dresses had crinoline skirts spreading wider and wider over petticoats so stiffened by whalebone or horsehair that they could stand alone.

At Maison Gagelin the days flashed by as the seamstresses worked on the dresses ordered for state balls and other social events. Marie had recently returned to the shop after having her baby, a fine boy, whom she and Worth had named Gaston. It was hard for Marie to leave him to another's care every day, and she often thought how wonderful it would be to live nearer the shop, but nothing was available to suit their modest income.

For Louise there was only one small cloud on the horizon. Turkey had declared war on Russia over a religious bone of contention, and Pierre held to the general belief that France might be drawn into the conflict in support of Turkey. In a Paris so carefree and lavish in the pursuit of pleasure it seemed impossible that war could intervene, and she tried to put the matter from her mind.

As for Pierre, he was spoiling for battle. Much as he enjoyed Paris and all that went with it, his training had geared him for war, and he had no wish to grow soft in a handsome and unbloodied uniform. One day when he was sent for by his godfather he wondered if he was to hear about a military posting, but the matter that the emperor wished to discuss proved to be as far removed from war as it could be.

The emperor was seated at his desk. With the habit he had developed whenever he talked, Louis Napoleon twirled one end of his waxed moustache. "My boy, I know you will remember my goddaughter, the delightful Stéphanie Casile." His eyes twinkled. "It appeared that the two of you became remarkably well acquainted last year at Fontainebleau."

Pierre frowned uncomfortably.

"Well, now Stéphanie is in Paris." The emperor raised his eyebrows to reflect the pleased surprise he imagined he had imparted with such news. "She is staying with the Duchess of Bassano, who has been preparing her for life as a lady-in-waiting at court. The empress is quite taken with my goddaughter and has decided to appoint her to be in personal attendance."

"An honour indeed," Pierre murmured.

"The duchess is bringing Stéphanie to the next state ball. I want you to meet the girl upon her arrival at the palace and partner her for the evening. That's not an arduous task, is it?"

"No, Sire," he replied stiffly. He rose smartly to his feet as his godfather got up to come around the desk. A fatherly hand was clapped on Pierre's shoulder.

"I am going to rely on you to see that Stéphanie is not lonely or unprotected while she adjusts to her new life in Paris. Now I'll keep you from your duty no longer."

Pierre left the building angrily. He had been clearly directed to dance attendance on Stéphanie for the next two or three months at least, and there was nothing he could do to go against that order.

On the evening of the ball, lights streamed into the Paris night from every window of the palace, making the edifice glow from afar. Five thousand guests had been invited, and the rue de Rivoli and the Quai des Tuileries were lined with equipages moving up to take their place in the forecourt. A never-ending stream of richly dressed people flowed through the marquee, where Pierre awaited the Bassano party.

At last their carriage arrived. He stepped forward, greeted the lady and her husband, and then turned to Stéphanie. He barely recognized her.

"We meet again, Pierre."

A grin spread across his face. She had positively bloomed since their last meeting. Her white-gold hair was worn in a huge coil at the nape of her neck, a circlet of flowers around it. Her gaucheness was gone. The brashness had melted away. She had even manipulated her wide skirt over the carriage steps with more grace than most women had managed upon their arrival.

"I'm honoured, Stéphanie. So you have come as you promised to conquer Paris."

She smiled impishly. "Yes, I have, so let this city beware."

With her heart beating wildly she went with him into the palace. The duchess had mercilessly given her instructions on how to walk, sit, smile, and conduct herself generally, and a dressmaker had produced a wardrobe to cover every occasion. Throughout the lessons and the endless fittings Stéphanie had known that it had all been building up to this moment when she would see Pierre again.

At her first sight of the Salle des Maréchaux, one of the Tuileries' magnificent ballrooms, Stéphanie caught her breath in awe. The ceiling seemed composed of waterfalls of crystal, thousands of candles glowing in the huge chandeliers. In the wonderful light the vast assemblage sparkled and glittered. The men who were not in uniform wore formal court dress, and every woman's skirt was shaped like a full-bloomed rose.

She was introduced to many people and attracted a great deal of attention. A new and lovely face was always a matter of speculation at a court where the empress had so firmly established the cult of beauty. Several of Pierre's fellow officers made a point of being presented, and Stéphanie flirted with them, hoping that Pierre noticed. It appeared that he did, especially since two or three of the officers gave him what seemed to be a congratulatory slap on the back at being with her.

At half past nine the emperor and empress opened the dancing, and soon Pierre took the floor with Stéphanie. He lost her to several partners afterwards, but claimed the supper dance. They did not take supper with the majority of the guests, however. They had been invited to join the emperor and empress with selected personages in another salon.

The royal couple left the gathering at midnight, Eugénie half turning to give the gracious sweep of the hand that was characteristically hers. The festivities would continue until the early morning, but the Bassanos were ready to leave, and Stéphanie had to go with them. "I feel the night has only just begun," she whispered to Pierre.

He consoled her. "There'll be plenty of other times ahead for you now."

Her eyes gleamed determinedly. "I hope so. I haven't come to Paris at long last to go to bed before dawn."

After the Bassanos' carriage departed, Pierre stood in the marquee and wondered where to pass the next few hours. He did not want to return to the dancing, and none of the diversions of the city held any appeal for him. Although Stéphanie had been beguiling, it was only Louise he wanted to be with.

Almost without thought he summoned a hackney cab and directed the driver to her address. In the mean and narrow street he alighted and looked up at the building where she lived. A candle showed at one of her windows. He entered the house and took the stairs at a run. He rapped at the door and Louise's voice answered cautiously. "Who's there?"

"I! Pierre!"

The door opened and she stood there holding a candlestick, a shawl over her white nightgown, her hair flowing down. "Whatever is the matter?" she asked anxiously, her eyes wide.

His heart almost stopped with love at the sight of her. Not one woman at the Tuileries that evening could have outshone Louise in her simple attire, her face beautiful in the candle's glow. He stepped into the room and closed the door behind him.

"I had to see you. Are you alone?" His swift glance had taken in the door standing open to Catherine's darkened room.

"Yes," she replied unthinkingly. "Catherine is still at work and will be until morning." She reached out an uncertain hand to touch his sleeve. "Are you going away?" she questioned tremulously. "Is that why you're here at this late hour?"

"No," he said. "Not yet. But maybe very soon." He put his hat on a chair. "I had to see you. I could not go another hour without telling you what I should have told you long ago."

220

She took a step backwards. The candle quivered in her hold, and he took it from her and set it down on the table beside them. Then he pulled her into his arms and held her against him, smoothing back the sweep of her hair. She kissed him, and the kiss seemed to go on for ever. When their lips parted, he reached for the key in the door, and she realized how far along the path to seduction she had gone.

"No!" She tried to catch his arm, but he merely crushed her tighter to him.

"I love you," he whispered. He swept her up in his arms and carried her through to the bed. She strained away from him, but she could not fight her own awakened passion and the tenderness of his caresses. Suddenly and gloriously she found herself lost and ardently submissive.

IN HER BEDROOM, Marie Worth regarded herself in the tilted cheval glass with dismay. She and her husband were to attend a ball being held in honour of the empress and her court, and he had designed a dress for her to wear. It was of pink tulle trimmed with purple ribbons, much too startling in its simplicity. And she hated it. Why did he always have to put her in something so new and different? She heard him coming up the stairs and steeled herself to request that she be allowed to wear one of her more conventional ball gowns. The door burst open and he entered, handsome in his evening clothes. In his hand he held high a posy of velvet pansies with floating ribbons.

"The final touch, my darling!"

To her complete horror he slipped the posy on its concealed comb into her curls, and its ribbons drifted down to her shoulder. Her voice and her tears burst forth in the same instant.

"I will not go to the ball with that tree in my hair!"

He threw up his arms in exasperation. Although they had often quarrelled in similar circumstances, he never failed to be keenly hurt that she of all people should dislike what he had created.

"It's not in the least like a tree! It's a simple cluster of superbly fashioned pansies."

"*Pansies!*" Marie stamped her foot. "I'm supposed to dance this evening, not push a country plough." Suddenly she dropped her face into her hands, sobbing helplessly. "Why can't you see that I would be the laughingstock of everyone present?"

221

He enfolded her into his arms, stroking her hair and kissing her brow. He spoke softly. "I decided on pansies because their simplicity is in harmony with the dress. Amid all the other women in their elaborate toilettes, you are going to stand out as an example of how beautiful a woman can look in a dress relying entirely on line to achieve elegance."

Worth won her around, as he always did, telling her that by the end of the week the dressmaking department would be getting orders for dresses exactly like the one she was displaying. "*And* with pansies for the hair," he added.

The municipal ballroom echoed the opulence of the Tuileries in its blue velvet hangings and silk-fringed swags. Acquaintances greeted the Worths on all sides. They had come to know many people in Paris, and invitations flowed their way, but far more were declined than accepted.

Worth insisted that he was too busy to give his time to events and people in whom he had little interest. Yet with their own close circle of friends he was relaxed and jovial and marvellous company. It was no wonder that Louise was pleased to be invited to join the Worths that evening with her escort, Pierre de Gand.

At last the empress arrived, wearing a dress of silvery gauze and a diadem of emeralds. As she and her entourage drew near, Pierre saw that Stéphanie was in the group. His enjoyment of the evening ended when he realized that she had spotted him. He felt duty-bound to pay her the usual courtesies, but he had no wish that she and Louise should meet. When Louise was dancing with Worth, Pierre threaded his way through the assemblage to the imperial party.

As he approached, Stéphanie turned from those to whom she was talking and held out her hand to him. "What a surprise! How clever of you to find out that I would be here this evening. Yes, I would love to dance." He spun her into a Strauss waltz, and she went chattering on as they rotated around the floor in the midst of a thousand or more couples. "You have rescued me from a most tedious evening."

"I'm afraid I can't be your knight to the rescue," he replied seriously. "Not on this occasion."

She pouted merrily. "Don't tease. You don't deserve to be promised every dance with me, but I'm prepared to forgive you."

"Stéphanie." He pressed her hand. "I'm not here by myself."

She stared at him, her cheeks scarlet. "The devil take your arrogance, Pierre de Gand! You let me make a fool of myself." He was prepared to suffer her accusation, but when she tried to fling herself away from him, his grip about her waist tightened.

"No one leaves me in the middle of a ballroom floor! You'll finish this waltz with me if it goes on for the rest of the night."

She would still have escaped him if she had not been aware of the gossip such behaviour would cause. At all costs she must do nothing to jeopardize her position at court.

On the final chord from the orchestra Pierre returned her to the empress's company. Eugénie spoke to him, and Louise, watching from afar, put a hand to her throat. "The empress is speaking to Pierre!" she exclaimed.

Somebody in the party said, "Why should she not, since he is the emperor's godson, after all?"

Louise looked at Marie for confirmation. "Is that true?"

Marie smiled and patted her arm reassuringly. "If the captain hasn't yet mentioned it, he obviously thinks it can make no difference. He's not a man to boast about such a matter, is he?"

"No," agreed Louise in a subdued tone. "He is not."

The music had begun again, and Pierre returned to her. Stéphanie tried to catch a glimpse of his unknown partner, but a host of dancing couples blocked her view. Behind her one woman asked another about the identity of the wearer of a pink tulle dress. The reply came promptly.

"That is Madame Worth, the wife of the couturier at Maison Gagelin."

"Would he have designed that dress, do you think?"

"She wears only his creations."

"How interesting." A pause. "Those pansies are enchanting."

Stéphanie looked at this Madame Worth dancing past. There was no doubt that in the unusual simplicity of her lovely gown she made everyone else look absurdly overdressed.

The empress left at her usual hour of midnight, and soon after, Louise and Pierre departed.

While they travelled across the city in a carriage, Pierre gave Louise a long-overdue explanation. "I should have told you before that my family became acquainted with the emperor and his mother long before I was born. Years later, while in exile in England, he honoured my parents and me by becoming my godfather. Perhaps you wonder why I've waited until now to tell you all this, but the chief reason was that I didn't want to alarm you unduly." His arm tightened about her. "Now I have no more to tell you about myself that you don't already know." His voice became amused. "Do you want to hear it all again? About my childhood? My horses?"

The fact was that Louise never tired of hearing anything about him, but she made a light, noncommittal reply, and with the matter apparently settled to his satisfaction, he began to peer through the window in impatience.

For the first time Louise noticed that they were not nearing her home, but were in an entirely different district. "Where are we?" she asked in bewilderment.

"You'll soon see. It's a surprise."

As they alighted in the rue Lenoir, she looked up at a cream-coloured stone house. The concierge admitted them and went ahead across the vestibule and up the stairs to light the way. On the first floor, Pierre took a key from his pocket and opened the double doors of an apartment. His footsteps rang on the polished floors as he put a lighted taper to one lamp and then another. Louise followed him as the flowing wicks rose to banish wave after wave of darkness. Finally, in a high-ceilinged drawing room, he stooped to light the logs in the marble fireplace and then turned around to face her.

"Well? What do you think of it?"

The furnishings were rich and comfortable amid the gleam of rosewood and marquetry. Letting her silken shawl slip from her shoulders, Louise went across to one of the room's tall windows to look out.

"Whose apartment is this?" she asked.

He came and stood behind her, drawing her against him. "It's yours and mine. The first home of our marriage."

She was overcome. "It must be the most splendid accommodation in Paris. I know we'll be happy here."

"All that remains now is to hand in my application to become betrothed and to hear when a marriage furlough will be granted. As soon as I know, we'll fix the wedding date." He drew her to a wing chair, where he sat down and took her onto his knees. He was full of plans for the honeymoon journey. They would take a long and picturesque route to the Loire Valley to see the mansion that would one day be theirs. He would teach her to ride. All his sisters would love her. And when they left the château they would continue back to Paris by the most leisurely means. Louise noted to herself that he did not name his mother among those who would welcome her into the de Gand fold.

Pierre then suggested that, while he would remain in his military quarters until the wedding day, she should move into the apartment with Catherine as soon as possible. He explained that the betrothed of a palace officer should reside at an address of some distinction and be suitably chaperoned.

Louise stiffened. "Don't ask me to say that I will move tomorrow or the day after that. I must choose the right moment to tell Catherine we are to wed. And I must ask Worth's permission for time away from the dressmaking department."

Pierre looked incredulous. "Time away? What do you mean? You won't be going back there once we are married."

She stared at him. "Surely you're not asking me to give up all I've been aiming for in the fashion world?"

He gave her waist an indulgent squeeze. "As my wife you'll have no time—"

She broke in. "Nearly all the leading couturières are married."

"No doubt, but they are women who have to earn their living. You will no longer be in that position."

"That's beside the point. As you know, I enjoy everything to do with the making of beautiful clothes, and in any case, to work hard is natural to me. I couldn't idle my time away all day."

He did not believe she could ever be idle, but he fully expected her energy to be channelled into the social pastimes enjoyed by women of his class. She had yet to realize how different her new life would be, and she must be won over to it with patience. "If it makes you happy to remain involved in fashion, so be it. But I'll not have you kneeling to pin the hems of women not fit to tie your shoe. You must have some authoritative post instead."

She kissed his brow. How dear he was, and how little he understood. There was no more disgrace in her pinning a hem on her knees than in a painter's kneeling to put a final brushstroke on a masterpiece. She shared Worth's attitude in seeing a lovely dress as an artistic creation.

"Let everything stay as it is for a while longer," she persuaded gently. "You and our love for each other will always come first with me."

225

LOUISE WAITED for the right moment to tell Catherine that she was betrothed. To her delight, Catherine laughed and cried and hugged her. "I could see you were in love," she admitted, wiping her eyes. "Shouldn't I of all people know the signs? Maybe for a while I didn't want you to tell me; I was a mite uncertain about letting you go. That doesn't mean that the day you marry won't be the happiest in your old Catherine's life."

Louise gave a little laugh. "I have more news. You and I are to move at once into the grand apartment where I'll be living when I'm Madame de Gand." She saw the change of expression in Catherine's face.

"Where is this apartment?"

"In the rue Lenoir."

"What! A fine fool I'd look going out of there to work!"

"I'll be doing the same. After I'm married, too."

Catherine was barely listening. She did not know how she would cope with the jealousy and perhaps the ridicule of her workmates when they heard of her new abode.

"I must have time to think," she said, and on that she remained adamant.

Pierre became impatient with Louise's delay in moving. He had not told her that he was withholding his application to become betrothed until she could give the rue Lenoir address, in order to avoid awkward questions.

Meanwhile, he found himself committed in an official capacity more and more to Stéphanie's company. She was now included frequently on drives with Eugénie when he was riding as escort. He noticed that her comely looks more than outshone the loveliest of the empress's other companions. It did not cross his mind that he was observing a beauty maturing through the effect of an all-encompassing love.

Stéphanie lived for the sight of him, and any glance, word, or smile was mulled over blissfully in what she now took to be his serious courtship. She could have had her choice of any number of young men showing an interest in her, but she wanted none of them. None was so dashing in uniform, so quick to share her sense of humour, or had such a dancing, wicked glint in his gaze. When she was with him she felt as if she were walking on air.

But, unbeknown to her, Pierre, unwilling to wait any longer, gave to his commanding officer his application to become betrothed

226

to Louise. He simply listed the rue Lenoir address as Louise's and made no mention of her work.

His interview with the colonel appeared to go without a hitch, but just when he expected him to sign the paper, it was folded and set aside.

"I'll see that your request is laid before His Majesty today."

"Is that necessary, sir?" Pierre asked stiffly, considerably alarmed. "The fact that I'm the emperor's godson has never been officially recognized in my army life. Why should this matter be an exception?"

The colonel looked well pleased. "Because of a special appointment that has come through. It is my pleasant duty to inform you, Captain de Gand, that you have been selected to take up command in the Cent-Gardes."

At any other time Pierre would have welcomed such extraordinary good fortune. The Cent-Gardes was an elite cavalry corps providing a bodyguard to the emperor, with duties that entitled them to military and social precedence over all other troops in the French army. He heard himself make some appreciative reply to the news.

"I congratulate you," the colonel continued. "Now you know why the emperor himself must approve your request to become betrothed."

There was nothing for Pierre to do but hope for the best.

Later that day, when the emperor picked up Pierre's application from his desk he smiled, stroking his goatee, until his eye alighted on the name of the bride-to-be. There was a look of intense displeasure on his countenance while he gave one of his equerries certain instructions. The application went into a drawer and remained there until a report was delivered into his hands a few days later. Then he sent for his godson.

"This betrothal is out of the question," the emperor said severely. "It is an unsuitable match."

Pierre stood as straight as if he were on the parade ground. "I beg permission to argue that point, Sire. I love the lady and want no other to be my wife."

Louis Napoleon picked up the report on his desk. "'Mademoiselle Louise Vernet has lived with a woman of questionable morals for many years, and has worked in the dressmaking trade since she was fourteen. The rent of the apartment given as her address is paid by a certain Captain de Gand." He tossed the report down. "Is she with child? Is that why you feel you must marry her?"

Pierre's eyes blazed. "No, she is not. I want to marry her because I love her."

Louis Napoleon became more sympathetic. "We have all loved women in our time whom we could never honour with our name or the privilege of bearing our heirs. Such a marriage as you have requested would put an end to your professional career and to your life in society." He observed the young officer closely. "Would you turn your back on the army, with your new position in the Cent-Gardes, at the very hour when your country stands on the brink of war?"

Pierre's jaw clenched. "Sire, I'm only asking to be allowed to marry. My loyalty to France is not on trial."

"I happen to believe that it is. Should you go against my wishes in this matter, it would be tantamount to treason."

"Sire!" It was an exclamation of vehement protest.

Louis Napoleon got up from his chair. "How else could I view such insubordination? By such a match you would degrade yourself, the de Gand family, and your association with me. I forbid the marriage that you have requested."

It had been a short, sharp tussle, but the outcome had been decreed from the start. Pierre stood pale and stricken, his white-gloved hand gripping the hilt of his sheathed sabre.

Louis Napoleon adopted a kindlier tone. "Don't think that your little grisette won't understand the situation. She will. Such women prove to be just as accommodating without a ring as ever they would have been with one. After all, you've already prepared a love nest for her, and I'm the last one to quarrel with that kind of sensible arrangement." He decided that the time had come to enlighten his godson as to the correct choice of a wife. "Be at ease now, Pierre," he urged. "I shall never refer to the difficult business again, although I must continue to speak for the moment on the subject of marriage. You do not have to look far to find a young woman of whom I know you are extremely fond, and who is fond of you in return."

Pierre stared at him. "I'm not sure that I understand, Sire."

Louis Napoleon paced leisurely about the room, twirling one end of his moustache. "I refer to Stéphanie. From the start I have been committed to finding her a suitable husband, one I could trust to

228

give her a fulfilled life in every sense, and it was only to be expected that I should have had you in mind." He did not add that Madame de Gand was of the same opinion that it would be a good match. "I'm exerting no pressure on you, particularly at this time when you are in the throes of a disappointment. I'm simply making my desire known."

"Perhaps the empress would not wish one in her entourage to marry so young," Pierre answered gratingly.

His godfather smiled. "The empress would be overjoyed. You would have her blessing and mine."

Pierre's resolve was unchanged. Whatever happened, he would not let Louise go, no matter that the few words of a marriage ceremony were to be withheld from their union. He loved her. She was his. And he would ensure that she remained his.

Four days later France and Britain made the expected declaration of war on Russia. All furloughs were cancelled, and since such matters as officers' betrothals were shelved for the time being, Pierre was able to postpone telling Louise what had taken place. She saw that he was depressed and, misunderstanding the reason, said that a little delay in the wedding was not important when they would be spending the rest of their lives together.

Louise lived in dread of Pierre's going to war. She knew as well as he that it was only a question of time before the sky-blue tunics of the Cent-Gardes were seen on the battlefield.

March became April, and she took every day that they could still be together as a bonus. They had boxes at the Opéra and the Opéra-Comique, went to every playhouse from the Théâtre-Français to the Bouffes-Parisiens, danced the night away at the Café Anglais, and took late suppers at the famed Véfour's. Pierre took great pleasure in defiantly flaunting her in places where he would be recognized.

Involved in such a round of pleasure, Louise used her ingenuity to vary her limited wardrobe, and was in luck when Worth let her have a black silk net overtop and skirt that a customer had rejected because of its trimming. He had seized upon the idea of creating glitter with black jet, which had never been used before. Unfortunately it was proving too bizarre for women accustomed to ribbons and feathers, but Louise had no qualms about it. When she danced with Pierre the jet sparkled and swung like diamonds, which was exactly the effect that Worth had wanted.

Louise thought that these must be the happiest days of her life, a time sprinkled with the lights of Paris, the glitter of jet, and the sparkle of champagne, a time of passion and tenderness and sweet words of love.

But one evening when Pierre arrived unexpectedly she felt a sudden stab of premonition.

"I have some important news," he said gravely.

She stood quite still. "Tell me," she said.

He traced the side of her cheek gently with his knuckles. "I'm leaving tomorrow for the battlefield. This is our last meeting for a long time."

She closed her eyes. Her head lowered as she struggled against tears. "I'm thankful for every moment granted to us."

"We have much to talk about. If anything happens to me—"

She looked up swiftly. "Don't say that!"

He smiled. "I'll put it another way. Nobody knows how long this war will last. Should you need anything at any time, my banker has instructions to let you have whatever you require. In the event of my death, you will be provided for until the end of your days."

A sob broke from her, and she buried her face against his shoulder. He stroked her hair, and then he delved into his waistcoat pocket and brought out a tiny velvet box. He snapped it open. Inside on crimson satin was a gold wedding ring and a diamond-set keeper to be worn with it. She could hardly speak, her voice coming in a barely audible whisper.

"I'll wear the keeper until you come home again."

"Wear them both for me tonight. Let me put them on your finger. I want to remember seeing them there. I want to know that you belong only to me."

They stood facing each other, the lamplight throwing their shadows across the room. He took her hand, and she watched him slide the gold band onto her finger. "I love you, my darling Louise. My own for ever more." The diamond keeper followed, a seal of love upon the ring of vows. He kissed her, and they clung to each other lovingly.

When he had left, Louise leaned against the door for a few minutes, torn by the parting. Then she sat down and removed the rings. She would wear them on a chain around her neck until Pierre came home again.

She did not see him leave Paris. At noon the next day she knew that the troop train was bearing him away to war. To the Crimea.

230

There were times when it seemed to Louise that Paris had forgotten the country was at war. Nothing stemmed its gaiety, its increasing opulence, its flamboyant imperial occasions. It was as if the whole city had become a brilliantly illuminated carousel.

More than a year had passed since Pierre had gone to war, and still the hostilities showed no sign of coming to an end. In contrast to the laughter and song of Paris, French soldiers had endured the rigours of a terrible Russian winter with inadequate clothing and insufficient supplies. Louise missed Pierre desperately and wrote to him regularly. She was grateful that Worth never allowed her a moment's respite at the shop. If one completed task left her with time on her hands, he gave her another. Yet it was not only she who was run off her feet. Worth and Marie worked as hard as anyone else. They were always first at the shop in the morning and last to leave at night, despite having to travel some distance.

Whether the proprietors realized it or not, Worth had become the very heart of their business. He was becoming known in commercial circles as an astute salesman who knew what he wanted, and it always had to be exactly right. Jet was now being produced widely for ornamentation, due entirely to his lead, and his inventiveness was spurring on the makers of *passementerie* to produce new kinds of trimmings.

Louise often thought it a great shame that the credit for everything Worth did went to Maison Gagelin. She wished she and Worth could go into business on their own, but although she had some tiny investments, her capital was not nearly enough to establish her at a good address. Sometimes, as customers chatted in the fitting rooms, Louise picked up scraps of financial information. On one occasion, a particularly pleasant woman had remarked on her husband's interest in the building of a canal at Suez, and Louise, plucking up her courage, asked if it would be a good proposition for

231

investment. The lady declared that it would be, and at the next fitting she passed on another investment tip. Louise often felt as though she were a squirrel, hoarding nuts for a winter that was still some distance away.

STÉPHANIE CASILE had made up her mind to patronize Monsieur Worth. She needed clothes that were warm and elegant and would travel well. Nobody knew it yet, but she had decided to visit Pierre in the Crimea.

She wrote to him often, bright and lively letters with news of people he knew, scraps of gossip that would entertain him, and accounts of anything amusing that had taken place. To judge from his replies, which came sporadically, he appreciated her correspondence, and although he did not use any endearments in his letters beyond sending his most affectionate regards, she understood that any unselfish man under constant threat of death through battle would not wish to tie a young woman with promises that could lead to heartache.

The idea of going to see Pierre had been in her mind for some time. She considered it grossly unfair that only the wives of a very few high-ranking officers were allowed to make the journey to visit their husbands, and she hoped that her godfather, the emperor, would ease the way for her.

Stéphanie did not disclose her destination to the couturier; she simply said that her travels would take her by sea and land, and she expected the climate to be bitterly cold. Madame Worth paraded garments that delighted her. Warm woollen dresses in glowing colours, evening gowns to shimmer magically over a practical interlining that would keep out icy draughts, a sturdy and elegant riding habit, and above all a handsome fur-lined cloak with a hood.

"Start at once, Monsieur Worth," she ordered recklessly, not considering that she would have a lot of unnecessary garments on her hands if her plans should come to naught.

Every fitting was spiced with excitement for her, and her joyous mood made her a welcome customer in the dressmaking department. Louise particularly enjoyed these fittings, and Stéphanie thought Mademoiselle Louise very pleasant company. Once, during a discussion of an opera they both knew, they burst into song, and this brought Worth into the room with such an outraged expression that they both collapsed with mirth.

Stéphanie had been laying the rest of her plans while her clothes were being prepared. She had located a widow who was to travel to the Crimea in order to bring her husband's remains home for burial, a privilege granted her in view of the late officer's gallantry in the line of duty. The widow, Madame Hélène de Vincent, was willing to chaperon Stéphanie.

"I will speak to thé emperor on your behalf if it proves necessary," Madame de Vincent offered. "In any case, you may tell him that your company would be greatly comforting to me."

The emperor heard Stéphanie out. "I love Pierre with all my heart, Sire," she concluded. "I beg you to grant this favour. Let me go to him. Please!"

"Have you asked the empress if she will allow you leave to embark on this romantic pilgrimage?" he inquired.

"No, Sire. I thought I should seek your permission first."

There was a long silence. She thought she would die of the suspense. Then she saw an unmistakable twinkle in his eye. "What are you waiting for? I suggest you make your request to the empress without further delay."

She gave a cry of joy, springing up and kissing his hand.

As the door closed after her he smiled to himself. Having lived a soldier's life in his younger days, he knew the effect Stéphanie's visit would have on Pierre after months of war. Things could not have worked out better.

The empress was harder to convince. She was pregnant, and having suffered two miscarriages she had to receive the greatest care and attention. She was unusually petulant but finally agreed to Stéphanie's request. "Be sure you are back by the time I am brought to bed. I want all my ladies near me."

Stéphanie sailed with Madame de Vincent early in November. The voyage proved to be pleasant; not only was the weather relatively calm in the Mediterranean, but the captain and officers of the supply ship were extremely attentive and good company. They disembarked at a bustling Black Sea port, where they were met by a Captain Desgranges, who offered his condolences to Madame de Vincent and greeted Stéphanie with an appreciative look.

"Is Captain de Gand not with you?" Stéphanie asked at once.

"No, but you will see him this evening."

"Does he know that I'm here?"

Captain Desgranges shook his head. "He was ordered only to

233

report to General Bosquet's headquarters, where he is to remain for three days." He smiled. "I envy him his delightful surprise."

With an escort of mounted lancers, Stéphanie and Madame de Vincent began their journey to headquarters on horseback, an army wagon trundling with their baggage in their wake. It was bitterly cold, and snow lay in drifts everywhere. They passed French troops under canvas, campfires making red-gold flares of colour as smoke curled skywards. Stéphanie was distressed to see how patched the men's uniforms were. Some soldiers draped blankets about themselves for extra warmth. There was a good number who had added Russian greatcoats and other articles of clothing, some of it cossack, to their attire, and she did not care to think about how those garments had been acquired.

General Bosquet's headquarters were in a large house that had changed hands twice before the French had taken the honours. It bore evidence of a past grandeur, but sconces had been ripped from the walls, and the furniture bore scars from sabres and swords.

"I must apologize for a certain amount of disarray in the decor," Captain Desgranges said wryly, "but I trust you will be comfortable, and General Bosquet will be honoured to have you join us at dinner."

In their bedrooms, which were adjoined with communicating double doors, the newly arrived travellers found two maids ready to wait on them. Hot tea was poured from a samovar; when they had finished their refreshment, the servants fetched hot water for the baths, and both visitors soaked away the tiredness of travel.

Madame de Vincent was soon clad in a silk dress of sombre black. Then she went to the chapel, where her husband's coffin had been placed. Stéphanie was shivering with nervous excitement as she dressed and arranged her hair into clusters of curls.

Wanting to make her entrance with as much impact as possible, she waited until she was sure that Madame de Vincent had joined the officers gathering with General Bosquet in the hour before dinner. She descended the stairs. At the archway leading into the room she paused, and all heads turned towards her. Silence fell as she stood there in a shining dress of copper silk, her fair hair gleaming and her smooth shoulders glowing white as alabaster. Her sudden appearance amid the squalor and misery of war brought a sense of disbelief to every man present.

General Bosquet stepped forward to greet her. "I bid you

welcome, Mademoiselle Casile. I knew your father well. A fine man and a courageous soldier."

Stéphanie never knew what answer she made. She had sighted Pierre. He was staring at her with a look of terrible amusement as if he saw some joke turned against himself. She felt lost and afraid, unable to comprehend his reaction, until he gave her a long, slow smile that left no doubt he was pleased to see her.

He approached her and said, "You are full of surprises, Stéphanie. I've never known quite what to expect of you since our very first meeting."

Her confidence returned, and a touch of mischief appeared on her face. "I hope this is the best surprise of all."

He chuckled and moved closer to her. "The very best. Nobody but you could manage to appear in a theatre of war as if you had come from a magician's hat, and secure three days of furlough for me at the same time."

She laughed delightedly, taking the arm he offered her. Dinner had been announced, and General Bosquet was leading Madame de Vincent into the dining hall.

Throughout the meal Stéphanie was the centre of attention, chattering away to all those around her, smiling and flirting and thoroughly enjoying herself. She had her darling Pierre beside her, which was all that mattered.

During the following days Madame de Vincent performed her duties as chaperon diligently. She was responsible for the girl's well-being and would not fail in her task, although she would have preferred not going along on walks through the village in the bitter cold, or exploring ancient fortresses of historical interest. Indoors she kept at a tactful distance whenever Stéphanie and her handsome beau sat talking together, but at all times she kept them within her range of vision.

She supposed that for them the time flew past, but for herself it dragged tediously. All she wanted was to be gone from this dreadful part of the world.

On their last night she slept fitfully, thoughts of the early start to be made in the morning making her stir restlessly. Then abruptly her eyes flew open and she sat up, her hair swirling about her shoulders. What had she heard?

She saw threads of candlelight touching the floorboards under the communicating doors. Was Stéphanie ill? Flinging back the bedclothes, she swung her feet to the floor, hurried across to the double doors, and flung them wide.

"Stéphanie! Are you . . ." Her voice died in her throat. Stéphanie, defiance in her face, sat against the pillows in her white nightgown, her legs drawn under her. Pierre was also on the bed, sitting on the edge in his quilted dressing robe, one bare foot on the floor. His expression was one of controlled exasperation, and neither of them showed any surprise. Madame de Vincent did not doubt that the creaking of floorboards had given ample notice of her coming. A gush of despair caused her to shriek, "Whatever would the emperor say?" Then as she collapsed into a chair and burst into tears, Stéphanie began to giggle.

At half past eight the next morning, General Bosquet and his officers and soldiers stood at attention and saluted the departing coffin draped in the tricolour. As Madame de Vincent rode ahead on horseback, the mounted lancers moved forward in escort. Stéphanie followed on a chestnut mare.

Madame de Vincent stared unseeingly ahead, thinking that the wretched girl, far from being consoling company, had only added to her ordeal. What if the emperor should find out about the previous night's shameful episode? Admittedly Stéphanie had finally appeared contrite at causing such upset. But it had been Captain de Gand who had soothed Madame de Vincent, inadvertently giving her a sharp insight into that persuasive charm of his that her charge had found impossible to resist. Yes, she could see how it had all come about, but she could not excuse either of them.

As for Stéphanie, she felt older and wiser, and for that alone the journey would have been worthwhile; but to have achieved the true purpose of the visit was a precious bonus that she hugged to herself in secret exultation.

STÉPHANIE FOUND LIFE IN PARIS gayer and more extravagant than ever before. The empress was glad to have her back. She was eager to show Stéphanie the forthcoming imperial baby's extensive layette, which was going on view to the public.

Among those who joined the long queue to see the exquisite display was Marie Worth. She was expecting another baby herself, and Louise, who had gone with her to view the layette, could not help contrasting Marie's daily routine with the rest and care that would be allotted to the empress. In his enthusiasm for work,

Worth often forgot that his wife tired more easily than usual. But Marie never complained.

One afternoon a well-dressed visitor arrived at the shop to see Worth, the circular package that he carried proclaiming his mission. A stream of inventors of crinoline expanders was making the rounds of the dressmakers. The man's back was towards her, but as Louise approached, she noticed something vaguely familiar about him.

"You wish to see Monsieur Worth?" she asked him.

He turned around, and bright, twinkling eyes regarded her. "Louise! Well, I'll be damned!"

She gave a gasp of astonishment. "Will Russell! Whenever did you come back to Paris?"

"An hour ago," he said, laughing. He gripped her shoulders and scanned her from head to toe. "You're a sight to see, my girl." His eyebrows lifted at finding no wedding band. "Not married, then? Are the men of this country out of their minds?"

"It won't be long before I am married," she confided, her face aglow. "It should only be a few weeks before an armistice is called in the Crimea."

Will grimaced sympathetically. "Your betrothed is involved in that mess, is he? Which regiment is he serving with?" He was impressed at hearing that the man she was to marry was of the Cent-Gardes. "Nothing but the cream of the regiments for you, eh?" He glanced about. "Where's Monsieur Worth? I'll get my business done, and then you and I will dine together."

"I'll find him for you." She started to hurry away, then paused to look back at Will. "You look so prosperous. I'm glad all appears to have gone well with you."

He smiled in acknowledgment as she disappeared in the direction of the fitting rooms. Things had gone well for him financially. He had opened a small dressmaking factory in London and installed his own patented sewing machines. After a great deal of hard work, he increased his business enough to move into bigger premises.

His marriage, however, had not gone well. He had been deeply in love with Ellen Moncrieffe. They had had a lavish wedding, and Ellen, ethereal in white satin and lace, had revelled in every minute. But to be a wife was a different matter. He had soon begun to see that she was one of those shallow women possessed of self-love. Emotionally she would give nothing, her heart as barren as her body appeared to be. A child would have brought some joy into

237

that house, where every lace curtain ruffle was starched and where every knob of coal would have been polished if it had been possible.

"Mr. Russell? I believe you wish to see me." Worth stood there, hands linked behind his back.

"How do you do, sir. I have come to Paris especially to show you my patented invention that nobody else has seen. I think you will find it of extreme interest."

"I doubt it," Worth replied. "I am sure you have a crinoline device to show me, and I have seen them all."

With easy arrogance which more than matched Worth's own, Will stood solidly and looped a thumb in his waistcoat pocket.

"You're a confident man to make such a boast, Mr. Worth. My invention is not a variation on heavy metal cages that almost pin a woman to the ground. It is made up of fine steel hoops attached by tapes and increasing in diameter from waist to hem. It is as light as a watch spring." His broad shoulders shifted casually. "However, if you are not interested I'll take up no more of your time."

Worth compressed his lips with some wryness. "Very well, Mr. Russell. I'll take a look at your watch-spring hoops."

As soon as Worth saw the invention he knew all his problems with the crinoline were solved. Not only would it relieve women of the bulky weight of petticoats and padding, but what a framework for his dresses it would be! He could scarcely wait to get it into the workrooms. "I want the bottom hoop to be six yards in circumference," he declared, visualizing the effect of at least ten yards of material over it.

"Six yards!" Will was surprised, but he did not question the order. "It shall be done."

That evening he called for Louise carrying armfuls of gardenias and a magnum of champagne, which he insisted on opening at once. Afterwards he took both Catherine and Louise to dine at the grand Maison Dorée.

Will had planned to leave Paris immediately, but since the next day was Sunday and Louise was free, he postponed his departure until that evening. He was interested in seeing the changes wrought by Baron Haussmann in the beautification of Paris, and in the morning he and Louise joined the promenading crowds.

"What grandeur!" he exclaimed at the architecture. He found the spaciousness everywhere equally remarkable, and declared that fifty carriages could be driven abreast down the Champs-Élysées.

238

He praised the newly laid out parks, the open squares, and the magnificence of the repaired Louvre.

In the afternoon he hired a coupé and drove Louise through the Bois de Boulogne, which had now become the grandest park of all, with its shrubberies, lakes, and sparkling cascades.

That evening they dined at an early hour. Then Louise went with Will to the railway terminus.

"I hope it won't be so long before we meet again," Will said. "Am I allowed to kiss the future bride farewell?"

Her eyes danced. "Everyone is allowed to kiss a bride."

But not as he kissed her. It was a repeat of the intimate kiss that had taken place long before in a dressmaker's workroom.

The guard blew his whistle, and Will released her and sprang up the steps into the train. His expression was serious as he waved to her while the train carried him away and out of her sight.

Louise was thoughtful as she left the station. She could not help but wonder what would have happened if a sharp-faced, vindictive woman had not intruded on those workroom premises so long ago.

IN LESS THAN A WEEK the first shipment of the Russell crinoline hoops was delivered at Maison Gagelin. Among them was one labelled as a gift for Louise. Worth was less than pleased at having to surrender one of the coveted number, but two days later there came the second of the many more shipments that were to arrive almost continually. He worked long hours, creating the largest and lightest crinoline dresses ever seen. Marie was the first to wear one of them, her now thick waistline disguised with a clever use of fringe on the jacket top. She declared that the inventor should be awarded a medal for freeing women from the cumbersome weight that had dogged the crinoline.

Marie was soon delivered of her second child, another son. He was welcomed with great joy and baptized Jean-Philippe. Then, just two weeks after the armistice in the Crimea, the empress went into a difficult labour, and it was not until the third day that she was delivered of a strong, lusty boy. Cannons were fired and church bells took up the rejoicing.

LOUISE HAD HOPED that Pierre would be home soon after the armistice, but in April she received a letter from one of his fellow officers saying that Pierre had been stricken by cholera. It seemed an eternity before word came of his slow recovery, and finally a letter from Pierre himself arrived. He wrote that as soon as he was able to travel he would be transported to his home in the Loire Valley for a long convalescence. She would hear from him constantly. He loved her with all his heart.

Throughout the summer letters came regularly from the Château de Gand. Pierre wrote that he had suffered a relapse and had been given extended furlough to go south for full recuperation. Louise was disappointed that their reunion would be postponed, but thankful that he was receiving every care.

At Maison Gagelin the autumn rush gave way to a mass of orders for the social events of the new year. The hooped crinoline was proving to be a great success, and Worth had some particularly beautiful petticoats made up that would ensure modesty if a skirt swung unduly. Imitators were producing similar hoops, but whatever was worn to support the skirt, one aim did not change, which was that crinolines should become wider and wider, a whim well matched to the mood of a city bent frenetically on pleasure.

One snowy night Louise was manipulating her skirt with care when she left the shop, failing to notice the man who waited beside a stationary fiacre. As she passed he caught her about the waist and swung her into his arms. Her cry was smothered by his rapturous kiss. "How I've missed you!" gasped Pierre, his lips barely lifted from hers.

Louise was deliriously excited. "Are you really here? I can scarcely believe it." She touched his face with quick, fluttering caresses, and he hastened her into the waiting fiacre.

He pulled off her bonnet and took her face between his hands. "Tell me you still love me as I love you." His voice shook. "I want to hear you speak those words."

She flung herself passionately across his chest. "I love you more than ever."

He gripped her by the arms and held her tightly. "Enough to defy the whole world if need be?"

"Yes, yes. What makes you ask that? Is something wrong?"

"No," he whispered. "Not now. Not any more."

They arrived at the apartment in the rue Lenoir. No one was there. Servants had readied it for Pierre's homecoming and then departed. Lamps glowed softly, and flames flickered and danced in every grate.

240

In his arms Louise responded utterly, exulting in his adoration of her. It was as if there were no world, no time, no night, no day. Only Pierre.

He was sleeping when she slipped from the apartment at dawn the next morning.

At the shop, Louise felt lightheaded and lighthearted, as if she had indulged in a champagne breakfast. It was during the afternoon, when she was clearing up after a fitting, that she became aware of the electrified atmosphere that accompanied the arrival of an important customer.

"It's that old terror, Madame de Gand!" said a *vendeuse*.

Louise walked to the draped doorway of the dressmaking salon where Worth had received the customer. There Madame de Gand was glancing about impatiently.

"I am to meet my son's betrothed here! Where is she?"

Louise was dismayed at being caught so completely unawares. Surely Pierre should have warned her that his mother was in Paris and ready to meet her. She drew in a deep breath and smoothed her hair. She had taken a step into the salon when Madame de Gand happened to glance in the opposite direction.

"There is Mademoiselle Casile now!"

Louise followed the woman's glance and saw Stéphanie approaching with some haste. "Your pardon, Madame de Gand," the girl implored. "I was early and decided to take a look at the new fabrics in the material department. I quite forgot the time."

"Never make excuses. Not even to me. It's undignified. Now tell Monsieur Worth what you want."

Stéphanie turned to him with shining eyes. "A wedding gown and a trousseau, Monsieur Worth. The most beautiful you've ever created."

His expression was guarded. "I'm honoured, Mademoiselle Casile. Am I to understand that the fortunate groom-to-be is Captain de Gand?"

"Yes, that is right. We are to be married in late summer."

Louise clutched the fold of the draperies as the room began to reel. She drew backwards out of the salon, her eyes shut as she fought for control. Then two of her fellow workers rushed forward and caught her as she collapsed into blackness.

Her faint lasted a long while. When she recovered consciousness she found herself lying on a chaise longue alone in a room with

Marie. Memory returned, and she jerked up from the pillow that had been placed under her head. "Is it true?" she questioned frantically.

Marie put aside the smelling salts and supported her with one arm. "I'm afraid so, Louise. The women have gone, but from what they said to Charles, it appears that Mademoiselle Casile has been visiting the de Gand residence during the captain's convalescence. A few days ago a private party was held there to celebrate their betrothal."

Louise covered her face, and her body was racked with sobs. Marie's own eyes filled with tears of pity for such distress. It had been what she had feared would happen all along, but Louise had been deaf to all words of caution. When she had opened Louise's dress at the throat, she had seen the diamond keeper and plain gold band on a chain. Louise had been betrayed by the oldest trick a man could play along the path of seduction. "Is there anything I can do?" she implored.

The answer was muffled. "Nothing. Nothing."

Marie left her for a while, and when she returned, the room was empty. To her amazement she found Louise once more at work, down on her knees adjusting the gathers of a dress. She was pale and her eyes were red-rimmed, but she appeared to be in complete control of herself. It was as if by concentrating on work she was forcing herself away from the abyss of despair.

Louise arrived home that night to find dark red roses delivered from Pierre, and a letter expressing regret that she had left him asleep when they had so much to talk about. He suggested that they meet the following night at the apartment.

The next evening Louise managed to arrive there before Pierre. She declined to give her cape and bonnet to the servants and went through to the salon to wait. Through open doors she could see a table laid for two, champagne in an ice bucket, and a floral centrepiece with candles. She understood now that the apartment had been planned all along for intimate tête-à-têtes. Astounded by her own gullibility, she was thankful that Catherine's indecision had kept her from moving in before Pierre's departure to the Crimea.

Suddenly she heard Pierre's voice as he spoke to a servant. She braced herself and faced him as he came into the room, closing the door behind him.

"*Chérie!* What a grand surprise to find you here already. Why are you still wearing your cape and bonnet? I'll take them from you."

She spoke before he could reach her. "I'm not staying. I've come to say goodbye. And to return these." She put the gold ring and the diamond keeper down on a small table.

He went ashen. "You have heard!" he exclaimed hoarsely. "But how was that possible? There's been no announcement—"

"The future Madame de Gand has ordered her trousseau from Maison Gagelin."

Pierre looked appalled. "My darling Louise—"

She shuddered. "Please! No more deceit!"

He threw out his arms. "You must believe that I intended to tell you the morning after our reunion."

She was suddenly seized with a terrible anger. "You should have told me before that night began!"

"No!" He grabbed her and pulled her close to him. "I thought to share a few last perfect hours with you before the time came for me to explain." His speech was bitter and emphatic as he told her of his application to become betrothed, and its outcome. "I had hoped that Stéphanie would meet someone else in my absence, but the emperor allowed her to visit me in the Crimea, a public showing of his approval of the relationship. Nothing less than a betrothal could follow."

Her eyes were desolate. "You knew when you left for the war that there would be nothing for us when you returned."

"No," he countered vehemently. "I had planned then that if I was lucky enough to come back unscathed, we should make a life together. This marriage is simply one of convenience. It will make no difference to us."

"No difference?" she echoed incredulously.

Pierre sighed. "If I had refused it, my service in the Cent-Gardes would have been at an end, and I would have been dismissed from the army without honour. Can you understand what that would have meant to me?"

She gave a bleak nod. "Yes," she whispered.

"Louise, I'll always think of you as my true wife, the only woman I'll ever love, and you shall always have whatever your heart desires." He reached out and took up the gold band from the table. "If you tire of this apartment, I'll buy any mansion you take a liking to, in the Faubourg Saint-Germain, perhaps, or—"

He took her hand and tried to replace the ring. "No! No! No!" she

243

cried. She pulled her hand away with such force that she knocked the ring aside and it bounced out of sight. For a few awful seconds she thought Pierre would strike her.

"Damnation!" he yelled, a pulse throbbing in his temple. "Does your love rely solely on a marriage certificate? Was it only a piece of paper that you wanted all along?"

She gave him a curiously pitying look. "If I had been told of the emperor's decision against our marriage, we could have talked about it together and found a way out. You could have resigned your commission with full honour, and we could have left France to live abroad. In America, or even Mexico."

"I couldn't have left our country during a time of war."

She gave a helpless shrug, not denying his patriotic loyalty, but because they had come to a point where they had nothing more to say to each other. He loved her, but not enough to give up everything for her as she would have done for him.

"I would have accepted your not being able to marry me, Pierre. There have been many before us and there will be many after us who will love and be prevented from marrying through circumstances beyond their control, but I can't share you. Can't you see that I couldn't spend the rest of my life waiting and hoping for an hour or a day granted now and again? I could never endure second place."

"You'll always come first with me," he protested fiercely.

She could scarcely bear the anguish in his face, and when she spoke, her voice almost broke. "For the sake of your marriage, and to enable me to start life afresh, we shall not meet again." Her words almost caught in her throat. "Goodbye, Pierre."

He did not attempt to stop her as she hastened from him, but when she reached the door his desperate voice rang down the room to her. "You haven't finished with me. It can never be over between us. You'll come back. You'll have to."

WORTH WAS in a dilemma. At Marie's request he had been prepared to spare Louise the fitting of the dresses for the Casile trousseau, but the bride-to-be had objected.

"I would like Mademoiselle Louise to be the one to fit my wedding gown and trousseau," she declared firmly. "Please see to it, Monsieur Worth."

The problem was solved by Louise herself when she caught word

244

of it. "I have been expecting to fit Mademoiselle Casile's dresses," she said to Worth without emotion.

He studied her for a moment. There was no denying that Louise had courage. At work she had continued as if she had nothing on her mind. She was just a little paler than before, with faint shadows under her eyes, and he sensed some indefinable change in her. "Thank you, Louise. I appreciate your cooperation, and I fully understand what it means to you."

She nodded and returned to her work. She found kind words and sympathy hard to bear. How Worth would deal with her later on she did not know. To date nobody suspected her secret, not even Catherine. She had managed on several early-morning occasions to reach the outdoor privy without the undue haste that would have attracted attention. She found it difficult to sleep, often pacing about her room as she tried to decide how best to cope with the new burden that had been laid upon her. Her first thought after realizing she was pregnant was to pack her bags and go to Will Russell in England. She knew that he would find employment for her. But, upon reflection, it seemed better to stay where she was and continue working for as long as she could.

The day came when Stéphanie arrived at Maison Gagelin for the first fitting of one of the forty dresses she had ordered. She was in her hooped petticoat when Louise entered the fitting room.

"How wonderful to see you again, Mademoiselle Louise," Stéphanie said. "Are you well?"

"I'm very well, thank you. I'm sure you will make a beautiful bride." She felt no personal enmity towards this amiable girl, but it was hard to be in her company.

"Look!" Stéphanie held out her hand proudly to show off a large diamond set in gold. "It's the de Gand betrothal ring. Did you ever see anything so grand?" She giggled. "Or so ostentatious! Pierre and I have all sorts of little jokes about it. He says he's marrying me because I make him laugh." She gave another infectious giggle. "That's only his jesting, of course."

"Of course," Louise agreed faintly.

"He is quite the handsomest man in Paris," Stéphanie said. "Women flock after him, you know."

Louise busied herself in unhooking the dress to be fitted. "I'm sure they do. As you say, he is extremely good-looking."

Stéphanie's eyebrows shot up. "Have you seen him, then?"

245

"He came here with Madame de Gand. It was quite a long time ago." Louise took up the dress. "Now if you care to stand still, Mademoiselle Michelle and I will help you on with this."

After the dress was on, Worth entered the room and expressed his usual dissatisfaction with every part of the garment, since perfection was impossible at a first fitting. Stéphanie was slightly in awe of him. He was so imperious, and quite merciless to the dress, keeping up a constant flow of instructions to his fitter.

It was after one of many fittings that Louise found an earring of Stéphanie's caught in a frill of lace. She hurried after her and reached her on the pavement.

"Thank you so much." Stéphanie took it gratefully. "It was my mother's. I would have hated to lose it."

Louise scarcely heard her. Too late she saw that Stéphanie had been met by Pierre at the shop's entrance. He stared at Louise, raking her appearance from head to toe and back again. She knew his thoughts, knew what he was demanding of her in a silence that boomed against her ears.

Quickly she withdrew and hastened back into the shop, hand pressed to her side. How much longer could she go on lacing herself in so tightly? She had eased her stay ribbons by a few centimetres, but was the present stricture still too much, endangering the baby? She wished there was someone from whom she could seek advice. Catherine, who now knew about the baby, was full of old wives' tales guaranteed to frighten a mother-to-be half out of her wits, and was not the one to consult.

As Louise re-entered the dressmaking salon Marie was modelling a dress for a customer. By chance their eyes met, and Louise saw concern sharpen Marie's glance. It came to her that Marie knew. She had guessed. It was as though a shadow had been lifted from Louise. Now she knew who would advise her.

Marie did more than give advice. She donated a pile of baby clothes that Jean-Philippe had outgrown, and she told Worth about the situation. With his permission, Louise made herself short jackets with scallops, similar to those he had designed for Marie when she was pregnant.

As week followed week, the dresses of the trousseau were finally completed. Louise approached Worth with a request to take up work in the sewing room, where there would be no risk of offending customers with her condition.

246

Worth agreed, then made his own request. "As you know, Louise, I do get customers ordering dresses for the advanced stages of the condition that you are now in, and to date it has been impossible to show them how a finished garment will look. Would you object to modelling these dresses for me? You would be veiled to spare you embarrassment. What do you say?"

She answered without hesitation. "I'll be glad to do it."

From that point on, her time was spent in the workroom, except when Stéphanie made a visit to the dressmaking salon or a pregnant customer came to order clothes. Then Louise, with a veil over her face, would pace slowly around the floor dressed in one of Worth's concealing creations. Word of Monsieur Worth's veiled lady spread like wildfire among those expecting a happy event, and the appointment book was filled daily.

Louise was thankful that she felt fit enough to continue working, although tiredness did overcome her at the end of the day. One evening, after climbing the stairs to her rooms, she paused to catch her breath on the landing. Gradually she became aware that she was not alone. She stiffened, knowing that Pierre was waiting in the shadows.

Quickly she put her key in the lock and shot through the door, but with a thud Pierre's fist blocked its closing and he was inside with her. She saw at once that he had been drinking; his eyes were bright and angry, his mouth set obstinately. With one hand he wrenched her cape from her and with the other jerked aside her silk jacket. Slowly his gaze rose from her waist to her face, his expression one of triumph.

"*Now* will you come back to me?"

She tugged the silk jacket from his grip, frightened and trembling. "No. You already belong to someone else. When I said goodbye to you I meant it. Now will you please go?"

He thrust his face towards her. "You're carrying my child. What can make us belong to each other more than that?"

"It's not your child. It's mine! Mine! Stéphanie Casile will bear you all the legitimate children you could possibly want. She's the one with whom you'll live your life, and with time you'll forget that you ever knew me." Sobs burst from her in a storm. "Get out!" she shrieked.

Pierre was dismayed. "I'm deeply sorry. Louise—"

She stumbled past him, pulled open the door, and turned her

face away. His expression was stricken as he paused. He half reached out to her, but then thought better of it and left.

She slammed the door shut and fell to her knees and wept.

STÉPHANIE CAME for the final fitting of her bridal gown. "This dress is surely your most beautiful creation, Monsieur Worth," she enthused as she admired her reflection in the mirror. The dress was light and ethereal, its satin complemented by the glow of flower clusters of pearls. She turned to Louise. For a long time she had been sure that the fitter was expecting a child, but since there was no marriage band on her finger, it was not a subject that could be mentioned. "You will be with me on my wedding morning to help me dress, won't you, mademoiselle?"

Worth spoke up. "We shall both be there."

Louise was dismayed that Worth had apparently forgotten the reason why she would not wish to help Stéphanie dress for the wedding. But any thought of evading the duty was dispelled when Stéphanie turned a frightened face to her when they were alone.

"I'm scared, Mademoiselle Louise. I love my betrothed so much, but I'm afraid that he's dreading the wedding day. When there's talk about it I see a kind of trapped look in his eyes."

"Hush! Hush!" Louise cried. "You must not say such things to me. You're nervous, as all brides are, but you can't confide your fears to a dressmaker's assistant."

"Why not? I've come to think of you as a friend. I have no one else who would listen to me kindly."

"Surely the Duchess of Bassano."

"No, she has never liked me very much. Once she called me a giggling little ninny, and that's what I am. No wonder Pierre regrets his promise to marry me. After all, I plotted and connived and trapped him into it—"

In desperation Louise put a hand over the girl's mouth. "Put all those foolish thoughts away. The period of a betrothment is always strained and often fraught with doubts, and it is the same for him as it is for you."

Stéphanie nodded, blinking back tears and wiping her eyes in a childlike way. "How sensible you are and how comforting." Impulsively she reached out to hug Louise. "If I had had a sister, I should have wanted her to be just like you."

On the eve of the wedding, Louise accompanied the huge boxes containing the bridal outfit to the Duke and Duchess of Bassano's residence, a grand edifice not far from the Élysée Palace. She placed the bridal gown on a wicker figure and smoothed out every frill and gather. She was about to leave when a maidservant came to say that Mademoiselle Casile wished to see her. Somewhat apprehensive, Louise followed the maid into the library.

Her first thought was that Stéphanie was ill. There was a thin look to her face and a bleakness to her eyes. She bade Louise sit down but remained standing herself, nervously drawing a handkerchief through her hands. "I should like to ask you an extremely personal question."

Louise's apprehension gave way to a sick dread. "I'll answer it if I can."

"Who is the father of your unborn child?"

Louise clasped the arm of the chair. "You have no right to ask me."

"I think I have every right!"

Louise tried not to show her inner qualms. "Perhaps you had better explain what you mean."

Stéphanie took a couple of paces in one direction and then the other before she came to a standstill, plucking at her handkerchief. "It appears that a new piece of gossip has just burst upon the Paris scene. It is said that the woman with whom Pierre was seen everywhere before he went to the Crimea has been fitting the garments of his bride. What do you say to that?"

Louise looked at her sadly. "I say that with all my heart I wish you had never heard such cruel talk."

"Do you deny that it is true?"

"The truth is that all is ended between Pierre and me."

"But the baby? Is it his?"

Louise's face froze. "I say once more that you have no right to ask such a question of me."

Stéphanie nodded helplessly. "I accept what you say. You have made me believe that I have nothing to fear from you. But how am I going to face everyone tomorrow, knowing how the scandal will have spread?"

Louise pitied her. "Gossip comes and goes," she said stoutly. "People will forget whatever they heard when they see how happy and radiant you are. Tomorrow is the day you have been longing for. Don't let anything spoil it for you. You're going to marry the man you love."

To Stéphanie it was as if she had been cast a lifeline. She *was* going to marry Pierre, and nothing else mattered. All men had affairs before they married, and she would make him forget Louise and all the others he must have known.

"I think it would be best if you didn't come tomorrow," she said. "Let Monsieur Worth bring someone else."

Louise was engulfed with relief. "I'll tell him that."

"Goodbye, Louise."

A MONTH and a half later, on the last day of October, Louise gave birth to a son in the presence of Catherine and a midwife. When the baby was laid in Louise's arms she looked at him with love. He was to be baptized Paul-Michel for no other reason than that she liked the name. And perhaps in her heart she wanted the letter *P* to be a link with the father he would never know.

CHAPTER SEVEN

A hired fiacre drew up at Maison Gagelin, and a young man stepped out of it and tipped the driver handsomely. He breezed through the door of the shop and snapped his fingers at an assistant. "Where can I find Monsieur Worth?"

As the assistant led the way, Robert Prestbury followed at a swaggering saunter, twirling his cane and glancing about him. What a difference between this opulent edifice and the interior of his father's London shop, which had a few potted palms, a handful of display dummies, and little else. Not even a comely young shopgirl to squeeze, but sour-faced harridans with pinched lips. They would be the first to go when he took charge of the Prestbury business. But before he could aspire to running that shop he had to prove to his ailing father that he was ready to clip his wings and take life more soberly than in the past.

Well, he had no choice in the matter. The legacy from his grandmother, which had given him two years of independence and extravagance, had finally run out, and he considered himself fortunate to be sent to a renowned Paris shop for training. He had visited Paris twice before, but he had been in the money then. The present position had been found for him through the kindly auspices of the silk merchant Allenby, an old friend of his father's.

Robert arrived at the dressmaking department and took a seat in a gilded chair. The salon was remarkably busy, with customers being attended to by *vendeuses* smartly dressed in black silk. He saw a tall, slim man approaching him in a black frock coat, his cravat folded immaculately and fastened with a pearl-headed pin, his waistcoat without a wrinkle. So this was Worth. Younger than he had expected. Early thirties. Distinguished and very serious. Robert rose leisurely to his feet. "This is indeed an honour, Monsieur Worth," he said with an easy, companionable air as he extended his hand. "I'm Robert Prestbury."

Worth ignored the outstretched hand. His eyes blazed. "This is not a club, Prestbury! I do not greet my employees in the salon as if they were customers of distinction. You were expected to report for work five days ago." He looked contemptuously at the natty check in which Robert was attired. "You will remove yourself from these premises and arrive suitably dressed in sombre black at the employces' entrance tomorrow morning at eight o'clock. You will also shave your upper lip. Moustaches are not permitted in this establishment. That's all for the moment." He turned on his heel and strode away.

Robert left the shop in high dudgeon. He had assumed that he would enjoy a privileged position due to Mr. Allenby's association with Worth, but it had been made clear that he could expect no favours. That evening he shaved off the light brown moustache that he had worn for a considerable time. Without it he looked younger than his twenty-four years. His face was solidly boned, with a square jaw and a well-shaped nose, and his hair had a tendency to fall silkily over his brow in a manner that women called "engaging".

The following morning he arrived on time and was surprised to find not only Worth already at the shop, but also Madame Worth. She was dressed in black silk like the other women on the staff, but in the height of fashion, her dress most elaborately flounced, her hair immaculately coiffed.

Worth looked Robert Prestbury up and down. The moustache had vanished, and the black frock coat had the correct amount of starched white cuff showing at the wrists.

"What do you know about materials, Prestbury?" Worth asked abruptly. "After all, that's where fashion begins."

"I know a good piece of cloth when I see it. Scottish tweed, broadcloth, serge, drill, waistcoat silk, and velvet."

"Well, that's a good beginning, but excepting silk and velvet, we deal with lighter fabrics here. Fashion is a living phenomenon, you know. It reflects the mood and environs of a society. Now!" Worth glanced about, looking for someone to whom he could entrust the newcomer for instruction, and he remembered that Louise was returning to work that day, almost a month after the birth of her child. "You shall meet Mademoiselle Louise. She is an authority on the quality of weave and design in a fabric."

It flustered Louise to be called forward, because she thought for a moment that someone had seen her smuggle Paul-Michel into the building. He was not yet a month old and needed to be put to the breast regularly, making it impossible for her to leave him with anyone else. There were a number of storerooms to the rear of the dressmaking department, and she had made him a bed in one of them, in a drawer set on a wide shelf. She could only hope that neither Worth nor the proprietors would discover that an infant was on the premises.

She was a good instructress, and Robert was soon able to judge the quality of fabrics and how they would drape or gather. Had he not been lazy, he could have come to excel in the business, but it was his nature to rely on guile and flattery to assure him an easy path.

Louise soon became aware that Prestbury stood too close to her and was always quick to take her arm when they passed through a crowded part of the shop. She discouraged his attentions and found it hard not to show impatience when he delayed her from slipping away to Paul-Michel.

Her footsteps were always light as she hastened to the tiny storeroom. A small window gave some illumination to the room, and on bright days the sun's warmth fell softly over her as she held her baby to her breast. Often she sang softly to him, smoothing his downy hair with her fingertips. When he had had his fill, she would return him with a kiss to his bed.

She went to and from the storeroom several times a day, week after week, always closing the door soundlessly behind her. She had no idea that her visits were beginning to be observed.

It had not taken long for Robert to hear from a couple of

vendeuses that Louise was what was known as a fallen woman and that she had recently had a baby. This information made her still more intriguing in his eyes. He was sorry when her supervision of his training came to an end.

One afternoon during a lull in the salon he slipped away into the corridor along which he had earlier seen Louise disappear; he was intent on waylaying her. Here and there a gaslight flickered, but soon the gloom deepened into shadows. Suddenly a door opened and Louise emerged. She gave a cry of alarm. "What are you doing here?" she demanded.

"I just came looking for you. Don't you want company to and from the storeroom?"

"What do you mean?" she blurted, fright in her eyes.

"Only that you must find it tedious running errands for the sewing room on your own."

"Oh, I see." She relaxed. "I don't mind it. Not at all."

He was watching her keenly. "I've missed our time together. Let me take you out to supper this evening."

She shook her head. "No, thank you. I'm going straight home."

He was piqued. Who did she think she was to turn him down? As she made to go on her way he stepped in front of her. "Come on, Louise. A pretty girl shouldn't hide herself away." He looked intently into her eyes. "And you're more than pretty. I would call you beautiful." Unable to keep his hands from her any longer, he reached out to grasp her.

"Don't touch me!" she cried, but he trapped her in his arms.

"Don't play games with me. We both know you like a little fun." He sought to capture her mouth with his own, but she twisted wildly in his arms and he let her go, glaring after her as she flew from him. He straightened his coat and returned to the showrooms, his mind entirely on Louise. It suddenly struck him that she had been empty-handed when she had gone to the storeroom, and empty-handed when she came out. How odd. How very odd.

UNBEKNOWN TO ANYONE else, Marie had been giving thought to that same section of storerooms, wondering if they could be turned into domestic quarters. More than ever she yearned to live on the premises. She did not know how much longer she could sustain the working days that kept her from returning home until late at night.

It was sheer chance that she happened to glance out of the shop-window one afternoon and notice that the family who occupied the apartment at the top of the building was moving out. She went at once to the office of the proprietors and asked them if the top flat had been re-let.

"No, Madame Worth. It has not," Monsieur Opigez replied. "Why do you ask?"

She leaned forward eagerly. "My husband and I would like to be the new tenants. For a long time we have wished to live on the spot. Not only would it make life much easier for him, but I should be at hand if there happened to be any emergency involving my children." She waited, her face alight with anticipation. Then her expression began to fade as she saw their aghast faces.

"Impossible! Out of the question!" they exclaimed in unison.

She could not believe her ears. "But what possible objection could you have?"

They looked both grave and shocked, and Monsieur Gagelin spoke with vehemence. "Madame Worth! Surely you can see that it is unacceptable for the *premier commis* of so grand a shop as ours to live on the premises like a common concierge! It would degrade his position and ours to allow such an unheard-of state of affairs."

She found their snobbery insufferable. That they should regard with contempt her simple request to live in all respectability five flights above the shop showed a complete lack of consideration. She answered their pomposity with spirit. "I fail to understand your attitude, messieurs." She tilted her head proudly and rose to her feet. "Charles Worth is a master and a genius. Nothing can taint such a man. He could live in a cellar or even above a shop and continue to command all respect. Good day to you."

She maintained her composure until she reached her husband's office. There she broke down.

"What is it, my darling? Whatever is the matter?" It all came out—her increasing concern for their children in her absence all day, her own tiredness, and the disappointment of having her request for the apartment turned down. Worth listened in silence, and made the decision that had long been in his mind. His employers had gone too far. They had put their own hideous snobbery before his wife and children.

That evening Worth called on a Swedish acquaintance whom he had known for a considerable time. He was welcomed with the offer of a Havana cigar, which he refused, and a glass of superb wine,

254

which he accepted. Otto Gustave Bobergh had been trained in the drapery trade in Sweden before coming to France, and he had worked for many years in a fashionable shop. Each man had often talked about how he would handle an enterprise of his own. Both had always been held back by lack of funds. But recently Bobergh's financial position had improved.

"I'm leaving Gagelin's," Worth said. "I'm going to open up a grand salon of *haute couture*, and I need a partner. Why not pool your resources with mine and come in with me? Somehow we'll raise the rest that we'll need."

Bobergh studied the perfect smoke ring that he had just blown. "What premises did you have in mind?"

"There's a suite of rooms that takes up the whole of the first floor at number seven rue de la Paix. The street is a quiet one, but a couple of high-class milliners do good business there. Moreover, the building is on the west side of the street near the opening into the Place Vendôme, with its exclusive properties. What do you say? Are you interested?"

Bobergh sat forward, a slow smile spreading across his face. "Extremely interested. Let's discuss a few more details."

They talked far into the night.

LOUISE WAS DEEPLY ALARMED the day she entered the storeroom to see one of Paul-Michel's blankets lying on the floor. She hurried to the makeshift bed and her heart stopped. The baby was not there.

As she whirled about in panic, Robert spoke tauntingly from a crate where he was seated in the gloom, holding Paul-Michel, wrapped in a shawl. "Is this what you're looking for?"

She ran to him with arms outstretched. "Give me my baby!"

"Wait!" Robert sprang up. "I don't know that you're fit to have charge of him. He was bawling his head off when I came in here."

"You were spying on me!"

"That's a harsh way of describing my interest in you. It'll do you no good to abuse me. What's to stop me from revealing your little secret to all and sundry?"

"Nothing! Go and report me if you must, but give me my baby!"

He hesitated, and then held the child forward. Louise snatched Paul-Michel to her and rocked him in the crook of her arm, speaking lovingly to him and drying his still tear-wet face with his shawl.

Robert regarded her with some embarrassment. He had thought, upon discovering the baby, that he had found a means of getting a hold over her. But he was mistaken. The girl could not be coerced. "Look here," he began. "I admire you for taking such a chance with your employment. I wouldn't think of telling anyone."

She raised her head, gratitude in her eyes. "Thank you, Monsieur Prestbury. I trust you to keep your word."

"Call me Robert."

She smiled. "Now if you would leave me alone with my baby, please, Robert?"

"Yes. Of course." He went from the storeroom much cheered by her smile. He had almost blundered the whole thing, but miraculously it had ended by putting him on a much better footing with her, giving him a clue as to how to proceed in the future.

WORTH WAS NOT entirely pleased with his protégé. Prestbury had the kind of polished manners that rarely failed to win sales, yet Worth was certain that he expended more energy in appearing busy than in actually working.

Prestbury was not Worth's only cause of irritation. Since he had given his notice to his employers, his relationship with them had deteriorated sharply. They became even more snobbish, treating Worth as if he were an ordinary employee whom they could well do without, instead of the *premier commis* who had made fortunes for them. It was their opinion that without their shop Worth would never have achieved anything, and would soon become nothing again. It never occurred to them that they were losing a great couturier.

IN THE RUE LEPELLETIER the coach taking the emperor and empress to a gala performance at the Opéra was escorted by mounted lancers and followed by two other equipages bearing members of the entourage. Stéphanie, seated beside Pierre in the carriage immediately behind the imperial couple's, looked out at the hundreds of people thundering forth cheers of loyalty and affection. She guessed that many envied the empress's seemingly perfect existence with her gallant husband and adored son. They could not know that the emperor had taken as his mistress the wife of his own foreign minister.

Were all husbands unfaithful? Stéphanie glanced at Pierre, who was gazing idly out of the window. Never would she give him cause

256

to stray. She loved him as fiercely and possessively after four months of marriage as she had done before, and had no reason to believe she had disappointed him in any way. On the contrary, he praised her ability to surprise him and make him laugh, a whispered comment from her at some dull official function always bringing amusement to his eyes. His past was over and done with. She, Stéphanie de Gand, was the one to fill his present and his future.

The wheels were slowing down, and through the window she saw the imperial carriage coming to a halt at the steps of the Opéra. She looked towards Pierre with a sudden rush of love and reached out her hand to him. Her impulsive gesture, causing her to turn from her window, saved her from serious injury, as in the same instant there came an enormous explosion from that side of the street. The impact sent her tumbling against him, the glass shattering and showering over them.

Stéphanie screamed, and Pierre hurled her down to the floor of the carriage. He threw himself over her as another bomb burst amid the terrified crowds. Total darkness descended as every gaslight in the street went out; then came the searing flash of the third bomb.

The air was filled with smoke as Pierre gathered Stéphanie up onto the seat. "Are you all right?" he demanded.

She nodded. "Yes, I think so." Then she shrieked at the sight of him. "What has happened to you?"

Pierre's face was streaming with blood from a cut on his head, but he was not conscious of it. "Stay here and I'll come back to you," he ordered. "I must get to the emperor."

If he is still alive, Pierre added grimly to himself as he swung out of the carriage. Lanterns were beginning to appear from the theatre, and beams of light showed the dead and injured lying about the street. Out of the smoke a man suddenly appeared from a narrow alley nearby, a pistol in his hand, and reached the imperial coach as Eugénie opened the door. Pierre gave a shout, hurling himself forward at the assassin, but gendarmes were there first and they brought the man down. Eugénie seemed almost unmoved by this attempt upon the lives of herself and her husband. The emperor had suffered only a scratched nose and, incongruously, a hole in his hat. She herself merely had a graze by her eye.

As she and Louis Napoleon alighted from the coach, she refused help and drew herself up, looking every inch an empress, and her voice was chill. "We have more courage than any assassin. Let all see that." The emperor seemed dazed with shock, but he accompanied Eugénie up the opera-house steps.

Pierre was about to fetch Stéphanie when his attention was gripped by a young woman leaning weakly against a building. He rushed to her. "Louise!"

He caught the unguarded look of love and relief in her eyes as she instinctively reached out to him. Then her hands withdrew in agitation. "You've been wounded," she said in confusion.

"It's nothing." He pulled out a handkerchief and wiped the blood from his brow. "What of you? What happened?"

"I was knocked over when everybody took fright." She jerked with shock as a lancer's bullet put an end to a horse's agony. Her lips quivered uncontrollably. "Those poor people! Oh, those horses!"

He moved to block her view. "I'll take you home."

"No, no. I'll be all right. Thank you for offering."

"One moment!" He looked down into her face. "Tell me. The child. What is it?"

A poignant look came across her face. "A boy."

"His name?"

"Paul-Michel."

His gaze followed her as she hastened away into the darkness. Then he returned to the carriage where Stéphanie waited at the open door. He supposed she had witnessed the whole incident. "That young woman had been knocked down in the crush," he said. "I thought I would make sure that she wasn't injured."

"I recognized her. She is a dressmaking assistant."

"Oh?" He dismissed the subject purposefully. "Take my arm. The others have already gone in."

Obediently Stéphanie placed her hand in the crook of his arm. She saw nothing of the performance. She had seen the look on her husband's face as he went to Louise. Any doubt she might have had as to who was the father of Louise's baby had gone.

THE DAY FINALLY CAME when Worth, wearing a new velvet-collared frock coat of impeccable cut, surveyed his redecorated premises at number 7 rue de la Paix. To celebrate his position as master in his own domain he had grown a large moustache, which Marie thought gave him an even more dashing air. She was equally delighted with her new home, the floor area being so spacious that they were able to have their own comfortable apartment adjoining the salons. Otto

258

Bobergh was content to be a partner in the background, dealing with the more mundane aspects of the business. His aristocratic Swedish connections had enabled him to raise the money needed without difficulty. An order for two dresses from the Queen of Sweden made an auspicious first entry in the order book.

The decor of the whole floor was luxurious, with gilded pillars and crystal chandeliers that cast sparkling slivers of light over ivory satin drapes and Louis Quinze chairs and sofas.

There was a staff of twenty. Louise had left Maison Gagelin to be Worth's premier fitter. And Worth was obliged through his word to Mr. Allenby to continue the training of Robert Prestbury.

Living on the premises was a great blessing to Marie. As before, a capable nurse had charge of her children, but both little boys were allowed to run at will in and out of the salons, where both staff and customers made a great fuss over them. If Marie ever wasted any time, it was in curling Jean-Philippe's silky hair about her fingers in an attempt to keep his baby ringlets beyond their natural span.

Paul-Michel also continued to thrive. One of Louise's neighbours, a responsible woman, had agreed to look after him while Louise worked. He was a chuckling, good-humoured baby, with his father's black hair and an unmistakable likeness in the eyes.

Louise knew that she could have seen Pierre often in the emperor's escort if she had gone to view any of the processions, but she avoided all sight of imperial public occasions, wanting to give her heart a chance to heal. Yet she did see him again some months after the bomb blasts. She had finally accepted an invitation to go to the Théâtre-Français with Robert. As the curtain went up on the second act, she was distracted by the arrival of two latecomers to a box. She felt her chest constrict. The woman with Pierre was a flame-haired demi-mondaine, her magnificent ivory bosom pouting out of its low décolletage. When the gaslights were raised for the intermission, Pierre and his courtesan had gone. Louise was filled with compassion for Stéphanie, and felt herself to be safely forgotten at last. Perversely, it only brought renewed pain.

Out of her sadness and loneliness she allowed Robert to kiss her that night, and in her yearning for comfort she responded to his kiss. Against her will, latent desires were stirred, reminding her that she was a young and passionate woman, long deprived of loving. But although she was fond of Robert, she did not want to become amorously involved with him.

EMPRESS EUGÉNIE had shown herself amazingly merciful towards the would-be assassin, Orsini. She felt that he should be allowed to live, but nevertheless he had gone to the guillotine. He had been an Italian patriot who had sought to spur France into revolution so that Italy might follow suit and throw off the yoke of Austrian dominance. Eugénie upheld the late man's dream of liberty and convinced her husband that the time had come for him to free Italy, a country he had learned to love in his youth.

Louise felt desperate when she saw the preparations going on around her: the influx of marching men, the patriotic slogans pasted on walls, the newspaper reports that emphasized Austria's tyranny. Pierre was brought constantly into her thoughts, and she turned more and more to Robert, who mistook her need for companionship for something deeper.

Louis Napoleon declared war against Austria at the end of April, 1859. The conflict was destined to be short and bloody. In early June there was a great victory over the Austrians at Magenta, and cannons were fired in Paris in celebration. Within days dyers were at work on a new shade, and soon Worth had bolts of a brilliant pinkish purple on display. Orders flowed in for dresses in magenta.

Even Robert was compelled by the rush of business to exert himself, something he did not care to do. He was even more disgruntled when he received word to return home at once. His father, whose health had improved once the worry of his son's future had been removed through Mr. Allenby's kindly intervention, had suffered a relapse. Robert had to go to him.

"I've two months left of my training," he said to Worth. "I'll be glad to return when matters are settled at home."

Worth sighed inwardly. He had been looking forward to seeing the last of the young man, whom he considered to be a spoiled weakling. He saw little hope for the Prestbury family business when Robert took over, but it would not be for lack of instruction. "Very well, Prestbury. Give my kindest regards to Mr. Allenby."

When Robert had left his office, Worth turned to some of his latest sketches on the desk. He was heartily tired of the crinoline. Women were obsessed with it, however, not seeming to care that it had proved to be a life hazard. Countless women had been burned to death when their huge skirts had brushed against an open fire or knocked over a lamp or a candle. Worth's mind was alive with ideas for new silhouettes, but for the first time female opinion was against him. How to break through? The problem would be solved if he could find a prominent woman who would wear a dress that was different. Why didn't he admit it? The woman he wanted to wear his clothes was Empress Eugénie herself. Wherever she led, the whole female world followed.

He lifted his head sharply as the boom of cannons resounded from the direction of Les Invalides. Another victory? He hastened out of his office and sent a junior staff member to discover the news. The lad returned jubilant. The war was over! It had lasted less than eleven weeks.

In August the victorious French troops returned home. On the long balcony of number 7 all of Worth's staff gathered to watch the great parade and throw flowers from the baskets of blossoms that had been thoughtfully provided. When the last row of bandsmen had passed, the emperor came riding alone at the head of the marching column, the gold of his cocked hat and his epaulets gleaming. In his wake came the mass of cavalry, every soldier bedecked with posies that had been thrust into their hands and speared on their rifles.

Louise threw the last of her flowers, and almost at once Robert brought her another basket. He had come back to Paris after only a short stay in England, and when he put his arm about her waist he was taking advantage of one of the few minor privileges that she now allowed him. "We'll be having our own celebration this evening, you and I," he reminded her.

"I'm looking forward to it," she answered with perfect truth. Paris in jubilation was a sight not to be missed.

That night all Paris danced in the streets. Every café was crowded: extra tables were put up everywhere and spread out onto the pavements. Robert and Louise dined magnificently. When they had been served coffee, he moved closer to her on the banquette seat and took her hand into his.

"Do you realize that I have entered the last lap of my time here?" he began. "Soon I'll be going back to England for good. The time has come for my father to retire." He paused. "I care for you very much, Louise. I'm asking you to come to England as my wife."

She was astounded. He had pursued her, but she had never imagined that it was with any true depth of feeling. "I wouldn't want to leave Paris, Robert. In any case, I have no thought of ever marrying."

"But you should, for your son's sake, if for no other reason. I'd be a good father to him."

She had to smile. "You don't like children. To my knowledge, you have never once taken Paul-Michel onto your knee."

"Is that any fault of mine? He cries and hides behind your skirts as soon as I come near, and who could wonder at it when he is closeted in a world of women." He saw he had made his point, for she looked quickly away. "You've long wanted a business of your own, and with me you shall have it. We'll be partners at Prestbury's, and you may make of it what you will."

She shook her head. "Please. I can't marry—"

He stopped what she was saying with a swift kiss. "I love you. I need you. Don't make me leave Paris without you." Then his mood lightened and he linked his fingers in hers. "Now, you and I are going to dance the night away." He summoned the waiter for the bill, and a few moments later he was whirling her around and around down the length of the Champs-Élysées. It was dawn before they arrived at her door, and there he kissed her again.

"Think about spending the rest of your life with me," he whispered. "This is how it could be between us always."

IT WAS A CLIENT who told Louise of a small suite of rooms available off the Boulevard des Capucines. Because the rent was low, Louise felt it was just the place for her to make a modest start on her own. It would give her a small salon and a workroom for Catherine, who would be her seamstress, and she would do the cutting and fitting herself. The rest of the space would make cramped but adequate living accommodation.

Robert was thoroughly taken aback by the news. "I can't believe Worth would let you go. He could never stomach a rival."

She laughed. "He has no rival, now or in the future, but I can make a niche for myself in my own right."

Robert's expression changed. "Then make that niche in London. At Prestbury's. That's what you'll do in the end, you know."

His grin was confident, making her wonder how to convince someone wholly used to getting his own way that in this matter he was not going to win.

The following Sunday started out much like any other. In the rue de la Paix the Worths set out with their children for a family stroll. From another direction Louise and Catherine were wending their way into the heart of the city, Paul-Michel trotting between them. Catherine was keeping up a swift pace, and when the boy began to drag on her hand, she looked at him with a rare show of impatience.

"Come along, Paul-Michel. You'll make us late to see all the horses and carriages at the Austrian embassy."

She knew he liked horses. For herself, all she wanted was to see Princess Pauline de Metternich, the young wife of the new Austrian ambassador, who that day was to attend her initial reception at the Palace of the Tuileries. She was reputed to be as ugly as a monkey and as fascinating as a siren.

Paul-Michel toddled on for a little longer, but when he tripped and fell, Louise bade Catherine go ahead. "We'll follow in a few minutes," she said.

Catherine needed no further encouragement. She hurried off, and Louise carried Paul-Michel into a nearby park. When his thumb went into his mouth she knew he would sleep, and holding him close to her, she walked slowly along a secluded, tree-lined path. She had failed to see one of the riders in the park dismount, hook the reins to a post, and walk towards her. But as he drew near, she froze to a halt. She forced herself to meet Pierre's eyes.

"Louise, I can't go on living without you," he said. His gaze lowered to the sleeping child. "Or without him." He bent his head and kissed his son's cheek. Then, as she stood paralysed, he curved his arms around both of them and his mouth took hers with a tenderness that seemed to settle all between them. It was as if she had no more will. He had defeated her in a vulnerable moment, and for the first time ever she was lost, and in being lost could turn only to him.

He drew her to a stone bench under the boughs. "A new beginning, my darling. Nothing that has gone before shall spoil the future. We must be together again, and it shall be only as you wish it and on your terms."

"I can scarcely believe this is happening." She was unable to regain her equilibrium.

"I have been watching out for you everywhere. Sooner or later I knew we'd meet again. There's so much to talk about, so much I want to hear. Where are you living now?"

"At the same address, but Catherine and I will be moving shortly." She told him of the rooms in the Boulevard des Capucines, and he expressed keen interest, praising her initiative.

"I should like to view the premises. May we meet there soon?"

They both knew the outcome of meeting alone. For her it would be a final and total commitment to loving him. She released a long-drawn-out breath. "The keys will be mine soon."

"Tell me the day and the hour. I'll be there."

Their meeting was arranged.

THE GILDED COACHES that made up Princess de Metternich's procession were approaching the Tuileries when the Worths were lucky enough to catch sight of them. They had a good view of the ambassador's wife as she alighted, and both were struck by her tremendous personal magnetism. When she had disappeared from sight, the Worths turned to each other, speaking at the same time.

"If only the princess had been wearing one of your dresses today, Charles!"

"That is a woman who would do full justice to my clothes!"

They chuckled, having shared the same thought, but the idea lingered in their minds long after that day had come to a close.

A few weeks later Worth and Marie stood in the doorway of number 7 rue de la Paix. Marie was dressed in a new outfit of bronze velvet, and in her arms she held a vellum-bound album.

"Good luck, my dearest," Worth said.

Marie smiled, putting her gloved hand against his cheek, and then she hurried down the stairs, bound for the Austrian embassy. At its gates she braced herself and walked through.

Pauline de Metternich dismissed out of hand the request of a certain Madame Worth to see her. It appeared that the young woman's husband wished to make her a dress, but she had never heard his name, and she had her own dressmakers of distinction. "Send her away," she instructed her lady-in-waiting, taking up the book she had been reading before the interruption.

The lady-in-waiting hesitated, the album in her arms. Impressed by Madame Worth's own elegant attire, she had glanced through the sketches. "May I suggest that Your Highness just look at the designs? I've never seen anything quite like them."

With the faintest of sighs the princess took the album onto her lap and opened it to the first page. The design that met her eyes was beautiful. She turned to the next page, and the next. Each appeared to be more ravishing than the last. "Show the caller in," she said decisively.

When Marie entered, the princess said, "Sit down, Madame Worth, and explain why you came to me."

"My husband and I saw you arrive at the Palace of the Tuileries on the day of Your Highness's reception, and he has talked ever since of how much he would like to make a dress for you." The princess displayed great interest, asking questions while all the time glancing at the album on her lap.

Finally she said, "I will have one day dress, and another for evening wear. If the dresses please me, I will wear the evening one to the state ball next week."

When Marie arrived back at the rue de la Paix, one look at her face told Worth that she had been successful. He caught her up and whirled her around in joyous triumph.

AMID THE FLURRY OF EXCITEMENT over the order from the princess, other customers had to receive the usual degree of attention. The day Stéphanie de Gand came for her appointment, Worth was waiting to greet her in the salon set aside for pregnant women. Stéphanie took a seat, and Louise was sent for.

The moment that Louise saw Pierre's wife sitting there, her delirious anticipation of the future subsided with a rush. "I should like Mademoiselle Louise to sit by me," said Stéphanie ingenuously, patting the seat of the chair next to her. "I wish her to fit my dresses as before, at Gagelin's."

As Worth signalled for the first dress, Stéphanie turned to Louise excitedly. "I can't tell you how happy I am that this good fortune has come to me. Pierre and I have had our little differences in the past, but that is over now." Her attention was caught by a dress of grey lace with magenta ribbons. "La! That's pretty! Would that be comfortable to wear right through to the last days, do you think, Louise?"

Worth glowered. "All my dresses are designed to that end, madame."

The session dragged on. As Louise sat there, her own new world fell slowly apart. Pierre was married to another woman who must make first claim on his time and affection, and soon the legitimate offspring of their marriage would supplant her own son. Her son. It stunned her to realize that she had not put him before all else during those days of feckless self-absorption. If she remained in Paris, Pierre would continue to pursue her, and how could Paul-

265

Michel grow up strong and self-confident in the taint of scandal that would come inevitably from any such affair? But it was not too late. There was still a path open to her.

She cancelled her option on the premises in the Boulevard des Capucines that day, and in the evening she accepted Robert's proposal of marriage. With time running short and many arrangements to be made, it was decided that they should marry on the morning he had been due to leave Paris, and they would catch the overnight Channel steamer to Dover.

She did not write the news to Pierre, but went instead to see him at the Tuileries. Pierre received her in a small waiting room in the military quarters, and she could tell at once that he was not entirely pleased to see her.

"Whatever brings you here, my darling?" he asked with a certain sharpness. "It's most unusual, you know."

"Since our meeting I've had time to think things over, Pierre. I have decided that there are many reasons why it would be impossible for us to take up our relationship once again."

He had gone quite white about the mouth. "Louise, have you decided to play the eternal coquette yet again? Heaven knows what you want of me, but I'll do anything to please you. However, it does not please me that you threaten to disrupt matters temporarily out of some headstrong whim!"

She spread her hands. "Pierre, I've come to tell you that I'm getting married. I'm going to England as the bride of a London man named Robert Prestbury."

He became very still. She had to turn away, stricken by the look on his face. Finally he spoke with quiet desperation.

"Don't match my folly with one of your own, Louise. You know that if ever two people were made for each other, we are."

She was shaking her head. "No, Pierre. It has to end."

She went blindly from the room. Later she could not remember walking home.

THAT SAME EVENING Princess Pauline de Metternich wore her first Worth gown to the state ball. It was a masterpiece of simplicity in white tulle, adorned with a single cluster of marguerites on the huge skirt. She stood out in that vast assemblage of ornate toilettes as if some specially directed ray of illumination followed her wherever she moved. The empress asked her who had made her dress.

266

Eugénie's brows lifted upon hearing that it was the creation of an Englishman named Worth, praised by the wearer as a new star glittering over all fashion.

Amused, the empress nodded her head. "This star should be beset with satellites. I am prepared to be one of them."

The Princess de Metternich promised that the couturier should call upon Her Majesty the next morning. She knew that in the future she would have to pay treble the figure she had paid for her Worth dress.

Worth was extremely busy when word came early for him to attend the empress at ten o'clock. Whatever the time of day, it was customary for gentlemen to wear evening dress when being received by her, but to Marie's dismay he refused to change out of his frock coat.

"I'm an independent tradesman," he declared with pride. "Not a lackey."

Marie watched her husband leave for the palace. Perhaps he was right to wear his frock coat. It suited him so well. It was also, she realized, a supreme arrogance. Worth, who believed himself to be so French, had never revealed himself more as an Englishman.

CHAPTER EIGHT

Before the pattern was cut for the empress's first dress from Maison Worth, Louise and Robert were married. Catherine, the Worths, and a few other friends attended the civil and religious ceremonies and went to the railway station to see them off. Louise waved from the compartment window, holding Paul-Michel in her arms. Robert, having imbibed a considerable amount of champagne, lounged back on the seat, waiting to take her onto his knee. But she remained looking out until the last spire and rooftop of Paris had disappeared from view.

Daylight had almost gone when they reached Calais, and it was cold and windy, with a wild, rough sea. No sooner had the steamer left the harbour than it began to pitch against huge waves. Louise was queasy; after supper she retired to their first-class cabin, leaving her bridegroom to brandy and a cigar.

It was a relief to lie down in the narrow bunk. She had left the brass hanging lamp burning brightly for her little son, who was sleeping in the opposite bunk. When Robert came stumbling in, he made such a clatter that Paul-Michel awakened, letting out a terrified wail as the wick was turned out and the cabin plunged into inky blackness. Louise put her feet to the floor to find her way to the child, but her nightgown was yanked from her as Robert rolled her back into the hollow of the bunk. Her son cried for a long while before he finally fell into a whimpering sleep.

When morning came, there was sun on the white cliffs of Dover, although the wind was still strong and rolling clouds scudded across the sky. On the train journey to London, Louise gazed out at the lovely Kent countryside, appreciating its acres of orchards. The suburbs of London were beginning to appear when Robert woke from the dozing that had made him silent company for most of the journey. He sat up, straightening his cravat and shooting his cuffs into place with a decidedly agitated air. To Louise he suddenly looked much like a schoolboy going home with a poor report. He cleared his throat twice in preparation for speech. Since landing at Dover he had reverted completely to speaking English, and she had replied in English. It was how it should be in whatever lay ahead, but she intended that Paul-Michel should never be allowed to forget his native tongue, and that they would always speak it when alone.

"There's something I have to tell you, Louise. Something I suppose I should have told you before we left France. You see, well, my parents believe that Paul-Michel is my child."

She merely considered that to be kindly intentioned of him. From now on her son would be his to all intents and purposes, and they had agreed that his name should be changed from Vernet to Prestbury.

"That was gallant of you, but surely your parents would be able to tell that Paul-Michel is far older than he should be according to the length of time you've spent in Paris. He was about four weeks old when you arrived at Gagelin's two years ago. They'll be expecting an infant of little more than a year old at the most."

He cleared his throat. "That's not the problem. I was in Paris before, you see. A couple of times; as a matter of fact I've told them that we met then. When I telegraphed to say that we were getting

268

wed, I added the lie that we already had a child from our union, which means they will assume that I have simply made an honest woman of you."

It was not a phrase she cared for, but she wanted to put him at his ease. "There's no harm in that," Louise said patiently.

"But my parents are so deucedly narrow-minded. I don't know what kind of reception you'll get. I felt I had to warn you."

So that was it. "I must hope that they will like me enough to take a charitable view. In any case, when they see Paul-Michel I can't believe they won't love him at once."

Robert looked unconvinced. "Don't bank on it. My father won't be proud of a grandson conceived out of wedlock, and my mother would die if the truth should ever come out. I believe you'll find that everyone you meet will have been informed that we were married secretly about three years ago."

Louise was thoughtful as she alighted in the great arched London Bridge station with Paul-Michel in her arms. She had been coerced into a false position and it went against her whole nature, but for Robert's sake she must go through with it.

A manservant from the Prestbury household led them to the family equipage waiting in the forecourt of the station. He drove them through the streets of London to a large, gracious-looking house with stone steps scrubbed white, the brass bellpull and boot scraper ashine in the sun. Watch must have been kept for the carriage, because the door was opened by a butler almost at once.

The interior of the house struck Louise as being very dark. It smelled of polish and linseed oil. Everything gleamed. It was not an atmosphere that welcomed children. The butler addressed her in almost perfect French.

"I trust you had a good journey, madame. It will be an honour to serve you in this house."

She was thanking him when a voice boomed from the head of the stairs. "None of that Bonaparte lingo under my roof! English is the language we use in this country, ma'am."

It was Robert's father, a thickset, short-necked man with a balding head, abundant side-whiskers, and an apoplectic complexion, more purple than red. He was leaning heavily on a silver-handled walking stick, looking down at the new arrivals. Robert went up the stairs to greet him nervously, leaving Louise and her child to follow.

By the time they reached the top step, Robert had accompanied his father into a drawing room, where his mother was seated in a high-back chair. Louise took Paul-Michel's small hand into her own, and they crossed the threshold.

"My dear parents," said Robert, "allow me to present my wife, Louise, and my son, Paul-Michel."

Verena Prestbury's thin lips compressed as her gaze went to the child. "It will not do," she stated coldly. "It will not do at all, Robert. I forbid you to tell anyone that you were married only yesterday. That is why your sister is not present at the moment. We had to spare Agnes the knowledge of your disgrace."

"Whatever you say, Mother," he replied quickly.

Mrs. Prestbury switched her scrutiny to Louise, taking her in from her elegant Parisian bonnet to the hem of her travelling costume. "I trust you are prepared to be a dutiful wife to my son. He has proved himself most honourable in marrying you."

John Prestbury was regarding Paul-Michel, and addressed him with a wag of the silver-handled stick. "One good Christian name is enough for common use. You'll be known as Paul now, and Prestbury when you go to school. Understand?"

Paul-Michel didn't like the cross man or the nasty lady, who had not smiled or held out her arms to him as ladies usually did. He wanted his mama to take him home, he wanted his Aunt Catherine to lift him onto her wonderful cushion of a lap. He turned his face into his mama's skirt and wept.

Later, in their bedroom, Louise upbraided Robert severely in a flow of French that released her pent-up outrage.

"How could you let them speak that way to me! I wasn't even invited to sit down. I want to move out of this house tomorrow."

Robert had stretched himself full length on the lace coverlet of the bed. "I'm sorry. Don't think I want to remain here any more than you do, but I'm afraid we'll have to for a while."

"Why?"

"Financial reasons for a start. I'm broke. In addition, my father expects me to look after my mother in this house until the end of her days, to say nothing of my sister Agnes, who is hardly likely to marry. I have to kowtow to his every wish if I'm to get my hands on Prestbury's when he dies. So for the present we must appear to be making our permanent home here."

Louise drew in a deep breath to calm herself. "You told me in

271

Paris that Prestbury's was already yours. You said we should be partners."

"So we shall. In time. Father's been given dire warning by his doctor to take life quietly, and with his irascible temperament that's virtually impossible."

She was furious. "Don't dangle dead men's shoes at me! I want no part of that. Let's start up on our own. We can both work hard and—"

"That won't do." He swung his legs from the bed and came across to put his arms about her. "It would take years to get going. It would have been different in Paris, where you have connections. In any case," he added, choosing a line of argument she would have to accept, "I'm committed by filial duty to Prestbury's." He did not care at all about principles, but he was not going to start from scratch with her when he had a ready-made business in his hands. And he was not going to jeopardize his share of inheritance when the old man died.

There was a tap on the door, and Robert went with ill grace to answer it. Immediately his expression changed to one of affability. "Agnes! How are you?"

Brother and sister embraced, and then Agnes came forward hesitantly. Her smile was singularly sweet, and her shyness so excessive that she stuttered when she spoke.

"I c-couldn't wait until teatime to m-meet you, dear sister, or to see my l-little nephew."

Louise could have wept tears of joy at this unexpected warmth in her chilly new surroundings. Paul-Michel recognized the same deep friendliness in the tones of the newcomer and did not shrink away from her. Soon he and Agnes were sitting on the bedroom carpet playing pat-a-cake, which gave Louise the opportunity to bathe and change after her travels.

Paul-Michel was fed his supper, and then Agnes introduced Louise and the child to Daisy.

Daisy was a pink-cheeked, smiling servant girl who had been promoted to the new position of nursemaid. Paul-Michel liked Daisy's red curls, and she had a big gap between her front teeth that he found fascinating. But he wanted his mama to put him to bed on this first night, and it was done. He did not mind her going downstairs when he discovered that Daisy was to stay by his cotside. He put his thumb in his mouth and slept.

272

Over dinner it became apparent to Louise that there had been a family discussion about her participation in the Prestbury business. Impressed in spite of himself with her extensive experience in dressmaking, John Prestbury was prepared to have her take an active role.

"It sounds as if you're not afraid of a bit of honest toil, and that's in your favour," he conceded. "There's an elderly female on the staff who's done the measuring-up for years, but her eyesight is failing, and you can take over. All the sewing is done by outworkers who call for it daily, and you can check that in and out." He frowned down the table at her. "I like my staff to wear plain black glacé silk. You do have a respectable black dress or two?"

"I have several."

Out of the corner of her eye Louise noticed Robert hastily taking a swallow of wine. He was as aware as she that what had suited Worth was going to prove startlingly elegant at Prestbury's.

"Good." John Prestbury gave a nod. "Robert can make a start at the shop tomorrow." He pointed with his fork at his son. "I expect hard work and a full sense of responsibility from now on. I didn't pay for you to train for two years in Paris without getting my just returns."

Robert looked decidedly strained. "I'll do my best, Father."

THREE DAYS LATER Louise made her first visit to Prestbury's. It was no great distance from the house, and the street where it was situated had briskly thriving businesses ranging from high-class grocers to good milliners.

As she slowed to a halt before the shop, all the apprehension that had been gathering in her caught sickeningly at her heart. The windows were crammed with cloaks, shawls, and mantles. But all the goods were black. Mourning black. Now she knew what Robert had not had the courage to tell her. Across the fascia of the shop the curly, gilded letters announced PRESTBURY'S MOURNING ESTABLISHMENT.

Robert had seen her crossing the road. He opened the glass door to receive her, his face uncertain. She entered without a glance at him. Inside, the blackness of the garments and the lengths of crape against dark walls made her feel as if she had entered a dungeon. Robert led the way to his office. There a cheerful fire burned in the grate, and the scent of cigar smoke was in the air. She did not doubt that a few minutes before he had had his feet up on the desk.

"Louise—"

She swung about and struck him hard across the face, her eyes blazing. "If ever you deceive me again, I'll leave you! I swear it!" He stood stunned into confusion while she jerked off her bonnet and removed her gloves. "But now we'll get to work. I want to examine every piece of merchandise in the place."

As one day followed another, she kept him working with her at a pressure that showed no sign of easing. At first he welcomed it, thankful that she had rallied in the face of what must have been a terrible blow to her, but then toleration began to give way to irritation. He had had enough of being run off his feet at Worth's.

"I'm going to visit the outworkers," she said to him at the shop one morning. "Your father will be coming in later, and you can let him examine the books and inspect the new arrangement of stock." All of Louise's improvements were credited to Robert, who had decided that his father would mistrust anything she initiated, no matter how much good it did the business.

For Louise, raising the standards of workmanship was the first point at issue. The sewing done by the outworkers was atrocious, and Louise was appalled by the conditions under which those unfortunate creatures laboured. She proposed letting the women sew on the premises, where she could supervise their work. But John Prestbury would have none of it.

So Louise did what she could with the garments that were sold, unpicking seams and resewing them herself to give customers a respectable fit, but all her skills in high fashion had to be shelved. Worth had often made dresses for those in mourning, but always with elegance. Those who came to Prestbury's bought garments that Worth would not have used as dusters.

Robert had visualized himself lording it at Prestbury's after his father's speedy demise, able to spend his time there or anywhere else he pleased while Louise managed everything and built up the business. But it was all proving to be very different. While John Prestbury continued to thrive, and looked set to become a centenarian, Louise served at a counter and measured garments. Meanwhile, Robert's chief occupation was making slight alterations in the books which could profitably line his pocket while escaping the eyes of his wife and his father. On the rare, busy occasions when he had to help serve in the shop, he loathed making himself agreeable to customers. Most of them wore the long faces suited to

274

the nature of their purchases, and he missed the flirtations that had made life so pleasant at Worth's. A married man in particular had to have some release from family routine, but in London, unlike the French capital, there was a prudish pretence that nothing existed beyond the propriety of the domestic scene.

Robert had hired four young women to replace staff members who had retired, and on their behalf Louise tried to get her father-in-law to waive his rule of glacé silk as the material for the staff dresses. The women had to supply these out of their own pockets, and glacé silk split and rotted easily, necessitating frequent replacement. Her suggestion of a more durable material was turned down at once, with her father-in-law informing Robert that Louise was to keep to her allotted duties and not interfere in business matters.

"She's an uppity creature," he told his son. "I saw that from the first. Don't be afraid to beat her if you have to."

Robert felt hatred for his father seep through his veins. He felt humiliated by the whole situation, and he let his pent-up exasperation fly forth at Louise.

"In the future, keep your mouth shut about Prestbury's. Haven't I warned you enough about it? Do you know what my father advocated? That I beat you. And I will if you don't toe the line."

Louise became so still and pale under his abuse that he drew back from her, contrite. For days afterwards the atmosphere between them was strained, and Robert wondered if everything would ever be quite the same again.

Meanwhile, he took unobtrusive note of the shopgirls' dresses. As Louise had said, the seams stretched thin, and the silk cracked at the elbows. One of the girls looked particularly shabby, and he had a word with her in the office. She was a pretty thing, very saucy, but all the ebullience left her when she was told to buy herself a new dress.

"I can't, sir," she wailed. "My wages won't run to it. When you took me on I'd been out of work for some time, and there's still arrears on my rent."

He regarded her coolly. "That is nothing to do with Prestbury's, Miss Ashcroft. You were given the job on condition that you obey the rules of the establishment."

She began to sob. "Maybe I could find a secondhand dress at the market. Give me a chance, I beg you, sir!"

He rose from his chair and came close to her. He rested a hand on her shaking shoulder and caressed it. "A castoff wouldn't do for Prestbury's," he said quietly.

A shiver of understanding went through her as she met his narrowed eyes. "I'd be real grateful if you think of some other way by which I might replace my dress, sir."

He smiled slowly, and crossing to the door, he turned the key. A week later Lily Ashcroft had her new dress.

LOUISE WAS ACUTELY HOMESICK, and it was a joy whenever a letter came from France. Catherine and Marie wrote frequently, their letters clearly indicating that Worth was making his fortune. Marie wrote of the complete redecoration of the salon and of orders that now came in from all over the world. The de Gands were never mentioned, except once with the sad news that Stéphanie had miscarried.

Louise was folding away a letter from Marie one morning when Robert came into the office. "What's that?" he inquired, nodding towards a neatly written sheet of foolscap on his desk.

"It's the outline of a plan I've worked out for Prestbury's. I believe that if your father could read it over, he might be inclined to consider it."

Robert perched on the desk and studied the paper. He knew Louise had already formed a nucleus of a few good outworkers under one roof, so she was sure of a properly produced garment to meet any customer's requirements. But her plan was to introduce some factory-made mourning clothes for Prestbury's middle-class customers. This would eliminate the mad rush to fill orders in a matter of days before a funeral, which in the past had allowed a lot of shoddy hand-sewing to slip through.

"This seems a splendid scheme," Robert endorsed cautiously. "I'll choose a congenial moment to put it before Father."

A few days later he told her that his father had agreed to the plan, and Louise could arrange to have a factory produce the garments.

She wrote at once to the Boston Street Factory, which had a good reputation. When she received a letter back from the owner, a look of surprise came across her face. The signature was that of her old friend Will Russell.

She took a hackney cab to Southwark, where the Boston Street Factory was located. It proved to be a large red brick building five storeys high. At a reception desk she asked to see Mr. Russell, and after a few moments' wait she was escorted up a flight of stairs to his office. Will had come to the doorway to await her, and as she came near she saw his eyes stretch wide with incredulity. He darted forward.

"My dear Louise! I can't believe it. The name I was given was Mrs. Prestbury."

Tears of joy filled her eyes. He swept her into his office, set her in a chair, then pulled another forward for himself. With elbows on his knees he leaned towards her, firing questions and shaking his head in the sheer wonder of seeing her there. She told him all that had happened, and when she came to her marriage he was suddenly restless, flinging himself up out of the chair. "Why didn't you write to me?" he demanded almost angrily. "I would have married you and been father to your son!"

She was taken aback. "But you are married—"

He groaned, running a hand through his thick, fair hair. "Of course you didn't know." He fixed her with a stare, his voice distant. "My wife died three years ago in childbirth. Six weeks later my infant daughter was buried in the same grave."

"Oh, Will." A cry of distress broke from her.

"The tragedy was that Ellen hadn't wanted a baby. She was terrified of childbirth, but selfishly I wanted a family and imagined that she would be happier with children. Her bouts of hysteria during her pregnancy were torture to me. Once she tried to throw herself from a window, and from then on she had a nurse with her night and day. When I lost her and the baby as well, all purpose in living seemed to leave me."

Louise grasped his hand in sympathy. "Dear Will, what bereavements you have known! How did you come through?"

He held her gloved hand in his. "There was always work." He gave a nod towards the papers and swatches of cloth on his desk. "Eighteen months ago I built this factory, and I have over two hundred hands working for me." His lips compressed. "Friends often ask why I don't marry again. I reply that I've drifted away from the domestic scene and feel more at home amid the snipping of scissors."

"Yet you say you would have married me." As she spoke she saw his gaze deepen.

"You have always lit fires in me, Louise," he admitted. "As long ago as when you used to tease me while I tried to concentrate on teaching you English." He looked down at her hand and felt her ring through the soft kid gloves. "Last time we met I asked you why there was no wedding band. I would that it were the same again." Then he smiled. "I'm thankful our paths have crossed once more."

She smiled back at him. "I am too, Will." Their hands still held. Both became aware of the retained contact at the same time, and he released his grip to let her slide her fingers away.

"I should like to show you around the factory," he said more casually. "I think you will find much here to attract your attention. For instance, I have a new invention to make buttonholes more speedily."

Still talking, he walked at her side as they went from the office. She found the tour interesting. Unlike most factories, the building was light and airy. Child labour was much in evidence, the children, offspring of the workers, keeping them supplied with patterns from the cutting tables. She was glad to hear that a thick soup was served to the young ones daily from the factory kitchen.

In the stockroom, Louise selected only the styles that she knew would be acceptable to Prestbury customers. When she was ready to leave, Will stayed her a moment on the factory steps.

"I want your word that if you should ever be in need of help again, you will summon me."

She nodded, thinking that for the first time since coming to England she did not feel alone. "Thank you, Will. I promise."

JOHN PRESTBURY stared at the calendar, trying to remember when he had last visited his shop. He found it difficult to remember anything these days. When his son had first taken over Prestbury's, he had made a point of calling in several times a week. But once he had crushed all interference from that French daughter-in-law of his and everything was running smoothly, it had been a relief not to go there more than occasionally. Any small effort tired him, and with tiredness came those cramping pains in his chest. Today, quite miraculously, he felt fine, and he longed to see the shop again.

He grunted as he heaved himself into the brougham. With such a long span of time having elapsed since he last visited Prestbury's, he could be certain of surprising his son and staff alike. He hoped that he would find Robert exerting himself. Nothing would be more pleasing than to know that Allenby had been right in saying that proper training would set the lad on the right path. John Prestbury sighed, peering out of the window. One more corner and a left turn would bring him to Prestbury's.

As the brougham drew up before the shop, he received such a shock that his mouth dropped open to a gape. One window held dresses in a range of colours that Prestbury's had never carried before. Mauve! Pale grey! Strong lilac!

He bounded out of the brougham and charged into the shop, thumping his walking stick. Customers were being served, making him hold back a bellow of wrath. He grabbed one of the offending garments from a stand and felt his eyes bulge. *Ready-made!* In *his* shop! Prestbury's, disgraced by factory rubbish only worn by the working classes!

He flung down the dress and glared about him. Louise was serving a customer, but he could contain himself no longer. Lurching across the floor, he brought up his stick and crashed it down on the counter in front of her. The customer squealed, and Louise stared at him as if he had lost his mind.

"Where's that husband of yours? In the office? Follow me!" He raised his hat to the customer. "Your pardon, ma'am."

With Louise in his wake he stumped to the office and crashed the door open. Robert leaped up.

"Father! What are you doing here? Whatever is the matter?"

"I'll tell you what's the matter!" Prestbury shook a fist under his son's nose. "Those goods in the window! How dare you!"

It was then that Louise realized that Robert had never shown her father-in-law all she had written down. John Prestbury knew nothing of the ready-mades that had come in from Will's factory. And the stockroom was full of them.

Her father-in-law wagged a furious finger at her. "You get off home! Don't you dare set your meddling foot on these premises again. Get out! Get—" He lost all breath as his chest suddenly exploded with pain. He felt himself slumping to the floor, saw Louise's frantic face as she snatched his cravat free and ripped open his collar. The last he knew was the cradling of the Frenchwoman's arms as she sought to save him from slipping away.

The funeral was well attended. Afterwards, the widow, her son, daughter, and daughter-in-law gathered in the library for the reading of the will. It was very straightforward. The house, the shop, and all else that John Prestbury had possessed went to his wife, and after her demise to his daughter, Agnes. Robert was not mentioned. Louise heard her husband's hollow groan of furious disappointment.

When they were alone he turned on her with hostility. "If I hadn't agreed to all your suggestions, we wouldn't be in this fix. You stuck in my father's craw. You're the reason he didn't leave me the shop."

She controlled herself with difficulty. To quarrel with him would solve nothing. "Suggest to your mother that she offer you a partnership. There is nothing to prevent her doing that, and it will give you equal status with her in the business and entitle you to a half share of the profits."

His eyes narrowed, and she could tell it was as good as settled. His mother might not like her, but she recognized Louise's intelligence. Robert answered her with a taunting challenge. "It will be up to you to prove what you can do with the business to make amends to me, won't it? I can't see Mother objecting to factory wear if the sales continue to increase as they have done lately." He made a mocking flourish, as if handing the project to her on his open palm. "Go ahead, my dear wife. Let's see how clever you really are. I'll remind you that I'm not moving from this house until we can afford a comparable establishment, so let's see how soon you can manage it."

She understood then exactly why he had married her. He had known that she would be useful to him. In trusting ignorance she had struggled to retain whatever had been good in their relationship and had sought constantly to keep the fondness for him that she had known, but now nothing was left. Her lips began to tremble and a sob burst from her throat.

Robert peered at her sardonically. "What's wrong? Don't you think yourself capable of success after all?"

She could take no more of his goading. "Yes! Yes! Yes!" she hurled at him. "I do! But I can't stay here as wife to you! I'm going back to Paris! I'm going home!"

He caught her arm. "If you go, you go alone. Paul is legally mine. He stays with me."

Louise closed her eyes. There was no escape. If she took Paul-Michel and fled, Robert would only have them brought back to him. Women had no rights, least of all over their children.

He released his hold on her, knowing that he had won.

A pattern of days and weeks followed during which business

improved and little else happened. One morning, when Louise left
the shop to pay her weekly visit to the outworkers, she bought a
newspaper which reported the latest news of Prince Albert's illness.
It merely stated that the prince consort's mild fever persisted, but
Louise had heard rumours that typhoid was suspected. She
contemplated with pity the queen's anxiety at such a time.

As she walked along, her memory drifted to her first days at
Madame Camille's, when she had asked why all the garments were
in sombre colours. She had been told that the court was in
mourning for King Louis Philippe's sister, but had it been the king
himself, they would have been up to their ears in black. She caught
her breath suddenly and swung about with a speed that sent her
hoops careening, intent on sharing with Robert the idea that had
come to her. As a shortcut she went through the gates normally
used for deliveries. Passing the window of the office, she glanced in
to see if Robert was there. What she saw turned her ashen. Her
husband and Lily Ashcroft!

She jerked away to press herself against the building. She began
to understand all manner of incidents that had been without
significance before. The smirks exchanged between the shopgirls,
and the whispering that had fallen silent at her approach. Lily's
uppishness and increasing tendency to answer back. The girl's
extravagances that were not in keeping with her wages.

Louise went back through the gates, amazed at her own
calmness. Out in the street, she hailed a cab and gave the address of
Will's factory. Once seated in his office, she put to Will the scheme
she no longer intended to share with Robert.

"And you're willing to risk every penny of your savings on this
gamble?" he questioned.

"Yes! More than that, I'm going to order on credit everywhere I
can, here and in France. But I'll need storage space and an outlet for
selling afterwards, retail and wholesale. Will you help me there?"

He grinned. "Naturally I'll help you. But why have you come to
me instead of sharing this venture with your husband?"

She flew up from her chair. "I will do nothing ever again in the
name of Prestbury! All goods for this venture will be ordered under
my maiden name."

Will rubbed his chin thoughtfully. "I see. There's just one
suggestion I'd like to make. The law doesn't recognize a married
woman's signature on a contract, but we can have a private

agreement of partnership drawn up. Then all can be conducted through my firm without any interference from outsiders."

She was at a loss for words, overcome that he should be willing to share the risk. They shook hands, then went to work.

Orders went forth to Manchester, Leeds, and Bradford. A telegraphed message went to Worth, who immediately dispatched all the jet trimming and black *passementerie* that he had available. As day followed day the condition of the prince consort appeared unchanged, while into the Boston Street Factory came bale after bale of funeral bunting, huge bolts of crape and every kind of black material, from softest velvet to strong broadcloth.

At home and at Prestbury's Louise went about her routine as normally as she could. The only significant action she took was to fire Lily Ashcroft. Robert shrugged when she told him what she had done. Lily did not have to work at Prestbury's to be available whenever he wanted her.

The news of the prince consort's death stunned the nation. It did not seem possible that the tall, serious man for ever at the queen's side was no more. Respect must be shown at once, and that meant the purchase of black clothes, black drapery for home and commercial premises, even black bows for family carriages and infants' perambulators. It soon became known among London retailers that the Boston Street Factory at Southwark had seemingly unlimited stocks of all that could be needed, and orders began to flow in. Soon London shimmered with funeral drapery.

The evening following the state funeral Louise saw Will at a dinner party. With Robert at her side Louise exchanged only the briefest of greetings with Will, but his eyes, very bright and twinkling, met hers frequently from across the table, and after dinner he seized the first opportunity to draw her aside.

"What's your dearest ambition?" he asked her with a quiet chuckle. "Is it still to open your own dress salon?"

She held her breath. "You know it is."

He was enjoying himself. "Anything else?"

"To buy a house."

"Then you can start looking at both kinds of property tomorrow. We're selling as fast as we can, and it will carry on for a long while yet." He glanced for a moment towards Robert. "As a matter of interest, how are you going to break the news to your husband that you have made yourself a tidy little fortune?"

Her lips twitched in a smile. "By announcing that I'm never setting foot inside Prestbury's again. I have gained my liberty, and never shall I surrender it."

He chuckled again. "You're a formidable lady, my beautiful Louise. Already I see London conquered."

Louise told Robert the news on the way home. At first his reaction was mixed. They had money at last, but weighed against it was the offence to his pride that she had done it without consulting him, and—nightmarish thought!—if the prince consort had survived, she would have lost everything.

"Whew! You took a chance! But you did it. You really did it. Naturally you've finished with Prestbury's. I agree with you. From now on you must concentrate on your own shop."

As they rode along, he thought about how he could get his hands on the purse strings. He had always fancied a stable of good horses, two or three fast equipages, and membership in an exclusive club. The future had never looked rosier.

LOUISE VIEWED several shop premises before she decided on one just off Regent Street. Workmen began installing fitting rooms, and she interviewed prospective employees for the salon staff. Long before the shop was due to open, she had sewing hands making up dresses of her own design. Worth had recently decreed shorter skirts for daytime wear, and Louise was following suit, dazzled by his brilliant stroke. It was a definite move against the crinoline shape.

A new family residence was chosen, facing a park where Paul-Michel could play with Daisy. Furniture was purchased, carpets laid, and domestic staff appointed. Louise had been lucky enough to find a French cook, and the meal on the first evening that she and Robert dined together in their new home made them feel as though they were back in Paris.

"Excellent, my dear." Robert touched his napkin to a corner of his mouth. "What an evening this has been." He glanced with satisfaction around the room, then returned his gaze to his wife. They were on amiable terms, and on this first night in their new abode he was in a high state of amorous anticipation.

He was pleased to have his own bedroom, dressing room, and bathroom. It meant that he could return home at whatever hour he liked without questioning, and the communicating doors of shining mahogany gave access to Louise's rooms. That night he tied the cord of his padded silk dressing robe and crossed the floor to open the doors. The handles did not move, and his face darkened as he realized they were locked.

"Louise! The doors appear to be jammed." He would give her a chance to redeem the situation. But no reply was forthcoming.

The next evening when Louise returned home, she entered her bedroom to find that Robert had had the lock removed from the communicating doors, which stood open. He leaned against the jamb, a satisfied smirk on his face. .

"How dare you!" she exclaimed furiously. "It will make no difference. I'll simply remove my possessions to another room."

"If you do, I'll send Paul away to school."

The colour drained from her face. "Are you mad? He's only four years old."

"You have my ultimatum. I intend to be master in this house."

She made him no reply, but turned her anguished face away. He knew he had won.

CHAPTER NINE

Louise's shop had been open for three years when she decided to take a trip to Paris. Her assistant, a Frenchwoman named Mademoiselle Brousseau, was dedicated to the business, and this allowed Louise more free time than she had had in the shop's early days.

It had not taken long for fashionable women to be drawn to Madame Louise de Paris. Before the first year was out, Louise had expanded her workshop and installed extra fitting rooms.

The royal wedding secured her success. The Prince of Wales took as his bride the beautiful Princess Alexandra of Denmark, and many of Louise's dresses graced balls and receptions held for the royal couple. If Worth's creations eclipsed hers, she felt it to be an honourable rout, knowing that at least she came second to the master.

284

Louise and Marie kept in touch through their letters, and although Worth had no time to read those that came from Louise, his wife passed on all the news. He had never been busier or happier. The Midas touch had entered into his fingertips, and Marie found herself with more jewels than she could wear. Her slightest whim was instantly fulfilled. She was seen at the grand social events of the season, frequently in the company of the Metternichs and other aristocratic personages. Her appearance was scrutinized from head to toe wherever she went, and only Worth was aware that at heart she was as shy as ever.

The domestic quarters at number 7 rue de la Paix reflected their steadily increasing wealth. Worth had had all the furnishing fabrics woven at Lyons, and he proved to be quite secretive about one material he had ordered. When it arrived he unrolled one bolt like a magician, throwing the rich cloth forward to billow like a river of red and gold.

Marie stared in amazement at the pattern of eyes and ears that shimmered over each rise and fall of the glorious stuff. "The material you've always talked about!" she cried. "The one you saw in the portrait of Queen Elizabeth when you were just a boy!" It was a tale she had heard many times.

He stood with feet apart, head thrown back. "It's mine at last," he said. He had always seen the design as his talisman; why should he not? He was as omnipotent in his own sphere as the great Elizabeth had been in hers. He was the one and only Worth, his the eyes and ears of the universe of *haute couture*.

Worth was making magnificent dresses for the masked balls that had become popular in society, and he was as dictatorial with them as with everything else he made. No matter whom a client had made up her mind to represent, he would silence her with an imperious gesture, put a hand to his head as he called upon inspiration, then tell the lady what he would make for her. He once gowned the empress as the wife of the Doge of Venice, in black velvet and scarlet satin. The Princess de Sagan was dressed by him as a peacock, the whole bird constructed in green and gold on her head, hundreds of peacock feathers in the train. Worth himself went to one ball in silken robes of his "eyes and ears" pattern, causing his own sensation. Requests by others for the same pattern were firmly turned down.

Marie enclosed a snippet of the "eyes and ears" material in a letter to Louise, knowing that she would be familiar with its origins. It slipped from between the pages as Louise opened the letter, and she smiled over it. Later that day she went to the National Gallery and stood before the portrait of the queen. Holding the shining material up to the canvas, she thought it might well have been cut from a fold in the regal gown.

Now, some months later, she was on her way to Paris with Robert and Paul-Michel. Robert would never have let her take the boy without him, since her son was the one hold he had over her.

Her relationship with Robert had deteriorated to the point where he always spoke tersely to her, and frequently with sarcasm. She sometimes felt that she had another child to look after, a feckless boy who would continue in his wayward role until the end of his days. How she could ever have imagined he would fulfil the role of father to Paul-Michel she did not know. It was Will who did most for the boy, taking him fishing, teaching him to play cricket, giving him his first riding lessons.

Marie met them at the station in Paris, her sons beside her. Eleven-year-old Gaston and eight-year-old Jean-Philippe were strong and healthy in appearance, although inwardly much embarrassed by the curls that their mother had crimped into their hair for the occasion. Paul-Michel noticed only that they were fellow boys. He pulled a twist of paper from his pocket and offered it.

"Have a piece of English licorice," he invited in faultless French. "If you stick bits on your front teeth, it looks as if they've been knocked out." The friendship was sealed.

Marie insisted that the travellers go with her to the salon, where a luncheon awaited them. The Prestburys had their baggage dispatched to the Grand Hotel, where they were to stay, with Daisy accompanying it.

The carriage swept through the gates to the inner courtyard of number 7. As Louise alighted, she saw that Worth's own monogram, gilded and gleaming, had been incorporated into the ironwork. But that was nothing compared to the grandeur of the interior. Floor upon floor was now given entirely to the business, and throughout there was a richness of Aubusson carpet and damask panelling and ormolu and marble.

The showrooms on the first floor each displayed a particular range of fabric or colour, black and white silks in one, green and blue in another, rose and coral in the next. In a long salon, mannequins, as

286

those who modelled dresses were now called, paraded in beautiful garments. If any client wished to see how she would look while waltzing in the Salle des Maréchaux, she had only to step inside a room filled with looking glasses and lights that simulated exactly the famous Tuileries chandeliers.

Luncheon was over when Worth appeared, full of apologies. "My dear Louise! To think I must snatch a greeting and rush back to work again." He kissed her hand, then twirled her around, looking her costume up and down critically. "Yes, yes. The skirt nicely flat in front, with a half-hooped crinolette at the back. Do you recall how it was once said that the full crinoline would never wane?"

"The whole world has followed your lead," she replied.

"Yes, it has," he agreed complacently. "What are your plans in Paris?"

"Well, tomorrow—"

"Tomorrow you shall go with me to the Tuileries. I have a new dress for the empress. You had best be here by nine thirty in the morning." He noticed Robert for the first time and extended his hand, then opened the double doors to depart.

The next morning Louise rode with Worth to the palace in his carriage. Once there, they walked in through the grand entrance, leaving the imperial servants to unload the huge box containing the empress's dress. Louise's heart contracted as she saw the familiar sky-blue tunics of the Cent-Gardes, but as she climbed the marble staircase she reminded herself that there was faint chance she would run into Pierre in that huge labyrinth.

They entered the empress's suite. Eugénie, at the age of thirty-eight, was at the zenith of her beauty.

"Show me my new dress, Monsieur Worth."

"I have had it made up in a Lyons silk brocade, Your Majesty." He motioned to Louise, who spread out the gown for inspection. "It has been specially woven, the unusual pattern only seen before in an antique Chinese shawl."

Eugénie stared at it, her dislike apparent. The soft beige background with the spread of flowers in yellows and corals and palest greens did not appeal to her. "It's like an old curtain. I'll not wear that!"

There was more to her hostility than mere dislike of the brocade. The city of Lyons had never been loyal to the emperor, and with the criticism currently being levelled throughout the country against both her husband and herself, the empress was sensitive about it. Worth brought his famous charm into play.

"This brocade is unlike any other made during the past thousand years. I can't imagine a combination of colours more suited to your titian hair. It will create interest everywhere and mean a full revival of the looms at Lyons almost overnight. After you have worn this dress, every fashionable woman in the world will want to possess a dress in Lyons brocade."

Eugénie shook her head, determined not to be won over this time. "I will not be seen in it. Take it away!"

Louise was astonished when Worth continued to argue with her. In the midst of the discussion the emperor entered the room. Worth immediately sought his support.

"I beg you, sire, to help me persuade Her Majesty to wear this dress." He explained his reasons with enthusiasm. "If the empress wears this, I'll be up to my ears in orders for Lyons brocade before the day is out."

Louis Napoleon studied the dress. "Hmm. Very fine." He drew slowly on his cigarette and gave his wife an encouraging nod. "It would be politic for you to wear it once, if never again. Renewed prosperity to any industry within the realm means benefit to France." The battle was won.

The days in Paris flew past for Louise. She completed a lot of business, ordered the latest in *passementerie* and other ornamentation, and visited with Catherine, spending as much time with her as she could. During the second week Paul-Michel was asked to join the Worths when they went to take up their summer sojourn at the mansion they had built outside Paris, at Suresnes. There the three boys had ponies to ride, trees to climb, lakes to swim in, and croquet lawns to enjoy together. Louise and Robert were invited to Suresnes to dine, sometimes in the vast conservatory filled with exotic flowers, or in the house, which was steeped in luxury and extravagance. Worth rode on horseback to the rue de la Paix each morning and home again in the evening, a dramatic figure in his tall top hat, his velvet coat-tails flying.

It was the empress's custom to give a large party for the prince imperial each year in the Tuileries gardens. Paul-Michel, as a guest of the Worths, was extended an invitation. He was reluctant to go, but Jean-Philippe assured him that it would be fun. The party lived up to all expectations. There were races and a treasure hunt, and a magician who produced rabbits from a hat. Paul-Michel told his mother about it when she tucked him into bed at the Grand Hôtel. It was their last night in Paris.

"Jean-Philippe and Gaston were presented to the empress, and I was, too. Then one of the officers came and talked to me. He had heard my English surname and wanted to know all about where I lived and about my parents. I told him I liked to ride, and he saddled up his cavalry horse for me. It's name is Sabre. I rode it around the courtyard." He frowned. "What's the matter, *Maman?*"

"Did the officer tell you his name?" she asked falteringly.

"Yes. Captain de Gand."

She turned so pale that he was alarmed, and pushed back the bedclothes to scramble forward on his knees and put his arms about her neck. "Is something wrong? Are you not well, *Maman?*"

She hugged him to her, hiding her face in his small shoulder. "Yes, yes. A little tired, perhaps."

After he was settled, she left him with Daisy and took a cab to have supper with Catherine. As soon as Catherine saw Louise, she knew that something was wrong.

"Pierre and Paul-Michel have met," Louise said.

Catherine listened to how it came about and tried to reassure her. "Think no more about it. Paul-Michel will soon forget about it."

Louise shook her head. "Paul-Michel will forget, but Pierre won't. Marie told me that after a third miscarriage, Stéphanie was informed that she would never be able to bear children."

Catherine lapsed into silence. There was nothing she could say to that. She could almost pity Pierre. Fate certainly extracted its dues most cruelly.

AFTER HER VISIT to France, Louise returned to work with renewed zest. She had become *the* couturière to dress debutantes who were to be presented at court. Hoops had now disappeared, and skirts were straight in front, with an abundance of draped and gathered fullness to the rear, which enabled Louise to give great variation to the debutantes' white gowns.

At times she had to suffer criticism of France. Since 1863 the British press had attacked the presence of French troops in Mexico, condemning the emperor's interference there. Louise found most worrying the rumours of a Prussian threat to the security of France. Since the short and bloody war executed by Prussia against Austria in 1866, it had become obvious that Bismarck was now the power in Europe, and Louis Napoleon, whose health was deteriorating, was in decline.

Louise felt keenly homesick when Mr. Allenby came to dine after visiting the great Paris Exhibition that had recently opened. Will, also just back from Paris, was among the friends she had gathered about her table to celebrate Robert's birthday. The guest of honour had failed to appear, and she had had to apologize for his absence. She had no idea where he was, or with whom.

Over dinner both Mr. Allenby and Will were encouraged by the other guests to describe the Paris Exhibition, which covered many acres and housed many wonders of the world. One of the highlights for both men had been hearing a new Strauss waltz called "The Blue Danube", conducted by the maestro himself. There was also talk on a more sombre note of the execution of Maximilian in Mexico, bringing the end to French influence in that part of the world.

After all the other guests had departed, Will remained in the drawing room. He held out a glass of cognac to Louise.

"Drink this. It will do you good. The evening has been a tremendous strain on you."

Obediently she took a sip from the glass and sank down onto the sofa. "I hope the guests did not feel uncomfortable. I tried to sustain an agreeable atmosphere."

"So you did. I'd say that nobody missed that husband of yours. How much longer are you going to put up with him, Louise?"

She glanced up uncertainly. "I'm not sure I understand you."

"I'm talking about divorce."

She closed her eyes and shook her head. "Robert would never allow me to divorce him. He has legally adopted Paul-Michel, and he would not hesitate to deprive me of my son. It is that threat and nothing else that stops me." Her voice quavered and she rose quickly to her feet.

Will watched her closely. "Are you saying that Robert loves you? Is that why he would never let you go?"

She had placed her glass on a side table, and now she ran a fingertip nervously around its rim. "No. He has never loved me. I'm his workhorse. With me to provide for him, he knows he can live in comfort until the end of his days."

Will reached out and closed his large hand firmly about her arm. "Is that all there is to your marriage these days?"

She looked away. "You have no right to ask me such questions."

"I have every right. Have I not known you for many years? Have I not loved you for as long?" His grip on her arm tightened, and he drew her to him.

Louise had not been held in such a loving embrace for a long time. Out of the chill of her loneliness she felt drawn by Will's warmth. A tremor ran through her as he bent his head to kiss her throat and lips.

"My love, my love," he whispered.

Slowly she lifted her head from his shoulder. "Will, my dear. It can't be. It can't be."

Robert's voice cracked like a whip from the direction of the door. "I'm mightily glad to hear it. A gentleman doesn't care to share his wife with every Tom, Dick, and Harry, you know!"

Louise had started at the sound of his voice, not with a sense of guilt but with revulsion at the insidious intrusion.

"Leave with me now," Will urged. "Fetch Paul-Michel and come in the clothes you're wearing. We'll sort the legal tangle out later." He took her hands into his own, not having taken his eyes from her.

Robert stamped across the room and, spluttering in rage, struck Louise away from Will with such force that she staggered back. "Damn you, Russell! Get out of my house!"

Louise gave a sharp cry. Her skirt had swept out over the coals in the fireplace, and flames were leaping up the taffeta. Will lunged forward and threw her to the ground, snatching the hearthrug and throwing it over the flaring fabric. It was all over in a matter of seconds, but when Will, still on one knee, would have assisted her to her feet, Robert leaned over and shook a clenched fist under his nose.

"Leave my wife alone!" His face was congested with fury.

Will stood up and grabbed him by the throat. "If you ever use violence on Louise again, I swear I'll thrash you within an inch of your miserable life!"

He released his hold with a thrust that sent Robert back onto his elbows. Then he helped Louise to stand. "I'll take you to your room. You can direct me."

He picked her up in his arms, ignoring her protests, and carried her upstairs, where he placed her on her bed. She was extremely white, and shaking from the whole ordeal. He would have rung for her maid, but she raised herself from the pillow. "Not yet. I'd rather

291

lie here quietly for a little while." Her eyes held his. "Thank you, Will. You've always been so good to me."

As Will left the bedroom, Paul-Michel appeared in his nightshirt, rubbing his eyes sleepily. When he saw Will his face lit up. "Hello, Mr. Russell. Have you come to the birthday party?"

Will smiled at him, ruffling his hair. "It's late, and the party ended long ago. You'd better get back to bed."

Downstairs, Robert had poured himself a whisky, and he took a mouthful of it as he stood in the doorway of the drawing room to watch Will depart. The scene he had witnessed between his wife and Russell was vivid in his mind. How much had gone before to bring them to the point of kissing under his roof? He would find out!

He left the drawing room and took the stairs two at a time. When he reached the landing he found his path blocked by Paul-Michel.

"What do you want?" he snapped. "Get out of my way."

"Happy birthday, Papa. This is my present."

A cane with an ivory handle carved into the head of a unicorn was being held out, a paper bow adorning it.

"Don't come to me with such rubbish!" Robert seized the cane, broke it over his knee, and hurled the pieces away. Bursting into his wife's room, he slammed the door after him.

Louise had just removed her ruined dress and was in her petticoats, the upper one trailing a scorched frill.

"You little whore," he said.

She stiffened. "You have no cause to use such a term to me."

"I happen to think I have. You and Russell have known each other for a long time. For all I know, he may be the father of your child."

"Think whatever you wish," she retorted, "but you are far from the truth. Who fathered my son is something you shall never know."

He walked to her dressing table and in a rage sent everything on it smashing to the floor. "Full of secrets, aren't you? Well, it's no use playing the innocent with me." He advanced slowly towards her. "I want to know how many times before tonight Russell has asked you to go away with him."

"Never!"

"I don't believe you." He made a rush at her and flung her backwards onto the bed. She gasped and struggled wildly, but he pinioned her down.

Then suddenly an ivory-handled piece of cane was beating at him.

292

To Louise's horror she saw her young son's contorted face and heard his terrified shrieking. "You're killing my *maman!* You're killing my *maman!*"

Robert pushed against the child's chest and sent him hurtling out of her range of vision. But she heard the sickening thud of his head and body against the wall. Her flailing arm touched the splintered end of the cane that had fallen onto the bed and her fingers closed around it. As Robert turned back to her she hit him across the face with the handle. He gave an awful yell, clapping his hand to the bloody wound, and she pushed him from her, scrambling free.

She saw Paul-Michel lying with his head propped at an angle against the wall. He was deathly white and his eyes were closed, but as she dropped to her knees and gathered him into her arms she saw he was breathing. Struggling to her feet, she ran from the room with him, calling to the servants. "Fetch Dr. Perkins at once! At once!"

For five days Paul-Michel lay in a coma, with Louise constantly at his bedside. She did not see Robert, but was told he had needed seven stitches in his forehead.

At last Paul-Michel opened his eyes, and Dr. Perkins assured Louise that from now on he would recover quickly. He advised her to get some fresh air and exercise.

Robert did not go out by day while his face was wrapped in bandages, and where he went at night Louise did not know. He did not speak to her until one evening, when he startled her by removing the bandage from his face. The ugly puckered wound made a gruesome sight. Robert gave her a mirthless grin. "I thought I would give you a sight of the damage you wrought on me." Then his face hardened. "Incidentally, I've decided that it's time for Paul to be sent away to school. He'll go to Fountleigh in Berkshire, which is my old school. The autumn term starts in three weeks."

Her son received the news of going away to school quite stoically. He did not want to leave his mother, but he would not be sorry to get away from the London house and the man who made it such a hateful place to live in. At least he knew Robert Prestbury was not his real father. Once, in a temper, Robert had called him a bastard, and when he had asked what the name meant he had been told. He had never talked to his mother about it, but he had to Mr. Russell. He was able to ask Mr. Russell anything.

Louise's heart sank when she took Paul-Michel to begin the term at Fountleigh School. It was a large, bleak building that reminded her of a children's prison. Paul-Michel wrote dutiful letters home, but it came as no surprise when the first words he burst out upon his return to London for the holidays were that he hated the school. He looked thin and wretched and had a bad cold, and his misery was not alleviated by Robert's anger at his poor school report.

At the end of the holiday it was hard for Paul-Michel to face going back to Fountleigh. He despised the injustices that he witnessed there, the bullying that was rampant, the birching, and the indignities. Most of all he resented not going to school in France. In spite of his English surname, he felt as French as his mother. Once back at school, he made up his mind to run away.

LOUISE HAD NEVER been busier. The rush of orders for debutantes' presentation dresses increased until Louise felt as if she were moving in an ocean of white silk and lace. She was in the midst of a fitting when she was told that her husband was in her office and wished to see her.

"Tell Mr. Prestbury that I'll be there as soon as I can," she replied, not at all pleased. Robert had become exceptionally aggressive of late, even though she had finally managed to purchase Prestbury's for him and had hoped that their life would run more smoothly as a result. In her office, she found Robert pacing.

"You certainly took your time!" he said with annoyance.

"I'm extremely busy. What has brought you here?"

He stubbed out a cigarette. "I need some money urgently."

Opening a drawer, Loise took out her purse. "I have about fifteen pounds. Is that enough?"

He crashed a fist down on her desk, making the papers fly. "Damn it! No! I need five thousand now and more later!"

She stared at him incredulously. "Whatever for?"

He scowled at her. "I've been playing the horses. I had a run of good luck for a while, but this past year it's been different. I haven't enough to pay the wages at the shop next Friday, and the bank is threatening to foreclose."

"You have borrowed on Prestbury's?"

"Yes, I've mortgaged it. Up to the hilt."

She passed a hand wearily across her forehead. "How much do you owe altogether?"

He did some reckoning and astounded her with the amount. As she shook her head, his expression became more belligerent. "Don't

294

pretend you haven't got it, because I know you do. This business is a gold mine."

She knew what the future would be if she gave in to his demands. He would continue along his self-indulgent path until every penny was drained away. All her hard work would be for nothing. She rested her fingers on the desk to steady their trembling. "Subject to your agreeing to a legal separation between us and forfeiting all control over Paul-Michel, you shall have your five thousand—"

"You're out of your mind! I'll never agree to that."

She continued as if he had not spoken. "To help bridge your debts, our home and its contents shall be sold. I'll ask Will Russell to purchase Prestbury's at a fair price."

"I've no intention of selling either the house or Prestbury's! You can draw on your business to provide what I need."

She took a deep breath. "That's not possible."

"What do you mean? All London knows it's a roaring success."

"I mean that officially I'm not at liberty to dispose of its income. The business is mine by a certain legal arrangement, and I intend to invoke its protection. I have always known that one day you would try to sap my livelihood for your own ends, so I put Paul-Michel's future and my own into a trusted friend's hands." Her palm slammed down on the bell on her desk. "Now at last I will be free."

If she had not rung the bell when she did, he would have used physical violence against her. She had seen it coming in the temper that consumed him, but the door opened almost instantly as the clerk from the outer office entered.

"I'm going to see my lawyers with Mr. Prestbury," she informed the man, taking her cape from the cupboard.

At the lawyers' office, everything was put into motion. The separation would go through without delay. Robert agreed that upon the settlement of his debts he would make no further claims against Louise. She drew up a bank draft for him to receive five thousand pounds. He took it with ill grace and hastened away.

Left on her own with the lawyers, Louise was advised to do nothing that might prejudice her case when it came to court. Separation hearings were always tricky, and she must not act rashly. She wanted to fetch Paul-Michel away fom Fountleigh, but that could appear to be going against her husband's good intentions of having the boy suitably educated. During the next few weeks she must tread the tightrope carefully.

Robert was alone at home one afternoon when an anxious junior master arrived from Fountleigh.

"I have the most serious news to impart, Mr. Prestbury," the young man began, twisting his hat. "Your son has run away from school. He went in the night. The police have been alerted and a search is going on." He thought the father seemed singularly unmoved. "If he should arrive here, the headmaster wishes to be notified immediately."

"If he turns up on this doorstep," Robert answered coldly, "I'll see that he is returned to Fountleigh by the next train."

When Louise arrived home that evening, Robert called to her from the drawing room. "The headmaster sent word that your son has absconded from Fountleigh. No one knows where the little wretch has gone."

She was shattered by the news and outraged that Robert had discovered no details as to how it had come about.

"I'm going to Fountleigh myself!" she exclaimed. "There'll be an evening train." She ran upstairs to her room, summoning her maid to her assistance, and within ten minutes she was being driven to the railway station.

After her departure, Robert went up to his wife's room. Ahead of him that evening lay the disagreeable prospect of informing his mistress that he could no longer afford her favours, and a piece of jewellery might help to sweeten the scene. From Louise's jewel case he picked out a diamond brooch. Then he looked into her reticule to see if she had left any money. He found only her tortoise-shell comb, and a ring of keys, which he quickly pocketed.

Lily Ashcroft was not in the best of moods when he arrived. "You're late," she told him sulkily.

"We've the whole night," he said, "and I have one or two surprises up my sleeve."

He told her to close her eyes, and opening them a moment later she saw him holding up a diamond brooch. She gave a shriek of delight. "Ooo! It's lovely. Give it here!"

He took her to a fancy restaurant and she wore the pin on the bodice of her dress. During the elegant dinner Robert drank deeply. After a while he took the ring of keys out of his pocket and laid it on the cloth. His speech was slurred, his grin a trifle foolish. "See those, my prett' Lily? They're keys to a wardrobe. A whole new wardrobe for you. I'm going to take you to it."

Out in the cool night air, he ordered a cab. At the dark entrance of his wife's shop, he unlocked the door and pushed Lily into the premises ahead of him. Lighting a match, he led her up the stairs to the showroom, where he lit the gas mantles. Dresses on display stands shone forth in the jewel colours for which Madame Louise had become known. Robert threw his arms wide.

"Help yourself, Lily. Anythin' you like is yours."

She could not believe her good fortune. "D'you mean it? Really? What's your wife going to say?"

He replied pithily as to how much his wife's opinion mattered to him. "Louise and I are separatin'. I should nev' have married her. Don't worry, Lily. Nobody'll ever know you've been here."

Still wary, Lily approached the nearest dress, but as soon as she handled the rich fabric, excitement took possession of her. She began to fumble frantically with the hooks at the back of her waist. "Undo me! Give me a hand!"

For a while Robert helped her in and out of the dresses, but soon he collapsed in one of the chairs, while Lily darted hither and thither in her petticoats. She laid the garments of her choice across a table, leaving a trail of discarded ones on the floor. She discovered more dresses in showrooms upstairs. Then she opened a door and gave a gasp. Dozens of exquisite white gowns shimmered on support figures, white linen spread under each. Slowly she traversed the room, enthralled by the delicate embroidery, the tiny flowerets of lace, and the sheen of woven ribbons. All these dresses for the high and mighty, created by the spiteful female who had kicked her out of Prestbury's. She began to breathe deeply. Her fingers, which were handling a pearl-decorated skirt, needled sharp nails into the fabric. There was a satisfying rip as she split the length of the skirt down to the hem. Then roughly she yanked at a sleeve, parting it from the bodice. She found some scissors, and within moments she set to work with them, a kind of sensual exultation accompanying the destruction. She could not have stopped even if she had wished it.

Robert awoke blearily when she shook him by the shoulder. "Go and find a cab," she instructed. "I'm ready to leave."

He was beyond helping her with the dresses, and she had to make two trips from the shop to the cab after bundling him into a seat. When she climbed in beside him he pawed at her, and she pushed him away, wanting to gloat over her spoils.

"Tha's no way to show gratitude for a memento," he growled. "I coulda left you with nothin'."

She glanced at him with a frown. "What do you mean?"

He managed to wag a finger at her. "Wha' I say. Can' pay your bills any more. Your pickin's t'night make final payment."

She understood at last, and clutched the diamond brooch. "I thought it too good to be true. This was your wife's, wasn't it? You're a miserable worm, Robert!"

He was past responding to insults. "You'll have to sell it. Rent owin'."

"What? How long since you paid my landlord?"

"Long time," he muttered. "Long, long time."

She grabbed his lapels and shook him. "What about the grocer? The butcher? My milliner?"

He blinked at her. "Sell th' brooch. Only way."

She screamed her outrage, pounding at him with her fists. Then she fumbled at the cab door. "You get out! Get out of my sight and never come near me again!" The cabby, hearing the commotion, hauled on the reins and jumped down from the box in time to break Robert's fall as Lily pushed him through the door. The driver held him until he regained some balance. "Awright, guvner?" The cabby looked up at his female passenger. "You getting out, too?"

"No, I'm not. Carry on." She slammed the door shut.

As the cab drew away she glanced back. Robert was stumbling in the road, shouting to her to come back. Then the cab turned the corner and he was swallowed up in darkness.

LOUISE RETURNED to London by an early train. Paul-Michel had not been found, and her hopes that he might have come home in her absence were dispelled at once by the anxious inquiry of the servant who opened the door to her. She dispatched a note to Will before going upstairs to bathe and change out of her travelling clothes. When he arrived she hastened downstairs.

"How good of you to come!" she exclaimed gratefully.

Will gave her a smile. "You know I'll do whatever I can. Now I just want you to talk about Paul-Michel. Anything that comes into your head. Maybe it will give me some clue where to look for him."

It was a release for her and a genuine aid to him. Before he left the house he bade her keep a good heart and go about her daily routine as best she could.

She was unable to find her keys when she was ready to leave for the shop. She went to ask Robert about them, but discovered that he was not at home. "When my husband returns, ask him if he has seen my keys," she said to her maid. Then she clutched the girl's hands in desperation. "And remember, send word at once if Paul-Michel should return."

Louise arrived to find the shop in a turmoil. Her assistant, Mademoiselle Brousseau, gasped out an account of the robbery of a number of dresses.

"What of the debutantes' dresses?" Louise demanded.

"I haven't looked there yet, madame."

Louise rushed up the stairs. When she opened the door to the salon that contained the white dresses, she was met by a sight worse than anything she could have expected. In stunned silence she touched each ruined gown, white beads and tiny pearls crunching underfoot. Behind her she heard Mademoiselle Brousseau wailing in lament. She addressed the woman without turning around, her voice toneless. "On no account must the police be notified." She spun about. "If a newspaper should report my apparent neglect in allowing this to happen, I'd be ruined!"

They rounded up every assistant and sewing hand to tidy the place and get the dresses back onto the stands. Then Louise addressed her staff.

"Your livelihood is at stake, and so is mine," she informed them crisply. "If we fail to deliver these court dresses on time, no debutante will ever come to this shop again. We have to replace those ruined dresses within fifteen days."

There was a chorus of protest. Mademoiselle Brousseau spoke for the staff. "Even if we all worked night and day, it would be impossible, madame. That embroidery! All that beadwork!"

"It can be done," Louise replied, "with extra hands. I'm sending to France for the best of them. In the meantime, we'll start cutting from scratch again."

A frenzy of activity began. After sending a postal dispatch to Worth, asking him to send her his best sewing hands, Louise set to at the cutting table. As she worked, she thought of Paul-Michel, her anxiety increasing while the hours went by with no word of him. At midnight she sent her workers home, and the next morning she was back at her cutting table at dawn.

The day passed the same as before. Robert continued to stay away from the house. It was early in the morning of the third day that the French sewing contingent arrived in cabs from London Bridge station. Louise organized them into various tasks. Before long every new arrival was busy with a needle.

Louise could no longer sleep at night, and by day she moved from crisis to crisis, ranging from a spool of special embroidery silk running out, to reassuring a debutante about a dress not yet sewn. On the eve of the last possible day for delivery, the workrooms erupted in a final explosion of flashing needles and pressing irons. In the midst of that madness Louise was told that a policeman wished to speak to her. She hurried to her office. One look at the constable's face told her that the news was bad.

"You'd best sit down, ma'am," he said. "It's my sad duty to inform you that your husband has been dead for several days. He was garrotted and his body thrown into the Thames."

She had to go with him to identify the body. Robert's pockets had been emptied of everything except a ring of keys, which were rusty from immersion in the water. When they were handed to her she recognized them instantly.

It was late in the evening when Louise finally returned to the shop. Robert's mother had received the sad news staunchly, but poor Agnes had needed to be comforted. Mademoiselle Brousseau, coming down from the busy sewing rooms, saw Louise leaning against a counter with her eyes closed in weariness.

"Madame," the assistant said gently, "I have good news."

Louise bestirred herself. "The dresses are done?"

"Almost to the last stitch. But it's better than that."

Slowly Louise's expression became suffused with hope. "My son?" she breathed.

Mademoiselle Brousseau nodded, brimming over with pleasure. "Mr. Russell sent word that Paul-Michel has been found and is with him at his house."

Louise raced out of the shop. When the cab dropped her off, Will hurried down the steps to meet her. She clutched him by the arms. "Is Paul-Michel well? Is he unharmed?"

Will smiled. "He's footsore and weary, but otherwise well. I picked up his trail after locating a cottage where he had been given a meal. I finally caught up with him on the outskirts of Calais."

"How did he get there?" she asked in astonishment.

Will led her into the house. "He stowed away on a French steam packet. He was trying to reach the place he loved best. Your son has spirit and initiative, Louise. Whatever you do, don't let Robert send him back to that miserable school."

"Robert is dead," she replied quietly. She told him what had happened as they went up to the room where her son had been put to bed.

Paul-Michel was fast asleep, his hair still damp from the bath that had washed away the dust of his travels. Louise sat down on the bed and leaned over to kiss his forehead. Then she started to sob. When Will began to stroke her hair she rose to her feet, reaching out blindly, and felt herself enfolded in his arms.

They left the sleeping child's room. In the hall, Will kissed Louise tenderly, and her hands slid up the nape of his neck to bury themselves in his thick curls.

He raised his lips fractionally from hers. "I love you," he said softly, "and I've wanted you since the day we met."

A smile touched the corners of her lips. "My darling Will," she whispered. "I knew it then and I know it now."

CHAPTER TEN

As the months went by, Will would not tolerate Louise's refusal to marry him. "What does it matter how long or how short a time you've been a widow?" he demanded. "I say forget the gossip, and let us be wed."

"You know it's nothing to do with that," she insisted. "I have told you that I'm never going to marry again."

"What about Paul-Michel? He and I like each other. And he needs a real family life."

"I married for that reason before, and I'm not doing it a second time." She drew in her breath.

"In any case, he will not be at home much in the future. I promised him that he could go to school in France as soon as he could read and write French. No boy could have worked harder. I've enrolled him in a school in Paris, where he will board weekly and spend Sundays with Catherine. He and I will have a little holiday there first."

"It's madness to go to France now," Will said. "Troops are mustering, and the Prussian armies are gathering on the border. War is likely to break out at any minute."

"I realize that, but the fighting would take place far away, on Prussian soil. There would be no danger in Paris."

"Don't be so complacent!" he stormed. "Do you think Bismarck would be trying to goad France into war if the country was as strong as she has been in the past? Wake up, Louise! Your glorious Second Empire is in its last days!"

France declared war on Prussia on July 19, 1870, shortly before Louise and Paul-Michel were due to depart for Paris. Will kept up his protests until the last minute, but any fears he might have implanted in Louise's mind vanished as soon as she saw the city she loved. The cafés still brimmed with life and merriment, and in front of the Madeleine the flower market blossomed with roses and heliotrope, jasmine, pinks, and verbena. Everywhere elegant women abounded, in tiny hats and sweeping dresses, watched by sauntering boulevardiers, who twirled their moustaches in the manner popularized by the emperor. On all sides there were soldiers strolling to see the sights before departing with him to the field of war. Louise and her son were driven past the Tuileries and on to Catherine's comfortable abode, where there was an emotional reunion with her old friend.

Their next call was on the Worths. Louise's visiting dress of striped blue and white Lyons silk was one of her most recent creations. It was superbly bustled in the line with which Worth had wooed women away from the crinoline.

As she mounted the staircase at number 7, she thought what a long way both she and Worth had come since they had first met at a garret door.

Marie was greatly excited to see her again, and Jean-Philippe and Paul-Michel picked up their friendship as though they had never been apart. The age difference with Gaston, now a handsome boy of seventeen, set him apart from the younger ones. Yet both Gaston and Jean-Philippe were able to discuss fashion with Louise on equal terms, their knowledge of *haute couture* deep-rooted from childhood.

Worth's business now occupied the whole of the huge building at number 7, and he employed over a thousand people. He greeted Louise wearing the velvet beret and flowing Rembrandt robe he

302

now donned during working hours. A genius in the garb of an earlier genius. It was all very fitting, and women loved it.

"Come to an Offenbach operetta with me this evening, Louise," Marie suggested a few days after Louise's arrival. "I'm sure you will enjoy it."

For Louise the merry music typified all Paris, and she applauded the songs and dancing with intense enjoyment. During the intermission some of Marie's acquaintances came into the box to greet her, and Louise was shocked to see that Stéphanie de Gand was among them. Marie was compelled out of politeness to inquire after her husband.

"He left Paris today to join the emperor at the Palace of Saint-Cloud. From there they will leave for the war." She took the seat beside Louise. "How well you look, and what a beautiful dress! You are the most successful couturière in London, I've been told. Are you on your own in Paris?"

Louise observed that Stéphanie had acquired a brittle poise and aplomb that had never been there before. "My son is with me," she replied.

"Indeed? He must be twelve years old now. I suppose you have been taking him to see the sights?"

"We have had quite a few excursions already, and the day after tomorrow we shall take a drive to Versailles."

Stéphanie smoothed the feathers of her closed fan. "Why not take him to Saint-Cloud instead to see the emperor and the prince imperial go off to war?"

Louise stiffened slightly, not sure if Stéphanie was taunting her. She kept to safe ground. "It doesn't seem right that the prince imperial should go into danger." Louise was remembering that the boy was only a few months older than Jean-Philippe.

"He has been trained since infancy to be fearless." Stéphanie saw that her party was drifting back to their seats, and as she made to go with them she looked back at Louise and said, "Remember what I said about Saint-Cloud. It would be a sight for your son to remember all his life."

After she left, Louise said to Marie, "Stéphanie wants me to let Pierre see his son. But I can't do it." Her fists were clenched on her lap. "I can't."

Marie sighed softly. "I think you should," she counselled. "He is off to war, Louise. He may never come back."

IT WAS A CLOUDY, sultry day when Louise and Paul-Michel arrived at the little thatched railway station that served the Palace of Saint-Cloud. Just after half past nine a line of equipages appeared from the direction of the palace. Along the route a gathering of local people raised the cry that had echoed so fiercely in Paris. "To Berlin! To Berlin! *Vive l'empereur!*"

Louise was shocked to see the change in the emperor. He looked sick and old, and she understood why the departure had been arranged quietly. In the carriage following his came the prince imperial, and with him were two officers. One was Pierre.

He saw her. His casual sideways glance hardened into a stare of disbelief, and he turned to keep his eyes on her as he passed.

In a few minutes he reappeared, coming towards her, and she saw that he was no less handsome than he had ever been. How could she have forgotten that his eyes were the exact grey-green of her son's?

"I never thought we should meet again," she said.

"Nor I, my dear." He kissed her on each cheek and they drew apart, seeing the past in one another's eyes. He stooped down to take Paul-Michel by the shoulders. "You've grown since I saw you last. Do you remember me?"

The boy nodded. "Yes, Captain de Gand. Do you still have Sabre to ride?"

Pierre chuckled, much pleased. "Yes, I do. It's a pity he's left for Metz, or I'd have had him saddled up for you."

"May I ride him when you come back from the war?"

"How long is your holiday? I'll try to get the Prussians beaten before you return to England." He smiled at what he had said, but Paul-Michel was intent on extracting a promise.

"I'm not going back to England, except for holidays. I'll be attending the Collège Saint-Nicholas in Paris."

"You will?" Pierre said slowly. "In that case you shall ride Sabre when the war is won. If we have your mother's permission."

She saw no reason to refuse. "Just as long as it's on a Sunday and Catherine has made no other plans. I'm returning to London as soon as Paul-Michel starts school."

Pierre straightened up, keeping a hand protectively on the boy's shoulder, and spoke to him again. "I expect you would like to have a look at the locomotive, wouldn't you?" Signalling to an official, he put Paul-Michel in his charge. Then Pierre and Louise began to stroll along the grass.

"What of your marriage, Louise? Are you content?"

She kept her gaze ahead. "I am widowed."

They took another pace or two in silence. "So you really have no personal ties to take you back to England," he said. "And Paul-Michel will be at school in Paris. I shall be there myself when this war is over."

His meaning was clear. He was asking her to remain in Paris in order that they might take up their life together again. She shook her head slowly, and he stilled her action with his fingertips, gently turning her face around to his.

"I refuse to accept that everything is at an end," he whispered. After a pause he said gravely, "Tell Paul-Michel who I am. I want him to know."

The discreet cough of an equerry interrupted them. "The emperor is about to board the train, Captain." Time had run out. Pierre kissed Louise's hand, took a step backwards, and saluted. Then he disappeared.

On the drive back to Paris, Paul-Michel was singularly quiet. Finally he said, "Captain de Gand is my father, isn't he?"

"Yes," Louise replied evenly. "He is. How did you know?"

"Well, when I found out what being a bastard meant, I asked Mr. Russell if I was his son. He said that he wished I was, but that my father was a courageous Frenchman, and I should be proud of that."

Louise closed her eyes for a moment. Dear Will. How like him to choose the right words. "Come and sit by me. I'll tell you all about your father." And as the last kilometres to Paris were covered, Louise felt that she and her son had been drawn closer to each other than ever before.

Five days later the emperor and his troops won a bloody battle on German soil. Champagne corks popped in Paris in celebration; but almost at once the tide turned. French soldiers were mowed down and scattered before the sweeping Prussian advance. Word began to leak out in the press of blundering, and resentment flared against the emperor with the tidings of each ignominious rout. Louise saw the whole city changing before her eyes, and the well-remembered smell of revolution seemed to hang in the air. The empress as regent acted decisively, declaring martial law.

Louise received an urgent telegram from Will asking her to return to England with Paul-Michel without delay, but she could

306

not have left even if she had wished it. Catherine had taken to her bed with a fever, and Louise was nursing her night and day.

Paul-Michel had scarcely started at his new school when he came home with his trunk one day and said, "The school is closing temporarily, *Maman.*" Then, seeing that she was bewildered, he added incredulously, "Haven't you heard the news? The emperor has surrendered. He and thousands of our troops have been taken prisoner by the Prussians."

Louise put her hand to her throat. "It can't be! It's little more than a month since the war started. We cannot be defeated!"

"It's true. The Prussians are said to be demanding the complete capitulation of France."

Two days later the streets of Paris were full of revolutionaries shouting and stampeding and tearing down the imperial eagle from gates and buildings. A dense crowd gathered in front of the Hôtel de Ville, where a provisional government was being formed. As the crowd was told that the Second Empire had fallen and France was a republic once again, a great shout went up. The mob headed for the gates of the Tuileries.

"Down with the empress! Long live the Third Republic!"

Inside the palace the shouts could be clearly heard, but Eugénie refused to leave. Stéphanie, shaking with fear, was among those waiting in the Blue Salon, while behind closed doors the empress's advisers begged her to take flight.

LOUISE WAS ALWAYS to remember that night as the one in which Catherine took a turn for the better. Her fever eased and she slept more peacefully. At dawn Louise rose from the couch in Catherine's room, and as she slipped on a robe, there came a jingling of the doorbell. She opened it to find Stéphanie de Gand held in the arms of a servant, her ankle bandaged. Silently Louise stepped aside to allow her to be carried in and put on a sofa.

"That was Dr. Evans's coachman," Stéphanie began falteringly when the man had left. "Dr. Evans is an American dentist who has risked his life taking the empress to Deauville to put her on a boat for England. We have been all night escaping from the mob surrounding the Tuileries, and somehow I have managed to sprain my ankle—"

"I'll put on the coffeepot," Louise interrupted kindly. "I can see you have been through an ordeal."

Stéphanie stayed on with Louise while her ankle healed. Paul-Michel was wary at first of his father's wife, but gradually, as Stéphanie's spontaneous nature shone through, he found her good company. They played cards and backgammon to alleviate her boredom, and he ran errands for her as well as for his mother. Every day Stéphanie scanned the newspapers that he fetched, first for any glimpse of her husband's name, and second for news of the military situation. Eventually she received word that Pierre was a prisoner of war along with the emperor, both of them housed in considerable comfort with other imperial officers.

Although the emperor had surrendered to the Prussians, the Third Republic had not, and the war was still on. Paris was being turned into a fortress, and Stéphanie made arrangements to get home to the Château de Gand. "I am to leave tomorrow," she told Louise. "I have asked for papers to cover you and Catherine and Paul-Michel. I want you all to come with me."

Louise shook her head. "Catherine couldn't possibly make such a journey. We must stay and face whatever comes."

"Then let Paul-Michel come with me. Everyone assures me it will be a long, hard siege. In the Loire countryside the boy will be safe. Surely this is what you would wish."

Louise could not refuse such a chance, but when Paul-Michel departed with Stéphanie, she fought to keep back tears. Two days later the Prussians completed their encirclement of the city and the telegraph wires were cut. The siege of Paris had begun.

Louise was among those who had to stand in long lines to get bread and other necessities. As the stores of food dwindled, butchers offered horseflesh or goat meat, while the very poor were reduced to trapping rats for the stewpot. Even the wild animals at the zoological gardens were slaughtered. As if there were not enough hardships, a very cold winter descended, and Louise had difficulty keeping the apartment adequately heated for the convalescent Catherine. Gradually whole areas of the city became bare of trees as the government allowed them to be felled for firewood.

New Year's Day of 1871 was no more than eight hours old when Charles Worth, ignoring the icy weather, took his family to church. They were just leaving when Jean-Philippe sighted a figure weighed down by a sack of kindling.

"There's Madame Prestbury!" he exclaimed. He darted across to her, and the others viewed her surprise and gratitude as he heaved

308

her sack onto his broad young shoulders. Marie was the next to reach her, and she insisted that Louise and Catherine move to number 7 rue de la Paix, where there was an adequate stock of coal and logs to see them through the winter.

"We've turned several floors into an emergency hospital," Marie said. "Most of the seamstresses are making bandages and hemming bed linen. Perhaps you can help nurse the wounded."

Louise smiled. "I'll do anything I can to help."

Marie's thoughtfulness saved both Louise's and Catherine's lives, because four days later, when the Prussians began to bombard the city, the house where Catherine had lived was destroyed.

It became obvious as days went by that no part of Paris was to be spared the shelling. Churches, hospitals, and schools were among the buildings flattened, and Louise was thankful that she had sent Paul-Michel to a place of safety.

On the whole, morale remained high, but gradually the Parisians began to look as pinched and bleak as the damaged city. Most of the population existed on bread, wine, and coffee; then bread began to get scarce, and a very real panic prevailed. Paris faced famine, but a last great sortie was to be made.

Louise stood with Marie at the window to watch the ragged array that marched off to meet the enemy. Hundreds of civilian volunteers, boys and elderly men among them, swelled the ranks of the National Guard, their provisions transported in a motley collection of hackney cabs and wagons. When the last of them had vanished from sight, Marie and Louise went to make beds in every available space for the aftermath of battle.

It was a defeat on a scale almost impossible to comprehend. It meant the capitulation of Paris. The wounded, mud-caked and dazed, returned to the city in a flood.

ON THE DAY the Prussians made their ceremonial entry into Paris to flaunt their victory, Marie and Louise drew down all the blinds. It was the same all over, the shops and cafés keeping their shutters up or displaying notices that Prussians would not be served. When six hundred German officers, resplendent in bright uniforms, rode down the Champs-Élysées at the head of a long column of cavalry and troops, the crowds watched in silent hostility. When the conquerors departed a few days later, they left in their wake a bitter sense of humiliation that roused certain sections of the people against the government. To avoid pressure from the population the government fled to Versailles.

Louise, eager for a reunion with Paul-Michel, paid no heed to fresh clouds gathering and wrote to him, saying she was looking forward to his immediate return. When his letter came, she tore it open eagerly, expecting to read the time of his arrival, but it was not there. Instead, he wrote of the horses he rode, his school, the new friends he had made. She reached the final paragraph:

> I do not want to return to Paris just yet, although I long to see you and Aunt Catherine again. Now that the emperor has gone to England to join the empress, my father is on his way home, and I should like to spend a few days with him before I leave. Please write and say that I may stay a little longer.

She wrote at once and gave her permission, suppressing her disappointment. But she realized that Paul-Michel was better off where he was when, soon after, the Communards, a group forming a revolutionary municipal goverment in Paris opposed to the Versailles government, seized power in a violent uprising. Everywhere in the city the red flag took the place of the tricolour. From Versailles, troops were sent in, and civil war broke forth in the bloodiest fighting the city had ever seen. The noise of rifle shot and cannon fire resounded night and day, and Louise felt that her countrymen had gone mad.

The government threw more and more troops into the fight to clear Paris, and the Communards were defeated. Order was finally restored to Paris, and the tricolour flew once again.

The city came back to life. Shopkeepers took down their shutters, and café owners set out tables and chairs under hastily patched awnings. Rubble was cleared from the streets, and the long task of repairing buildings began.

Louise found an apartment on the Champs-Élysées with a balcony from which Catherine could watch the world go by. A middle-aged widow accepted the post of housekeeper and companion. At last Louise felt free to journey to the Château de Gand to get Paul-Michel, and she wrote to tell him she was coming.

THE DRIVE LEADING to the château was a mile long, and Louise was driven past lush lawns and a wide lake to the forecourt. She had expected Paul-Michel to come running down the steps to meet her,

310

but he did not appear. She was aware of an uncomfortable thumping of her heart as she was shown into a richly furnished room, where Stéphanie awaited her.

"How pleasant to see you again, Louise. My thoughts were with you all through the terrible siege and through the ordeal of the Commune. Do sit down. I have ordered refreshment."

Louise sat on the edge of a chair. She could not quell her sense that all was not as it should be. "How is Paul-Michel?"

Stéphanie was quick to put her mind at rest. "He is bouncing with good health. He would have been here to meet you, but I wanted the opportunity to talk to you first, so he has taken his usual morning ride with Pierre."

"Paul-Michel rides well," Louise remarked with pride.

"Indeed he does. He's a born horseman." Stéphanie paused fractionally. "Just like Pierre. In fact, the likeness between them becomes more marked every day."

A tray of coffee and small almond cakes were brought in. The conversation did not resume until the coffee had been served. "When you see Paul-Michel," Stéphanie continued carefully, "he will make a request of you. I implore you for his sake and for Pierre's to grant what it is that he will ask."

Now everything was clear. Louise knew beyond a shadow of a doubt what would be requested. She put down her cup with deliberate care. "I'll not give up my son."

Stéphanie leaned forward, her hands held out imploringly. "Don't make a decision until you hear what he has to say."

Louise could only stare. "I'll not give him up," she repeated.

There was a sound of running footsteps. Paul-Michel burst into the room. "*Maman!*" he shouted joyously. They hugged, laughing and talking and questioning each other. When at last they drew apart, Stéphanie had gone from the room. Louise glanced at the clock on the mantel.

"There's a train leaving at three o'clock. If you will collect your belongings, we can catch it easily."

He frowned, wandering across to the coffee tray. Absently he helped himself to a rose-coloured almond cake and bit into it. "I'd like to talk a bit first."

"We can talk on the way—"

"*Please!*" he interrupted.

She sat down, trying to keep her expression bright and unconcerned. "The principal of your school in Paris is willing for you to start there again."

"That's it." He heaved a sigh. "I don't want to leave my present school. I'm getting on well, and I've made lots of friends."

"That would mean staying on here," she replied faintly, "and I'm sure we can't impose any longer on the generous hospitality you have received."

He answered indignantly. "It's not hospitality. It's *home*. Madame Stéphanie told me that when I came here with her. And my grandmother said the same when she told me all about my ancestors in the portraits in the gallery. I belong to this house."

Louise drew a shuddering breath. "What does your father say?"

Paul-Michel said quietly, "He wants me to stay. And he would like to have my surname changed to his. But I must have your permission, given willingly."

She looked down at her hands to hide her anguish from him. "I'm at a loss. I can't seem to think what to say."

He came and crouched down in front of her to look up into her face. "I'd come and see you in London. I'd spend holidays with you. You're always so busy that you wouldn't miss me."

She saw then what little time she had ever spent with him. If ever fate decreed that she should bear more children, she would never make the same mistake again. She had sacrificed the very relationship that she treasured most in her struggle to gain independence for herself and freedom for him. Now he had found his roots. He had cemented the filial tie between a son and father that she had always wished for him. She raised her head slowly and smiled.

"I give you permission to stay with your father. As you say, I never seem to have time for anybody or anything when the rush of the season is on. But with your holidays to look forward to, I'll arrange time off from business; that will give me much-needed holidays, too." She became more animated. "We'll go wherever you wish. To the seaside. To the pyramids. To the moon!"

He burst out laughing, and she with him. "Yes, we'll do that, *Maman*."

For a little while, she thought. Then he would seek out those of his own age for holiday companionship, and rightly so. At the moment she must think only of keeping a smile for him.

He saw her off, riding in the brougham as far as the gates, then waving to her until she was gone from sight. She had seen how deeply he felt this moment of parting, but her smile had remained intact. Only now did she lean back in the seat and weep.

At the station, a porter found her a first-class compartment, and she took a corner seat and rested her head wearily. Suddenly the door was jerked open; Louise gasped as Pierre flung himself into the seat at her side.

"How could you leave without a word?" He pulled her into his arms. "Louise, Louise. Do you think I don't know what a sacrifice you have made? I'll do everything in my power for our son." He kissed her with a kind of frenzy. Along the train there came the sound of doors slamming in preparation for departure. She pulled away.

"You mustn't come to Paris with me! Please get out while you can."

He looked into her eyes. "There will be other times. Remember what I said to you at Saint-Cloud? You are going to stay on in Paris, aren't you?"

"No," she said. "I'm going home. To England."

The guard's whistle blew. The locomotive billowed forth steam. Pierre rose to his feet and stood staring at her, his mouth tightening. Abruptly he swung the compartment door open and sprang out as the train began to move. She had a last glimpse of him through the window. His face bore the same expression as that of their son at the moment of goodbye. He could not bear to see her go.

A week later she was due to leave Paris. She had ensured that Catherine would want for nothing and was receiving the best of care. She went by way of the rue de la Paix to the railway station. In the Place Vendôme the column with the statue of Napoleon, which had been smashed down by the Communards in their rampage of destruction, had not yet been restored. Louise remembered a popular saying, that the statue should not have been of Napoleon but of Worth, for all he had done for fashion and for Paris itself.

At number 7 she found that everything appeared to be just as it had always been, but as Louise went through the sumptuous showrooms she knew it was not quite the same. The Palace of the Tuileries was a burned-out shell, and never again would Worth go there with wonderful dresses for the beautiful Eugénie to wear and dazzle the world. The age of the Second Empire had also been the age of Worth.

Marie came to meet her. "So you're really going," she said,

threading her arm through Louise's. "Don't let it be too long before you come and see us again."

Worth was busy working on a dress for the president's elderly wife, the new first lady of France, who never appeared in anything but black. He broke away to give Louise a small gilded box that he was entrusting to her for personal delivery. Lifting the lid, he showed her a bouquet of French violets on a bed of damp moss.

"For the empress," Worth said, "from her loyal and devoted couturier."

The skies over the white cliffs were a soft English blue as the Channel steamer put in at Dover. Louise stood at the rails, a wisp of sea breeze fanning a few tendrils of her hair. Will waited on the quayside, a tall, broad figure with feet set squarely apart, hands clasped behind his back, his mouth compressed and smiling. An unmistakably triumphant smile. He and Paris had done silent battle, and he had won.

She went down the gangway to him. Will had been as much a part of her life as Pierre had ever been. There was no easy time ahead for him with her. How could there be, when she was no more pliable now than before she went away, and he was not one ever to be satisfied with second place in any woman's heart? She did not fear the struggle that lay before them. It was what life and love were all about between a man and a woman. And Will was a man among men.

Rosalind Laker

Small, dark-haired, totally feminine, Rosalind Laker looks just the way a best-selling author of romantic novels should look. And clearly she enjoys her work, the research as well as the writing. "It's the fun of living in one period of history and then another," she says, and her eyes shine as she describes the thrill of visiting number 7 rue de la Paix and seeing Worth's initials, CW, still entwined in the ironwork beneath the balcony. Since Miss Laker had studied the history of costume at college, she found the life and work of the great couturier a particularly enticing subject. Worth's great-grandson, Maurice Worth, was extremely helpful to her in gathering information for her book. When she first met him in Paris, she found that he bore a striking physical resemblance to his great-grandfather and seemed also to have inherited his reputed charm. Maurice is the head of Worth Parfums, Maison Worth having terminated its dressmaking business in 1956.

"Charles Worth was a truly admirable man," Rosalind Laker points out. "He had a social conscience that was way ahead of his time. He paid his workers a living wage and looked after their welfare. In fact, he endowed two hospital beds for their use and continued paying for them throughout the siege of Paris." This was remarkable in an era when child labour was widely accepted.

Miss Laker lives in West Sussex with her tall, attractive Norwegian husband. They are the parents of two grown children, Susan and Paul, and the proud grandparents of Paul's baby daughter. They love to visit their four-hundred-year-old farmhouse in Norway, which has the traditional turf roof, covered with wild flowers in summer. Its lyrical mountain setting provides the peace and beauty a busy author needs for relaxation and renewed inspiration.

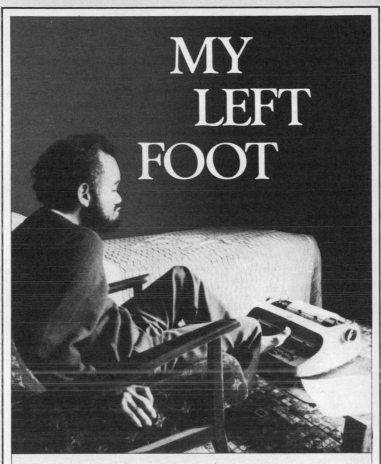

MY
LEFT
FOOT

A CONDENSATION OF THE BOOK,
WITH ADDITIONAL MATERIAL, BY

Christy Brown

ILLUSTRATED BY ERIC STEMP
PUBLISHED BY SECKER & WARBURG

A
CLASSIC
OF OUR
TIME

Until Christy Brown was five, his mother was the only person who had faith that inside the tortured body of the little victim of cerebral palsy was an intelligent, sensitive being. Unable to speak or control his hands, Christy then suddenly discovered that he could communicate—but only through his left foot. Thus he started on the long and difficult road which led him from the poverty of his home in Dublin to a distinguished career as a writer.

Christy Brown's moving story is not only a tribute to his own courage, but also to the remarkable and loving determination of his mother, who with the rest of the large and lively Brown family played a vital part in the miracle of Christy's triumph over disability.

My Left Foot was first published in 1955. Now, to mark the Year of the Disabled, we are proud to present a special edition of this classic autobiography, with extra chapters written by Christy Brown exclusively for readers of Condensed Books.

CHAPTER 1

I was born in Dublin on 5th June 1932. There were nine children before me and twelve after me. Thirteen of us survived infancy, and mine was a difficult birth, I am told. Both mother and son almost died.

It was mother who first noticed that there was something wrong with me. My head had a habit of falling backwards whenever she tried to feed me. She attempted to correct this by placing her hand on the back of my neck to keep it steady. But when she took it away, back it would drop again. My hands were clenched nearly all of the time and were inclined to twine behind my back; my mouth couldn't grasp the teat of a bottle because my jaws would either lock together tightly, or they would suddenly become limp and fall loose, dragging my whole mouth to one side.

Very worried by this, my mother and father sought medical advice. There was indeed something disturbingly wrong with me. Almost every doctor who examined me labelled me a hopeless case of cerebral palsy: I had suffered brain injury at birth, with the result that I was unable to control or coordinate my movements.

Very little was known about the condition at that time. Most of the doctors simply told mother gently that I was mentally defective and would remain so. Yet, in spite of all the specialists told her, she would not agree that I was an imbecile. She had nothing in the world to go by, not a scrap of evidence, but she was convinced that, though my body was crippled, my mind was not.

But my mother wasn't content just to say that I was not an idiot. She set out to prove it, not because she felt any rigid sense of duty, but purely out of love. I was *her* child, and therefore part of the family.

At this time she had five other children to look after in our little council house in Kimmage. There were my brothers, Jim, Tony and Paddy, and my two sisters, Lily and Mona, all of them very young, just a year or so between each of them. She was determined to treat me on the same plane as the others, and not as the "queer one" in the back room who was never spoken of when there were visitors present.

While my father was out at bricklaying earning our bread and butter for us, mother tried slowly, patiently, to penetrate beyond the thick curtain that hung over my mind. It was hard, heart-breaking work, for often all she got from me in return was a vague smile and perhaps a faint gurgle. I showed no sign of intelligence. I could not speak, nor could I sit up without support, let alone take steps. But I wasn't motionless. I seemed indeed to be convulsed with movement, wild, stiff, snake-like movement that never left me, except in sleep. My fingers twisted and twitched continually, my arms twined backwards and would often shoot out suddenly this way and that, and my head lolled sideways. I was a queer, crooked little fellow.

Mother told me how one day when I was five she had been showing me pictures out of a big storybook and telling me the names of the different animals and flowers that were in them, trying without success to get me to repeat them. This had gone on for hours while she talked and laughed with me. Then at the end of it she leaned over me and said gently into my ear:

"Did you like it, Chris? Did you like the bears and the monkeys and all the lovely flowers? Nod your head for yes if you did, like a good boy."

But I could make no sign that I had understood her. Her face was bent over mine, hopefully. Suddenly, involuntarily, my queer hand reached up and grasped one of the dark curls that fell in a thick cluster about her neck. Gently she loosened the clenched fingers, turned away from my curious stare and left the room, crying. It all seemed hopeless.

All I remember of that time is lying on my back in the kitchen or, on bright warm days, out in the garden, a little bundle of crooked muscles and twisted nerves, surrounded by a family that loved me and that made me part of their own warmth and humanity. I remember I was lonely, that I longed to run about and play with the rest, yet was separated from them as though by a glass wall. I remember too how, suddenly, in a moment everything was changed.

I can see and feel the whole scene as if it had happened last week. It was the afternoon of a cold, grey December day. The streets outside glistened with snow; the white sparkling flakes stuck and melted on the windowpanes and hung on the boughs of the trees like molten silver. Over all, the dull, murky sky stretched like a dark canopy. Inside, all the family were gathered round the big kitchen fire that lit up the little room with a warm glow and made giant shadows dance on the walls and ceiling.

In a corner Mona and Paddy were sitting huddled together, a few torn school primers before them. They were writing down sums on an old chipped slate, using a piece of yellow chalk. I was close to them, propped up by pillows against the wall, watching.

The chalk was a long, slender stick of vivid yellow. I was fascinated by it as much as if it had been a stick of gold. Suddenly I wanted desperately to do what my sister was doing. Then, without thinking or knowing exactly what I was doing, I reached out and took the stick of chalk out of her hand—*with my left foot*.

I do not know why I used my left foot. Although I had displayed a curious interest in my toes at an early age, I had never attempted before this to use either of my feet in any way. That day, however, my left foot, apparently of its own volition, reached out and took the chalk out of my sister's hand. I held it tightly between my toes, and, acting on impulse, made a wild sort of scribble with it on the slate. Next moment I stopped, a bit dazed, looking down at the stick of yellow chalk stuck between my toes, not knowing what to do with it next. Then I became aware that everyone had stopped talking and was staring at me silently. Nobody stirred. Across the open hearth, his face lit by flames, sat my father, leaning forward, hands outspread on his knees, his shoulders tense. I felt the sweat break out on my forehead.

321

My mother came in from the pantry, a steaming pot in her hand. She stopped midway between the table and the fire, feeling the tension flowing through the room. She followed the stares and saw me, in the corner, the chalk gripped between my toes. She put down the pot.

Then she crossed over to me and knelt down beside me, as she had done so many times before. "I'll show you what to do with it, Chris," she said, in a queer, jerky way, her face flushed as if with some inner excitement.

Taking another piece of chalk from Mona, she very deliberately drew, on the floor in front of me, the single letter "A".

"Copy that," she said, looking steadily at me. "Copy it, Christy." I looked about me at the tense, excited faces that were turned towards me, frozen, eager, waiting for a miracle in their midst.

The stillness was profound. I could hear water dripping in the pantry, the ticking of the clock on the mantelshelf, the soft hiss and crackle of the logs on the open hearth.

I tried again. I put out my foot and made a wild jerking stab with the chalk which produced a very crooked line and nothing more. Mother held the slate steady for me.

"Try again, Chris," she whispered in my ear. "Again."

I did. I stiffened my body and put my left foot out again, for the third time. I drew one side of the letter. I drew half the other side. Then the stick of chalk broke and I was left with a stump. I wanted to fling it away and give up. Then I felt my mother's hand on my shoulder. I tried once more. Out went my foot. My hands were so tightly clenched that my fingernails bit into the flesh. I set my teeth so hard that I nearly pierced my lower lip. Everything in the room swam till the faces around me were mere patches of white. But I drew it—*the letter* "A". There it was on the floor before me. Shaky, with awkward, wobbly sides and a very uneven centre line. But it *was* the letter "A". I looked up. I saw mother's face for a moment, tears on her cheeks. Then my father stooped down and hoisted me onto his shoulder.

I had done it! It had started—the thing that was to give my mind its chance of expressing itself. That one letter, scrawled on the floor with a broken bit of yellow chalk gripped between my toes, was to be my key to mental freedom. It was to provide a source of relaxation to the tense, taut thing that was me which panted for expression behind a twisted mouth.

CHAPTER 2

Having taught me to draw the letter "A" with my foot, mother next set out to teach me the whole alphabet. She was determined to make use of the opportunity so miraculously presented to her.

My memory of the way she set about this is quite clear. She would bring me up into the front bedroom any day

she wasn't too busy with the household, and spend hours teaching me one letter after the other. She would write down each letter on the floor with a piece of chalk. Then she would rub them out with a duster and make me write them down again from memory with the chalk held between my toes. It was hard work for both of us. I remember the first thing I learned to write was my initials: "C.B." I was tremendously proud of myself when I could do this.

Slowly, very painfully, I ploughed through the whole twenty-six letters with my mother, and gradually mastered them. One thing that gave mother great encouragement was my ability to listen and watch attentively when she was sitting by my side giving me lessons.

Knowing the alphabet was half the battle won, for I was soon able to put letters together and to form little words. After a while I began to know how to put words together and form sentences. But it wasn't as easy as it sounds. Often mother would be in the pantry cooking the dinner when I'd give a howl to make her come up to see if I had spelt a word correctly. If I was wrong, I'd make her kneel down, her hands covered with flour, and show me the right way.

Mother had by now seven other children to care for besides myself. Fortunately she had a real ally in my sister Lily. She was the eldest and the little mother of the circle, a small, wiry kid with flowing black curls and flashing eyes. She could be a proper little angel when she liked, but she wasn't very angelic when she was roused. She realized mother's tough situation quickly and busied

323

herself looking after the others so that mother could spend more time with me. She washed and dressed the smaller ones and made sure the bigger ones washed behind their ears every morning. Perhaps she was a shade too zealous, for often Jim or Tony would slink,-shamefaced, into the kitchen, bearing testimony to little Lily's earnest housewifery in the form of swollen ears or black eyes.

I could not speak intelligibly, but by now I had a sort of grunting language which the family understood more or less. Whenever I got into difficulties and they couldn't make out what I was saying, I'd print words out on the floor with my left foot. I was now going on six, and able to sit up alone and crawl about from place to place on my bottom. I wore no shoes or any other kind of footwear. I hated having·my feet covered, just as any normal person might feel if his hands were tied behind his back.

In our house the great thing was food. To us children mealtimes never came too soon. We'd all wait patiently till mother laid the table, then we'd make a beeline for it, I scrambling between the others on my bottom and usually managing to get there first by throwing myself across a chair to show it was engaged till some of the bigger ones would lift me onto it. Then the fight began—to see which one of us would outdo the rest in eating. I couldn't feed myself, of course, but that didn't stop me from taking a very active part in those contests. My mother or father would sit by me and feed me. Their hands often became tired from the simple process of lifting the bread and butter and putting it into my mouth.

After tea, if we decided not to go out, we would get together and have a game of hide-and-seek, or maybe blind-man's-buff. Someone would get an old scarf, tie it over the eyes of whoever had been chosen, and the game would be on. Everyone would run about the blindfolded figure, laughing while he sought to catch hold of a flying arm or wriggling leg, and all the time he would be buffeted around the room by "friendly" shoves. It wasn't a gentle game.

Sometimes the part of the "blind man" would fall to me. I'd pause a moment, waiting to catch the least sound of an intaken breath or a giggle that would indicate where someone was hiding, then, very cautiously, I'd crawl in the direction of the sound, pushing myself along on my behind. Then out I'd shoot my left foot, toes tensed to catch the leg of young Peter's trousers or the hem of Mona's frock. When I caught someone I'd drag them towards me and wrap my legs around them till they gasped, "I—give in!"

324

As time went on I began to depend more and more on my left foot for everything. With it I learned to break down some of the barriers that stood between me and the others at home. It was the only key to the door of the prison I was in.

It was my habit when I had written something down on the floor, to spit on it, rub it out with my heel, and then to write it down again from memory as I did when mother was teaching me. One day when I was about six and a half a local doctor came to visit my brother who had sprained his wrist while playing a game of rugger. After coming downstairs the doctor saw me writing on the floor with some chalk between my toes. He began to ask mother questions about me and, being anxious to show him that I understood all that was being said, she put me up on the table and invited him to ask me to write something for him. He thought for a moment, then he took out a ledger from his bag, offered me a big red pencil and asked me to write my name in the book. I took the pencil between my toes, pulled the book towards me, steadied myself, and slowly wrote my name on the flyleaf in big block-letter capitals.

"Amazing! I'm astonished, Mrs. Brown. It really is—" he began. Then he stopped in surprise, and mother blushed in confusion, for I had spat very deliberately on the page and was trying vigorously to erase what I had written, not understanding why the pencilled letters wouldn't come off as easily as chalked ones!

The doctor brushed my mother's apologies aside with a laugh, patted me on the head and told me I was a great chap. He visited me often after that and followed my progress keenly for many years.

Meanwhile the family was multiplying steadily. I was growing, too. My body was filling out and so was my mind. Mother wanted above all to make me equal with my sisters and brothers in every way possible, and, as I could not go to school, she did all she could to lessen the consequences of that disadvantage herself. But she hadn't much time to do this daily, for she already had her hands full struggling to carry us all through times of unemployment, illnesses and many other worries. She found it difficult to smile at times, though somehow or other she always managed to do so.

When mother was busy I worked on by myself, trying to make out new words whenever I came across them. One day I had been trying particularly hard to master a new word that I had come upon in Peter's schoolbook. At last I got it and turned to mother, who was sitting in a chair by the fire nursing my baby brother Eamonn. It was evening, the dying April light made a pattern on the floor and shone on the polished top of the little mahogany table, showing up the crack that zigzagged across its surface. I sat crouched in a corner of the sofa, Peter's book before me and a pencil in my left foot. Many times I had looked over appealingly to where mother sat, despairing of making this word out by myself. But, seeing her rocking gently in the chair, holding the baby closely against her breast, I had turned my face away again, feeling in a vague sort of way that somehow or other I must work out this one word for myself.

A few minutes later I gave a whoop of triumph that made mother start. "What is it, Chris?" she asked. "You'll waken the baby."

But I didn't care. In my own queer, grunting way I told her to come over to me at once.

"A new word, is it?" she said as she came across and sat down on the edge of the sofa, the baby asleep in her arms.

I grinned and, taking up the pencil, wrote down the word which had puzzled me for so long. When it was done I looked up into her face for her approval, and saw she was staring silently at what I had written on the margin of the page. She remained so still and thoughtful for so long that I became anxious and nudged her with my foot. She turned, placed her hand upon me and smiled.

The new word which I had learned to write was—M-O-T-H-E-R.

CHAPTER 3

By the time that I was seven I was beginning to associate with children of my own age through the help of my brothers. They took me with them when they went out to play in the streets, pushing me along in a rusty old go-car which they called my "chariot". Some of the best years of my life were passed in that battered old crock, which creaked and groaned as they raced me along in it. Everybody joked about it. But to me it was something lovable, almost human. It seemed to have some queer dignity of its own that nobody but I could appreciate. I called it Henry.

Very soon I too had pals, boys from our own neighbourhood who were young enough to accept me as one of themselves without asking any questions. Indeed, many of them regarded my affliction as some queer sort of symbol of superiority, so that they treated me with deference in a strange childish way.

I had now improved so much that I could sit up in Henry without having any pillows behind my back to support me. I took many a fall on those rides, when the car would topple over as it was pushed round a bend at full speed. But I grew to be quite adept at falling in such a manner that all I ever got was a bruising and a scrape or two. I got a huge thrill out of it all.

In Henry I tasted adventure, and excitement, too. The others took me with them everywhere, even to the local cinema every weekend. I would go in perched on the back of my big brother Jim. I noticed how the other kids would stare at me and how Jim would tell them to "scram", but I didn't think about it because I didn't see why I shouldn't be perched on my brother's back. I had always gone about on somebody's back ever since I could remember.

Summer came. The poor little row of forget-me-nots along the wall came out bravely, and the big tree in our neighbour's garden next door was covered with leaves of light green, the moss on its bark shining with little gems of dew. Outside on the streets the flies buzzed over the garbage bins and flickered about the heads of dogs sleeping on doorsteps.

It was too hot and sweaty for the cinema. So my brothers took me for long "walks" out into the suburbs of Dublin, or up into the Phoenix Park where we'd spend the day lying on the grass and then go down into Donnelly's Hollow and light a fire and make tea in a rusty old billycan, munching sandwiches and telling stories.

It was all great fun, going on those little outings. People would sometimes stop and stare at me as my brothers wheeled me along, but I didn't worry about it because I had no idea why they stared. Perhaps at the back of my mind I knew that there was something wrong somewhere, but it frightened me, so I tried not to think about it. I just wanted to be happy. And my brothers saw to it that I was.

I remember a trip we took out into the country beyond Dublin one day. We set out at about ten on a bright warm Sunday morning in September. Old Henry had been specially oiled and polished up the night before and in consequence he was groaning a little less fiercely. Peter stuffed his schoolbag with sandwiches and a nine-penny bottle of sauce. Two bottles of milk were pushed beneath the cushion of my car. They bruised my behind every time the go-car jolted. There were five of us, Paddy and Peter, two pals and myself. We all had our Sunday clothes on and Peter had dowsed his head with hair-oil he'd pinched from Tony. "I'm like Clark Gable now, aren't I?" he said.

A few hours later we were camped on the bank of a mountain stream. I sat on the bank, fascinated as I looked down into the sun-flecked water and saw little fish flitting like shadows in and out between the waving green moss on the bottom. A bunch of these little silvery creatures gathered right below me round a slanting shelf of rock. Quickly I thrust my left foot into the water, thinking I might catch one of them between my toes. But I was ignorant of fish's habits, and they darted away in a flurry of streaks and ripples to the opposite bank.

Towards evening we set out for home, but by the time we had got halfway we were very hungry. Our grub had run out two hours earlier, and we still had a long way to go.

"I'm starving," Peter complained, his shoulders drooping.

"Shut up, so am I," growled Paddy in return, striding on.

We were all losing our tempers when suddenly, on coming round a bend in the road, we saw before us a big country house with wrought-iron gates in front and a wall all around. The whole front of the house was covered with fruit trees. The branches hung over the walls, drooping with apples and pears. We stopped abruptly.

We looked first at the fruit trees, then at one another.

Peter looked around cautiously. "No one's near," he said.

We all looked at Paddy. He was the eldest among us. Paddy shuffled from one foot to the other, cleared his throat, and said with a desperate solemnity, "Seventh—thou shalt not steal!"

"Sissy!" shouted the others, making a dash for the wall. One of them bent down, legs braced, while Peter got up onto his shoulders. He reached the fruit and dropped it to the third one, who stood below holding out his coat as a blanket.

Paddy couldn't stick it any longer. He pushed my car over against the wall and climbed onto the side of it so that he had only to reach up his arm to touch the red apples and yellowish-brown pears.

"All right, that's enough—don't be greedy," said Paddy when

they'd gathered a handful of apples and pears. They climbed down and sat on the grassy margin of the road to eat the fruit.

"It'll do us till we get home anyway," Peter said, feeding me with a pear.

Then we caught the sound of footsteps approaching along the road just round the bend. Peter crept to the corner, peeping round it cautiously. Then he came running back, breathless. "Suffering duck—it's a copper!" he panted.

Paddy turned green. He seemed powerless to move.

"Run for it!" said Bob, leaping to his feet.

"Can't leave Christy here, can we?" Peter broke in as the steps came nearer. Then he had an idea. "Quick," he said, turning to the others. "Put all the stuff under Christy's cushion!" There was no time for questions. In a matter of seconds they had picked up all the fruit, half dragged me out of the go-car, dumped the stuff beneath the torn old cushion, and then pushed me in on top of it.

The policeman walked round the corner and came towards us slowly. "Evening, lads," he said smiling. He patted me on the head. "Out late, little man, eh? 'Tis almost eight."

The other four tried to keep calm, but they fidgeted uneasily.

"Take him home now, boys," said the friendly policeman. "Don't tarry any longer. Cheerio." With that he left us, going slowly up the road the way we had come.

They waited till he was out of sight, then they took out the apples and pears. They weren't pretty to look at.

"Aw—put 'em back!" Paddy growled when he saw them. "God didn't like us stealing them."

So, very sadly, they dumped the sticky mass of fruit back over the wall of the big house, and we started on our way home again. We got there about ten at night, feeling as empty as air.

We were in better spirits the next day, when Tony and Jim took me along to watch them swim in the canal not very far from our house. The day was warm and sultry.

We got to the canal and found a big crowd of children gathered there. The air was filled with the sounds of laughter and screams as they splashed about, covering the roadside with spray.

My two brothers placed me at a point where I could see all that went on. Then they changed into swimming togs and took a dive into the water. I looked on, amid all the noise and excitement, feeling hot, sticky, and a little jealous.

Suddenly I felt the same way as I had felt on that day when I first drew the letter "A"—a queer eagerness, an unconscious determination to do what the others were doing. I wanted more than anything else to go into the water.

Tony climbed out onto the bank, his body glistening and his hair clinging to his forehead. I gave a yell, and he came up to me. In my own queer grunting language I told him I wanted to have a swim.

"G'wan—you're kidding me!" he said laughing. "You'd drown!"

I insisted.

"All right then," he said. But when my eldest brother Jim heard, he said he'd have nothing to do with it.

"Give me your togs then," Tony demanded. "He can't go in in his pelt!"

He took me behind a bush and undressed me. Jim was very big and fat so his togs had to be wrapped round me a few times and pinned at the back. Finally, however, Tony got me ready and carried me down to the bank. He stopped and looked at me.

"Still want to go in?" he asked.

I grinned and nodded my head. Maybe I was afraid, but I was also too stubborn to give in now.

Tony pulled a branch off a tree, dipped it into the water and waved it over my head, saying an "Our Father" over me. Then he caught me under the arms, and swung me into the canal!

I gasped as I felt the cold, icy water rush over me; everything melted into a watery blur. I was beneath the water for a second, rose, went under again, rose once more and expected to go under for the third time. But I didn't. Instead, I lashed out frantically with my feet, and next thing I knew I was simply floating along like one of the white swans further up the river. I kept kicking my feet out vigorously and remained sailing on top of the water. I heard a burst of laughter coming from the bank, and a few moments later Tony swam up beside me and steered me towards the towpath, where Jim hauled me ashore. I lay there panting but triumphant.

"You'd lick Christopher Columbus any day!" said Tony.

That was my first swim. It wasn't my last, for I had many others in a little rocky stream which we discovered in a wood. Often I would lie on the bank while the others were swimming or picking blackberries. Sometimes I would fall asleep there. I was happy. I looked out on the world noticing everything except myself.

Then one day my go-car broke down: the axle snapped, the seat collapsed and nobody could do anything with it. It was put away in the coalhouse to rust.

I was lost without it. It wasn't just that I missed the old car so much. It was that my brothers could no longer take me with them when they went out to play. I was thrown upon myself at last. That queer idea that there was something wrong which had entered my mind sometimes before now loomed larger.

A few days later I was sitting in the garden playing toy soldiers with my brothers when along came some of our pals, carrying fishing-nets and jam jars on a string. They suggested we should all go fishing. There was an excited rush for rods and tackle.

They all crowded at the gate, ready to go. Then Tony forgot something and came back for it along with a pal. As he was going down the path again I looked up at him dumbly, appealing silently.

He stopped. "Sorry, Chris," he said, not looking at me. "We'll bring you back lots of pinkeens." He moved away quickly.

"Pity about him—" began his companion. Tony gave him a shove. Then they ran on to join the others. I was left alone in the garden. I looked down at my hands twisting and turning.

CHAPTER 4

The bottom had fallen out of my world. Everything was different. I'd sit at the window in the kitchen and gaze out at my brothers as they played football on the road outside. Sometimes some of them would smile and wave in at me. I'd try to wave back, but when I lifted my arm it would shoot out sideways and bang against the window frame. Then I'd throw myself onto the sofa and bury my face in it.

At last I realized just how helpless I was. I was now ten, a boy who couldn't walk, speak, feed or dress himself. I was "different" from others.

I couldn't reason this out or even think clearly about it. I could only feel it deep down, like a thin sharp needle that worked its way through all the fancies and dreams of my childish mind till it tore them to shreds. Up to then I had never thought about myself. Now it was different. Now I saw everything through the eyes of a cripple, a cripple who had only just discovered his own affliction. I was for the first time conscious of myself.

I looked at Peter's hands. They were brown, steady hands with strong, square fingers, hands that could clasp a hurley firmly or swing a chestnut high into the air. Then I looked down at my own. They were queer, twisted hands with bent, crooked fingers, hands that were never still.

I began to hate the sight of those hands, and I soon came to hate and fear a mirror too. It let me see what other people saw every time they looked at me—that when I opened my mouth it slid sideways, making me look ugly and foolish, that when I tried to speak I only slobbered and gabbled, that my head kept wobbling from side to side, that when I'd try to smile I'd only grimace and pucker up my eyes so that my face looked like an ugly mask.

One day, in tears, I climbed onto my bed, reached up my left foot to the little mirror that hung on the wall and knocked it off its peg. Mother, hearing the crash, rushed up the stairs. I just pointed with my foot to where the shattered glass lay.

"That means seven years of bad luck," she said.

After a few weeks mother managed to buy me a new car, a proper invalid chair this time that had a padded seat and rubber tyres. "Now you can go out again," she told me happily. I said nothing.

The next day my brothers, eager to "show off" my new wagon, took me out into the streets once more.

"We'll call it Sylvester," said Peter grandly.

That day they took me to watch them play a football game. It was just like old times, all the "gang" around me, but I couldn't laugh with them as I used to. I hid my face whenever anybody strange passed me by, but I couldn't help seeing how they'd glance at me, nodding their heads significantly as they went on up the road. They went right through me, those looks from people in the streets. In the space of a few weeks, since my old go-car had broken down, I had become as different in mind as I now knew I was in body.

After that day I went out no more, except, perhaps, once or twice a year. My brothers didn't understand what made me such a stay-at-home. They appealed to me again and again to go out with them, but I just shook my head and smiled at them.

332

Mother noticed the change in me and knew the cause of it. In an uncanny way she could feel what I felt. She saw now that I was nearly always sad, moody and shut up in myself, and knowing the danger of letting loneliness stay with me, she devised little pastimes for me, like writing out stories from the newspapers into cheap six-penny jotters with a lead pencil held in my left foot. She'd go over them to see if I had copied them down correctly. The writing would be dreadful: huge, scrawling capitals sloping down the page with no punctuation between them.

Still, though it helped to lighten the days for me, it could not take away that awful dissatisfied feeling that was beginning to take root in my heart. I wanted something else—something that would give me a chance to expend the nervous energy, the mental tension that welled up inside me.

Then, that Christmas, Paddy got a box of paints from Santa Claus. I got a box of toy soldiers, but the moment I saw Paddy's paints with all the wonderful colours I fell in love with them. I was fascinated by the little solid blocks of blue, red, yellow, green and white—and the long, slender fuzzy-haired brush. Later in the day I sat and watched Paddy as he tried to make some impression with the paints on a piece of white cardboard torn from an old shoe box, but he only made a mess. In a queer way I felt annoyed with him—and a bit jealous.

"Blow—I can't use these things!" he grumbled, flinging his brush down. "They're only for girls."

I saw my chance. Pushing my box of soldiers towards him with my foot, I asked him in grunts to "swop" them for his paints.

"Done!" exclaimed Paddy, glad to get rid of such a sissy's toy.

I put the paints away till all the excitement of Christmas was past. Then one quiet afternoon when there was nobody in the kitchen but mother and myself, I took out the little black box and laid it on the floor in front of me.

Very solemnly, I picked up the brush between my toes, wetted it in my mouth, then rubbed it on one of the paint squares—the bright blue one which I liked best. I next rubbed the brush against my other foot—and saw a blue spot on it when I took it away.

"It works!" I managed to exclaim, my face hot with excitement.

"I'll get you water," said mother, going into the pantry and coming back with a cupful which she put on the floor beside me.

Then she tore some paper out of Peter's sum-copy. I dipped the

333

brush into the water and rubbed on some vivid red paint. Then I steadied my foot and, while mother looked on intently, painted on the open page before me—the outline of a cross.

I grinned triumphantly up at her. I remembered how, on that day five years previously, we had sat together on the floor, almost in the same spot, while I shook and sweated as I drew with my left foot for the first time. There was no sweating or shaking now. I did it quite smoothly. I was holding a painting brush, not a broken piece of chalk, but it meant the same thing—I had discovered a new way to communicate with the outside world.

As time went on I became more and more devoted to my little box of paints. I painted all sorts of crazy things, from a sketch of Peter's face to dead fish lying in the dustbin. Then mother managed to buy me more paints and brushes, along with drawing books. After the first few weeks of uncertainty and awkwardness, I settled down contentedly with my new pastime, alone in the back bedroom.

I didn't know it then, but I had found a way to forget some of the things that had made me unhappy. Above all I learned to forget myself. I didn't miss going out with my brothers now, for I had something to look forward to each day.

I had a feeling of pure joy while I painted, a feeling I had never experienced before, which seemed almost to lift me above myself. I would sit crouched on the floor for hours, holding the brush between my toes, my right leg curled up under my left, my arms held tightly at my sides. My paints and brushes were around me, and I would get mother or father to tack drawing paper to the floor. It looked a queer, awkward position, with my head almost between my knees and my back as crooked as a corkscrew. But I painted my best pictures in this way, with the floor as my only easel.

Then one day, when I was about eleven, mother became ill and was shifted to the Rotunda Hospital, where a few weeks later, she gave birth to her last child, thus completing the total of twenty-two. She remained very ill after my smallest brother was born and we were all in a terrible state at home. With mother away the house seemed to go dead. I didn't even paint now; I had no interest in anything because I thought mother was going to die.

I was huddled up on the sofa one cold night in December when a knock sounded on the front door. Father, who was sitting by the fire holding a newspaper closely in his hand, too worried to read it, got up and went into the hall to answer it.

I heard voices at the hall door, but I was too worried and upset to listen. I had just turned over on my side, burying my head in the corner of the sofa when the door was opened and I heard father and someone else come into the kitchen.

"This is Christy," father said.

Then I heard a girl's voice saying, "Is he asleep?" In a dazed way I looked up at the visitor, blinking a little. The light hadn't been switched on yet, but by the light of the street lamp outside I saw that my visitor was a young girl, perhaps about eighteen. She was slim and tall and lovely—the most beautiful girl I had ever seen.

"Hello," she said, smiling a lovely smile. "My name is Miss Delahunt. Your mother told me about you."

I tried to say something, but I only made the same queer grunting noise that I always made when I tried to speak. The girl just smiled and sat down on the edge of the sofa. She told me she was an almoner's student at the Rotunda Hospital, that she had met mother, had heard about me and my paintings and so had wanted to meet me. Also she had another motive in coming. Mother was very worried about how we were getting on without her, so she had decided to come out and get me to write mother a little note. "Will you do that for me?" she asked.

Father lifted me onto the table and, holding the pencil between my toes, I wrote on the back of an old envelope: "Dear Mom. Don't worry. All OK. Lots of grub. Get well soon. Christy."

Miss Delahunt left, but promised to come again. I went to bed that night feeling dizzy.

Next time she came I got a big surprise, for she brought me a whole load of paints, brushes and drawing books, along with the good news that mother was improving and would be home soon.

Meeting Katriona Delahunt was an event which for me had a unique chain of consequences. I was too young to notice if my heart misbehaved itself in any way, for at that age I centred my interest more in my left foot than in any other part of me, yet I suppose my feelings were much the same as those of any other young chap with the least bit of imagination in him. Although at first I got confused and self-conscious when Miss Delahunt visited me, I gradually became calmer and began to look forward very excitedly to the days when she would come. I'd get mother, now home again, to comb my hair very carefully, instructing her to put as many "waves" in it as she could.

I still couldn't talk, but somehow speech didn't seem to matter an awful lot when I was with my new friend. We had a way of understanding each other without consciously expressing ourselves.

My mind began to stretch itself. I began to feel a little more, think a little more and therefore to know a little more. As I became further attached to painting I felt happier and more tranquil within myself. Yet it wasn't just painting that made me so happy; that in itself would not have been sufficient. It was the fact that I painted, not just to please myself, but to please someone else. I painted very badly. All I could do were horrible little landscapes with great lumps of brown and green scattered all over the paper and a huge sticky sea of blue for the sky. But Miss Delahunt always spoke of them as if they had been great masterpieces, and with this encouragement I began painting better and with more confidence.

One December day a few weeks before Christmas I was flicking over the pages of the *Sunday Independent* with my foot when I saw the announcement of a Christmas painting competition for children. There was a black-and-white reproduction of the picture that had to be coloured, showing a gay ballroom scene with Cinderella and Prince Charming in the middle of the floor, surrounded by men in skin-tight stockings and doublets and ladies in flowing skirts. Over their heads swung great chandeliers. I was so attracted by the picture that I seemed to see it all finished and glowing with colour as I stared at it. I called mother in from the pantry and showed her the news about the competition.

"Try it," she said.

I did. I painted the picture that same afternoon and I did it better than I thought I would. I made Cinderella quite a glamour girl, with pink cheeks, golden ringlets and a beautiful blue dress. Her white satin slippers peeped daintily from under her gown, like two little mice. I painted Prince Charming's uniform a bright purple and as an artistic touch I decided to bespatter it with tiny spots of yellow in imitation of gems.

I was satisfied when I had finished the picture, though I didn't want to have anything to do with the competition itself because I didn't think I stood a chance. But I couldn't refuse when my "dream girl" said I should enter it without delay.

I really thought it was all a waste of time and I soon forgot about it. I just went back to painting in the ordinary way happy that at least I had pleased Miss Delahunt by doing what she had asked me.

Then, on the following Friday morning, there came a knock on the front door. Mother was in the pantry washing some clothes. She came in to answer it with her hands covered with soap suds. I happened, for a change, to be perched on the big round table in the kitchen painting, with all my paints and brushes around me.

Mother answered the knock and found a newspaper reporter along with a photographer from the *Independent* who had come to see me. It transpired that Miss Delahunt had told the newspaper that one of the pictures sent in to their office was done by a boy who painted with his toes. They had been a little sceptical and decided to send out one of their reporters to check on it.

When the reporter and photographer came into the kitchen I was just putting the finishing touches to a tropical South Sea island in a blue lagoon, complete with waving palms and golden brown beaches. Hearing the door being opened I looked up; the two press men stood and stared across the room at me. I became confused and went on painting quickly.

"It's true!" I heard one of them exclaim in an awed whisper.

They asked mother many questions about me, and she told them my history. All the time this was going on I painted on quietly. At length they took a photograph of me painting at the table with a brush between my toes. It was my first photograph.

The next Sunday morning I was lying cosily in bed with Peter, halfway between sleep and wakefulness, when father burst into the room and pulled me up into a sitting position.

"Look—look!" he said, waving a copy of the *Sunday Independent* before my face. "See—you've won!"

It was true. There, on the centre page, was a photograph of a little boy in short trousers, his thin legs bent beneath one another, his eyebrows cocked up rather snobbishly, and by his side one twisted hand held tightly to keep it still.

I was brought down to the kitchen where all the family were eating breakfast and talking excitedly about my success. As father carried me into the room everyone stopped speaking at once. Mother laid down the teapot she was holding and came up to me.

"Never stop trying, Chris," she said as she kissed me.

And my "dream girl"?—she came later in the day. She took my hand in hers and kissed me, too, saying she was proud of me.

My left foot and I had done it again.

CHAPTER 5

Thirteen—and still very much the boy artist who hadn't yet come to know his own abilities sufficiently to make use of them. Painting became everything to me. Through it I made articulate all that I saw and felt, all that went on inside the mind that was housed within my useless body.

I saw more with my mind than with my eyes. I'd sit for hours sometimes, alone in my bedroom, just sitting and staring into a world of my own. When I went into one of those daydreams I forgot everything else: the loud voices in the stuffy little kitchen below . . . Peter trying to play the mouth organ on the doorstep . . . the high shrill voice of the ragman in the street outside . . . .

I didn't go out at all now. I didn't even play in the house with my brothers. This puzzled them at first, but they slowly began to accept the new kind of relationship. They even seemed a little in awe of their crippled brother. I didn't become a stranger to the rest of the family, of course, because with so many of us all living together in the same house that was impossible. But I had come to live more within myself.

And yet, withdrawn as I was from the ordinary life of a boy, the life of the streets, I found that my heart was still miles ahead of my body in development. I lost it again, good and truly this time. Another "dream girl" had come into my vision, not as tall and beautiful as my old one, but more my own age. She was called Jenny and she lived a few doors away. Jenny was small, energetic, gay, with a mass of brown curls framing her pretty elfin face, and lovely green eyes: she could start a riot among all the boys on our street just by using those eyes.

I worshipped Jenny from afar, that is from my bedroom window. It made me lazy in my painting, for whenever I heard her voice in the street below I'd crawl over to the window and sit on the bed, gazing out at her as she ran and skipped with the other girls. One day she looked up at me. I felt my face grow hot and made to draw back, but at that moment she smiled, and threw me a kiss before running away down the street, her dark curls flying and her white dress blowing in the wind.

That night I tore a page from an old jotter and, holding the pencil in my shaking toes, I wrote a passionate little note to Jenny. I told her in the note that I thought she was the prettiest kid on our street and that I'd paint her lots of pictures if she'd let me. Then, in a hurried postscript, I told her that I loved her "lots and lots of times".

I got one of my younger brothers to deliver it, and I waited for him to come back in excitement and fear, not daring to hope that Jenny would reply. In a half an hour's time he returned—with a note from her tucked up his jersey! I took the note and read it eagerly over and over again. She said she'd come and see me in my backyard the next day. I felt myself go hot and cold in turn. Then I threw myself back on the pillow, my heart jumping crazily.

I kept the appointment next day, all "done up" with Tony's deluxe hair grease actually dripping down my forehead. Jenny was very sweet. We sat and looked over some of my paintings, and she gave a little gasp of admiration at each one. I was shy and awkward at first, but Jenny was either very innocent or very tactful, for she didn't seem to notice anything queer about me, but talked on gaily to me about games and parties. I liked her for that.

We became great pals, Jenny and I. We never said a great deal to each other, but we exchanged innumerable little notes each week and she'd steal over to see me every Saturday night. I was secretly proud that I, a cripple, had made friends with the prettiest girl in our neighbourhood. I often heard Peter saying fervently that he'd do anything to be her favourite "beau".

Then one Saturday he came upon Jenny and me as we sat together in the backyard, our heads very close to one another, looking at some old story book that Jenny had brought along. I got red in the face, but Jenny didn't move. She just lifted her head, smiled at my brother briefly, and bent over the book again. Peter gave me a murderous look and went into the house, banging the door after him.

That evening, before she left, Jenny sat very quietly, toying idly with the book, a frown creasing her forehead and her lower lip pushed out. After a little while she got up, hesitated, then suddenly knelt down on the grass beside me and kissed me very tenderly on the forehead. I drew back, surprised, bewildered, for she had never kissed me before. I opened my mouth to try and say something, but at that moment she sprang to her feet, her face flushed and her eyes wet with tears, and rushed from the garden.

She didn't come for weeks after that, although I fairly bombarded her with notes. I often sat up in my bed at night, thinking of her and the way she had kissed me. I felt very melancholy and alone. Why doesn't she come, I asked myself, as I tossed restlessly in the dark, hearing Peter snoring comfortably at my side.

My fourteenth birthday came, and among my birthday cards there was one written in Jenny's childish hand; but still she never came to see me. I often saw her from my bedroom window playing in the streets below, but she never looked up once.

To hide my disappointment I painted furiously for the whole of every day, painting crazy little pictures that had neither pattern nor theme. They were just haphazard slices of my boiling mind dashed onto the paper wildly and recklessly.

Then one day as I sat disconsolately in the backyard with my back against a soapbox I heard a step close by. I looked up wearily . . . . It was *Jenny!* She stood a few feet away, at the entrance to the yard, her slim, childish figure outlined against the white wall behind her, vividly bright in the June sunshine. She was looking across at me, but—it was with a *look of pity*.

I knew then, as I came to know many times later, how bitter and crushing a simple look of pity can be to someone like myself who needs something other than sympathy—the strength that only genuine human affection can give to the weakest heart.

I lowered my head under her pitying gaze, and without a word being said Jenny turned slowly and left me to myself in the yard.

I became different after that. For a few blissful weeks I had allowed myself to dream that I was a normal, ordinary boy who thought himself "in love" with the sweetest girl in the whole neighbourhood and who was foolish enough and vain enough to think that she cared for him in return. Now all that make-believe was at an end, but the bitterest realization of all was that I had tricked myself into believing that my affliction didn't matter.

In the excitement of meeting Miss Delahunt, the novelty of painting, and the dreamy enchantment that came with Jenny, I had almost forgotten myself. I had come to believe that there was no "difference" between myself and other people, except in my own mind. It was a pleasure to lose myself in such a dream world, but it made coming back to reality all the more violent and bitter.

I now was poised between the blissful ignorance of childhood and the awakening pain and frustration of adolescence. I longed to be ignorant and happy as before. But I knew childhood had gone. I had seen the hopelessness and futility of my future that day in the backyard when a child gazed on me with a look of pity in her eyes.

I COULD NO LONGER run away from myself, I had grown too big for that. And now in a thousand ways, as the family grew up one by one and became—to me—strange self-supporting adults, I saw and felt the terrible *narrowness* of my own existence.

Lily had married, so too had Tony. Jim was the next to join the married ranks, and I suspected Paddy was courting from the way he tried to lecture Peter on how to go about getting girlfriends. Mona went dancing every night and was nearly always in the wars with father because she didn't agree with him that eleven o'clock was late enough to be out. Peter would soon leave school and go to work as a bricklayer, like Jim, Tony and Paddy. Father was quite determined that his sons should become bricklayers like himself, not stopping to find out if they had thought of taking up any other occupation.

Father now looked rather aged. His beautiful mop of fair hair had gone and the only remaining signs of it were two tufts on his temples which looked exactly like little balls of grey wool stuck on with paste. Yet he was still as tough as nails, with a pair of hands that were gnarled and hardened by the lifting of concrete blocks and the constant twisting of the trowel. He might bawl at us, but I knew he was rather proud of us all too.

Mother still looked almost the same as she did when I was a child, unconquerable. Perhaps she was a little stouter and her black hair was slightly streaked with grey, but she had the same smile, the same sparkling blue eyes and lightness of step.

She was, as always, a tremendous well of inspiration to me. Although we now had many quarrels, there was a queer, almost uncanny link between us that could make the one wince at what the other felt. She knew that I was feeling my own position in life more acutely as I got older, and she sought to soften the reality of it a little, to give me her own strength and spirit, if only by showing me that I wasn't alone. She was something more than a mother to me; she was a comrade in arms.

Katriona Delahunt was also a great help, someone quite apart from my own path of life who made me realize the necessity of trying to rise above the ordinary standard of thought and activity around me. To my adolescent mind she spoke of something so beautiful and elevated that I wondered sometimes if she wasn't some lovely illusion that would suddenly vanish away.

So I went on painting my little watercolours, painting things I had never seen, but only imagined, like village scenes, ships, and so on. But now even painting couldn't satisfy me. I still *liked* it, but I had ceased to *love* it. There was some new need in me that couldn't be expressed just by putting bright colours onto paper and working them into a pattern. I needed a broader medium.

Then suddenly one day I had an idea. I had always been fond of writing letters, mostly to Katriona Delahunt. But now I decided to try something more ambitious, not just letters, but stories. I hadn't read much before this. Books were rare in our house. Bread was thought more important. Still, I had lots of ideas crowding my mind which I couldn't express through my paints and brushes. I would try and pin them down on paper through the use of words.

Immediately I got a sixpenny jotter and began to write. I hardly knew what I was doing. I just sat there, writing down whatever came into my head. It was a crazy jumble of words, sentences and paragraphs that hadn't the least relation to one another. It was just like mixing my paints and letting them all run into one mass of colour. I played with words like a child fascinated by a new toy, writing them down and then looking at them in a sort of wonder.

Later I tried to weave them into a pattern, just like I did with my paints. Finally I started to put thoughts behind what I wrote, so that in a little while they were not merely words but ideas.

I had first learned to write with my toes when I was five years old, but I had to wait till I was almost seventeen before I realized that it could give me the key to a new sort of life, that with it I could explore new realms of thought and build for myself a world in which I might live alone, independent of others. Just as Peter and the rest built their houses with bricks, so could I now build, not just a house, but a whole world of my own. From then on writing became my only real interest, and a pencil was seldom out of my foot. I wrote stories about the American Wild West, based mostly on memories of my childhood days at the "pictures". The characters in them were tobacco-chewing, gun-slinging men who rode all day and drank all night, and girls with streamlined figures and roving eyes who never seemed to do anything except kick up their legs and drink gin. Often I'd start a story with about twenty characters in it, but about halfway through I'd become confused and wouldn't know what to do with them all, so I'd let them all be shot in turn till only about two were left. My jotter would become a graveyard.

Then I started to be sentimental and wrote wistful little tales based on a "boy-meets-girl" theme. These were full of wishful thinking, and although I enjoyed the actual writing of them they always left me sad when I remembered that I would never experience such things myself.

My emotional life had already begun to emerge. What had been mere childish whims were now adult needs. I was a cripple but that didn't mean that I didn't want the things that made up the everyday lives of other fellows: football, dances, beer parties and girls.

Then the final calamity happened. One day when Katriona Delahunt came to visit me, I saw something sparkle brightly on her finger as she placed her hand on the chair that stood in a shaft of sunlight. It was a diamond engagement ring. A few minutes later she held out her hand with a blush and showed mother the ring, asking her if she liked it. After mother had congratulated her she turned and showed it to me. I grunted and turned my head away.

"Don't make a sour face," she said to me with one of her special smiles. "I'll still come to see you after I'm married."

She was married some months later on a fine June morning in the University Church. I was brought down by mother in my wheel-chair. There was a large crowd of Katriona's friends present, but as she and her husband came out of the church she saw me and a bright smile lit up her darling face. I had no resistance against that.

She was now Katriona Delahunt no longer, but Mrs. Maguire, a very nice name, but it was a long time before I could get used to it. I met Mr. Maguire. He was kind, but I was very jealous.

I remembered how sad I had been as a child when I first found out that I was "different" from other people. I thought the world had ended for me then. But only now was I beginning to feel the full significance of that "difference". As a child I had cried bitterly when I became conscious of my own crippledom. I didn't cry now—I hadn't the comfort of tears. All my agony was inside.

On the night of my seventeenth birthday I got up from the sofa where I had been lying and managed to make my way out into the back garden. I was hot and wanted a little air. I crawled over and sat down on a broken piece of plank under a tree. It was June and the air was filled with the scent of flowers. I could hear the least sound, from the twittering of birds in the branches above me to the honking of car horns in the distance. The moonlight made a pattern on the ground in front of me through the waving branches of the stunted old tree I was sitting under. The back window was a square of yellow light and the sound of voices came to my ears from the kitchen within.

It was a beautiful night, calm, gentle, yet alive. As I looked about at all that was normal and perfect around me, I asked myself for the hundredth time why I was made different, why I should have been given the same feelings as other people along with a practically functionless body that not only denied me the right to live a normal life, but also made me sick at the sight of myself. What prospect had I of being anything else other than the cripple who painted with his toes? People always thought it was a marvellous thing that I could paint, but what difference did it make? I only wanted to be ordinary, like everyone else. I used my left foot simply because I couldn't use my hands, but it did not make me feel proud. What was I but one of God's practical jokes? My life seemed without purpose or worth. I was imprisoned within the walls that I now felt closing in around me. I longed passionately to break loose and escape.

CHAPTER 6

Whatever little willpower I might have had seemed to be ebbing away from me. I came to dread the thought of having to face another day. Worst of all, I began to feel that there was something cruel and senseless behind my affliction. If I thought of God at all, it was only with a sense of resentment. I prayed each night with the others, but I did so automatically, without putting any thought or sincerity behind what I said.

Then one day Katriona Maguire came to me and said, "Christy, what about your going to Lourdes?"

All my life I'd heard people talk of it and I felt a strong wish to go there, partly for the adventure of travelling and partly because, despite my lack of interest in religion, I had the hope deep down that a miracle might happen to me.

"Yes," I said. "But . . . what about the money?"

The trip would cost £34. The people organizing the pilgrimage helped me out by giving £10 towards the fare; the next day mother touched my very old aunt for a "fiver". That was just about as far as we could go.

"Well," said Mrs. Maguire, "I'll get the rest somehow. I'll invite round all my friends and make them play bridge for something tremendous, like five shillings a hundred, and see that they all lose and send you to Lourdes with the proceeds." She smiled her enchanting smile, and I knew it would be all right. It was.

For hours before I left I was very jittery. This was my first trip abroad, and I would be travelling without anyone I knew. Would the people understand me? How would I get my meals? Even at seventeen I still had to be fed, dressed and washed and father looked after all my natural functions. I was nearly helpless—except for my left foot.

Mother saw me off at the airport with Mrs. Maguire and her husband, who drove me out there. I was lifted into the plane by two sturdy ambulance men, and put on a seat next to a window, much to my joy. Everything was done so efficiently, and all was so nice and cosy inside the plane that I quite forgot to worry. The doctor was nice, the priest was nice and the nurses were nice, especially one with dark eyes and fair hair. "Cherry Ripe" I called her.

Soon we were flying out over the Irish Sea, and I looked at my fellow pilgrims for the first time. On the seat next to me sat a girl of nineteen, her bright auburn hair framing a pretty smiling face, though one lined with pain. Her legs and spine were paralysed. She told me her name was Màire and that she came from County Wicklow. She talked about books and films and her sister who went to dances and told her about them afterwards. I thought she seemed happy in spite of everything. But later I heard her sigh wearily and saw her pass a hand across her forehead as if in a gesture of pain. "Please God," she said, "I'll walk again some day. And then I'll go to my first dance." She died at Lourdes two days later.

There was a little chap from Kerry who'd lost the use of both legs as well as his right hand a few weeks before. All he could talk about was the cow he used to milk on the farm. We all made fun of him, because he talked with a country brogue, but it didn't bother him, and he went on talking about "Nellie", his cow, and how he would milk her again when he got better.

There was the smiling little girl, deaf and dumb, clutching her big doll tightly. Right behind me lay a young woman who had contracted tuberculosis after the birth of her first baby a year ago. She lay prone on a stretcher, pale and worn, moaning feebly now and then. A few days before we were due to return to Dublin she died, still in great pain.

As I saw those people each with his or her own suffering, a new light began to dawn upon me. Not only were all those people afflicted, but their handicaps were worse than my own! I felt as if I had been blind all along and that only now was I seeing with my eyes and feeling with my heart the plight of others whose burdens were so great as to make mine seem nothing in comparison.

At last our plane touched down and we were in France. We were placed in an ambulance which took us along long winding roads to the convent where we were to stay during our seven days' pilgrimage. This was in the little town of Lourdes itself.

As our van drew into the square before the convent I caught my first view of the famous Basilica and beautiful Rosary Square. The long, slender spire with its golden cross rose sheer up into the brilliant blue sky, and from within the depths of the chapel came the rhythmical chant of a choir singing a hymn to Mary.

We were lifted from the ambulance, put into chairs like Chinese rickshaws and wheeled into the convent. In the ward everything was cool and bright, but towards night I began to feel very lonely and forgotten. I tried hard to pray, but I kept thinking of home and my parents. I was just about to hide my head under the blankets and give way to tears when the door opened and the night nurse came in. My heart gave a leap—it was "Cherry Ripe" again, a cluster of golden curls peeping coquettishly from beneath her stiff white nurse's cap. She went from bed to bed, making sure we were all comfortable. She arrived at my bed, smiled brightly and asked if I would like to be tucked in some more.

"Oh, yes," I said, although I was as tucked in as could be.

"There we are," she smiled as she doubled the edges of the sheets under the mattress. The last thing I remember as I went off to sleep was her smiling as she bent over me to pull the clothes up over my shoulder. I slept soundly that night.

Next morning we were brought down to the famous Healing Baths, where already there were big crowds of various nationalities assembled, all waiting to touch the wonderful waters of the underground spring over which the modern baths were built.

As I waited my turn, I looked about me. There must have been close on three hundred people gathered in the small forecourt. Nearly three-quarters of them were in wheelchairs like myself— legless, armless, sightless, some looking like living corpses as they lay under the newly risen sun. Among them all, I felt very small and insignificant.

Then it was my turn to go in to be bathed. I was wheeled in, sat on a wooden bench and stripped naked by two Frenchmen. All the cubicles in the building were of marble, the "bath" being a deep, square cavity hewn out of the floor itself, with steps leading down to the water. On the wall opposite hung a simple wooden crucifix with prayers inscribed in Latin beneath it.

I was lifted gently by each arm, carried down the steps and then lowered into the water slowly. The two men above me recited prayers in French, and then I gasped as I felt the cold water go over my head. They lifted me out and one of them held a small cross to my lips for me to kiss.

It may have been pure fancy, I don't know, but after I had got out of that water I felt as if I was reborn; it was like stepping out from a tomb into the light of day.

That afternoon I saw the Grotto for the first time. As I was wheeled down the broad road leading to the Shrine, throngs of pilgrims passed me by and the air was filled with a dozen languages. Everyone had a common purpose that day, to pray and to hope.

When I arrived at the Grotto I could see nothing but a multitude of people kneeling before it with bowed heads.

Soon I was at the altar rails along with the others in wheelchairs. I timidly lifted my eyes up and gazed on the marble statue of the tall, beautiful Lady in the blue robe, with the little peasant girl kneeling before her, her hands clasped in ecstasy. From her niche hewn out of the solid wall of rock, Mary gazed serenely down on the vast gathering of her children who now knelt at her feet and gave her their sorrows as well as their love.

I prayed and I prayed that I might be cured.

That night, as dusk descended and shrouded the surrounding hills in a veil of mist, thousands gathered in the Rosary Square for a torchlight procession from the Basilica to the Shrine. The entire façade of the beautiful Basilica was illuminated, sparkling vividly against the black velvet of the night sky.

As we wended our way through the little town on the road to the Grotto the crowd lifted their voices and sang "Ave Maria". The notes rose and fell on the soft night air and echoed back from the nearby hills. Thousands more lined the route, all holding lighted candles, flickering in the gentle breeze.

In contrast, the Grotto itself was in darkness, save for a single candle on the marble altar. The crowd, still singing, knelt in a semicircle round the Shrine, the flames from their candles lighting up the scene and sparkling on the crown of pearls circling the Virgin's head.

It was the most beautiful moment of my life.

CHAPTER 7

Lourdes left a lasting impression on my mind. I saw that, far from being alone and isolated as I thought myself to be, I was merely one of a brotherhood of suffering that stretched over the whole globe. Yet once I was at home again, away from the glory of Lourdes and from all the things that had made me forget myself in that first rush of communion with others, an awful sense of loneliness and disappointment began to creep in upon me and play havoc with my thoughts.

One Thursday evening, about seven days after my return from Lourdes, I was sitting at my window gazing gloomily out into the gathering autumn dusk that was slowly covering the street outside in a dark purple haze. In the kitchen behind me I could hear the sausages frizzling in the pan as mother got the dinner ready with all the children chattering around her.

Suddenly from out the corner of my eye I saw the headlights of a car piercing the deepening twilight as it came round the bend in the road. It stopped outside our door. A man stepped out, paused to peer uncertainly at the number of the house, then opened the front gate, came up the steps and knocked at the front door.

Hearing the knock, mother went to answer it. I heard her speaking to someone at the hall door, and a moment later she came back into the kitchen with the strange man.

"This is Christy," she told him as they entered.

I looked up at him as he stood smiling down at me. He was a well-built man with grey-green eyes, eyes that, while they looked at me, seemed at the same time to look *into* me.

He sat down on a chair close by and told me he was a doctor who had seen me before as a baby. Somehow he hadn't forgotten me, and had started to look for me a few days ago.

"Christy," he said in his deep, pleasant voice, "there is a new treatment for cerebral palsy. I believe you can be cured—but only if you are willing to try hard enough with us. You must *want* to get better before anything can be done for you." Then he leaned forward, his eyes steady on me, "Will you try if I help?" he asked.

"Will I try!" I thought.

I couldn't speak. I could only stare. But he must have read the message in my eyes, for he stood up, satisfied, came over to me, put his arm round my shoulders and said: "Right! We'll start tomorrow."

He said he would send out one of his assistants to examine me and devise a special line of treatment, as the method was to treat each patient individually. I would be treated at home, as they hadn't as yet formed a special clinic of their own.

He stood up to go, then paused. "By the way," he said with a slow smile, "my name's Dr. Collis." With that he left.

As the door closed upon him, I turned and looked at the faces around me. They were all lit up with excitement. Father was so overjoyed that his hand trembled as he poured me out some tea and Peter, good old Peter, put two spoonfuls of salt instead of sugar into his cup.

But it was at mother that I looked most of all. There was a quiet air of joy about her that meant more to me than if she had thrown her arms about my neck and wept with thanksgiving.

And I—what did I feel at that moment of my life, the moment I had so longed for and dreamed about? For a while I didn't feel or think of anything. It was too much for me to grasp the idea that I could be cured at last. I listened in a trance to all the others talking excitedly around me. I couldn't distinguish a word. I sipped my tea absently each time father lifted the cup to my lips.

It was later, as I sat round the fire with mother and father when the rest had gone out, that I started to think about the news I had heard that day, and only then did the reality of it come to my mind. I had gone to Lourdes joyful and full of hope. A week later I had come home, a little shaken and maybe a little wiser, but disappointed. Everything had seemed just as it was before. Then, even while I was still thinking bitterly about it, a doctor had suddenly come in and told me that I could be cured! In a very few words he had changed the pattern of my whole life; he had given me something to fasten my aspirations to at the moment when I was sure that there was nothing but empty and fruitless years before me.

To me, because of all it meant and brought to me later, it then seemed, and has seemed since, nothing less than a beautiful little miracle, because it created faith where before there had been only bitterness and disillusion. It showed me that in the great Plan of life we all matter, and that I too had a part to play, no matter how small it was.

That night, before I went to sleep, I prayed a prayer of thankfulness—and repentance for having doubted.

THE DOCTOR who came next day to examine me was a young man, tall, handsome, with a certain military bearing that impressed even while it subdued me a little. He was slow and deliberate in his movements and his whole manner suggested an easy confidence. I felt myself liking him at once. His name was Louis Warnants.

Dr. Warnants drew up a special line of treatment that consisted mostly in certain physical exercises which I could carry out myself at home. This, he told me, was only a preliminary test. If he saw that I was responding, no matter how slightly, he would then put me to a much harder routine.

After that Dr. Warnants came once a week. Each time he came he made me go through the exercises while he looked on, taking careful note of the ones I found most difficult to do and pointing out to me where I went wrong.

Everyone at home used to rush about and fall over themselves
every Sunday afternoon when the hour approached for Dr.
Warnants to come. They were all a little in awe of him, for although
he was a nice gentleman and his manners impeccable, there were
no half measures about him; he took his job very seriously.

It was very difficult for Dr. Warnants to treat me in the house
because the only room available was the kitchen, and that was much
too small. During exercises, when I stretched out my leg, it would
bang against the firegrate, and when I turned round on my stomach
my head would be under a chair and my legs beneath the table, so
that each time I lifted my head it'd get a resounding smack.

"You're too big, Christy, or this room's too small," he said.

"I think it's a mixture of both, doctor," said mother.

At the back of the house there was a bit of waste ground which
everybody at home had tried to cultivate but in vain. True, they had
succeeded in raising cabbage and turnips there once in a while, but
after a time they all seemed to wither and die.

Now, mother had a sudden brainwave. It would help both Dr.
Warnants and myself greatly if we had a room to ourselves. So,
mother thought, why not build that room on the ground at the back?
Ah, but the money—there was always the question of money! By
making unobtrusive little inquiries among father and the boys, she
was able to estimate that the cost of the building materials would be
a cool £50.

Still, she would not let this defeat her. She was determined to put
her ambitious notion into practice. So for several weeks she plunged
secretly into cash-gathering: borrowing, selling, visiting the
pawnshop, looking up well-to-do old uncles and aunts.

When she had netted about £20 she decided to make a start. She
knew it was useless putting the matter to father, for he'd oppose it
on the grounds that the "Authorities", a favourite word of his,
wouldn't allow it because the house we were living in was subject to
certain rules of a body of people known as the City Corporation.

So mother decided to take matters into her own hands and start
immediately herself. She went out one afternoon and ordered a
hundred concrete blocks, four bags of cement and two bags of
mortar, "For a start," she said!

The stuff arrived the same day. Poor father almost collapsed when
he came home from work that evening and saw all the concrete
blocks piled up neatly in the front garden. He staggered up to the

door and said in a sort of hoarse whisper to mother, "What's the idea?"

"Oh, I forgot to tell you," said mother casually as she put his dinner on the table. "I'm going to build a house for Christy in the back garden."

"My God!" said father, staring at her. "Do you want us all to be evicted? Do you realize what the Authorities will——"

"Yes, yes, I know all that," said mother quietly. "But do take your dinner now, like a good man, or it'll be cold on you."

Father next resorted to a plan of non-cooperation, saying that he wouldn't set one block and that he'd advise the four other bricklayers in the house to have nothing to do with it either.

Mother just smiled and said: "Very well, if none of you will do it, I'll build it myself."

They all laughed at that—the idea of a woman building a house.

Next day mother rose particularly early, got breakfast ready very fast, sent the six younger children off to school and got through all the household work during the morning. Lunchtime came and went as usual.

At about four o'clock that afternoon I became aware of peculiar sounds coming from the back garden. Very curious, I managed to stumble to the pantry window and I looked out.

There was mother, on her knees on the grass, a bucket of cement on one side of her and a jug of water on the other. She held a trowel in her right hand. She was looking proudly at the line of blocks she had already set out before her.

That evening when she had served dinner and tea, she went quietly back to her work in the garden. A few minutes later, father went outside and saw her. He stood stock still, then slowly approached the growing wall. He touched it with his foot. "What's this?" he asked.

Mother looked up. "I'm building Christy's house," she said.

Father said nothing for a minute or so, he just watched. Then his hand went out; he pulled it back. His upper lip twitched a bit; he paused . . . . At last he said, "Look-it! You're doing it all wrong, woman. Where's your foundation?"

"I knew I was forgetting something," mother answered rather crossly.

By this time the other four bricklayers had gathered round.

"Look-it, boys," said father, turning to them. "Your mother's trying to do *our* work!"

"Terrible," said Paddy, shaking his head disapprovingly at the row of blocks. "You haven't even got them level, mother!"

"That's women for you," said Peter, "always trying to be like men. Go back to your dishes, ma."

"Well, if it's a man's job, get on with it," she said. She just stood up and wiped her hands on her apron. Slowly she turned and left them. As she passed me she smiled.

The five bricklayers stood and looked at each other.

"C'mon," said father. "Let's start."

So they built my little house. The work went through many vicissitudes and it looked at one time as though it would never be finished. The thing that held us up most was money. Mother's £20 had been used up quickly and we seemed to come to a standstill. Then mother managed to scrape together another few pounds and the work was resumed. They appointed me foreman, and from time to time I pointed out to them what way I'd like certain parts of it built and where I wanted the fireplace, the window and the door.

By degrees the place began to take shape; the chimney was up, the window panes were in and the walls were plastered. Then piece by piece the furniture was moved in—a divan, a bed, a few chairs and a table. My brother-in-law, a sawyer, made me a handsome little bureau in which to hold some odds and ends. Lino was put down, wallpaper put up and curtains hung. In a few days more the electric light was installed. It was ready at last.

It was originally intended only to make a sort of exercise room of it, where Dr. Warnants might treat me undisturbed. As time went on, however, I slowly converted it into both a living room and study, where I ate, read, wrote and slept. I got bookshelves put up for me which were gradually filled.

Thus at last I had really broken away from the noise and busy life of the house. I could live in comfortable solitude and paint and write as much as I liked in perfect freedom. In summer, I could sit by the open window and read, the only sound being the happy chorus of the birds in the trees outside, and when the winter came it was even more pleasant, for then I'd sit by the fire in the dark and watch the red glow dance on the walls and fall on the backs of books on the shelves, making their gilt lettering stand out in the gloom.

My reading was still rather limited, my chief companion being Charles Dickens. I read six or seven of his books in very quick succession, and my special favourite was *David Copperfield*, which I read three times with unabated eagerness.

It had been largely through my father, that strange inarticulate man, that I had gained entry into the world of books. He was a generous man and never failed to give us our pocket money at the weekend, no matter how hard the times might be, and they were usually very hard indeed. The amount of pocket money meted out varied according to our ages. My weekly dowry came to one shilling and sixpence, an enormous sum in my eyes, with—to his everlasting credit—no concession to my crippledom. The others usually spent their money right away, going to the pictures, buying comics or illicit cigarettes, but I stored mine like a miser until over a couple of months I had accumulated quite a little nest egg. Then I would send away for books, mostly from Thomas Nelson in London and their famous list of Classics—Sterne, Trollope, George Eliot, Stevenson, and of course Dickens, who became a god to me. Through these books a door was opened, and my "education" began. To this day I believe it was better than any school could hand out. Without being priggish about it, I still believe that had I been able to go to school to be "educated" I would never have had a single original thought in my head or written a single original word. So my physical handicap, while being something of a straitjacket, became in time almost an asset. From being a mere fly on the wall I became almost overnight an eagle, and all through the one shilling and sixpence pocket money my father gave me and the magic it helped me buy.

CHAPTER 8

Dr. Warnants and I were able to make better headway now that we had more space for my exercises, but this treatment was still very crude and slow. One day Dr. Collis came and told me that he had

354

decided to send me over to London to see his sister-in-law Mrs. Eirene Collis, who was a well-known specialist in cerebral palsy. He wanted to get her opinion as to whether I was likely to respond to a full-scale rehabilitation programme.

I would travel to London by air with mother. Dr. Warnants, who had gone over ahead of me, would meet us at Northolt Airport and drive me to Middlesex Hospital.

I realized then that everything depended on Mrs. Collis's verdict. If she decided I was too far advanced a case to benefit from treatment, then I would be back to where I was before Dr. Collis found me, back to the old life of inactivity and hopelessness. If, on the other hand, she should conclude that I would respond favourably to treatment, then my life would have some ultimate worth and value. I could begin to break down some of the walls that stood between me and an ōrdinary existence.

I was at the crossroads.

We all expected mother to be excited, and indeed a little nervous, for this was to be her first air trip, but she took the prospect of flying quite calmly.

"Might as well die in the air as on the ground," she summed it up. Next day she went out and bought a new hat, a tiny black satin thing with a huge plumage of feathers and a dark veil.

Father looked at it critically from all angles, and scratched his head. "Hmm . . . very—er—artistic. What's it supposed to be?"

"Too bright," Peter chimed in. "People will start calling you Mrs. Peacock."

In spite of this, mother wore her new hat the day we flew to London, and smiled triumphantly when Dr. Collis said he liked it.

We arrived at Northolt at eleven o'clock on a bright, cold January morning. Dr. Warnants was there to meet us and hoisted me across his shoulder and into a waiting taxi. I didn't like this mode of travelling on a person's back. It made me feel foolish. I would much rather have crawled to the taxi.

I looked out of the window as the car wound its way through the London traffic, seeing the big jostling crowds outside the huge shop windows, the ceaseless stream of red buses and motorcars and cyclists. Over all rose the sounds that issue up from the heart of a great city every moment of the day. Then the car pulled up outside a huge stone building with a great many steps leading up to it—the Middlesex Hospital.

We were taken up in a lift to a consulting room to wait for Mrs. Collis. Dr. Warnants smiled as he helped me into a chair.

"Scared?" he asked me.

I shook my head just to give myself courage.

"You are, you know," he continued, looking at me. "You're scared stiff, but you're too stubborn to admit it. That's good."

Mother was perfect, she just sat calmly looking through some magazines that were on the table, munching ham sandwiches she had brought along with her. This was the first time she had ever been outside Dublin, and yet she seemed as calm and cheerful as if she had been at home in the kitchen cutting bread for tea.

I knew very well that inwardly she was feeling and thinking the same things as myself, that she understood as well as I how my whole life would be ruled according to this interview. Without as much as speaking one word, she gave me a part of her own courage and strength to face up to it.

Suddenly the door behind me opened. I looked round and my eyes were drawn at once towards a small thin woman with greying hair, handsome face and light, springy step—Mrs. Collis. In her presence my doubts and apprehensions soon vanished, because there was something about her slow smile and complete naturalness that made me feel secure.

"Sorry I'm late," she said, sitting on the edge of the desk and lighting a cigarette. For a few moments she just sat chatting about things like the weather, the cost of cigarettes and Mr. Churchill. Then she slid off the desk and strolled over to me.

"How old are you, Christy?" she asked me, and when mother attempted to tell her my age she held up her hand and said politely: "Let Christy tell me himself."

I managed to grunt that I was seventeen.

"Seventeen?" said Mrs. Collis. "Seventeen years a cripple is quite enough for anyone. Don't you think it's time you did something about it?" I nodded my head in agreement. "Yes, so do I!" she said. "Well then, let's see if we can make anything of you."

I was stripped and put lying on the couch while Mrs. Collis examined me, helped by Dr. Warnants. I didn't understand what they were talking about most of the time. I caught words like "cerebrum", "basal ganglia", "incoordination", and many other mystic-sounding words which were unintelligible to me.

When the examination was over they helped me on with my

356

clothes again. After that Mrs. Collis, Dr. Warnants and mother withdrew to the further corner of the room to speak among themselves for a while. I sat alone on the couch, my heart beating quickly, waiting desperately for the verdict. It was as if I were on trial for my life.

At last Mrs. Collis came across the room slowly and sat down on the couch beside me.

"Well, Christy," she said. "You haven't come to London in vain. I can find no reason why you shouldn't be cured eventually."

My heart gave a leap of pure joy. All the old bitterness and heartache was changed now into an all-pervading happiness that lit up my face and made my heart dance wildly.

"Yes," continued Mrs. Collis. "You can be cured if you are prepared to do lots of really hard work over the next few years. But—" here she paused, looked steadily at me, and went on—"you must first make a big sacrifice—you must resolve never to use your left foot again."

My left foot! But that meant everything to me—I could speak only with that, create only with that! My left foot was the only workable thing in my whole body. Without it I would be silent, powerless.

"Yes, I know it's tough," she said, interpreting my thoughts. "But it's the only way out. If you continue to use your left foot you may one day become a great artist or writer with it—but you'll never be cured. You'll never walk, or talk or use your hands, or lead a normal life."

She explained that, although the use of my foot was good for me mentally since it had provided an outlet for my imprisoned mind to express itself, if I could no longer use my foot I would then have to concentrate on making some use of the rest of my body. All very logical, I thought. But there was such a big difference between *thinking* about those things and actually carrying them through! It wasn't just a question of tying up my poor old left foot. It went far deeper than that. I felt as if I was about to lock myself up and throw away the key.

Still, what could I do but make the "deal"? If I took the chance and "cut off" my left foot, as it were, then I'd enter into a completely new mode of thinking and acting, and that in itself would be something worth any sacrifice. It would be frightful, but it might bring victory in the end.

"I will," I said—and they were the clearest words I had ever uttered.

She took my hand and pressed it, her eyes alight. "Good boy. It's not going to be easy. You must put your whole mind behind the work we're going to give you, and even then it will be slow, terribly slow, especially at your age."

We flew back to Dublin that night and were met at the airport by Dr. Collis. He told me that he had recently succeeded in forming a Cerebral Palsy Clinic in Dublin, and the Knights of Malta and the St. John Ambulance Brigade had agreed to provide transport to bring the crippled children to and from the clinic for treatment. I was to start attending it on the following Monday morning.

"There's nothing you can't conquer, Christy," he said to me, putting his hand on my shoulder: "And remember I'm with you all the way."

But I knew then that my first task was to conquer myself, and that the real battle was only beginning.

I WAS VERY EXCITED at the prospect of going to the clinic, but on the memorable Monday morning, when the St. John's ambulance pulled up outside our door, I glanced at it from the window apprehensively. I had always thought of ambulances as in some way connected with funerals: sombre, spirit-chilling things, full of bleeding bodies.

However, the driver was a cheerful, smiling man who helped father to lift me. That made me a little less afraid. As I sat down on the seat I looked about at my fellow-patients. I saw that I was very much the oldest amongst them. On the stretcher before me lay a small child, not more than a baby, with stiff arms and bent, crooked legs and a head that lay at a queer angle to the rest of his body. Beside him sat a little girl with bright golden hair and very large eyes. She was very pretty, but her legs were thin and misshapen with protruding bones, and her restless, shaking hands were like my own, but smaller and more fragile. She kept smiling the whole time, and trying to brush her fair ringlets out of her eyes. On the seat next to me a little child lay, completely inert, with set, frozen features that were expressionless but for her eyes, which moved restlessly and inquiringly around. Those two eyes were the only living things about her—they were like two lighted windows in a dark house.

At last the ambulance drew into Merrion Street and came to a stop outside a big stone-grey building. I caught sight of Dr. Warnants coming down the steps and felt reassured when I saw him again. I couldn't walk, and there was no sign of any car or chair to wheel me into the building. I looked at Dr. Warnants, and he looked back at me.

"I'll have to do the strong-man act again, old boy," he said with a shrug of his shoulders. Then he gripped me round the legs and threw me over his back. As he carried me up the steps I saw a little gold plaque on the wall which was inscribed:

"Dublin Orthopaedic Hospital."

That sounds bad, I said to myself. I wonder what that awfully big word means anyway?

From my position over Dr. Warnants's shoulder I couldn't see my surroundings very well, but from a constant view of the floor I knew that we were passing right through the building. We went down a flight of stairs, walked along a corridor, opened a rickety old door at the end, and came out into daylight again.

"That's one journey," said Dr. Warnants in between pants. "Now for the other."

I could see there was grass on either side of the gravel path I was being carried over, and by lifting my head from its downward angle I got a view of a long, narrow wooden building, single-storied, which looked like a gymnasium hut. As we approached it I heard sounds of children's voices.

The doctor pushed open the door and went in, still carrying me over his shoulder. The moment we entered the full force of the noise hit me with an almost physical sensation. Children were crying, roaring, screaming, banging toys and anything they could find against the walls and floor, kicking their legs in the air, crawling and wriggling like crabs over one another. It was awful. I looked about me as Dr. Warnants dumped me on the floor and wondered if I had been taken to the wrong place, for I saw that there was not one child there over three years of age.

"No treatment this morning, Christy," said Dr. Warnants with a smile. "Just relax and look on."

Looking on was treatment in itself. It was an education in human suffering, a new, rather frightening experience for one who, until lately, had never seen life beyond the walls of his own home. In the light of this altogether new aspect of life which now lay before me, the things I had seen at Lourdes were only a shadow. The afflicted people I had met there were all adults, some in great pain, of course, with nothing but wrecked lives behind or before them, but still quite capable of understanding their own affliction. But here there was no reasoning, only helplessness, and near-horror in the form of twisting, twining babies with crooked little limbs, mis-shapen heads, distorted features, some lying huddled on the floor, inert and motionless, like empty sacks thrown carelessly here and there around the room. Others were convulsed with wild, endless movement, their little hands clenched, their legs bent and locked together as if in a vice, their heads awry.

Suddenly I realized for the first time what I myself had looked like as a child.

I could easily have pitied them, but I did not, for I remembered how bitterly a look of pity had hurt me once. Instead of pity, I began to feel an affinity with those children, a link that enabled me to see and to *feel* the real personalities which lay behind the grotesquely working faces and tense taut limbs. I saw that I was not the only one who was shut away behind prison bars.

After about a week at the clinic, during which time, as Dr. Warnants put it, I was being "conditioned", I was slowly initiated into the mode of treatment. I found that it was similar to that which I had been receiving at home, except that the exercises at the clinic were more intricate—and a lot more arduous to perform. At first, to be quite truthful, I felt rather silly doing them among a roomful of kids—like an elephant among a lot of kittens.

Often, as I pulled myself along on my stomach in amongst the children—this was all part of the exercises for I wasn't allowed to move about on my behind as I used to do—I'd stop suddenly, as though becoming aware of my surroundings for the first time, look slowly around at all the twisting and inert forms lying about me on the floor, at the face of Dr. Warnants as he bent over the children, and ask myself:

"What am I, Christy Brown, doing here? Why am I in this queer place, instead of writing in the bedroom at home?"

I still hadn't become accustomed to the "outside world" as yet. I still couldn't grasp the reality of it all—the fact that I was now a part of this new and fast-moving world of people and places.

Many times, as I sat hunched on the floor staring unseeingly before me, I'd feel a toe nudging me from behind. I'd start and look around, and there'd be Dr. Warnants, standing above me and smiling. "Daydreaming again!" he'd say. "Snap out of it, old boy! There's a job to be done, you know."

Yes, I knew there *was* a job to be done, and quite a job too. A job that wouldn't be done in a year, two years, or even five years—a job, in fact, that would take a lifetime.

THE FIRST JOB I had to be taught at the clinic was to relax. That may sound easy, but I found it the most difficult part of the morning's work. To relax one's muscles completely, to make them as limp as wet paper, it is necessary to relax one's mind first. That is something I find nearly impossible. I have a very restless mind, and I am always intensely aware of the scene around me: the noise, the interplay of light and shade, people's expressions, the inflections of their voices.

Working under the physiotherapists that formed the staff, first at the Merrion Street clinic and later when the clinic moved to bigger premises, I learned to walk in specially-made skis, and to make more use of my hands. I learned to mould shapes out of plasticine— they usually turned out to be the most unshapely shapes imaginable!—manipulated dumbbells from one hand to the other, and so on.

Speech has always been one of the biggest obstacles in my endeavour to make ordinary contact with people. It has been the one aspect of my handicap that has caused me the bitterest pain, for without speech one is practically lost, curtained off from other people. Writing is all very well, but there are some emotions that cannot be "felt" through the written word alone. I would rather have an hour's fierce argument with a pal or a few moments of soft chatter with a girl than write the greatest book on earth. Now, however, I began to speak more. This was due to the special treatment I received from the clinic's speech therapist, Dr. Patricia Sheehan. Dr. Sheehan told me that I had got into the habit of breathing anyhow, in jerks. That wouldn't do, she said. I would never speak properly unless I learned how to control my breathing.

The first breathing lesson I had was—blowing bubbles! One morning Dr. Sheehan brought a little tin box filled with soapy water, took out from her pocket a tiny metal ring with a handle on it, dipped it into the water and then told me to blow away the watery film that had formed inside the ring. I looked at her, thinking it was a joke. But I saw she was serious, so I took a breath, pursed my lips and blew. Immediately a perfect hail of vapoury balls began falling about me from all angles. I started to hum "I'm Forever Blowing Bubbles."

361

Then it became a little tougher. Along with my friend John, another adult patient attending the clinic, I was taught to deepen my breathing in rather a novel way: by blowing water through a tube from one bottle to another. The two bottles were airtight, and the rubber tube ran from one into the other. One of the bottles would be filled with coloured water and the plan was to blow the contents of the full bottle through the connecting tube into the empty one and gradually fill it.

It sounds simple, but I found it very hard indeed. I puffed and puffed till I was red in the face, but only a miserable few drops of water trickled through into the empty bottle. John's turn came next and in a matter of seconds he had blown all the water from one bottle into the other, for John had a first-class pair of lungs.

As time went on I became a little better at the water-blowing business, and I found after some months that my speech had improved considerably: I took greater care to make certain I articulated each word slowly and distinctly and to say what I wanted to say calmly. Now I can speak quite well if only I take my time about it and do not get flustered when I cannot get out a word clearly.

In time I came to regard the clinic as being in some way a part of me, a necessary part of my life. It had its doctors and its persons in white, it had its long corridors and cool marble walls. It had all these, but something else besides. It had *spirit* as well as efficiency, genuine human warmth as well as cold scientific precision. The people in the cool white coats had very warm hearts, and in their job a warm heart is an invaluable asset. It counted just as much as their medical skill, for theirs was not an ordinary straightforward job because theirs were not ordinary patients, but human beings faced with many huge problems, problems which cannot merely be summarized under the heading "physical".

We who are handicapped need confidence and friendliness as well as, if not more than, medical treatment. It is not only our muscles and limbs which bother us—sometimes it is our minds as well. A child with a crooked mouth and twisted hands can very quickly and easily develop a set of very crooked and twisted attitudes both towards himself and life in general, unless he is helped to an understanding of them. Life becomes to him just a reflection of his own "crookedness", his own emotional pain.

In the clinic, it was different. Here, we were "among our own", surrounded by people with handicaps similar to, and often worse than, our own, and we saw that our old "difference" is not so different after all. From thinking of ourselves as outcasts and burdens on others, we slowly came to realize that there are people who understand, people who have actually dedicated their lives towards helping us and bringing us to a greater understanding of our own, so that in the end something splendid is wrought out of our affliction.

CHAPTER 9

My experiences at the clinic lifted a curtain from before my eyes, as though I had at last found the key to something that had puzzled and tormented me for a long, long time. It wasn't just something about myself, but about all who had a life similar to my own, a life bounded by high walls on all sides. It had taken years to find, but now I was positive that I had discovered it at last, and suddenly I wanted desperately to communicate it to others.

But—how could I express what I wanted to say? My hands were of no use to me; they were still twisted, powerless to hold or control anything. Nor could my lips utter the thoughts which were whirling round in my mind like swarms of impatient bees, because I still wasn't able to speak any sort of intelligible language outside the family circle.

What about my old friend, my left foot? Could I not use that now?

No! That was impossible. I couldn't go back on my promise to Mrs. Collis. And I knew that if I started to use my left foot again I would be standing in the way of my own recovery.

It seemed I had reached a dead end; everywhere I turned the way was blocked. I felt as anyone would feel with their hands and feet tied and a gag in their mouth.

Then suddenly I had an inspiration. I was sitting in the kitchen one afternoon thinking how I could find a way of putting down all I wanted to say onto paper when I noticed one of my brothers writing at the table. This was Eamonn, just twelve years of age.

I leaned forward and asked him what he was doing.

"Trying to write a composition," he answered with a sigh.

I could see, by the scowl on his face, he wasn't enjoying it very much. The idea of him sitting there writing and yet not knowing what to write about, and me sitting there by the window, my brain teeming with ideas and yet not able to hold a pen in my hand, almost made me want to run amok!

I saw my chance. I told him I'd help him—on condition that he'd do something for me in return.

"Sure I will," he said confidently. "What do you want me to do?"

"Write for me," I told him briefly.

"But I can't even do my own writing!" he protested.

"Fool," I replied. "You'll just hold the pen and I'll tell you what to put down."

My brother was very doubtful about this idea; he felt there was something "fishy" at the back of it. But at the same time he wanted to get that composition right, so in the end he agreed.

When we were done with his homework we went out to my study, got a ninepenny jotter out of the drawer, sat down at the table and looked at each other.

"What d'ye want me to write down for you?" asked my brother innocently, the pen poised in his hand.

I looked out the window at the branches of the trees waving against the bright spring sky, thought a bit, then turned back to look at my young brother's inquiring face.

"My life story," I told him.

Poor Eamonn let his pen clatter down on the table. "Your . . . what?" he asked.

I told him again, and this time he was quite silent.

I was eighteen when I began that first attempt to write my autobiography. It was a ponderous piece of work, a veritable forest of seven- and eight-syllabled words. In my inexperience I imagined it my duty to try and imitate Dickens's style of writing—with the result that I used words and phrases that would have tied up anybody's tongue in a matter of seconds. I still wonder why neither my brother nor I had a nervous breakdown during the writing of that tremendous first attempt. It dragged on and on like a stream of molten lead. My poor brother had written almost four hundred pages of manuscript before I saw that if I went on like this the book would go on for ever.

Its title typified the whole. I called it "The Reminiscences of a Mental Defective"! I meant that to be a nice piece of irony, a sort of punch on the nose for the doctors who had doubted my sanity at the age of five.

The language, if impossible, was gorgeous. Instead of calling myself a cripple and leaving it at that, I spoke of myself as being an "unfortunate item of mortality". Likewise I was also adept at using completely abstract words to express my essentially simple ideas, words like "inconceivability" when I wanted to describe a thing that couldn't happen. I used the word "materialistic" very often when what I really had in mind was something thoughtless and gay, so that I could have said my brother Peter was a materialist because he preferred dances to Dickens!

All this, of course, didn't mean that I didn't know what I wanted to say, but the trouble was that I didn't know *how* to say it. I seldom expressed one individual thought in a single sentence—I required three or four sentences before being satisfied that I'd really expressed my meaning.

I knew there was something wrong somewhere, for before I'd begin dictating, my thoughts would be clear enough, but the moment I began trying to dictate them they'd all go haywire, like fallen leaves blown to and fro by the wind. I found it hard to catch and hold on to them. I became mad at my own stupidity.

I called myself a fool; I called my poor brother a fool. In fact, I called everyone in the house a fool—because I couldn't write as well as I wanted to! The longer the "book" dragged on the more irritable I became. If anything got in my way I'd just lift my foot and kick it violently. I'd get so annoyed that sometimes I wanted to burn the whole thing and put it out of my sight, but by this time I had spent more than a year at it and I couldn't bear to admit, even to myself, that all that work had been in vain. I felt that I could write a good book, if only—if only . . . .

That was it! If only I had someone to advise me, to show me how to write clearly. I needed a guiding hand; I needed someone not only with brains but with a heart as well. But where could I find this somebody, this fairy godfather? I could think of no one. It seemed as if I'd have to carry on by myself as best I could.

Then one day, as I was sitting moodily by the window in a bad temper, too disgusted with myself even to dictate any more, a name suddenly flashed across my mind: "Collis!" Without waiting to think, I yelled for Eamonn, made him get a postcard from the drawer and sent it to Dr. Collis immediately. I was very abrupt.

"Dear Dr. Collis," I wrote, "I'm trying to write a book. If you don't mind, please come and help me. Christy Brown."

It was only after the card had been posted that I began to think about what I had done. I hadn't seen the doctor for over a year, not since I had come back from London. I didn't know much about him, except that he was the founder of the clinic, but I had liked him from the moment I saw him. I hadn't felt any awkwardness in his presence, and that was unusual, because even with people I knew quite well I always felt out of place.

But, after all, he was only a doctor, wasn't he? He might be the nicest man in the world, but what good was that if he couldn't help me to write? Apart from being a nice man, who was he?

It was only later that I found out that he was not just Dr. Collis— but Robert Collis too, the author of the famous play, *Marrowbone Lane*, which described the appalling conditions of the poor of Dublin in the forties. From the proceeds of that play he founded the Marrowbone Lane Fund to help meet the many needs of the working class.

The next day I was in my little study, sitting by the fire reading old Dickens, when the door opened suddenly and Dr. Collis marched in, carrying a large bundle of books under one arm. He dumped the books on the bed, and came over and sat down on the chair at the opposite side of the table. "I got your SOS this morning. So you're writing a book. Well, let's see it."

I had the manuscript in an old leather case under the bed. He pulled it out, put on his glasses and began reading.

As he read the first page I saw him raise his eyebrows. He read the second and the third, and each time his eyebrows went higher. Then he threw down the copy on the table.

"What the hell!" he said. He looked at me keenly to see if I could take criticism and understand. I forced myself to keep a poker face. He smiled. "The language you use may have been popular in the reign of Queen Victoria, but . . ."

My heart sank within me as I heard this. It seemed I was back to where I always had been, wanting to do things and not knowing how. My dreams were too big to come true. How could I ever write a book—I, who had been shut up all my life within the four walls of my home and who had never as much as seen the inside of a school?

I sat with my head bowed as Robert Collis turned over more pages of that awful manuscript. Sometimes he grunted to himself. Then suddenly he stopped and sat upright in the chair. I looked up in surprise. His face was smiling with approval.

"Good!" he exclaimed excitedly. "One sentence here stands out like a rose among a lot of weeds. It shows me that you could write if you knew how. That's what I wanted to find out."

Then he got up and had a look at the few books I had on the shelves. He shook his head. "To write good modern English one has to read modern English, Christy. Dickens is all very well, but . . . literary taste, like all other tastes, changes."

Then he showed me the books he had brought me, and spread them all out on the table: six volumes of a collection of famous literature from all over the world.

"These will show you how English should be written," he said.

He told me that writing was as difficult an art as painting, and to master it one had to practise and cultivate a style of one's own. He told me that, no matter how difficult I found it, I had one good thing in my favour—I *wanted* to write. To do a thing really well, one had to like doing it.

"Christy," he said, leaning forward with his elbows resting on the table, "all this—" pointing to the bundle of copies "—hasn't been in vain. It has given you practice at thinking out ideas. Now, if you still want to write your story—?" He paused and looked at me questioningly. I nodded my head vigorously.

"Right, then," he went on, "If so, you must begin the whole thing again!" Now he began to talk.

I listened as I had never listened before, that evening and many following, and he taught me so many things in so short a time that for a few days I was rather dizzy, like one who suddenly comes upon a treasure chest of jewels and is blinded by their light. In the light of all that I learned from him I saw the many mistakes I had made. But he was very patient; he came out to me, sometimes twice and even three times a week. He showed me how to write in a simple way without using any grand phrases; he taught me the technicalities without being technical; he was a good critic and did not let my situation soften his criticism. But he believed I could become a writer and that gave me the confidence I needed.

Soon I started to write the second version of my autobiography, still by dictation. My scribe now was Francis, my thirteen-year-old brother, quite different from Eamonn, who just wrote down what I said without thinking, like a writing machine. Francis thought about what he was writing. After we had finished, he would sit down quietly and read over what he had written down for me, sometimes asking me questions about the grammar, the meaning of words and so on, questions which I was hard put to answer at times. One night I asked him what he thought of a chapter which we had just finished. He thought for a while, then said very solemnly, "It's all right, but you'd want the dictionary beside you when reading it!"

I wanted to throw the table at him, but he just sat there, not a smile on his face, his hands folded placidly in his lap. I was furious, but I knew there was something in what he said.

The second effort at writing the book came out much better than the first. The theme was more clear-cut, the construction more orderly and the thought behind it more mature. I hoped for a while that it might do, but still Dr. Collis shook his head.

"Better than before," he said. "But still too literary. Scrap it and start over again. This time you can make it, I know. We all rewrite our stuff till we get it right—third time lucky."

I pretended to smile, but actually I swore to myself as I contemplated the awful piles of useless manuscript.

One December night Dr. Collis came into my study and sat down on the seat opposite me. He said nothing for a while, but just sat warming his hands at the fire. Then he pushed his chair away a bit and looked up.

"Christy," he said, "I've been thinking about your future. You have talent for original work. The problem is how best to develop it. How far have you got in your education?"

My education! It was practically nil. The only bit of education I'd ever had was learning the alphabet from mother at the age of five. I had gone on from there the best way I could on my own, teaching myself to read and to learn all I could from books.

"Not very far," I managed to say.

"Education is invaluable," he said, "and in your case I think it is essential. You couldn't attend a school or university in the ordinary way, so I'm going to ask the Marrowbone Lane Fund to put up the money to get a private tutor for you."

A few days later he came and told me that he had found the ideal sort of man to school me, a Mr. Guthrie, who taught in one of the large national schools quite close to my own home.

"I think you'll get on well together," he said. "He's the sort of tutor any boy would wish to have.

The very next evening my new tutor arrived, a stocky, fresh-complexioned man of about middle age, with keen blue eyes and a humorous mouth. His whole face seemed lit with a keen intelligence and a keener sympathy. I took an instant liking to him.

"Hello, Christy," he said in a deep resonant voice, coming forward and shaking hands with me. "I'm delighted to meet you. I hope we'll be partners from now on."

And that was the way of it. Mr. Guthrie began at once to show his skill by breaking down quietly and confidently all the barriers that naturally stood in the way. He made me feel as if ours was a partnership in a big and difficult job.

He came two evenings a week, each session lasting for about two hours or more. When the official "programme" was over for the night he would stay on for a while and we'd discuss things like psycho-analysis, or the philosophy of Bertrand Russell, or the poetry of Yeats, so that, apart from the ordinary lessons, I learned a great deal. And, of course, those talks greatly helped me to speak clearly and confidently.

When I was first introduced to mathematics, I couldn't write down the figures myself, so I called yet another brother, Seàn, to service, as Francis had more than enough work to do on the next version of the book. Besides, Seàn was pretty good at maths in school and he proved to be a good help to me—almost too good a help, in fact, for soon I found myself letting him do all the "dirty work", tackling the hard core of the stuff while I just corrected the answers!

Latin I took to at once. I fell in love with the elegance and beauty of the language, its smoothness and neatness of expression. My reading also became more comprehensive. Discovering the beauty of Shakespeare gave me an almost physical sense of joy. Often while in the middle of one of his plays I'd pause, breathless, and wonder at the incredible loveliness of his imagination and the soundness of his reasoning. It seemed to me he had revealed the mind of man, as no one has before or since.

Yet sometimes, on nights when I sat in my study at home supposedly reading Caesar or making out problems in geometry or arithmetic, I'd suddenly stop and start thinking of all the girls I could have met, all the girls I could have danced with and perhaps made love to, like my brothers. It wasn't easy, then, to sit in a chair and try to read Caesar's campaign in Gaul, or even Shakespeare. I still had a "pain in my mind". I was just twenty years old. I wanted other company besides books. I wanted to know the joy of climbing a mountain on an early spring morning or of strolling home in the moonlight along rain-washed city streets with a beautiful girl by my side.

I remember one evening when I felt particularly isolated and jealous of Peter and Paddy, who had gone out with their pals. I was left alone, I was sick of reading. For a time I sat morosely doing nothing. Francis came in for dictation. He sat down, took out his pen and waited.

I knew I had something to say, but it wouldn't come. I looked down at my hands, useless as ever. Then suddenly I remembered my left foot.

"Get to hell out of here, Francis," I shouted.

Poor Francis looked at me as if he was going to cry.

"Go on," I said. "Out—"

He got up and, looking at me over his shoulder like a frightened rabbit, slipped out of the room. Then I flung myself onto my bed, tore off my left shoe, ripped off my left sock with the other foot, seized a pencil between my first and second left toe and began to write.

I wrote and wrote without pause, without consciousness of my surroundings hour after hour. I felt a different person. I didn't feel frustrated any more. I was free, I could think, I could live, I could create . . . . Suddenly the door opened and the doctor came in. I stopped, tucked my left foot under me and tried to grin at him and said something about "a cold evening". He sat down by the fire and began to talk about ordinary things. After a while he came round to the subject of the book.

"So you had to call out the old left foot again," he said. I pulled it from under me rather sheepishly. "Dictation is not quite enough is it? Well, I understand. We won't tell Eirene Collis. But don't use it except when you must."

I felt released, at peace, I could be myself sometimes anyway. And if I couldn't know the joy of dancing I could know the ecstasy of creating.

370

CHAPTER **10**

One of the most exciting days of my life came about in an unusual way.

Dr. Collis had been one of the first medical staff to enter the notorious Belsen concentration camp. There he found and later adopted a small dark-skinned Hungarian-Slovak boy. He was very ill when the doctor found him, and later the old place in his lung got bad again and he had to have a big operation in the Chest Hospital in London. Burl Ives, the American folk singer, had met him in Dublin before and taken a great liking to him. So he used to visit him quite often in the Chest Hospital.

One afternoon Dr. Collis was in London consulting with the surgeon about the boy. They came into the ward and found a regular concert in full swing. Burl Ives had everybody laughing and singing. Suddenly Dr. Collis got an idea and asked him if he would give a concert in Dublin in aid of cerebral palsy. Burl Ives agreed immediately.

On returning to Dublin the doctor came out to see me and told me what had happened. "The idea is," he said, "that Burl Ives will sing and I shall make an appeal for cerebral palsy. But I think it would be much more to the point if you did."

"Me," I said. "How . . . ?"

"You've finished your first chapter, about the letter A and your mother," he said. "If I were to read them that, they'd know much more about cerebral palsy from the inside than if I was to talk to them for an hour. But you must come along with me and sit beside me so that they'll know it's your work and not mine."

I thought a moment. I had visions of sitting before a large audience and seeing hundreds of questioning faces peering up at me, noting my queer movements, my twisting hands and crooked mouth. I hesitated. He read my thoughts.

"You can take it?" he said.

"OK," I said, "I can, of course——"

But I felt scared.

Arrangements went ahead at great speed. The occasion was to be sponsored by the Ireland-America Society and many distinguished people were invited. A huge, lovely room seating over five hundred people was taken at the Gresham Hotel, tickets were issued, and notices were put up in the press. The whole city knew about it, but in no quarter more than in our house. All the family said they must come. It seemed to me that if the whole family and friends got free tickets they could easily fill the whole hall and there wouldn't be much left for cerebral palsy!

The day arrived. All that morning our house looked like a public house on Saturday night with everyone bumping into one another and all talking at the same time. Mother got a loan of a fur coat from a friend and tried it on. "What do I look like?" she asked, taking up different poses as she stood in the centre of the kitchen.

There was a hush in the conversation at the table as we turned round to view our model. Nobody spoke. None of us wanted to commit ourselves on such a difficult question. At last Peter picked up his newspaper and said casually, his eyes intent on the page:

"I see a bear escaped from the zoo last night . . . ."

Mother did not condescend to hear this remark, and, getting out her London hat, put it on in front of the mirror.

Father too broke out. He had bought a new suit and a funny sort of hat that seemed to be a cross between a trilby and a bowler. He looked extremely smart.

They then started to dress me up in a dinner jacket which they'd got out on hire between them without telling me anything about it. Despite my protests I was squeezed into it grimly by Peter and Tony. "Have to look proper," they said.

The taxi arrived punctually and we set out like a royal family in a carriage and pair. Only half a dozen of us could be crammed into it, so the others went by bus: about a dozen and a half or so, not to mention a whole retinue of friends and other relatives who followed after. It was like a regiment on the march when they all set off down the street together, linking arms.

At last we reached the hotel. The show hadn't started yet and the curtain hadn't gone up. I was put in a chair on the stage beside mother and father. From the other side of the curtain I could hear the people talking and shuffling as they settled into their seats. I knew there was a huge crowd in the hall and that the curtain would rise any second now. I felt awful. I saw that I had been placed on the right of the stage, the centre being left vacant except for chairs which were now being occupied by the president of the Ireland-American Society, the film producer, Mr. John Huston, and Dr. Collis.

Then I caught sight of something very remarkable through the small door at the side of the stage. All I could see at first was a huge expanse of gold waistcoat and green trousers. Then the rest of their owner came into view. I thought I had never seen anything so enormous and resplendent before. The man must have stood over six feet high and weighed over twenty stone. He had a smiling moon-like face, small eyes and a pointed beard. He carried a guitar across one shoulder. He seemed to me fantastic, like a giant out of a fairy-story, amidst the crowd of ordinary mortals. This was Burl Ives.

The next moment the curtain went up and the show was on. I gripped the sides of the chair and tried to hold myself rigid. All I could see was a huge white blur of faces staring up at me. I felt myself go hot and cold in turn. I was conscious of every involuntary movement I made, no matter how slight, and my own awareness of them magnified them into painful conspicuousness. It seemed as if I was under the lens of a microscope so that not one movement I made could escape detention. I felt the old panic rising within me.

Then Burl Ives began to sing. He had a wonderful, soft, mellow voice with a humorous twist in it and his style of singing was artful and droll. I just shut my eyes and listened to his singing and half forgot my stage fright.

Soon I was laughing like everyone else as he sang "The Blue-Tailed Fly" and "Mr. Frog Went A'Courting". Finally he had everyone singing with him:

"There was an old woman who swallowed a fly.
Now I don't know why she swallowed a fly—
Perhaps she'll die . . . ."

I found myself singing like everyone else in the hall.

I laughed so much that I'd quite forgotten everything else. After several encores he finally withdrew and the president of the Ireland-America Society announced that Dr. Collis would address the audience on behalf of the Cerebral Palsy Association.

The doctor got up and went to the microphone. The crowd before him were still in a jovial mood laughing and talking. It wasn't going to be easy to interest them.

He took my manuscript from his pocket and placed it on the stand in front of him. "I'm not going to make a speech," he said. "I'm not even going to make an appeal. I'm just going to read you something that will give you an inside view of a person crippled with cerebral palsy. The first chapter of Christy Brown's autobiography here—" he held out his hand towards me "—written with his left foot."

Then he began to read. For the first few minutes there was still a good deal of noise in the audience, people shuffling their feet, and coughing. Gradually, however, as the doctor read on, movement and noise ceased; there was complete stillness. I looked down at the faces before me, but now they were no longer just questioning faces with peering eyes, but intent friendly faces full of interest. They were listening . . . !

I was still taut as a telegraph wire, but after a while I too began to listen, and as I did so my tension left me. I forgot my queer hands twisting and twining in my lap. I forgot my crooked mouth and shaking head. I listened . . . was this true, me sitting on a stage with mother and father before a huge audience, listening to a description of my own childhood? Had I really written all that stuff? It seemed as if I was dreaming.

Suddenly I became aware that the doctor had stopped speaking. There was complete silence in the big hall. I saw somebody in the front row crying. I looked aside at mother, sitting upright, her eyes glistening. I looked at father; he was twisting his hat in his hands; he looked at me in a new way. Still there wasn't a sound. Then Dr. Collis walked across the stage, laid his hand on my shoulder and helped me to my feet. And the cheering broke out . . . . It went on and on and seemed to cover us like waves of the sea.

Suddenly somebody from the audience brought forward a huge bouquet of roses. The doctor stooped and took them. He walked over towards mother. He held up his hand. The cheering stopped. "Red Roses for Mrs. Brown!" he said. "For you, Ma'am!" and he handed the bouquet to mother with a bow.

Mother took the bouquet, looking like a Queen Mother, as if she was quite used to roses every day of her life. Standing beside her was father, his shoulders drooping and his bald head bent forward. As mother laid the flowers across her arm I heard her say in a loud whisper out of the corner of her mouth:

374

"Straighten up, Paddy, can't yer!" Father stiffened but dropped his hat. Then Burl Ives came on again. He began to sing our own Irish folk songs.

Now I could relax and enjoy it completely. I was at peace, happy. I lay back in my chair while my old left foot beat time to the rhythm of the tune.

EPILOGUE 1

I was eighteen when I began *My Left Foot* and twenty-one when I finished it. I thought then it was the story of my life, and that I was a writer, but it was really only the starting point of my life, and I had a long way to go and a lot of despair to face before I could even remotely consider myself a writer.

When that first slim book was published in 1955, I was suddenly catapulted from obscurity into the limelight. I was no longer an unknown cripple living in some concrete corner of Dublin suburbia, but a famous writer. I could not quite believe it had happened, that so many people around the world were interested in reading about me. Strangers were writing me warm, affectionate, admiring letters, telling me how much they had liked my book and how in so many ways it had helped and inspired them in their personal lives. I was being feted, nothing less than that, and it was heady stuff. If I could achieve all this with my first book, what would I not achieve with all the others that would surely follow? The horizons seemed limitless.

The reaction of my family when *My Left Foot* finally came out was rather muted, restrained, as if they could not quite take it all in. They were glad for me, proud of me, but shy almost of allowing their feelings to show too much. Sadly, my father had died just the year before after a massive stroke, so he was not there to share in my success, but in the few months before he died he showed an increasing interest in my writing and even went so far once as to say that some day I would be a credit to them all. For him to even say that was something of a victory in itself. My mother's character was different: she was careful not to over-praise me in case it gave me a swelled head—a very likely possibility, I must admit.

Meanwhile I was still going to the clinic. I had started treatment a bit too old for any dramatic improvement to come about, but I continued to attend the clinic for six years or more. I liked the camaraderie that existed there. As well as that, my speech had greatly improved under the guidance of Dr. Patricia Sheehan, who became a lifelong friend. Under her tutelage, I learned to form words and soon whole sentences, even to make myself understood by strangers, which again opened up new ways of communication for me, though I was always to prefer the written word to the spoken one.

There was to be no spectacular change in my physical condition, and in my heart I had expected none; yet there had been a change in my outlook, a subtle one, for seeing others at the clinic far more severely handicapped than myself had inevitably brought about a change in me, and though my moments of self-pity were never quite to disappear altogether, they became less frequent.

During this vital period of my life, when I was still struggling to come to terms with both my disablement and my growing adulthood, the most important figure, apart from my mother, was Dr. Collis, who was, as the saying goes, my guide, philosopher and friend. Our relationship was to last up unto his death at the age of seventy-four.

He himself became a world-renowned child psychologist and paediatrician; yet he watched over me like a wise gigantic eagle watching over its fledgling, and in a way he treated me as a son. He followed every step of my career and was tremendously proud when my books became well known throughout the world. The sad irony was that he had a severely retarded son of his own, with little or no hope of improvement, and I know that this was one of the great sorrows of his life.

Robert Collis died in what I believe to be a singularly fitting, almost poetic way; he was passionately fond of animals, especially horses, and one mild-mannered day while out riding he suffered a massive coronary, fell from his horse, and died among the wild beautiful gorse and soft grass of his beloved Wicklow hills: a perfect close to a strong, humane and selfless life. His death saddened me, but not too hurtfully, because in my heart I knew it was the sort of end he would most surely have chosen for himself, and that is something not many of us are granted.

After the euphoria following the success of *My Left Foot* had abated somewhat and I could look about me with clearer eyes, I made a very painful discovery; I was not the great young writer I had imagined myself to be. The words were still there, but they no longer came forth at my beck and call, they lay huddled at the back of my mind like a sullen mutinous army, refusing all orders to come to attention. I was alarmed and astonished. What had happened? It had been hard enough before filling jotter after jotter with mangled sentences with a pencil held between my toes while at the same time trying to control the involuntary movements of my body; but the words had come, in a wild stampede at times, almost leaping up out of the pages at me. So what was happening now? The more desperately I tried to put down my thoughts and ideas on paper the more they eluded me.

Thanks to the publicity about *My Left Foot* I was now the owner of an electric typewriter, given to me by a well-known business gentleman in Dublin, which took most of the physical labour out of my writing; but even this magical machine did not help to release the flood of words. Images and pictures flashed tantalizingly before my eyes, but were gone before I could catch them; it was as if the words simply refused to be pinned down upon the page.

In my own quarters at the back of the house, I slept, read, and vainly tried to work, sometimes into the early hours of the morning. I would crouch forward in the armchair, flick on the switch of the typewriter and wait for the floodgates of language to open; but all that I heard was the mechanical purr of the typewriter on the floor at my feet, a black ugly hooded creature spluttering inanely away; whenever I hit the keys in desperation all that came back was an asthmatic cough and on the page a stream of unintelligible hieroglyphics.

I began to pine after the days of pencil and jotter; there had been a certain reckless freedom then, when I would dash all my thoughts down in a crazy jumble and cross out those that did not fit with one arrogant swipe of the pencil or coloured marker. Now it had all changed and I seemed to be at the mercy of this machine at my feet, purring away with a strange mechanical life of its own. From being a generous gift it became an ill omen.

I began to retreat into myself. I wanted to be alone with my misery. I was convinced that nobody could help me but myself; of course I could not explain any of this to the family. This inability to share my feelings with others had never troubled me before; on the contrary, it had acted as a spur to make me concentrate more on my writing. I did not shun company, but neither did I mind being alone, as long as the words came. Now it was different; being alone now was akin to being locked away in a vault.

More than ever I envied my brothers and sisters their broad carefree freedom, their easy alliance with the outside world. I knew that they too suffered times of uncertainty and pain, but I was too wrapped up in my own tribulations to consider anyone else's plight save my own. If I could not be a writer I did not want to live. It was as simple as that.

It dawned on me slowly that my real enemy was the almost instant success I had achieved with that first book. If things had been just that little bit harder, I would have been a lot more prepared for the sheer daily grind of work. What had seemed like a miracle had turned out to be a confidence trick, a sly pulling of wool over my eyes.

I was of course being impossibly melodramatic, but I was in no mood to weigh things up calmly. Without my having to put it into words, it was my mother who finally guessed the cause of my peevish behaviour, and who broached the subject with her usual briskness.

"What's the matter with you lately?" she asked me one day, as she laid the table for dinner, bustling about the kitchen in her usual way. "You've a face on you that would turn back a funeral."

At first I tried to evade the question, but she would have none of it, and at last I blurted out something of what seemed then to me to be the truth of the matter.

She paused and blew back some wisps of hair from her face. "Finished you say you are, is it? Thrown in the towel already?" She stood before me, hands on hips. "Well, that beats everything!" She sat down in the chair opposite me, smoothing down her apron. "Well, me lad, let me tell you something—I never reared a jibber!"

I winced, for a "jibber" was the name we gave to a shirker of hard work, a no-hoper. It raised my hackles.

"Good," she said upon hearing my angry retort to the contrary. "So what are you going to do about it? Where's your backbone, for

378

the love of God? Nothing comes easy in this world. You have to fight for every scrap and morsel, and you're no different from the rest of us." She got up again impatiently and resumed her task. "Do you think your poor father liked being a bricklayer, or any of your brothers, out in all weathers? They did not, but it is their job, and putting words together is your job. So get on with it and stop feeling sorry for yourself." She slung the dinner plates out on the table as if she were dishing out a round of cards, with restrained impatient energy. She shot me a glance over her shoulder, at once tender and challenging. "I know it isn't easy, son, but you've had your miracle, and now it's time for hard work."

Her logic was unsophisticated, but unanswerable, and it made me ashamed of myself. I swallowed my dinner meekly, and as soon as I could crawled back out to my study, full of new resolve.

That night I gave the typewriter one hell of a battering, but in the morning, exhausted as I was, I felt pleased with what I had written for the first time since *My Left Foot* came out.

EPILOGUE 2

What came out of my head via my much maligned typewriter in the months and, indeed, years that followed was a queer assembly of things—at first all pitchforked together but then gradually assuming a sort of order and shape. It was a bit like weeding a garden; I was weeding out my ideas and putting them in an erratic but discernible line, row upon wobbly row. After a while, since nobody had ever accused me of being shy or modest, I struck upon the bold notion of sending some of my stuff to the Dublin newspapers; there was at that time in the *Evening Press* a daily short story taking up roughly half the centre page or so, and I decided to have a go at that allegedly sacrosanct space.

Once again the results amazed and elated me. Not only did the editor accept my first offering, but even negotiated with my London publishers to serialize *My Left Foot*, and it proved quite a hit with its readers. After that I wrote short stories for the *Press* more or less regularly for about two or three years. The subject matter was optional, but mostly the stories were cameos dealing with some aspect of everyday life. They printed at least one of my stories each week, at I think five pounds a time, which later shot dramatically up to ten pounds, and on such a regular basis this was very satisfying indeed, since it put me on a par with my elder brothers, who were earning a weekly wage. There was also the extra bonus of seeing my name in bold print—it always gave me a thrill. There was a definite distinction, at least to my mind, between writing a book that went round the world, and writing something weekly for your home patch; it was at once more insular and more demanding.

At this time, too, poetry was streaming out of me, but for a couple of years I kept the results hidden in a small wooden box under my bed, shown only to one or two trusted friends when infrequently they came to visit me in my "hideout" at the back of the house. One of these was a girl from the "black North" of Ireland whose uncle happened to be a famous poet. I had met her at the clinic when she was there on some sociology course, and she reappeared several years later, married by then and with two kids to prove it. I at length showed her some of my poems, and she liked them so much she wanted to show them to her famous uncle. I shied away from that as if from fire, but such was her enthusiasm that I was persuaded to send half a dozen or so poems to a periodical that was popular in Dublin at that time; they printed two, and eventually I met the editor, a stout-hearted fellow who looked a bit like a miniature version of Dylan Thomas and had almost the same capacity for beer-swilling. He was kind enough to print many more of my poems in his magazine before it folded, like so many others before and after it. But at least my voice had been heard as a poet, if an embryonic one, and when other poetry broadsheets briefly flourished for a while my poems somehow found their way into these too.

Soon some of the young poets in Dublin began to visit me; we would either have a drink in my study or else they would push me in my wheelchair down to the local pub, where we would talk our heads off all evening, being heroically objective and self-critical while at the same time dying to proclaim our own genius. I talked as loudly and as foolishly as the others; I had found that once I got

380

involved in a conversation that really interested me, my speech defect almost disappeared and people could understand me quite well. So the poets of past and present came in for either an eulogy or a hammering when we sucklings gathered in back rooms or smoky bars; we were intoxicated more with our own high-flung rhetoric than with the beer we incautiously gulped down, I with the aid of the plastic straws that latterly had proved such a boon in my consumption of all things liquid.

I enjoyed these meetings tremendously; they lifted me out of myself, and in passing put a keener edge to my writing as I was put in touch with the current ideas of my contemporaries. This woke many things in me that had lain dormant—dim perceptions, small sudden discoveries within myself, things that I would at a later stage in my life put into poems and novels and paintings. I did not realize then that a simple conversation with friends could surface so many years later as something meaningful, prophetic and touching.

Painting too became a more and more important part of my life, though it was never to usurp writing. At first I had used water colours or poster paints, painting mostly from imagination, since there was very little to see in Kimmage other than the front and back of houses. But water colours did not really suit my temperament; they "ran" too fast for me and if I was not quick enough the end result would be an unholy mess of colours. I tried my foot at some drawing, too, and wasn't too bad at it, but that really did not satisfy me either—it was too finicky for my liking, and too flat. So I "graduated" to oils and found an immediate affinity with that medium. I slapped on the paint thickly with rare abandon, and soon learned to use my brushes the way other artists used palette knives to create a realistic, three-dimensional effect. It was exhausting physically, and at the end of the day I found that I had more muscles in my body than I had ever imagined. I painted mostly portraits, not of real people, but completely out of my head, and since I had no formal training I suppose my style could have been dubbed "primitive", with everything out of proportion—the eyes huge and staring, overhanging brows like promontories, the nose bulbous or razor-sharp, the mouth sloping, twisted in a grotesque grin or snarl.

God knows what a psychiatrist would have made of those early efforts of mind, dredged up from some black hole in my subconscious! They certainly alarmed the family; my mother was especially struck by the eyes I painted, and used to say they followed her around the room. I also painted city scenes, reflections of tall leaning dilapidated tenements in the sunset waters of the River Liffey against lurid skies, and the occasional landscape and still-life with flowers or fruit. Then I began experimenting with female nudes, which alarmed the family still more; they would not look directly at them. They would mutter something like "Not bad, not bad at all," averting their eyes all the time from the huge melon-ripe breasts, protruding belly and large provocative buttocks shamelessly on display. "Who's your woman?" a curious brother would ask, and upon hearing my reply that it was just something out of my head, he would declare, "You must have one hell of a head, mate!"

With my book and a scattering of poems I had made a bit of a name for myself, but I certainly had no visions at all of any future as a painter and did it merely as a diversion. Then one day a big man with a beaming face arrived at our house; he had heard of my painting activities, and had come up from Cork to see me. His name was Seàn Feehan, a retired captain in the Irish army who ran a thriving publishing house called the Mercier Press; he also happened to be the Irish representative of the Disabled Artists' Association, which he explained operated throughout the world as a fulcrum for handicapped people who painted with either their feet or their mouths. It sponsored their careers, exhibiting and printing their work as illustrations for calendars or Christmas cards, which it sold and distributed in almost every country, paying a monthly stipend to the artists, varying in amount according to how long they had been members of the association and of course how well their work sold. Captain Feehan was impressed with what he saw of my pictures and asked me if I wanted to join the association, starting as a student member at a fixed salary each month; I cannot quite recall the exact sum, about twenty-five pounds or thereabouts, but of course I jumped at the opportunity and was duly accepted into the DAA. I was elated at the thought that now I would be actually earning money as an artist and it did wonders for my self-esteem and also my painting. Once again fortune had smiled on me.

Seàn Feehan and myself became—and remain—great friends, sharing something of the same rumbustious and slightly salacious sense of humour and outlook. An integral part of the DAA's campaign to promote its aims and keep the coffers full was to organize painting tours and exhibitions up and down each country where the artists themselves lived, giving demonstrations of their skill before the assembled audience, and soon I was travelling all over Ireland by car, usually accompanied by one of my brothers as helper, painting in town halls, hotels, in large cities and small country towns and villages, working away at my easel in front of curious onlookers. It was hard work, for we would start off sometime during the morning, have a break for lunch, and continue until four or five in the evening; then came the drive back home to Dublin which might take several hours. For the most part I enjoyed it and found the whole experience stimulating and rewarding. At times I must admit I felt distinctly uncomfortable painting in front of people; some of them made comments and asked questions that were disconcerting, but through sheer necessity I learned how to accept and cope with all this. I became a full member of the DAA, with a greatly improved monthly salary which was to become my main, and at times, only, source of livelihood.

Eventually I met the founder and guiding genius of the association, Eric Stegmann, a German who had been born severely crippled but who had overcome almost insurmountable obstacles to become a famous artist and sculptor, working only with his mouth, and finally launching the DAA. Eric Stegmann surely is a genius in the true sense of that much battered word; he exudes enormous energy, and has a stone-wall determination to conquer every barrier that gets in his way; one can almost *feel* the life-force flowing out of him. We became firm friends almost at once, and it has stayed that way ever since; he does not speak English, I do not speak German, and still we make ourselves understood to each other whenever we meet. He remains one of my small band of heroes, one of the major inspirations of my life, and I shall for ever be grateful to Seàn Feehan for bringing me in contact with such a man.

My mother was naturally delighted with all this, and more than ever proud of the fact that I was now financially independent and recognized as both writer and artist. It was all she had ever dreamed of, all those years, and it was coming true before her eyes. A lesser mortal would perhaps have given up on me, but not she; despite all the signs to the contrary, despite all the dire warnings from doctors and psychologists in the early days that I would never amount to anything, she had never wavered, had never lost faith in me, had continued to insist that in spite of my outward appearance I was as normal as the rest of her thirteen children. Indeed, she always

383

believed that I was better than "normal", that I had something that set me apart from the others, some inner force that she perceived quite clearly even in the days when I could not talk and all my physical movements were wildly erratic and uncontrollable.

I had been by her side practically all my life, as the others grew up, went to work, fell in love, got married, had children. We were more comrades, friends, than mother and son; she knew my thoughts and feelings better than I knew them myself, even if she could not put them into words. She knew my light side and my dark side, my elations and depressions, my secret hurts and hopes. I did not have to use any stammering words with her, because she knew what I was feeling, knew the things that were stirring in my head and heart. There was just nobody like her in the whole world.

And then I slowly became aware that she was sick, very sick, and had been for some years. In my gross self-absorption I had hardly noticed the change in her; now it was all too obvious. There was a lethargy about her as she went about the housework; she was in turn both flushed and then deathly pale, her cheeks were sunken, her eyes lacked the old lustre.

After my father died she had gone out to work as a cleaner with Dublin Corporation, more as a chance to get away from the monotony of the house rather than to earn money, a chance to meet other people and have a joke and chat with them, for she was a born mixer, a great talker, quick and witty. But now she was not able to work except the few mundane chores about the house. She loved her glass of stout in our local pub; it brought her in touch with most of the neighbours, but now she spent more and more time in bed. She vomited quite often and suffered acute abdominal pains which she put down to "wind". But it was not wind; it was stomach cancer.

At last she was persuaded to go into hospital, and she was operated upon almost immediately. It was the first in a series of four operations, and all within five weeks. It was plainly hopeless; it was the end; we all knew that, though we tried to keep it from ourselves, from each other, not wishing to admit the inconceivable. The cancer had spread like wildfire, and the operations had been mere desperate efforts to prevent it from spreading further. She was in severe and constant pain, but her spirit never gave out; she remained cheerful, inquisitive, wanting to know how things were at home, if we were all getting along with each other. She was connected up with all sorts of tubes and bottles hanging above her

384

bed, and would joke about them, saying she must look a sight, "something from outer space". We watched in mute misery, made ashamed of our unspilt tears by her humour and gaiety, her soft comforting words, her gallantry.

She died early one August morning, without complaint, leaving the doctor who had attended her in tears, moved by her courage. When we all went to the hospital to see her that bright and terrible morning she had a tranquil expression on her face, not exactly a smile, more of an intent and interested look, as if she were in deep conversation with someone and was putting across her own point of view. She was just a month short of her sixty-eighth birthday, but her spirit was ageless. She truly made a mockery of death.

A few months later I wrote:

"Only in your dying, Lady, could I offer you a poem.

You were a song inside my skin
        a sudden sunburst of defiant laughter
spilling over the night-gloom of my half awakenings
        a firefly of far splendid light
dancing in the dim catacombs of my brain.
        Light of foot and quick of eye for pain
you printed patterns of much joy upon the bare walls of my life
        with broad bold strokes of your Irish wit
flaming from the ruins of your towers.

    Only in your dying, Lady, could I offer you a poem.

With gay uplifted finger you beckoned
        and faltering I followed you down paths
I would not otherwise have known or dared
        limping after you up that secret mountain
where you sang without need of voice or words.
        I touched briefly the torch you held out
and bled pricked by a thorn from the black deep rose of your courage.

    From the gutter of my defeated dreams
you pulled me to heights almost your own.

    Only in your dying, Lady, could I offer you a poem.

I do not grieve for you
       in your little square plot of indiscriminate clay
for now shall you truly dance.

O great heart
    O best of all my songs
        the dust be merciful upon your holy bones."

EPILOGUE 3

After mother died things at home in Kimmage changed. The central force that had held us all together was no longer there, and we began to drift apart. Little tensions became major ones, we became wary and suspicious of each other for no rhyme or reason. It was a sad experience, but in retrospect I suppose it was inevitable. We were all quite different in our approach to life; and the camaraderie we had known as children began to crumble now that we were young men and women. I do not think any of us wanted to break apart from each other—it just happened.

The death of our father had not affected us in the same way. For a time we were sad and bewildered, but we carried on much as before. It was different when our mother died; there was this sense of absolute loss, a deep grief that was wordless and terribly wounding. We had only ourselves to rely on now, and consequently we became more self-absorbed, the lines of communication became thinner.

I continued to write, and just two years after mother's death, the book—a novel—that I had been trying to write for so long was finished and came out in 1970. It was called *Down All The Days*, and it became almost an immediate success and was translated into fifteen languages. At last the years between were over.

The book was to lay the foundation for most of my life afterwards, paving the way for what one might almost call a second career. I had been just twenty-two when my first book was published; I was now thirty-eight and with a lot more experience of life and of people and with a lot more knowledge of myself.

This book was a mixture of fact and fiction, and it surprised some people that I could have written it at all, so different was it from *My Left Foot*. The two books might have been written by two different persons, as indeed they were, for of course I had been maturing, saddened and enriched by life, tougher and much more objective, more prepared to look truth squarely in the face. It was a book that was terribly hard to write; it was bound to hurt others, especially members of my family, and it did, to my regret, but I had to write it or burst. I had the feeling that my mother would have given it her blessing. I had often talked about it with her before she died, so she knew most of what I was putting into the book and she was neither dismayed or angry. I was denied the one thing that would have made my success complete—her own pleasure in sharing it with me.

My editor at my English publishers, David Farrer, also had great belief in me as a writer; he had been instrumental in having my first book published so many years ago, and had always kept in touch with me. When at last I submitted the manuscript of *Down All The Days* to him, he knew at once that at last I had written the book he always had expected of me. Being the professional that he is, he was now sparing with his words, but he could not disguise the fact that he was excited by what I had written, and together we hammered out the script into its final shape.

It soared off like a rocket, an eruption of words, images and feelings so long suppressed, penetrating those "shades of the prison house" that had attended the growing boy: that boy was now transformed into a sceptical man capable of judgments which seemed harsh at times; but which were infused with conviction. It scared the hell out of me when I finally saw it in print, when I realized the better half of my life was in the hands of total strangers. I was still rather naive and did not wholly comprehend the hidden minefields of publication. It was a delight and a danger that I would have to live with when I started to write other books in the years that followed, in poetry as well as prose; I was leaving myself wide open to attack from the people most involved with my life. For better or worse I was holding a mirror up to them, not out of spite or

387

malice, but from a deeper need to know them as human fallible beings like myself, stripped of artifice. In the process I learned more about myself than about anyone else. It was like scouring the spirit inside of me, everything out in the open and no holds barred.

The aftermath was unexpected, to say the least. I was invited to appear on the David Frost TV show, and I did. I found the man utterly charming and winning, putting me completely at my ease, but that was nothing compared to the single unexpected event that followed, which was to alter my whole life, my whole world.

After the David Frost show, we were all feeling rather euphoric, and my brother Seàn organized a party to celebrate. He had lived in London for quite some time and had a very nice flat in Holland Park. Seàn is very artistic and he and I had much in common; I had given him a few of my paintings, which to my gratification he had framed and hung on the walls. Anyway, he threw this party, or "hooley" as we call it in Ireland, and a lot of his friends showed up. Pretty soon the flat was overflowing with them. They all appeared to be enjoying themselves, but they were strangers to me, and soon I grew restless and a little lost. The party seemed destined to go on into the early hours, and I looked about me with very jaundiced eyes indeed, thinking uncharitably that the whole thing was a silly circus signifying little.

And then I saw her. She was sitting across the jam-packed room from where I sulked on a settee, morosely sipping my drink through one of my invaluable plastic straws. I could not take my eyes away from this blonde and very beautiful girl. The whole clamorous scene melted into insignificance.

Later on I beckoned to Seàn and asked him who the girl was, lifting my foot and pointing her out.

Seàn gave me one of his wicked grins. "Oh, that's Mary, a great friend of mine. She likes your paintings."

A few moments later she was sitting beside me on the couch. In my excitement I babbled some high-faluting nonsense about Yeats and James Joyce and a host of other writers I admired. In her calm gentle voice she told me of her own favourite authors which included many of my own. My speech impediment intruded not at all, she understood every word I said, and for almost the remainder of that night we just sat and talked to each other, though I did most of the talking while she listened, grave and intent, her marvellous blue eyes upon me, her silky hair falling softly on her shoulders. I had always been acutely susceptible to pretty girls, but I knew instinctively that this encounter was something entirely different, that it marked the most important moment in my life.

Back home I could not get her out of my mind—not that I wanted to. An instant affinity had sprung up between us. She had promised to write, and soon we were corresponding regularly. I told her of all my hopes and plans for the future in full certainty that she would understand, and she did, completely, every time. I tried to write poems about her, but seldom succeeded, for she herself was the best poem I could ever write, the best story I could ever tell. Slowly my letters to her took on a more intimate, impetuous tone, became more fervent and importuning. I had fallen desperately in love.

Her own letters to me told me what I most wanted to hear—that she cared deeply for me and thought about me almost as much as I thought about her. Yet at the same time she was a bit wary, as if not to raise my hopes too much. Like myself she was inwardly lonely despite having so many friends, despite the warm affection and admiration in which other people held her; but unlike me she did not allow her loneliness to engulf her. There was a certain quiet fortitude about her which I admired but could not emulate. She was aware of what was happening between us, but she was wiser than me and knew the pitfalls of human emotion much better than I did. Yet she could not indefinitely deny the beautiful bond that had been forged between us almost from the moment we met.

A few months later the unbelievable happened—she came over to Ireland on holiday. She loved the country, had relatives in County Kerry, and had in fact been born in Killarney. She had been reared and educated in London, but I think her heart had always been in Ireland.

I was by now living in a very nice bungalow on the outskirts of Dublin with my sister Ann, her husband and two young children; I had bought the house from the proceeds of the success of *Down All The Days*. Mary came to visit me before continuing on her holiday. On seeing her my heart jumped; she was more lovely than ever, and more than ever I was in love. She greeted me with her usual gentle shyness, and for most of the time we studiously avoided looking at each other.

Later that same never-to-be forgotten evening we had a few drinks, played some records, talked about inconsequential things; my sister and her husband were there along with a few friends, for which I was secretly glad, because I was still very tense, and knew Mary must be feeling pretty much the same. Slowly I relaxed, determined that I would say what I had to say before the evening was out even if it dashed all my hopes.

As she was about to leave and go back to her hotel, I wheeled myself up to her. "Er—could I—um—see you alone for a minute before you go—please?" I asked.

"Yes, if you want to," she replied calmly.

I wheeled myself into an adjoining bedroom, and she followed. I swivelled around in my wheelchair almost before she had time to sit down.

"Well," I said, with a singular lack of grace; "how about it?"

Not surprisingly she looked rather mystified. "Pardon?"

"You know," I said. My voice was peculiarly clear despite the commotion inside me. "Us. You and me." My heart was thumping ponderously by now. "I mean—will you marry me?"

She did not answer at once, and I was on the rack, waiting, for my world to begin or end. I could not see her face clearly in the gathering dusk, for we had not turned on any lamps. Then she came up to me and, stooping, kissed me gently on the forehead. No words were necessary. My real life had begun.

*Christy Brown and his wife Mary in 1981. This year
they attended the first performance, in Dublin, of a play based on*
Down All The Days, *and Christy has just completed a new novel.*

TROJAN TREASURE

A condensation of book by
ROBERT L. FISH

Illustrated by Daniel Brown

Published by Doubleday, New York,
under the title "The Gold of Troy"

There was no doubt about it: the offer was genuine. Someone was selling the fabulous treasure Heinrich Schliemann had found a century ago amid the ruins of ancient Troy. The treasure that had vanished without trace after World War II. The treasure that any collector in the world would pay a fortune to own.

For Ruth McVeigh, the new director of New York's Metropolitan Museum of Art, it was the chance of a lifetime: an opportunity to crown her already brilliant career by acquiring the unique collection for the museum. There was just one problem: the treasure was stolen property.

Who was the thief? Why had he waited almost thirty-five years to sell the gold of Troy? And why were both the CIA and the Soviet secret police so interested in the sale?

With the help of a handsome Russian archaeologist, Ruth set out to search for answers—and found herself following an eerie and perilous trail.

BERLIN—April 1945

THE fighting had reached the western edge of the city; the shattered buildings, the burning trees of the Grunewald, the dangling telephone wires, all testified to the ferocity of the battle. The troops under Captain Mikhail Sudikoff had borne their share of the attack, and the captain heard with relief from his radioman that his battered company was to retire for rest to a bunker at the Berlin zoo, now firmly in the control of the Russians.

The bunker lay like a huge blister on the crater-pocked area of the zoo; the last of the many paintings that had been stored there by the Nazis were being removed. The Russian lieutenant in charge of this operation smiled at Sudikoff. "It's all yours," he said, and climbed on the truck bearing the paintings away.

The organization of the bunker fell to Sudikoff's elderly quartermaster, Sergeant Fedor Kolenko, who had been a university professor before the war. As a start, he set up a first-aid station and field kitchen. Then he assigned Corporal Sokolov and Private Boldin to go through the many rooms and warrens of the huge bunker and make an inventory of food, liquor, and anything else of value left behind either by the retreating Germans or by the Russian troops who had liberated the paintings.

"Anything you find, you bring back here!" Sergeant Kolenko ordered. "Understand?"

The two nodded and went off. They followed the many passages of the bunker to their ends, finding little more than comrades settling in. There was no sign of food, and they were about finished when by pure accident Private Boldin kicked at a pile of rubbish and discovered a small recess hidden in the wall behind it. Apparently the recess had once been covered with plaster, but the plaster had crumbled under the heavy bombardment. The corporal bent down and studied the interior of the cavelike opening. Then he reached in and dragged a small trunk into view.

The two men examined it. It was less than three feet long, with an old-fashioned rounded top, a small traveling trunk of an earlier era, made of wood and inexpertly covered with a malodorous artificial leather. Bands of copper—greenish now—had been riveted around it to give it the appearance of security, and someone had fastened a heavy padlock through its cheap hasp. Corporal Sokolov pulled his bayonet from its sheath, slid it through the hasp, and with an easy twist removed it entirely, padlock and all. For a moment he hesitated, afraid the trunk might be booby-trapped, but the temptation to open it was too great. He tipped the lid up, stepping back quickly. There was no explosion. Then both men stepped forward and stared inside.

There were four packages of approximately equal size. Corporal Sokolov, after returning his bayonet to its sheath and putting his rifle aside, picked up a package and began to unwrap it. The contents were protected with exceptional care, the outer wrapping being of fine suede, the inner one of sheet after sheet of tissue. The corporal's hopes of a rich discovery began to increase, but when he peeled away the final sheets of tissue, his face fell. All there appeared to be were some buttons and beads made from what seemed a poor-quality brass. With a disappointed grimace he unwrapped a second package. While its contents were made up of larger pieces, the same inexperienced labor and inferior material had apparently been employed.

Roughly Sokolov wrapped the pieces in their original coverings, thrust the packages back into the trunk, and closed the lid. "We'll take it back to the sergeant," he said. "Maybe some of the guys will want some of this junk for souvenirs."

The trunk was not very heavy, and the two men had no trouble carrying it back to the room adjoining the captain's quarters, where they set it on the floor before Sergeant Kolenko. The sergeant looked at them quizzically.

"It's all we found," Corporal Sokolov stated.

"I see," the sergeant said, and he raised the trunk lid. He knelt down, opened one of the packages, and stared at its contents. He unwrapped a second package, then rapidly the last two. His hands began to tremble. With an effort he kept his face expressionless as he stood up and carefully closed the lid.

"Where did you find this?" he asked.

"In a little hole in the wall," said the corporal.

"That will be all," the sergeant said. When the two soldiers had left, he sighed deeply and then walked into the captain's quarters. Sudikoff was lying in a hammock which the sergeant had found for him in the bunker. He was staring at the arched ceiling.

"Captain," the sergeant said, trying to keep his voice steady. "Captain, have you ever heard of the Schliemann treasure?"

NEW YORK—April 1979

As ON every working day, Dr. Ruth McVeigh spent the hour between nine and ten in the morning—when the Metropolitan Museum of Art opened to the public—in a walk around her newly acquired domain, basking in the heady feeling of achievement. She had been the director of the museum for two months now, the first woman director in the institution's history, and it was more than a sense of power that made her daily inspection so rewarding; it was the knowledge that she was fully capable of administering the vast galleries with their wealth of rich treasures.

Ruth McVeigh was a tall, handsome, in fact extremely beautiful woman. She had lustrous, dark brown wavy hair; dark, almost sloe-shaped eyes; full lips; and extremely fine features. Men instinctively turned to look at her in passing, but Ruth McVeigh seldom noticed their attention; her life was dedicated to archaeology, learned from her earliest days from her father, the noted archaeologist James McVeigh. Her childhood had been spent chiefly in exotic places with uncomfortable climates and strange tongues, where he and his crews had chosen to dig. After her mother died, Ruth—an only child—worked beside her father in the field, becoming more and more committed to the earth and the many wonders hidden beneath it.

She obtained the college and graduate school degrees necessary to advance herself in her chosen career. Even her marriage—to one of her professors—was entered into, consciously or unconsciously, from a desire to wed herself closer to her field by a union with a man whose knowledge she believed to be greater than her own. It did not work. For one thing, her husband showed a surprising lack of passion; for another, she recognized early on that he was a book scholar, many chapters behind her in both perception and experience.

After her father's death, her ambition did not waver. She spent four years in Egypt, digging at various sites in Luxor, three as an assistant curator at the Cleveland Museum of Art, and another three as a curator at the Smithsonian. Now, at thirty-four, Ruth McVeigh had found her niche as director of the Metropolitan Museum. The new job kept her amply busy, and more than compensated for the lack of male companionship in her life.

Today, as she moved through the high-arched corridors, nodding to the guards in their blue uniforms, her eyes subconsciously searched for any sign of vandalism by the previous day's visitors— there had been nearly thirty thousand—or any exhibit that seemed the least bit out of place. After her tour was complete, she walked into the large rotunda near the main entrance. She smiled at the eight receptionists in their octagonal station, and was on her way to her office when one of the women called to her.

"Dr. McVeigh, there is a package for you. It came yesterday, at closing time. You had left, so I kept it for you."

The woman handed her a flat package roughly five inches square and an inch deep. Ruth McVeigh noted that it had been carefully wrapped in brown paper, bound tightly with twine, and closed by red wax seals. Her name was machine printed, rather than handwritten or typed. Someone has gone to a lot of trouble, she thought as she turned the package over. There was no return address. She looked up, puzzled.

"Did you happen to notice who left this for me?"

The woman shrugged. "You know how crowded the desk is at closing, Doctor. All I remember is a hand reaching through the crowd and laying the package down. Why? Is it important?"

"No, I was just curious." Ruth McVeigh smiled. "Thank you."

She walked toward the staircase that led to her office, considering the package as she went. The outer wrapping appeared to have been carefully glued shut. Were the contents so fragile or so valuable, then? But if they were, would they simply be laid on a desk with no message and no return address?

She reached her office, nodded to her secretary, and went inside to her desk. Inserting her letter opener carefully at one corner of the package, she pried loose the wax seals. There was an inner wrapping, which she removed with equal care. Inside was a box. She removed the cover.

Inside was another box. For a moment she wondered if a practical-joking acquaintance had sent her one of those sets of nesting boxes that end up containing something quite useless. With a sigh she removed the cover of the inner box and found a letter clipped to a translucent envelope through which she could see photographs. Taking the envelope and the letter out of the box, she noticed something else at the very bottom of the package, something that was wrapped in cotton batting and appeared lumpy. She peeled away the cotton and stared. There was a small ring inside. With a frown she picked up the letter and began to read it.

When she had finished she stared at the ring for a moment, then reached for the telephone, pressing the button for her secretary. "Marge, would you ask Dr. Keller to come in? And ask Jed Martin to come along, too."

Replacing the telephone, she removed the photographs from the envelope and studied them intently. Well, this day, certainly, had not started off in the usual manner, and she had a feeling that many of the days to come might be different, too, as a result of this strange package. After a few moments there was a rap on the door and Dr. Robert Keller and Jed Martin entered.

Dr. Keller was in charge of special projects at the museum. He was a large, handsome man in his late forties, whose rumpled clothes looked as if they had been slept in. He sat down, dug a pipe from one pocket and a sack of tobacco from another, and methodically began filling the pipe.

Jed Martin, in sharp contrast, was a short, thin, and very dapper man with small, birdlike eyes. He was dressed this morning in a spotless laboratory jacket over a conservative vest and neatly pressed trousers. He was the curator of Greek and Roman antiquities. He also chose a chair and asked impatiently, glancing at his wristwatch, "Well, what is it, Ruth?"

Dr. McVeigh picked up the letter. "This came in a package that was delivered after I had left yesterday. There is no salutation, and no date, and, for reasons I'm sure you'll understand when you've heard the letter, there is no signature." She began to read.

"The enclosed ring is from the collection of gold objects discovered at Hissarlik in The Troad in Turkey by Heinrich Schliemann and his wife, Sophia, in early June of 1873. The entire collection, consisting of approximately nine thousand separate items, and with a net weight of approximately eighty-six hundred drams, will be offered at auction to selected bidders, of whom you are one, beginning September first, 1979. Instructions for submitting secret bids will be furnished before that date.

"The attached photographs will prove the authenticity of the statements made herein. Further proof can be obtained by examining the enclosed specimen from the collection. No opening bid below fifteen million dollars will be considered."

Ruth McVeigh put down the letter and looked up at the two men. Robert Keller had stopped puffing on his pipe. Martin was staring at the director incredulously.

"What absolute and utter rot!" Martin said. "The Schliemann treasure! It's been in the hands of the Russians for years! Everyone knows that!" He picked up the photographs Dr. McVeigh offered him and leafed through them, then tossed them back. "Someone got hold of Schliemann's book, had some duplicate pieces made up, and then took photos of the fakes." He fished the ring from the box. "And this"—he hesitated a moment—"well, I expect he did read up enough on the subject to know that the rings Schliemann found were made from gold wire."

"You will, however, check the ring for authenticity." Dr. McVeigh's tone made it an order, not a request.

"Of course," Martin said. "We'll check it for age, for purity of gold content, for the rare earths found in the gold of that day, and everything else." He snorted, eyeing the small ring malevolently. "The Schliemann treasure! Really!"

Bob Keller had resumed puffing on his pipe and was staring thoughtfully at the ceiling. "You know," he said slowly, "I've wondered for years if the treasure really *was* in the hands of the Russians." He watched the pipe smoke waft its way upward. "We know that Heinrich Schliemann donated it to Germany toward the end of the 1870s. His wife, Sophia, wanted it to go to Greece, which was her home country, and since she was almost certainly the one who first spotted the treasure, her word might have carried some weight. But in those days"—he cast a mischievous glance at Ruth McVeigh—"the man of the house was the boss. So the treasure went to Germany, where it remained in some museum or other until the Second World War. Then, for safekeeping, it was hidden in a bunker at the Berlin Zoological Garden. And that is all we know."

"Not quite," Martin said. "We know a lot more. We know that the Americans foolishly allowed the Russians to capture Berlin, including the bunker under the zoo. And we also know the treasure has never been seen since. Are you suggesting, Bob," he asked sarcastically, "that there is no connection between those two facts?"

"I'm only saying we don't know," Keller pointed out mildly. "If the Russians have had the Schliemann treasure since 1945, why haven't they ever exhibited it?"

"Because they have no legal right to it," Martin said triumphantly. He came to his feet, holding up the ring and reaching for the photographs. "It's a fake, a swindle, and if you'll let me get on with it, I'll prove it!"

"Do that," Ruth McVeigh said.

As Martin darted out the door, Bob Keller knocked the dottle from his pipe and said quietly, "All right, Ruth, let's get down to it. Suppose Jed and his laboratory find that the ring is from the era of Troy, and that the best photographic analysis indicates the pictures are genuine. And suppose an individual is actually offering the real Schliemann treasure for auction." He paused. "Question: Who is going to bid on it?"

Ruth frowned. "What do you mean?"

"Exactly what I say." Keller shrugged. "I know that we won't, and I seriously wonder whether any other museum will. Jed Martin was right when he said the legal ownership of the Schliemann treasure is definitely in doubt."

"If it's in doubt—" Ruth began.

"Wait." Keller held up his hand. "Look, Ruth. I know your history as an avid collector. We all are, or we wouldn't be doing what we do. But the Metropolitan Museum of Art does not, I repeat *not*, touch anything in the least dubious as to ownership. You know that as well as I do. It's merely the prospect of a battle for acquisition that made you forget it. Temporarily, I assume."

Ruth McVeigh smiled noncommittally.

Keller looked at her in frustration. "The Turkish government could present a case for ownership because the treasure originally came from a section of that country. Or if not the Turks, then the Germans, or possibly even the Greeks. But if the title is not crystal clear, our board of directors will never give you permission to bid on something like this, and no other museum in the world will bid on it either. Whoever is offering it to museums is an idiot. To private collectors, possibly. But museums? Never. You see—"

He paused as the telephone rang. Ruth shrugged her apology for the interruption and raised the receiver. It was her secretary.

"Dr. McVeigh, you have an overseas call from Dr. Armando Lopez in Spain. Will you take it?"

"Of course." There was a short wait and then the familiar tones of Dr. Lopez, an old acquaintance of both Ruth McVeigh and her father. The doctor was curator of Greek and Roman antiquities at the National Archaeological Museum in Madrid.

"Ruth, my dear one, how are you?" He spoke in his usual English, which Ruth always referred to as Obscure Florid. "The new position runs itself along well?"

"Very well, thank you. And you?"

"At the best." There was a brief pause. "Ruth, a most unusual affair has lifted its head. By private messenger a package comes with a letter inside of it together with some photographs and two buttons. They are of *oro*. This letter—"

"I'm sure I know what it says," Ruth said to speed the conversation. "My letter had a ring in it. Purportedly from the Schliemann collection."

"Ah? But they would never overpass such a prestigious museum as the Metropolitan. I wonder which more museums receive this letter. Possibly you know?"

"You're the first I've heard from, but I expect to hear from others. Dr. Lopez, are you convinced of the genuineness of the offer?" Ruth asked.

402

"Our laboratories are checking in deep, of course, but for me, I have no doubts. I know these buttons. I did my study in Berlin, and—how do you say?—I cut my tooth on that collection." There was a pause. "So, my dear one, will the Metropolitan bid?"

"Will the National Museum bid?"

Lopez laughed. "Now we are friends no longer, but competitors." His laughter faded, his tone became sad. "Alas, the question of legal ownership forms itself into a complication. And also there arises the question of money. Our small museum does not have the funding of the wonderful Metropolitan."

"No museum sits around with fifteen or twenty million dollars in its bank account waiting for something to buy," Ruth said, trying to sound equally sad.

"But you are possessed of such wealthy patrons, my dear one!"

"And there are no longer any wealthy Spaniards since Franco?"

There was another pause. "Ah, well, a shameful pity that the question of ownership prevents us all from bidding, is it not? But there it is. Well! We must meet someday soon and speak of many things. And please to take good care of yourself, my dear one."

"I shall do my best. And you do the same."

She hung up. Bob Keller raised his bushy eyebrows inquisitively. "I gather another museum has also received a letter and photographs, plus a sample from the collection."

Ruth smiled mischievously. "Dr. Armando Lopez of the National Archaeological Museum in Madrid is not the most able dissembler in the world," she said. "He told me his museum wouldn't bid on the collection, but I know he will be working day and night to find some way to raise the money."

LONDON—May 1979

"IT's quite insane, Maurice, I agree," Sir Clifford Edgerton, the director of the British Museum was saying into the telephone. Dr. Harold Gordon, the curator for Greek and Roman antiquities, sat beside his desk, listening politely. "Fifteen million dollars merely as a starting bid. That's over seven million pounds! Not that it really makes any difference. Obviously the British Museum has no intention of getting involved. Oh, yes, I agree that whoever sent those letters has the real collection in his possession. Our laboratories have made quite sure of the authenticity of the piece we received. And I admit that if the title were clear . . . but of course it isn't. Ah, well . . . What? Yes, indeed, we really must get together one of these days!"

As he hung up the receiver, he turned to Dr. Gordon. "That Maurice Dupaul! Saying that the Louvre has no intention of bidding, when I would wager every penny I possess that his bid will be the first out of the starting gate! Really!" He heaved a sigh. "One can't trust a soul these days! Dupaul will bid through some private collector, and the two of them will gloat over the collection in secret! *If* they get their hands on it. Ah, well . . ."

NEW YORK—May 1979

THE meeting of the board of directors of the Metropolitan Museum was not going well, and Ruth McVeigh realized that it was her emotional presentation, set against the cold, businesslike attitudes of the board members, that was at fault. Bob Keller had reported the full facts regarding the legal aspects of acquisition. Now Ruth McVeigh was making a final attempt to get her point across.

"You all seem to be under the impression," she said, shaking her head at their obtuseness, "that if we do not bid on this acquisition, the treasure will remain where it is, in the hands of a person who was foolish enough to try and sell something that wasn't rightfully his. That is ridiculous. Believe me, the collection will be sold, under one guise or another, to a museum. I would not be surprised to find—if we do not bid—that we were the only museum invited to participate that did not do so."

"And what will the buyers get for their money?" someone asked disdainfully. "A collection they cannot exhibit, a collection they will not even be able to acknowledge!"

"For the time being, perhaps," Ruth said angrily. "But I have a strong conviction that anyone, museum or private collector, who gets this collection will find very good arguments not only for keeping it, but for exhibiting it as well."

404

Someone on the board yawned audibly. Ruth McVeigh clenched her jaw. This was, she knew, her last chance. Different tactics were needed, and now she kept her voice emotionless, under rigid control. "Mr. Chairman, members of the board, is the problem here the legal ownership of the collection, or is it the fifteen million dollars? If, for example, it were a matter of one million dollars, or half a million, would you be more willing to chance the question of legal ownership?"

Dr. Keller raised a hand. "Definitely not," he said flatly.

Ruth looked from one face to another down the long table, weighing an idea that had come to her and finding it more and more to her liking. Suddenly she was sure she could convince them to try it, and her tone became more confident. "Suppose we were able to get the fifteen leading museums in the world, say, to put up one million dollars each, or thirty museums to contribute half a million each, and to agree that the treasure would then be owned jointly by all of us. And suppose those museums were to include the Turkish, the Greek, and the German—all the possible claimants to ownership—and that they also agreed not only on sharing ownership but on a schedule for each one to exhibit the treasure."

There was silence as this new concept was explored. Then Bob Keller shook his head. "The claimants would never agree."

Ruth persisted. "How do we know unless we ask them?"

"Exactly what are you suggesting, Ruth?" asked the chairman.

Ruth McVeigh took a deep breath. "I'm suggesting that I arrange a meeting of the leading museum directors at some central location—maybe London—where we can all discuss the auction in detail. If we can cooperate, at least the question of finances can be overcome. And, in the absence of competition, we can keep the price down to the original figure—fifteen million."

She looked around the table again. Everyone was listening carefully now. "As to the question of ownership, most of the major claimants are precisely the museums least able to finance a bid. Such a proposition certainly should interest them—to have at least partial ownership rather than none at all."

She had finished. There was silence; then a hand was raised. The chairman nodded.

"Mr. Chairman," the man said, "I move that Dr. McVeigh be given instructions by this board to pursue her suggestion."

"Second!"

"Any discussion?" Silence. "If not, all in favor?"

There was a chorus of ayes.

"Opposed?"

Another silence. The chairman tapped his gavel. "Motion carried. I will see Dr. McVeigh tomorrow to make arrangements."

WASHINGTON, D.C.—May 1979

SPECULATION in the press regarding the mysterious auction of the Schliemann treasure had caught the attention of the federal government, and a meeting to discuss the matter had been arranged between Frank Mayberry of the State Department and Thomas Wilson of the CIA. The meeting took place in Wilson's office at CIA headquarters in Langley, Virginia, and Mayberry led off. A tall, thin man, he spoke softly but effectively.

"I assume, Tom," he said, "that you've been reading about what the newspapers call the Auction of the Ages?"

"It would be difficult to miss," Wilson said. He was a gray-haired, stocky man in his late fifties. "What's State's interest in it?"

"Potentially, this auction poses a very serious question," Mayberry replied. He paused for a moment. "Tom, do you honestly believe the Schliemann treasure is in Russia?"

Wilson seemed surprised at the question. "Yes. The OSS investigated after the war, and I was part of that investigation. There was an agreement between the Allied powers that all art treasures found would be turned over to an Allied commission for disposition when the war was over. I would say in general that the other Allies kept their part of the bargain better than the Russians. The Schliemann treasure was hidden in a bunker under the Berlin zoo; the Red Army took the city, including the zoo, and the treasure hasn't been seen or heard of since."

"You never made representations to the Russians?"

Wilson smiled wryly. "Of course we did. They said they didn't know what we were talking about. Treasure? What treasure?" He frowned. "The only conclusion we were able to come to was that the treasure went to the Soviet Union. We think it's still there."

"Then," Mayberry asked, leaning forward a bit, "do you think this auction is being conducted by the Russian government?"

Wilson shook his head. "Why would they sell it? The collection has far more intrinsic than monetary value. And I'm sure that they don't need fifteen million dollars to balance their budget."

"Precisely," Mayberry said seriously. "And *that* is State's interest in the matter. *Why* are they selling it, after having it for over thirty years?"

Wilson thought a moment. "Suppose Russia had the treasure until recently, when some enterprising thief simply stole it, carried it quietly out of Russia, and is now offering it for sale."

"What then?"

"Then the CIA would be very interested, too," Wilson said. "If Soviet security can be breached so easily, it would definitely be in our interest to know."

Mayberry nodded. "Agreed. Then both of us seem to have a stake in this affair. You'll do something about it?"

Wilson sighed. "I suppose we'll have to." He came to his feet, holding out his hand. "We'll be in touch, Frank."

When his visitor had left, Tom Wilson reached for his telephone. "Personnel? Find me someone who knows something about archaeology, preferably someone who is familiar with the Schliemann collection. Sure, I suppose a free lance would be all right for this one."

LENINGRAD—May 1979

A MEETING was in progress in the Leningrad offices of the KGB— the State Security Committee—of the Soviet Union. Present were Colonel Ilya Berezhkov, head of the Leningrad section, Major Serge Ulanov of the scientific section, and Ulanov's superior from KGB headquarters in Moscow, Colonel Vasily Vashugin. Through the tall windows of the office, the spires of the Fortress of Peter and Paul sparkled in the spring sunshine.

Vashugin, a rugged, gray-haired man, was speaking thoughtfully. "The question is simple. Why has the American OSS—CIA now, of course—after all these years of secrecy over their theft of the Schliemann collection, suddenly put it up for auction?"

Ulanov stirred in his chair. He was a stocky man in his early sixties with a shock of short white hair that seemed to stand on end. "I wonder if it really is the CIA that is offering it for sale." He paused to light a cigarette. "They don't need fifteen or twenty million dollars; they have an almost unlimited budget."

Vashugin was watching him with narrowed eyes. "So?"

"It is possible that someone other than the CIA is offering it. If so, then they must have managed to steal it from Langley, or from wherever the CIA has been holding it."

Vashugin was nodding his head slowly. "I see. Are you suggesting that someone was able to breach the security of the CIA?"

Ulanov shrugged. "It seems at least a possibility."

Berezhkov wrinkled his forehead in thought. "I'm not so sure. Let's not underestimate the CIA. When they were the OSS, they managed to steal the collection from under our noses. They were the only ones who could have arranged the forged papers and everything in those confused days."

"Yes, we're fairly certain of that," Vashugin said, recalling the ancient investigation in his mind's eye. "We're positive the man who forged the papers that released the collection from Russian custody was Pettersson, the Swedish forger. Our experts studied the documents, and there was no doubt he was responsible. In addition, Pettersson answered the description of one of the men who took the crate off the train at Bad Freienwalde; he and his companion wore black suits and white shirts, to look like government agents. We were the NKVD then. The idiot conductor admitted the other man looked quite Anglo-Saxon, and I believe he was American. Where did Pettersson disappear to? He didn't go to Denmark or Sweden, because we looked long and hard for him, so he must have ended up in Langley, Virginia." He shook his head. "No, I don't underestimate the CIA."

"They managed to convince the world that we have the collection ourselves," Ulanov said dryly. "Possibly in the basement of the Hermitage Museum here in Leningrad, I expect." He shook his head, almost in admiration, and crushed out his cigarette. "But I cannot see the CIA behind this auction. They wouldn't handle it in this open fashion, any more than we would."

"I agree it's possible that someone else has the treasure," Vashugin said, and suddenly he smiled broadly. "That would be something, eh? Someone robbing the vaults at Langley?" His smile disappeared. "So what do we do about this auction, and the meeting next month in London?" He looked at Ulanov, who was closer to the archaeological field than either of the two colonels.

"To begin with," Ulanov replied slowly, "I should think we would want to enter this auction ourselves. If only to discover who is selling the treasure, and—if it isn't the CIA—how they got their hands on it. And to what extent it reflects weaknesses in the CIA security system. And how that knowledge can be of use to us."

Berezhkov leaned forward. "And as to the meeting in London?"

"I suggest we attend. I'm sure there will be many there who have not been officially invited. I'll go, and I'll take along Dr. Gregor Kovpak, of the Hermitage. He's quite knowledgeable, I hear. And we'll see what we can learn."

Vashugin thought it over and nodded. "It's a logical first step." He rose, indicating that the meeting was over.

Dr. Gregor Kovpak was a tall, handsome man in his middle forties whose expertise in archaeological matters was acknowledged throughout the world. At the moment, however, Dr. Kovpak was in the Zoological Museum of the U.S.S.R. Academy of Sciences, engaged in something far from his true field. He was attempting to produce imitation bones to complete the authentic ones he had accidentally discovered on the Ruthenian slopes of the Carpathians while engaged in an archaeological dig. When the project was finished, he hoped to have assembled the first skeleton of a baby dinosaur ever found in the Soviet Union.

He frowned as the telephone rang, wiped his hands on his lab smock, and picked up the receiver with two fingers.

"Gregor?" It was Alex Pomerenko, director of the Hermitage Museum. "Would you come to my office?"

"No, I can't! I'm casting baby dinosaur bones and my hands are full of plaster of paris!"

"Those bones have waited seventy million years—a few minutes more won't hurt," Pomerenko said. "And we pay your salary—not the Zoological Museum. Right now, Gregor. It's important."

The director hung up the telephone to avoid further discussion. Kovpak stared at the receiver in frustration, and then also hung up. After washing his hands and combing his thick curly hair, he shrugged off his smock and pulled on his jacket. Museum directors! he thought blackly as he stamped out the door.

He crossed the Neva River via the nearest bridge, entered the Hermitage, and climbed the steps to the director's office. He found Alex Pomerenko standing by the window. Seated before the wide desk was a stocky man with a pure white crew cut.

"Major Ulanov," Pomerenko said, "this is Dr. Gregor Kovpak. Gregor, Major Serge Ulanov."

In mufti, Kovpak noted as he sat down. Most probably KGB. What can the State Security Committee want of us poor scientists at the Hermitage?

Ulanov lit a cigarette and came right to the point. "Dr. Kovpak," he said, "what is your professional opinion of this proposed auction of the Schliemann collection?"

"Auction?" Kovpak frowned, surprised at the question, then looked apologetic. "I've been busy with a special project and haven't been paying much attention to the journals lately."

Major Ulanov filled him in. Then he asked, "Who do you think has had the Schliemann collection all these years?"

Kovpak grinned. "I haven't the faintest. But all my colleagues are convinced that we have it here at the Hermitage. Why? Doesn't anyone know who is offering it?"

"No," the major said. "It's a blind auction. So far."

Kovpak frowned again. "But you must have some ideas—"

Ulanov leaned forward. "In our opinion, Doctor, the treasure has been in the hands of American intelligence since the end of the war. However, I think someone has been clever enough to steal it from them, as they stole it from us. And we are extremely interested in learning how. We think you can help us."

Kovpak's eyebrows went up. "Me? How?"

"First, through your knowledge in the field. Second, there will soon be a meeting in London of museum directors from around the world to discuss this auction. We would like you to attend."

"I'd be very willing, except I'm in the middle of a project—"

"Gregor!" Pomerenko said threateningly.

Kovpak sighed. "All right, but I'm not . . ." He paused.

Ulanov smiled. "An intelligence agent? Well, I am. And I'll be with you." He crushed out his cigarette and rose to his feet. "Gentlemen, thank you."

410

BERLIN—April 1945

"THE Schliemann treasure?" Captain Sudikoff said. "No, Sergeant, I never heard of it." He smiled at his elderly quartermaster, of whom he was fond. "Should I have?"

"I suppose not," Sergeant Kolenko said. He was aware of the captain's lack of university education, but he had a profound respect for the younger man nevertheless.

"What exactly is this treasure of yours?" asked the captain.

"One of the most valuable collections in the world," the sergeant replied, his voice unconsciously taking on the tone of a professor at his lectern. "It is supposedly the treasure accumulated by Priam, king of ancient Troy at the time of the war with the Greeks. Homer . . ." He paused. "You know who Homer was?"

"We're not totally ignorant in the provinces," the captain said dryly, and smiled. "I know who Homer was."

"Good," the sergeant said, and once again he became the professor. "It is assumed Homer lived in the ninth century B.C., give or take fifty years. Prior to his time, history was handed down from generation to generation by word of mouth, as legends. Homer, in his *Iliad* and *Odyssey*, related these legends of events that had taken place five or six centuries earlier, and until relatively recent times people assumed that the stories were simply products of his imagination. However, one man, Heinrich Schliemann, was convinced that Homer's tales were historical fact."

"And?" the captain asked.

"And Schliemann proved it," the sergeant said triumphantly. "He discovered the site of ancient Troy, where Homer had said it was. He also discovered Priam's golden treasure. This was in 1873, over seventy years ago. Then he donated the treasure to a museum here in Berlin. And when the bombing began, it was decided the gold would be safer hidden under good, strong concrete. So, in a bunker under the zoo—"

Now the full import of what he had been hearing suddenly struck the captain. "What? No!"

"Yes, sir," the sergeant said, grinning widely. "The treasure is outside your quarters right now."

411

The captain's eyes narrowed. "I can't believe it. Bring it in and let's have a look at it!"

"Yes, sir!" The sergeant went out and returned dragging the trunk by one handle. The door to the office was closed, the trunk's lid thrown back. Captain Sudikoff stared as the sergeant carefully unwrapped each bundle and spread out the contents on a bench.

"That's gold?" the captain asked.

"Yes, and almost pure, too. To make the fine wire used in some of the delicate ornaments they had to work it very soft; they didn't have the tools or the techniques for doing such work unless the metal was soft and almost pure."

The captain seemed dazed as he stared at the golden bracelets, beads, masks, buttons, ornamental singlets. "What do we do with this stuff, now that we've found it?"

"You remember the order," the sergeant replied. "Art treasures are to be turned over to the Allied art commission for disposition."

Captain Sudikoff snorted. "Nonsense! Turn something this valuable over to whom? To the Americans? Who delayed helping us in the war until we had almost bled to death? No! You know the Allied commission will never give it back to Germany!"

"But—what will we do with it then, sir?"

The captain thought a moment and then smiled. "I'll do what every good army man would do in the same circumstances," he said. "I'll pass the decision up the line."

BERLIN—May 1945

HITLER was dead, the war was finally over. Those Germans who were in uniform, or whose papers looked too recent to be genuine, were on their way to prison camps. Of those left behind, some had been conscripted for clearing the rubble from the streets of Berlin. Among them was an old man named Hans Gruber. He was uneducated and knew nothing of politics, but under the Nazis he had felt a part of something important.

Before the bombings began, Gruber had been a porter in the zoo. When the need for bunkers arose, he had willingly helped construct one for the Schliemann treasure. It had been he who

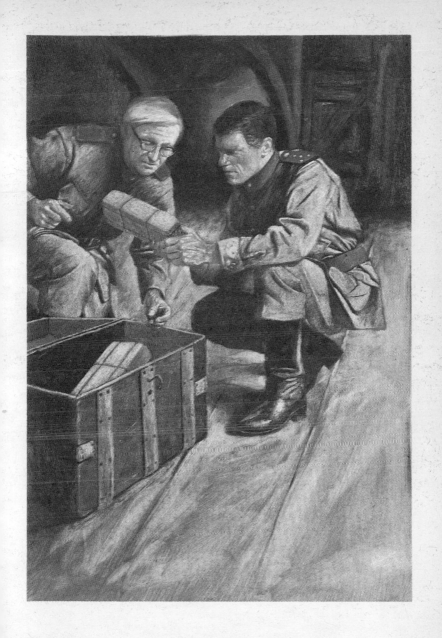

had plastered over the hole in the wall to conceal its location. Now, as one of the workers assigned to the gargantuan job of clearing the rubble, Gruber was aware that the treasure had been discovered. Each day, as he lined up with the others to receive his shovel, he would peer past the issuing quartermaster and see the trunk in one corner of the captain's room. Its hasp had been repaired and rope had been wrapped around it in profusion. He could not understand why it had not been removed to a safer place. But it never occurred to him to do something about it.

Until one day, while piling broken building stone into a truck, he noticed that a new member of the work crew was a former SS major named Kurt Schurz. Gruber walked over to him, amazed to find him alive and free, not in prison as a war criminal.

"Major—" he began, but the other man glared him to silence. Gruber dropped his voice. "I'm sorry. I didn't think. Don't you remember me? Hans Gruber. I was a porter at the zoo when you brought that trunk. I plastered over the hole."

"I remember," Schurz said shortly. "What about it?"

"The Russians found it, and it's in the captain's quarters."

"So?"

Gruber wet his lips. "I thought maybe you could figure out how to get it away from them. It's valuable, isn't it?"

Schurz laughed—a short, humorless laugh. "It's more than valuable. It's invaluable. What do you suggest, old man? That I just go in and ask for it? Say it's an antique trunk that has sentimental value for me? You're a fool."

"I just thought—"

"Don't think," Schurz said harshly. He turned and walked away.

Although he had admonished the old man, Schurz could not help but think about what he had said. What a coup it would be to get the treasure from under the noses of the Russian pigs! They were probably waiting now for orders to move it. Schurz stopped dead in his tracks. What if the orders should come *from us!*

The practical problems of such a scheme at once became apparent. First, there was the matter of locating the man he needed before the real orders came through. After work Schurz hurried toward the small bar where he went for an occasional drink. He slid into an occupied corner booth.

"Pettersson," he said in a low tone. "Is he still around?"

414

"I think so," someone said. "Why do you want him?"

"Business," Schurz said. "How do I get in touch with him?"

"Where are you living?" the man asked.

"In the Hermann Göring Strasse. Number eighteen, first floor, in back on the right. Make it fast, can you? It's very important."

"Important for you? Or for the party?"

"Both," Schurz said as he stood up.

THREE nights later Jan Pettersson appeared at Schurz's room. He was a very thin, extremely tall man with a sad, horselike face. A shock of bright yellow hair was tucked under a ragged stocking cap. Schurz sat his guest down, brought out a bottle of vodka, and asked Pettersson why he was still around.

"My face," Pettersson said wearily. "My height. My hair. The Allies are looking for me. It is easy enough to forge papers"— Pettersson had forged all the pound notes and the dollar bills printed in Germany—"but at every border crossing they want me for a war criminal. Can you imagine? Me, an artist! It's only a question of time before I'm caught." He took a healthy drink from the bottle. "They told me it was important, so I came."

"It *is*," Schurz said, and leaned forward. "I can get you out of the country with me. We'll have to take a small crate with us—"

"A small crate? What will be inside it?"

"A treasure in gold. All you have to do is to forge some papers. In Russian. Can you do it?"

"Of course."

"Good!" Schurz took a deep breath and then thought a moment. "Do you have money—pounds or dollars? We need a boat. It's the only way to take the gold with us. I know someone who can arrange one for us on the Baltic, but I need dollars."

Pettersson took another drink. "I've got plenty of money," he said. The vodka was making him expansive. "I insisted on payment in real American dollars before I forged the foreign currency."

"You'll be repaid," Schurz said flatly. "With interest."

Pettersson looked at him. "How can I be sure?"

"Because I say so." Schurz was beginning to get irritated. "Besides, you want to get out of Germany, don't you? As you say, it's only a question of time before they pick you up, and then—" He drew his index finger across his throat.

415

Pettersson winced. "Where will we be going?"

"Sweden," Schurz replied. "We can both be safe there."

Pettersson wet his lips. "And rich."

"And very rich." Schurz wondered that a man as clever with his hands as Jan Pettersson could not realize that he would never get off the boat alive.

The tall Swede nodded and leaned back. "All right," he said. "What papers will you need, and what do you want them to say?"

THE Russian courier was about to descend the bunker steps when he felt a tap on his shoulder. Turning, he stared suspiciously at the ragged figure who had stopped him. "What is it?"

The man smiled obsequiously and held out a small bundle of official-looking papers. "You dropped this." He pointed to the dispatch bag and then to the ground.

"Oh." The soldier understood the gesture if not the language. He shoved the papers into the dispatch bag. "Thanks." He turned and trotted down the bunker steps.

Behind him Schurz returned to his shovel. All he could do now was wait. And hope that the real orders for the disposition of the treasure would not come through in the next two days.

In the bunker below, Captain Sudikoff looked at the orders. "About time!" he said with a combination of relief and irritation. "How did we ever manage to win the war with all this bureaucracy? Three weeks to get a simple answer to a simple question!" He studied the orders again. They were written in a crabbed longhand and signed with an indecipherable scrawl, although the name of General L. Schvichev was clearly typed below.

The captain summoned Sergeant Kolenko. "We've finally gotten our orders to ship out that treasure of yours," he said, smiling.

"Oh?" the sergeant said, interested. "To the Allied art commission, I suppose?"

"To Russia," the captain said. He tapped the instructions. "The orders are clear enough. They want the treasure protected against any contingency. They want it placed in a case made of thin steel. The case is to be fitted inside a wooden crate, then nailed shut and banded with steel for shipping. Is that clear?"

"Bands for shipping," the sergeant said, busily scribbling the instructions on a piece of paper.

416

"And tear up that paper!" the captain said testily. "This matter is to be kept completely secret. Nothing in writing."

"Yes, sir." The sergeant tore the paper into shreds, dropped them into an ashtray, and lit them with a match.

Referring to the instructions again, the captain continued. "The box is to be marked 'Captured Medical Equipment' and is to be shipped out on the train that leaves at six tomorrow evening from the Stuttgarter Bahnhof for Leningrad. It is to be placed in the baggage car—*not* in any of the freight cars—and it is to be released only to a Colonel Boris Golobev, or his representatives, on written identification. Those instructions are to be given to the train officials verbally, understand?"

"Yes, sir!" said Sergeant Kolenko. He left the room, secretly pleased that the treasure was going to his own country.

To KURT Schurz, the scene of total confusion at the Stuttgarter Bahnhof was very reassuring. Trucks were drawn up before the gaping doors of freight cars, discharging every imaginable type of matériel; officers with lists were frantically attempting to keep track of what was being loaded into the cars. Soldiers being reassigned were milling about trying to locate their units. Above it all, the sun's late afternoon rays crept through the spaces which bombs had blasted in the station's roof. Pacing on the platform by the six-o'clock train for Leningrad, Kurt Schurz hoped that amid all this frenzy he and his tall companion might pass unnoticed.

At his side Pettersson shuffled along resignedly, almost as if he were walking to his execution. If the Russians were actively looking for him, Schurz thought dourly, that guilty look on the horse-like face would be enough to guarantee capture.

Both men were dressed in neat black suits, dark polished shoes, white shirts, and dark neckties, and each wore a black homburg. The outfits, purchased on the black market, had cost nearly as much as the boat Schurz had arranged for in Warnemünde on the Baltic coast, or the car he had set up to meet them in Bad Freienwalde. To make these arrangements, he had sought out members of ODESSA—the organization dedicated to keeping the Nazi Party alive—but while they were devoted to the cause, they had wanted as much as they could get for taking chances.

Freight-car doors were now being slammed shut, and a Russian train official stood looking at his watch. Schurz scowled. Where was the crate? On the rapidly emptying platform he and the abnormally tall and tragic-looking Pettersson were beginning to become noticeable.

The official was staring pointedly at them now, gesturing for them to board. Schurz put one foot on the lower step of the car and paused. The official began walking purposefully in their direction. And then, at last, a large truck came charging through the makeshift entrance of the station, blasting its horn. As the official turned and moved toward it, the truck stopped and three men descended from the cab. Two of them went to the back and dragged a heavy crate to the tailgate while the third, a sergeant, spoke to the official. After a few minutes of conversation, the latter nodded, then jumped onto the baggage car; the crate was carried over to the car and shoved in, and the door was closed. Trying not to show his relief, Schurz tugged at Pettersson's sleeve, and the two climbed aboard.

The conductor assumed that the black suits and homburgs marked them as NKVD men and glanced at their identity cards only perfunctorily. Without words he led them to a compartment and was about to leave when Schurz pinched Pettersson painfully through his sleeve. The tall man remembered his instructions.

"Bad Freienwalde. Advise us when we're near," he said in Russian, trying to keep his voice from breaking.

"Right," the conductor said, and slid the compartment door shut.

"Now what?" Pettersson asked nervously as they sat down.

"Now we keep to the plan," Schurz replied. "We get off at Bad Freienwalde and take the crate with us. And try not to look as if you were climbing a scaffold."

"It'll never work."

"What do you mean? It *is* working!" If only he himself spoke Russian and didn't need the services of this monstrous idiot any longer! "When we get to Bad Freienwalde, just say what you were told to say." Pettersson opened his mouth to reply, but Schurz said coldly, "Keep quiet now."

The two leaned back, Pettersson wondering how he could possibly say his little piece to the Russian official in the baggage car without stammering and giving the whole show away.

Outside the train window the shadows darkened across the bat-

418

tered city and its outskirts, starkly silhouetting the jagged ruins of buildings. It would take time, Schurz thought, but with the help of such treasures as the Schliemann gold, he and the party would return and rebuild all this.

It was not long before the conductor put his head into the compartment. "Bad Freienwalde in five minutes."

The two men nodded and got to their feet. Pettersson took a deep breath, and at Schurz's urging led the way to the baggage car. The official recognized the two men from the platform, and his expression froze into polite immobility.

Pettersson wet his lips nervously. "A crate . . ." He swallowed the next words and pointed to the box near the outer door.

The official had been expecting to be approached about the mysterious crate, and he was only too happy to be rid of it—and of the NKVD. Still, there were the necessary formalities.

"You have the proper papers?"

Pettersson managed to find them in a pocket and hand them over. The Russian checked them carefully. Satisfied, he nodded and began to wrestle the heavy crate to the doorsill.

At that moment the train came to an abrupt halt. The door slid back, and a dark, important-looking military sedan appeared out of the blackness, coming to a stop across from the door. The headlights were extinguished, and a man, also dressed in dark clothes but wearing a peaked cap instead of a homburg, stepped out and approached the train. Between them, he and the official managed to get the crate down and carry it to the car.

Schurz followed quickly with Pettersson, and they climbed into the rear seat, where they could hear the sounds of the crate being stored in the trunk. The driver returned to the front seat and the headlights came on, revealing on the front fenders the small flags of a general officer. The motor started, and the car slid off into the darkness. Behind them, Schurz and Pettersson could hear the engine's whistle as the train began to move again.

There was silence in the sedan for a moment, and then Schurz burst into laughter, clapping his hands in glee. *They had done it! They had actually done it!* He looked over at Pettersson, squeezed into a corner of the seat.

"Well?" he demanded triumphantly.

"We're not there yet."

Oh, my God! Schurz thought. Well, at least there was the satisfaction of knowing that before long he would be finished with this pessimistic clown. Once the lights of Trelleborg in Sweden could be seen from the boat, one stab, and then he would weight the idiot's body with the chains he had asked to have put aboard.

He leaned forward and, pushing back the glass between the driver's seat and his own, spoke in a low voice. "*Heil* Hitler!"

"*Heil* Hitler!"

"Any trouble?"

"No. Only the car must be back before dawn. The general will be with his girl friend till then. Any trouble at your end?"

"Not so far," Schurz replied. "You spoke to the boat's captain?"

"Yes. He was here two days ago. His boat's the *Linderndsee*." The driver turned his attention back to the road, and they sped through the darkness toward the Baltic coast, four hours away.

THE BALTIC—May 1945

THE outskirts of Rostock rose about them in the dark; they raced through the cobbled streets and took the road that headed to Warnemünde, eight miles away. Schurz and Pettersson had napped during the journey; now they both came awake.

The car crept past the deserted Warnemünde ferry dock, not yet back in operation, and took a side road that led past more docks hung with nets. The sudden gleam of a flashlight, instantly extinguished, gave them direction. A moment later they pulled up before a small boat swaying against its mooring lines at dockside.

A man emerged from the shadows as they climbed out of the car. Schurz and the driver wrestled the crate out of the car's trunk and across the narrow gangplank to the deck of the boat. This done, the driver returned to the car and drove off toward the main highway south. Schurz and a dazed Pettersson followed their contact forward and belowdecks.

Inside a tiny, closely curtained cabin the man lit a small lamp connected to a gas bottle. Then he turned to face the two of them with a smile on his bearded lips. Schurz returned the smile. "Hello, Captain Sneller. It's been a while."

"Hello, Major. It has, indeed."

Schurz sat down on a swivel chair. Across from him Pettersson sank down on the cabin's single bunk, his head in his hands. Sneller considered the tall man and looked at Schurz queryingly.

"A touch of nerves," Schurz said disinterestedly. "How do you like being a fisherman, Captain?"

Sneller shrugged lightly. "I was a fisherman before I was a U-boat captain," he said with another smile. It quickly faded. "Major, do you think you can make it across in this boat with only—?" He jerked a thumb in the direction of Pettersson, who was not paying much attention to their conversation.

"I could do it alone," Schurz said confidently. "I've had experience with boats."

"If you say so, Major. There's enough gasoline to get you there, and there's a full container of gas here for the lamp." Sneller cleared his throat. "Now, there's the matter of the balance of the money. . . ."

"No problem," Schurz said expansively. He leaned over and, taking a wallet from Pettersson's inner pocket, extracted some notes and handed them over. "Any schnapps on board?"

"There's plenty in the locker, there." Sneller pointed. "Now, I'll show you the controls on the bridge."

The two men left the cabin and climbed to the deck. A short companionway took them to the small bridge, where blackout curtains had been strung over the glass before the wheel.

"There's the engine starter," Sneller said, shining his flashlight on a button. "Next to it is a choke, and here is the accelerator."

"Good. And what about patrols?"

Captain Sneller moved to the chart table at the left of the wheel. "Here's where we are: Warnemünde. The Danes have a fleet of four patrol boats in this area. They come from the north and the west, arriving alternately right on schedule, three hours apart. They all turn at Gedser lighthouse"—he indicated a small spit of land in Denmark directly across a narrow arm of the Baltic from Warnemünde—"and then go back the way they came." He glanced at his watch. "It's a little after one now. It will take you an hour or so to be off Gedser. If you leave now, you should be well out of sight of the next patrol boat; it's due at the lighthouse at four."

Schurz nodded. "In that case we'd better be off."

"I would say so." Sneller led the way back down the companionway and jumped to the pier. "Good luck. *Heil* Hitler!"

"*Heil* Hitler!" Schurz whispered as Sneller unwound the ropes. When the *Linderndsee* had drifted clear of the dock, Schurz started the engine and headed out of the estuary to the sea. As the first slight wave of the Baltic lifted the prow, he took a deep, shuddering breath, feeling himself begin to tremble.

He had done it! He had actually gotten away with it! He felt a sudden desire to sing at the top of his voice, but he knew how sound carries over water. And he still had about seventy miles to go to reach Trelleborg; in this boat, that would mean at least six hours. Time to sing or yell when he had reached his final destination. Forcing himself to think only of the present and the many miles to go, he settled himself at the wheel while the *Linderndsee* headed steadily out across the water.

BELOW, in the small cabin, Pettersson heard the sound of the engine starting and knew that it was a death knell for him. There was no doubt in his mind that Schurz had no intention of allowing him to live to share the treasure. Why, then, had he come along? Pettersson did not know. He knew only that he was tired of hiding, tired of running, tired of being afraid, tired of everything.

Should he kill Schurz before Schurz killed him? But what then? He could not go back to Germany, and in Sweden his family and friends thought him a traitor. And what would he do with the treasure if he had it? He had no idea how to turn it into cash. Yes, it was better to let Schurz kill him; it was the one solution to his pain, a pain that had no source and therefore no cure.

By whatever method Schurz planned to kill him, it would certainly be easier to take, he thought, if he had some of that schnapps the captain had mentioned. He got to his feet and opened the locker. There was enough there to drink oneself to death, if one had the time, he mused. Unfortunately, he always either got sick or fell asleep before he had had anywhere near enough to cause death. It was a pity. It would have been the ideal way to cheat Schurz of the satisfaction of killing him. Still, one could always try. He took a bottle back to the bunk with him, opened it, and drank deeply.

The schnapps was not even half finished when he had to suppress a deep yawn and knew he would never make it. Life was so unfair! Tears rolled down his cheeks. A man of his talents, and he couldn't even choose his own way of dying!

He looked around the cabin, his reddened, swollen eyes taking in the effects one by one, until they spied the lamp. *The lamp!* He set the schnapps at his feet and moved unsteadily to the table where the lamp stood. He studied the bottle of gas and then looked at the steady flame burning within the glass chimney. He smiled and then began to giggle. Reaching over to the reservoir, he slowly turned the valve, watching until the flame disappeared and the cabin was in total darkness. Now Pettersson opened the valve all the way and sniffed at the aperture over the chimney. The sudden wave of dizziness that washed over him convinced him that the gas was pouring out. He groped his way back to the bunk and sat down, feeling for the schnapps bottle on the deck. Finding it, he raised it to his lips. Just one more drink and then to sleep, he said to himself. He lay back on the bunk, inhaling deeply, and smiled at the thought of Schurz's surprise and disappointment.

THE Danish coast guard cutter *Elritse* was not a large vessel; her only weaponry was an old forty-millimeter Bofors cannon at the prow. Her mission was to prevent smuggling and—more important in the eyes of her skipper—the illegal entry of the hated ex-Nazis. When not stopping and searching suspicious-looking ships, Captain Eric Hansen was meticulous about maintaining a rigid schedule of patrol.

Tonight, however, it was certain that no schedule would be maintained. A bit of flotsam had caught in the ship's propeller, twisting it badly. The makeshift repair by the ship's engineer had taken an hour, and the slow speed required to avoid damage to the propeller shaft had brought the *Elritse* off the Gedser lighthouse a good two hours late. Captain Hansen was about to abort his patrol and return to base for permanent repairs when there was a whistle from the speaking tube on the bridge. He picked it up. "The captain here."

"Lookout, sir. A small boat, two points off the starboard bow, distance about four miles. Running without lights, sir."

The small boat Hansen picked up in his night glasses seemed a perfect example of a smuggler's vessel; undoubtedly its crew had expected the patrol to be long gone by now, on its return trip. Hansen had always known that holding a rigid schedule was foolish, but orders were orders. And now, when he was sure he had a smuggler in his sights, here he was with a crippled ship! Still, the smuggler didn't know that.

Hansen picked up the speaking tube. "Lookout . . . signal that boat to lay to and await our boarding party."

"Aye, aye, sir." The flashing light on the lookout platform went into action.

Captain Hansen again trained his glasses on the boat. Was it possible it was not a smuggler? It did not take any evasive action. But neither did it reply to his order to lie to. Hansen set a course to intersect the other's path and ordered a shot fired across its bow.

On board the *Linderndsee*, Schurz was dozing. The steady drone of the engines and the hypnotic rising and falling of the boat had finally induced a lethargy beyond his control. His head had come to rest between two spokes of the wheel, fortuitously holding the boat on course. He was dreaming of his days as a lieutenant. Suddenly it seemed that someone was playing a flashlight across his eyes. He started, awoke, and then sat erect, frightened by the loud *boom* of a cannon. Ahead of him, unbelievably, he saw a spout of water rise in the air.

Confused, Schurz tried to make some sense of what was happening. There, approaching him, lit up like a Christmas tree, was what had to be a coast guard cutter! He glanced quickly at the chronometer. He was less than an hour from Warnemünde! How did the damned patrol boat happen to be here now?

The cutter was no more than two miles off. If he turned and ran, he knew they could easily send him to the bottom with a well-placed shot from their cannon. As if to prove the point, another waterspout rose even closer to him, the *boom* reverberating over the water. He pulled back the throttle in a token of surrender.

Vitally important now was that the treasure not fall into enemy hands. Schurz hastily lashed the wheel to keep the boat from swinging, and ran down the companionway to the crate on the deck. Looking frantically for some kind of orientation, he saw the brilliant arc of the Gedser light. He swung about, searching for another marker to make a triangulation, and saw a few lights from a village, strung along a dock of sorts. It would have to do.

Someday, somehow, he would come back to recover the treasure. He bent to the herculean task of raising the crate to the rail, but the strain was too much. The cutter was now only a mile away, and he could barely budge the heavy steel-bound box. He paused, panting, thinking furiously, and then looked up. Pettersson! Schurz dashed down to the cabin and shoved open the door.

No light! So the big ox was sleeping, eh? Well, he'd wake him in a hurry. A sudden dizziness seemed to bother Schurz, but he put it down to his lack of sleep. No time now for such ailments, he told himself sternly, and reached into a pocket for a match. . . .

FROM the log of the Danish cutter *Elritse*, entered by her captain, Eric Hansen:

23 May 1945: . . . At 0205 encountered small boat running without lights off Gedser light. Flashed orders for it to lay to and, when it did not obey, fired several shots across its bows. In our crippled condition it could have outrun us, but unaware of that fact, it elected instead to self-destruct. The *Elritse* cruised the spot where it blew up. There were no signs of survivors or anything to indicate a cargo so precious that the smuggler would blow up his boat rather than submit to search.

GEDSER—January 1979

WINTER storms on the Baltic are not uncommon, but the one that raged down from the north that day in late January surpassed any of the long, bitter season. Knud Christensen, standing at the window of his farmhouse outside Gedser, stared with concern out over the sea. Ahead was a wall of white, sweeping over gray waters lashed by wind. The small dock at the end of his property was barely visible, with the high waves washing over it. Christensen was worried about his younger brothers, Niels and Gustave. They were both seasoned fishermen, but this storm had come up so suddenly that any boat caught in it would be in danger.

It was odd in some ways that Knud had not taken to fishing. As a boy of fourteen he had been the one most at home in or on the water, the best swimmer, the best diver. But as he grew older, he realized he preferred the quiet, almost stolid life of farming. Sailing and fishing at times required instant decisions, which he was ill equipped to make. Now, at twenty-eight, he knew he had made the right choice. Farming allowed a man time to think, to ponder problems in depth. Today, however, Knud wished he had gone with his brothers; in a storm of this magnitude, muscle was needed as well as brains.

The snow ceased as suddenly as it had come, but the winds seemed to intensify. Under the probing beam from the lighthouse, huge waves could be seen falling with fury on the shore. Christensen strained his eyes, but in the darkening overcast it was impossible to distinguish any boat.

A knock on the door brought him hurrying to the front room. Jens Krag, a neighbor and a fisherman, came in, shaking water from his sou'wester. Knud stared at him blankly, wondering at the visit. Then, slowly, the other's silence, his expression of misery, brought understanding.

"Gustave . . . Niels . . . Where are they? What happened?"

Krag stared at the floor, unable to look into Christensen's gaunt face. "The weather looked threatening," he said, speaking hesitantly, "but the herring were running, we were netting them like mad, and nobody wanted to leave until we had filled our lockers. When the storm really struck, we all pulled our nets and headed in. We were off the lighthouse when the blizzard hit, and we couldn't see a thing. Then suddenly the snow stopped, and I saw I was almost on top of your brothers' boat. They were in trouble. The engine must have failed. They were bouncing around completely out of control. Then . . ." He paused.

Christensen's eyes were cold on Krag, as if blaming the man for surviving when his two brothers had not. "Then?"

"Then I saw Niels starting to raise sail—"

"*Raise sail? In that sea?*"

"He had to try something, didn't he?" Krag swallowed. "Anyway, the wind caught the sail and—and the mast snapped. It threw Niels overboard and he was swept away."

Christensen's voice was like doom. "And Gustave?"

Krag swallowed again; he knew Knud's special feeling for the youngest brother. "The wind took the boat into a trough, swinging it, tangling Gustave in the shrouds, and then it seemed the boat

426

just opened where the mast had split the deck, and—and the next thing she was gone, just like that." He avoided Christensen's eyes. "I'm sorry, Knud."

"Sorry . . ." Christensen was staring through the window at the blackness beyond. It was his fault that they had foundered. They had discussed the need for a new engine, but Knud had said the farm requirements came first.

Krag was moving to the door. "I have to be going."

"Wait." Christensen's features seemed carved in granite. "Do you know where the boat went down?"

"Fairly close," Krag said. "We could see both the light and the harbor entrance. She wouldn't drift much with her lockers full, and it's too deep there for the waves to cause much undersea movement. As soon as it's calm, I can locate the place for Pastor Rasmussen to hold a proper service."

"A proper service," Knud repeated, and turned without another word to climb the steps to the bedroom.

ON THE following Sunday morning Pastor Rasmussen stood in his small dory as it bobbed lightly on the calm sea. Grouped about him were the boats of the other villagers; Jens Krag had brought Knud Christensen. The air was bitter cold but still on this fine morning. Some of the mourners had brought hothouse flowers; others, small wreaths they had woven from fir boughs. At the final sad words of the service, they leaned over the rails of their boats and tossed their offerings into the sea. There were a few moments of silence, all eyes following the drifting flowers, the men aware that but for the grace of God they, too, could be under the sea with the floating wreaths above them. Then Pastor Rasmussen started his outboard, and the other boatmen followed suit, slowly heading back to the village.

Krag moved to his boat's controls, happy to be standing no longer beside his silent passenger. He pressed the starter, revved the engine, and swung his wheel in the direction of the harbor. Then he became aware that Christensen had moved with him.

"Jens, pull into my dock," Knud said. "I have to get my diving gear. Then I want you to take me out again."

"*What?*" Jens Krag stared incredulously at him. "That's crazy! What do you think you'll find?"

"Gustave."

"But you couldn't live five minutes in that water! This is January, and it's eighty feet deep there!"

"I'll get my gear quickly," Knud replied as he reached over to steer the boat toward the Christensen dock. That service was for you, Niels, he said silently to the waves. But Gustave shall rest in Gedser cemetery, beside our mother and father. I shall recover his body and see he has a proper burial on land, in a place where I can go and mourn when I want.

The engine was cut and Knud stepped onto the dock, warped the boat's rope to a bollard, and walked briskly toward the house. Jens Krag watched with a feeling of dread as Knud soon came tramping back down the path, laden with his gear. The man was totally insane.

"I'm not committing suicide," Knud said quietly, seeming to read the other's mind. "I have compressed-air equipment which is good for well below a hundred feet. And I've worked in cold water. I've got a wet suit and a good lamp. I'll be all right."

Jens Krag sighed and headed out to sea. At the approximate location he slowed and allowed the boat to drift, checking in his memory the position of the lighthouse tower and the harbor entrance as they had appeared the day of the storm. "I think it was about here," he said.

Christensen climbed into his wet suit and flippers and strapped on the compressed-air tank. Then he picked up his lamp and walked to the railing. He put the breathing tube in his mouth, leaned over backward, and let himself fall into the water.

It was cold, shocking, numbing. Despite his wet suit, and despite his great strength and fanatical stubbornness, Knud Christensen realized that in that icy sea he had only minutes to locate his brother's body. He sank like a plumb, brought to the bottom by the heavy weights he had attached to his belt.

The beam from his electric lamp cut weakly through the dark waters, illuminating only a small patch before him. He began a circular search, gradually increasing the diameter of his circles, but the rocky bottom displayed only the normal detritus of an area in sight of land: discarded food cans, broken fish crates, a sunken skiff with a torn bottom. Christensen forced himself on.

The deadly cold suddenly seemed to abate. Knud had a sense

of increasing comfort—of warm torpor, in fact—and he knew he was rapidly coming to the end of his endurance. One final circuit, he promised himself sleepily.

Then he came awake with a start. Ahead of him, looming out of the darkness, was a wreck, but it was larger than the small Christensen fishing vessel. As he swam closer, he realized that he had actually come upon the wreckage of two boats that were now locked together on the rocky bottom. The nearer one obviously had been down for many years; he circled about it. His progress was momentarily blocked by a small wooden crate perched between two rocks. He pushed against it, and its rotten exterior fell away, revealing an inner metal shell. He swam on to the other side of the tangled wrecks. And there, faintly visible in the dimness, was the body of his brother Gustave, hanging from the shrouds, seemingly relaxed, as if it had come to terms with this grave beneath the sea.

Christensen forgot the strange metal case in an instant. He dragged his knife from his belt, swam over the crushed gunwale, and hooked a leg about the stub of the mast. He forced himself to slash at the rope above his head, knowing his time was rapidly running out. The rope seemed to be made of steel; his knife seemed merely to be sawing at it uselessly. And then Knud saw the rope part. The corpse seemed to hesitate a moment, as if reluctant to leave the safety of the shrouds, and then began to rise slowly. Knud remembered the weights at his waist and flipped open his belt buckle, feeling weights and belt fall away. Then he was free and rising, his brother's arm clasped in his numb hand.

Jens Krag saw Knud surface with his lifeless companion. In seconds he brought the boat near to drag the semiconscious man aboard, but Knud insisted that Gustave be taken out of the water first. Then he blacked out.

He awakened, sputtering, the warm bite of aquavit in his throat. He was aware that he was alive and lying on a bunk. The boat was tied at the dock and Krag was sitting next to him, a beaker of spirits in his hand. Knud tried to sit erect, but Krag gently pushed him down. "His body's on deck," Krag said quietly.

Christensen fell back. Now, at least, one brother would have a decent burial in the cemetery on the hill next to their mother and father. Now Knud would be able to sleep a little.

GEDSER—April 1979

SPRING came early and swiftly to the Gedser peninsula that year, but the regular, untroubled sleep that Knud Christensen had promised himself did not materialize. Though he deliberately tired himself out during the day preparing for the spring planting, the nights often brought nightmares. He would be swimming underwater, searching. In the dim light Gustave could be seen, locked helplessly in the shrouds, staring at him intently, as if pleading with him to hurry. But a box stood in Knud's way, and whenever he tried to swim around it, it blocked him anew. Somehow he would have to remove that damnable metal case if he ever wished to reach Gustave.

One morning, after another nightmare about the metal case, Knud knew he had to bring it up, if only to exorcise whatever devils were forcing him to picture the youngest brother just beyond his reach. He considered the matter carefully. Jens Krag would be glad to take him out in his boat, but then Knud would have to share whatever he salvaged. No, he would bring the case up alone, at night. He could reach the spot easily in his dory and be down, up again, and back home without involving anyone else.

The following night Christensen put on his wet suit, attaching a new belt and weights he had purchased. He took the rest of his gear and a hundred feet of rope and carried them down to the dock. He hitched the extra rope to the anchor, climbed into his dory, untied it, and reached for the oars.

When he judged he was close to the wreck, he picked up the anchor and tossed it overboard. Then he put on his compressed air gear, clipped his lamp to his belt, and leaned backward over the gunwale, falling silently into the sea. The water was still cold, though not as cold as it had been in January, and he knew he could not stay down long. He followed the anchor line to the bottom. There he hooked the extra rope into his belt to be sure not to lose the line that led to the surface and the dory, and began his search. After he had reached the limit of the rope, he pulled himself back to the anchor, raised it, swam ahead, and placed it in a new spot, then resumed the search.

He was about to move the anchor a second time when he saw the tangled wreckage of the two boats ahead of him, saw the glint of his light reflected from metal, and knew he had found the case.

Setting down his lamp, he put both hands to the task of shifting the box. Even though its weight was greatly reduced underwater, it was too heavy to lift. Knud paused, thinking. He cut the anchor loose and thrust the free end of the line through the steel bands that still girdled the box, making a sturdy knot that held the case firmly. Then he unhooked the rope from his belt and, with a strong thrust of his flippers, grasped the line and drew himself upward.

He climbed into the dory, slipped off his gear, and began hauling slowly on the anchor line, bringing the case up from the bottom. Beneath his feet the dory dipped dangerously, and Christensen knew he would never be able to bring the case aboard without capsizing. When the side of the box bumped gently against the bottom of his boat, he looped the line tightly around a cleat and bent to the oars. It was hard rowing, but the steel bands held, and the case was still with him when he nudged the dock.

Christensen secured the boat and then waded through the shallow water out to his prize. With his knife he cut the line, leaving enough slack to wind about his thick arm and allow him to tow the case to land. There, assuring himself that if there was anything of value in the box it would go toward a memorial to his brothers, he bent and with all the strength of his large body picked up the case and staggered toward the house. He dragged his prize across the sill and closed the door behind him.

After lighting a lamp, he found a cold chisel and a maul and began to cut through the steel carefully. When he had removed a large enough panel, he reached in, felt around, and brought out four packages. Spreading them on the floor, he opened them one by one.

Each was wrapped in some type of suede, and inside, in tissue paper, were a huge number of beads and buttons and little circlets of wire, all made of a metal Knud didn't recognize. He stared at his find, wondering what on earth it was and why it had been so carefully packaged and boxed. It seemed doubtful that the contents could possibly have enough value to compensate him for his arduous effort by enabling him to replace his discarded anchor

432

and to erect a modest memorial for his brothers. Still, someone had gone to great trouble to preserve the stuff.

Whom could he ask about it? Pastor Rasmussen was by far the best-educated man in the village, but his training was largely ecclesiastical. Per Baunsgaard, the blacksmith? He might recognize what metal the stuff was made of, but he was a noted gossip. It was a problem.

Deciding to sleep on it, Knud packed the pieces back into the box and went to bed. When he woke at dawn, he knew exactly the man to help him solve his problem—a distant cousin his mother had often mentioned to him named Arne Nyborg. He was a professor of something or other at the University of Copenhagen. Knud decided to go and ask his advice. He had never met the man, but he was sure that would make no difference.

Whistling, he started to dress.

COPENHAGEN—April 1979

FROM the window of his small office at the university, Arne Nyborg, associate professor of Danish history, stared sourly at the pretty coeds hurrying past in their tight skirts, books in arms. For some reason he never seemed able to impress them. His hints that their favors might be returned in the form of better grades were met by blank stares or barely concealed smiles of derision.

If he had money, Nyborg assured himself, it would be different; his short stature, his tendency toward obesity, and his advancing baldness would be forgiven. Or, if he had an international reputation, like some members of the faculty, then there would be, he was sure, no problem with girls. But at thirty-two Arne Nyborg had very little money. And as for scholarly attainment, of the few papers he had written, all but one had been refused publication by the university press. The world was against him, and that, the professor thought, was a fact.

Just why the world should take this unfair attitude was beyond him. So he was considered strict in class. Why shouldn't he be? Who did anything for him, that he should do anything for others? He had heard it said snidely, behind his back, that he was also unintelligible in class. That simply was a lie. The truth was that he was as bright as anyone on the faculty.

He became aware that his intercom was buzzing, and with a scowl he flipped the switch downward. "Yes?"

"There's someone here to see you, Professor," his secretary announced. "He says he's a cousin of yours. Knud Christensen."

Nyborg frowned at the intercom. Christensen? It seemed faintly familiar. Distant relatives of his mother's, he recalled. Fishermen, weren't they? What on earth could a fisherman cousin want of him? Money, of course. These country yokels thought that if you lived in Copenhagen you were rich. Little did they know!

"Tell him I can't see him. I'm busy."

"Yes, sir." But before Nyborg could push the intercom switch her voice came back. "Professor, Mr. Christensen says he'll wait."

Damn! There was no escape from this peasant, who undoubtedly was rawboned and reeked of fish. He steeled himself and glowered at the intercom. "Tell him to come in."

The door opened and Nyborg coldly considered the man who stood there. Christensen, dressed in his Sunday best, was certainly big, if not rawboned, with a thick head of curly hair. He did not smell of fish, although this, Nyborg thought sourly, would not get him one penny. Christensen carried a small cloth bag and was smiling uncertainly.

Nyborg did not offer him a chair. "What can I do for you?"

"I thought . . ." Christensen paused and looked around, then sat down on the chair by the desk. He opened his bag and brought out a piece of metal. "I thought you might be able to tell me if this had any value."

Nyborg frowned. What was this? A new way to ask for money? He took the piece and studied it without much interest. Finally he looked up at Christensen with a puzzled air.

"Where did you get this? Do you have more?"

"I have a few more pieces with me. There're lots more at home." Christensen hastily brought out the rest of his samples and laid them on the desk. Nyborg looked at them, his interest piqued. They were undoubtedly very old.

"Where did you say you found them?"

Christensen began, "Well, you see . . ."

When he had finished explaining, he looked down at his sam-

434

ples and then up at Nyborg. "Do you think they have any value?"

Nyborg bent over the pieces, now studying them intently. There was something vaguely familiar about one of them, a small, slightly curved mask with open eyeholes. The metal, he was sure, was gold, and he tried to recall where he had read about something like this. It would come back to him in time, but meanwhile caution was clearly indicated—he must be careful not to give Christensen any information. Some of these country types were shrewder than they looked.

"Value?" He shook his head. "I doubt it. I'm afraid you probably found something somebody threw away. These pieces are obviously made of some inferior alloy. See how easily they bend. Still," Nyborg added, as if trying to put the best face on the matter, "I won't say they're totally worthless, at least not until I've seen the rest of what you found. Can you bring it to me? Or would it be less trouble if I were to come to you?"

"Could you come back with me today?" Christensen asked anxiously. "I live in Gedser. It's only a few hours by train."

Don't rush, Nyborg told himself sternly. "Today? I'm afraid not," he said. He flipped through his appointment calendar, being careful not to let his visitor see that the pages were blank. "Ah! How about a week from Sunday?"

"Not before?" Christensen could not hide his disappointment.

Nyborg flipped the pages again, then reached for a pencil and crossed out something. "I'll postpone that," he said, as if making a great concession. "I'll drive down Saturday. If you leave these pieces with me, I can try to find out what they're made of."

Christensen stood up with a sigh. "Until Saturday, then. Anyone in Gedser can tell you where I live." He walked to the door and then stopped, twisting the empty bag in his hands. "And thank you for your time," he said sincerely, remembering his manners.

Nyborg waved away the thanks gracefully.

It came to Nyborg at three o'clock in the morning. He left his bed and padded to the front room of his small apartment. Switching on a lamp, he searched the bookshelves for the book he wanted, drew it down, and flipped the pages until he reached the right section. *There it was!* A picture of the very mask that was now locked in his desk at the university! And that diadem with the owl's head at the end of each of the hanging chains—the owl's head of Athena! My God! Was it possible? He felt himself begin to tremble. Was the Schliemann treasure in the hands of a stupid fisherman from Gedser, when the entire world was convinced it was in Russia someplace?

Nyborg fell into a chair, his mind churning. He tried to think clearly. Saturday was four days away; could he wait that long to go to Gedser and verify that the treasure was indeed the Schliemann collection? Suppose the fisherman took what he had to some metal dealer who would recognize the material as gold! But if Nyborg went down to Gedser any sooner, wouldn't the man be suspicious? What excuse could he give for arriving tomorrow?

Then an even greater problem forced itself into his mind. Eventually, if Nyborg got his hands on the treasure, the world would know that the Schliemann collection had been found! There would be newspaper articles. Pictures would be shown. With all the publicity, Christensen would hear of it. And when he did, what would his reaction be?

A cold, eerie feeling gripped Nyborg. There was only one solution. He came to his feet, moving to his bookshelf again almost like a marionette. This time he took down his pharmacopoeia. He would require a poison that could be introduced in liquor, for he was sure that a man like Knud Christensen drank. There were certain drugs which should never be taken with alcohol. A strong dose of one of those in a bottle of liquor . . .

THE pharmacist cautioned him not to drink anything alcoholic while using the sleeping pills, and Arne Nyborg assured him he was quite aware of the consequences. He next stopped by his office to advise his secretary that he had been taken ill and would not be able to conduct any classes that day. Then he drove his old Volvo to the bank and withdrew two thousand kroner, which left his balance woefully thin, but this was no time to be niggardly.

His next stop was at a liquor store. Again he decided not to be cheap and purchased an expensive bottle of whisky; his coldly calculating brain told him that the pills he had purchased might well cloud a clear liquid like aquavit, which a countryman like Christensen probably preferred, but would be invisible in the amber color of Scotch whisky.

436

He then got back into his car and started for Gedser. At a rest area he pulled off the road, opened the bottle, and dropped in the pills. Recapping the bottle, he shook it to dissolve the drug, and then turned back onto the highway for Gedser, forcing himself to concentrate on what he would do when he had the treasure.

He had no doubt that if he turned it over to the authorities his fame would be great. It would mean advancement and the publication of a paper that no university press would turn down.

On the other hand, if he kept it, he would be in possession of a fortune, but how on earth could he go about making a decent sum of money from it? He could scarcely put an advertisement in the papers offering the treasure for sale. Still, there simply *had* to be some way to get at least a portion of its great value for himself. Think of the pleasures that could be purchased with such unlimited funds—all the places he could go, all the girls he could have! But first he had to get his hands on the treasure.

It was late afternoon when Nyborg finally arrived in Gedser. Knud Christensen was fixing a harness when Nyborg pulled into the driveway. The sound of the ancient car's asthmatic wheezing brought Christensen to the doorway of the barn.

"Professor Nyborg? I thought—"

Nyborg shrugged a bit self-deprecatingly. "I found it was impossible to break my appointment for Saturday," he said lightly. "But since I had made a sort of promise to you . . ." He smiled.

"Good! Good!" Christensen said, pleased at the professor's sudden appearance. He tilted his head in the direction of the house. "The things are in there."

He led the way inside, lit a lamp, and dragged the heavy steel case from the closet. He fished out the four packages and carefully unwrapped them, making small piles of their contents. He then looked up at the professor anxiously.

"Well? What to you think?"

Nyborg could scarcely keep his hands from shaking as he reached for a small gold cup. He studied it with outward disinterest, but inside he was chortling, for he was positive he was actually looking at the missing Schliemann treasure; the night before, in Schliemann's own book *Ilios*, he had seen a drawing of that same cup. He put the cup down and picked up a necklace, certain as he did so that the beads would number seventy, exactly

437

according to Schliemann's description. He now knew that he would never turn this find over to any authorities for mere academic credit. It was worth a fortune, mountains of money!

He tossed the necklace down carelessly. "I'm sorry," he said, managing to look a trifle chagrined. "I had your pieces checked by our engineering laboratory and discovered, as I suspected, that they are a tin alloy, the cheapest sort of costume jewelry. I had hopes that some of the stuff you had here might be of better quality, but it all appears to be—well, to be frank, junk."

Knud's face fell. He shook his head disconsolately.

"I can understand how you feel," Nyborg said sympathetically. "Tell me—ah—cousin, what do you plan to do with these things?"

"I have no idea. Try to sell them to the local church bazaar, I suppose. Or for scrap."

Nyborg frowned, as if considering the problem. At last a possible solution seemed to occur to him. "I can make a suggestion. I have a collection of curiosities, of junk, if you will. Conversation pieces, you know. If you would be interested in selling these to me, they might be amusing to some of my friends—" He hurriedly raised a hand. "I couldn't pay very much, of course, but then the stuff isn't worth anything. Still, I would pay more than you could get from the church bazaar."

Christensen's eyes brightened. "How much?"

Nyborg thought a moment. "Well," he said, "you went to a lot of trouble diving for this stuff. That alone ought to be worth something. What about—say—a thousand kroner?"

Christensen took a deep breath of relief. A thousand kroner! Certainly far more than the stuff's value as scrap. It would buy a new anchor, and while it wouldn't also pay for a memorial for his brothers, it would at least make a down payment on some sort of metal cross to replace the crude wooden one he had set up over Gustave's grave.

"That's very generous," he said, and held out his big hand. Nyborg gripped it. Knud swallowed, as if ashamed, after such generosity, to be asking. "I don't suppose—"

"You mean, can I pay you now? Of course," Nyborg said lightly. He brought out his wallet and separated a thousand kroner from the sheaf of bills there, allowing Christensen to note his affluence. It did seem a shame to be wasting a thousand kroner on a man who would soon be dead, but Nyborg did not intend to wait to recover the money. There was no alternative. He handed it over.

"Thank you!" Christensen could not believe his good fortune.

"There's one thing, though," Nyborg said, almost as an afterthought. It had occurred to him that he didn't know how fast the poison would work, and he didn't want the oaf running to the neighbors and telling them of his good fortune. "I should not like my university colleagues to think me a fool for spending that much money on worthless jewelry. So I would appreciate it if we could keep this business—well, just between the two of us."

"Of course! I haven't even told anyone that I found the box." Christensen bent to rewrap the pieces. Nyborg did not stoop to help him, but when the packages were ready, he did deign to carry two of them out to the trunk of his car.

"I say," he said as he closed the lid. "Do you like whisky?"

"Very much!" Christensen replied, and then seemed to realize the lack of hospitality the question implied. "I never offered you a drink! I'm sorry. Let me get you—"

"No, no!" Nyborg waved the offer away. He tapped his stomach and smiled regretfully. "Doctor's orders. No alcohol. But someone gave me this rather fine imported stuff, and I thought you might care for it." He reached into the car and brought out the bottle. "Have some now. To . . . well, to sort of seal our deal."

Knud Christensen grinned as he looked at the label. "Well! I haven't seen anything this fine for a long time. This will have to wait for a proper occasion."

"No, no!" Nyborg said, and cursed his stupidity for buying an expensive brand. "Have some now and tell me how it is."

"It's good. I don't need to prove that." Christensen smiled gratefully. "It won't go to waste, I promise." He held out his hand. "And I want to thank you for everything."

Nyborg stood and stared, incapable of thinking of any way to get the clod to drink the whisky. Then he shook hands briefly and climbed into his car. With a frozen face he drove from the yard.

If the oaf didn't drink the whisky today, Nyborg was sure he would drink it one of these days, certainly before any news of the treasure ever got out. And, of course, he had the idiot's promise not to mention the deal to anyone. It was about as much as he could have hoped for.

Except for the fact that Knud Christensen had not drunk the doctored liquor in his presence, one might have thought the professor would be a happy man. After all, he was in possession of a veritable king's ransom. But in the week since his return from Gedser all it had meant was the added expense of two large bank safe-deposit boxes, where he had put the treasure, plus a complete loss of appetite, and even, possibly, the loss of his job. He simply had to get his mind back onto his history lectures and away from thoughts of the treasure sitting idle and to all intents and purposes worthless in the bank.

One morning he stared at his students without seeing them and then wordlessly left the classroom and walked unsteadily to his office, where he fell into a chair and pressed his head into his shaking hands. What to do? How to dispose of the treasure? A solution had to be found quickly, or he was going to have a nervous breakdown. He reached into a desk drawer and brought out a bottle of aquavit. He took a long drink and could soon feel the alcohol begin to relax him. . . . If only he had money! Then, he was sure, any number of solutions would press themselves upon him. Suddenly he sat erect. *Of course!* The answer was simplicity itself. It was true that he himself had no money, but there were others in the world who did. What he needed was a partner; someone who had not only money but contacts, and brains as well. Someone with nerve and a touch of the gambler in him.

Someone like Count Axel Lindholm, for example.

Even as the thought came, Nyborg knew it had been a burst of pure genius. Lindholm was a trustee of the university, and Nyborg had met him on several occasions. Rich as Croesus, they said. Certainly Lindholm Castle, on the outskirts of Ringsted, forty miles away, seemed to bear that out. Nyborg had seen parts of it when the count had permitted tours. Set on two hundred acres, its crenellated towers and more than a hundred rooms were filled with untold wealth in the form of paintings and statuary.

It was rumored that the count had been asked to leave the consular service after an affair with the wife of a diplomat. Moreover, Lindholm was a known gambler; the Copenhagen newspapers often mentioned his presence at Monte Carlo or Las Vegas.

Yes, the count was exactly the man to help Nyborg solve his problem. In fact, Lindholm probably wouldn't even want money for his help. With his wealth, he didn't need it. He'd probably do it just for the sport of it.

Nyborg got to his feet, staggered, and sat down again. Better sober up, he told himself sternly. Tomorrow, when you have your wits about you, go to Lindholm Castle and start the ball rolling.

RINGSTED—April 1979

THE following day Count Axel Lindholm was at home in conference with his lawyer and old friend, Erik Trosborg. "Axel," the lawyer was pleading, "why can't you realize that the estate is entailed? It is not yours to dispose of as you wish! You simply cannot sell off pictures, or statuary, or anything else."

Count Lindholm shrugged. He was a handsome man in his late forties, with the build of an athlete, sharp, clean features, a cleft chin, icy blue eyes, and light brown hair. He flicked ash from his thin cigar and smiled coldly at his friend.

"I need the money," he said simply. "Blame it on inflation."

"Or gambling. Or women."

"Now there you are being unfair," Lindholm said a bit reprovingly. "My women do not cost me an öre."

"Not in hard cash. Only a Mercedes for this one, a dress shop for that one!" Trosborg said in despair. "You simply cannot keep this up!"

"My dear Erik," Lindholm said with no attempt at apology, "do you have any idea how much it costs just to run this place? A butler who also does duty as chauffeur and valet, a cook and an assistant, five maids, and a housekeeper?"

"I have a perfect idea," Trosborg said dryly, "since I handle the bills. Axel, you have an income from this estate that would enable the most extravagant man in the world to live in total comfort. You simply must learn to live within that income. You might even consider working. It's not a crime, you know."

"Well, it should be," Lindholm said, and smiled.

"I mean it, Axel. You're considered an expert on art. I'm sure you could get a few well-paying purchasing commissions, if you were to let people know you were interested."

Lindholm laughed. "And have all my friends realize the depths of my degradation?"

Trosborg rose to his feet and held out his hand. "I don't agree with your philosophy, but it's your life. Take care."

They shook hands, and Lindholm watched his friend leave the room. Then he crushed out his cigar, his smile gone. This money thing, or the lack of it, was the very devil!

He was about to go in to lunch when Wilten, his butler, appeared at the door. He was a large man with cold, unexpressive eyes. "A . . . person to see you, sir. He says he is an acquaintance. A Professor Nyborg. Of the University of Copenhagen."

Lindholm frowned. He seemed to remember Nyborg; they had met at a few university functions when the professor had managed to introduce himself. A rather disgusting example of the human animal, as the count recalled. Fat, short, balding, verbose, and stupid, always ogling the women. What on earth was he doing here? And just when lunch was about to be served. François, the cook, would be most perturbed.

Still, Count Lindholm prided himself on always being polite to his inferiors. Such dissembling had often proved profitable. "Ask him in, Wilten. And tell François lunch will be delayed."

When Nyborg appeared, the count got to his feet smiling, as if he had lacked suitable company all morning and was pleased that Arne Nyborg had appeared to answer the want.

"Ah, Professor. It's good to see you again."

"Thank you!" Nyborg gratefully accepted the chair the count waved him to and stared in awe at the luxurious appointments of the private study. What exquisite taste! He was brought back to earth by a polite cough from his smiling host, who had also seated himself.

Nyborg wet his lips, took a deep breath, and began. "You know, I'm sure, of the Schliemann treasure, sir?"

"Yes," Lindholm said, wondering if he was to eat a delayed lunch because this idiot wished to discuss art objects. "Before the war I was fortunate enough to see it at a museum in Berlin. May I ask in what connection you are inquiring about it?"

Nyborg swallowed. "I—I have it. In my possession."

The count's smile disappeared. "Are you sure you know what you're saying?" Lindholm was convinced he was dealing with a

442

man who was mentally unbalanced. "I'm sorry, but I'm afraid—"
"Please!" Nyborg's tone was pleading. "I'm quite serious." He
reached into a pocket, brought out a tissue-wrapped packet, and
opened it. He handed the count a diadem. "Have you ever seen this
before, sir?"

Count Lindholm took the diadem carefully, examining it in detail. It certainly looked genuine. His interest was fully aroused.
"Where did you get this piece?"

"Well," Nyborg replied, confident now that the count would
believe his concocted story, "I'm sure you know the treasure has
been in Russia since the war—"

"And I thought it was still there."

"Well, sir, it was stolen." Nyborg raised a hand hastily. "Oh,
not by me! It was stolen by a man who worked in the Hermitage,
in Leningrad—and he defected. He got as far as Copenhagen and
he needed money desperately to go on. He came to me at the university and offered it for sale. At first I was sure it was a hoax—he
wouldn't tell me how he got it out of the museum, or even out of
Russia. But when I examined the pieces, I knew they were genuine.
So I—I bought the collection."

"I see. And may I ask just why you're telling me all this?"

"Well, sir," Nyborg said earnestly, "the fact is, I'm like the man
who stole the treasure. I've got it, but I don't know what to do
with it. It cost me all the money I had in the world—fifty thousand
kroner. But I thought it was worth it."

"I'm sure," Lindholm said dryly. One of the world's greatest
collections for the price of a Volvo! "Do you wish to resell it?"

"No, no!" Nyborg said hastily. "I thought"—he hesitated—"I
thought we could be sort of partners, sir. That you might be able
to figure out how both of us could make some money from it."

Lindholm contemplated the man before him with outer calm,
but inwardly his mind was racing. Nyborg would not be so foolish
as to bring a hoax to a trustee of the university. It would mean his
job, if not worse. And if Nyborg actually had the treasure, there
was indeed a fortune to be made. Enough, in fact, to enable the
count to return to the style of living he had been forced to abandon.

Lindholm smiled genially. "If the collection is genuine—and
that, of course, I shall have to verify—then I think I might be interested." He laughed. "Oh, not for the money, you understand, but

for the sport of it. I think it might be rather a lark, you know?"

Nyborg was thrilled. "Do you have any idea, sir, of . . . of just how we . . . you . . . might . . . ?"

Lindholm waved the question away airily. "I'm sure there are many means of disposing of so desirable a collection," he said absently. Reaching into a nearby cabinet, he found a bottle of rare brandy, filled two glasses, and held one out to the professor.

Nyborg could hardly believe it; he was drinking cognac with Count Axel Lindholm! He raised his glass in response to Lindholm's gesture of a toast and sipped. My Lord, it was good! To think that with money one could drink this ambrosia every day of the week!

"How much, do you think?" he asked.

"Please don't worry about that," Lindholm said with an air of sincerity. "Whatever monies result from selling the treasure, I assure you will be yours. I have all the money I need. What I don't have is some project to occupy my mind. But first, when may I verify that the treasure is authentic?"

"Right now, if you wish." Nyborg finished his drink. "It's in two safe-deposit boxes at my bank, the Handelsbank, in Copenhagen. The bank is open, and it's only an hour from here."

Lindholm knew he had a lot of thinking to do. He stood up. "Shall we say tomorrow, instead? Suppose I meet you at the bank at eleven." He walked his guest to the door, then made his way toward the dining room.

There, for once, Count Lindholm's mind was not on the food. He barely noticed the overdone introductory omelet, François's revenge for tardy diners; he was considering more important things than his lunch.

Nyborg would present no problem. In his youth Lindholm had volunteered as a mercenary in Africa, and he would not have the slightest compunction about eliminating a person as distasteful as Arne Nyborg, should the need arise. Nor would selling the treasure be a problem. With his contacts, he could certainly arrange an auction among the top museums of the world. It could be conducted without revealing his identity or anything else. In one way or another they'd all manage to bid. Yes, the affair would be a lark—in addition, of course, to rescuing his finances from the pit in which they now were.

LONDON—June 1979

THE conference room of the Gramercy Arms Hotel in Park Lane was slowly filling up. Ruth McVeigh, at the head of a long table, watched her colleagues file in slowly and take the places marked for them with individual name cards. At each place was a small console furnished with an earphone and buttons that would provide instant translation in any one of five languages.

Many of those present were friends, but seated along the wall were some people she did not recognize. One man, dressed informally in a dark jacket over a white turtleneck sweater, seemed faintly familiar. She leaned over to a former colleague from the Cleveland Museum of Art and spoke in a low voice.

"Tim, that man along the wall, the one sitting next to the man with the stiff white hair. He looks familiar. Do you know him? I expect he's from some small museum. . . ."

Casually Tim Rubin looked across the room. He turned back with a wicked glint in his eye. "Oh, he's just a nobody named Gregor Kovpak, from a nothing place called the Hermitage."

Ruth's eyes widened. Of course! She had seen Gregor Kovpak's picture in the journals often enough. She had visited the Hermitage several times and knew it to be one of the finest museums in the world. Was it possible that the Russians were behind the auction? Well, whatever reason had brought Kovpak, Ruth McVeigh was glad she would have a chance to meet him.

She became aware that Tim Rubin was speaking to her. "He's very good-looking, isn't he? I might mention that Kovpak is a widower. That's the good news. The bad news is that, as I understand it, he's not interested in any entangling alliances."

Ruth felt her face flush. "Tim, you're an idiot! I'm not interested in Dr. Kovpak other than to meet him. I've read his papers and I think he's brilliant."

"As well as good-looking and single," Tim murmured, but Ruth had turned away. The room was now full. People were settling down. Ruth reached for the gavel and tapped it several times. The noise abated and people began slipping on their earphones and pushing the appropriate buttons. Ruth stood up with a smile.

"My colleagues in the field of archaeology: This introductory session will be short, as we all are tired from our travels. We are here in connection with the auction of the Schliemann treasure, whether or not we as individual museums have been asked to bid. I am sure there have been many discussions at your respective museums regarding the legal title to the treasure. I believe it would be best, therefore, before we make any concrete proposals, to open the floor for a general airing of views."

A hand shot up at once. Ruth nodded to a rotund man with pince-nez. He rose to his feet and spoke in German.

"I am Dr. Wilhelm Kloster, of the Museum Dahlem, in West Berlin," he said in quiet, courteous tones. "The Schliemann treasure, as we all know, was stolen"—he turned to look directly at Kovpak—"from a bunker under the Berlin zoo. Our charming chairperson has mentioned the problem of legal ownership. There is no problem at all, my friends. The treasure belongs to Germany."

He paused to sip some water. "The treasure was taken to the Berlin zoo from a museum which, though destroyed during the war, was located in what is now *West* Berlin. The treasure was given to that museum by Heinrich Schliemann himself, and it remained there, *unchallenged as to ownership*, until the last war, when, as I say, it was removed for safekeeping and subsequently disappeared. It now seems that the treasure has been found. Logic and law state unequivocally that it should and must return to its proper home at the Museum Dahlem in *West* Berlin. And may I add"—the small eyes behind the pince-nez glittered threateningly—"that we shall take whatever steps are necessary to see that our rights are not trampled upon!" He sat down abruptly.

Another hand had been held high during his final words, and Ruth called upon its owner. A heavyset man with a pockmarked face and a fierce-looking mustache stood up.

"My name is Dimitrios Jacoubs," he said, "and I represent the Greek government." He spoke in French, as Greek was not one of the languages available on the consoles. "I should like to take you back to when the treasure was discovered. It was brought to Greece and remained there for some years before it was given— without the right to give—by Heinrich Schliemann to a German museum. I say without the right to give, because the discovery of this treasure was a joint effort by Schliemann and his wife, Sophia

Engastromenos, a Greek. And Sophia desperately wanted the treasure given to Greece. Her desires are fully recorded, and I have the documents here for anyone who wishes to examine them. I will close by saying that the Greek government intends to pursue this matter to the fullest. Thank you."

A man who had been holding up his hand almost from the beginning of Jacoubs' statement got up at Ruth's nod. He was tall, with swarthy cheeks and black hair. He also spoke in French.

"My name is Suleiman Abbas," he said, "and I represent the archaeological museums of Istanbul. All of you must be aware that the Schliemann treasure was taken from Turkey illegally. The firman—the permit issued by the Turkish government to Schliemann to dig in The Troad—specified that all finds were to be examined by a representative of the Turkish government, and that a division based upon mutual agreement would be made. Actually Schliemann carried the treasure from the site by subterfuge—under his wife's skirts, according to the story—and later smuggled it from Turkey to Greece. I am sure that all of you are aware not only of the illegality of this smuggling but also of the United Nations stand on art treasures—that they belong to the country of origin. Heinrich Schliemann is considered a sort of genius, but he was, in fact, a mere thief."

Mr. Abbas turned to address the head of the table. "Dr. Mc-Veigh, the Turkish museums believe that nobody should bid in this farcical so-called auction, because the treasure should be turned over to us, from whom it was taken."

He pushed his chair back and walked with dignity from the room. There was a moment's silence at his unexpected departure; then everyone wanted to speak at once. Hands flashed in the air, waving frantically; people called into the console microphones for attention. It was bedlam, and the rapping of Ruth McVeigh's gavel made little difference. She waited a moment, then reached for her purse and took out a police whistle. Turning the volume dial on her microphone to its maximum, she blew the whistle with all her strength. The shrill sound brought immediate quiet.

"I think we've had enough discussion for today," Ruth said. "We will meet here again at ten tomorrow morning." She switched off the microphone and, sliding her papers into her briefcase, turned to leave. She found herself facing Dr. Kovpak. He was smiling.

447

"Hello," he said. "My name is Gregor Kovpak, and I just wanted to tell you I thought you handled that near riot in style."

His English was excellent, tinged with only the slightest of accents. Ruth also noticed that he was tall, had brown eyes, very white teeth, dark curly hair, and a wonderful smile.

"I also wanted to tell you," Kovpak said fervently, "that I've read most of your papers and enjoyed them very much. And finally, I want to congratulate you on your recent appointment at the Metropolitan."

"Thank you," Ruth said. "I had no idea you would be here, or I would have seen to it you were seated at the table, with a translation console."

Kovpak shrugged lightly. "It was no problem. I speak both German and French." His expressive face was now curious. "What did you think of your meeting?"

"Hectic, I would call it. What did you think?"

"Amusing," Kovpak said, and laughed. "Very amusing."

"Amusing? In what way?"

"It's too long a story to go into here. Besides, it's too near the cocktail hour. Why don't I meet you in the lounge in, say"—he consulted his watch—"half an hour? And afterward perhaps we could have dinner together."

Ruth hesitated, then smiled and nodded. "Half an hour it is." She held out her hand to be shaken. "On second thought," she said, "let's make that an hour." She wanted time to find that little perfume shop in Shepherd Market. . . .

JAMES Newkirk remained at the press table, writing in his notebook. He was a tall, heavyset, muscular man, who carried credentials as the cultural reporter for the Paris office of the *International Daily Gazette*, and he worked at the job. What he was writing now, however, was a report he would transmit to the CIA in Langley, Virginia, later that evening.

Newkirk had recognized Gregor Kovpak at the session. He had expected that the foremost archaeologist in the Soviet Union would be attending and that he would be accompanied by a KGB official; undoubtedly that was the white-haired man who had been at Kovpak's side.

But the interesting fact was that Kovpak was not seated at the

448

main conference table. If the Russians were behind the auction, one would think they would have arranged to be at the main table, if only to dissemble. It was also interesting that as soon as the meeting ended, Kovpak had made contact with Dr. Ruth McVeigh. Surveillance of the two was clearly indicated. Someone would also have to keep an eye on the white-haired KGB man.

Finished with his scribbling, Newkirk came to his feet and innocently followed Ruth McVeigh and Gregor Kovpak from the room as they left, still chatting amiably.

MAJOR Serge Ulanov was lying on his bed reading a copy of *Playboy* when Gregor Kovpak came into the adjoining room. The major got up and walked through the open connecting door. He sat down in a chair and watched with interest as Kovpak opened a dresser drawer and examined a white shirt with a critical eye. Satisfied, Kovpak laid the shirt on the bed and walked over to the closet. He took out his only suit and laid it, too, on the bed, then went back to the closet to make a selection between the two neckties there.

The major smiled broadly. "Getting dressed for dinner with the handsome chairperson, I assume? You certainly work fast."

Kovpak laughed. In the few days the two men had been together, he had grown to like the stocky KGB man. "Major, you'll become an investigator yet, coming to such accurate conclusions so quickly." He suddenly frowned. "Incidentally, so there won't be any misunderstanding, may I say that you're not invited to this dinner date of mine."

"I'm disappointed, but really not surprised," Ulanov replied. "Besides, I have my own date tonight. One of the press reporters." He lit a cigarette. "Of course, he's also CIA. A free lance, not a regular, but still . . ."

"You're having dinner with a CIA man?"

"He doesn't know about it yet. And," Ulanov added, "if I'm careful, he won't know about it at all."

Gregor shook his head. "How do you know he's CIA?"

"The same way he either knows, or at least strongly suspects, that I am KGB," Ulanov said calmly. "We try to keep track of each other's agents on a job. That's the way the game is played."

"And why is the CIA here?" Kovpak asked.

"Possibly to prevent us from learning what weakness in CIA security allowed the treasure to be gotten out of Langley. Or possibly for some other reason we know nothing about. By the way," Ulanov said as he stood up, "let me make a suggestion. There's a good restaurant just down Curzon Street that I'm sure Dr. McVeigh would enjoy very much."

Kovpak had put on his suit jacket and was examining himself in the mirror. "Why do you want me to take her to that restaurant?"

Ulanov sighed. "My friend, you're overly suspicious. Leave that to us security people."

"All right, I'll take her there," Kovpak said shortly. "But I really do not like playing these cloak-and-dagger games, Major."

Ulanov shook his head as if hurt by an unfair accusation, and with a smile he turned and walked back to his room.

RUTH McVeigh, too, was studying herself in the mirror. She liked what she saw, aware that the gown was cut to flatter her full figure. It would be a shame, she thought, if Gregor Kovpak returned to Leningrad without knowing that Ruth McVeigh was more than just another archaeologist, that she was also very much a woman. She winked at herself in the mirror and left the room.

Gregor Kovpak was waiting for her at a small table in a corner of the dim lounge, and he rose as Ruth paused in the doorway. He could sense the eyes of almost every man in the crowded room turning toward her as she made her way to his table. He hurried to pull out a chair for her. Watching her sink gracefully into it, he sat down himself, wondering at a sudden feeling of gaucheness. It's been too long since I was with a woman, he said to himself; certainly with one this lovely or talented. A waiter appeared, and Gregor turned to Ruth inquiringly.

"A martini, very dry," she said.

"The same," Kovpak said. He waited for his companion to open the conversation, but she was looking about the lounge. Their drinks were served, and then they spoke at the same time.

"I—" she said.

"You—" he began.

They laughed; the ice broken, Gregor began to relax. It's simply dinner with a fellow archaeologist, he told himself. Forget that she's beautiful. He raised his glass in the gesture of a toast and

450

Ruth responded. They both sipped; then Gregor set down his glass. "I was going to say that you look very attractive in that gown."

"Thank you," Ruth said. "I was going to ask what you meant this afternoon when you said the session had been amusing."

Gregor's initial feeling of clumsiness was slipping away. "What I found amusing," he replied "was that although the three arguments presented appeared logical on the surface, all were basically invalid. What did you *think* I meant?"

"I thought you found it amusing because—" Ruth hesitated and then decided to be frank. "Well, because you thought the auction was a hoax, and because you knew the treasure was in Russia."

"You thought that?" Gregor Kovpak shook his head. "No," he said gently, "the treasure is not in Russia, nor has it ever been. That is the truth. And as for the auction being a hoax, I'm quite convinced it is genuine. But the meeting was a waste of time."

"Why do you think that?"

"Because of the people you are dealing with," Gregor said quietly. "All of them want the treasure for themselves. If they were rational, they would agree that each museum put up a portion of the asking price. They would buy the treasure jointly, and then decide how each museum would exhibit it in turn."

"That's exactly what I said to our board of directors!" Ruth said triumphantly. "And that is the proposition I intend to present to the conference tomorrow morning." She felt exhilarated. "So you agree that's the best way to handle the matter?"

"Not at all!" Kovpak replied. "I said that is what would happen if you were dealing with rational people. But you are dealing with fanatics, collectors. Do you honestly believe the three who spoke today are going to relinquish their claims for a small share of something they believe is totally theirs? And then to be told that they might not be able to exhibit the treasure for ten or fifteen years?" He shook his head decisively. "They will never agree."

Ruth, too, shook her head. "I think you're wrong."

They finished their drinks. Signing the tab, Gregor said, "There's a restaurant on Curzon Street that's been recommended to me. We could walk over and try it, if you don't mind."

"I don't mind at all."

They found the restaurant easily, and it was not crowded. They were seated, ordered their meal, and looked at each other in silence. Ruth could see the admiration in Gregor's eyes, and wondered if he could see the same in hers. She decided it was time to say something and picked the first thing that came into her mind.

"You said just now that the arguments of those three people were invalid," she said. "On what basis?"

"Simply because they were." He suddenly grinned. "On the same basis you could claim the treasure for the Metropolitan. After all, Heinrich Schliemann was a citizen of the United States at the time he discovered Troy; not of Germany or Greece." Then, his grin disappearing, he added, "The only valid arguments for ownership would have to come from Russia."

"*Russia?* You're joking."

"I'm quite serious," Gregor said. "Schliemann spent the last part of his life searching for Troy. The thing that enabled him to do this was money that he made from selling war materials to Russia—at what even an American would call unconscionable prices—during the Crimean War. So, it was Russian money that financed the discovery of the treasure in the first place." He paused as their meal was served. "A second argument for my country's claim to the treasure is, of course, that it constitutes the legitimate spoils of war."

"You also said," Ruth reminded him, "that the treasure wasn't in Russia and never had been."

"That's right." Gregor shook his head ruefully. "We discovered it in a bunker in Berlin, and it was stolen from us with forged papers on May twenty-second, 1945. It got as far as Bad Freienwalde, a small town that's not very far from Berlin. There it just disappeared."

It made sense, Ruth McVeigh thought. If the treasure had been in private hands all these years, then an auction could be explained. It was like a mystery story, and Ruth had always enjoyed them. "Didn't your people make any effort to locate it?"

"Of course," Gregor said, and then waited as the wine he had ordered was poured. Looking around, he suddenly remembered they were probably being watched. All but a few of the tables were now occupied, but no one seemed to be interested in them in the slightest. The only single person was a man seated well out of earshot, engrossed in a book. Kovpak put the matter of spies out of his mind and returned to their discussion.

"There was an investigation of sorts at the time," he said quietly. "They did figure out that a man named Pettersson, a Swedish national, was the one who forged the documents. He also fit the description of one of the two men who removed the crate from the train. But after that"—he shrugged—"nothing."

The detective in Ruth was aroused. "If one of the men was Swedish, isn't it likely that they took the treasure to Sweden?"

"They could have gone anywhere," Gregor said. "It was nighttime. They put the treasure in the trunk of an official-looking car and drove off. Where they went, nobody knows." He could scarcely tell Ruth that the Russians believed the car had belonged to an American general, and that the treasure had undoubtedly ended up in the hands of the OSS. It would cheat her of romance.

"Anyway," Gregor added, "this auction proves that *no* museum has the treasure. Can you picture us allowing the Schliemann collection to be diminished by the pieces this person—whoever he is—sent out as proof he had the genuine treasure? I would not have let loose a single button. Would you?"

Ruth laughed. "Never in the world."

"Case closed," Gregor said with juridical solemnity, and they began their meal, gazing at each other in contentment, satisfied that they had established a certain rapport.

A waiter carrying a tray with a whisky bottle and glasses paused before the door of room 1123 of the Gramercy Arms Hotel. Had he been observed, it would simply have appeared that his gloved hand tapped on the door and rested there a moment, as if awaiting permission to enter. But the glove held against the door actually contained a tiny microphone, connected by a thin wire running up the waiter's sleeve to a small amplifier concealed behind his right ear by his stylishly long hair.

Satisfied with what he heard—the sound of a man moving about, the rustle of a newspaper—the waiter returned to the floor pantry. He was prepared to watch the door of room 1123 and repeat his charade every fifteen minutes until the occupant went to sleep or left the room—or until a call from James Newkirk advised him his task was complete for the evening.

As the waiter watched, an elderly gentleman with a dark raincoat over his dinner jacket, his top hat awry and a silly look on his flushed face, came out of a side corridor and staggered toward the elevator. When the drunk had disappeared, the waiter walked down the corridor again with his microphone. This time he heard the creak of a bed, followed by an extended belch. Russians! the waiter thought, and walked sedately back to the pantry.

He was a young agent, and he had no idea he had been listening to a tape recording—two hours of fine sound effects, prepared by Major Serge Ulanov for any curious ear.

In the lobby, the elderly drunk found himself a comfortable chair, sank into it gratefully, and seemed to close his eyes. But through slitted lids he saw Gregor Kovpak emerge from the lounge with Ruth McVeigh and escort her through the lobby to the street. And a moment later he was not surprised to see James Newkirk, a thin book under his arm, turn away from his contemplation of the activities board and casually move off in the same direction. With a sigh the elderly gentleman heaved himself to his feet and tottered out into the night air.

Ahead of him he could see Newkirk turning into Curzon Street. The elderly gentleman paused in the doorway of a darkened storefront, removed and collapsed the top hat, and tucked it into his waistband. He took a simple cap from a pocket and donned it, then wrapped a scarf around his throat. His appearance now completely changed, he continued toward Curzon Street and the restaurant to which he had directed Gregor Kovpak. He had selected it because it was easily observed from the shadows; its low curtains permitted a view of the interior. In the crowded dining room of the Gramercy Arms it would have been impossible with the same anonymity to watch Newkirk and discover what he was up to.

Through the restaurant window Major Ulanov could see Gregor and Ruth sitting in a booth, ordering their dinner. He watched Newkirk enter the restaurant. Ulanov frowned when Newkirk refused a table close to Kovpak's booth in favor of one across the room, quite out of earshot of the booth. The American ordered something, and immediately fell to reading his book, paying no attention to Gregor Kovpak or Ruth McVeigh.

Suddenly Ulanov's frown disappeared. He walked down the street until he located a telephone booth. He dialed, and after identifying himself to the person who answered, he gave some instructions and hung up. Then he replaced the cap with the top hat and removed the scarf and tucked it into a pocket. Once again the elderly gentleman—though far less under the influence—he marched back to the Gramercy Arms.

He sat down in the lobby and leaned back, again half closing his eyes. After a while he saw Gregor and Dr. McVeigh enter and move toward the lounge. The elderly gentleman remained in his pose for thirty minutes, after which he got up and made for the elevator. As he did so, another man, crossing the lobby in a hurry, bumped into him, causing him to stumble and fall. Apologizing, the other man helped him up and brushed him off. Ulanov waved the matter off and continued to the elevator.

In the hallway on the eleventh floor Ulanov nodded at the floor waiter, who was just retreating to his pantry, turned into a side corridor, and entered the first room on his right. He then entered his own room through the connecting door and turned off the tape recorder. From now on he would play himself.

From the pocket of his coat he withdrew a slim volume deposited there by the man who had bumped into him. Outwardly the book had the appearance of a new best seller. Inside, as Ulanov had suspected, it contained an exceedingly small tape recorder with a minute amplified pickup. Aimed toward Gregor's booth, it had undoubtedly recorded the conversation there.

Ulanov grinned in satisfaction and took the machine into the bathroom, where he ran the water noisily into the tub, meanwhile playing the tape. Nothing he heard gave him a clue about the treasure or the auction, but he had at least come into possession of a recorder far better than anything the KGB technicians had come up with. Very clever, those Americans. Ulanov hoped Newkirk had not been too badly hurt.

FROM a safe telephone in the American embassy in Grosvenor Square, James Newkirk was making his report to Thomas Wilson in Langley, Virginia. He was also nursing a colossal headache.

"They took everything," he was saying bitterly. "Two thugs. One hit me with something. They got my watch, my wallet, the book—"

"You mean that recorder we flew over to you? That was a prototype; we don't have another." Wilson did not sound pleased. "Well, anyway, what did you learn?"

"Nothing, sir," Newkirk said unhappily. "The entire conversation was on the tape."

"Do you think the Russians had anything to do with the recorder being taken from you?"

"Not unless they have more men here than I think they have. I'm sure there's only one KGB man here, a white-haired man registered as Dr. Sverdlov."

"A crew cut? A man in his sixties?"

"Yes, sir. That's him."

"His name is Serge Ulanov," Wilson said. "He's pretty clever."

"But I'm sure he wasn't involved. I had a man outside his hotel room all evening; the waiter bit, you know, sir. He assured me Ulanov never left the room."

There was a moment of silence as Wilson digested this report. He was far from sure that Ulanov had had nothing to do with the mugging. Muggers took wallets and watches, of course, but how many would bother taking an innocent-looking book? And if Ulanov was on to Newkirk, maybe Newkirk should be replaced. But that would take time, and he was the only one available in the area with the requisite knowledge of archaeology.

"All right," Wilson said wearily, "stay with it. Keep an eye on Ulanov and Kovpak. And," he added dryly, "try not to get mugged in the future." He hung up.

With a heartfelt sigh Newkirk put his pounding head in his hands. There were times he wished he was only a reporter.

GREGOR Kovpak could not sleep. It was pointless, he tried to tell himself, to think of Ruth McVeigh as anyone other than a fellow scientist whom he had come to know and respect through her writings and whom he had been fortunate enough to meet at last. But he could not recall an evening he had enjoyed more, certainly not since Natasha had died eleven years ago. Still, there could never be anything between Ruth McVeigh and himself. So think of something else.

But heavens, Ruth was beautiful, intelligent, and—well, fascinating. He and Natasha had never had children. If he and Ruth were married, would they . . . ? What a ridiculous thought! One dinner with a woman and he was imagining her as married to him! And raising a family, yet!

456

He rolled over and stared at the wall. He must stop thinking about Dr. Ruth McVeigh and think about the Schliemann treasure and what Ulanov had said about its probable whereabouts. But precisely how had it gotten from Bad Freienwalde to Langley, Virginia? Where could one go from Bad Freienwalde? Gregor, yawning, realized that his knowledge of East German geography was sketchy, so he let his thoughts return to Ruth, the warmth of her smile, and her faint but unforgettable perfume.

RUTH McVeigh was tired this morning, and she knew she looked terrible, because she hadn't slept either. She sat at the head of the conference table, staring at the chairs along the wall, noting Gregor's absence, while the delegates filed in and took their places.

Where was Gregor? Didn't he know how much she wanted to see him, to look at him, to find out if last night had been real, or if her imagination had given it dimensions it did not have? Where was he? Possibly he knew the utter hopelessness of their ever being anything but friends and had taken off for Leningrad to save both of them the embarrassment of a further meeting.

As on the morning before, she became aware that Tim Rubin was speaking to her. She turned. "Excuse me. What did you say?"

"I said, what's the matter with you? You look like three days in the city morgue." Tim was studying her with concern. "Why don't you go up to your room and lie down and let me handle this?"

"No, I'll be all right," Ruth replied stubbornly. She just wished Gregor Kovpak were here. She looked at her wristwatch and stood up, rapping the gavel. Slowly the meeting came to order. She pulled the microphone toward her and began.

"Ladies and gentlemen, we saw in yesterday's statements the diversity of opinion as to the ownership of the Schliemann treasure, and I am sure that others here are prepared to offer similar arguments. But if we allow this meeting to dissolve into controversy, the treasure will never be purchased at a reasonable price."

She paused; her audience was watching her suspiciously. Well, she thought, here's where we discover if Gregor was right.

"My suggestion is simplicity itself—that all the museums who are interested share the cost of the purchase price, and also share the exhibition privileges, on a basis to be determined. To begin with, this method would—"

"*No!*" It was Kloster of the Museum Dahlem screaming into his microphone, his face red. "*It cannot be!* You are very generous with something that belongs—"

Ruth rapped her gavel for order. The response was quite the opposite. Bedlam broke out, with everyone wanting to speak at once; some were on their feet, shouting. Ruth looked at Tim Rubin helplessly. He hesitated a moment, then searched beneath the table for something and grinned as he found the master electrical plug connecting the consoles. He pulled it from its socket, and suddenly the booming sounds from the ceiling speakers disappeared. The noise that before had seemed threatening seemed merely foolish now. The delegates stopped to look at one another and then, with what seemed to be sudden accord, picked up their papers and briefcases and began to file from the room.

Tim and Ruth watched them go. She took a deep breath. "Well, at least it's over."

"And the horse race is on again." Tim squeezed her hand and walked quickly away.

Ruth looked around the now-deserted room and rose to go. Well, Gregor had been right after all. She had just wasted her time and everybody else's. And what had she gotten out of it? She had met a man she had instantly felt a deep liking for, and he had not even bothered to try to see her again.

She rode the elevator to her floor, walked into her room, and went to the window to stare out, thinking. The meeting had been a disaster, but the important thing was that the Schliemann treasure was still being held somewhere, by someone. Where had it been taken after it was removed from the railroad car at that Bad something? According to Gregor, the Russian officials had made some sort of an investigation at the time. But perhaps today, with the turmoil of the war long past, someone with the time and energy could actually find out what had happened to it. Certainly whoever was offering the treasure for auction must have done exactly that. And what that unknown person had been able to accomplish, someone else should be able to duplicate. If, in the process, one could confront that unknown—then one could undoubtedly make a deal to buy the treasure. And what museum, faced with the pos-. sibility of possessing the treasure, would fail to come up with the required money, despite any alleged scruples?

458

She stared off toward Hyde Park, with its lawn chairs and playing children, but she barely saw them. If only Gregor were here to help her, she was sure they could dig up some clues. . . .

Forget Gregor Kovpak, she told herself sternly. What woman in her right mind would feel this way about a man she had met less than twenty-four hours before? It was ridiculous. She picked up her purse and marched purposefully toward the door.

RUTH climbed the steps to the landing where the map room of the British Museum was located, and rang the bell. An elderly uniformed guard studied her reader's card and allowed her to enter.

In the file section Ruth consulted the notebook containing listings for German maps and located one, dated 1945, of northern Germany and southern Scandinavia. She filled out the necessary call slip and handed it to the girl at the desk.

The clerk started to leave the room, then returned. "I thought that number was familiar," she said. "I'm afraid you'll have to wait. That map is in use by that gentleman in the corner."

Ruth looked across the room and felt a shock, a tingling that seemed to start at her toes and run up her entire body. Gregor Kovpak was at a table in the far corner, studying a large map. Ruth walked over and stood behind him.

"Hello."

He swung about, his eyes widening in surprise, and then hurriedly rose, smiling with pleasure. "What are you doing here? What about your conference?"

Ruth made a small grimace. "The conference is over. A monumental failure. So I came here to see where the treasure could have gone to, from that Bad whatever."

Gregor nodded, trying to keep the profound admiration he felt for her from becoming too apparent. Suddenly he remembered his manners and pulled out a chair for her.

"Here, sit down." He sat beside her, thinking, What should I say now? Obviously he couldn't tell her that she was wasting her time, that the treasure had been in Langley, Virginia, all these years. Still, he didn't want to waste an opportunity to spend the day with her. "So you're a detective, too," he said. "I'll make a deal with you. I'll share my map with you if you'll have lunch with me."

"It's a deal," Ruth said.

459

"Good." Gregor leaned over the map, pointing, hiding his pleasure at her acceptance. "There—that is Bad Freienwalde, almost due east of Berlin."

Ruth looked disappointed. "If they were planning on taking the treasure to Denmark or Sweden, which seems to me logical, especially since one of them was Swedish, that's not the most direct way to the Baltic ports."

"The treasure ostensibly was on its way to Russia, and the trains that went to Russia did not go by way of the Baltic ports," Gregor said. "That may have been the reason."

Ruth felt a bit sheepish. "So where do you think they went from Bad Freienwalde?"

"Let us assume, as you said, that the two men went to either Denmark or Sweden as the first step in going—wherever they eventually ended up."

Ruth glanced up from the map. "You don't think they stayed there?"

"Look at it this way," Gregor said. "The police in those countries searched for them hard and long, and without success. Therefore it seems likely they moved on."

Ruth considered the logic of this. "But they still had to get to either Sweden or Denmark before they could move on. And if we're going to follow their trail—"

Gregor's eyebrows quirked humorously. "*We?*"

Ruth reddened a bit. "I mean me. I have my vacation coming, and I think it might be fun trying to trace just exactly where the treasure did end up."

"And you think you can do it? With the trail nearly thirty-five years old?"

"Well," Ruth said, "someone else did it, or there wouldn't be an auction. Then so can we! I mean, I!"

"We," Gregor corrected gently, thinking what it would mean if they could travel together, even for the short time it would take for her to realize she was on a wild-goose chase. "I can spare a week. And," he added disingenuously, "you may be right."

"You sound dubious," Ruth said, but she was happier at that moment than she had been for a long time.

Gregor returned his attention to the map. "Let's consider the ports they might have left from."

"There's a place—Warnemünde," Ruth said, pointing. "That's the closest point to Denmark."

"It's a possibility," Gregor admitted. "Or Sassnitz. That's the closest to Sweden."

"But the farthest from Bad Freienwalde," Ruth pointed out. "Besides, Denmark is a much better jumping-off place. From Sweden where could they go? Norway? It's easier to get there from Denmark. Finland? It was under Russian domination. Russia itself? Obviously they didn't steal the treasure from the Russians just to take it to Russia."

She was probably right, Gregor thought with amused admiration. The CIA man would have taken Pettersson to the States by way of Denmark and then England. And Warnemünde would be a logical place for them to be met by a high-speed cutter. Still, Gregor had to make it look as if there were a choice. He wanted his travels with Ruth to last as long as possible.

He looked at the map again. "Of course, their decision as to which port to leave from would depend on the state of the roads at the time."

Ruth looked at him, her eyes shining. "Right! That means that the man who was with Pettersson had to be either a German or a Russian. Who else would know the state of the roads? Only the Germans, who had retreated down them a short time before, or the Russians, who had advanced over them."

Gregor had to concede that it was a good point.

"And," Ruth went on, "the entire thing must have been planned— the theft, the car, and then, naturally, a boat. Now who had access to boats in the Baltic along the German coast at that time? German fishermen, that's who. And who had access to cars in eastern Germany at that time? Germans, of course—or Russians." She paused, her mind racing. "It was night, you said, and the car looked official. It was probably the German chauffeur of some Russian bigwig, who took a chance on using the car because the man who was paying him, the man with Pettersson, was a former officer of his and they were both from ODESSA. . . ."

Gregor laughed in pure enjoyment. Then he shook his head in admiration. "What an imagination!"

Ruth smiled. "You see? We've made progress already. We know that a German and Pettersson stole the treasure. We know they

461

left Germany from Warnemünde, probably landing"—she looked at the map—"somewhere near Gedser, and from there—"

Gregor interrupted her. "We *know?*"

"Well," she said, "we're pretty sure, and that's better than not knowing at all."

"I suppose so. In that case, it's been a good morning's work." Gregor looked at his watch. "Which deserves a good lunch. At which time we can plan our trip in pursuit of the Schliemann gold!" He made it sound very dramatic.

Well, Ruth thought, it is dramatic! Or it could be.

FROM his position in the telephone booth, James Newkirk had a perfect view across Piccadilly into the Aeroflot Soviet Airlines ticket office. He waited until a certain attendant at the counter was the only one unoccupied with her phone. Then he dialed rapidly.

She answered at once. "Good morning, Aeroflot, Sonia speaking. May I help you?"

"Good morning," Newkirk said. "Does Aeroflot have a direct flight from London to Kuibyshev?"

"I'm afraid not. You have to change in Moscow."

"I see. Well, what equipment flies from Moscow to Kuibyshev?"

"One moment." There was a pause. "It's an Ilyushin, the Il-18."

"That's a prop job, isn't it?"

"Yes, sir, but it's an excellent airplane."

"If I have to get there in a prop job, I'll have to think about it," Newkirk said, and hung up.

He stepped from the booth and strolled to White Lion Yard, where he would meet Sonia at a small restaurant. He considered with pride the code he had developed with her. Kuibyshev meant he wished to meet for lunch at one o'clock. The bit about propellers indicated where they would dine.

At the restaurant he was ushered to a quiet booth and ordered a whisky and water for himself and a very cold Finnish vodka for Sonia. He came to his feet a few minutes later as she slipped quickly into the booth. She inspected herself in her compact mirror, and wasting no time on gestures of friendship, she drank her vodka in one steady gulp, then rapped her glass on the table. The waiter appeared at once, then hurried to the bar.

Sonia did not consider herself an enemy agent; she merely gave information to Newkirk or whoever appeared with the proper identification and the money. The information was innocent enough, for she was not in a position to know anything critical, and she was positive she would have refused to pass any on if she had known it.

"What do you want now?" she asked coldly. "This will have to be quick. We're rushed. The British Airways strike, you know."

Newkirk perused his menu as he answered her. "Two men. Their names are Gregor Kovpak and Serge Ulanov. They arrived in England on Aeroflot from Leningrad a few days ago. I want to know when they are leaving and where they are going. And whether either of them will be accompanied, and if so, by whom."

Sonia nodded. "Get me another vodka, please."

SERGE Ulanov, a cigarette in one corner of his mouth, reclined on the bed in Gregor Kovpak's room with his copy of *Playboy* while he waited for his compatriot to return. Suddenly he looked up. Someone was fumbling at the lock of the room. Sliding silently from the bed, Ulanov moved to the door. With a quick motion he flung it open, and almost went over backward as Kovpak, his arms laden with bundles, nearly fell over him.

"Thanks. I was having trouble opening the door with my arms full."

"Oh," Ulanov said, feeling a bit foolish, as Kovpak unloaded his burdens on the bed. "Which reminds me, I also want to do a bit of shopping before we go back."

"Before we go back," Kovpak repeated. "That is one of the things I want to talk to you about, Serge. You see, I think we should start to do something here about this auction of the Schliemann treasure. Certainly the Hermitage must bid on it."

"Are you trying to say you aren't going home with me now? If it's a question of spending a few more days in London with Dr. McVeigh, we can go back together next week."

Gregor reddened slightly. "I'm not thinking of staying in London. I'm thinking of a trip to East Berlin. To see the Bode Museum."

"And when do you plan on leaving for East Berlin?"

"I—tomorrow morning, I suppose. We—I mean, I haven't made any plans yet."

"I see," Ulanov said, and decided to take Gregor off the hook.

"Well, in that case, all I can do is wish you a pleasant journey. And if, by chance, you happen to run into Dr. McVeigh at the Bode, please give her my best regards." He gave Gregor a friendly wink and went into his own room.

Watching the older man close the door behind him, Kovpak heaved a sigh of relief. He had thought it would be tougher than that to shake the old boy. The last thing he wanted was to be under surveillance while traveling with Ruth. He began unwrapping the packages of new clothes which he hoped would make him appear, at least in her eyes, more like a man of the world.

MAJOR Serge Ulanov telephoned the London manager of Aeroflot from the office of the military attaché at the Russian embassy, where he made all his official telephone calls. "Two people, Alexis," he said quietly in Russian. "A Dr. Gregor Kovpak, a Russian national, and a Dr. Ruth McVeigh, carrying an American passport. Of course, they may not be traveling by Aeroflot, but in any event I'm sure your computer can find them. Going possibly to East Berlin, but not necessarily. Sometime tomorrow morning, I'm fairly sure. . . . What? . . . Yes, I'll hold on."

He leaned back and waited. Soon he brought his attention back to the telephone. "What line? . . . LOT? I see, the Polish airline . . . leaving Heathrow at eleven fifty tomorrow, arriving at Schönefeld airport, in East Berlin, at thirteen twenty-five . . . flight two eight six, nonstop . . . and with a car rental waiting for them at the airport. . . . Wait a minute, Alexis, let me think."

Ulanov sorted things out in his mind; then he smiled a broad smile. "All right, Alexis, this is what I want you to do. Call Dr. Kovpak and Dr. McVeigh at their hotel and inform them that, unfortunately, flight two eight six has been overbooked, but that you have managed to book them on a slightly later one. Pick out a flight like that and let me know. I'll wait."

He leaned back again for a few minutes, and then paid attention to the telephone.

"What? Excellent. What line is it? KLM to Amsterdam and then to East Berlin on Interflug? Never heard of them, but so long as their planes don't fall down. Now hold one of those seats on the LOT flight for me. Well, of course. What do you think this whole charade was all about, anyway?"

He hung up, thought a moment, and then placed a second call—to Colonel Franz Mueller of East German security in Berlin. After a wait, a voice came on the line, and Ulanov identified himself.

"Major!" Mueller sounded delighted. "When did you get in?"

"I'm in London, but I'll be in Berlin tomorrow, early afternoon. I need your help. I get to Schönefeld at thirteen twenty-five on LOT flight two eight six. I want to be met by two cars. I—"

"*Two* cars?" the colonel asked.

Ulanov explained. "I want to be very sure we do not lose the people we will be trailing, and if one car has to be left, to trail them on foot, I want another car handy. I want both cars completely nondescript—nothing official about them—a good driver with each, and a good man with the driver in the second car." He thought a moment. "Is it possible to arrange for some sort of telephonic communication between them?"

"Of course. Would I do as the man with the driver in the second car? I assume you'll be with the driver in the first."

"Excellent! Oh, one more thing. The man we will be trailing is named Gregor Kovpak. He's a Russian. He's arranged for a rental car at the airport. Is it possible to put some sort of bug in that car?"

"Certainly. Major, will we be requiring arms?"

Ulanov laughed. "No, Kovpak's not dangerous. But you might bring along some beer and sandwiches. It may be a long drive."

"Oh? Where to?"

"All I have is a silly hunch that I'd be ashamed to tell you about," Ulanov said. "I'll see you tomorrow." He hung up.

NEWKIRK made his way through the evening crush to the bar. He got the barmaid's attention and ordered a triple vodka for Sonia, a half-pint of lager for himself.

"Now," he said as he placed the drink before her. "What have you been able to learn?"

"You're lucky I worked late tonight. Gregor Kovpak's schedule was changed a little while ago. He was to leave on the LOT plane for East Berlin tomorrow, but he was put on another one that connects in Amsterdam and arrives later."

"Ulanov, too?"

Sonia shook her head. "No, he's taken one of the seats in the LOT plane."

Newkirk wrinkled his forehead, trying to digest this odd information. "So they aren't traveling together. But they are each, I suppose, traveling alone?"

Sonia giggled. The triple vodka was getting to her; he had no idea how much alcohol Sonia had consumed since their lunch. "This Gregor Kovpak—he must be some man, huh? He's traveling with a woman, a Ruth McVeigh."

Newkirk considered this revelation. Obviously Ulanov had arranged the change in Kovpak's flight in order to get to Schönefeld ahead of him, in order to follow him and McVeigh when they arrived. That was certainly interesting: a surveillance by the KGB of one of Russia's top scientists! Why? The involvement of the American, McVeigh, had to mean that the affair concerned the Schliemann treasure. Well, if the treasure was of such interest to the KGB, then it had to be of equal interest to the CIA.

A new thought came to him. "Sonia, did Kovpak arrange to rent a car at Schönefeld?"

"Yes." She yawned deeply.

Which simply meant that he, Newkirk, had to get to Schönefeld airport before any of the others, and rent a car. Then, when Ulanov took off after the two archaeologists, Newkirk would fall in line and find out what there was to know.

Better catch a cab to Heathrow now, he thought, and take the next plane to West Berlin. He took Sonia's arm. "Come on. I'll take you home."

She scowled at him. "Take your hands off me! The pub doesn't close for almost an hour. I'm staying right here."

Newkirk sighed. "I'll see your money is mailed to your home." He stood up and walked away quickly.

DENMARK—June 1979

FROM the small balcony that jutted out of the sheer walls of Lindholm Castle the view was spectacular, and Professor Arne Nyborg luxuriated in it. In the distance the sparkling spires and glistening rooftops of Ringsted could be seen, and the land between was filled with bucolic meadows and intermittent stands of pine and birch.

466

Stepping back a bit, since heights always affected him, the professor turned and walked into Count Lindholm's study.

Lindholm poured brandy for him. "Wonderful!" Nyborg said, still amazed at having been invited to several meetings in this sacred aerie. "And what a view! It never wearies, Count!"

Lindholm chided him. "After the time we've spent together, and when we are partners in a most audacious scheme, you still call me Count? May I call you Arne?"

"Of course! Certainly! Absolutely!"

"Then you should call me Axel." Lindholm smiled.

"If you wish . . . Axel," Nyborg said, and thought his heart would burst. He was on a first-name basis with Count Axel Lindholm! Who would have believed it? Still, why shouldn't Axel be his friend? After all, he had brought the count a proposition to challenge any man's sporting blood, his spirit of adventure. And he, Professor Arne Nyborg, would get the money! He wriggled in his chair. "Axel, how is our . . . audacious scheme . . . going?"

"Very well," Count Lindholm said. "You recall the letters that went out to the various museums?"

"Of course. But they said that bidding would start September first. Why the delay? That's over two months away."

Lindholm looked at him evenly. "To begin with, I wish to give ample time for the matter to be thoroughly publicized. The meeting in London that ended in such discord did a good deal for our cause. It brought the question of legal ownership—or lack of ownership—to the fore. That should result in even more bidders. And the various museums need time to raise the money to bid."

"So . . . how do you plan to conduct the auction?"

Lindholm took a panatela from his humidor, held a match to it, and puffed it into life. "On the twenty-fifth of August an advertisement will appear in the personal columns of newspapers in the major cities of the world. This advertisement will state that, beginning on September first, a telephone conference call has been arranged for twelve noon, Greenwich time, which any interested museum or individual can join upon request to the international telephone company. The major news services of the world may also connect without cost. The conference call will last one hour each day for three consecutive days—"

Nyborg had paled. "That will cost a fortune!"

467

Lindholm shrugged lightly. "Fifty or sixty thousand dollars is all, I should judge. Surely no great sum, in these inflationary times, for the fun of an auction like this."

"But if you conduct the auction, won't you be identified?"

"No, I shall merely be a listener," Lindholm replied. "The auction will be conducted by someone from Switzerland, from an unlisted number. Actually, from an apartment I maintain there. That someone will be a person of confidence whose voice is unknown." The unknown would be his butler, Wilten, but there was no reason for Nyborg to know that. "I shall be listening on an extension in an adjoining room. Whoever is the high bidder at one o'clock on September third will be declared the winner."

The professor bobbed his balding head in profound admiration. He looks like an idiot doll on a string, Lindholm thought.

"But what about the delivery of the treasure? And the payment?" Nyborg asked, a frown suddenly crossing his face.

"The height of simplicity," Lindholm said. "The winner of the auction will be directed to place the money in escrow in Switzerland. It will be released from escrow and deposited in a numbered Swiss bank account when the high bidder confirms that delivery of the treasure has taken place, or when the delivery is reliably reported in the press."

"And the delivery itself?" Nyborg asked.

"The treasure will be discovered in a suitcase at an airport in the baggage-claim area of a given flight. The number of that flight will be divulged to the winning museum, together with the fictitious passenger's name that will be on the suitcase, as well as the proper claim-check number. The newspapers in that city will be told where and when they can witness the denouement of the Auction of the Ages—at Kennedy, or Orly, or wherever. Then the money will be released from escrow to the account."

Nyborg set his snifter of brandy down. He could see no flaw in the scheme. It was brilliant! He leaned back in his comfortable leather chair, his tiny hands clasped across the bulge of his belly, and tried to picture what it would be like to have a minimum of fifteen million dollars in his possession! Over *eighty million kroner!* His mind boggled at the thought. He would have to show Count Lindholm his appreciation and get him a nice gift. Something personal, man to man. A gold cigar lighter, possibly. He became aware that he was being addressed, and looked up from his reverie with a start. "I beg your pardon?"

Lindholm was smiling. "I said, I envy you your composure. Here you are, with a fortune almost in your hands, and all of it depends on a very dubious location in a bank. I tell you," the count went on, his voice dripping sincerity, "I'd be as nervous as a witch."

Nyborg was confused. "Nervous? Dubious location?"

"These bank robberies," the count said knowingly. "Getting more and more prevalent. And daring, too. I'm sure you recall that case in Monte Carlo where bandits put a gun under the bank manager's nose and made him open the vault. Then they planted an explosive that popped open the doors of all the safe-deposit boxes on the wall, just like that." The count snapped his fingers. "But then I'm undoubtedly exaggerating the danger! Banks are robbed every day without their vaults or safe-deposit boxes being disturbed. I really shouldn't even have raised the subject."

"No, no! You were quite right! If there's a safer place—" The pudgy professor looked about at the valuable carvings on the shelves, the rare paintings on the walls. "Count—I mean, Axel— how do you keep your things from being stolen?"

"I have the best vault, plus one of the most complete alarm systems in Denmark. Believe me," he went on patronizingly, "if you entered the castle without Wilten deactivating the system, you would be overwhelmed with sirens, bells, and general bedlam. In addition, the Ringsted police would be here in moments, guns drawn." It was true, and the count still resented Erik Trosborg's having insisted upon the alarm system. Without it, Lindholm might have faked a burglary and raised some needed money.

Nyborg's eyes were round with wonder. "You mean, all the doors and windows are wired?"

"Everything," the count said wearily as he stifled a yawn and leaned over to crush out his cigar. He had obviously been continuing the conversation only out of politeness. Now he came to his feet. "My dear Arne, I'm sure you will forgive me, but I had a late evening last night, and I'm afraid I need a bit of rest."

"Of course! I understand," Nyborg said. He got up and moved toward the door. There he paused, unable to leave with the issue unsettled. "Axel—I wonder—I know it's an imposition—I mean—" Nyborg stumbled into embarrassed silence.

"Arne, my dear fellow!" said the count. "Is there something I can do for you? Nothing would give me greater pleasure!"

Nyborg relaxed. He should have known Count Lindholm would not let him down. "Well, what I thought was—since the castle is so well protected—well, we might keep the treasure here, rather than in the bank. It wouldn't take up much room."

"Keep the treasure here?" The count rubbed his chin, staring at the floor in deep thought. "I hadn't considered it before. The vault, of course, is out of the question. Too many people have access to it. Still, I suppose we could keep it here in my study. Nobody comes in when I'm away." He thought a moment more and then looked up. "Actually, now that I think about it, it's a brilliant idea. I must congratulate you, Arne."

Nyborg's face flushed with pleasure at the compliment. "Let me see, today is Friday; it's too late to get to the bank. Next week is graduation week, and on Monday I really must be at the university. But Tuesday I'll definitely be here. Say, five o'clock?"

"Fine!"

"And thank you, Count—I mean, Axel! Thank you!"

"It is nothing," Lindholm said modestly, and held out his hand. Nyborg shook it enthusiastically, then hurried to the door.

Lindholm watched it close behind the dumpy professor and sank back into his chair with relief. Now, in case of any trouble, the treasure would be here at the castle. After all, bank safe-deposit boxes could be opened with court orders.

The count poured himself more brandy and stared contemplatively at the balcony the professor always favored on his visits. In four days Nyborg would bring the treasure here. Lindholm smiled coldly as he lit another cigar.

EAST GERMANY—July 1979

It was a beautiful Sunday, the first day of July. The small car that Gregor Kovpak had rented at Schönefeld airport was performing well, and traffic on the autobahn was light. Best of all, in Kovpak's mind as he drove, was the fact that the lovely Ruth McVeigh sat beside him, looking as if she were enjoying herself.

470

A mile or so behind the small car, Major Serge Ulanov relaxed in the passenger seat of a battered Zis, alternately drinking from a bottle of beer and consulting a road map spread out in his lap. His driver, a plainclothes *Volkspolizei* detective named Wolper, spoke for the first time since they had left the airport.

"They've turned, sir. Onto route two."

Ulanov consulted his map. Route 2 was a minor road that left the autobahn, skirted the Polish border, and would eventually take them to Bad Freienwalde. His hunch, then, had been correct. Ruth McVeigh was intrigued by the story Gregor had told her in the restaurant the first night they met, and she was now trying to trace the treasure from where it had last been seen. Kovpak, fully aware that she was wasting her time, was simply taking advantage of the opportunity to be with her. The poor fool is falling in love, Ulanov thought, and obviously nothing can come of it.

He drained his bottle of beer as Colonel Mueller's voice came over the intercom speaker.

"Major, I think you have company. When you left Schönefeld, and before I picked up your trail, another car came out of the airport parking lot and turned after you. I dropped back and gave him plenty of room. When you turned onto route two he followed. I thought that was enough of a coincidence to advise you."

Ulanov had a pretty good idea who it was. "What can you see of the car and the driver?"

"It has West Berlin plates," replied the colonel, "and the man driving seems to be fairly tall. Heavy head of hair and wearing glasses."

"His name is Newkirk," Ulanov said. He thought a moment, then spoke into the microphone. "Colonel, pass that car. Then pass me and take up following Kovpak and the woman. Discreetly, of course. I'm sure they're going to Bad Freienwalde. I'm going to turn back to the autobahn and head into Berlin."

"Taking your friend Newkirk with you, I gather. By the nose."

"Or giving it a good try. Get in touch with me later at the Stadt Berlin Hotel."

FOR some miles James Newkirk had been concentrating on following Ulanov's car. He frowned as the Zis swung off to the left onto a route that Newkirk knew would take them back to the autobahn. Was it possible that Ulanov suspected he was being followed, and was merely taking diversionary action? But if Ulanov was trailing Kovpak and the woman, how could he be going anywhere except where they went? Could it be that *they* were taking diversionary action, suspecting *they* were being followed? It was very possible, Newkirk thought. He shrugged and followed the battered Zis onto the autobahn heading south.

Soon the city of Berlin grew about them, new apartment houses appearing in monotonous similarity along both sides of the road. Newkirk drew closer to his quarry, aware that it would be easy for Ulanov to evade him in the sprawling warren of the metropolis. But the driver of the car ahead gave no indication that he knew he was being followed.

It was growing dark, and Newkirk leaned forward to put on his parking lights. The Zis entered Unter den Linden, Newkirk still keeping up easily on the broad avenue in spite of the heavier traffic. Then the Zis suddenly turned left into a side street that led toward Checkpoint Charlie, the double-guarded gateway between East and West Berlin.

Newkirk sat erect, worried now. Could Kovpak and McVeigh be heading for West Berlin with Ulanov behind them? If so, by the time he got through the well-known delay at Checkpoint Charlie, both Ulanov and the two archaeologists would long since have disappeared.

But that was exactly where Ulanov's car was going! He saw the Zis turn sharply into the checkpoint entrance and draw up to the barrier manned by the East German police. The husky driver exhibited papers and spoke earnestly to the guard, then put the car in gear and turned behind the high wooden wall that separated the check stations of the two republics. Newkirk hurried his car forward, then sat in frustrated impatience as the guard checked each entry in his passport before finally waving him through. Newkirk stepped on the gas, hoping the American checkpoint would detain Ulanov long enough for him to be able to resume the chase.

As he swung his car around the wooden wall toward the American post, he saw the Zis blocking the narrow roadway. Its driver stepped out and moved toward him in the white glare of the floodlights that lit up the restricted area. Newkirk saw Ulanov slide behind the wheel of the Zis and pull the car out of the way of traffic. The driver, in the meantime, came up to the window of Newkirk's car, holding his identification card in his hand.

Newkirk realized he was still in East Berlin, but he had no fears, since his papers were in order. "Yes? What is it?" he asked equably.

Wolper's face might have been carved of granite. "I am a sergeant in the *Volkspolizei*. Please step down. I may have to search you." He tilted his head in the direction of the East German barrier, invisible behind the intervening wall. "You failed to declare any of our currency you might have."

Newkirk was suddenly aware of the trap into which he had been led. He got out of the car slowly. "There's no need to search me. I do have some of your marks. I bought them at Schönefeld, in case I needed gasoline. I'm sorry, but the man at the barrier didn't ask about them and I simply forgot. I'll go back now and turn them in for West German money."

"No," the sergeant said. "You have attempted to smuggle currency into West Germany. Turn your car around and follow me." As he spoke, he allowed his jacket to swing open; a revolver in a shoulder holster glistened momentarily under the lights.

"But this is ridiculous. Who would want to smuggle money out of East Germany? Outside this country your marks have no value." He took one look at the sergeant's rigid face and sighed. "All right," he said.

"You say you are a newspaper reporter?" the magistrate asked.

"You have my press credentials on your desk, with my passport," Newkirk replied.

"You did not exchange your currency in accordance with the regulations. Is that correct?"

Newkirk heaved a great sigh. "May I make a telephone call?"

"Of course. All rights are respected here."

Newkirk went to the telephone, and when at last he was connected, he knew exactly what he wanted to say. "Hello, Mike? This is Jim Newkirk. I'm in East Berlin. That's right; the *Volkspolizei* headquarters. Some silly mix-up with the currency regulations, but I'm afraid I'll have to miss Aunt Betty's birthday party. Tell her I'm sorry. And get somebody from the paper's legal staff to get me out of here, understand?"

"Aunt Betty's birthday party!" Ulanov said with a grin, and ordered another beer. He and Sergeant Wolper were having dinner at the Stadt Berlin Hotel, and calls from Colonel Mueller's security office were being relayed there.

The sergeant put down his stein of beer and wiped foam from his lips. "Aunt Betty's birthday party?" he asked, mystified.

"To advise his control that he stepped into dung," Ulanov said. "We use Uncle Vanya's fiftieth wedding anniversary, ourselves." At that moment the headwaiter appeared again with a telephone. The call was for Ulanov.

"Major? Colonel Mueller here. We're in Rostock, up near the Baltic. Kovpak and the girl are staying at the Warnow Interhotel here. So am I."

"They went directly to Rostock?" Ulanov asked.

"No. As you surmised, they went to Bad Freienwalde, but they didn't even get out of the car. They consulted a map and then took the road to Rostock. After they checked into the hotel, they got back in their car and drove off to Warnemünde. That's about eight miles, along the estuary to the Baltic."

"I see. And exactly what did they do when they got there?"

"Well, Major," the colonel said, "that is what is so curious. They drove along the docks slowly, and then stopped and got out of the car and just stood there, facing the sea. Then they burst into laughter. Yes, they laughed like idiots. And there wasn't anything I could see to laugh at. Then they got back into the car, still laughing, and returned to the hotel, where at the moment they are eating dinner in the restaurant. They put their car in the hotel garage, and I have my driver watching it so they won't go anywhere without my knowing."

"Good." Ulanov thought a moment. "Book me a room at the same hotel. We'll leave in an hour."

As Gregor drove along the road leading to Warnemünde and the sea, Ruth McVeigh leaned back and closed her eyes, trying to picture the kind of dock they should look for—one with small fishing boats, the sort of dock Pettersson and his unknown accomplice would have sailed from. In her imagination it was a sort of Winslow Homer scene, with wrinkled fishermen sitting around weathered shacks in sou'westers and puffing on their pipes.

474

The car came gently to a stop. "Warnemünde docks," Gregor announced. Ruth opened her eyes, and as they climbed out, she stared about her incredulously. For miles in each direction were huge dock cranes, looking like giant prehistoric birds. Behind them, instead of quaint fishing shacks, were large concrete warehouses surrounded by mountains of cases, crates, and casks. Instead of small fishing boats at the docks, there were huge ocean freighters. And the only living creatures to be seen were the sea gulls soaring overhead above the gray, choppy sea.

Gregor looked at Ruth, feeling sorry for her: it was obvious that this could never have been the port from which the two thieves had sailed with the treasure in 1945. Ruth's face wrinkled as if she were fighting tears, but instead a huge peal of laughter came. Gregor stared at the huge cranes and then he, too, saw the humor in it, and both of them whooped. Still laughing, they climbed into the car again and Gregor put the car into gear, starting back toward Rostock.

As Ruth wiped her eyes, Gregor asked, "Tomorrow, would you like to drive to Sassnitz? It isn't very far, and they might have gone from there to Sweden, you know."

Ruth shook her head. "No," she said quietly. It had come to her that falling in love was painful, and the sooner cured the better. "Don't humor me. I know when I'm wrong. It was only a dream in the first place, a silly notion."

There was a long silence and then Gregor said suddenly, "It wasn't silly." Entering Rostock, he kept his eyes rigidly on the cobbled streets. "I doubt if anything you ever did, or ever could do, would be silly." He knew that now that the quest was finished, both of them would be leaving for home very soon. Time was slipping away; he had to say something that would at least hint to her how he felt, pointless as it would be. He wet his lips. "Ruth, do you know that you are very beautiful?"

"Thank you." She turned to stare out the car window. They were already approaching the hotel. She had to speak now or keep quiet forever. But she knew she could not leave him for good without his knowing. She spoke without looking at him. "You said before that I could never do anything silly. Well, I have. I've fallen in love with you."

His hand jerked wildly on the wheel and the car bumped the

475

curb by the hotel entrance before he brought it to a stop. He felt completely confused. "You—what?"

There was quiet, almost resigned amusement in her voice. "I said, I've fallen in love with you. Madly."

He shook his head as if to clear it, running his hand through his thick hair. "But—that's impossible!"

"Improbable, maybe, but unfortunately not impossible." She opened the car door and got out. She bent down and looked at him unsteadily, willing herself not to cry. "Thanks for going along with my idiocy about the treasure. I'll say good-by now. I can get a plane to Berlin and fly home from there."

He took her hand and pulled her back into the car, a gleam of pure happiness in his eyes. "My darling Ruth," he said quietly. "I never dreamed of such a thing—me, at my age! And you, the loveliest thing in the world! Wait—" She had begun to tug her arm free. He let her go but spoke quickly. "Why do you think I'm here, chasing after something we probably couldn't find even if we knew where it was? I'm here because I wanted to spend as much time with you as I could before we had to go our separate ways. Just to look at you. Just to know you were near me."

He smiled a bit wryly and touched the lapel of his suit. "I'm wearing these clothes because the salesman told me they made me look like a man of the world, which is ridiculous, but I wanted to do it for you. Why do you think I look and talk like an idiot when I'm with you? I've been in love with you almost from the minute I met you."

Ruth stared at her hands, clasped tightly in her lap. She had never felt so happy in her life. "And now?" she asked softly.

"Now," Gregor said, "I shall put the car away in the garage until morning, after which we shall have dinner."

"I'm not hungry," Ruth said in a small voice.

He reached over and took her hand. "Then we shall merely have wine—after which we shall go to my room. . . ."

THEY made love with a passion that Gregor had thought a thing of the past, and that Ruth had never known. Afterward they lay quietly, holding hands like children, reveling in their feeling for each other.

"And now," Gregor said, attempting lightness, "as they say in

476

the novels, we get married and live happily ever after." It could be, he told himself fiercely. Why not? He turned to Ruth, trying to sound convincing. "You will love Leningrad; it's a beautiful city. We shall work together at the Hermitage, and excavate in strange places together, and "

Ruth kissed him. "Darling, you're dreaming. I couldn't live in Russia. I've worked all my life to get where I am, and I couldn't give up my job." A thought came—another dream, she knew—but she had to voice it. "Why don't you come to New York?"

He grinned, but it was a tight grin. "My darling Ruth! I couldn't leave the Hermitage. It's the greatest museum in the world, and the antiquities section is largely my work. Besides, I have a baby dinosaur—"

Ruth leaned over to kiss him again. Oddly enough, she felt relaxed. "My darling," she said, "neither of us can leave what we have, but now we both have something extra, something we never had before. I will always love you, I'm sure of that, and I hope you will always love me. We will meet at archaeological congresses, and discuss our respective papers in dull, scientific terms, and then when we're alone—" She kissed him once more. "But now, for reasons I cannot imagine, I'm hungry."

IN THEIR growing wonder at their love, Ruth and Gregor consumed their meal with little idea of what they were eating. The only other person in the dining room at that late hour was a military-looking gentleman drinking schnapps with beer.

Over coffee and brandy Ruth suddenly said firmly, "It wasn't always like that."

Gregor stared. Ruth, he realized, would be fascinating to live with. Her mind went off at odd angles without warning. "What wasn't always like that?"

"Warnemünde. I mean, there were probably fishing docks back in 1945." She stared at Gregor thoughtfully. "And the sea was pretty choppy today, wasn't it?"

There was humor in Gregor's eyes. "Is there a connection?"

Ruth leaned toward him and said with conviction, "Darling, do you want to know what happened to that fishing boat with the treasure on it? It sank! In a big storm!" Ruth leaned back triumphantly. Why hadn't it occurred to her before? "That's why the treasure hasn't been seen or heard of all these years! Or Pettersson and the man with him! They've all been at the bottom of the sea!"

"And exactly who discovered the treasure and is putting it up for auction now?" Gregor asked with gentle sarcasm. "Was it a fisherman or an archaeologist?" He grinned. "Ruth, with your imagination, you should be writing books."

"Well, it could have happened," Ruth said. "Where could we find out about storms on the Baltic thirty-four years ago?"

Gregor smiled and shrugged. "I have no idea."

"Probably not here in Germany," Ruth said, sipping her coffee. "Things must have been a mess at the time. Do you think they might have records of storms and wrecks anywhere else? Possibly in Denmark?"

"Possibly," Gregor conceded. A trip to Denmark, while it would be a further waste of time as far as the treasure was concerned, would be a great excuse to spend a few more days with Ruth, and he did not wish to think beyond that point.

"I know an influential man in Denmark," Ruth said. "When I was at the Smithsonian, in Washington, he was in the diplomatic corps, and we used to run into each other at parties. He's a count— Axel Lindholm."

MAJOR Serge Ulanov rolled over in bed and tried to orient himself. Ah, yes. Rostock and the Warnow Interhotel. He yawned and consulted his watch. Almost noon. Well, he had had a decent night's rest for a change, and apparently the lovebirds had as well, since there had been no word from Sergeant Wolper or the colonel. He had just started to dress when the telephone rang.

"Major? Colonel Mueller. Kovpak and the girl are still here. We've kept an eye on their car. They haven't even come down to the restaurant."

"Not yet?" Ulanov sounded puzzled. "What rooms have they?"

"Four ten and four twelve. Why?"

"Meet me in the lobby," said the major curtly. He depressed the telephone lever and raised it again, asking the operator first for one room number and then the other. A sense of unease gripped him as each telephone rang in turn without being answered. His suspicions solidifying, Ulanov hung up and finished dressing. Then he strode to the elevator.

478

"Drs. Kovpak and McVeigh," he said to the girl at the desk in the lobby. "Their rooms do not answer."

The girl consulted some cards. "Oh," she said, "they both checked out early this morning."

"*What?*" said Colonel Mueller, who had joined Ulanov at the desk. "Their car is still in the garage!"

"Yes, sir. You see, it's a rental car, and we're an authorized agency to accept delivery. They turned it in this morning when they checked out."

"How did they leave? By cab?"

"I don't know, but they each had a small bag when they left. They might have taken the tram. It runs by the bus and railroad stations."

Where had Kovpak and the woman gone? Ulanov wondered. Checking on the trams, the cabs, and the stations would be quite a job. Then a plan came to him. Why not? After all, despite its occasional failings, the CIA was far from a helpless giant. His eyes twinkling, he looked up at Colonel Mueller.

"There is a man named Newkirk," Ulanov said, "being held at *Volkspolizei* headquarters in Berlin on charges of attempting to smuggle East German marks into West Germany—"

"So that's how you handled it!" said the colonel. "Excellent! Is he an enemy agent?"

"What he is," Ulanov replied, "is a poor, misguided newspaperman, and in thinking about it, I am ashamed of the trouble I have caused him. In my opinion, the German security forces should let him go. However, since Mr. Newkirk has a habit of getting into trouble, I believe you should keep a very careful watch over him. Advise me at once if he leaves the German Democratic Republic."

"Yes, sir." Colonel Mueller hesitated. "Will you be coming back to Berlin with me, sir?"

Major Ulanov sighed. "I suppose so." Duty was so difficult, he thought. He had hoped to see the circus that was playing on a dock across the street from the hotel. Its colorful banners and cheerfully painted wagons appealed to the Russian in him.

IT WAS two days before Major Ulanov's plan bore fruit. Lying on the bed in his room at the Stadt Berlin Hotel, he received a call from Colonel Mueller.

"Newkirk spent a good part of yesterday at the American embassy," the colonel reported. "He ate alone, made no other contacts, and went to bed early at his hotel. Today he returned to the embassy—"

"To find out if the tentacles of the famed CIA had managed to unearth Kovpak and McVeigh in the meantime."

"Probably," the colonel said. "Because right after that he went down to the railroad station and bought a ticket to Copenhagen. His train leaves at six tomorrow morning."

"Copenhagen, eh?" Ulanov said. "Get me a ticket on the train for the day *after* tomorrow. And check Copenhagen hotels and find out where Kovpak and the girl are staying." He hung up, pleased that Newkirk and the CIA had done his work for him. With luck, they might eventually tell him what Kovpak and McVeigh were up to.

DENMARK—July 1979

Count Axel Lindholm had been surprised and delighted to hear from Ruth McVeigh. In Washington he had done his best to convince her that she should spend a vacation with him, and despite her repeated amused refusals, he was determined to renew his efforts now that she was in Copenhagen. After all, *she* had called *him*. That had to mean something.

The count had arranged lunch for two in an intimate booth at one of his favorite restaurants, the Spinderokken. He had arrived early to advise the maître d' exactly what food was to be prepared and how he wished the wine chilled, and to see to the flowers for the table.

As Ruth entered the restaurant, the count felt a small flush of pleasure; she was even more beautiful than he remembered. He started forward, both hands outstretched, and then paused, his smile tightening a bit. A man had come in behind her, obviously accompanying her. A rather handsome man, the count thought, and somehow slightly familiar. But Count Lindholm had not been a diplomat for nothing. He smiled brilliantly, bent over Ruth's hand and kissed it. Then, straightening up, he looked at the intruder.

"Ruth, it's a very great pleasure. Who is your friend?"

"Hello, Axel. It's good to see you again. I want you to meet Dr. Gregor Kovpak." She turned to Gregor. "Darling, this is Count Lindholm, whom I've being telling you about."

The two men shook hands a bit warily. Lindholm led the way to the booth and instructed the maître d' to set another place. He waited until Ruth and Gregor had sat down beside one another. Then, seating himself across from them, he said brightly, "I've heard of all you've done at the Hermitage, Dr. Kovpak, and it's an honor to have you as my guest. And Ruth, of course, is an old friend. A very dear and close friend."

"Dear Axel," Ruth said gently, "I hope you and I will always be friends, but that is all we ever were. Gregor and I are in love."

"May I congratulate you both." The count's beaming expression lingered, but behind it he was deciding that now the luncheon should be used to elicit information that might be helpful in the auction. "I'm very glad to have this chance to talk with you both," he said earnestly. "I've read about the London conference, of course, but the Danish newspapers were vague as to the details."

Ruth smiled sadly. "The less said about it, the better. There undoubtedly will be more bidders now and the price of the treasure will go very high."

Count Lindholm looked properly sympathetic. "That's too bad! This cannot be welcome news to the Metropolitan."

"It isn't. Axel"—Ruth leaned a bit closer to him—"Axel, suppose I were to tell you I have a good idea of where the Schliemann gold might be."

"*What?*" Count Lindholm recovered instantly, but his heart was beating much faster. "What do you mean?"

"I mean I think it never reached Russia in 1945, but ended up in Denmark instead. With your help I think I can prove it."

"With my help? How?" Lindholm's mind was racing. Had Nyborg lied about how the treasure had come from the Hermitage?

Ruth was prevented from answering by the arrival of their food. They gave the excellent cuisine the homage it deserved by refraining from any serious conversation, although Count Lindholm's mind continued to churn. What if she were on to something? When coffee and brandy arrived, he turned to Ruth. "You were saying I could help you. In what way?"

481

Ruth put down her demitasse. "Do you know anyone at the Danish Admiralty?"

"As a matter of fact, I do," Lindholm replied. "He's head of naval intelligence. What do you want from him?"

"There must be records at the Admiralty of storms and ship-wrecks in the Baltic."

"I'm sure my friend can get that information for you. But why would you want it?"

Ruth smiled. "That's a secret, at least for now." She glanced at her watch. "Would it be possible to get hold of him today?"

Lindholm forced a laugh. "Impatient as ever! I'll see what I can do." He disappeared in the direction of the phone, and returned shortly, smiling. "He's in his office. I'll take you there."

As he led the way from the restaurant to his car, where Wilten sprang to open the doors for them, Count Lindholm wondered how much Ruth knew or suspected. He hoped he would learn the answer soon, because he had an appointment later that afternoon with Professor Nyborg.

AT THE naval station on the waterfront, the young ensign was determined to give the beautiful lady all the help he could—and not just because those were his orders. The ledger from the 1945 weather archives was open on his desk, and he began leafing through it.

"May twenty-second and twenty-third, I believe you said." He smiled. "Ah, here we are. Good weather both days over the entire western Baltic."

To his surprise the lady did not seem pleased with the information. "Good weather? You're sure? No storms?"

The ensign checked the reports again and then looked up, slightly puzzled by her reaction. "No, ma'am. Full moon, no cloud cover, calm sea."

Ruth spoke to Gregory disconsolately as Count Lindholm drew closer to catch every word. "It looks as if I might be wrong," she said. But she turned again to the ensign, still not ready to give up. "Do you keep records on things like reported wrecks, or ships asking for assistance? As far back as 1945?"

"Oh, yes, ma'am." While they waited for him to get the files, Ruth and Gregor wandered to the window. They could see tourists taking photographs of the Little Mermaid, the famed character in the Hans Christian Andersen story, whose statue sits on a rock at the harbor's edge and symbolizes Copenhagen for many people. In a low voice Gregor said, "Ruth, let's forget the Schliemann treasure and simply enjoy ourselves? Copenhagen is so beautiful."

He broke off as the ensign came back with another ledger and opened it. "There were no ships asking for assistance on those two days, ma'am, but maybe this will help. These are copies of the logs of our patrol boats for those years. Here is one for May twenty-third, 1945, from a ship named the *Elritse*."

Ruth, Gregor, and Lindholm came up behind the ensign and looked over his shoulder. Lindholm translated. "It says, 'At 0205 encountered small boat running without lights off Gedser light.'" He continued on to the end. "'There were no signs of survivors or anything to indicate a cargo so precious that the smuggler would blow up his boat rather than submit to search.'"

Ruth was beaming. "That's it! *That's it!*"

"Darling," Gregor said with some impatience, "that was probably someone running explosives or illegal arms. The chances of that having anything to do with what we're looking for are—well, it's impossible."

"It isn't impossible! I tell you that's our fishing boat!" Ruth turned to Lindholm. "Axel, isn't Gedser that little point of land just across from Warnemünde?" When he nodded she said, "I thought so. Gregor, darling, we'll rent a car and drive there tomorrow." She smiled at the ensign. "I don't know how to thank you!"

Again leading the way to the car, Lindholm was trying to make sense of what he had heard. Obviously Ruth McVeigh believed the treasure had been aboard a small boat that had exploded near Gedser. If this was true, then the gold had been found and had somehow fallen into the hands of Arne Nyborg. And now it was about to be delivered into his own. Ruth McVeigh's idea was a distinct possibility, and a very dangerous one for Axel Lindholm.

As they got into the car, the count turned to his guests. "I really cannot allow you to hire a car tomorrow. I insist that you use Wilten to drive you to Gedser in my car. Would nine in the morning be all right?"

Ruth smiled. "You're very sweet. Thank you, Axel."

When they drew up at the Plaza Hotel and Ruth and Gregor disappeared inside, Lindholm climbed into the front seat beside his chauffeur. As they started back to Lindholm Castle, Wilten raised his eyebrows inquiringly. Lindholm nodded. "Trouble!" he said heavily. "There's a good possibility that Nyborg was lying to me about how he got the treasure."

"You're seeing him shortly. Will you ask him?" There was none of the normal servant-master relationship in Wilten's tone. Clearly the two shared a long history of roguery.

Lindholm shook his head. "He would only deny it. But if he has lied to me, maybe Ruth McVeigh will be able to trace the treasure to him."

"But the trail will stop there, won't it?"

"Maybe, or maybe not. In any event, I don't believe in taking chances. You will be driving them to Gedser tomorrow morning. Keep your ears open. If they pick up any clues that may lead them to Nyborg, I expect you will know what to do."

Wilten smiled faintly. "I know what you mean."

FROM the small balcony that jutted from the wall of Lindholm Castle, the count watched as Professor Nyborg's old yellow Volvo came rattling up the long drive. Five o'clock; the professor was on time. Count Lindholm walked back into his study and sat down, calculating coldly.

In a few minutes there was a timid rap on the door. The count walked over and opened it. Nyborg, puffing from his climb up the stairs with his bulky package, came in and carefully set the bundle on a chair. "I truly appreciate this, Count Lindholm—"

"Axel," Lindholm corrected him almost mechanically, bending over the bundle. "Shall we see what we have here?"

"Oh, certainly." Professor Nyborg opened it reverently. "It's all there," Nyborg said, wetting his thick lips. Everything he had always wanted in life was represented by this jumbled dullish yellow pile. He watched the count check the pieces, rewrap them, then stow the bundle carefully in a large drawer of a cabinet. He locked the drawer and pocketed the key. Nyborg smiled tremulously and then—as Count Lindholm had been sure he would—moved toward the balcony to enjoy the view.

How perfectly he plays his part, Count Lindholm thought as he reached for the brandy and carefully filled two snifters. Noiselessly

484

he stepped toward the balcony with the glasses, prepared to call out to the professor and then seem to stumble, at the same time splashing the burning liquid into those wide, inane eyes. Then he would quickly push the temporarily blinded man over the low parapet. He opened his mouth to call out, and then froze!

There was a loud banging on the study door and it was rudely flung open. Lindholm swung about, the brandy sloshing in the two glasses. His chef, François, stood there glowering, with his assistant's ear pinched painfully between two fingers.

The infuriated chef was sputtering. "This idiot! Cumin in the vichyssoise! I shall not tolerate it! Yesterday it was paprika in the lobster bisque! You must send him away at once, sir!"

Lindholm fought down the wave of blind fury that had swept over him at the interruption. But the damage was done; the moment had passed. The professor had come back into the study as a result of the clamor, lifting a glass from the count's hand as he went by. Lindholm walked to his desk as if in a trance and pressed a button. Wilten appeared in moments, quickly took in the tableau, and gently led the chef and his assistant from the room.

"I'm afraid I must go, Axel," Nyborg said, and emptied his glass. "Tomorrow is graduation and tonight we rehearse the procession." He moved to the door. "I can't thank you enough," he said sincerely, tilting his head toward the cabinet containing the treasure. Then he left.

Count Lindholm sank into a chair. He felt let down, deprived. It had been so close! Still, there would be other opportunities as far as Professor Arne Nyborg was concerned. But if Ruth McVeigh and Gregor Kovpak were to become a threat, the opportunities in their case might be far more limited, and any possibilities at all would have to be exploited, no matter the cost. He would have to discuss the matter with Wilten in great detail that evening.

WITH the glass between front and back seats closed, Wilten was driving Ruth and Gregor south from Copenhagen along the coast highway. As they neared Gedser, they saw stone farmhouses with sharply sloping roofs; the farms ran down to tiny docks at the edge of the water. A lighthouse stood on a slight rise. Sailboats were scattered about the small harbor, and on the Gedser dock men could be seen repairing nets, smoking, and talking.

Ruth turned to Gregor. "It looks like what I expected at Warnemünde. This is where we finish this business."

Which, Gregor thought a bit sadly, is what I'm afraid of.

Ruth slid the glass divider open. "Wilten, I want to stop at that dock over there." As Wilten brought the car to a halt, she asked him, "Do you suppose these men speak English?"

"Oh, yes, miss. Almost everyone in Denmark speaks English except possibly the very old folks. It's taught in school."

"Good!" Ruth said. She got out of the car and marched off toward the nearest group.

The men looked up, surprised at the sight of the beautiful woman, and one by one they came to their feet. The oldest stepped forward. "Miss? Is there something . . . ?"

Ruth took a deep breath. "There was a ship sunk off the Gedser light in May 1945. It was probably a small fishing boat. Does anyone recall it?"

The spokesman shook his head. "I wouldn't know anything about that, miss. I was in the Royal Navy in 1945."

Ruth looked at the others questioningly. One by one they shook their heads. She began again with a smile. "Well, do any of you remember anyone trawling around here in the past few months, bringing up a box of some sort?"

The men looked at each other and again shook their heads. "Nobody trawls near the light, miss," said the spokesman. "Lose their nets if they did. Bottom's a jumble of rocks."

Ruth was getting a bit desperate. "Perhaps you remember someone diving?"

One man suddenly spoke up. "That Knud Christensen. Didn't you take him out diving, Jens?"

Jens Krag stepped forward. "Yes, I did. Last January. He was diving for his brother's body," he said quietly. "Both his brothers went down in a storm off the light. Never found Niels, but Gustave's body was tangled in ropes. Knud found it and brought it up." His voice became philosophical. "Knud hasn't been the same since. Going to lose the farm if he doesn't wake up—or starve first."

"Where does Knud Christensen live?" Ruth asked quickly.

Jens Krag pointed down the road. "Back the way you came. Name's on the mailbox."

"Thank you." Ruth gave them all a brilliant smile and walked back to the car. She told Gregor what she had learned. "Let's go visit this Christensen," she said. "Maybe he saw something when he was diving. At least he was on the bottom of the sea near our boat." She looked at Wilten, who had been listening. "Back down the road, please, Wilten. I'll tell you where to turn in."

KNUD Christensen sat in his living room wondering why he had wasted a good portion of the money he had received from Professor Nyborg on anything as silly as a new anchor. He hated the sea for what it had taken from him, and he knew he would never go out in the boat again. Nor had the cross he had bought with the remainder of the money been a wise purchase. Vandals had torn it from its base in the cemetery and twisted it beyond repair.

What Knud Christensen had really wanted to buy was a granite stone with a large cross on top, and a polished panel on the face, with the names of his brothers and his parents engraved on it. He thought about such a monument constantly, taking time from chores that needed doing. But he knew it was an idle dream. Stones like that cost more money than he could ever earn.

He looked up at the sound of an automobile braking in the gravel of his driveway. He rose heavily to his feet, opened the front door, and watched a woman and a man get out of the car. His first reaction was to close the door in their faces. Let strangers leave him in peace. But there was something about the woman's friendly face that reminded him he had not always been the recluse he had become in the six months since he had lost his brothers. His voice, however, came out low and hard.

"You want something, ma'am?" he asked suspiciously.

Reaching the open door, Ruth looked past him into the gloomy living room and gave him her warmest smile. "We should like to talk to you a bit. May we come in?" And she moved forward in such a way that Christensen had to take a step backward. She seated herself on a sofa, and Gregor joined her.

Christensen sat down in a chair across from them. "All right," he said abruptly. "Who are you and what do you want?"

Ruth again took the initiative. "My name is Ruth McVeigh and this is Dr. Kovpak. We want to talk to you about what happened last January off the Gedser light, when you dove to recover your brother's body."

Knud Christensen scowled. Why should these two want to talk about Gustave? Obviously it was the box he had brought up that they wanted to talk about. But how did they know about it? He had been alone, and he hadn't said anything. Had the professor? Or had somebody in the village become suspicious because of the money he had spent on the cross and the anchor? Then a frightening thought came: Maybe there was something in that old sunken wreck besides the box, something of greater value—like drugs, or gold bars! And they thought he had it! He knew these two would never believe he had gone back just that one time to investigate that sunken wreck. But he must try to convince them; if he failed, they might take him away—away from Gustave and his family. The only thing to do, then, was to deny—deny everything.

"I dove to bring up my brother's body," he said, his face rigid. "That's all I dove for and all I brought up. Not another thing." He rushed on compulsively. "And I can explain the new cross in the cemetery, too. It was just welded steel with some gold paint on it, but I didn't have much money after I bought the anchor. He didn't give me very much, but then it wasn't worth very much." Sweat stood out on his brow. "I never brought up any box. I'll swear to it if I have to." He stared at the two confused people.

Gregor looked at the huge man. "Listen to me," he said sympathetically. "We are not here to cause you any trouble. Please believe me, we are your friends." Christensen stared dully as Gregor went on. "This is what happened. You dove for your brother's body and brought it up. While you were diving, you saw another sunken ship, an old one, and a box that had been there since the old boat sank. You brought that up as well. You opened it and inside you found a treasure in gold—"

"No!" Christensen shook his head violently. So that was what they thought he had found! "There was no gold treasure! Only a lot of beads and buttons and crude necklaces. And some masks, and a lopsided cup, I think. He said that what I found was junk." Christensen looked at Gregor sadly. "If you're looking for a treasure, it's still down there at the bottom of the sea."

"He?" Gregor asked softly.

"A cousin of mine, a professor at the university in Copenhagen." Christensen smiled in remembrance. "He's a nice fellow. Gave me a thousand kroner for the stuff."

Ruth and Gregor exchanged stunned, unbelieving glances.

"What's the name of this cousin of yours?" asked Gregor.

Christensen shook his head. "I can't tell you that. I promised I wouldn't. You see," he said, explaining, "he'd look foolish if anyone knew he paid that much money just for junk."

Gregor took a deep breath. "Mr. Christensen, that was not junk. It was a collection of archaeological artifacts made of almost pure gold that was discovered by a man named Schliemann at Troy, in Turkey, over a hundred years ago. The treasure has been missing for the past thirty-four years. You found it."

Christensen, his forehead wrinkled, was trying to understand. "It wasn't junk? It was worth more than a thousand kroner?"

Gregor smiled. "It is worth millions of kroner."

Christensen pressed his head into his hands. Millions of kroner made little sense to him. He could not picture that much money, although he knew it was a fortune.

"Look," he said earnestly. "Do you know how much a good block of granite is worth? One big enough to go across four graves? Maybe this high?" He stood, towering above them, and placed his hand across his chest.

Gregor did not understand how granite had come into the conversation, but there was no doubt that the man was dead serious. "I'm sorry, but I have no idea."

Christensen turned to Ruth, who could only shake her head. The giant sighed and turned back to Gregor. "I don't want a lot of money. I just want a piece of granite that big. Including the engraving," he added hastily.

"I understand," Ruth said quietly. "You want to build a memorial to your family, and to the brothers you lost. If you will tell us the name of that professor cousin of yours, I will guarantee you a reward of one hundred thousand kroner. That should be more than enough for your monument."

Christensen looked miserable. "I can't. I promised."

"I'll tell you whom you promised," Ruth said angrily. "That 'nice fellow' cheated you. He knew exactly what you found, and its value. In fact, he is offering the treasure for auction to the leading museums of the world, asking a fortune."

"Arne Nyborg cheated me?" Christensen looked stunned.

"Yes," Ruth said, and glanced swiftly at Gregor. The name had not been lost on Kovpak. Ruth got up and opened her purse. "Here are two thousand kroner on account, from the museum I direct, the Metropolitan Museum of Art in New York. I promise you'll get your stone, no matter what happens to the treasure." Ruth placed a small pile of notes on a table.

Gregor also came to his feet. "Thank you, Mr. Christensen. You'll get your monument, and more."

Christensen did not respond. He seemed stunned and watched dully as his two visitors left.

He took a deep breath. Cheated . . . ! And not just him. The entire Christensen family had been cheated of their granite memorial. And after cheating him, the man had presented him with an expensive bottle of Scotch whisky, of such good quality that he had been keeping it ever since for a special occasion. . . .

He stumbled to his feet and lumbered into the kitchen. Reaching to the top shelf of the cupboard, far to the rear, he drew the bottle down from its hiding place and carried it to the living room. There he sat down and stared at the two thousand kroner on the table.

A proper event . . . ? What was a proper event?

In the rear seat of the car, the glass divider once again closed after Wilten had been instructed to return them to Copenhagen, Ruth and Gregor stared at each other in total disbelief.

"It isn't possible!" Ruth said, her voice tinged with awe.

"But it's true. A farmer! Diving for his brother's body! And finding . . ." Gregor could hardly voice the words.

"I've been playing a game," Ruth said in a dazed voice. "I never actually thought . . ." She squeezed Gregor's hand as the car unexpectedly slid to a halt at a gasoline station. Wilten's voice came through the speaking tube. "Fuel." He got out, told the attendant to fill the tank, and then walked around to the rear. Beside the twin doors of the rest rooms was a telephone booth; he entered, dropped a coin in the slot, and dialed.

Count Lindholm had been awaiting the call anxiously. "Yes?"

"Wilten here," and he began to recount all that had happened at the Gedser dock and the conversation after his passengers came out of the farmhouse—he had kept the speaking tube open.

"Did they mention Arne Nyborg?" Lindholm asked.

"No, sir."

The count took a deep breath. His mind had been racing, all through Wilten's report. "I'm sure they discovered something! The treasure had been under the sea, just as the woman suspected, and now they know how it was found. That lying Nyborg! Now they'll find him, and he'll lead them to us. But you know what to do about them. We discussed it last night. And when you're through with the police, get back here as soon as you can."

"Right." Wilten hung up. Returning to the car, he paid for the gas, started the engine, and pulled back onto the highway. In the rearview mirror he could see his two passengers, holding hands tightly, looking at each other in silent wonder.

Soon Gregor became aware that the car was slowing down again. He leaned forward as they left the highway and came to a halt on a dirt road which led down to the sea. "Why are we stopping now?" he said into the speaking tube.

"I'm afraid one of the rear tires is losing pressure, sir," Wilten answered. "I'm just going to check it."

"Oh." Gregor sat back and watched Wilten move out of sight behind the car. He was about to say something to Ruth when the heavy car began to move, rolling down the slope; gaining momentum. Ahead he could see where the dirt road ended in a turnaround guarded only by a low stone wall; beyond that was a sheer drop to the sea, churning and frothing over the rocks below. He swung around, staring through the rear window. Wilten was running after the car, his hands outstretched, screaming, "Oh, my God! I forgot the hand brake!"

Ruth was sitting rigid, white-faced. Gregor tried the door handles of both rear doors; *they were locked!* Ahead, the edge of the cliff was coming closer and closer as the car picked up speed. Abruptly Gregor leaned back in his seat, raised his feet, and jammed his shoes through the glass divider. Forcing his way headfirst through the shards of broken glass, he slithered across the front seat. Under the dashboard he found the emergency-brake handle and pulled on it with all his strength. The car shuddered and swayed from side to side. Gritting his teeth, Gregor held on. Slowly the car responded, finally coming to rest with a jarring thud against the stone wall of the turnaround, one wheel crushed by the impact.

For several seconds Gregor stayed where he was, trembling.

Then he opened the driver's door and rolled out onto the ground just as Wilten came panting down, his face white as he considered Count Lindholm's reaction to the failure of his mission.

"Thank God!" Wilten said, trying to catch his breath. "Count Lindholm will never forgive me! You might have been killed!"

Gregor got up and opened the rear door. Ruth still sat rigid inside, unable to move. Gregor turned back to Wilten, his eyes narrowed in fury. "The doors wouldn't open from inside!"

"Oh, no, sir! They are locked, controlled from the front seat. For safety reasons, sir. Count Lindholm often sends his car to take orphans on picnics, and you know children, sir—" He brought out a handkerchief. "Your cheek, sir. It's bleeding."

Gregor took a deep breath, bringing himself under control, and accepted the handkerchief. It had been a nasty accident, but both he and Ruth were alive. "What do we do now?" he asked.

Wilten gestured toward some people who had seen the incident from the highway and were beginning to come down the road. "I'm sure one of them will give you a lift into the next town, sir," he said deferentially. "You can rent a car there. I'm terribly sorry for this, sir. I'll stay with the car. If you could send a wrecker . . . ?"

"I'm sorry, too," Gregor said, feeling sympathy for the unhappy Wilten. "It was one of those things. We'll tell the count that."

"I would appreciate it, sir," Wilten said, although he did not appear any happier. "Count Lindholm will be very upset about this. Very upset . . ."

COPENHAGEN—July 1979

In his corner of the Plaza Hotel lobby, Major Serge Ulanov waited glumly for the arrival of Dr. Gregor Kovpak. The major had arrived in Copenhagen that afternoon from Berlin only to be told, upon using the Russian embassy phone to report to Colonel Vashugin in Moscow, that one week of his vacation had already been deducted and that the director of the Hermitage had been asking when Dr. Kovpak would be returning.

"I don't understand," Vashugin had said sternly, "what kind of game you and Kovpak are playing, but the two of you had better have your last expensive meal, take your last shopping spree, and enjoy your last stay in Europe's most comfortable hotels—and get back home! And when you arrive, Major, I hope you have a better story than you've given me so far! Good day!" Ulanov's ears still rang from the sound of the telephone being slammed down.

Now, sitting disconsolately in the hotel lobby, Major Ulanov was forced to admit there might be justice in the colonel's attitude. He had started out to discover how the CIA's security at Langley had been breached, but he had become distracted by the antics of Ruth McVeigh and Gregor Kovpak. They probably had simply and stupidly fallen in love, and in so doing had led him a merry chase all over Europe. And he, in pursuing them like an idiot, had only run the risk of a demotion.

He looked up as the doors of the Plaza opened, but it was not his quarry. It was a sour-looking James Newkirk who entered and took a chair commanding a view of the main entrance.

As far as Ulanov knew, Newkirk had had no more success with his mission than he had had with his. And if Langley was anything like Moscow, then Newkirk had probably also been reprimanded for wasting time and money. On a sudden impulse, Ulanov got to his feet, walked over to a chair beside the American, and sat down.

"Mr. Newkirk? . . . My name is Ulanov," the major said. "I believe we are both following Dr. McVeigh and Dr. Kovpak to discover what they are up to. I personally believe they are up to nothing, but I could be wrong. It has occurred to me that, possibly, if we were to pool our efforts we might get further."

Newkirk looked at him as if he were insane. "I have no idea what you are talking about," he said stiffly. "I happen to be a reporter for the *International Daily Gazette*, and you, sir, are a complete stranger to me."

Ulanov sighed and stood up. "Of course," he said quietly. "My suggestion was ridiculous."

He turned and walked back to his seat in the corner, wondering at the crazy impulse that had led him to approach the CIA man. But at least the matter was out in the open; they would no longer have to trail each other from a distance. With this thought relieving his depression, he leaned back to wait for Kovpak.

"MY IDEA is this," Ruth said as they entered the southern outskirts of Copenhagen in the car they had rented near the scene of the accident. "We get Nyborg's address from the phone book, and tomorrow morning we walk in on him and tell him we know he has the treasure and can prove it. We tell him that either he gives it up without any fuss, in which case the Metropolitan will see that he gets an ample reward—or, if he refuses, that we will go to the authorities and he'll end up in jail. And get nothing."

Gregor smiled across at her. "And you expect that once you hand him that tough ultimatum, he'll drag the treasure out from under the bed and lay it at your feet?"

"Well," Ruth said stiffly. "What do *you* think he'll do?"

Gregor shrugged. "He'll deny knowing what you're talking about, and say that Knud Christensen is a crazy cousin who suffers from delusions. And that there is no proof that he sold him anything for a thousand kroner."

"Well," said Ruth irritably. "How would you handle it?"

"I'd use a completely different approach." He raised his hand quickly. "I'm not objecting to your trying your way first; but when it fails, as it will, then I get a chance to try mine."

Ruth reached over to squeeze his hand. "All right, darling," she said as Gregor pulled the car up to the Plaza Hotel entrance. "If my method doesn't work, you can try yours. I promise."

MAJOR Serge Ulanov watched the two lovers enter the elevator oblivious to anything except themselves. He then got to his feet reluctantly. He knew Gregor Kovpak would be angry with him for interrupting what obviously was the equivalent of a honeymoon for two people who could never marry. But duty is duty, he thought, and he might yet save his job. He walked to the elevator bank just as James Newkirk approached. Newkirk waited stiffly, paying no attention to the man at his side. When they entered the first car that appeared, Ulanov pressed the button for his floor and looked at Newkirk inquiringly.

"Same floor," Newkirk said brusquely. Ulanov nodded and stepped back. They rode up in silence, left the elevator together, and walked down the hall. Newkirk stopped at Ruth McVeigh's door and frowned at Ulanov. But Ulanov continued on to Kovpak's room without breaking stride. He knocked on the door and waited for Kovpak to open it.

To Ulanov's amazement, Kovpak smiled broadly when he saw him. "Serge! Just the man I wanted to see. But what on earth are you doing here?"

"I've been following you and the girl," Ulanov replied, walking over to the bed and dropping down on it.

"Following us? But why?" asked Kovpak, closing the door.

"It seemed obvious to me that when you left London for Berlin and then went to Bad Freienwalde, you were trying to trace the Schliemann treasure. The treasure and its connection with the CIA is, after all, my assignment, so I thought that if I followed you I

495

might learn something. Instead," he said bitterly, "I managed to lose you both in Rostock and got the worst reprimand of my career for wasting my time—"

"You haven't been wasting your time." Kovpak grinned. "We found the Schliemann treasure!" He sat down on a chair near the bed. "It was at the bottom of the sea all these years. A man in a town called Gedser found it when he was diving for his brother's body. He didn't know what it was, and he sold it to a professor named Nyborg, for almost nothing."

Ulanov was staring. "You mean the Schliemann treasure hasn't been in Langley?"

"It hasn't been anywhere except on the bottom of the sea," Gregor said impatiently. "We haven't located it physically, but if you know how to tap a telephone, we soon will!"

"The professor's telephone, I assume. Why?"

Kovpak leaned forward. "There is absolutely no way a European professor could finance anything as expensive as this auction. Nyborg must have a confederate, someone with money, and undoubtedly this confederate has the treasure."

Ulanov nodded. "I see. And if we can frighten Nyborg sufficiently, he's going to telephone this confederate—"

"And you're going to be listening in," Kovpak said flatly. He reached for the telephone directory and quickly found Nyborg's phone number and address. He asked the hotel operator for an outside line, dialed the number, and waited stolidly. Then he came to life, smiling brightly into the receiver.

"Hello? Professor Nyborg? My name is Gregor Kovpak, of the Hermitage Museum in Leningrad. What? . . . You have? That's very kind of you, I'm sure. The reason for my call, Professor, is that on a recent expedition I discovered some bones which proved to be those of a baby dinosaur. Now, I have just come across a history paper of yours, and it impressed me greatly. Since I find myself in Copenhagen, I would really like to discuss with someone of your background the era when those tiny bones were laid down. I'm sure it could make a great joint paper, if you would be interested. . . . Tomorrow morning would be fine. . . . No, no! I'll come to you! Nine o'clock? . . . Excellent!"

He hung up and smiled at Ulanov, who was shaking his head. "How did you know he'd written a paper?"

496

"He's probably written twenty and had one published," Kovpak said with a faint smile, glancing at his watch. "And now you'll have to excuse me, Serge. I have a date with Dr. McVeigh."

WHEN James Newkirk knocked at Ruth McVeigh's door he did not receive the same kind of welcome that Gregor Kovpak had given Serge Ulanov.

"Yes?" she asked curtly.

Newkirk brought out his wallet and showed her his government ID card. "My name is James Newkirk. I'm with the CIA. I'd like a minute of your time." He pushed past her, closed the door, and motioned her toward a chair. "Have a seat, Dr. McVeigh."

Ruth sat down, not pleased with the interruption. She wanted to shower and dress for her date with Gregor. "All right," she said coolly. "What do you want?"

Newkirk sat down opposite her. "Dr. McVeigh, what do you know of this man you've been traveling with—Gregor Kovpak?"

"What business is that of yours?"

Newkirk shrugged delicately. "America is my business, Dr. McVeigh. The fact is that you are an American citizen traveling with a Russian national. We would like to know the reason for this possibly treasonous act."

"Mr. Newkirk, do you have a warrant for my arrest?"

He smiled coldly. "Why, Dr. McVeigh? Do you feel you deserve to be arrested?"

Fuming, Ruth jumped to her feet. "Get out!"

Newkirk felt he was finally getting somewhere. An interview like this, had he conducted it earlier, might have saved him several days in an East German jail, not to mention several severe reprimands from Langley.

"Dr. McVeigh," he said quietly, "I can have you brought to the American embassy here in Copenhagen on suspicion that you are dealing with a hostile intelligence service, and we can continue the questioning there, if you prefer." She has no idea my threat is completely idle, Newkirk thought with satisfaction; I have no authority to take her to the embassy or anywhere else.

Ruth glared at him, speechless. Here she was, with the Schliemann treasure practically in her hands, and this person—who claimed to be a CIA man—had chosen this particular moment to

497

appear and create a nuisance. A thought came. "Mr. Newkirk, may I see your card again, please?"

"Certainly," Newkirk said courteously—courtesy was always best once a suspect had decided to tell all. He handed over his wallet, opened to the proper cellophane slot. Ruth extracted the ID card as if to examine it better. Then she began to tear it into pieces.

"Hey!" Newkirk said, outraged. "You can't do that!"

"I just did." Ruth smiled at him pleasantly. "And now, if you don't leave at once, I shall call the hotel security staff."

Newkirk clenched his jaw and stood up. Never in his life had he seen a more blatant confession of involvement in some nefarious scheme! He walked to the door with the air of a man who was far from intimidated by the mere loss of his ID card. "We shall meet again, Dr. McVeigh."

"I hope not," Ruth said, and watched the door close behind him.

PROFESSOR Arne Nyborg tucked his only clean sport shirt into the pants of his best suit and considered himself in the mirror. Not bad, he thought with a smile; a fitting co-author of a paper with Dr. Gregor Kovpak of the famous Hermitage Museum. My, how things had changed in a few months!

When the bell rang he hurried to the door and held it open, frowning slightly as he saw two figures instead of one. Then he felt a shock as he recognized Dr. Ruth McVeigh of the Metropolitan Museum in New York! Her picture had been in the newspapers often enough during that conference in London. Suddenly he had a cold feeling that this meeting had nothing to do with dinosaurs. Still, how could anyone possibly connect him with the Schliemann treasure? He forced a welcoming smile and ushered his guests into the shoddy living room.

"Dr. Kovpak? And you are Dr. McVeigh; I recognize you from the papers. This is a great honor. Can I get you some coffee?"

"No," Ruth McVeigh said abruptly, looking at him with distaste as she sat down on the sofa. Gregor moved about the room, looking at the copies of paintings on the walls. Nyborg tried to appear insouciant, but his heart was beating rapidly.

"Let's not waste any time," Ruth began. "You have the Schliemann treasure and we know it. Your cousin Knud Christensen told us all about it."

498

Professor Nyborg tried not to panic. Somehow this woman had located Christensen, and the stupid oaf had talked. He had *not* drunk the doctored whisky! *Why* had Nyborg bought an expensive bottle? A cheaper Scotch would have been gone long since, and the talkative, dim-witted farmer with it! Still, it was obvious that these two knew nothing of Count Lindholm and the true location of the treasure. This thought calmed Nyborg instantly, and he assumed a look of startled incredulity. "I beg your pardon," he said.

"Please do not try to look innocent," Ruth said scornfully. "If you don't want to spend the rest of your life in prison, you will admit you have the treasure and we can go on from there."

Nyborg stared at her, looking perplexed. "How can I admit something that isn't true?"

"Let me put it to you in simple words. I will guarantee that the Metropolitan Museum will pay you a hundred thousand dollars for the treasure. If you accept my offer, I will see that you are paid in cash and that nobody beyond the three of us will ever hear of it. If you refuse, I'll have no choice but to go to the authorities and see that you are arrested. Not only for attempted extortion—that's all your auction amounts to—but also for failing to report the discovery of a treasure found in Danish waters."

Nyborg sighed in frustration. "Madam, of course I have heard of the Schliemann treasure. But the idea that I have it is absurd."

Ruth looked at him triumphantly. "Then how do you explain Knud Christensen and the story he told us?"

"I never met my cousin Knud Christensen. Perhaps he enjoys making up stories. Or perhaps he is mad. But whatever he told you, if it involved me in any sense, it is false."

"Knud Christensen said he was diving for his brother's body last January off the Gedser lighthouse, and—"

Nyborg threw up his hands. "Please! This insanity must end! Those waters in January would kill any man in minutes! Madam, I have no idea what your purpose was in coming here with this ridiculous story, but you will please leave now, or I shall have to call the police." He stood up, swung the door open, and waited.

Ruth stared at him, furious. The fact that his words had come so close to Gregor's prediction did not lessen her frustration.

Gregor dropped his inspection of the inferior reproductions on the walls and walked over to Ruth. "I believe the professor is well within his rights, Ruth," he said quietly. "You have no proof of your charge. Why don't you go back to the hotel and wait for me? I should like to speak to Professor Nyborg for a few moments on the subject I came to discuss with him, before you insisted upon accompanying me here."

Ruth opened her mouth to retort, and then remembered her promise, though she held little hope for Gregor's success. She stood up. "Don't do anything foolish, darling," she said under her breath, and without glancing at Nyborg she walked through the door he was holding open.

The professor, still wearing his assumed look of bewilderment, turned to Kovpak. "I can't imagine where that woman ever got such an odd idea—"

"Oh, I can," Gregor said cheerfully, taking Nyborg lightly by the arm. "Why don't you sit down and let me explain this entire affair to you? I think I can make you understand."

He lowered the paunchy Dane to the sofa and pulled a chair close to him. Now Nyborg's bewilderment was quite genuine.

"You see, Professor," Gregor went on benignly, "I did not disagree with Dr. McVeigh on her facts or her conclusions, but on her methods. If I gave you any other impression, I'm sorry. I know that you have the treasure, and that you would never release it on the mere threat of prosecution by the authorities. Why should you? The proof that you have it is tenuous, and Knud Christensen's story, coming from a man shattered by the death of his family, would never convince even the most receptive jury. However"—Gregory was now smiling—"I believe that under the methods of interrogation that are fortunately available to me, you would be more than willing to tell us exactly where you have hidden the treasure."

Nyborg's lips were white. "But I tell you, I don't have—"

"You don't have the treasure?" Gregor's smile disappeared. He looked sad. "That would be a pity. Because you will suffer—that is, be interrogated—for nothing, until it is too late, I'm afraid."

"You—a noted scientist—are threatening to torture me?"

"The word I used was interrogate," Kovpak said chidingly. "And I certainly wouldn't conduct the interrogation. With my lack of experience, I would botch the whole thing and lose you before—" He seemed to notice that his words were disturbing the professor and he went on apologetically. "There is a KGB man in Copenhagen trained in this sort of thing. He could probably make you last for days. I'd be lucky if you didn't die on me in a few hours."

He got to his feet, towering over the shaken professor.

"I will give you until noon today to decide if it is really necessary to go to such extreme limits. I am at the Plaza Hotel. If I do not hear from you by noon, you will be in the hands of the KGB by twelve thirty. There is no escape, Professor!"

Gregor walked to the door, turned to give Nyborg one last cold look, and left, closing the door firmly behind him. Then he hurried down the stairs to the basement of the building.

Alone in his living room, Arne Nyborg shivered. This Kovpak was the very devil! There was no doubt the man meant every word of his threat. But even if he told him that the treasure was at Lindholm Castle, he would never be believed, especially if the count should deny it, which he was bound to do. And the idea of accepting a mere hundred thousand dollars for the treasure was galling, after his appetite had been whetted with thoughts of at least fifteen million. There must be some way to avoid the torture and to go ahead with the auction Lindholm had planned. The thing to do now, he suddenly realized, was what he had been clever enough to do when the question of disposing of the treasure had first presented itself—ask the advice of Count Lindholm.

Nyborg walked unsteadily to the telephone and dialed the familiar number. But before the telephone at the other end had rung more than twice, there was a heavy knock on his apartment door. He frowned. Who could that be? Cursing, he put the receiver back on the hook and went to open the door.

In the basement of the apartment building, Kovpak watched as Ulanov and a large blond man listened patiently to their headsets. Suddenly Ulanov winked at Gregor. "He's dialing. . . ." The major scribbled some numbers on a pad and showed them to the blond man, who read them, nodded, and then left the basement.

Ulanov returned his attention to his headset and then scowled. "He hung up without waiting for his call to be answered."

"Maybe he decided to go see the man instead of calling him," Kovpak said. "I'd better get out to my car."

"There's no need to rush," said Ulanov. "I have a man outside

who'll advise us when your professor leaves the apartment."
Kovpak slipped on the headset abandoned by the blond man, and
he and Ulanov resumed the vigil. After more than thirty minutes
of silence Kovpak said irritably, "I have no idea why Nyborg isn't
calling someone! Or rushing out to see someone! I don't like this."
"Well, we'll have an address and a name in a few more minutes,"
Ulanov said commiseratingly.

There was a sound at the head of the basement steps, and Ulanov
assumed the attitude of a faithful telephone repairman, but it was
the blond man who reappeared, out of breath. "It took longer than
I thought," he said, "but here it is. The call was made to a place
called Lindholm Castle in Ringsted. A Count Axel Lindholm lives
there."

"*Lindholm!*" Gregor stared at him for a moment, then his jaw
hardened. "So that car accident was no accident! That murdering
scoundrel!" Speaking aloud to himself, he glared at Ulanov, not
seeing him. "It makes sense when you think about it. He's important enough to have the necessary contacts all over the world.
He has the money to finance the operation, and he has the charm
to get a nincompoop like Nyborg to hand the treasure over to him."

Ulanov had been listening politely. "I don't know who this
Count Lindholm is, but if you believe he has the treasure,
shouldn't we be on our way to visit him?"

"We certainly should. Let's go!"

They climbed the basement steps and walked quickly out to the
car. Gregor studied a highway map for a moment and then put the
car in motion. "We'll ask for Lindholm Castle when we get near
Ringsted," he said. The white-haired major nodded.

In a car parked some distance behind them, James Newkirk was
pleased to see them moving at last; he had been sitting in the hot
sun ever since he had followed Ulanov there from the Russian
embassy early that morning. At this point, Newkirk did not care
if the men in the car ahead knew he was following them. He had
no idea what Kovpak and Ulanov had been doing in the apartment building, but there was no doubt something was up, and
James Newkirk meant to know what it was.

As Kovpak entered the highway to Ringsted, he glanced rou-
tinely in the rearview mirror. Without turning his head he said to
Ulanov, "We're being followed!"

"Oh?" Ulanov looked over his shoulder and then turned back. "That's just Newkirk." He bit back a yawn. "That CIA agent I told you about in London. Don't pay any attention to him."

Kovpak swung around, staring at Ulanov in disbelief. *"You mean he's been following us since London?"*

"No, no!" The major shook his head. *"I've* been following you. He's been following *me*. Then in Germany I lost you but found him. I let him find you for me. Then I followed him." He shrugged. "Now he's following both of us. It isn't important." He leaned back, closing his eyes. "Try not to use the horn too much. I'm going to take a nap before we get there."

DENMARK—July 1979

COUNT Lindholm was in a foul mood. Wilten was in the count's poor graces, and under those circumstances everyone on the staff suffered. The chef, who was serving the count's late breakfast on the terrace of Lindholm Castle, recognized that this was no time to skimp. He had outdone himself with the blueberry crepes, but the count was chewing on one as if it were a mere pancake.

Wilten approached with a telephone, and Lindholm looked at him as if he were a stranger. "There is a person at the other end of the line this time, I hope?" The last caller had hung up before he could speak.

Wilten swallowed. "Yes, sir. It's—it's that McVeigh woman."

Lindholm took the telephone from him, cupping the receiver while wondering what Ruth McVeigh could have to say. She had called the day before about the accident, explaining that it had not been Wilten's fault.

He forced a smile into his voice. "Hello, Ruth! How good to hear from you! I'm so sorry about yesterday!"

"No, forget that," Ruth said. "Axel, I'm worried about Gregor." She sounded desperate. "I don't know where he is. We were at this man's apartment—"

Axel Lindholm felt a sudden chill. "What man's apartment?"

But Ruth's mind was on her story. "—and Gregor told me to go back to the hotel and wait for him, so I did, but Gregor never came. Finally I went back to the apartment, but nobody answered the bell. I'm afraid Gregor might have used force, and—"

"Ruth, *whose apartment?*"

"You wouldn't know him. His name is Arne Nyborg."

"Ruth, hold on a moment." Count Lindholm cupped the receiver in one damp palm and thought furiously. Damn Wilten for failing to eliminate the two of them the day before, and double damn that fool Nyborg! First, because he had lied about where he had gotten the treasure; second, because the idiot was probably running to his protector, Axel Lindholm, at this very moment! And with Kovpak undoubtedly right behind him! There was no time to lose.

Lindholm uncovered the telephone receiver. "Ruth, stay at the hotel. I'll be there as soon as I can."

Lindholm hung up and jumped to his feet. "Wilten!"

"Sir?"

"Call Kastrup Airport. I want the first flight out—on any line—to Rome, Amsterdam, London, Paris, Madrid—anyplace so long as it's not in eastern Europe."

"Yes, sir."

Count Lindholm hurried upstairs to his rooms. He took a suitcase from his wardrobe, then went to the study. Removing the treasure from the cabinet drawer, he hastily stuffed the bundle into the suitcase. Then, suitcase in hand, he trotted down the stairs and moved at a brisk walk to the stables, where four of the stalls had been requisitioned for his cars. He selected the fastest—a Ferrari open-topped two-seater—wedged the suitcase into the narrow space behind the driver's seat, and climbed in. Gunning the engine, he roared down the driveway that twisted its way through the parklands of Lindholm Castle.

When Kovpak stopped at a gasoline station to ask directions, Newkirk stopped on the highway a few yards behind him. As Kovpak pulled away, Newkirk started up as well. Soon Ulanov was telling Kovpak, "You'd better slow down. That looks like the castle gate ahead." He started to lean back as Gregor braked to turn into the castle grounds. Then suddenly he lunged forward, pointing. "*Look out!*"

A small, open-topped roadster was shooting around the final curve of the wooded drive and heading directly for them. Gregor swung the wheel as hard as he could. At the same moment the driver of the roadster saw their car and tried desperately to avoid a collision by hitting his brakes. The Ferrari skidded wildly, caromed off a tree, and crashed head-on into one of the huge stone piers that anchored the open gate. Bouncing back several feet, it stopped, with steam spouting from its radiator.

Gregor brought his car to a shuddering halt, inches from one of the huge trees. For a moment he sat there, his hands shaking. Then he and Ulanov were out of the car, running to the roadster. It was obvious that the driver had died instantly. He lay as if sleeping peacefully, his head to one side against the shattered dashboard.

Gregor looked at Ulanov. "That's Count Lindholm."

"He was going somewhere in a great hurry," Ulanov said dryly. He studied the interior of the car and then reached down, dragging the suitcase from behind the twisted seat. Laying it on the ground, he opened it and unwrapped the bundle. He looked up. "Would this be the treasure you've been talking about?"

Kovpak crouched beside him. "Yes." Behind them Newkirk came hurrying up. He stared with wide eyes, first at the dead man and then down at the open suitcase.

Ulanov closed the suitcase and handed it to Kovpak. "You'd better take this and get going," he said evenly.

Kovpak hesitated. In a few minutes the place would be swarming with police, and anyone with one of Count Lindholm's initialed suitcases in his hand would have many questions to answer. The faint sound of a distant siren convinced him. Without another word he ran for his car. Newkirk made a move to go after him, but Ulanov threw himself around the tall man's legs, bringing him down. He held him tightly by the ankles as Kovpak jumped into the car, started it, and turned toward Copenhagen.

Newkirk kicked himself loose and stared after the car, knowing he could never catch it. "Ulanov," he said heavily, getting to his feet, "I'm going to beat you to a pulp. For East Berlin—"

"Wait a minute," Ulanov said hastily, holding up a conciliatory hand, and Newkirk paused, one fist cocked. "I know that you people have always thought that we Russians had the Schliemann treasure. Well, we were sure you had stolen it from us. Now that we can prove that neither one of us had it"—he shrugged—"well, we've both completed our investigations successfully, haven't we?"

Newkirk slowly opened his fist and dropped his arm. The KGB man was right. Newkirk could now demonstrate that Russian security had not been breached, which meant that the KGB would not go about changing its systems and the CIA would not have to discard all its findings on those systems. Not bad for a lowly free lance! That credit alone could bring Newkirk advancement, possibly even a change to a New York paper. In that light, Ulanov deserved a pat on the back, not a beating. Newkirk smiled and held out his hand. "I'm sorry. You're quite correct."

"That's all right," Ulanov said magnanimously as he shook hands. "By the way, you recall the recorder you carried in that book in London? I don't suppose you happen to have any spare tapes?"

Newkirk stared at the man, speechless, and then plowed in, swinging, just as a police car came roaring up, siren screaming.

An hour had passed since Ruth's call to Count Lindholm, and she was more worried than ever. She was about to telephone the castle again when there was a sharp rap on the door. She opened it to see a large, balding, moon-faced man, a complete stranger.

"Dr. McVeigh, I am Inspector Ib Rodhe." He presented his police identification. "May I come in?"

"Of course." Ruth let him in and closed the door, her heart pounding. "Something's happened to Gregor Kovpak, hasn't it?"

The inspector sank into a chair. It was obvious from his puzzled look that the name meant nothing to him. "Dr. McVeigh, I understand you placed a telephone call to Lindholm Castle a little over an hour ago. Is that correct?"

"Yes, I did. Why?"

"Count Lindholm was killed in an automobile accident only moments later. I was wondering—"

Ruth was staring at him in shock. "It's my fault," she said miserably. "He was hurrying to get here."

"No, ma'am. According to the butler, Wilten—who informed us of your call—he was on his way to the airport."

"The *airport!* But that's impossible!"

"I'm afraid not, ma'am. I have known men like Wilten before. While his master was alive I have no doubt that Wilten would have lied for him. But with his master dead there was no reason for him not to give us as much of the truth as he knew. He said that after your call he was instructed to telephone the airport and arrange a ticket for the count on the first flight out of the country."

"*What?*" Ruth was looking at him with unbelieving eyes.

The inspector took out a notebook and consulted it. "Wilten then said, and I quote, 'Count Lindholm hurried upstairs to his rooms. When he came down he had a suitcase.' I asked Wilten if the suitcase had contained clothes, and he said he had checked his employer's wardrobe and no clothes had been taken." The inspector went back to his notebook. "He said, 'I surmise, sir, the suitcase contained something that Professor Nyborg brought to the castle a few days ago. He and the count were quite secretive about it.'"

Ruth looked at the inspector incredulously, trying to comprehend what she had heard. Then something occurred to her. "Do the police have this suitcase now?"

"No, ma'am. There was no suitcase in the car. There were two men fighting furiously when the police arrived. One was an American named James Newkirk, who claims to be a newspaper reporter. The other was a Russian, Serge Ulanov, who says he's an assistant curator at the Hermitage Museum. We have them both in custody. Now, about your telephone call, ma'am—"

"It's a long story," Ruth said wearily, and recounted the entire history of locating the treasure. "It appears that Professor Nyborg and Count Lindholm have been working together."

The inspector looked at her shrewdly. "And now the treasure is gone. And this Gregor Kovpak is also gone. Is that the story, ma'am?"

Ruth glared. "I know what you're thinking, but you're wrong! Something has happened to Gregor, or he would have been here by now. I'm worried! I left him at this Professor Nyborg's apartment, and now the apartment telephone doesn't answer, and—"

"Well, then, we can go to the professor's home and see if we can find out where your Gregor is."

He led her from the room and downstairs to the hotel lobby. An unmarked police car with a driver was waiting outside. They climbed in and Ruth gave the professor's address.

When they arrived, the inspector rapped loudly on the door to Nyborg's apartment. There was no answer. The driver, who had accompanied them upstairs, reached into his pocket for a bunch of keys. In a moment he unlocked the door and stepped back.

Pushing it open, Inspector Rodhe stood looking inside while Ruth peered around his shoulder. Then she screamed. A man lay sprawled on the sofa, his face suffused with blood, the marks of strangulation clearly visible on his neck.

"That's Professor Nyborg," Ruth gasped.

"I suggest you wait for me in the car," the inspector said politely. The driver led Ruth down the steps as the inspector entered the room and closed the door behind him.

Ruth sat in the police car, stunned. Oh, Gregor! she thought despondently. Why had he used force? My darling, my love, a murderer! At this moment he was undoubtedly hiding someplace. And he had done it for her, because of her greed for the treasure! It was all her fault, the death of Nyborg, the death of Axel Lindholm, the fact that Gregor was a murderer. The guilt would lie on her conscience for the rest of her days. . . .

She looked up. Inspector Rodhe was coming from the apartment, pushing a manacled figure ahead of him. It was Knud Christensen, looking at her dully, not recognizing her at all. The inspector ushered him into the front seat next to the driver and climbed into the back beside Ruth.

"He was in the kitchen, drinking aquavit," the inspector said cheerfully. "Gave me no trouble at all. Kept saying Nyborg had cheated him, and the next thing he knew he was holding the man by the neck." He looked compassionately at the silent figure beside the driver. "I don't believe he's all there."

Ruth felt a wave of relief, followed by a flush of shame that she could have thought Gregor capable of killing Nyborg. But if Gregor was not involved, where was he?

"About this Gregor," Inspector Rodhe said gently. "I made a call from the apartment upstairs, for when something valuable connected with a case disappears, and when a person connected with the same case also disappears, I tend to believe they very well might be together."

Ruth stared at him. "What do you mean?"

"I mean," the inspector said in the same gentle voice, "that a man named Gregor Kovpak took a Scandinavian Airlines nonstop flight for Leningrad less than thirty minutes ago. He was carrying a very expensive suitcase; the young lady who checked him in remembered it because it was so elegant."

508

NEW YORK—August 1979

THE three weeks of vacation Ruth McVeigh had taken in Paris had done nothing to lessen the combination of grief and anger she felt whenever she thought of Gregor Kovpak and the Schliemann treasure. Her visits to the Louvre, once one of her greatest pleasures, were dull now, and no amount of time spent in boutiques buying clothes seemed to assuage her bitterness. Realizing finally that a vacation could not resolve her problem, she cabled the Metropolitan that she would be back the following Monday.

The plane trip home seemed endless, with her mind constantly dwelling upon the hurt she had suffered at the hands of a man who had taken advantage of her, pretending to fall in love with her and capping his caddishness by stealing the treasure. What could she do now to even the score? Surely there had to be a way to press charges, possibly through the State Department to the Cultural Commission of the Soviet Union—although if they were anything like Gregor Kovpak, they would probably deny any knowledge of the treasure. And how could she prove her case? Knud Christensen had been put in a home for the mentally ill. Count Lindholm was dead, and so was Professor Nyborg. To the police, all Gregor Kovpak had stolen was a suitcase. What it contained, they did not know. *But she knew!*

Proof or no proof, she would see to it that the entire world would learn what a cheat Gregor Kovpak was, despite his great reputation! She would spread the word through every archaeological society, every professional journal; she would blacken his name so that he would never dare show his face anywhere!

She arrived at Kennedy airport early in the morning, tired but determined. Dropping her suitcases off at her apartment, she took a taxi at once to the Metropolitan Museum.

She stalked past the receptionists and the guards without seeing them, pushed through her office door, and then stopped dead, her heart in her throat. There was a man inside, looking out the window, and his shoulders and back were achingly familiar.

He turned and smiled, his pleasure at seeing her evident in his eyes. "Hello, Ruth."

"Gregor!" She sat down abruptly. "What are you doing here?"

He shrugged, as if his presence were the most natural thing in the world. "I'm in love with you. You are in love with me—or you were a while ago. I thought we might get married. I've defected from my country—with the help of a good but slightly battered friend, a retired major—and I've requested asylum here."

"But—but, what about Copenhagen . . . ?"

"Ah, you mean my sudden departure with that suitcase?" Gregor grinned, then put on a straight face. "Ruth, suppose I told you that when I got to Leningrad that suitcase was empty?"

Her anger returned. "I wouldn't believe you!"

Gregor persisted. "But suppose that even if there had been something of value in that suitcase—which I am not in a position to verify—I honestly believed it belonged in Russia. And suppose I thought that you might be willing to take me instead. . . ."

She stared at him a moment and then smiled, ruefully at first and then with happiness. "I don't have much choice, do I?"

"I'm afraid not." Gregor frowned slightly. "Incidentally, where have you been? When I returned to Copenhagen you had already left. I stayed on in Denmark because I had to arrange for a large granite monument. Knud Christensen will be allowed to visit it frequently once it is completed."

"Oh, Gregor!" She rose to her feet and came into his arms.

But even as they kissed, Dr. Ruth McVeigh, director of the Metropolitan Museum of Art, was trying to figure how she could exhibit the Schliemann collection, if only on loan. And for a decent period of time, not just for a few miserable weeks or months.

THE announcement of the coming marriage of two famous archaeologists, Dr. Ruth McVeigh, of the Metropolitan Museum, and Dr. Gregor Kovpak, lately of the Hermitage, was the first story to be covered for New York's leading newspaper by its new reporter for cultural affairs, Mr. James Newkirk.

Robert L. Fish

As we were going to press we learned, with deep regret, that Robert Fish had died of a heart attack, at the age of 68.

When he was interviewed a few months ago he told us that unlike most authors, who start writing at an early age, the urge to do so came to him only when he was forty-eight. He had always been a "maniac mystery reader", and on one rainy afternoon twenty years ago he decided to try writing one. He was then working as an engineer in Rio de Janeiro.

He sold that first short story to *Ellery Queen's Mystery Magazine* for one hundred dollars. Although the celebration afterwards cost him three times that amount, the event was one of his fondest memories. Afterwards he won three Edgar awards from the Mystery Writers of America. Among his thirty-five books, some have been made into films, notably *Mute Witness*, re-titled *Bullitt*, starring Steve McQueen.

Fish's second career, as an author, became as successful as his first, though he still found engineering exciting—the two careers "were just perfect together". He had graduated as an engineer in 1933 in his hometown of Cleveland, Ohio and moved to New York to work on the Triborough Bridge. Soon afterwards he married a Cleveland girl and took part in the first surveys for the World's Fair that opened in New York in 1939. Being an engineering consultant gave him the opportunity to travel, which he loved. He and his wife moved twenty-two times—to places as different as Brazil, Spain, England and Belgium—before finally settling in Trumbull, Connecticut, where he died at his home.